ROBERTA G
Romantic Times Award

"When a novel of historical romance has Roberta Gellis' name on it . . . readers know they're getting a meticulously researched, expertly told story full of passion and adventure."

—Waldenbooks' *Lovenotes*

MASQUES OF GOLD

"DELIGHTFULLY IMAGINED . . . [A] RICH TAPESTRY OF DETAIL."

—*Publishers Weekly*

FIRES OF WINTER

"A MASTERPIECE . . . FANTASTIC AND FASCINATING . . . Roberta Gellis transports readers into the hearts and minds of her hero and heroine."

—*Rave Reviews*

"THE BEST A BOOK CAN BE . . . I DARE ANYONE NOT TO BE HOOKED!"

—*Affaire de Coeur*

A TAPESTRY OF DREAMS

"SPLENDID . . . AGLOW WITH COLOR, ROMANCE, AND RICH IN HISTORICAL DETAIL!"

—Jennifer Wilde, author of *Angel in Scarlet*

"FIRST-RATE ROMANCE IN AN INTRIGUING HISTORICAL SETTING."

—*New York Daily News*

THE ROPE DANCER

"AN EXQUISITE NOVEL FROM THE PEN OF A MASTER STORYTELLER."

—*Rave Reviews*

"AN EXTREMELY ENTERTAINING AND DELIGHTFUL TALE."

—Rebecca Brandewyne, author of *The Outlaw Hearts*

Books by Roberta Gellis
from Jove

A TAPESTRY OF DREAMS
FIRE SONG
THE ROPE DANCER
FIRES OF WINTER
MASQUES OF GOLD
A SILVER MIRROR

A Silver Mirror

By

Roberta Gellis

JOVE BOOKS, NEW YORK

A SILVER MIRROR

A Jove Book/published by arrangement with
the author

PRINTING HISTORY
Jove trade paperback edition/November 1989

ISBN: 0-515-10135-4

Jove Books are published by The Berkley Publishing Group,
200 Madison Avenue, New York, New York 10016.
The name "JOVE" and the "J" logo
are trademarks belonging to Jove Publications, Inc.

PRINTED IN THE UNITED STATES OF AMERICA

10 9 8 7 6 5 4 3 2 1

Chapter 1

"You are making too much of it, Joanna," Barbara said idly, watching the dancing shadows the rose leaves made as a soft breeze stirred them.

The pretty patterns of the shadows made the warm, sweet-smelling garden even more pleasant, Barbara thought. Although the manor house beyond the garden wall was far more comfortable than her father's great keeps, where the walls breathed damp cold that called for a fire even in high summer, the hall could not compete with a garden seat in the middle of May.

"I do not think I am making too much of Guy's behavior." Joanna's voice broke into Barbara's thoughts.

"I can make Guy wish he had let me be," Barbara snapped. "It was only because he was my father's guest that I felt I must be polite to him."

Barbara was beginning to wish she had found some excuse other than the unwelcome attentions of Guy de Montfort for her sudden visit to Kirby Moorside. The walled manor was the favorite retreat of her uncle, Hugh Bigod. Could she not have said simply that she wanted a few weeks there in her aunt's company? No, she could not; despite their fondness for each other Joanna would never have believed her.

"No, you must not do that," Joanna Bigod said. "You would

make Guy hate you. And his father is so indulgent. It would be dangerous. You must tell the earl." Her soft voice trembled a little.

"I could not." Barbara spoke equally softly, now remorseful for her previous sharpness. She knew Joanna was harping on Guy's behavior because she could not bear to be silent and think. Then Barbara's distinctive brows drew together in surprise. It was not like Joanna to give bad advice, no matter how distracted she was. "You know my father," Barbara said defensively. "He would—"

"I did not mean Norfolk." Joanna shuddered slightly at the idea of the reaction of her brother-by-marriage. "I meant Leicester," she added hastily.

"Tell Leicester that his son Guy is pursuing me with dishonorable intent?" This time Barbara's brows rose as high as they could go in disdain. Because they were thick and grew straight across without a curve above her dark blue eyes, they made a distinct, burnished chestnut circumflex within her forehead.

"You do not know that Guy's intent is dishonorable."

There was no inflection at all in the soft voice, and Barbara was about to ask what kind of idiot Joanna took her for when the real implications behind the remark burst on her. Barbara's eyebrows went down again into a straight, thick line that nearly met over her handsome nose, and she looked at her aunt-by-marriage with considerable respect.

"You mean I should go to Leicester and warn him that I am not a good match for his son," Barbara said slowly, getting interested in the subject herself. The earl of Leicester had grown so powerful in the last few months that she knew she must be wary. "That would do if I were trying to avoid young Simon, since his father will not take less than a palatine estate for his namesake, but what if he does not think me too far below the despicable Guy? It is true that I am only a natural daughter with no more than small property in France; however, I am also the earl of Norfolk's only child. My father is not likely to have another, and everyone knows he loves me. In Leicester's opinion I might do quite well enough to bind papa more tightly to his cause."

"All true, but do you think Guy would be willing to marry you even to please his father and ensure Norfolk's support?" Joanna's lips twitched, but only once.

Barbara knew her aunt very well, however, and her own eyes brightened with mischief. "Of course not!" she exclaimed, and then burst out laughing and rose from her seat to embrace Joanna. "How clever you are, my love! Guy will only accept a wife with great wealth, but Leicester will never admit his son's greed. Naturally the fond father will ask if I am really what his dear sweet child desires. The dear sweet child will assure his doting papa that he would not accept me on a platter, even stuffed with pigeons, and papa will then wonder how I came by my puffed-up notion and warn Guy to avoid me lest I cry that he had made me an offer and then withdrawn.''

''Surely Leicester will warn both young Simon and Guy so that you will not—in your 'puffed-up notion' of importance—begin to speak of having a choice between the two brothers.''

Barbara was accustomed to her aunt's subtle way of giving instructions. She wondered with a flicker of amusement whether her forthright uncle had ever come to understand how he was being manipulated. As Hugh came into her thoughts, her glance dropped to the row of little gold and green shields that Hugh's wife was stitching into a neckband. Some were already adorned with the red lion *passant guardant* that watched the enemy from her uncle's shield. Barbara looked away hastily and, having given Joanna a brisk hug, returned to her end of the bench and picked up her own embroidery. She would not think of war. It was better to think of Leicester's sons.

''Young Simon is not spiteful and vicious like Guy.'' Barbara shrugged. ''He is only spoiled and lazy, but still, God save me from such a choice.''

''Taking a husband would save you more finally,'' Joanna said.

Allowing the sleeve cuff she was decorating to drop into her lap before she had taken a stitch, Barbara stared at her Uncle Hugh's wife. The one unfailing support she had had in resisting a second marriage during the first few years after she returned from France had been Joanna's. Of course, her father had not really wanted her to marry. Even seven years ago in 1257 the political situation had been so volatile that Norfolk had feared any choice of husband he made for her would be the wrong choice. However, it had been Joanna who soothed away his concern that he was being selfish and reassured him that what was right for him politically was also best for Barbara. Why was Joanna urging marriage now?

There was more color than usual in Joanna's face, but she kept her eyes fixed on her own work when she added, ''I have learned at long last that first loves may be sweet memories but are not always best, as a rich stew is really more satisfying than a honeyed comfit.''

Barbara made a choked, wordless protest, but her angry denial of any ''first love'' jammed in her throat. She had had a first love; to deny it would be a lie, and she could not lie to Joanna. But was it a lie? It had been so long ago, a child's fancy, long forgotten. She shifted uneasily on the bench and her foot touched the basket that held her embroidery silks, pushing it into a ray of sunlight. The fresh green leaves of the rose trees, even with their branches clipped and bent to form a bower over the bench on which the ladies sat, provided only a dappled shade. Now the light glinted back at Barbara from the basket, making her turn her head to clear the dazzle from her eyes and reminding her of the small polished silver mirror that lay with her matching comb in the basket. Barbara frowned.

The juxtaposition of Joanna's remark about a first love and the reminder of the silver mirror in her basket made her more uncomfortable. Nonsense, she thought, when one has hair like mine, one needs a comb and mirror. Her hand went up and sure enough, tendrils of her thick, curling hair had worked free of her crespine and barbette and would have to be combed and tucked away again. The mirror Alphonse had given her was small and pretty and convenient to carry, that was all.

The silence was growing marked. Joanna had stopped working and was staring blindly across the garden toward the open gate in the garden wall. Barbara's throat ached. Her uncle had been gone three weeks. News was due—overdue.

''My distaste for a second marriage has nothing to do with my first husband,'' Barbara said hastily, knowing she was talking nonsense but needing desperately to say something, anything, no matter how silly. ''You know I never even met Pierre de le Pontet de Thouzan le Thor. I told you we married by proxy and he died on his way to consummate our marriage—more than two years later. I was so far from loving him that I almost decided to fly to England to escape him. Why should I marry a second time and become some man's chattel?''

Joanna had been about to say that she was not referring to Barbara's late husband, but the last word startled her so much she asked instead, ''Am I Hugh's chattel?''

Barbara made a dismissive gesture. ''Yes. You just do not realize it because Uncle Hugh is Uncle Hugh. In any case our situations are entirely different. You were a very rich widow with young sons to protect. You had to have a strong man to fight for you. I am an aged virgin with a small manor in France ably administered by an honest and faithful clerk and overseen by that most selfless and honorable of all monarchs, Louis the Ninth.''

Joanna had started to giggle when Barbara called herself an aged virgin and continued to do so at Barbara's description of the king of France. Not that it was untrue. In fact, Louis of France was so virtuous that he was rather dull. Barbara thought him easy to deceive too, because she herself had managed to do it, but that was typical of Barbara.

Still chuckling, Joanna glanced across at Hugh's niece, seeing her for a moment as if she were a stranger. Nothing in Barbara's appearance betrayed either her age or her virginity. Possibly because she had not been subjected to ten years of childbearing, as most women of twenty-four had been, Barbara's body was as lithe and slender as that of a young girl. But her manner was not in the least virginal; it was assured, almost bold.

No, Joanna thought, the boldness was more in the way Barbara's face was made than in her manner. She was not beautiful; her features were too large and strong for beauty, but she had a fascinating face. The eyes, responding to the sunlight of the bright May morning and to Barbara's joining her aunt's laughter, shone blue instead of the dull black or sullen slate gray they often appeared. The wide, mobile mouth, its lips when she was sad or serious almost as free of any curve as her brows, had curled upward at the corners, bringing the center of the long upper lip down into a temporary bow that was eminently kissable.

The laughter did not last long. The two women glanced at each other, feeling guilty for having forgotten in a private jest how dangerous the outside world had become.

Joanna sighed. "Oh well," she said, "this is not a good time to be choosing a husband—unless you would consider going back to France. And that would solve your problems with young Simon and Guy de Montfort. I know you hate France, my love, but you must have seen the war coming. Why did you not go with Queen Eleanor last September, Barbara?"

"I could not!" Barbara exclaimed indignantly. "Father was so angry at Uncle Hugh. Surely you did not think I would run for safety when I feared at any moment I would need to thrust myself between them physically to keep them from one another's throats. Why, oh, why, could they not agree on whom to support?"

"Because," Joanna said dryly, "Hugh believes that if God chose Henry to be king, only God has the right to order the king's behavior."

There was a brief silence, in which Barbara made a wordless sound, half amusement, half despair. Then Joanna went on. "Is it more reasonable to believe that it is right for any group of men who are strong enough to bend the king to their will? That way lies chaos."

"Oh Joanna," Barbara sighed. "The king himself creates chaos."

Joanna sighed too. "As you well know, Hugh has done his best to guide King Henry away from his errors. The attempt was not a success. The king flew into a rage and dismissed Hugh from his service."

But her voice had changed over the last sentence into a dreamy softness, almost a purr of complacency. It was a most unsuitable tone for the words. Barbara, who had picked up her work and begun to set stitches, dropped it again and turned her head. "So that was why Uncle Hugh would not come to the meeting father wanted. You were the one who calmed him. I will lay odds that if you had not—"

"I never speak to your uncle about political matters," Joanna said. "It is not my place."

"Pish-tush," Barbara snapped. "I suppose you would not try to stop him if he were going to do something stupid or dangerous."

"No, I would not. He would do what he thought right anyway and only be more miserable because of my tears and entreaties."

"Joanna!" Barbara exclaimed, quite exasperated.

Joanna smiled. "Your uncle never does stupid things."

"Never does stupid things!" Barbara echoed. "What do you call his responding to King Henry's call to arms after the way he has been treated? Uncle Hugh should have spat in the king's face instead of going off to fight Leicester in his behalf. Henry is a selfish, petty, spiteful, vindictive, spendthrift—"

"But he is the *king*," Joanna interrupted softly. "God chose Henry, and only he has the right to rule."

But Joanna's eyes had filled with tears and she put her work aside and slid across the bench. Barbara put a sheltering arm around her aunt's shoulders. The sun had slipped behind a cloud, and a breeze was fluttering the leaves of the rose trees, which was reason enough for Joanna to shiver. But Barbara knew her aunt was not cold; Joanna was frightened. Barbara was frightened herself. She could not bear to think of her uncle and the two armies that might even now be rushing at each other somewhere in the south.

Joanna had slipped her arm around Barbara's waist, and the two women clung together. In a war, no matter who won, Barbara thought bitterly, the women always lost. And Joanna's situation, with her sons on one side and her husband on the other, was heart-wrenching. Was everyone in England so torn apart? Did everyone have some dear one who supported the king, as did her Uncle Hugh, and another who was sworn to the earl of Leicester, as was her own father? There must be no battle, Barbara thought desperately; surely someone would find a way to make peace. She clutched Joanna closer, and Joanna shuddered again.

"Let us go in, you are cold," Barbara said.

"No." Joanna found a smile, released her grip, and sat back, but she did not move away or reach for her work. "The sun is coming from behind the cloud now. And it was not cold that made me shiver. I was thinking of the king."

Their glances met and shifted guiltily because of the unspoken thought in both minds: Henry III of England was old. Why could he not die? Why did he live on and on, bringing misery to all? Barbara thought again of what she had said, and it was true. The king *was* selfish, petty, spiteful, vindictive, and spendthrift; unfortunately he was also both more and less than that. Henry was more in that he was clever, often brilliant, in devising political expedients to escape the consequences of his blunders and to thrust the blame for them onto others. He was less in that he was basically weak and had, despite his fifty-seven years of age, a kind of hopeful innocence that seemed to prevent him from learning from his mistakes. Barbara bit her lip. It was the weakest part of the king's nature that was the most dangerous; that hopeful innocence made even Henry's worst enemies wish to help him and protect him.

The bitten lip did not dam speech for long. Barbara burst out, "How can Uncle Hugh allow himself to be seduced over and over by that man?" And then she choked on a sob that was half laughter. "How can I be so stupid as to ask, when Henry does the same thing to me too, each time I speak to him."

Joanna's lips almost curved into a smile and then drooped again. "The king is not an evil person. His faults are those we all understand too well. Those he loves, he loves too much, so he is blind to the wrong they do. He is of expansive spirit, generous, and gives away what he should not; then when he feels the pinch he seeks a way to get back what he gave so blithely. He is easily frightened and under duress promises what he knows is wrong."

"He is not fit to be a king," Barbara snapped. "He needs a governor, and you know it."

"That does not make it right to govern him," Joanna said slowly. "It was by God's will that he was crowned. It is not for us to question God's will. If His holy purpose is served in some way by our suffering, then we must endure with patience."

Barbara jumped up and stamped her foot. "You cannot tell me Hugh believes all that. I know he agreed with my father when Leicester first urged the barons to accept the Provisions of Oxford, and he knew quite well that the purpose of the Provisions was to govern the king."

Joanna shook her head. "To help the king govern. That is the difference between what happened when the Provisions were first signed and now. In 1258 the king was willing to accept the Provisions. Henry was truly distressed when he learned of the terrible abuses that had crept into his government and desired that they be amended. But the king became dissatisfied with the reforms over the next three years."

"You mean he missed his greedy and accursed lick-spittle relatives more than he cared about his kingdom," Barbara retorted. Then she bit her lip. "Not that I care. I only care for papa and Uncle Hugh. Good God, I know Leicester is just as seductive as the king, but could not my father and Uncle Hugh at least have been seduced by the same man?"

"Neither Henry nor Leicester had much influence on Hugh's decision. In the beginning Hugh supported the Provisions of Oxford with all his heart. But when he saw how they were being used, not only to cure ills but to overturn the natural order, how the king's right to rule was being taken from him, against the will of God, by Leicester and his party, Hugh had to side with Henry. I do not think the king seduced Hugh. He is not easily seduced—"

Joanna stopped abruptly and blushed; Barbara saw the blush with her eyes, but it meant nothing to her at the moment. She was remembering her father's admission that many of the barons had not realized where the Provisions of Oxford must lead if they were fulfilled to the letter. Papa himself had not understood the full ramifications until the king's will had conflicted with the Provisions three years after they had been sworn to by all. Then her father had been forced to decide whether his oath stood above the will of a bad king or whether the anointing of a weak man as king set that man above all oaths, as Joanna claimed. Papa had decided one way; Hugh had decided the other.

Barbara slowly sank down on the bench again. Three years earlier her sympathies had been with her Uncle Hugh's Royalist point of view, but she now knew her father was right about the king being unfit to rule. Henry had not only bent the Provisions of Oxford but had arranged for the pope to declare them null and void. And then, as in the past, the king had repeated every mistake that had brought him into conflict with his barons in the first place. Henry had interfered with the special court sessions meant to redress judicial and financial abuses, and he had recalled his Lusignan half brothers, who had caused such turmoil by their cruelty and rapacity.

When Hugh was dismissed from his office by the king, Barbara had been distressed and asked leave of the queen to visit her uncle. She had not told her father where she was going because she had been afraid he would either forbid her to visit Hugh or urge her to plead with Hugh to oppose the king again, which Barbara felt would be cruel at such a time. But her visit had been brief. Her uncle was not brokenhearted, as she had feared; indeed, Hugh had looked well and rested for the first time since the Provisions had been signed.

Relieved and delighted, Barbara had gone on to Framlingham Castle and confessed to her father that she had been at Kirby Moorside, Hugh's favorite manor. Norfolk forgave her when she told him that Hugh seemed settled into private life without regret, but he would not agree that she should end her service with the queen. She was a clever chick, her father said, and her eyes and ears at court were useful to him. Unless Eleanor dismissed her out of spite over his opposition to Henry, her father insisted she continue to go to court for her regular months of service and be meek and listen, even if she had to bite her tongue when Eleanor criticized him.

More than three years had passed without giving Barbara much reason to worry about Hugh's withdrawal from participation in the king's government. Even though matters had gone from bad to worse, Hugh had kept himself quietly retired. She knew he was not happy about the state of the realm, but because her father and her uncle quarreled each time they met, she had seen less and less of Hugh and Joanna.

Serving at court was horrid. When Hugh and her father were summoned at the same time—and the king seemed deliberately to demand they attend him together—they seemed to Barbara to be a hairbreadth from drawing knives on each other. Nor was her life much easier when her father and uncle were absent. The king's sycophants said offensive things about Norfolk when he was not there, and the courtiers who were of Leicester's party made bad worse by trying to protect her. Leicester himself had sullenly retired to France, riding a high horse of pride, after Henry had seized the reins of government again. But the barony in general seemed sunk into apathy, allowing the king to go his own way, except for stubbornly refusing to help him extricate himself from his increasing financial woes.

Then a quarrel between Henry's son, Prince Edward, and his steward Roger Leybourne had been blown out of all proportion, and in the past year the barons had again combined and risen against the king. Edward had acted like a stupid hothead at first and temporarily lost the support of the lords of the Welsh Marches, who had been his most faithful friends. In their initial rage, the Marcher lords had asked Leicester to return to England and lead them. There had been some minor battles in the west, and the king had withdrawn to London. But even there he found no real support. Instead of being protected, the king had found himself trapped in the Tower of London, and the people of London had stoned Queen Eleanor's barge when she tried to leave the city.

Terrified by the violent hostility of the Londoners, who had always supported him in the past, the weathercock king had again promised everything to everyone and, as soon as his tether was relaxed, had gone back on his promises—and the weary round was about to be danced again. There were differences, however. Although the king had not changed, everyone else had. This time Leicester seemed to have made up his mind to fight. King Henry would have been helpless, but Prince Edward had learned a sharp lesson too and had made his peace with the Welsh Marcher lords—but he had made peace with his old friends in order to make war on Leicester. Not all desired war, but so much harm had been done, so much bitterness aroused, that few were able to keep their balance.

Barbara's hands were again idle, even though she held her needle poised over the sleeve cuff she was embroidering. She was recalling miserably that even her father, who knew it was wrong to fight, had said bitterly that he could only hold back so long.

"They will call me a coward," the earl of Norfolk had mumbled, half turning his head from Barbara in shame after his chaplain had read him the earl of Leicester's letter and he had waved the man away. "But it is wrong to bear arms against the king—and yet, Leicester has tried everything else."

"You are no coward," Barbara had cried. "No one will even think it, papa. If more men had your good sense and no one on either side would fight, there could be no war."

Her passionate remark had brought a faint smile and a rough hug, but then Norfolk had straightened and stood looking out of the window at the teeming rain, one hand still resting on Barbara's shoulder. At last he had said, "If it comes to battle, Leicester will win, you know. If I thought he needed my help, I would go, but he has men enough and is a far better soldier than any who support Henry."

That was the first time Barbara remembered thinking beyond the fact of the danger in fighting to the results of a great battle won or lost. Until then fighting between the two parties had been raids and skirmishes—tests of strength, perhaps, but with no major effects. She had cried out, "It will not come to battle. It must not! But—but if it does and Leicester wins, what will happen to those who opposed him? What will happen to Uncle Hugh?"

"I will do my best for him," Norfolk had said slowly, "but I do not know how much influence I still have. Leicester is not pleased with me.'' He shrugged and his lips twisted. ''You heard his letter. He thinks me not sufficiently committed to the cause. But if Hugh will remain quiet, I know Leicester will leave him in peace.''

Barbara's relief over those words, and her gladness that her father wished to protect his brother despite all their quarrels, had made her smile and say ''Surely he will. I am very certain that Uncle Hugh is sick of King Henry and his lies and excuses.''

It had been a shock when her father shook his head and said, ''I wish I were sure. I am afraid that Hugh, thinking as I think—that the king is the weaker—will answer Henry's call to arms. Also, he may hope to serve as peacemaker.''

''Then you must go to Uncle Hugh. You must stop him.''

''I dare not go, chick.'' Her father's scarred knuckles had stroked her cheek. ''First because Hugh would not listen to me. Second because I might be accused of some conspiracy with him. Guy de Montfort did not come here only to carry a letter from his father. He asked some strange questions of my steward and master-at-arms.'' He hesitated and looked down at her and suddenly smiled. ''But you can go to talk with Hugh.''

Barbara had left the very next day for Kirby Moorside despite the continuing rain. She had a head full of reasoned arguments supplied by her father to convince Hugh it was his duty to refuse to respond to the king's summons to arms. She had been too late; Hugh had been gone when she arrived.

Remembering, a wave of cold passed over Barbara and she glanced up, but the sun was still shining. She did not speak, only swallowed hard, laid down her work, and took Joanna's hand in hers. At least, she thought, she had had sense enough not to tell Joanna the real reason why she had come. That could only have added to her aunt's fear for Hugh. The tale of wishing to escape the lewd attentions of Leicester's younger sons had been the first idea to pop into her head because Guy had made a nuisance of himself whenever he contrived to catch her away from her father. Now the memory of her father's remark about Guy's ''strange questions'' came together with her fear that her uncle might be imprisoned or his lands confiscated, and she suddenly wondered how a victory for Leicester might affect her. Might she be considered a spoil of war, particularly if she were taken here, in an ''enemy'' household? Might Guy believe that evidence gathered against her father could be used to silence Norfolk if she were despoiled?

Barbara uttered a gasp of laughter as she realized how fear could inflate one's self-importance. Her father held wide lands from which many men and rich supplies of grain could be mustered, and he commanded many miles of the eastern coast that could be used to land mercenaries from the Continent if he did not oppose the landing. If Guy was trying to find evidence to accuse her father of disloyalty, it would be so that another governor could be set over Norfolk for those reasons, not because that spoiled child desired her. Probably he had only reached for her because she was there and he, like so many others, could not believe that she neither wished to take the veil nor used her single state to lie with any man at any time without the interference of a husband.

"Tell me," Joanna said, squeezing Barbara's hand. "I would like a cause to laugh, even at myself."

Because she had been thinking about Guy's clumsy attempts on her, Barbara recalled Joanna's last words and her blush. She realized that something had happened between her aunt and uncle. When she had been part of their household, Joanna and Hugh had been comfortable together but more like polite acquaintances than devoted husband and wife. Though both had done their marital duty and produced children, nothing in their relationship, even three years ago, could have called a blush to Joanna's cheek.

Add to that blush Joanna's urging a second marriage on her and Barbara decided that whatever had happened was very good. It was also none of her business, Barbara thought, so all she said was "It just came to me that young Simon was not really trying to seduce me at all and Guy, that idiot, was only after me to imitate his brother."

"I do not believe it," Joanna said with a smile. "You have never come to see that you are now a very attractive woman, no longer a scrawny child with features too big for her face. Why do you say Simon was not interested in you?"

"Because he was only ardent when Aliva le Despenser was there to see him," Barbara replied, her brows going up in challenge.

"And Guy?" Joanna asked. Then before Barbara answered she went on, "Do not be a fool, my dear. Make a chance to speak to Leicester at the first opportunity. Even if Simon was trying to make Aliva jealous, Guy is the kind who is enraged by refusal. If you leapt at his offer, he would soon be bored and forget you, but if you deny him, he will desire to break your will. Now a word from his father hinting that you have taken his advances too seriously will let Guy turn away from you with contempt. He will enjoy the notion that he is scorning you and depressing your pretensions, so no ill will will linger in him."

"But I would like to arouse ill will in that nasty, vicious— Oh, I cannot even think of a creature I would soil with comparison,"

Barbara protested. "I was about to call him a toad, but I rather like toads. They have such beautiful eyes."

"You like all animals," Joanna chuckled. "I have seen you avoid stepping on an ant or a slimy worm."

"You would not see me avoid stepping on Guy," Barbara remarked tartly. "Slimy or not, worms are very interesting. Guy is not." Then she caught the anxious expression on Joanna's face and sighed. "I suppose you are right, but I do not need to think about it while I am with you. Guy will not come here."

"No."

The sudden flatness of Joanna's voice made Barbara wish she had stopped after admitting that Joanna was right about telling Leicester as soon as possible that she believed his son was growing too enamored. She had meant only that Guy was not interested enough in her to pursue her all the way to Yorkshire, but it was clear that Joanna had taken the remark to mean that Guy would not come to a manor of his father's enemy. And before Barbara could think of how to explain, Joanna spoke again.

"But I do not think you should be here with me." Her voice trembled just a little. "I have done very wrong to allow you to stay so long. I thought it could not matter for a few days. Hugh was only just gone and you were such a comfort to me. But I have been a coward to cling to you for three weeks. You must go back to your father. It would look very bad for him if—"

Her voice stuck on the next word and Barbara rushed desperately into speech. "There is no reason at all to drive me out, Joanna. You are just trying to punish me by exposing me to Guy because I will not take your advice and rush off to France to choose a husband."

Barbara expected a denial and a heated defense, but her aunt did not respond other than by an urgent pressure on Barbara's hand and a sharp gesture for silence. Joanna's head tilted and her whole body stiffened in an attitude of listening. Barbara's breath caught. She heard it too, now that the sound of her own voice did not fill her ears. Very faintly from beyond the palisade and moat she heard the thud of horses' hooves and a thin ringing of metal harness. Armed men were passing outside of the manor's defenses.

Chapter 2

Barbara snatched up her work basket as she leapt to her feet and then felt a fool, for there was nothing in it that could protect her. The thought made her feel even more foolish; the troop that had passed was small and could not be dangerous even to the lightly defended manor house. Nonetheless, for a moment she was rigid with fear, staring blankly at the wall until all hint of sound faded. In another moment her panic eased. Barbara became aware that she was standing beside Joanna still clasping the basket to her. She put it down on the bench, picked up the sleeve cuff she had been embroidering, folded it, and tucked it in with the thread, the comb, and the silver mirror.

"Shall we go in?" she asked, turning to her aunt.

Having recovered from panic herself, Barbara was shocked to see how pale Joanna had become. She put a hand under her aunt's arm to support her, but Joanna's voice was quite steady when she said, "No, I left word that I would be in the garden. The guard at the gate will send any messenger here."

Messenger? Barbara did not repeat the word aloud. A messenger did not come with an armed troop, and Joanna knew that. But perhaps the men were only passing the manor. A distant shout—the hail of the guard at the gate, Barbara was sure, although she could not make out the words—ended that brief hope and the faint flicker of expectation that it might be her uncle coming home. The guard would not have questioned him.

"Perhaps you should go in," Joanna said. "No one need know you are here."

"I will not." Barbara's response was immediate. "We are witness for each other if any abuse is offered."

Joanna did not reply, and Barbara guessed she had not listened; she was not afraid for herself or for Barbara. Neither moved or spoke again until Hugh Bigod's old master-at-arms came through the open gate in the inner garden wall and hurried toward them. Barbara could feel Joanna's arm stiffen in her hand as she braced herself, and her own heart sank again, for she thought the old man looked frightened.

As soon as he was close enough not to need to shout, he said, "My lady, the earl of Norfolk begs admittance."

"Father?" Barbara exclaimed, feeling an instant of joy and relief. But then she had to tighten her grip on Joanna, who wavered on her feet, and both joy and relief fled.

"Yes," Joanna whispered, clutching at Barbara, and as the man came forward, his head cocked to show he had not heard her, she nodded.

"Yes," Barbara repeated as she steadied Joanna. "Bid him enter and come to us here as quickly as he can."

She helped her aunt to sit down and stood beside her, one arm around her shoulders. She could think of nothing to say, no comfort to offer. Tears stood in her eyes and then began slowly to trickle down her cheeks. If her father had come, the news must be very bad, worse than confiscated estates. Uncle Hugh must be in prison or hurt or—or dead.

"Hugh is safe, whole and safe."

Norfolk's rough bellow, the words shouted from the entrance gate in his eagerness to give good news, was like heavenly music. Barbara ran forward to embrace her father. Joanna, who had bounded to her feet, was barely a step behind.

"It is not all good news," the earl warned, sliding his left arm around Barbara's waist and taking Joanna's hand in his right.

"He is not wounded?" Joanna asked, and when Norfolk shook his head, she smiled with clear-eyed joy. "Then I do not care for any other bad news. If he is taken prisoner, I will find ransom for him. I have my jewels and my own lands to draw upon—"

"You will need no ransom. Hugh is fled to France."

"To France—" Joanna looked around as if surprised at finding herself still in the garden instead of packing. "Then I will go—"

"You will not!" Norfolk exclaimed, dropping Joanna's hand. "Fool of a woman! I thought better of you, Joanna. There are more important considerations than your desire for your husband's company."

Color flooded into Joanna's face. "What would you, of all men, know of that consideration?" she asked in a voice Barbara had never heard her use before.

"I know there has been a major battle at Lewes," Norfolk roared, "and that any hope the king will ever again rule by his own sweet will, throwing plums to his favorites, is over for good."

Pure shock at the cruelty of Joanna's remark—for her father's long unhappiness in his marriage and his attempt to free himself from it was public knowledge—had held Barbara silent. It was totally uncharacteristic behavior; Joanna was never cruel. Nor was she ever sharp-tongued, but now Barbara saw her draw breath, clearly to answer as angrily as her father had spoken. Before even more unforgivable words were said, Barbara pushed Joanna back and stepped between her and Norfolk.

"Joanna!" she cried. "Look at my father's clothes and his eyes. He has been riding night and day—have you not, papa? He has come to protect you and to protect Uncle Hugh as well as he can. You must listen to the whole story before you decide anything. Let us all go in so father can sit down and have some wine."

"Joanna," Norfolk said, moderating his tone, "King Henry and Prince Edward are now Leicester's prisoners. In fact, nearly every important supporter of Henry has been taken prisoner. If you go to Hugh in France, your lands will be swallowed up by Leicester's followers. I intend to lay claim to Hugh's property; after all, it was my mother's first—but I could offer no reason for taking yours."

"My son Baldwin will be released from prison now," Joanna said angrily. "Will he not be favored with my lands if I go to France? Surely he deserves at least that, since he suffered imprisonment in Leicester's great cause. Or is the high and pure earl of Leicester so little different from the king he blames? Are you telling me that Leicester too will only gift his own sons and his powerful supporters with the prizes he wrests from those who fought honestly for what they believed right?"

"At least his sons have roots in this land," Norfolk began hotly, but stopped when Barbara took his arm, turned him about, and gave him a sharp push.

"Go in, I beg you," she cried. "I will be on your heels." And then, turning to Joanna, "What ails you? Can you not see that you are the only one who can safely try to win permission for Hugh to return? If my father or even Baldwin interceded in Hugh's behalf, his loyalty would come into question at once. You are no threat, and Leicester will think it right and proper for a wife to try to arrange for her husband's pardon. Come, Joanna, gather up our sewing, then go and lie down for a little time and recover from your fright. I will see to my father's care. His temper will also be better for a rest, a clean gown, and a cup of wine."

Joanna raised her hands to her face for a moment and uttered a stifled sob, but she dropped them and turned back toward the bench where they had been sitting. As soon as she was sure Joanna would do as she had asked, Barbara ran quickly after her father. She caught up with him outside of the garden; he was staring at the handsome stone manor house from which a thatch-roofed walk extended to the kitchen building. Voices and laughter drifted from the latter, mingling with the occasional bark of a dog from the kennel attached to the near side of the barn and stable across the courtyard and the distant clang of the blacksmith's hammer from his shed just beyond the pens for animals fattening for slaughter.

"Hugh has done well with this place," he said when she took his arm.

"It is a great favorite with all of us." Barbara tugged at him gently, and he walked with her toward the house. "One can see out across the hills from the windows of the hall. Come, you will feel better when you have shed that mail and filled your belly."

"Will I?"

"Of course you will." She hugged his arm affectionately to her side. "You know you are always cross when you miss a meal, and I am sure you have missed more than one, coming in haste from Norfolk."

He raised a hand to pull at a thick curl that had snaked its way through the net of gold silk that, as usual, was losing the battle of controlling her hair. "I have not missed any meals, but I admit they were not such as I cared to linger over."

"Well, that is the same," Barbara said, releasing his arm so he could climb the narrow stair to the open door. "Go up, papa, do. As soon as you have eaten, you will see that matters could be worse."

He laughed harshly at that, but climbed the stair without any other reply. Normally Barbara would have taken him into Joanna's solar, but her father and her aunt would be better apart for a while and Joanna's bed was in the solar. Thus, Barbara gestured to one of the dozen or so menservants, who were busy about various duties in the hall. The man hurried to her and began to help the earl remove his mail while Barbara ran across the hall into the solar. There she opened a clothes chest from which she drew a surcoat and tunic, a fine linen shirt, and thin, footed woolen chausses.

Norfolk was stripped to shirt and hose when she came back and was standing at a window with its shutters open to the sweet spring air and sun. He shook his head when she asked if he wanted a bath, and continued to stare out toward the hills, bright green with spring growth beyond the plowed fields, until the manservant brought a basin of water for washing and a towel.

Turning at Barbara's touch, he pulled off his shirt and scrubbed his broad, hairy torso with the washing cloth, then let Barbara dry him and slip the clean shirt over his head. When she had tied the sleeves, he pushed off his undergarments under the shirt and sat down in the short window seat. The manor house was a substantial building, but its walls were nowhere near the ten- or twelve-foot thickness of a keep's. There was room in the inlet bays that held the arched windows for only a single wooden seat on either side.

As Barbara knelt to pull off her father's chausses and fit the feet of the fresh pair on, he turned his head sharply. Barbara looked up also and saw Joanna pass among the workers and idlers—who sought suddenly to look busy—through the hall and into the solar.

"What the devil has got into her?" Norfolk asked his daughter.

"I am not sure, papa." Barbara pulled the fresh chausses up to her father's knees, letting go when he took the garment from her and got up to draw it up to his waist. "But . . ."

He looked down. "But?" he echoed, making clear that he wanted to hear any idea Barbara had, which was not always the case.

"I think she has fallen in love with Hugh."

"Fallen—"

The word came out in a roar, and Barbara jumped to her feet and put her hand over her father's mouth.

"You silly filly," he went on, but much more softly. "She has been Hugh's wife for twenty years. Is it not a little late for 'love'? You have been reading those stupid tales again and are growing addle-witted."

"Papa—"

"*Merde!*" He turned away toward the window again. "If I had known that Queen Marguerite would take it into her head to have you taught to read, I would never have left you with her in France. You are spoiled. And I am at fault too. I should have married you properly as soon as I brought you home, instead of allowing you to—"

Barbara put her hand on her father's shoulder. "Now, papa,

you are not at fault. We have talked before of the complications of getting me married because my lands are in France and I am in King Louis's gift. Forget about it. I have been content, and I am not dreaming of love. I know it seems strange to say that Joanna has fallen in love with the husband she has had for twenty years, but I have good reason to think so. In any case, she is different from when I lived with her and Uncle Hugh. She never really cared then whether he was with her or not. Now she cannot bear to be parted from him. Papa, would it really matter so much if she went to France?"

Norfolk turned around, but he did not answer his daughter's question at once, remaining silent as Barbara pulled on and laced his tunic, slipped the tabard-style surcoat over it, and fastened that with a supple leather belt. He glanced at his sword belt, which lay across the opposite window seat, then around at the hall, but there were only unarmed servants about. His men at the gate and in the courtyard would make sure now that no armed men came in to attack him, and he let his sword lie where it was.

"Now you listen to me, chick," he said at last. "I came here for a double purpose, only partly for Hugh's good. The other part is for the good of the realm—as *I* see it. I swear to you that I love Hugh and do not wish to see his property despoiled. I intend to have it whole and safe for him on the day he can win a pardon for his misguided support of Henry. But I also intend to make a pardon his only way back to England."

"But what has that to do with Joanna?" Barbara asked. "She . . . Oh, dear sweet Mary, will you hold Aunt Joanna hostage for Uncle Hugh's behavior?"

"Yes," Norfolk said, then laughed suddenly at the stricken expression on his daughter's face. "But I promise you I do not intend to hang Joanna if Hugh works for an invasion or even leads one. In fact, I will take an oath to keep Joanna safe, protect her and the younger children and her lands—by force of arms, if necessary—if she should be declared a traitor for her husband's crimes, and—"

"Oh, thank you, father," Barbara burst out before she thought. An instant later she drew in an appalled gasp and cried, "Papa! You are a monster!"

"So?"

"You know that will tie Uncle Hugh's hands even tighter because then whatever he does will get you in trouble too."

"Not whatever he does. If he strives for the settlement that Leicester has proposed, which will include pardons for all those who will accept the Provisions of Oxford, no one will be in trouble."

"I will be in trouble," Barbara pointed out. "If Uncle Hugh and Joanna suspect I told you how important they have become to one another, they will both hate me forever."

"Nonsense. What you said has nothing to do with my decision." He frowned and shook his head when she started to speak, then raised his brows. "Chick, did you not promise me something to eat when you lured me in here?"

Barbara turned to look for an idle servant to send for food, only to see Joanna coming toward them leading a manservant carrying a small table and a maidservant with a laden tray. She had been aware of movement in the hall, but there were always people coming and going so neither she nor her father had paid any attention. When Barbara did not answer him, Norfolk looked out into the hall and also saw Joanna. His lips thinned.

"My lord, forgive me," Joanna said softly, curtsying low. "I did very wrong to missay you and—"

"Stop that bobbing up and down," Norfolk said irritably, gesturing at Joanna to rise, "and do not be more of a ninny than you must. We have been brother and sister for more than twenty years. Do you think I do not understand that you are at your wit's end with worry? And you might consider that I am fond of Hugh also. Sit."

He gestured for Barbara to remove his sword and belt from the seat opposite to him, and she picked it up and leaned it against his thigh, knowing that he seldom let the weapon out of his sight, even in his own great hall. As the servants set out the food, Joanna seated herself and Barbara pointed at a stool, which was carried to her father's side. His hand went to his breast when he saw the platter held slices of meat as well as a large wedge of cheese, but he was not wearing an eating knife. Before his head turned, Barbara had the knife out of its sheath on his sword belt and the hilt under his hand.

"Thank you, chick," he said. He drew the blade across the meat, folded the strip, pinned it together with the knife point, and stuffed it in his mouth. "Do you want to talk now, Joanna," he asked thickly, "or do you want to make ready to leave first and listen to my explanations later? Leave you must, before one of your neighbors hears that Hugh is proscribed and decides to take this place. I have troops on the way to all Hugh's properties to hold them, and I will leave my troop captain here with some of the men. That should be enough to safeguard this place under my claim—but only if you are gone from it."

"Will you not let me go to Hugh?" she asked. "I will leave the children with you. I will take nothing—"

He laid down the knife. "No. There are many reasons, Joanna, but even if I were willing you could not go. The ports are all closed. Leicester will let no one in or out of the country except those he chooses to present the settlement he is offering. Would you rather be in his keeping than in mine?"

There was a moment of silence during which Barbara held her breath and Norfolk picked up his knife again with a slight clatter. He had, rather savagely, hacked off a hunk of cheese and speared it on the knife point when Joanna drew the back of her hand across her wet cheeks.

"He would at least be more polite to me than you are." She uttered a watery chuckle. "Likely he would convince me that I had wanted to be in his keeping from the beginning or that it was best for everyone, even Hugh and me, if I was."

"If you ran for a port," Norfolk said sourly, "you would never see Leicester. You would be a name on a list, perhaps shackled with other prisoners for months before he knew you had been taken. But if you prefer him as host, I will take you to him personally—"

"Oh no, Roger." Joanna put out a pleading hand. "I was only trying to make a little lightness out of my heart's heaviness." Then, on an indrawn breath, she added, "I had not thought I might be taken and kept as a prisoner. Will Hugh think of that?"

"Not unless he has reason to believe you would try to get to him." He stopped abruptly as color crimsoned Joanna's cheeks and cast a swift glance at Barbara.

She caught the quick glance and cursed herself for mentioning the new bond that seemed to have grown between Joanna and her husband. "Hugh will be worried sick if he does not hear from Joanna in any case," she said. "Did you not yourself say, papa, that you had come to prevent an attack on Kirby Moorside when news of the battle spread? Hugh might fear that. I will say this. If you bring Joanna to Leicester, he will let her send a letter to Hugh."

"I am sure he will. I am less sure that what is in the letter will be much comfort to Hugh."

"But it would surely prevent Hugh from trying any desperate act to save me." Joanna clasped her hands. "Roger, please let me go. I know you can put me in a fishing boat in some tiny village—"

"Curse you, woman! Use the brains God gave you, if He gave brains to any woman!"

Barbara stood up. She was agonized for Joanna, whom she

could see was in terror that Hugh would try to come to her rescue and be hurt. And if Hugh had become as besotted as his wife, for all Barbara knew Joanna might be right. She was frightened for her father too, because he might be ruined and become an outcast to both parties if Joanna, who was cleverer than he guessed, grew desperate and escaped.

"Papa cannot let you go, Joanna," she said. "Unless you plan to murder every man, woman, and child in this area, it would be easy to discover that he came here before you left. Then he would be in deep trouble. Leicester might call him a traitor. Still"—Barbara turned to her father—"I think Joanna is right, papa. Somehow word must be sent to Uncle Hugh that she and the younger children are all safe."

"Not through me," Norfolk said. "Leicester will be busy enough not to give any thought to Joanna, and I would like matters to remain just so. He is no fool. He must have eyes and ears set around Queen Eleanor, and it is to her in Boulogne that Hugh will go, I suppose. Through those eyes and ears, Leicester will surely hear if Hugh has had a letter from Joanna. He would blame me for that, and I do not know whether my temper would hold through another visitation from young Guy—"

"Guy!" Barbara exclaimed. "Perhaps he is the answer to this problem."

"Guy only makes problems. You stay away from him," Norfolk growled and addressed himself with more attention to the food before him.

"Barbara—" Joanna began warningly, but Barbara shook her head and her aunt fell silent.

With eyes that hardly saw, Barbara watched her father eat another slice of meat and a third of the cheese, washing down both with draughts of wine. A muddle of thoughts had filled her head when her father said Guy's name. The first, come in a flash, was that Leicester's victory at Lewes would make Guy's attentions harder to avoid. Her father would almost certainly be deeply involved in government business again, which would mean many messages from and meetings with Leicester and his sons. Almost simultaneously the word "court" had brought to mind her father's saying that Queen Eleanor was not at the French court but living in Boulogne, where news of her husband and England could come across the narrow sea every day. Atop those ideas was her awareness of Joanna's misery and Hugh's and the hurt their fears for each other might do her father. At which point, a clear solution had appeared in her mind. If she went to the queen in Boulogne, she would be safe from Guy; she could calm all Hugh's fears; Joanna, knowing that, would cause her father no trouble; and she herself would not need to go near the French court, where she might see Alphonse—not that that mattered at all.

"That is the excuse I could use to go to France—my need to escape from Guy," she said.

"What!" Norfolk roared, slamming his knife down on the tray so hard that the table teetered and Joanna had to reach out and steady it.

"Now do not lose your temper, papa. Guy is no danger to me, but it is true that he seemed much struck with me when he was at Framlingham. I did not encourage him and paid no mind to his babbling. I know you do not like him, and to speak the truth, papa, I cannot endure him. He is a nasty little creature."

"*His* babbling! What are *you* babbling about?"

"What I am trying to tell you is coming out all backwards because I do not want you to fly into a rage."

"Why do I feel that I am about to have a ring slipped through my nose?" Norfolk asked the wall above Joanna's head. Then he looked sidelong at his daughter.

Barbara smiled at him. "Father dear, you know I am not so clumsy as to let you catch a hint of it when I am about to cozen you. I only want you to listen to me without oversetting the table."

She began with a much expurgated version of Guy's pursuit, emphasizing the sweet words and moonling looks rather than the crude attempts at physical seduction. What emerged was a picture of a very young man besotted with an older woman. She explained that she had not earlier thought it worthwhile to mention the matter; with Queen Eleanor in France, she would not be going to court and felt she would be able to avoid Guy until he forgot about her.

"But I cannot bear him, papa," she repeated, "and with Leicester grown so great by this victory, perhaps Guy would think he could have me. Then you would have to refuse . . . You would refuse, would you not? Guy would not make a good husband. He is vicious and mean."

Norfolk's gesture stopped her. "I would refuse. So. You have the ring in. Do not waste my time. Let me see in which direction you want to pull me."

Barbara put a placating hand on her father's shoulder. "If you refused Leicester's offer of his son, there would be ill feeling. Guy is a third son, but I was born outside the marriage bond. So if you went to Leicester and said you did not think a natural daughter good enough for his son and that I had ideas above my station, Leicester would be grateful to you and would not take offense. And you could urge that I be sent away to France, out of Guy's way, so he would be safe from me."

"And I might choke on the words."

"To keep Uncle Hugh quiet, father? Surely you could eat a small piece of pride for your brother's good."

"I could eat a large piece of pride—if I felt sure the meal would end with that subtlety." He turned his head to look first at Joanna, who was staring at him with tear-filled eyes and had folded her hands as if in prayer, and then out of the window again, where a four-ox plow team was coming down a lane between two fields.

Joanna shifted her eyes to Barbara and silently mouthed, "Thank you, my love."

Barbara barely moved her head to acknowledge that she understood. Now that her father had taken up the idea, she knew that she must not intrude herself into his deliberations in any way. Sometimes she could urge his thoughts in one direction or another, but he was now suspicious of being manipulated and would reject everything out of hand if he felt prodded.

"The queen asked you to accompany her to France in September, although she knows you hate France—why?" Norfolk asked suddenly.

Startled by the change of subject, Barbara answered without thinking, "I do not hate France, I . . . Oh, that does not matter anyway. I think Queen Eleanor only wanted to protect me. She has been so fearful since those Londoners stoned her barge. She thought she was offering me a haven."

"And you refused her favor. Was she not angry?"

"No, not at all." Barbara looked down at her toes. "I gave her a fanciful reason for wishing to stay, but one with which she was content. I have served her a long time and know what she will believe."

"So she would welcome you if you went to Boulogne?"

Now Barbara followed the direction of her father's thoughts. "I am not certain," she admitted. "I have heard that she has been growing more and more bitter. If she feels I am more loyal to you than to her, she might refuse to take me back into her household."

"But you have no reason to believe she would reject you without at least one meeting?"

"I am sure Queen Eleanor would receive me," Barbara agreed. "Taking me as a lady again might be . . . doubtful."

"If she does not, you could lodge with Hugh," Joanna said.

Barbara looked anxiously at her father, but he nodded to that abruptly and dismissively, and said, "I cannot say to Simon that I want you to go to France. He must think of that for himself."

Joanna bit her lip and Norfolk stared at her sightlessly, thinking about the problem. After a little while, Barbara giggled suddenly and said, "I think I can manage that. I will tell Guy's mother of the grip I have on her son—"

Norfolk choked. Leicester's wife was King Henry's own sister and far prouder than her husband. Leicester might actually welcome Barbara as a wife for his third son, but his wife would never agree and, fortunately, Leicester loved her deeply and would never force her to accept Barbara as a daughter-by-marriage.

"Clever chick," Norfolk said, grinning. "You had better come with me to London and flaunt your conquest of Guy in his mother's face before I speak to Leicester. I agree. If you do that, you will be on the next ship out of England."

Chapter 3

Alphonse d'Aix cursed under his breath and leaned closer to the window of the bedchamber of his lodging in Paris, hoping the slight increase in light would help him decipher his brother's scrawl. He knew the trouble was not in the dull gray light of the rainy morning, however; nor was it actually in Raymond's writing, although Alphonse was convinced it had grown worse over the years he had been receiving information and instructions from his brother. As political affairs had grown more complex, Raymond's letters had grown more obscure. There was always the chance that King Louis would ask Alphonse to show him a letter—the king was Raymond's overlord and had a perfect right to ask—and Raymond wished to be sure there was nothing that could make trouble in what he wrote.

That left Alys's letter. Alphonse had no complaint about the clarity of either the handwriting or the news Raymond's wife sent, but her written French was barbarous. And this letter was worse than ever before. He could barely make out every third word. Alys spoke perfectly clearly, Alphonse thought, gritting his teeth and applying himself again to her letter. Why could she not write in civilized French? And what she said was quite mad—that he was to save her father? Alphonse was ready to do all he could for William of Marlowe, of whom he was very fond, but William was in England and he was in France.

Alphonse had heard of King Henry's defeat and capture at the battle of Lewes, but he had been indifferent, not believing the battle could have any personal relevance. At the time the news had come, he had seen the deep interest it aroused in King Louis only as an opportunity to free himself gently from a mistress who had begun to talk of ridding herself of her husband. He had never given a thought to Alys's family in England. The conflict between Henry III and his barons had been going on for many years. William of Marlowe had been involved in it only as an aide to King Henry's brother, Richard of Cornwall, who had been trying to make peace between the parties. Why should William need to be "saved"? And what kind of help could Alphonse give?

The answers to those questions could no doubt be given by the man who had brought the letters and had been named by Alys as John of Hurley, the younger son of Marlowe's second wife. Alphonse gritted his teeth again; John was waiting in the solar to speak to him, but in spite of the real affection he felt for Alys and her father, Alphonse could not simply agree to any request John made.

After making out most of Alys's frantic plea, Alphonse realized that Richard of Cornwall had somehow been forced to join the fighting at Lewes. If so, of course Richard would have fought for his brother, King Henry, and William would have supported Richard, which meant that Alys's father might be in serious trouble. But if Richard was no longer the chief negotiator of peace, it was almost certain that both parties would turn to King Louis to take up that burden.

In that case, Alphonse knew he would need to move carefully if he wished to enlist King Louis's influence on William of Marlowe's behalf. Louis would take his role as arbitrator of a settlement between the earl of Leicester and King Henry most seriously and would refuse to act in the interest of any individual unless that action was presented to him as a part of a larger, satisfactory solution to the problem as a whole. Alphonse feared that John of Hurley might be nearly as hysterical as Alys's letter. He might demand instant action to free his father, and Alphonse was sure that would do more harm than good.

Sir John of Hurley, once page and squire to Hugh Bigod and now his sworn man as well as his friend, had followed Hugh to war and into exile in France. As the minutes passed, John glanced uneasily around the richly furnished chamber to which he had been led. The servant who had come to the door and taken him up to the solar had politely gestured him toward a cushioned chair flanking the raised and hooded hearth. But John, splashed to the thighs with mud, had declined to take a seat, knowing he would transfer the mud to the beautifully embroidered cushion.

He wished now that he had found an inn and a bathhouse before he came so he could have presented himself more decently to Alphonse d'Aix. Clearly Alphonse was a more delicate and elegant gentleman than John had expected. He had assumed Alphonse would be much like his brother, Raymond, comte d'Aix, who was, despite his high station, a man's man who hardly noticed such things as silken cushions or what he wore, except to be sure his armor was sound.

When he decided to come to Alphonse as soon as he arrived in Paris, John had not stopped to consider that Alphonse had spent nearly all his life as a courtier. He felt that his message was of desperate urgency; whether Sieur Alphonse would feel the same, John was less and less certain as more minutes passed and the gentleman did not come forth from his bedchamber to greet him. John could not help wondering how convincing he could be to a courtier in his present condition. He could not smell himself—his nose had become accustomed to the stink of his own sweat and his horse's—but he knew the aroma with which he was filling the room was not delicate.

"I am very sorry to take so long, but I still have great difficulty reading Alys's letters."

John turned from the fire into which he had been staring to examine the man who had finally bestirred himself to come from his bedchamber. Alphonse was as dark as Raymond; he looked darker because his eyes were black rather than blue-gray, and his black hair surrounded his face more closely. John was surprised by the features, which were larger and harsher than Raymond's. As if to compensate for that, Alphonse wore his hair longer, curling over his forehead and ears almost to his shoulders in back.

The voice was deep and pleasant but rather languid, as if the urgency and terror in Alys's letter meant little to Alphonse, and his expression was bland, totally unreadable. John did note that his speech carried much less of the accent of the south than did Raymond's, which made John wonder whether Alphonse's remark about his difficulty in reading Alys's writing was true.

"She was upset," John said, making a strong effort to keep his voice steady and not bellow with rage. "We do not know whether her father and my brother are dead or alive. We do not know what will happen to my mother and my sister-by-marriage, to our lands—"

Alphonse frowned, strode forward, and clasped John's forearm. "I was not making light of the matter. I really did have trouble reading Alys's part of the letter, and I felt I should because she often adds important details to what Raymond says. Raymond can be vague so the letter can be shown to anyone. No one ever asks to see what my sister-by-marriage wrote. Please sit down, Sir John. You must be very tired."

"I am in no condition to sit down without befouling everything I touch. If you will tell me whether you will try to obtain a meeting with King Louis for me, I will find a lodging and make myself decent."

"Lodging? Why seek a lodging?" Alphonse was truly startled; he had not been at all put off by John's stink or appearance and was shocked that Alys's brother-by-law would doubt his welcome. "Surely you will stay here with me," he went on. "Alys will kill me if I let you wander loose around Paris. And as to the meeting, I have already sent my servant with a request for an interview with my aunt, Queen Marguerite, and with the king."

Alphonse smiled when John laughed shakily. He had told John the literal truth, but his note to Queen Marguerite had been sent in the hope and conviction that the court was no longer in Paris. And his servant, Chacier, had been gone long enough now that he was nearly sure the hope was well founded. Alphonse liked John's open, expressive face, but he was very glad he would not need to present it to King Louis, haggard and filled with fear as it was even when John laughed. He needed time to convince John that a raw, emotional appeal would not work with King Louis as it would with King Henry. Not that Louis was hard-hearted. On the contrary, he was easily moved; however, experience had shown him how often strong feeling led to error, and he had become suspicious of his own sympathy to any cause other than God's.

Responding to the warmth of Alphonse's smile, John realized he had been a fool. Alphonse's comical expression of dismay when he mentioned Alys was also irresistible. John knew just how he felt. "Forgive me," he said. "I am so tired and distraught myself that I am like the man who planned to borrow an ax. You remember, he struck down him from whom he wished to obtain it without even making the request because of a slight he himself imagined while planning how to ask for the tool."

Alphonse knew the story—only in the version he had heard it was a knife the borrower wanted. He nodded. "I understand your impatience," he said, "but we can do nothing right now, not even stand with those who have petitions and wait King Louis's notice. I must discover where the king and queen are."

"You mean King Louis and Queen Marguerite are not in Paris?" John exclaimed.

"I do not know," Alphonse admitted. "When I heard about the battle at Lewes, I realized that King Louis would be fully occupied with the problems of the English for some little while and I thought it would be a good time for me to go home, so I asked for leave. I had an . . . ah . . . personal matter to attend to before I left for Aix, however, and it took me out of the city for more than a week. Yesterday and today I was packing and putting my affairs in order—"

"Good God! What am I to do?"

"Take heart." Alphonse put his hand on John's shoulder and shook it gently. "Surely if the court has gone out of Paris they have moved north to be in easier reach of news from England. I will come with you instead of going home. You will lose no time. You would have had to cover the ground anyway. And one piece of good luck brings another. We can follow the court as soon as you are rested. You are fortunate to catch me here at all. I am all packed and ready to leave. I would have been on the road for Aix by dawn tomorrow."

"No wonder you were not overjoyed to see me." John sighed. "I am sorry to have spoiled your leave. Perhaps it would be sufficient for you to give me a letter—"

"Even if it were, I would not think of it," Alphonse said. "I must go with you. Quite aside from the fact that I am very fond of William and Aubery myself and most anxious to hear what has befallen them, do you think I would dare show my face in Aix without news of them? Alys would tear me in shreds and Ray would stamp on the remains." He shook John's shoulder again as John put a hand up to his head. "Come into my bedchamber with me and take off your mail. You will have to change into more suitable clothing if the court is still here, and you must eat and sleep before you go farther if it is not."

He drew John after him toward the back of the house where a partition had been raised to provide a chamber for private business. Because it was smaller than the main room, it was also warmer and Alphonse had his bed there and his clothing. Leaving John near the hearth where a small fire had burned down to coals, Alphonse threw open a chest and pulled out a set of clothes, which he tossed onto the bed. He felt considerable relief when John took off his sword belt and untied the hood of his mail, which he seemed to have forgotten to do when he came in. Apparently, Alphonse thought, John could still think rationally and had accepted his reasoning. Nonetheless, he was glad when he heard the door in the outer chamber open and close, indicating that his servant had returned. He called out to the man to come in.

"Queen Marguerite and the king are gone to Boulogne," Chacier said. "I caught the Lord Steward just as he was sending off a packet and he put your request for an audience into it gladly, so the queen will know you are coming."

"Excellent," Alphonse said heartily. "The messenger will take three days to Boulogne, unless the news is very urgent—"

He paused and looked at Chacier, who shook his head. "I doubt it, sieur. From the look of the Lord Steward and the way he was placing scrolls in the pouch, I would say it was ordinary court business."

"Very well, then we can start tomorrow morning and arrive in Boulogne only a few hours after the messenger, our horses being the better."

"Not mine," John said, passing his hand down his face. "I fear I have ridden the poor beast close to death."

"That is no problem," Alphonse assured him, smiling. "I can provide you with a mount."

He was delighted that John had not demanded they leave at once and outride the messenger. At the moment he could not decide whether John's reasonableness was owing to common sense or to the sudden reluctance that comes when one approaches a long-sought goal and realizes it may not be what one desired after all. But later, when they were talking while having an evening meal together after John had slept a few hours, Alphonse learned that John was accustomed to the working of a court. He really knew quite well that it was impossible to thrust oneself into a royal presence without warning and with a private problem.

Thus it was not at all difficult, as they rode north the next day, for Alphonse to make clear to John the problem with King Louis's character. Both the discussions of the best way to approach King Louis and the fact that they were riding—doing something—soothed John. He did not beg to travel through the dark each night, recognizing that Queen Marguerite would need time to arrange an audience for them with her husband so that it would do no good to arrive before Alphonse's letter. By the time the walls of Boulogne were in sight, John had lost the frantic, desperate look that had so disturbed Alphonse and had begun to speak of more practical subjects—like the fact that Boulogne was packed like herring in a barrel.

"You may lodge with us," John told him. "Queen Eleanor found a house for Hugh in the town—unless you think that lodging with Hugh Bigod would prejudice King Louis against your appeal for William."

"He will not ask where I am lodging," Alphonse said. "And I

will be glad not to need to pitch a tent in a field or ride twenty miles before dawn each time I come to court. I doubt I could find lodging closer, with those who came from England and Louis's people filling the town. Usually my aunt includes me among her household for lodging when she travels with the king, but I told her I was going home."

"Good God," John said, "I hope Hugh still has the house."

"Louis is not the kind to demand his people be given the room of other noblemen—" Alphonse began.

John cut him short with an impatient gesture. "At least he would have the right. No, I was not thinking of Louis. We had some trouble with King Henry's half brothers, Guy de Lusignan and William de Valence. They insisted on having the place Queen Eleanor wished for Hugh—"

"The Lusignans." There was little expression in Alphonse's voice, but the corners of his full lips, which usually seemed to curve upward in a slight smile, drew back, making his mouth into a straight, hard line. "I will see to them if need be," he went on, shaking his head as John began to protest. "I do not think you fear them, but one must respect the wishes of one's king. Louis, I know, dislikes them for many reasons and will not be sorry to see them . . . ah . . . encouraged to leave Boulogne."

John laughed. "In a general way, I agree with you. Aside from Henry himself, there must hardly be a man alive, whatever his party, who would not be glad to see the backs of all that brood of vipers, but I must say that in this case we were grateful to them. Hugh really preferred a smaller lodging—he was very short of money, of course—and he wanted to be somewhat farther from Queen Eleanor—"

John stopped short in confusion, but Alphonse echoed his laugh. "That, too, I understand. Eleanor is my aunt, and I love her, but she has grown harder and more demanding as her husband's troubles have multiplied. And for any reasonable man, who can see that Henry's troubles are mostly of his own making, it must be very hard to deal with her. As to the money—"

"Raymond has taken care of that," John said quickly. "And Hugh and I will cover your expenses too, of course. In fact, if I had not been half out of my wits, I would never have let you pay our scores—"

"Zut!" Alphonse laughed again. "Do not be so foolish. All the money is coming from my brother's purse anyway. So what does it matter who pays it out? And my expenses? What expenses? I will not have any if I lodge with you. Moreover"—Alphonse's eyes brightened—"if we are here some weeks, someone will get up a tournament in a neighboring town, and I will make a handsome profit on all the young fools in the area who want to try to overset me."

He held up a hand as John was about to speak and rose in his stirrups, pointing ahead to what seemed to be a mob around the gate they were approaching.

"What can have happened?" John groaned.

"Nothing, except an unusually rich market," Alphonse answered soothingly.

He turned to gesture his servant ahead toward the gate to make sure with a small bribe to the guards they were not delayed there. But it was not the guards who put obstacles in their path; the guards were caught somewhere among the shouting, milling throng, and Chacier never found them. Fortunately, John and Alphonse did not wait for the servant to return but forged ahead, picking their way around the outer fringes of angry farmers and carters, whose confused and frightened oxen balked and backed and started forward just when it was least expected and most inconvenient.

When men, beasts, and carts became more tightly packed, Alphonse and John laid about them with the flats of their swords, which quieted most of the protest at their pushing through ahead of others. They found Chacier staring in perplexity at two carts that had locked wheels and jammed in the narrow passageway that pierced the thick wall. The oxen were bawling and bumping into one another in the dark tunnel, trying to escape from the carts and each other, and the farmers on the far side of the gate were exchanging blows and recriminations.

"You will have to go around to another gate, sieur," Chacier said.

"Nonsense," Alphonse replied. "How do I know it will be any better than this?"

On the words, he handed his reins to John, loosened his foot from his right stirrup, and slid from his saddle to the top of one cart, using his sword to brace himself upright. Unfortunately, just as he stood erect, the ox attached to the cart chose to back up, and Alphonse lost his balance, pitching forward onto a heap of unwashed and well-fertilized vegetables.

Alphonse's remark and the voice in which it was uttered silenced the mob nearest the gate, and they remained quiet while he got to his feet again and worked his way to the front. Having studied the situation for a moment, he leaned down and cut the leather traces that held both oxen to their carts. One being a little ahead of the other already, both were able to lumber forward without hindrance when Alphonse smacked them smartly on the rear with the flat of his blade.

Their emergence from the gate drew the attention of their masters, who left off their quarrel to pursue the beasts. Meanwhile, Alphonse had clambered back and gestured the nearest men to him. The gesture being made with his bared blade and Chacier standing by whip in hand encouraged cooperation. John had been struggling not to laugh—until he had to dismount and get his horse and Alphonse's out of the way. He was soon splashed with dung and mud himself, and much less inclined to find the situation exquisitely humorous.

Now that the oxen were no longer pulling forward, it was no great feat to draw the carts back out of the gate, and John and Alphonse were first through. The streets were almost as crowded as the gate, however, which made John remark despairingly that he was sure Hugh would be gone and they would never be able to find him with the city so crowded. But Alphonse had recovered his good temper and retorted with laughter that, if so, he was going to lie down in the gutter to sleep, since he had no longer anything to lose and it would be better than trying to battle their way out of the city again.

Neither awful prognostication came true. As they worked their way past the market area, which spread out from the port, and climbed the hill toward the castle at the top, the streets grew somewhat quieter. John's conviction that the crowding was sure to have displaced his lord was proved wrong at last when Hugh's own manservant opened the door to them and welcomed them in with considerable enthusiasm, despite their dirt. He apologized for leaving them to make their way up to the solar themselves while he helped Chacier unload the baggage animals and showed him where to take the horses. With the town so full, it was impossible for foreigners to get servants, he said somewhat bitterly. John clapped him on the shoulder and replied that he could forgive him anything just for being where he was and gestured for Alphonse to precede him up the stair.

"Oh no," Alphonse said. "I freely relinquish to you the courtesy due me as a guest and the honor due me as the son of a count. You go first and explain our condition."

His intention was to give John a chance to say a few words to Hugh Bigod alone, not to explain why they were both soiled with well-manured mud but to allow Bigod to make mental arrangements for what might be one unexpected guest too many. Thus Alphonse climbed the stair in a leisurely fashion, entering the large front room when John was about halfway across, moving toward a solitary figure just rising from a chair near the fireplace. In the same instant that it became clear that the figure could not be Hugh Bigod, John let out a yell of "Barby! Barby!" and leapt forward.

Alphonse stopped as abruptly as if he had seen Medusa instead of Barbara de le Pontet de Thouzan le Thor. She had run toward John when he called her name and they were now embracing. With a small shocked intake of breath, Alphonse removed his hand from his sword hilt. He had no right to her; he had been fool enough to turn away the love she had offered him so artlessly when she was a child—a scrawny, almost ugly little girl. And look at her now. Alphonse swallowed hard and took a deep breath. In any case, he reminded himself bitterly, she was doubtless no longer the widow of de le Pontet de Thouzan le Thor. In the seven years since he had seen her she must surely have remarried.

At least she had not married John of Hurley. That was clear enough. There was nothing of husband and wife in the rough hugs of joy they had exchanged, and they had backed away from each other without the smallest lingering of physical pleasure in touching. John's questions about his brother and father-by-law had burst out at once, and she was answering, assuring him that all was well with William of Marlowe and Aubery of Ilmer.

"They are not shackled or in a dungeon," she said. "At least William is not. He was with Richard of Cornwall. I saw Richard and William in London and William looked too well and easy for me to believe that Aubery was hurt or harshly treated."

John bent his head and murmured, "Thank God. Thank God. I could not have borne to have escaped, leaving them to die." He then laughed aloud and struck Barbara gently on the upper arm. "Now we can work to free them." But after that he frowned, relief providing time for him to become puzzled. "What the devil are you doing here?"

"My father sent me, of course. Surely you do not think he would leave poor Hugh to wonder what had happened to his wife and children. Joanna is safe at Framlingham with the two younger children, and father sent his men to hold Hugh's lands. With any luck, everything will be safe for Hugh when he comes home."

"And when is that likely to be?" John asked, his voice gone cold.

"Do not begin to argue with me," Barbara snapped. "I am not afraid to warm your ears as they deserve. What do you men care for anything beyond your own pride and your precious 'right'? Uncle Hugh too! Did he give a single thought to Joanna's suffering when he agreed to go to war?"

John made pacifying gestures. "Do not eat me, Barby. I am no more free to do my will than you are. When did you come? Are you staying here with us? Where is Hugh?"

Hugh Bigod! When Barbara referred to him as Uncle Hugh, Alphonse at last connected John's lord with Roger Bigod, earl of Norfolk. Because Alphonse never thought of Norfolk by his personal name, he had not realized Hugh Bigod must be the earl's brother. But he could not stay in the house while she was there. He had no idea how much seeing her would hurt. If someone had named her to him, he would have said he had almost forgotten her. It would have been a lie, but he had not ached with missing her for years.

Only the anger and contempt in her voice when she spoke of men's pride had carried him back to the day when the news of Thouzan le Thor's death had arrived. Overnight Louis had received a dozen requests for her in marriage. There had been the same anger and contempt in her when she called those men ghouls. And so he had run back to Aix to hide himself, afraid she would class him with the "ghouls" who desired not her but the pretty estate that had become hers when her husband died. Why should she not? How could she know how much he had come to love her over the two years she had been Thouzan le Thor's wife in name only? He had been very careful to treat her with proper courtesy—and what else could he do? Pierre de le Pontet de Thouzan le Thor had been his friend. He had been fulfilling Alphonse's own conditions in not claiming his wife until she became fifteen years of age—

"Man, have you turned to stone?"

John's voice, quite loud, as if he had spoken more than once, startled Alphonse out of old regrets and led him to new ones. He realized with disgust that he had not heard her answer to John's questions, but he forced himself forward in response to a beckoning gesture.

"I promise Barby will not faint over a little dirt." John went on, with just the hint of a quiver, as if he were carefully hiding his amusement over Alphonse's reluctance to come closer.

"No, of course not," Alphonse said, somewhat relieved to discover that John's conception of him as a man too much dedicated to fine clothes and elegance had hidden the blow he had received. "Nonetheless, I cannot be other than offensive company in my present state. If madame will give her permission, I will go below and change my clothes."

Alphonse spoke as easily as if the utter blankness of her face had not turned the knife in his heart. His years as a courtier had taught him to expose only those emotions calculated to gain an end, so his dark eyes were half lidded, concealing pain, and his lips slightly curved. The expression of indolent indifference infuriated Barbara enough to dissipate the paralysis that had stricken her when John pointed out the guest he had brought with him.

"Madame!" she exclaimed. "You cannot have forgotten me completely in only seven years, Sir Alphonse. You always called me Barbe. Have I changed so much?"

"Not so much that I do not recognize you," he said, "but enough so that I would not dare use your name without permission."

"Oh, of course you two must know each other," John put in quickly, hoping Barbara would control her quick temper. "I forgot that Barby was Queen Marguerite's lady for four years. That was before she came to live with Hugh."

John was annoyed with Barbara, believing that her pride had been pricked because Alphonse had not recognized her at once. He turned more toward Alphonse, blocking their view of each other slightly, and pinched her arm to remind her that they needed Alphonse's goodwill.

"We know each other very well indeed," Barbara said, smiling slightly now. "My father put my affairs into Sir Alphonse's hands when he brought me to France in 1253 and had to leave almost at once to join King Henry in Gascony. And Sir Alphonse was always very kind to me, which is why I was so surprised when he addressed me formally. Madame, indeed!"

"Good God, Barby, it is no sin to be polite," John remarked, but he spoke lightly, adding, "Well then, I will leave you to renew your old acquaintance while I go and tell Hugh my news."

It was safe enough and might even be profitable to leave them alone, John thought. Barbara's voice and manner had become more cordial. Barbara could charm birds off trees when she wanted. Without waiting to see if either of them would object, John started toward a door at the back of the room.

Barbara put out her hand. "Surely we are still good enough friends for you to call me Barbe again?" she said.

She was very much ashamed of herself for jumping down Alphonse's throat. He had made it clear long ago that he did not return any feeling warmer than friendship. It was not fair to blame him for being distantly polite after her absence of seven years. The years had all dropped away for her the moment she saw him, but she had no reason to be angry because they had not dropped away for him.

"Of course," Alphonse replied.

He was actually somewhat annoyed at her insistence on being treated as an old friend. That would make it very difficult for him to avoid an intimacy rapidly growing too painful to endure. Also, he would have liked to know her current husband's name in case the man had accompanied her. Alphonse was afraid that if he did not prepare himself, he would take the man by the throat instead of being polite when they met. His immediate problem, though, was his need to discover if she was also Bigod's guest. He was about to ask, even if she thought him mad to do so, but she spoke first, suggesting that they sit down and turning to her chair by the empty hearth.

He sat down opposite her, glad that his rear was less bedaubed than his front, and remarked, "You will think me a fool for being so surprised to see you that I did not hear what you said to John, but—"

"I was surprised too," she said, "which was much more foolish. I should have known you would be in Boulogne when I found King Louis and Queen Marguerite here."

As she cut off his second attempt to discover where she was lodging and whether her husband was with her, Alphonse forgot all about how much he desired Barbe and recalled instead how infuriating she could be. "I do not always follow the court," he pointed out. "And I have little interest in English affairs because they usually do not affect my family. This time you would not have seen me if John had not caught me in Paris just before I started for home."

"John? What have you to do with John?"

Alphonse cleared his throat, wondering uneasily how long he would need to continue this inane conversation before he could either leave or get back to the subject in which he was interested. "It is rather complicated," he said. "Raymond, my elder brother, now comte d'Aix, married an Englishwoman, Alys of Marlowe, and my niece, Raymond's eldest daughter—not Alys's child—oh, curse it!"

"I am not sensitive about being a bastard," Barbara remarked, easily picking out the cause for his embarrassment over an otherwise harmless statement. She also made herself smile, although she was hurt again because he seemed to remember so little about her. "Whatever else he has done right and wrong, at least my father made that easy for me."

Alphonse shrugged. "We have talked about this before, and you know I consider you very sensible—"

"You did remember!" Barbara exclaimed.

Alphonse smiled faintly, although he had to bite his tongue to stop himself from calling her a fool for not seeing that he remembered everything about her. Instead he raised his brows and said, "At least you are sensible on that subject."

Barbara was so shocked at the cruel reply, which seemed to her a plain warning not to hope he cared about her, that she gasped. His voice faltered, and he seemed about to say something more gentle. She feared she would burst into tears if he did that, and turned her head away.

He seemed to understand, for after a brief check he rambled on, "After all, the sin your father and mother committed is nothing whatsoever to do with you. However, Fenice, my niece, married William's son-by-law so that my family is bound closely to the family at Marlowe. If you add to that the fact that King Henry is our uncle-by-marriage—Raymond's and mine, I mean—it was natural for John to seek help from Raymond and for Raymond to ask me to do what I could not only for William and Aubery but for Henry's cause too."

"I hope no help will be needed," Barbara said. "I have just come—the day before yesterday—from England. The earl of Leicester has sent proposals for peace. If they are accepted this long misery will be over."

She was able to speak quite calmly by then. Barbara had made little sense of what Alphonse said, but his explanation had given her time to recover. He was not cruel, she told herself. Alphonse was never cruel. He was trying to protect her from herself, as he had all those years ago when she had flung herself at him. She had not known then that half the ladies of the court, some of them great heiresses, panted after him like bitches in heat because he was one of the great tourney champions—and was said to be as skillful with his lance in bed as on the tourney field. If she had only known—but no one had spoken of such things to her; they had thought her a child because her breasts had not yet budded, and she had not guessed how he drew women because he was not particularly handsome.

If she had known, Barbara reminded herself, she would have understood he acted out of simple kindness, a desire to comfort one he thought of as a child, when he supported her through her first misery of being, as she believed, however wrongly, cast away by her father. Barbara now knew she had interpreted wrongly Alphonse's reasons for explaining that only great love and fear for her safety had forced her father to leave her with Queen Marguerite. But in 1253, as she recovered from the shock of being "abandoned" in the French court, she had assumed she had been sent there to be married. And, because her father said he was placing her affairs in Alphonse's hands and that she was to go to Alphonse for help if she needed it, she also assumed that if she liked Alphonse, he would be chosen as her husband. He had even carried her sleeve in a tourney and given her the prize—her silver mirror.

He had not even laughed at her when she offered her love, only said gently that he could never look so high for a wife, for she was an earl's daughter and he only a landless younger son. She was to have a much better husband than he, he had told her then, a rich count who would settle on her her mother's lands. Kind. Alphonse was always kind. It would have been far better for her if he had not spared her feelings but laughed and called her a fool as her father would have done.

Chapter 4

"My dear Sieur Alphonse, do forgive me for not coming out to welcome you as soon as John told me you were here, but I was so eager to hear his news that I took for granted your good nature."

Hugh Bigod's voice interrupted Alphonse's surprise at Barbara's statement, which seemed to imply, no matter how unlikely, that she had brought peace terms to Hugh from England. Both he and Barbara stood up, and as Hugh took his hand, he made a polite disclaimer of any offense taken. However, before he could say that he was sure Hugh's house was too crowded to absorb another unexpected guest, Bigod pressed his forearm and turned to smile at Barbara, saying, "I will keep the new arguments against Leicester's proposals Queen Eleanor has sent, if that will not inconvenience her." He shrugged and added, "I will need some time to find answers that will content her."

"You may keep them. I am sure those copies are for you, but is there something I can tell her that will induce her not to insult Leicester's emissaries? I do not think any harm will be done to Prince Edward, but I do believe that total confiscation of property and other very harsh measures will be taken against Leicester's enemies if arbitration for peace is not begun."

Hugh sighed. "I can think of any number of things I would *like* you to tell her, but—"

"Uncle!"

Barbara's lips curved with amusement at the exasperation in Hugh's voice and Alphonse set his teeth. He had forgotten something about his Barbe; he had forgotten how sensual her mouth looked when a half-smile bowed the lips—or he had never noticed before. There were so many reasons to want her, like the obvious lighthearted mockery behind her now solemn expression.

"I shall tell the queen that you do not consider me fit to carry messages."

"Do not you dare!" Hugh exclaimed, half laughing and half concerned. "Eleanor will not realize you are accusing me of thinking all women empty-headed. Our poor queen has had too many shocks and sorrows, love. Her sense of humor is sadly worn away. She might think I meant that you were a rebel at heart and not trustworthy."

This time Barbara sighed. "I fear she thinks that already and has invited me to join her household so that she can watch me."

Bigod frowned. "You must not allow your sympathy for Eleanor to bind you to her if—"

Barbara laughed, interrupting him. "Uncle, you always see the best in me. I am not nearly so self-sacrificing as you believe."

"Then accept Queen Marguerite's invitation," Bigod urged. "I understand she has offered you a place with her. You will be more comfortable in the French court where Leicester has as many friends as King Henry. I would have you here, love, but Queen Eleanor would take offense."

"I may join Queen Marguerite," Barbara temporized, not yet willing to commit herself. "But so far I have mostly been with Prince Edward's wife, and you know what a sweet soul she is. Princess Eleanor is frightened, too, since Edward offered to be hostage for his father's behavior. She needs someone a bit livelier than the lachrymose ladies the queen has appointed to attend her."

A desire to attend Prince Edward's wife, young Eleanor of Castile, was a reason no one would question for Barbara to remain nominally a member of Queen Eleanor's household. Hugh Bigod's expression softened immediately, as Barbara had known it would. Everyone adored the gentle Castilian princess and wished to make as easy as possible her exile and her separation from the husband she so obviously worshiped. And what Barbara said was perfectly true, but she had other reasons for wishing to delay her decision about whether to remain where she was or move to

Queen Marguerite's household. Her father would expect her to garner information, and Barbara did not yet know whether what she could learn in the English or the French queen's household would be more useful. Nor, though she wished to serve her father, was she at all certain she wished to be useful to Leicester's cause.

Her other reason for indecision had a sudden broad smile on his face that Barbara could not at first understand. Then she realized Alphonse expected to stay with her uncle, and was pleased to learn that he would not need to share a lodging with her.

"Well uncle," she said, "I have stayed long enough for a loving reunion and for you to decide that the questions raised by the queen are too weighty to be answered without long consideration. It is time for me to go back."

Hugh drew her to him and kissed her fondly. "I would bid you stay longer, but perhaps young Eleanor needs you. John will see you safe, love, and you can tell Queen Eleanor that he is returned from Aix. If she wishes to speak to him, John can explain better than I could what the comte d'Aix can and cannot do." He looked purposefully at John, who had groaned. "You can explain how Lord Raymond's hands are tied by the fact that Marlowe, his father-by-marriage, is a prisoner and might be mistreated in revenge for any overt action on Lord Raymond's part." John groaned again, and Bigod smiled very slightly. "You can also point out that Sieur Alphonse has already come to discover whether William of Marlowe can be freed for ransom."

"Ransom?" John echoed. "But Richard of Cornwall must already have offered to pay my father's ransom, and my father no doubt refused to leave him. It is my brother Aubery who will need ransom."

"Why did I teach you to be so honest?" Hugh sighed. "If you are not asked a question, do not answer it. Doubtless Queen Eleanor will be glad to hear that the comte d'Aix favors us enough to send his brother to help us."

"You had better phrase that another way, John," Alphonse said. "Raymond and I are both Queen Eleanor's nephews, after all. Say Alys has made herself ill and forced Raymond to promise he would do nothing to endanger her father."

"I will step on John's toes if he opens his mouth too wide," Barbara said. And then to John, "Come along."

Usually John was impervious to her teasing and temper, and Barbara did not give him a thought during the time it took the servants to bring their horses and for them to ride farther up the hill toward the castle. Before Barbara realized how rude she had been, she and John had reached the area between the castle walls and the church which enclosed several houses. These had been lent to Queen Eleanor when it was known that Edward's wife, Princess Eleanor, and a party of her servants would join the English queen in Boulogne. When she had spoken as if John were a feebleminded child, Barbara had been aware only of her need to get away, to be free of the flickering glances Alphonse cast at her. She did not understand why he should look at her as if he could not help it and then pull his eyes away, but she felt those glances, like butterfly touches on her skin, although no physical source for the sensation existed.

It only occurred to Barbara as John helped her down from her mare and told the groom who took the horses to unsaddle her mount, but not his, that he had not said a word to her all the time they waited for their horses at Hugh's house and rode through the town. The knowledge that she had offended him lowered her spirits even further. It took considerable effort not to burst into tears, but that would have made John feel worse. And it was not John's fault that Alphonse found her company unpleasant, Barbara reminded herself severely—even if John had brought him to Boulogne.

''Do not be angry with me, John,'' she said, touching his arm as they walked toward Queen Eleanor's lodging. ''I did not mean to offend you. I am out of sorts.''

''I am aware of it,'' he said, keeping his voice low. ''Are you worse off here than you wanted Hugh to know?''

''You mean is the queen unkind to me? No. I told the truth about being much with Edward's wife, Princess Eleanor.''

John stared at her for a moment and then drew her around beside the stone stair where they were half hidden. ''I know something is eating you, Barby. If I can help, let me know. I am as eager as you to spare Hugh any further worry, although your good news about his wife and his lands has made a new man of him. It is kind of your father to protect Joanna and try to save Hugh loss when they have been so sharply at odds for so long.''

Barbara laughed. ''Oh, papa loves Hugh,'' she said, while looking around for anyone close enough to overhear, and continuing in a lower voice when it was clear no one was interested in them. ''But it is not all for love that he acted. Do not underestimate my father because he has a red face and a loud voice. He is a clever man, and subtle. Do you not see that he has put Hugh under a deep obligation? By shielding Hugh's wife and lands from any threat of harm, thus tying Leicester's hands with regard to any hold on Hugh, papa has made *himself* guilty of any act against Leicester Hugh might commit. How eager do you think

Hugh will be to take part in an invasion of England when he knows his brother is likely to lose his own lands if he does?"

"By God's—"

Barbara's hand flashed up and stopped John's mouth. "Do not blaspheme!" she hissed. "King Louis is a little mad on the subject of dismembering the Lord to express surprise or disapproval and does not hesitate to order a whipping for the highest lord as well as the meanest peasant. Usually out of his hearing none pay mind to his harmless lunacy—except those who desire a mean revenge on some enemy and carry an accusation to his proctors—but Leicester's friends watch to carry word to Louis of any fault in King Henry's supporters, and of course Queen Eleanor's friends watch Leicester's friends, and—"

John took her hand away from his mouth. "I will be careful. I should have remembered the trouble we had over blasphemers during the peace negotiation in 1257." Then he looked quizzically at Barbara. "Thank you for warning me—and for pointing out your father's purpose. With whom do *you* stand, Barbara?"

"With Joanna," she said sharply, "and Princess Eleanor and all women who are driven from their homes with their babes in their arms because you men cannot decide how best a realm should be ruled." She bit her lip. "Come, let us go in before I scold you again for what is not your fault. You have told me already that you do not follow your own will in this matter."

Barbara turned away quickly, wondering if John had guessed her passionate answer, though not a lie, was not all the truth. How could she tell the truth, she thought as she climbed the stair to the open door of the great hall, when she did not herself know where her loyalty lay? King Henry was impossible, generating debts and confusion and injustice, yet to have him ruled by Leicester as she had seen him in London surely was a sin against the sacred order God had established. Her father had been as uneasy about it as she.

The steward's clerk, who had been writing on a small lap desk near one of the two windows, looked up when the voices of the ladies near the other window stilled briefly. He set aside his work and came to meet Barbara and John as they entered the hall, squinting because they were hardly more than silhouettes. The light from the small windows gave poor definition against the brighter light that came in from the open doorway behind them. However, he slowed his hurried stride when he recognized John as Hugh Bigod's man and offered a polite greeting. Barbara recited her message—that her uncle craved some time to examine the queen's suggestions and begged Eleanor not to take any action until he could talk with her.

She pretended she did not see the way the clerk's mouth tightened, simply going on smoothly to throw John to the wolf by saying he had come with news from Aix. After all, Queen Eleanor could not really eat John, no matter how furious she was with him for telling her that Raymond was not about to appear with a huge army or large chests of gold with which to hire mercenaries. The queen had no power over John, and he could go back to relative peace in her uncle's house. On the other hand, the poor clerk might be devoured alive for announcing that Hugh Bigod had not come to support Eleanor's attempt to circumvent any hope of peace.

As the clerk, with a much lightened countenance, turned away toward the circular stair behind the eating dais that led to the solar, John said softly, "The poor devil looked quite frightened when you told him Hugh was not coming. Is the queen so much changed?"

"You have not seen her?"

"No. I left for Aix before she arrived in Boulogne."

Barbara nodded but did not answer at once, moving to stand in the window behind the bench where the clerk had been working, well away from the ladies and passing servants. "She has not accepted this last turn of fortune very easily," she murmured to John, who had followed her. "For one thing, she blames herself for the battle at Lewes and its outcome. I believe she had been writing letters urging Henry to take stronger action against those who opposed him."

"What a fool!" John muttered. "She has too much Provençal pride. What leader did she think we had to stand up against Leicester?"

"Prince Edward."

"Not until he learns to control his temper," John said furiously. "If Edward had not been so desirous of avenging the insult the Londoners gave his mother that he chased them for hours, leaving our flank naked—"

He stopped and swallowed and Barbara put a hand on his and squeezed. The clerk was approaching, beckoning to John. "I will leave you then," Barbara said.

John cast an astonished look at her, and Barbara remembered she had implied she would accompany him into the queen's presence when she said she would step on his toes if he opened his mouth too wide. He had no doubt been counting on her to do just that—not perhaps step on his toes but to warn him subtly if he was saying what he should not—and he had expected her to ask the clerk if she could accompany him. But Barbara felt she could not. She had kept her personal distress submerged, but

Queen Eleanor was sure to ask about Alphonse, and Barbara did not feel able to talk about him, or even listen to John and the queen talk about him, without bursting into tears. She had to be alone to consider what she should do about Alphonse.

As a small compensation to John, she walked with him toward the stair, holding him back a little as the clerk went up. "Do not say anything about how long you have been in Boulogne," she whispered. "Be sure to bring attention to your muddy condition to show the haste with which you were sent to bring her news. She does not like to be the last to be informed." And before she could stop herself, she added, "And when she asks why Alphonse did not come with you, tell her he was nearly fainting with exhaustion and did not wish to affright his aunt with his weakness."

John could not repress a chuckle. "He will kill me."

But before Barbara could reply, Alphonse himself came into the room, newly dressed in a sky blue tunic over which he wore a loose rose-colored surcoat, its huge armholes, which stretched from shoulder to hip, bordered with intricately gold-embroidered strips of ribbon. A little round cap of matching rose, similarly embroidered, perched on his luxuriant black curls, just a bit askew. Barbara choked between laughter and tears. It was remarkable how that tiny tilt to his cap gave Alphonse's elegant appearance an air of breathless hurry.

He looked toward them at the sound, and Barbara was momentarily lifted on a surge of hope. There were other people in the hall, none of them deliberately silent. Why should he be able to pick out her laugh . . . ? But she shut out the thought without completing it, and Alphonse's expression was hidden by the glare of the light behind him. There was nothing to be read in it, however, even after he hurried across the room to them and Barbara could see him clearly.

"Go up to the queen," he said to John. "Do not say I am here. I will follow you in a few minutes. Quick, before the clerk comes back to see what is delaying you." Assured of support from someone who knew Eleanor well, John hurried up the stairs and Alphonse turned to Barbara. "In the name of God," he said, "why are you here in France?"

There was such urgency to the question, which as far as Barbara could see was totally unimportant, that she hesitated, seeking a hidden meaning. Alphonse glanced up the stair and back at her impatiently. Finally, still without understanding why her presence in France was important, she said, "My father sent me to prevent my uncle from throwing away his lands, and perhaps his life, in a wild attempt to protect his wife."

"I thought you said you brought Leicester's latest peace terms."

That was the last thing Barbara wanted to hear. It brushed away the thin spiderweb of hope she had been weaving again. Apparently he had misunderstood what she said earlier and had seen some political purpose in her coming to France.

"No. Oh no," she said. "I only came with William Charles, the king's knight. The earl of Leicester would not think of entrusting such a mission to me."

"Then you will be returning to England as soon as you can, I suppose," he said. "You will want to rejoin—"

"Sieur Alphonse!" The clerk's voice, high with surprise, cut off what Alphonse was about to say. "Oh," he went on, turning to go into the queen's apartment again, "my lady will be overjoyed to see you."

"*Merde!*" Alphonse muttered, his full lips suddenly thin with fury, but he was far too well trained in diplomacy and far too aware of Queen Eleanor's delicately balanced temper to delay even a moment. He pushed past Barbara and pounded up the stairs.

She stood staring after him until he disappeared through the doorway of the queen's chamber. Some emotion had flickered briefly in Alphonse before he mentioned his expectation that she would soon go back to England. It was gone too fast for her to tell whether it was sadness or gladness, but if her purpose for being in France was not political, why should Alphonse care whether she left or stayed? Surely he could not fear that she would throw herself at him again like a foolish child? Nonsense. They had been together at court for years after that and she had never been more than properly polite.

And why had he been so angry when the clerk interrupted their conversation? "You will want to rejoin—" he had said. Want to rejoin whom? Her father? She loved papa dearly, of course, but to feel any urgency to rejoin him was ridiculous. She had gone home with him after he came to negotiate the peace treaty with France in 1257 only to avoid all the ghouls who wanted to gobble up the estate that became hers when Thouzan le Thor died. Any one of them was willing to swallow her with the lands, like a bitter pill wrapped in the sweetmeat of her manor and farms. Alphonse knew that. She herself had told him of her disgust, and it was Alphonse who had suggested to her the device that prevented King Louis from choosing a "good man" to be her second husband.

A smile curved Barbara's lips for an instant. Only King Louis would have taken seriously her plea that he not give her in marriage because, though she did not yet feel a call to the cloister, she did not wish to close that door to salvation either, and wished to remain celibate until she was sure. But Alphonse had told her to say that, so he knew she felt no desire to be a nun. And then he had been called home to Aix and had not returned to court until after her father arrived in France and agreed to take her home. He acted when he first returned from Aix as if he found her desirable, but then, when he heard she was going to England, he had suddenly gone away again to fight in a series of tourneys.

Barbara went slowly outside and stood at the foot of the stair for a moment while duty to Princess Eleanor pulled one way and desire pulled another. She glanced over her shoulder at the open doors of the church and then blushed. In a time of so many great troubles, would it not be a sin to pray for a solution to her very small problem? Surely God and his saints should not be badgered about one girl's stupid inability to master her own heart. So she started toward the smaller house that had been assigned to Eleanor of Castile, but her need to be away from everyone made the idea of idle conversation horrible, and she set out instead for the kitchen shed to get some apples.

The poor things were very brown and wrinkled, but Frivole would not mind. Feeling better already, Barbara made her way to the stable. She peeped in, but only the huge bulk of battle destriers showed in the dim light, and she did not enter. Around to the back there was an area between the building and the outer wall closed off by a gate where the lesser beasts, the palfreys and roncins and light mares, were kept. Barbara's fluting whistle drew the attention of all the horses, and several began to move toward the gate. Two were roughly shouldered aside, another nipped sharply as Frivole took precedence.

"Tchk," Barbara said, as she held out one apple on her open palm. "You are supposed to be gay and flighty, not a shrew."

Frivole snorted so emphatically that the apple was nearly blown away, and Barbara laughed. She knew quite well that the snort was not a response to her words, but it seemed so like an arrogant reply that her spirit lightened. She went on talking to the mare, who nodded her head, often at comically appropriate moments. Within a few minutes a groom came out of the stable and asked how he could serve her. He looked at her strangely when she bade him go away and said she had just come to visit her mare. Men often came to examine their destriers, which were very valuable animals, but few women rode other than pillion, and even those who could ride usually did not know one animal from another. But it was clear from the way the mare pushed her head into the lady's breast that she was accustomed to fondling by this woman, so he shrugged and went away.

Barbara gave Frivole a second apple, rubbing her nose and stroking her neck. Eventually she laid her cheek against Frivole's head, circled the mare's neck with her arm, and sighed. If she had married and had a household of her own, she could have had a more convenient pet, a dog or cat. But at court such an animal caused endless trouble, and to leave it behind to the uncertain care of people like her father's kennelman—a good man but totally contemptuous of a dog that had no purpose but to love a mistress—was impossible. The poor creature, loved and petted while with her, lonely and even mistreated by being forgotten when she was away, would go mad.

The stable cast a shade across the yard behind it. It was cool, Frivole was plainly enjoying being petted, and Barbara lingered, leaning against the fence and thinking about a more settled life. But though she complained often about the inconveniences of court service and might have preferred a more gentle and considerate mistress, like Princess Eleanor, Barbara had to admit to herself that she enjoyed the excitement of life at court. She did not think she would care to exchange her life for Joanna's, living retired and busying herself with babes, a dairy, a stillroom, weaving, and embroidering—in short, a woman's life. As a retreat from too much intrigue, Kirby Moorside was a desired haven; as a full-time residence, she would soon regard it as hell.

"I knew I would find you here."

Barbara was so startled that she tried to right herself and turn around at the same time. The combination of her sudden movement and Alphonse's voice, which was tight with tension, made Frivole throw up her head. Barbara's hand slipped from the mare's nose so that she banged her elbow on the top rail of the gate, while the twist of her head to look at Alphonse brought her headdress right under Frivole's mouth. Never loath to try what was offered, Frivole seized Barbara's fillet and pulled. Both fillet and the net that held her hair promptly came off as Frivole backed away, and Barbara's chestnut mane tumbled down her back and around her face.

"*Peste!*" Barbara cried, leaping up and grabbing for Frivole's prize.

Unfortunately, with her hair in her eyes, her hand went wide of its target and slapped Frivole's neck, thus further startling the mare, who turned and trotted away. And because she was reaching out over the gate, Barbara came down on the rail on her belly with enough force to knock the breath out of her and leave her teetering dangerously, her feet on one side, her head on the other.

Alphonse seized her by the hips and hauled her back, holding her against him as she gasped for air.

"Is it I or the horse who is a pestilence?" he asked.

"Frivole! My crespine!" Barbara cried despairingly, ignoring the facetious question as the mare tossed her head, sending the net, its beads glittering, flying through the air into the trodden dust of the yard.

Laughing, Alphonse set her aside and leapt over the gate. The horses all trotted away and he picked up the net and shook it. "Since you do not think me a pestilence, I have saved your crespine. Do you want the fillet too?" he called back.

"You are surely a plague, if not a pestilence," Barbara retorted. "No, I do not want the fillet. That idiot mare is chewing it."

She brushed back her hair and reached for the net as Alphonse came over the gate, but he held it away and said, "No, if I give it to you, you will run away again. I have some questions I want answered."

"I! Why should I run away?" Barbara asked with as much indignation as she could muster. She held out her hand imperiously. "Give me my crespine. Do not act like a naughty child. It does not befit a man of your age."

He shook his head, but he was no longer laughing. "Is it true that you have come to gather information on the invasion that Queen Eleanor hopes will free her husband?" he asked. "She said she will not allow you to return to England because she fears you have already learned too much and will pass the information to Leicester."

"I assure you I have not made the smallest effort to learn what I should not," Barbara said angrily. "Give me the net."

"I was not accusing you of spying deliberately," he said. "But—"

"No one hereabouts would need to spy deliberately," Barbara snapped. "Every mouth, including Queen Eleanor's, pours forth a steady stream of information. But I assure you, the earl of Leicester has friends better placed than I to send him important news."

Alphonse sighed. "I am making you angry, and I do not mean to. You must understand that I cannot help being partial to my aunt's cause any more than you can help being attached to your father's. I was only trying to discover if helping you would truly hurt Eleanor and Henry. But I cannot bear for you to be unhappy, Barbe. If you are very eager to go back to England, I will try to arrange it through Marguerite and Louis."

"I would love to know why you are so eager to be rid of me. Is this some ploy of Queen Eleanor's to get me out of Boulogne before I learn something she does not want me to know? Or do you have some private reason? Unfortunately for you, it does not matter. I must stay in France for a while whether you and the queen like it or not. Give me my net and I will go away and promise to avoid you—''

''Like a plague?''

Alphonse laughed and held her crespine behind his back. Barbara could see that the tension had gone out of him, but she could not guess why. Because she was staying in Boulogne? She tried to crush that hope, and told herself it was more likely because she had promised to avoid him.

''Sieur Alphonse—'' she began with rigid formality.

''Tell me why you came,'' he murmured, coming closer, ''and why you *must* stay.''

Barbara stared up at him, transfixed between rage and tears. His playful manner and the relaxation she had seen in him when she said she planned to remain in France had made her feel he had a special interest in her, despite her efforts to remember that he had never wanted her. And now there was something in his posture, in the low, deep voice, which touched her like a caress, that woke sexual desire in her and implied it in him. But the words! The words were pure politics! Queen Eleanor must be completely mad with suspicion and had set him to *seduce* the truth—which she had already told—out of her.

''You know my reason for coming,'' she said. She had intended to sound cold and angry, but her voice trembled. She was furious at him for playing such a role at his aunt's request, and at herself for responding so violently that she could hardly keep from flinging her arms around him. Her anger made her say, ''The reason I cannot go back is that Guy de Montfort, Leicester's third son, has decided he would like me to be his whore, and I wish to give him some months to find a more delectable—and willing—morsel.''

Alphonse stared at her; his mouth opened, closed, opened again to emit a harsh croak. Then dark color came up under his skin and he looked away. ''Is there no one to protect you?'' he asked stiffly.

''Give me my net,'' Barbara repeated, barely preventing herself from sobbing with fury.

''Is your husband afraid to offend Leicester's son?'' he asked, as if he had not heard her. ''Or—''

''Husband!'' Barbara exclaimed. ''Have you forgotten me completely? My husband has been dead for over eight years. Do you expect him to rise from his grave to fight Guy de Montfort when he could not be bothered to come to court to meet me?''

"Dead for eight years?" Alphonse echoed. "You mean you never married again?"

"What is that to you?"

"Barbe," he cried, "you need fear nothing and no one. I will protect you. I—"

"Thank you very much," she interrupted with icy formality, "but having been born a bastard and seen the bitterness that grew between my father and mother, I have a strong aversion to placing myself under any man's protection outside the bonds of marriage."

Alphonse gaped and words he did not seem able to form gurgled in his throat. A bitter satisfaction filled Barbara. That lecher was too accustomed to having foolish women leap at his invitations in the hope of seducing him into marriage. Marriage had been her mother's hope too—and her mother had almost succeeded—but with regard to women her father was a simple soul compared with Alphonse.

"Barbe—"

"No!" She cut him off again. "Why the devil should I prefer being your whore to being Guy's?"

"No. No. Not that. I love you—"

"I have been assured that when they first came together my father loved my mother also, and she him. Besides, if I had not concealed Guy's pursuit from my father for political reasons, he would have protected me. And if you think the word 'love' makes whoring more or less—"

"Will you be quiet!" Alphonse bellowed. "My offer of protection had nothing to do with inviting you to my bed. I am your knight; you are my lady. You have had the right to my protection ever since I carried your favor in that tourney many years ago. But if you feel that my challenge to Leicester's son will in some way be damaging to you, then I offer myself as husband, not lover"—he stopped shouting abruptly and held out the hair net to her, going on very softly—"if you will have me. I have loved you for a very long time, Barbe. Will you have me?"

"Of course," she said, snatching the crespine from his hand and dancing out of reach. She called back over her shoulder, "Have I not been passionately enamored of you since I was thirteen years old? Surely eleven years of constancy should be rewarded. If you can get King Louis's approval, I will be delighted to be your wife."

Chapter 5

The little devil believes I was jesting, Alphonse thought. It would serve her right if I went to Louis and asked for her. He rubbed the back of his neck fretfully, settled his cap more squarely on his head, and went to the front of the stable to order a groom to bring his horse. When he was mounted, he did not ride back to Hugh's house but out into the countryside, where he soon found a meadow whose thin grass could support only a few sheep. Those were at a distance, and Alphonse dismounted, tied his horse, and sat down in the shade of an outcrop of rocks.

Somewhere during the ride, although he had not been conscious of thinking at all, he had decided to launch an all-out campaign to get Barbara for his wife. Had there been any truth at all in the teasing remark that she had loved him since she was thirteen? He knew she had thought her father had decided on him for her husband and had allowed herself to feel she loved him then, but she seemed to have recovered very easily when he pointed out how unsuitable he was. But had she really recovered or simply been too proud to show what she felt once he made it plain he did not desire her?

Alphonse laughed softly. What a fool he had been not to see what she would become—not that she had the kind of beauty over which the romances raved, but beauty was nothing. It seemed to him now that the more beautiful a woman was, the more likelihood existed that she would bore you to death every minute your shaft was not in her sheath, and the brief pleasure of futtering was never worth the hours of boredom that preceded and followed it. Barbara was different. The spirit in her and the bright mind that loved intrigue as much as he did somehow combined with her odd features to ravish him. When her eyebrows went up and made a little pointed tent on her forehead, his knees felt like jelly and his sword and hangers heated almost painfully.

"Stupid," he muttered aloud and shifted position, his body having responded immediately to the appealing subject of Barbara's thick, shining eyebrows. No, he would not imagine how it would feel to brush his lips over them and down her long nose to that wide mouth whose every movement—and it was very mobile—presented a sensuous invitation.

Sighing with exasperation, Alphonse wondered at his inability to control his wayward fancies. It never happened with any other woman. For many years he had been as easily able to send away as to call forth the image of his current mistress—or any other woman. As a curative, Alphonse asked himself sternly whether the feeling Barbe had been concealing from him was not love but hate. That idea cooled his heated body, but though he dwelt on the notion, it did not gain in reality.

He asked himself whether his self-love was preventing him from seeing the truth, but he did not think so. Barbe had never acted like a woman scorned—a horrible condition with which Alphonse had experience despite all his care. And it was to him she had come for help when the marriage to Thouzan le Thor had been proposed. She had been in despair when her father agreed to it, had threatened everything and anything to escape the match. But she had become calm and reasonable when he pointed out the advantages of being married to a rich man who had promised not to take her from Queen Marguerite's care for two years, and she had accepted his promise to protect her from her husband if she could not like him after they finally met.

Nor did she come to hate me later, Alphonse thought. The proof was that she had come to him and reminded him of his promise to protect her when Pierre sent word he was coming to consummate their marriage at last. By then Barbe did not need his protection; any number of other men would have been glad to kill Thouzan le Thor for her. Alphonse probably would have done it himself, despite the fact that he knew Pierre and liked him. But she did not ask that of him, only that he agree to escort her to England to her father if she found her husband distasteful.

And of course the question had never arisen, because Pierre had died of a fever on the way to Paris.

Should he have joined the mob of men who rushed to Louis to propose themselves or their sons as husbands for Barbe as soon as news of Pierre's death came to the court? No, that had not been a mistake. He was sure of that because it was again to him Barbe had run for help, reminding him that her father had bade her come to him when she needed advice. She had been cool when she asked if he could think of a way to save her from the "ghouls" who wished to batten on Thouzan le Thor's death leavings, but Barbe was always cool—except to men who pursued her, and to them she was freezing cold. Her teasing and laughter and clever hints about court intrigue or how to manipulate people were only for "friends," male or female.

However, it might have been a mistake not to follow her to England, Alphonse thought. She had seemed to respond to his tentative approaches when he returned to court from Aix almost a year after Pierre's death. But when he tried to discover whether that warmth meant she looked on him with favor, she had told him—so lightly—that she was going home to England with her father. Alphonse had been hurt and angry, thinking himself rejected, and had gone to fight off his spleen in tournaments. By the time he had begun to wonder whether he had not taken offense at innocence rather than rejection, she was gone.

At that time Alphonse had felt there was no sense in presenting himself to Norfolk as a suitor. He was no match for Barbe; although she was not Norfolk's heiress, she was his only child and his fondness for her made her a valuable prize. Certainly there was no need for the earl of Norfolk to urge his daughter to make so unequal a match. Had Alphonse had time to woo Barbe so that she would plead with her father to accept him, Norfolk might have considered him favorably. He had also assumed Norfolk took her with him because he already had in mind a marriage far more suitable than the virtually landless younger brother of the comte d'Aix. However Barbe had not married at all, and considering her father's fondness for her, that could only have been because she was unwilling to marry.

Alphonse drew his shapely lower lip between his teeth and gnawed on it. Could it be that she had no taste for men at all? But it was he who had suggested that she say she wished to live celibate for a time to save her from a second marriage immediately after Pierre's death. Barbe had not thought of that device herself. Besides, if she had really wished to live celibate, all she needed to do was tell King Louis she wanted to be a nun. He would have done all in his power to satisfy that desire. No, Barbe had no inclination for the cloister. But that did not mean she had any inclination for marriage either.

Had he a right to try for marriage if Barbe was happy living under her father's protection? Alphonse uttered a soft obscenity. He did not care! She had become a fire in his blood. He would make her happy. He had to try for her at least—and at once, before anyone else at court realized she was still a widow.

So after all the thinking, he had come again to what he had decided without thinking at all, but he was no nearer to how to achieve his purpose. It was hopeless to ask either Marguerite or Eleanor for help. Both his aunts would think Barbe a bad match and present him with great heiresses more suitable to be his wife. Nor could he go directly to Louis. That good man would certainly not press Barbe to marry him against her will . . . unless some greater good for all would come from the arrangement. That was something to think about when he knew more of the political situation than he could learn from Queen Eleanor's narrowly prejudiced view. Hugh Bigod and John of Hurley could tell him most of what he would need to know. And Eleanor might support his request to marry Barbe if he said he could thus control her, and possibly her father through her.

No, that would not do. To approach Barbe through others would only make her angry and disdainful. If he convinced her that he did love her and took seriously her agreement to marry him, she would keep her word and become his wife. She would be angry at being held to a promise made in jest, but not nearly as angry as she would be if he tried to work his will on her through others.

Barbara fled from Alphonse without heed, across the courtyard and through the great hall of Princess Eleanor's house to the stair that led to the women's quarters above. She had not taken five steps into the chamber when her maid's voice, shriller than normal with alarm, checked her.

"My lady! What has befallen you?"

The speed with which Clotilde had separated herself from the gossiping knot of maidservants clustered not far from the entrance to the large room in which all the ladies slept and the fright in her voice brought Barbara to her senses. She forced a laugh and explained what Frivole had done. Clotilde, who was not unfamiliar with the damage to Barbara's clothing caused by her fondness for animals, tch'd and clucked but busied herself with putting her mistress to rights, allowing Barbara's thoughts to slip back to the subject that was consuming her.

She had been far more shocked than Alphonse by the answer

she had made to his proposal. When she opened her mouth, Barbara had intended to make a lighthearted joke comparing the two frivolous creatures who had snatched her crespine, implying that Alphonse was as thoughtless as Frivole. The jesting tone had been true to her original intention, but the words . . . She had accepted his offer of marriage! An offer she had shamed him into making!

The shock faded slowly as a much more important notion took hold of her. Alphonse *had* intended to seduce her. His reaction to her accusation was proof of that. And if he intended to seduce her, he found her attractive.

Her first reaction to his seductive voice and manner had been hurt and rage because she leapt to the conclusion that he had made the advance on Queen Eleanor's order, but second thought had cured her of that notion. It was possible that Eleanor had suggested seduction to him, but Barbara had known Alphonse for years, and he was no meek performer of anyone's will but his own. If he had not wanted to seduce her, he would have convinced his aunt that it was the wrong thing to do and that it was Eleanor who was turning him aside from a disastrous idea. Barbara had seen him work that magic—had he not worked it on her to make her agree to marry Thouzan le Thor? Only good had come of that, but . . .

That was not important. The significant fact was that Alphonse had decided to seduce her on his own—or Queen Eleanor's suggestion had coincided with his own wishes. Whichever was true, he now found her desirable—desirable enough to say "I love you." Barbara's breath quickened and she reminded herself sternly that his saying the words did not mean he did love her. No doubt he felt that the declaration was required at the beginning of every affair and he said it by rote. Then was it fair to hold him to an offer of marriage forced out of him by shame?

Barbara considered the question while her maid recombed her hair. She held the silver mirror, the tourney prize he had faithfully given to an ugly child made still uglier by constant weeping with homesickness. Later she had learned that he had a beautiful mistress who had quarreled with him for not carrying her favor in the tourney and for bestowing the mirror she desired on "an ugly child." But Alphonse was always faithful to his word, even when that word was only meant to draw a smile by asking for a child's favor to carry in a tourney. She had been so ignorant that she had pulled the scarf from her hair and given it to him at once, not realizing he was jesting. But Alphonse had not laughed at her. He had taken the scarf and thanked her and kissed her hand as gravely as if she were the most beautiful lady in the land.

So he would keep his word and marry her if she did not offer to release him from his proposal. Was it fair to bind him to words forced from him? By a path of reasoning similar to Alphonse's, Barbara came to the same conclusion: that she would make him so good a wife that he would, in the end, be content. She had wanted him for years; now, having seen him again and felt pangs as sharp and eager as those of great hunger, she was ready to admit the truth. There was no use in lying to herself anymore. She had refused to marry only because she desired no man but Alphonse.

He would not regret the marriage, Barbara vowed. But there was another problem: Would she regret it? A confirmed chaser of women does not change his ways because the priest pronounces him a husband. Adultery would only be a little pebble piled on the mountain of sins of fornication Alphonse had already committed. If he loved her and vowed to be faithful, there was a chance that he would cleave to her, forsaking all others. But that was not a vow into which she could—or even wanted to—trick him. Real hatred would grow out of such a trick, the kind of hatred that existed between her father and his wife. Barbara shuddered.

"It is growing cooler," Clotilde said, laying the comb on Barbara's knee and bringing a short cloak from the chest that held Barbara's clothes. "And I have told you many times, my lady, that you must let me make the crespines larger. I cannot stuff all your hair into this net, and there are holes in it."

Barbara allowed her maid to slip the cloak over her shoulders. She had changed from her sturdy riding dress into summer silks because she had run all the way from the stable and arrived hot as well as disheveled. Now that the evening breeze had brought a slight chill with it, she did not need to explain why she had shivered. Nonetheless, Clotilde's care for her was soothing, and she smiled slightly; she and the maid seemed to have this argument about her hair at least three times a week. Besides Clotilde's comment had broken her train of thought, which was a welcome interruption.

"But I do not like my crespines to hang halfway down my back," she said, "and they would if you made them longer. For now, plait my hair and wind it around my head."

"Plait it," Clotilde grumbled merrily, "as well plait ten hanks of yarn. Why does the good Lord put all the hair in the world on one person's head? Could He not spread it about? I can think of ten ladies who would benefit from a handful or two—and a few who would like to pull it out themselves."

"What? Already?" Barbara exclaimed, alert to Clotilde's oblique hints. "I cannot have offended anyone yet."

"Were you not in the queen's hall this afternoon with two handsome and richly dressed young men?" Clotilde asked. "Did you not ignore the ladies there and fail to join them? And did not Alphonse d'Aix, Queen Eleanor's own nephew, ask for you when he came from her chamber and set out to find you without even nodding to the other ladies? Do you call that being inoffensive?"

Barbara groaned slightly and shook her head without bothering to answer. She had forgotten that any gentlewoman in the hall might know Alphonse because of Queen Eleanor's long stay at the French court. And the maid was right to warn her. Gossip was Clotilde's specialty; she gathered it and passed it with equal assiduity and both were often of great value to Barbara. In fact, the maid was invaluable in many ways, for she was brave, strong, and clever—and heart and soul Barbara's own with no ties or loyalties to any other person. When she reminded Barbara of Alphonse, however, Clotilde's company became painful. Barbara had suddenly remembered that the maid had been another gift from Alphonse. She waited impatiently for Clotilde to finish pinning a fresh fillet over her hair, pushed the silver mirror into her hands, and walked swiftly toward the stair.

The servant who had come with Barbara to France in 1253 had been her nurse, an old woman and very unhappy in her new environment. Her fear and grief at being parted from her family had added to Barbara's misery. How he had discovered it Barbara never found out, but one day Alphonse had brought Clotilde, only a few years older than Barbara but far wiser in the ways of the world, lively and laughing and eager to serve a young lady at court. As soon as Barbara had grown accustomed to Clotilde, he had arranged for the old woman to go back to England and her children.

The memory of that kindness made Barbara feel more guilty about binding Alphonse to a marriage he had not really sought. She knew she must not even consider trying to make him change his way of life. Then there was only the choice of releasing him from his request to marry her or living with the knowledge that she would share him with other women.

Sickness and fury churned so strongly in Barbara that she paused at the foot of the stair she had descended. For a moment she looked sightlessly out over the hall, which took up almost the whole lower floor of the house. Servants passed to and fro, but Barbara was so accustomed to their presence and their many activities that she regarded them no more than she did the stools and benches standing here and there.

A high and delicate titter of laughter—no servant's voice that—finally drew Barbara's eyes toward the open window at the far end of the room. There sat the ladies, grouped around Princess Eleanor. Among them, Barbara knew, were several, quite placid and contented, whose husbands were well known to seek entertainment abroad. Perhaps some hid suffering, but just as many, Barbara was sure, were well pleased to be relieved of marital attentions they found distasteful.

Perhaps theirs was the wiser way, Barbara thought. Look at poor Eleanor, who adored her husband with good reason, for Edward was gentle and loving to her and very faithful. Her face was pale and drawn and her eyes dark ringed, although her lips were curved into the form of a smile and she nodded now and again to remarks made to her. Barbara's mind flashed back to Joanna, to the pain and anxiety she suffered since her relationship with Hugh had changed. Perhaps it was worse to love one's husband than not to love him.

"You do look better, Lady Barbara," a sharp voice called. "When you came in your disarray gave me some very strange ideas."

Barbara started forward toward the ladies, smiling sweetly at Lady Jeanne, who belonged to the French queen's household. Another attack on her reputation demanded all of Barbara's attention and left no room for musing on subjects that sent shivers over her skin. She blessed Clotilde, too, for having warned her about the jealousy among the ladies. Somewhere inside her she had been making ready, half expecting trouble. A few of the women, like Lady Ela seated to the left of the princess, her gaze fixed on nothing and her hands idle in her lap, had a real cause to be bitter. Lacking a better outlet for their fear for their menfolk, who had fought for the king, such a woman might feel a desire to torment the daughter of Leicester's ally. But Lady Jeanne simply enjoyed pricking a victim. Barbara did not mind at all; she was an expert at knife-play with sharp words.

"Your ideas could not have been as strange as the true reason, Lady Jeanne," she said merrily as she paused just beyond the seated women. "My mare, who has a playful disposition, snatched my fillet from my head and my crespine with it."

"No, no," Lady Jeanne said, "you cannot get away with that excuse. I saw you come in from riding earlier."

"Yes." Seeing the sudden tension in the way Princess Eleanor looked at her, Barbara recalled that she might be thought to have carried back a message from Hugh Bigod. "I came with John of Hurley, my Uncle Hugh's man. Sir Hugh needed more time to study the message sent by Queen Eleanor, and John had come with news from Comte Raymond d'Aix. I went back to the stable yard after John was taken to the queen to see that Frivole had been properly cared for."

"Do you not trust Queen Marguerite's servants to tend your horse?" another French lady asked indignantly.

"She does not trust any servants, even her own, about the care of her mare." Princess Eleanor spoke more sharply than usual.

The princess was indifferent to the implication that Barbara had been disheveled in a sexual encounter. For one thing, Princess Eleanor was not fond of malicious gossip; for another, she had known Barbara for a long time and was certain she would never have run through the hall as she had if her condition had anything to do with a man. More important, the princess had questions she wanted answered. She had lived in courts all her life, however, and she spent one sentence to placate Lady Jeanne, because she was aware of the need to be particularly gracious to ladies sent to attend her by the French queen, who was her hostess.

"Lady Barbara is famous—or is it infamous?—for cosseting her animals," the princess said, trying to smile.

Although the princess had supported her statement, Barbara was aware that the purpose was not to save her but to cut off further remarks on a subject in which Princess Eleanor was not interested. And her expression, when she looked at Barbara, held reproach for Barbara's long delay in coming to her.

Barbara dropped a curtsy and seated herself on a bench near the princess at which Eleanor had gestured. "I am sorry, madam, I do not know what news John of Hurley brought," she said, answering the expression rather than the words. "He was so anxious about his father-by-law, who had been taken prisoner with Richard of Cornwall, and asked me so many questions about Sir William, whom I had seen in London, that he gave me no chance to ask what news he brought from Aix. And I am not sure he would have told me if I did ask, partly because I am a woman but also because of my father's alliance with Leicester. But I am sure, madam, that Lord Raymond d'Aix will do what he can to help Queen Eleanor."

"But *what* will he do?" the princess murmured, her eyes filling with tears. "King Henry's letter threatens Leicester will hurt my darling Edward if Queen Eleanor does not stop gathering men for an invasion of England. Will Lord Raymond bring an army?"

"No one will hurt Prince Edward," Barbara said, not for the first or, she expected, the last time. "I swear to you that my father would never countenance that—nor would anyone else, not even Leicester himself. I do not know how King Henry came by such a notion. Madam, you know I saw the prince in London myself, well and strong, at several sessions of the court before I sailed for France. He was guarded, yes, but not chained, and he was treated with honor."

"Do *you* favor an invasion?" Lady Jeanne asked cynically.

"No, of course not," Barbara replied, a flick of her brows expressing her disdain for so cruel and clumsy a question. "How could I favor what would endanger my father and my uncle both?" she asked, and then added, "Besides, I am certain that King Louis will find a way to reconcile the parties if only both will have a little patience."

"Reconcile?" Lady Ela echoed, pricked out of apathy by indignation. "You would like that, would you not? Are we, who are loyal to King Henry, to have no recompense for the ill done us? My house in London was burned. My husband lies wounded in prison. Great harm has been done to all those who fought for what is right."

Aware that her own family had lost little, Barbara could not be pert. She shook her head and looked down. "There has been hurt on both sides," she said. "It is my hope and my comfort that King Louis will find a middle path that will avoid further war."

"War is terrible, terrible," the princess said, and stood up. "Pray pardon me. My babe was fretful this morning. I must go and see that she is well."

Barbara's heart sank right into the suddenly hollow pit of her stomach. More than half of all babies born died before their second year, but for this babe to sicken now, after Princess Eleanor had been driven from Windsor where the child had been healthy, would be another blow, almost certainly fatal, to the frail hope of peace. If the infant died, the harsh treatment Princess Eleanor had received would be blamed. Neither Eleanor nor Edward, whose ferocity could be frightening and whose memory for injury was very long, would ever forgive the death of their firstborn child. Then Barbara drew a deep breath. She had seen the baby herself after dinner. The child had been crowing happily then, and Eleanor's face had been free of strain until Barbara had recalled her to present troubles. Likely, Barbara thought, Eleanor had gone to her baby in search of comfort rather than out of anxiety.

The idea immediately brought Alphonse back to her mind because he was the only man she associated with marriage, and children could only be had, as far as Barbara was concerned, within marriage. She sat staring at the chair from which Eleanor had risen, paying no attention to a voice in the background, until a Frenchwoman prodded her.

"Lady Barbara, do you not hear Lady Jeanne ask how your mare gained so strong a hold on your affection?"

Barbara swept her eyes over the company and allowed her mobile mouth to twist in distaste. "I am fond of my mare because she does not ask me stupid questions. My country is at war with itself, a princess I love is suffering, and you think my love for a horse is of grave importance?" She sighed. "I am not in the mood to play your games, Lady Jeanne. I will say this and no more: I am not a stupid woman and I do not have a lover. If I did, however, and tumbling him had caused my disarray, I assure you I would have managed to find a private place to set myself to rights rather than run through the hall where all could see me."

There was a shocked silence, which was broken by a brief chuckle from Lady Ela. "I think you must be greatly distressed by something," she said. "It is not at all like you, Barbara, to apply a bludgeon when you could draw blood with a poniard. Do not lose your sense of humor. You may have need of it." And then she turned away deliberately to speak to another.

Barbara did not hear more than the words addressed to her. It was most excellent advice, she thought, and though she knew it was almost a threat on the political level, coming from the source it did, she sincerely wished she knew a way to take it on the personal level. Whether she released Alphonse and thus lost all chance of him forever or kept him to his unwilling offer and looked forward to a life of ignoring his mistresses and remarks about them from such kind ladies as Lady Jeanne, she would certainly need her sense of humor. Surely it would be better to release him, she thought. She would thus save herself the agonies of jealousy and of fear for any danger he might face.

Even as the logical ideas formed in her mind, she was struck by a pang of loss and came to a startling conclusion. She had not been as content as she told herself she was during her years in England. She had been empty and wanting; only now when she had seen Alphonse again and felt all of herself alive and awake did she realize what she had been lacking. And if she did not fill that emptiness now—her skin grew cold—it would be in her forever.

To have him, even partly, and to have his children—surely that was worth suffering the green fever. If she kept the peace, if she did not rail at him for playing with other women, surely he would grow to love her, to depend on her. But what if he did not? What if he sent her to Aix to be out of his way? No, she could bargain about that, and anyhow, if they could not live together, if she found it too hard to bear his unfaithfulness, she could always go back to her father in England. So she would keep him to the offer he had made. At least she could sip some of the honey of that beautiful mouth and play with the curls in his private places, which must be even blacker and glossier than those on his head. Unless he was so furious with her for tricking him into a proposal that he would not even consummate the marriage. No, that was silly. Why should he leave lying what was freely offered and would cost him nothing?

The thoughts went round and round, back and forth, and Barbara came no closer to a decision than she had been when she first ran back to her lodging. Before the long day ended, she regretted bitterly her use of the bludgeon. She would have been glad of any diversion from her thoughts, but Princess Eleanor stayed in her own chamber with her infant daughter and none of the other ladies would speak to her.

One piece of good came out of her misery. She was exhausted by the endless turnings of her mind and the images of eternal unhappiness she painted for herself. So when she was free to go to her bed, one pallet among the long row of pallets in the women's quarters—the large influx of ladies with two queens and a princess having exhausted the available cots—Barbara fell asleep before the first two tears she allowed herself to shed rolled from her eyes.

If she dreamed, no memory of the dreams haunted her, and the rest did her good in that she regained some control of her thoughts. At least when she woke she was able to ignore the problem of what she would say to Alphonse if he repeated his proposal and to consider instead what she should do if he did not approach her at all. If he avoided her, should she accept that and lose even his friendship, or should she approach him and make clear that she had taken his offer only as a jest? But would that save their friendship? She heard Clotilde's voice and guessed that she had asked what her mistress wished to wear. Barbara asked in turn about the weather.

What should she wear? If she dressed like a lady ready to receive a lover and he did not come, the women would tease her to madness, especially after her rudeness the previous day. She would have no armor against their cruelty, which had only amused her before. Now for the first time the barbs would strike a sore place in her heart. But if she wore no finery and he did come, that would be an insult.

Clotilde asked a question, and Barbara, having forgotten completely the question and answer already exchanged, again thought the maid had asked what dress to prepare. To avoid an answer,

Barbara asked what the weather was like, realizing only when Clotilde looked at her very strangely that she had already asked and been answered. In desperation, Barbara, who still did not know whether it was sunny or raining, had got as far as saying, "I will wear—" without having the faintest idea what words would follow, when a little page came up and whispered to Clotilde, who cocked her head in a puzzled way, following the child with her eyes as he ran off, before she turned to Barbara and said, "I am called below, my lady. May I go?"

The respite was so welcome that Barbara gave permission without once thinking how strange it was that Clotilde should be summoned. The maid had no family, for her mother had died before she came into Barbara's service, and she was, like her mistress, a love child. Nor was it likely that Clotilde had retained any friends in France over the seven years she had lived with Barbara in England. However, all Barbara felt was relief that Clotilde's quizzical gaze had left her, and the relief made it possible for her to go to her chest and take out a dark gold tunic and a bright blue silk gown of especially fine fabric. By omitting all jewelry and the embroidered collar she usually wore over the low, wide neck of the gown, she felt she had struck a fair compromise.

The decision had been made just in time, for Clotilde came back wearing no expression at all, which Barbara did not notice until the maid said, "Sieur Alphonse is waiting below to take you to mass."

Chapter 6

Alphonse had a better day than Barbara because he spent it talking to Hugh Bigod and John of Hurley about the situation in England. He had prepared a full salt cellar in his imagination to have sufficient pinches of salt to sprinkle on what he expected Sir Hugh to say about Leicester's ingratitude and selfishness and the king's long-suffering. What he heard seemed to him instead a measured and impartial recounting of the quarrel between the king and his barons, with Leicester more sinned against than sinning—although Hugh did state that Leicester's abrupt manner and tactlessness had added to troubles already present.

"I do not know the answer," Hugh said, staring down into the wine in his cup after the evening meal. "King Henry's extravagance and the greed and cruelty of his half brothers constantly incite rebellion. We can have no peace in the realm while these offenses continue, and war is bringing us all to ruin. Yet, Henry *is* the king; it is his *right* to rule and to choose those he wants to be his councillors and officers."

"Is it not time," Alphonse asked, "for Prince Edward to take a greater part in the government? I have heard that his father is more willing to take his advice than that of many others. I know the prince from the tourney field, both as ally and as adversary, and I liked what I saw. He had a cool head in the joust and in the melee, was generous to those of his party without extravagance, and was fair to the defeated. He lives up to his rank, too, but with no unnecessary display.''

''Edward may be cool on the tourney field,'' John said bitterly, ''but in battle, where it counts, his temper leads him into disaster.''

Hugh put his hand on John's arm. ''It was a special case,'' he explained to Alphonse. ''At Lewes Edward held the eastern flank and, unfortunately, opposed the troops from London. When he saw their standard, he forgot everything except the attack on his mother. The Londoners broke so easily, he must have thought the entire battle would go the same way. After all, he probably saw Richard of Cornwall's banner going forward up the hill and believed Leicester's center had also been destroyed. So he chased the Londoners.'' Hugh sighed.

''He chased them until the battle was lost,'' John said sourly.

Alphonse shrugged. ''A bad time and place for a mistake, but I have seen worse mistakes made in battles that were victories in the end. And you may put too much blame on Prince Edward. Leicester has exceptional skill as a battle leader. There is this too. I have known the prince from when he first began to fight in tourneys, and I have seen him make mistakes—but never the same one twice.''

Hugh smiled. ''That is a strong hope for the future. God give us all strength to live through the present without wounds so deep and bitter that they can never be healed. I have no right to complain, since I am the least injured of any by this trouble. My brother may curse me and shake his fist at me, but he has placed his own body and honor between me and any loss. That was what Barbara came to France to say—that my wife is safe and her only anxiety is for me, her only grief our separation.''

Another silence fell. Alphonse, suddenly reminded of Barbara, had his need for her doubled and redoubled by what he saw in Hugh Bigod's face when he spoke of his wife. Nor did Alphonse fail to notice that Hugh had not even mentioned what nine out of ten men would have put first—that his property had also been protected by his brother. From the long discussion of English affairs, Alphonse had come to a good understanding of Hugh and knew carelessness about material matters was not characteristic of him. Only in this case, the value of the woman was so great that everything else paled to nothing in comparison.

''I knew your niece when she was fostered by my aunt, Queen Marguerite,'' Alphonse said with outward calm. ''I was much surprised to learn that she had not remarried.''

But Hugh did not answer. His eyes were on the little wine

remaining in his cup and there was something in his face so private that Alphonse looked away.

"I should imagine Lady Barbe would be much sought after," he said to John. "Years ago, when Norfolk brought her to my aunt, he put some business into my hands, and I thought at the time that he was fond of his daughter. That alone should make her a marriage prize, and though she is not a great heiress, her manor at Cruas is not poor."

John laughed and then said softly, "She was sought after, but she refused all offers, and Norfolk would not force her to marry. You might call him doting rather than fond, but he has had so evil an experience of marriage I could hardly blame him. And poor Barby was caught in the middle. Norfolk had never agreed with his wife, Isabella, but she still blamed Barby's mother for being the instigator of the earl's attempt to free himself from his marriage to her, and she hated Barby for that. And to speak the truth, I do not think it was all sweetness and light between Norfolk and Barby's mother, either. She must have pressed him hard before he became willing to try to set aside Isabella, who is the sister of the king of Scotland. Then Barby's mother died in childbirth. All in all, one can see why Barby might be reluctant to marry."

"One can," Alphonse agreed dryly.

"Still," John said philosophically, "my mother was not happy in her first marriage, but she tried again and is more than content with Marlowe. Of course, we all knew William for many, many years before he married my mother. And although I often could have murdered King Henry, I must say that Barby had an example of a very happy marriage when she served Queen Eleanor. Whatever his faults as a king, Henry is a model husband, and Eleanor loves him dearly. Anyway, Norfolk left the matter of marriage to Barby and she refused every man, no matter whether he wooed or did not woo her. She railed against how women are made chattels and said she did not wish to be ruled by a man simply because he was bigger and stronger than she."

John started to say something else, but broke it off when Hugh rose and bade Alphonse good night. Alphonse replied, raising a hand in farewell to John, who followed his master to help him to bed.

The tale of Norfolk's unhappy marriage gave Alphonse a twinge of guilt but did not change his decision. He would hold Barbe to the promise she had made, and then he would teach her that marriage could be a happy state. He refilled his cup and emptied it twice more before he rose from the bench to seek his own cot while he planned what to do. Decision made, he told Chacier to wake him at first light as he was undressed.

Although he woke several times during the night, with a pounding heart, having dreamed each time that he was too late for something, Alphonse thought he was perfectly calm the next morning when he sent his message up with Clotilde. For a few minutes after she had gone to her mistress he was tense, half expecting her to reappear with a refusal from Barbara, but as the time stretched, he became more confident and moved from the middle of the hall to lean on the wall beside the stair. From there he would see Barbe before she saw him and could speak before she did.

Still, if the words he had planned to say had not been already fixed in his mind when Barbara appeared, he would have been struck mute. Each time he saw her, he was overwhelmed anew by an intense pleasure, which surprised him. The first time, he had assumed the reaction to be a result of surprise. When he had spoken to her near the stable, he had told himself the pleasure was owing to finding her fascinating even when he was not surprised. Now he acknowledged that he had felt the same pleasure at seeing her for years before she left France and that the delight she gave him had little to do with her physical appearance. Moreover, he suspected it would last all his life. In the moment he had hesitated she stood poised on the lowest step looking for him. He saw her stiffen with doubt when her eye did not find him, and he stepped forward and put his hand on her arm before her quick temper could rise.

"No, do not speak," he said. "What we say to each other now must be in a place where there can be no jesting and no lies."

She turned her head; he saw that she was unnaturally pale and had to bite his tongue to keep from promising he would not hold her to a promise she clearly regretted. That would be stupid, he told himself as he led her toward the church. She would be far better off married to him than unmarried. If he could never reconcile her to being a wife, he would give her her freedom. Then she need never fear that some great necessity could force her into a worse marriage.

Barbara balked slightly at the dark entryway to the church, but Alphonse went forward and she, too, stepped out of the silvery light of a gray early morning into the deeper gray inside the church. He seemed to feel her presence; although he did not turn his head to look at her, he took her hand as she entered a step behind him and led her out of the center aisle to the right. Near the wall and opposite one of the wide pillars that supported the roof and partially hid them from others in the church, he stopped and turned to face her.

"I am very sorry to hold you to a promise you made in jest," he said, "but I love you very much, Barbe, and I think I can reconcile you to being my wife."

Barbara peered at his face. "Please say that again," she whispered. It was not that the light was so poor that she could not see; she simply could not believe her ears and wanted to make sure his lips were moving in the right pattern to form the words she had heard.

Alphonse's square chin came forward and his lips thinned. "Very well, but this time I will speak the same truth without courtesy. I intend to hold you to your promise to marry me, and I am not at all sorry about it. I am delighted that you have fallen into a trap of your own digging. No doubt my offer seemed comical to you, who have been sought by others far more wealthy and powerful. No doubt also you were more cautious in your answer to those you feared to scorn, but I want you too much not to close my hand on you when you have fallen into it."

"You want me?" Barbara repeated, fastening on the words most important to her. "No, you do not—"

"Yes I do!"

His voice echoed in the almost silent building, the priests not yet having entered to begin the mass, and they both started and looked around. However, there were only a few people, well forward in the church, who did not seek the source of the remark. All kinds of business were carried on in a church, especially any that might require oath-taking, and raised voices were not unusual.

"Why would I take you into a church and insist that you marry me if I did not want you?" he went on in a tense but lowered voice.

"Because you have great pride and I shamed you by accusing you of wanting to make me your whore."

Alphonse stared, wondering if he would spend all the rest of his life being enthralled one moment and exasperated the next. "Idiot!" he exclaimed. "Would I make such a suggestion to you if I did not want you? Do you think I am so ill able to find a willing woman that I urge to my bed even those I find detestable?"

Barbara giggled. She felt divided into two parts, one on the surface, aware of how ridiculous the conversation was, and another beneath, in which an enormous joy was growing. But Alphonse had stiffened with indignation at her wordless reply.

"And I wish you would not call a spade a shovel with such

frankness,'' he added. ''There are more polite ways of referring to an irregular arrangement between lovers. To call every woman who forms a bond outside of marriage a whore does not become you, speaks ill of your charity, and makes me think poorly of the English court for not having cured you of such crudities of language.''

Barbara giggled again. For a moment she was back in a time when her hurt over Alphonse's rejection had become so much a part of her that she was no more aware of it as a burden than of the weight of her hair. Over the years she had been married to the absent Thouzan le Thor, Alphonse had become a lively friend and a wise, if irascible, teacher. So when she spoke, the words were a blend of the joyful heart and the amused mind.

''And am I to spend my life with a man to whom I cannot speak the truth, as I see it, in plain language? Did you not just call me an idiot? I did not take offense.''

''But to say I intended to make you a—'' Alphonse began then choked back the rest of his remark. Suddenly he chuckled. ''You are quite right,'' he said. ''A wife must be able to speak as she likes to her husband in private, so to me you may use the word 'whoring' if you think of courtly love that way—but not in the court, and not in Louis's hearing or I will murder you. Now that is done with, and do not try to start a new subject again. Do you promise, in this place, to marry me?''

''Alphonse—''

''You have already given your word. Will you be a coward and go back on it?''

She was silent for a long moment, then shook her head. ''I do not wish to go back on my word. I only—'' She intended to explain that the answer she had given him in the stableyard had come from her heart, that the laughter had been an accident, but he gave her no chance.

''And do you swear, before God, in His own house, that you will appeal to King Louis and to your father to accept me as your husband?''

''Yes,'' she said, and then, realizing that the joy inside her had become so great that she would die if she first gave it free rein and then discovered it to be false, she added, ''but—''

''No 'buts.' You promise you will speak to the king and to your father as if our wedding were the dearest wish of your heart?''

''Not until you answer one question,'' Barbara insisted. And before Alphonse could object she asked, ''Why did you first offer your 'protection' instead of asking me to marry you if you wished to marry me?''

The look of angry refusal—of what Barbara could not guess—

was replaced on Alphonse's face by an expression of astonishment, which melted into a smile. "I thought you were married already. I tried four or five times to discover the name of your husband, but you seemed not to wish to speak of him. Well, how was I to suspect that your father had not arranged a marriage for you?"

There was a vague noise at the door of the church. They both glanced toward the central aisle and saw that the priests and their acolytes were entering.

Alphonse drew Barbara a little closer, speaking softly and quickly but determined to finish what he wanted to say. "And Sir Hugh gave me no time to ask any questions after you and John left to see Queen Eleanor. He said, and I knew it was true, that she would be terribly hurt if I did not appear. So I changed my clothes for an excuse to be late and followed. Then when I found you near the stable and you spoke of your reason for remaining in France, I thought your husband was trying to push you into accepting the Montfort boy to curry favor with Leicester. But I told you the truth. You could have had my protection without coming to my bed. Nonetheless, you agreed to be my wife and I will keep you to your promise. I love you, Barbe."

The chanting had begun by then, without the usual hum of conversation and movement to blur the sound. The quiet was a warning that King Louis was in the church. Neither Barbara nor Alphonse found anything peculiar in a greater reluctance to offend the devout king with inattention to the mass than to offend God. The king was closer, and the result of his anger would be more direct. Together, they moved quietly toward the center aisle of the church and some way forward. As they stopped, they glanced at each other, recognizing that their thoughts were so much in tune that they had acted in concert without a word or sign needed.

Alphonse was filled with an enormous sense of relief. If Barbe wished to be seen with him at mass, it was very likely that she intended in good faith to ask King Louis to permit her to marry him. Had she hoped that the king would provide a way for her to escape her promise, she would have stayed near the wall where Louis would have been unlikely to notice her. After that, full of gratitude, Alphonse gave his attention to the service, sincerely praying for forgiveness for the many times he had not done so.

The wisdom of showing themselves to King Louis also passed through Barbara's mind, but her response to the mass was otherwise the result of endless repetitions. Her mind was fully engaged with the secular miracle she had experienced. She went over and over every word Alphonse had said, savoring her joy.

He had said he loved her; he had said he wanted her. At first it was enough to cherish the idea and to glance at him as he knelt and rose with her, catching fragmentary views of his black curls, the stubble of dark beard on cheeks and jaw, the strong nose and bold cheekbones, his gleaming dark eyes. But he did not look at her. Barbara was not hurt; it was clear that he was truly attending to the mass and she was not such a fool as to be jealous of his love of God. But the withdrawal that did not hurt reminded her that one might come—despite his present declaration of love and need—that would hurt.

How did one hold a man? She had never tried, never had any reason to want to hold one. She reviewed in her mind the men she knew to be faithful to their wives, but none of them seemed ever to have been a hunter of women like Alphonse. And then the word "hunter" provided a clue. In hunting a doe, the pleasure was in the chase. The kill itself was nothing, and the dead thing that remained was only meat for the table. It was the chase that was thrilling. So if Alphonse went from woman to woman, was it not because having "killed" his prey he lost interest in the dead meat?

Yet a wife, because she was bound to her husband's will and bed, was, by definition, dead meat . . . Only, he had believed she was laughing at him when she said she had loved him for eleven long years. From everything he had said, he believed he was forcing her into marriage—or, if not forcing, at least urging an only partly willing woman to accept him. Then let him believe it. There was no need to tell him the truth. Let him hunt *her* love.

Barbara choked back laughter. She would not hurt him by seeming resentful, but she could admit she was tired of refusing suitors, tired of being torn apart between her father and her uncle, and that, after consideration, she had decided that being bound to an old, familiar friend was the least of the evils that might attend marriage. Oh, what fun she would have, leading him a wild dance—and what pleasure she would give him, yielding a smile here, a kiss there. He would feel he was winning a rare prize.

Barbara was so busy planning into the future that she was still kneeling, seemingly absorbed in prayer, when King Louis, coming back up the aisle and nodding right and left to bowing courtiers suddenly stopped in front of Alphonse.

"Ah, Sieur Alphonse," he said. "Marguerite told me you had asked to speak to me, but I had forgotten in the press of business."

His voice startled Barbara out of her reverie. She jumped up only to sink down again into a deep curtsy when she saw who was speaking. The movement attracted Louis's eye, and he stared for a moment, then said, "Lady Barbe? Is it you?"

"Yes, sire." Barbara smiled and dipped again. "How kind of you to remember me after all these years."

"I see you have not taken the veil after all," he said with mild disapproval.

"No, sire," Barbara replied, looking down at her toes. "I knew it was best, but I could not subdue my heart to the cloister. There was a different desire buried too deep in it." She looked at Alphonse.

Louis sighed. "It is true that God takes pleasure only in willing sacrifices." Then, although Barbara had bowed her head in acceptance of the gentle rebuke, he seemed to remember how her eyes had gone to Alphonse and also looked at him. "Does your business with me concern Lady Barbe?" he asked, frowning but sounding relieved.

"Yes, sire, but—but not altogether."

"If you have an appeal to make because of the trouble in England, I must tell you that I can give you no answer. I cannot undertake to listen to any private pleas until King Henry's affairs are settled."

"I understand that, my lord, but if you could find a few moments for Lady Barbara to speak to you on a personal matter, we would be most grateful."

The king looked from one to the other and Barbara said, "You are my overlord for the manor of Cruas, sire."

Louis nodded. "If it is to do with Cruas, I will see you at the evening meal."

Barbara curtsied, Alphonse bowed, and the king passed on and out of the church.

"That was clever, bringing in Cruas," Alphonse said, urging Barbara back into the side aisle, "and I am glad too that you made plain you no longer wished to become a nun."

"Yes, well, I was thinking how I could explain why I had not married all these years," Barbara said coolly. "If I do not find a better reason before this evening, I will tell him I thought I would take the veil because you refused me and I did not wish to marry any other man." She shook her head and smiled as Alphonse seized her hand. "But do not allow the notion to take too strong a hold on you. It is not true."

Alphonse frowned. "It is not safe to lie to King Louis, Barbe. He is cleverer than you think."

She shrugged. "Then give me a better reason to offer him for my sudden request for permission to marry you. He cannot read inside my heart, and appearances will support what I say. I did not marry in all the years after Thouzan le Thor died, and I did accept you when you asked me." A smile of pure delight began to form, but Barbara managed to tighten her lips against it, which gave her mouth a peculiarly flat, hard look. "Even if I did not expect to be taken at my word."

"I will not release you." Alphonse's voice was firm, but his dark eyes were large and sad.

"I do not wish to be released," Barbara assured him with a little more warmth than she meant to show. "Women have not the same kind of pride as men. Had taking you as my husband been horrible to me, I would not have agreed for the sake of keeping a promise I did not mean to make."

"But you did agree." Most of the tension lines had eased in Alphonse's face and he smiled as Barbara nodded.

"Although I spoke in jest," she said, "I did give the matter some thought last night—and it seemed to me that, old friend that you are, there might be advantages to marrying you."

"Advantages you did not see before I asked?"

There was a growing assurance in his voice and Barbara began to feel worried. It might not be easy to keep this man, who surely knew too much about women, off balance.

"I never thought of it before you asked." She took her hand out of his. "I am hungry, and Princess Eleanor will wonder what has become of me if I do not break my fast with the other ladies. And it has just occurred to me that if you go and break your fast with Queen Eleanor, you would be able to tell her about these plans. I do not think she can forbid the marriage, but she does have some claim on me as a lady of her household."

"Well thought of. If Queen Eleanor goes weeping to Marguerrite that I have stolen her lady without consideration for her, I will have both my aunts around my neck." Alphonse recaptured her hand and tucked it into his arm. He seemed about to say something but did not, his brow furrowing in thought as he led her to the door of the church.

"A word of warning," Barbara said as they stepped out into the rosy light of a beautiful morning.

She paused and looked around. A cool breeze had driven away the stench of festering filth, and the colors of the garments of the ladies and gentlemen making their way toward their morning meal in the great hall were luminous in the early sunlight. Barbara could not help wondering whether it had really been gray and sticky all yesterday or if the shadow in her soul had befouled the weather.

"Warning?" Alphonse repeated a trifle stiffly.

"If Queen Eleanor thinks I desire you," Barbara said, "she

might try to prevent our marrying. She is usually kind, but just now she is so hurt and frightened herself that I fear she wishes to strike back at the world. And I am the daughter of Leicester's ally."

A trace of anxiety made Barbara's voice too flat and Alphonse cocked his head at her. "I will tell her that you have accepted me because you wish to use me as a defense against the unwelcome advances of Guy de Montfort."

"She might believe that," Barbara agreed slowly. "If more important matters have not driven it from her mind, she will remember that I was annoyed by Guy's attentions."

She pursed her lips, as she considered Queen Eleanor's reaction. The temptation when her lips formed a bow was too great. Alphonse caught her chin and kissed her. She stood rigid, not resisting but responding no more than a statue. He stepped back, angry at himself for going too fast, and turned his head, thus missing the way Barbara put her hand on the wall behind her for support. When he looked back she did not seem to have moved at all and she simply stared at him without any expression.

"Well," he said briskly, pretending he was not distressed by her lack of response, "Aunt Eleanor is so bound up in her own woes just now that I do not believe she will think of any objections. If she does, of course, I will point out that, as a younger son, I have little of my own, and your manor of Cruas is rich, well managed, and convenient to my property. If you remember, that was how I knew Thouzan le Thor. The income will make a welcome addition to my purse—a sound reason to choose a wife."

"Yes, of course," Barbara said vaguely.

Alphonse blinked with shock; he had expected a violent reaction to his casual remark that the income of her manor would be a welcome addition to his purse. He had said it only to take a little revenge on her, to bring a little life into her frozen face. But her eyes had no color at all, and they were so wide open that a rim of white showed all around the dark irises.

"Barbe—" he began, his head suddenly full of horrors. Fathers could be too fond or some other man could have hurt her. But a kiss? In a public place? How could that freeze her with fear?

She did not wait for him to find soothing words. "I am so hungry," she said, looking past him. "I will go now. No, do not come with me. Go and speak to Queen Eleanor."

Chapter 7

Barbara's parting words let Alphonse breathe again and lifted the horrors off his spirit. If she was urging him to speak to Eleanor, she intended to marry him no matter what she had felt when he kissed her. Now that he could think, he realized her voice was too calm for her stillness to have been caused by revulsion. It was more as if she had suddenly remembered something so overwhelming that she had lost all consciousness of the present time and place.

Another man's kiss? Alphonse, who had not been a prey to jealousy since his first love had betrayed him when he was still a silly boy, suddenly felt the fangs of the green-eyed monster. Why had she yielded without a struggle to his demand that she keep her word and marry him? Not because she cared about being forsworn—she had made that clear. Had Guy de Montfort done more than pursue her? Had he caught her and had his father sent her to France to bear the child in secret?

Having asked himself this melodramatic question, Alphonse began to chuckle. How ridiculous. When one came to bear a child secretly in France, one did not come in the company of a princess and present oneself to two queens. Besides, it was more likely that Leicester would welcome a marriage between his third son and Norfolk's only child, even if his lecherous son would not. In any case, Leicester would not take a chance of mortally offending Norfolk in the present political situation by rushing his betrayed daughter into exile. Barbe was not a ditchling seller of favors, not even a common knight's daughter. Had she been with Guy's child, Leicester would not only have agreed to marriage, he would have insisted on it. And between them, he and Norfolk would have found lands enough to cram into the maw of young Guy to make him willing.

Alphonse went briskly down the steps, shaking his head over the way love turned a man's mind to thin gruel. The most important aspect of his last few minutes with Barbe was not that she had not responded to his kiss—what could he expect her to do in the church porch? It was significant that she had urged him to go to Eleanor and smooth the way to their marriage. He was hungry, too, and it occurred to him that he had to see Hugh as well as his aunt Eleanor. Hugh clearly loved Barbe very much, and she almost certainly returned that affection; thus, Hugh Bigod would be a strong ally and a bad enemy in persuading Barbe to take her vows with joy.

In any case it was useless for him to rack his brains about Barbe's reaction. Most likely she had only been surprised, and perhaps shocked and annoyed, that he should kiss her in public. No doubt when the shock passed, she would suddenly remember what he had said about her manor and demand a promise from him signed in blood that he would not interfere with the way the manor was managed and would turn the income into her hands. He chuckled once more as he climbed the steps to the hall of Queen Eleanor's house.

Alphonse was right only about Barbara's remembering what he had said about her estate after her shock passed. When she did remember, all she felt was a rush of pleasure at how clever he was. To hear that Barbara would be deprived of the income of her dower property probably would seem like a "fitting punishment" to Eleanor. The queen was not a cruel woman; she would herself have protested if she thought Barbara would be reduced to rags or starvation, but she would know that the deprivation would not be severe. Alphonse would provide Barbara with everything she needed—all the proud lady would need to do was ask. When Barbara thought of that, she smiled. She knew Alphonse did not want her income. Either of his aunts could have provided him with a far richer wife. But it would indeed seem appropriate to Queen Eleanor for the daughter of a rebel to lose her "freedom."

However, when Barbara first brushed by Alphonse and walked

quickly to Princess Eleanor's house, she was in no state to consider the question of her dower rights. All she wanted was a place to sit down before her shaking knees gave way, and the only thought in her head, as she slipped into the hall and braced herself against the wall, was that it must have been a special dispensation of mercy that left her so surprised when Alphonse's lips touched hers that she felt nothing. Only after he had removed his mouth from hers did desire flood her. God knew what would have happened if they had not been in the open church porch. That and the memory of the people passing, although all she could see was his face, had allowed her to resist the urge to kiss him back.

If she had, her whole plan would be in ruins; she would have betrayed her love for him. Or would she? Barbara knew from what she had heard—it was quite surprising how many ladies offered her confidences in the hope that she would spill her own secrets in return—that love and lust did not necessarily go hand in hand. Barbara had listened and looked wise, but she had had no secrets to tell. Now she regretted her lack of experience with lust. Too fearful of being caught in the trap that had held her mother, she had avoided kissing in corners and assignations in the woods. Her amorous activities had been confined to words, looks, and sighs exchanged in public. That had been amusing, but the faint stirrings of excitement had been easily quelled, nothing like the attack of ravening hunger, the heat, hollowness, and fluttering in her belly that had sprung to life at Alphonse's kiss.

She had even told him she was hungry. Barbara suddenly giggled, but then sobered. Could she allow him to see her desire for him, or would that end his "hunt" for her love? There would be nothing funny about losing his interest and his desire for her. Barbara knew she needed advice, but there was no one she could ask. Queen Eleanor had held her husband, but King Henry was no lecher. He lusted after beauty in art and music not in women.

Princess Eleanor . . . Barbara considered the princess. Prince Edward certainly loved her. His voice and expression changed when he spoke to her or she to him. Eleanor had been married to Edward as a child of ten when he was fifteen, so he could not have fallen passionately in love with her at first sight, as in the romances. And although fathers did not hide daughters from him, as in the stories that were told of his grandfather, King John, Edward certainly had played with the ladies of the court and with others less elegant. Yet after he married Eleanor, his gallantries to women, except for common politeness, had ended. Why? What had Eleanor done? I could ask, Barbara thought—not why Edward was faithful; the princess would say it was her husband's great kindness and perfect nature. I could ask what Eleanor does to make her husband happy; the princess would be delighted to talk about Edward.

Barbara started forward into the hall without noticing that the ladies who had attended mass with the princess and the queen in her private chapel were coming in at that moment. One collided with her and exclaimed, "Oh, I am sorry. Did I hurt you?"

"Not at all," Barbara replied, although she had cried out in surprise. "I should have looked where I was going."

Her voice drew the attention of Lady Jeanne. "You have missed mass," she said severely. "The princess noticed your absence."

"I attended mass in the church," Barbara said, smiling sweetly. "Thank you very much for mentioning Princess Eleanor's concern. I will go to her at once and explain what happened."

On her way to make her curtsy to Princess Eleanor, who was seated at a table set up on the dais in the hall, Barbara gathered up bread and cheese and wine, which she could eat while standing. For fast-breaking only the princess's table was set up; others ate indoors or out, seated or standing, as best suited the tasks of the day.

As she had assumed, Barbara had no trouble inducing Princess Eleanor to talk about the early years of her marriage to Edward. In fact, the princess was so eager to recall those happy years that she invited Barbara to sit down beside her. Unfortunately Barbara soon found that what Eleanor had to tell her was of very little value to her; she would have had to become a different person to take the advice. Eleanor was by nature sweet, gentle, and yielding; Barbara knew she was more tart than sweet, and she had been told often enough that she was abrasive and stubborn as rock.

One piece of information Eleanor provided *was* very interesting. Barbara knew the consummation of the princess's marriage had been long delayed because of Eleanor's youth. Now, bright-eyed with joyful memory, which had temporarily relieved her present fears, Eleanor rambled on about her husband's kindness, saying at last that it had made him hesitate to ask of her more than she wished to give. But Edward had finally confessed he was displeased with her passive yielding when they coupled. Not that he wished her to refuse, she admitted, with a faint, genuine smile; he wanted her to participate.

She had, of course, spoken her doubts about sins of the flesh, Eleanor whispered confidentially, but Edward had told her that what he asked was no sin, for he did not ask it for the sake of pleasure. God bade all his creatures to be fruitful and multiply, and that was especially the duty of the heir to a throne. Some priests did not understand, he had pointed out, that unless she helped, she would not get with child.

Five years had passed between the consummation of the prince's marriage and the conception of his first child, but Barbara had heard too much talk among women to believe their active participation was needed to get them pregnant. Barbara's doubt must have shown on her face.

The princess leaned even closer to her. "But it was true," she said earnestly. "There was no sin in it, for what my dearling taught me to do made his seed come forth more strongly and so I did get with child."

There were a number of odd noises in the background that Barbara knew quite well were smothered laughter and, possibly, strangled cynicisms, but she paid no heed. It had occurred to her that desire might be quenched in a man of tender heart—and Edward, while not in general soft-hearted, was certainly tender toward his wife—by what seemed like fear or indifference. Also, a few actions beyond simple compliance, especially those that might seem accidental at first, might lend spice to what would be to Alphonse too common and familiar an activity.

So Barbara asked eagerly, "What was it that your husband desired of you?"

But, recalled out of her own sweet memories, Eleanor looked troubled. "Is it fitting that I tell you such things, you who are a maiden?"

Barbara made a quick calculation. Alphonse must have already broken the news to the queen, so it was safe to tell the princess even if she rushed right out to talk over the idea with her mother-by-marriage. Princess Eleanor would be pleased to receive the confidence, and she would have something pleasant about which to think and gossip.

"I ask," Barbara said, lowering her voice even further, although neither of them had been speaking loudly, "because I may not be a maiden very long," and explained about her French property and being in King Louis's gift.

Eleanor smiled again, this time with a touch of archness. "And you have no one at all in mind that you would like to marry?"

Many thought of the princess as simple, but Barbara reminded herself that Eleanor's nature was simple, not her mind. "I did not think of marriage at all when I came back to France," Barbara replied quite truthfully. "Then I only wished to escape Leicester's son, whose attentions I knew could not be wholesome for me."

The princess stiffened and drew back. "You did not wish to marry a de Montfort?" she asked with a lifted brow. Clearly she thought Barbara was lying to make herself seem less a rebel. "I heard that Guy's mother felt you were not the equal of her son."

Barbara smiled. The disdainful remark, made deliberately to quash her pretension, was the princess's revenge because she thought Barbara took her for a gullible fool. "Madam," she said, "I am sure that is true, but the question of marriage did not arise. Guy never suggested he wanted me for his wife, and I had no desire at all to be any de Montfort's whore. You know well enough that I was born out of wedlock. That state is not a happy one, even for such as I, loved and recognized by my father. I will never lay that burden on a child of my body."

"I am very sorry," the princess whispered. "I did not know Guy planned such evil." Tears rose in her eyes. "I never guessed any of them planned such evil. I thought Leicester a kind and honorable man, and yet—"

"But he *is* kind and honorable, madam." Barbara hastened to interrupt before Princess Eleanor converted Guy's lechery into a murderous intent toward Edward on Leicester's part. "Leicester is too fond a father to see ill in his son," she explained, "so he assumed Guy's intent was marriage. That is why he sent me away. He wished to spare both his son and me any pain. But when I came here, an old friend, who took care of my affairs years ago when my father left me here in France with Queen Marguerite, discovered my problem. He suggested that I would be safe from molestation as his wife. Also, his lands and mine march well together, so I agreed that if King Louis was willing, I would accept his suit to me."

"A friend of your father's?" The kind princess began to look worried again. She knew she had been greatly favored of God when her brother found a royal match for her with a prince only five years her senior. Sixteen years separated Queen Eleanor and King Henry, and there were marriages far more disparate than that. Some were happy despite the difference in ages, but others were not.

It was easy to read the train of thought that must follow the question the princess had asked, and Barbara smiled again. "He is not as old as my father, and, madam, I am maiden in body, but not in years."

"Then you desire—" Eleanor looked a little shocked at what she had been about to say. No woman should desire anything but to be obedient to her guardian or overlord. "I mean," she amended herself, "you are satisfied to accept King Louis's decision in this matter?"

"I know Sieur Alphonse to be kind, and I am comfortable with him," Barbara said carefully, and was rewarded by a warm smile.

Princess Eleanor approved heartily of friendship and comfort as the basis of marriage. "So I would accept him," Barbara went on, "if he is King Louis's choice, but—"

She was hesitating, seeking a way of saying, without shocking the princess, that she would not accept any other man even by God's decree, when Queen Eleanor's clerk bowed to the princess and said his mistress wished to speak to Lady Barbara. The princess nodded and Barbara rose without the smallest reluctance to follow him. On this most perfect of all days, the coincidence of the clerk's appearance just in time to save her seemed right and natural.

The feeling that nothing could go wrong that day upheld her, even though she was surprised by the sharpness of Queen Eleanor's attack. Later she laughed at herself for being such a fool, but the searching questions the queen asked drew her mind firmly away from the yearnings of her body and the vague worry about how to bind Alphonse to her and reminded her of her coming interview with King Louis. She spent the rest of the day, when not forcibly called from her thoughts by the need to eat and answer conversation sensibly, planning what to say to him. She considered many approaches but came back each time to Louis's essential goodness and to Alphonse's warning that it was dangerous to lie to the king.

Had she known that Alphonse would not be allowed to accompany her into King Louis's presence, she would have come earlier to the conclusion she reached anyway: that she must tell Louis the truth—but carefully. Alphonse himself had not expected to be excluded and had begun to protest to the squire who summoned her to the audience, but Barbara stepped forward at once and put her hand on his arm.

"My lord," she said, "the king is very wise. You know and I know that we are in perfect accord and what I wish to say will be said freely of my own will whether you are there to hear me or not, but how can King Louis know this? You were with me, and you asked for this audience. Might I not fear to tell the truth in your presence? Will I not be more likely to say what is truly my own desire if the king can assure me of his protection in private?"

Alphonse looked angry and worried, but Barbara pressed his hand and shook her head infinitesimally, and he recalled that further protest would do harm. He stepped back and let her go, oddly relieved after his surprise passed that she would break the ice of Louis's fixed notion. The idea surprised him again, considering his doubts about her real willingness to marry him, but he had been reassured by her steady look and serious expression.

* * *

Inside the small chamber that King Louis used for private business, Barbara saw a table had been set beside the king's great chair. At right angles to the table, most convenient for easy talk, stood a stool. Barbara let her breath trickle out with relief; apparently the king had decided her business could be conducted without formality. No clerk with a writing desk was there, and the squire who had brought her into the room looked briefly at the table and then went out again.

Barbara looked at the table, too. On an exquisite gold plate before the king lay untouched a thin wedge of cheese and an even narrower slice of meat pasty. Beside the plate stood a precious glass goblet filled with wine so pale that Barbara knew it was more than half water. As Barbara rose from her curtsy, Louis gestured toward a longer table against the wall and bade her take what she wished for her own meal. She would have to serve herself, he said, smiling, since she had requested privacy. Barbara thanked him for his consideration, assuring him that serving herself was no burden.

The selection offered, Barbara was glad to see, was far broader than Louis's own ascetic taste. She helped herself liberally. She was not hungry, but she wanted to demonstrate the fact that she would not enjoy the meager diet of a convent. She had already silently displayed her lack of fitness for a life of renunciation by wearing her richest clothes. Her tunic was a glowing orange, the outer gown a deep gold with sleeves so wide their ends trailed nearly to the floor. Her fillet and crespine glittered with jewels, long golden earrings set with sapphires hung from her ears, and elaborately worked bracelets ringed both arms over her tight tunic sleeves. The bracelets shone in bold contrast to the blue lining exposed by turning back the wide sleeves of the golden gown.

On a fine silver platter, she placed a selection of cold meat, two cheeses, and a good piece of the pasty. Nor did she add any water to the cup of wine she poured and carried back to the table. Balancing plate and cup carefully, she began another curtsy, but desisted when King Louis laughed, pointed to the stool, and told her to sit and stop bobbing up and down.

"You are making me very suspicious," he said, smiling kindly. "I do hope that you have not discovered any fault in the bailiff I charged with the management of Cruas."

"No, indeed, sire," she replied. "I suppose I should not have said only that you were my overlord for Cruas, but I did not know how to compress my request to you into few enough words. I am afraid I must go back many years to explain."

"Very well." Louis sighed. "If you must, you must."

He broke off a bit of cheese and chewed slowly, while Barbara reminded him briefly how her father had brought her to France and placed the problem of getting back her manor of Cruas in Alphonse's hands. "It was through Cruas that I became friendly with Sieur Alphonse and came to depend on him. I came back to France recently, sire, to escape the attentions of Guy de Montfort. When I met Sieur Alphonse again in my uncle Hugh Bigod's house, the years melted away and I told him my trouble. He offered at once to marry me to secure me from molestation. And when he did, I understood at once why I could not accept any other offer."

"Ah, you love him!"

But Barbara did not fall into the trap of using that word. She knew that Louis distrusted emotions, and love, except of God, most of all. She smiled faintly.

"If you mean that I grow faint and cannot speak in his presence or turn red and shake all over, as told in some lays and romances, I do not. Sire, I am not at all certain what is meant by love. I know comfort; I know friendship; I know what I feel for my father and for my uncle, and I know that I repose equal trust and affection in Sieur Alphonse. I have not found in all these years another man, other than those of my blood, of course, in whose hand I could put mine. I do not wish to take the veil. I do wish to have children, and Sieur Alphonse is the only man to whom I am willing to trust my own body and estate."

Louis looked at her with some surprise. "That is a most sensible view. Trust and affection are, indeed, a sound foundation for marriage, and children are a holy and natural desire in any woman."

Barbara bowed her head. "Sieur Alphonse and I are suited by birth, by estate, by age, and by long knowledge of each other. So I would like formally to ask for permission to take Sieur Alphonse as my husband."

"I cannot answer you at once, Madame Barbe," Louis said thoughtfully. "I must look at the grant of Cruas and give a little thought to Sieur Alphonse's lands and overlord. But without making any promise, I do not see any reason why I should withhold permission. Is Sieur Alphonse also waiting to speak to me?"

"Yes, sire."

"Then if you have eaten your fill, Madame Barbe, you may send him in to me."

Chapter 8

Alphonse leaned on the crenel in the battlement of Dover Castle and looked down and to the west where lay the town of Dover. Despite the fine harbor in the mouth of the river—ah, yes, the Dour—the town had an unfinished, temporary look to it. Well, that was no surprise when one remembered that it was constantly overrun by enemies in any conflict. Always the party that had power and the party that desired it both wanted Dover. Whichever side held the keep, the other came and overran the town—a rather pointless action, since town and harbor were within range of the castle's weapons and were thus useless.

Swinging around so that his broad shoulders were supported by the merlon, Alphonse looked across to the other towers. Overrunning the keep was another matter entirely. Unless there was treachery within, Alphonse could not think of any way to take Dover keep without two armies—one to loose during fruitless attacks on the great castle, the other to be decimated while fighting its way in. He had been so awed when he first saw the huge walls and buildings crowning the shining cliffs that he had forgotten both his frustration and his *mal de mer*.

The *mal de mer* was gone, of course, but the frustration was growing. He and Barbe had come to England with Sir William Charles, who carried a letter from King Louis stating his willingness to mediate a peace. Barbe had asked to come to explain in person to her father about her wish to be married; although she did not need his permission, King Louis being her overlord, she was afraid Norfolk would think she had been forced to take Alphonse for some political purpose. She wanted to see her father to tell him she was truly happy and the agreement to marry had been of her own free will.

Alphonse no longer saw the towers, though his eyes stared at the one closest. Barbe's desire to put off the actual marriage until she could talk to her father seemed reasonable, but it had wakened all his suspicions. And she had gone to Louis with the request, without telling Alphonse first. King Louis had been delighted. Her desire fitted perfectly with a private purpose of his own—a purpose in which Alphonse was involved—so he had been most willing to send them to England ahead of the agents who were to be his negotiating team.

Unfortunately none of their plans had worked properly. When they landed in England, they had become virtual prisoners in Dover. They were not chained or held in the black bottom floor of the keep; they were treated with courtesy and had every luxury Dover could supply, but they were not free to leave. Alphonse could not accomplish either the French king's purpose or his own. Sir William Charles had not been permitted to carry Louis's letter to King Henry. The letter was sent on—to whom, Alphonse was not ready to swear—by Richard de Grey, the castellan of Dover and an ardent supporter of Leicester. Barbara's letter to her father had also been taken by Grey.

Without moving his head, Alphonse checked the presence of the two men-at-arms who followed him everywhere. They were a pair of fools, bored and always off guard; he could have killed both in the time between two breaths. Then he almost laughed aloud. That was surely an extreme cure for his frustration—and it would not even accomplish its purpose. The worst thing he could do was to prove to Grey he wished to escape when he had nowhere to go.

Even if he could get Barbe into Dover town without those damned guardsmen, would she be willing to write again to her father? She had refused to ask for a special license to travel in the letter she had asked Grey to send to Norfolk. She had not even told her father that she was holding off her marriage, which she desired to take place as soon as possible, until she could see and speak to him. All she had written was that she was back in England and desired his approval of her betrothal to Alphonse d'Aix at his convenience. Alphonse had been furious about the lack of urgency, but she said she was afraid that her letter would be read and misinterpreted by Grey, and perhaps by others as well. And no matter what she wrote, would Norfolk come for them himself or send them a pass to travel?

Alphonse uttered an irritated sigh. From what Barbe told him about the somewhat strained relations between her father and Leicester, a passport issued by Norfolk might not be honored. And Norfolk could not come himself; he was no doubt responsible for the defense of the east coast against invasion—and being watched. Alphonse straightened and paced around the battlement until he was looking out to sea. It was that cursed invasion that Queen Eleanor and the king's half brothers were so set on that had caused the trouble. That invasion was probably the only subject that the queen, Lusignan, and Valence had ever agreed on—but Alphonse could not believe the invasion would be successful or that it would ever take place.

Eleanor and the king's half brothers had agreed on battle rather than bargaining but on nothing else. There was too much bitterness, too much desire for revenge, too much greed—and, as far as Alphonse could tell from the few days he had been in Boulogne, a complete lack of common sense about how to manage an invasion. Hugh Bigod could have organized it for them, but none of them trusted him because his wife and lands were under his brother's protection and Norfolk supported Leicester. And Bigod did not believe an invasion could succeed at this time and had not hidden his relief at being ignored.

King Louis could also have supplied the organization that was lacking, but he had remained strictly neutral, aside from advising Eleanor to wait for the outcome of his negotiation with Leicester before committing herself and her limited funds to a war. Queen Eleanor, however, had rejected the idea of negotiation totally, and had used every shred of influence and every device to gather men and money for the invasion. Alphonse sighed again. He had hardly recognized his aunt when, on a hint from Louis, he reminded her of Henry's letter warning that invasion could bring disaster to him and her beloved son, Prince Edward. She had laughed at the reminder, saying that Leicester had neither the strength nor the courage to harm Henry or Edward.

Eleanor was wrong about that, Alphonse thought, staring sightlessly at the moving gray water. Leicester did not lack strength or courage for any purpose. He had too much honor to violate the terms under which prisoners had yielded. Leicester might have made the threat, however, hoping Eleanor, who loved both her husband and her son, would be frightened and give up the idea of invasion.

Alphonse was annoyed with himself because he had not

guessed that, with rumors of invasion rife, he and Barbe would be held at Dover. In fact, he had not given political matters a thought. His head was full of the need to get to Norfolk and obtain his enthusiastic support by explaining to him how much he loved Barbe and how indulgent a husband he would be to her.

"Thin gruel," Alphonse said aloud.

"What, my lord?" one of the guardsmen asked.

Alphonse laughed and shook his head. "Nothing. An idle thought spoken aloud."

He was almost tempted to tell the man that thin gruel was what desire for a woman could make of a man's brains, but he did not want to be regarded as demented as well as untrustworthy. He cursed himself briefly, but silently this time. He and Barbe had been in Dover less than two weeks. If they had been married, or even lovers, he would not have cared if they were immured in the place for months.

Why did Barbe have to be so terrified of yielding her body before marriage? They were betrothed; for most women that was good enough. Did she intend ever to marry him or was all of this some kind of elaborate ruse? Ridiculous! What kind of ruse? For what purpose? She had certainly enjoyed his caresses and responded avidly the one time he had managed to get her alone. They were all but coupled when she suddenly pulled away frantically, almost hysterically. And here in Dover, where they could have found an empty wall chamber and shut out the guardsmen, she would not come near him except in company.

Barbe had given him a reason, and a good one, for refusing to share his bed. She said she would not bear a child out of wedlock and that betrothal was not enough in such parlous times. She was right. Alphonse knew it, but suspicions that her real reason was different troubled him and his frustration sent him to walk the walls, ready to tear out his hair.

Alphonse did not even dare go into the town without her to work off his rut on a whore. Barbe already knew too much about his past habits; she had made a remark or two about expecting him to be discreet and not shame her. He had tried to explain that if he had her he would desire no other, but she had raised those thick brows into their enchanting peak and bade him make no promises he would regret. Certainly to go whoring in Dover with two thick-headed and probably loose-mouthed guardsmen on his tail would not be wise.

Part of his problem was that he had been too sure of her once he discovered how cleverly she had paved the way for their marriage with King Louis. Alphonse's first meeting with the king had been very short. Louis had asked him whether he was aware of

Lady Barbe's request to him to sanction a marriage between them, and when he said he was indeed aware and had proposed the idea himself, the king had given him a summary of what Barbe had said.

"Lady Barbe has good reasons for accepting your offer," Louis had said then. "What is not so clear to me is why you made the offer."

"Because I desire her for my wife," Alphonse replied without pretense. "I have desired her for many years, since shortly after I, like a fool, suggested to Queen Marguerite that the simplest way to settle the matter of the manor of Cruas was to arrange a marriage between Thouzan le Thor and Lady Barbe."

Louis said nothing, but the doubt was clear in his eyes. Alphonse shrugged irritably. Usually he found his reputation as irresistible to women an advantage; it made his prey so curious they were easy to catch, but he was annoyed by the king's lack of perception.

"I do not play at courtly love with young and innocent maidens, sire, for they might not know the game and be hurt. Moreover, Thouzan le Thor was my friend. The marriage was by my advice. Surely you cannot believe that because I had made a mistake, I would shame my friend and make a life of misery for his wife."

"No, you would not," Louis said. "You are a man of honor." His disapproval of the general frivolity of Alphonse's life did not blind him to the fact that his wife's nephew lived by a strict code.

"I did not ask for her after Thouzan le Thor died," Alphonse continued, "because she told me she was not willing to consider a second marriage at that time."

After a pause, Louis nodded. "I do not remember the terms under which Lady Barbe holds the manor," he said, "and I must examine them, particularly since you are your brother's vassal for other lands, but I see no reason to discourage your suit at present. I will give you my decision and we can talk about terms and fines in two or three days."

Although Alphonse had guessed that Louis wanted the few days to consider more than the fate of Cruas, foremost in his mind was the proof of Barbe's willingness to marry him. He had been further lulled by Barbe's eagerness to spend that first evening with him, just the two of them in a quiet corner of Princess Eleanor's hall. He had obtained the princess's permission to have his lady's help in preparing a letter to his brother, who was his overlord. Barbe had been so serious and intent in devising arguments to convince Raymond she was a good match that Alphonse had not bothered to explain that he expected no protest from

Raymond. His brother had himself married for love and had come near a falling-out with his father over the bride he had chosen.

Raymond would be easily pacified, having long given up any hope that Alphonse would marry for money or influence. And Barbe was a good match for a younger son. The manor at Cruas was adequate; Norfolk might be of use to Alys's family in England; and Barbe's liking for and familiarity with court life would be a definite advantage. Alphonse's only doubt was aroused when he mentioned to Barbe that Raymond might commit himself so heavily in men and money to Queen Eleanor's invasion of England that he might be pinched when it came to paying the fee for Louis's goodwill.

"Then tell Raymond he will be wasting his men and money," she had said.

Since Alphonse had been glad of the excuse to express his doubts to his brother about the abilities of those planning the invasion, he simply agreed. He was troubled for a moment by the intense way she had spoken, however. So strong an opposition to the invasion seemed to mark a passionate attachment to the rebel cause. Then he had dismissed the problem as irrelevant. He and Barbe would live in France where she could feel as strongly as she liked without any consequences. Only the next day, when they had ridden out together, had he discovered that Barbe would not marry without her father's approval.

When Louis summoned him as promised two days later, Alphonse found that he had again been thinking too much of love and had lightly dismissed what should have worried him. Louis had said at once that there was nothing he could see to prevent the marriage and had named a fine that, although higher than Alphonse had expected, was not outrageous.

"I will pay, of course, sire," Alphonse said, "but I am afraid I will have to ask for time. As you know, I have little of my own. In other times, my brother would have provided the sum, but I fear he may have committed all that he can afford to Queen Eleanor. I have written to him, but I will not have any reply for another month."

Louis looked at him for a moment and then said, "You have written already? I had not expected you to write to Raymond before you had my leave to marry."

"I am very sorry if I offended, sire." Alphonse was surprised. The king was not ordinarily proud and did not ordinarily demand ceremonial politeness. "I hope you will forgive my eagerness. As I explained, I have waited many years and I am impatient of delay now. I sent my messenger as soon as I could because Barbe insists that if you agree she must still obtain her father's consent. She knows it is not his right to interfere, sire, but she loves him and he her. And considering her reason for coming here, I will not allow her to go to England alone."

"I am not offended." Louis paused and then added, "In fact, both problems—I mean that of Madame Barbe's desire for her father's approval and that of your brother's thin purse—might be solved if you are willing to undertake a task for me."

"I am always ready to serve you, sire."

Louis laughed. "You almost look as if you mean it, but I know you too long and too well, my dear Alphonse. I can smell the wariness in you. I will not force this duty on you. I do not believe you could perform it if you were reluctant. I will say only that it concerns Prince Edward and depends somewhat on my remembering that he admired your skill on the tourney field. Is my memory correct?"

"Yes, my lord, it is," Alphonse replied. "And I liked the prince. He is young and rash—or was, before so many misfortunes befell him—but I thought him clever and practical also and not likely to make the same mistake twice."

"Would he trust your word if you told him something?"

"Yes, sire, he would."

Louis laughed again. "Do not look so troubled. I am not going to ask you to tell Edward any lies. In fact, quite the opposite. I want you to tell him the exact truth and discover his private feelings."

"But, sire," Alphonse protested, "my exact truth may not be the same as yours."

"I understand that. I will tell you what I want you to say to Edward. Then you may add what you like."

"If I may say I am your messenger and only repeat your words, I am very willing," Alphonse said. "But I am not at all sure I will be allowed to see him."

"You will have the best chance of anyone. Edward is in the keeping of Leicester's eldest son, Henry de Montfort, whom you also know."

"Yes. We often companied together—with the prince. God help them. It must be a bitter cud for both to chew for the friend now to become the gaoler. Edward has too much pride to swallow his fate easily, especially since he has no one but himself to blame, and Henry must feel the rage and anguish because he is a fine man and, I believe, truly loves Edward."

Louis nodded with satisfaction. "You have made a point that has been troubling me. Leicester is clever, but I am afraid he has underestimated the prince's stubbornness and temper. No doubt one of Leicester's reasons for choosing his eldest son to be Edward's gaoler was his trust in young Henry and his desire to be sure that Edward was carefully watched without being mistreated. But another reason for Leicester's choice may have been his hope that their past affection would make Edward more inclined to listen to Henry. What I fear is just the opposite—that Edward has taken as an insult what was meant to be a kindness."

"That is by no means impossible," Alphonse agreed.

"You understand that King Henry is not a young man and the trials that he has undergone may have affected his health. There is no sense in mediating a peace between the king and Leicester only to have King Henry die and Edward repudiate everything because he is too bitter to accept any terms except the earl's abject surrender. I want to know how deep the gall has eaten into the prince's soul, and I want him to know that I will make no peace if he cannot accept peace. I will trust you to judge how much you may say if you cannot speak without being overheard."

Alphonse nodded. "I will do my best. As a friend of both, I can ask Henry de Montfort to let me visit Prince Edward. He will allow it, unless Leicester has ordered that the prince be refused all visitors. As betrothed of the daughter of Norfolk, I might be thought favorable to Leicester's party, so I might be allowed to see the prince in private. But I do not see"—Alphonse smiled—"how this can help my brother's thin purse. Most likely I will need to extend my stay in England to see Edward, which would cost Raymond more."

"I will remit the fine for freedom to marry—in return for service rendered."

Alphonse met Louis's eyes squarely. "Barbe could be of help to me. I know she was allowed to speak to Edward at court, and she has been serving Princess Eleanor. She could give Edward assurance as to the princess's and his child's well-being as well as of the kindness you have shown them."

Louis smiled. "And for that you would expect me to remit Madame Barbe's fine also." Then he frowned thoughtfully. "Actually, it is well thought of, Alphonse. Edward cares deeply for his wife. To have small, intimate questions answered might well ease his heart and make him more patient of other troubles." The king nodded. "Very well. Cruas is only a manor and I will not lose much by remitting that fee also."

Then Alphonse had bowed and thanked Louis sincerely. Now, remembering, he frowned out at the sea, noting absently the black dots that had appeared as some of the fishing boats made their way in. He had made a good bargain with King Louis, but if Barbe was a strong rebel she might well be angry, not so much over his undertaking a commission from King Louis but because he had committed her without asking. Surely she would understand that he had had to make the suggestion just then. Later, Louis would probably not have agreed; only at that moment, when he had already decided to remit one fine, would he be swept along and remit the other.

He had planned to tell her, but there had been no time for explanation. Having acknowledged his thanks, Louis had announced that a betrothal ceremony would be carried out before dinner and he and Barbe should be ready to leave for England the next morning. Alphonse remembered the king's shrug and the hand he had raised to stem any protest. The quittances for the fines and a letter requesting that he be allowed to travel freely with his betrothed wife in England would be brought to his lodging.

Once more Alphonse sighed. He should have told Barbe on the boat, he thought. Why had he been so reluctant? Now she would be angry . . . unless he could somehow use his other task to explain how he had become involved in gathering information for Louis. He had not left the king when Louis plainly expected to end the interview. Despite the moment being wrong, Alphonse could not neglect his promise to John of Hurley.

"There is another favor I must ask if we are to leave tomorrow, sire," he had said reluctantly.

A short pause followed, then Louis said, "Ask." But his voice was less friendly.

"This is not a great matter, sire, and will not touch your purse," Alphonse began somewhat apologetically. "My brother's father-by-marriage, Sir William Marlowe, was taken prisoner with Richard of Cornwall. My brother's wife is making herself sick over her father's well-being. Would you write a letter requesting permission for me to see Sir William and pay his ransom?"

"Raymond cannot pay your marriage fine but can pay Sir William's ransom?" Louis's question was sharp.

"The ransom is nothing to do with my brother, sire," Alphonse assured him hurriedly. "I doubt Sir William would accept any offer to pay his ransom. He and Richard of Cornwall are childhood friends, and Sir William has been allowed to remain with his lord. I know he will not accept freedom until Richard himself is set free, unless Richard has some task for him and orders him to go. In that case, of course, Richard will pay Sir William's ransom."

Louis frowned. "Then what is the purpose of this letter I am to write?"

"To pacify my sister-by-marriage, sire. Her father almost died of wounds taken in battle some twelve or fifteen years ago and she has never gotten over it. I can send her a copy of your letter, which will convince her that Raymond and I are doing all we can for her father."

The king's frown cleared. He now recalled that the comte d'Aix's wife did not come from a great family. Sir William had little wealth or power of his own and was not even King Henry's man. A request for favorable treatment for him could be made on humanitarian grounds and would have no political overtones.

"Very well," Louis said, "so long as I am not made responsible for the ransom and Sir William, if he is ransomed, swears to take no action against Leicester's party, you can have your letter." Louis put up a hand as Alphonse bowed. "But Prince Edward and Richard of Cornwall will not be kept together. You are to do my business first if you can—even before you go to visit Norfolk."

One of the black dots had changed to a cockleshell of a ship. Alphonse watched it disappear into the town dock. He felt one of the guards move closer and turned his back on sea and dock to walk around to the other side of the tower, which overlooked the outer wall and the great ditch. Because of the height of the outer wall, Alphonse could not see the ditch, only the edge of the road that went around the keep and trailed dustily over the headland until it disappeared in a small wood.

He had done his best to obey King Louis's order, Alphonse thought. He had written to Henry de Montfort at the same time Barbe had written to Norfolk and Grey had accepted his letter, but he had had no more answer than Barbe had had from her father. Because all the letters had been sent on to Leicester himself? That seemed— The thought broke off suddenly as Alphonse sensed movement and turned sharply, his hand on his sword hilt. The sword was half out of its sheath when the intruder stopped abruptly and said, "Alphonse!"

"I beg your pardon, my love." He laughed. "That is not the weapon I wish to brandish at you."

Color flooded into her face, and then, to his delight, she said, "Your chance to show me your pride and joy may be coming closer. There is a messenger come from London, and he had a large packet. I have a letter from my father and there is one for you from Henry de Montfort."

"What does your father say?"

Barbara looked at him meaningfully. "I do not yet know. The clerk who was sorting the packet put those two aside. I came to fetch you at once so you could read both letters."

She meant, Alphonse thought, that the clerk did not realize she could read and therefore did not try to hide the contents of the packet from her. And she had come away partly to let him know and partly to give Grey a chance to open and read the letters addressed to them if he wished to do so.

"How clever you are, my love," he said, and then with spurious innocence, "How strange it is that all our answers should come at the same time."

"Not so strange," she answered, the angry slate gray of her eyes suddenly brightening to a lighter blue with amusement at the game they were playing. "My father," she went on sententiously and most untruthfully, "would never think of inviting us to come to him without gaining the earl of Leicester's approval. And I am sure Sir Henry de Montfort would wish to let his father know that a close friend of his had come to England and was taking the daughter of an ally to wife."

"True," Alphonse agreed. "How unfortunate that Leicester was called away to Wales just when King Louis was brought to agree to be mediator."

As he spoke, the jest lost its humor for Alphonse, and his lips thinned. Even if Norfolk's letter was an invitation for him and Barbe to come to him, it might not be honored, and Leicester was just as far away as ever. There might be more weeks of waiting before Norfolk's consent could be obtained.

Barbara saw his anger and put a placating hand on his arm. She was in no doubt as to the real cause of his bad temper and was growing frightened by the way he had begun to avoid her over the last few days. Had she taken the right path when she insisted on being a wife before she gave Alphonse the right to love her? It was true that their betrothal had been hasty, but it had been complete and formal, announced in the chapel of the castle and witnessed by King Louis, Queen Marguerite, Queen Eleanor, and Princess Eleanor as well as her uncle Hugh Bigod and the king's half brothers, Lusignan and Valence.

God knew few betrothals had more illustrious and more conscientious witnesses. She had no fear that Alphonse would fail to marry her, but when he had taken her to a sheltered spot in the garden and began to caress her, she had had to fight him off. It was either that or tear off his clothes and leap atop him. Even a whore would not do that, nor would the boldest and lewdest of his mistresses. Her lust for him was shameful and would surely disgust him. Or if it did not, it would expose her need for him and remove any check on his interest in other women.

"Leicester did not go to Wales to spite us," she said, her eyes pleading for patience. "It is not the earl's fault that the lords of the Welsh Marches did not honor the oaths they swore when they were freed after Lewes."

Alphonse put his hand over hers and became aware that it was trembling. Why was she so concerned? "The fault may lie with neither Leicester nor the lords Marcher," he said, deciding then and there that he would tell her nothing about his plan to meet with Edward until he could wean her away from what he considered too great a sympathy for Leicester's cause.

"But when Grey explained why we were to be held here at Dover—that Leicester and the earl of Gloucester too were in Wales—did he not tell us that the Marcher lords had refused to give up the prisoners taken at Northampton and had attacked Leicester's allies in the west?"

"I fear those prisoners are the bone of the contention," Alphonse said smoothly, tightening his grip on the hand that was trying to slip out from under his. "When a man is taken in battle, his captor has a right to ransom. The custom is very old and very strong, and a defeat of the captor's allies does not diminish his right. He might agree to exchange his prisoner for another captive out of love or duty, or he might agree that his prisoner be yielded in return for his own freedom, but the mere fact that his party were the losers in a later battle is no reason that his captive should be freed on command without payment of ransom."

"Did the Marchers not agree to free the men they captured at Northampton in order to regain their own freedom?"

Barbara was only partly aware of what she had said. She had stopped trying to extricate her hand, and warmth seemed to flow into it from Alphonse's touch. That warmth was spreading insidiously through her body, making her wonder whether it was worthwhile to torture them both for the uncertain purpose of fixing her betrothed's attention on her. What proof did she have that seeming cool and indifferent would spur Alphonse into a more intense pursuit?

Alphonse, seeming to look only at her, managed to cast quick glances over her head and shoulder, noting the position of his two guards and the one who had come with her. They were far enough away, he thought, not to hear clearly what was said, especially if he kept his voice low.

Leaning closer, as if to say a word of love, he asked, "Did they?"

At first, because she thought he was about to kiss her, the question seemed meaningless to Barbara. She stared fixedly into Alphonse's face for a moment before she realized he had used the movement of his body as an excuse to lower his voice and recalled that they had been talking about whether the Marcher lords had agreed to give up their prisoners as one price of their freedom.

"So I heard when I was at court," she replied.

Her fixed, challenging stare made Alphonse even more determined to shake her attachment to Leicester's party.

"Perhaps you have been told only what your friends thought it safe for you to know," he said.

As he spoke, Alphonse pulled gently on Barbara's hand, drawing her nearer. Although she yielded to the pull and even leaned against his shoulder, allowing him to turn them both so their backs were to their guards, the fear that he could feel her desire for him made her suspicious. She rallied her scattered wits to say sharply, "And you will tell me only the truth and all the truth?"

Alphonse laughed and slipped his free arm around her waist. "Do not be a goose! Even if I were mad enough to wish to do it, how could I possibly know all the truth? The information I have comes from my aunt, Queen Eleanor, who must surely be the most prejudiced person involved, and from King Louis. I do not believe him to be prejudiced—"

"Except, perhaps, in his belief of the rights inherent in kingship?" Barbara suggested. Her voice still had an edge, but there was more amusement than anger in it.

"He does not forget the duties either," Alphonse reminded her.

"Very true, which is why King Henry's barons are forced to put constraints on him while King Louis's barons obey him without argument."

"Not completely without argument," Alphonse said, chuckling. "There are groans and growls and howls of rage in France too. Nonetheless, I do not mean to deny your point. I was about to say that I may be no nearer the truth than you. I must suppose both Queen Eleanor and King Louis have told me what they wanted me to know and no more."

He drew her still closer, bending as if to kiss her. Barbara drew in her breath, not quite sure whether she was about to pull away or respond, but his voice came softly instead. "But think, Barbe. If what you know is from the point of view of Leicester's party and what I know is mostly from King Henry's point of view, will we not come somewhere near the truth if we put what we know together?"

The warm breath tickling her ear made her shiver, even as tears of disappointment stung her eyes because he was still only trying to hide their conversation from the guards. All she could manage was "Is it safe to talk about this?"

"We must," he murmured, "but it would be better done in private, and perhaps we can make more sense after we see what is in our letters. I think we have idled away time enough here." He straightened up, but pulled her even tighter against him as he added, less softly, "And you are cold, I think. Let us go down to the hall."

Chapter 9

Both clerk and letters had disappeared from the hall when Barbara and Alphonse entered it. Neither of them was surprised, but before they could decide whether to betake themselves to a window seat and pretend ignorance or ask about the letters, a servant came forward and asked them to come into the castellan's chamber. There the letters were given to them and Sir Richard de Grey politely offered the services of his clerk to read to them. As politely, Alphonse refused, remarking that he was a good clerk himself, it being the custom in the part of the country from which he came for the nobility to learn to read and write.

"The better to compose verses to our ladies," Alphonse said, smiling. "But sometimes it is useful for other purposes. And I will read Lady Barbe's letter to her, since it concerns me most closely."

A flicker of irritation was barely hidden by a curt nod, but Grey handed Alphonse both letters without any further remark. Alphonse was surprised by this sign that Grey had not examined their contents and hoped he would learn them from his clerk, but that seemed to be true. A close examination of the seals in the privacy of his chamber showed no sign of their having been lifted.

"If he was so interested, why did he not look?" Alphonse said to Barbara as he handed her Norfolk's letter.

She, to his surprise, had followed him into the room and shut the door in the guards' faces without hesitation. He guessed she was too intent on whatever news had come to worry about anything else, but fate seemed against him. When he had schemed and planned to get her alone, she had been as adroit as a fish in slipping out of his grasp. Now that he wished she would go off alone to read what her father said, she wished to share the news. Not that he was uninterested in Norfolk's letter, but he wanted time to consider the best way to handle whatever Henry de Montfort had written.

"Now I think of it," she said somewhat absently, while breaking the seal on her father's letter and unfolding it, "Grey might well hesitate to open a letter from Henry de Montfort." She looked up for a moment. "Leicester's sons are precious to him, and Henry is pure gold in the earl's eyes. If you should complain to Henry and Henry should speak to his father, Leicester might be angry. He might even believe Grey was spying on him rather than trying to protect him."

"Nonsense." Alphonse was still turning Henry's letter in his hands, a little reluctant to open it in Barbara's presence. "Sir Richard de Grey has proven himself loyal."

Barbara did not answer, but after she had eagerly scanned the parchment, she let the hand holding it drop and uttered a sharp sigh of impatience. "He says *nothing*!" she exclaimed, and proffered the letter to Alphonse.

The disappointment in her voice wiped everything from his mind but the fact that Barbe seemed as eager for her father's approval as he. But as he reached out to embrace her, she thrust the parchment into his hand. By then the sense of what she said had penetrated and he looked down at the letter, noting the neat cursive lines of a scribe's hand. Norfolk had not written it himself. After he had read it, he looked up again, black eyes intent.

"He does not say nothing," he remarked. "He says you have chosen well. Surely that is permission for us to marry, Barbe."

"I suppose it is," she said, but the eyes that met his were full of tears. "But here? Without a person I know to attend me? I wanted to see him. Oh, Alphonse, something is very wrong, very wrong. Papa cares for me. He would want to speak to me, to see me married."

Alphonse did not answer immediately. The tearful protest did not make him angry because he did not think it was an excuse to delay their wedding. He sensed something wrong in Norfolk's stiff reply himself, recalling the man's real affection for his daughter.

"Do you think he did not write this?"

"No, not that. I recognized his clerk's hand, and as for the exact words, he hardly ever says more than 'tell her this or that' when he bids the clerk write to me or anyone else, except the king, perhaps. But why did he not tell us to come to Framlingham or Orford to be married where I could have Joanna with me?"

"You are afraid he is in deep trouble with Leicester," Alphonse said slowly, then shook his head. "No, if that were true, Grey would have opened his letter. That he did not touch it at all can mean only one of two things: Either your father is above suspicion—and we do not believe that to be true for good reasons—or he is still too powerful to offend."

"Why did I say Orford?" Barbara muttered and snatched back the letter. When she had reexamined the heading, she smiled. "You must be right, for he wrote from Orford, and that is a royal castle. Leicester would have demanded my father give up Orford if he really distrusted him and could enforce the order. But I still do not see why papa did not bid us come— But you have not yet read what Henry de Montfort wrote. Perhaps that will explain. Henry is more in his father's confidence than anyone else. What does he say?"

To hesitate about opening the letter now would amount to screaming aloud that he did not want her to know what was in it, so he broke the seal and read, bursting out after a few minutes, "We are freed!"

"To go to my father?" Barbara asked eagerly.

"No, to Canterbury. Wait, let me finish."

"Canterbury?" Barbara murmured to herself.

At first she was disappointed, but after a moment she smiled. I will be married in the cathedral, she thought. The archbishop is in France, but someone else will marry us. Whom do I know in Kent who could come to attend me? She wandered away and sat on the chest that held Alphonse's clothing to think about the women who lived in Kent.

Meanwhile, Alphonse had breathed a sigh of relief. Henry de Montfort's letter was delightfully discreet. After an apology for the long delay in replying, for which Henry gave no reason, he urged Alphonse to come at once to Canterbury, where the court was gathering for discussions with King Louis's emissaries. Henry de Montfort himself expected to be there by August 12 "in company with Prince Edward." Although he said no more on that subject, Henry expressed his joy about Alphonse's betrothal and warm praise of Barbe. In fact his expressions of delight were so warm that Alphonse reread them. He did not remember telling Henry about his long and hopeless desire for Barbe; he had never told anyone . . . unless he had spilled something when drunk?

''We are to join the court in Canterbury,'' Alphonse said, dismissing the puzzle of Henry's enthusiasm. ''Apparently arrangements have been made to meet with Louis's emissaries in Canterbury some time after the twelfth of the month.''

''I thought you told me that the meeting was to be here in Dover on the eighth,'' Barbara said, drawn from her pleasant, if inconclusive, thoughts.

''That was what King Louis told me, and why he sent us off in such a rush—'' Alphonse barely prevented himself from gasping at what he had let slip, but he went on quite smoothly, ''I suppose Leicester sent word after our departure to put off the meeting. He would not want Queen Eleanor and the king's half brothers to learn of the Marcher lords' rebellion. That would be an open invitation for an invasion.''

Somewhere in Barbara an alarm sounded, but it was faint and far away. She ignored it, diverted by what came foremost to her—the fact that the whole court would be at Canterbury. ''Perhaps that was why my father did not tell us to come to Orford. He must be coming to Canterbury.'' She laughed. ''He thought we knew all along.''

''I hope so, Barbe, but do not set your heart too much on his being there,'' Alphonse warned. ''He might have guessed we would be at Canterbury but could not promise to meet us. He might not be able to leave his post if the threat of invasion seems immediate.''

He gave no sign of his relief. Seemingly she had not noted the hint that Louis had a private purpose in sending them to England. He could not understand why he was unable to keep any thought private from Barbe. He had always trusted her and admired her cleverness, but the present situation should have made him more wary, and by habit he did not blab anything to women.

Barbara had hesitated over his warning, but shook her head. ''Canterbury is not far from Orford. He could come by coastal boat in a day.'' She jumped to her feet. ''I will write to him at once and beg him to come and to bring Joanna—'' The brightness of her face dimmed. ''No, I must not ask that. Even if Leicester himself is not there, one of the others might demand that my father give Joanna up to him.''

Alphonse laid both hands gently on her shoulders. ''But Norfolk may have reasons about which we know nothing to remain on his own lands. If he cannot come, will you make me wait, Barbe?''

She hesitated, not wanting to seem too eager and troubled because her father might be hurt. ''Let us see what my father answers.''

"His answer might take long to come if the letter you write today takes the same route as the one you wrote when we first arrived."

Her thick brows drew together. Alphonse had provided her with a salve she could use to soothe her father's wounded feelings—if he was wounded by her marrying without his support. "If there is no letter and papa has not come by the fifteenth, and if King Henry will give his permission, we can marry before the court is dismissed." She smiled. "I would like to be married in the cathedral with the court in attendance."

"Barbe—"

She stepped back, stiffening as he reached for her. "There is a problem more immediate than my agreement," she said. "Before we make more plans, I think we had better discover whether Grey will let us go."

That reminder was as effective as a bucket of cold water in cooling Alphonse's flush of heat. He nodded briskly and went to open the door, quickly marshaling arguments and veiled threats to induce the castellan to free them, and then considering the problem of how to get to Grey if he tried to use delay as a weapon. In the event, none of Alphonse's devices were necessary. Although Grey was clearly angry and uneasy, he merely nodded when Alphonse told him that Henry de Montfort had bidden him to join the court in Canterbury and that he and Lady Barbe wished to leave the next morning.

The castellan's sullen acquiescence, without even a request to see Henry de Montfort's letter, was virtual proof that Henry must also have written to Grey. Alphonse was delighted, nor was his satisfaction diminished at all when Grey said that he would be sending a guard of ten men-at-arms to see that they arrived safely.

"By all means," Alphonse answered with a sunny smile. "I gather that is most necessary in this country now."

What Grey would have replied to that subtle insult remained forever lost because Barbara appeared at that moment with a letter in her hand. "I have written an answer to my father's letter," she said, looking down her long, elegant nose at Grey. "I wish this to go direct to my father at Orford rather than being sent to the earl of Leicester first."

The castellan made a wordless protest and Barbara's brows went up. She sniffed disdainfully.

"Please understand, Sir Richard, that I have nothing to hide and no objection to Lord Simon seeing what my father and I have written, but the matter is wholly personal, concerning only my marriage to Sieur Alphonse. To make matters simpler for you, I have brought the letter open so that a copy could be made and sent to Leicester if you so desire. However, if you do not send my answer direct to my father so that he can come to Canterbury for one day to give me in marriage, I will be very angry and very bitter."

Grey turned puce, and Barbara lifted her head still higher, struggling mightily not to laugh at his reaction. In a way she was sorry to pretend contempt for what she knew the man felt to be his duty, but she had considered a variety of ways to get her letter directly to her father and this seemed the only practical method.

"If you will be good enough to have your scribe copy the letter," Alphonse suggested, "it would allow us more time to oversee our packing."

"Canterbury is only some six leagues distant," Grey protested. "The court will not arrive until the twelfth. What is your hurry?"

Barbara and Alphonse looked at each other and then back at Grey. "I do not wish to sleep in the gutter," Alphonse remarked, as Barbara said, "Queen Eleanor is in France, and I will have no place among her ladies. Sieur Alphonse and I must seek lodging. It is late for that already."

Sir Richard started to speak, then changed his mind. Barbara thought she caught a flash of an odd expression, but she could not define what it meant and was not even certain she had seen anything. In any case he did not interfere with their departure early the next morning. Indeed, once they were out of Dover, the captain of the guardsmen assigned to them showed himself most eager to get them into Canterbury town as quickly as possible.

Barbara almost made a fool of herself twice—once by remarking on her surprise about the captain's desire for an early arrival at Canterbury and again by very nearly suggesting that since the day was fine, bright but not too hot, they might take the coast road to Richborough before turning inland. Both her mare Frivole and Alphonse's great gray destrier, Dadais, were in need of exercise, prancing and lunging in their eagerness to run after being confined for so long. Barbara was completely in sympathy with the animals. She too had had enough of confinement. Fortunately the way the guard surrounded them as soon as they emerged from the gates of Dover Castle reminded her that there must be armed encampments along the cliffs that they should not seem eager to see, and she held her tongue.

Other things struck Barbara as peculiar and made her uncomfortable. The roads were unusually quiet. She would have expected the way to be blocked more than once with supply wagons hauling salt fish and grain and with herds of sheep and cattle and gaggles of geese being driven in to feed the influx of people expected for a gathering of the court. Several times she began to mention the matter to Alphonse, but changed the subject because of the close attention their voices brought from the captain of the guard.

Nor was there any crush at the gate when they arrived in Canterbury well before the time for dinner. Nonetheless, the guards at the gate that fronted the Dover road were tensely alert, and Alphonse had to show them Henry de Montfort's seal before they were allowed to enter the town. The anxiety implied an overcrowded situation of incipient violence, but Watling Street, from which one could go left to the castle or right to the cathedral, was all but deserted.

Barbara could not imagine what Alphonse was thinking. His expression was bland and bored, his black eyes half lidded. However, he signaled to Chacier, who promptly turned into the first crossroad, drawing the packhorses in behind him. Before anyone could react, Alphonse pulled Dadais to a stop across the entrance to the street, and said to Barbara, "Let us find a place to eat, my lady."

The remark caused an instant renewal of an argument that had arisen several times before. The captain of the guard Grey had sent with them wanted them to seek lodging in the castle, and he now assured them that a fine dinner would be waiting for them in the keep. Apparently he had been told to use any means but violence to get them there; however, in their case nothing but physical force could have succeeded. Both Alphonse and Barbara suspected that, once in, they might not so easily come out again. Neither had anything to gain by obeying the order or to lose by disobeying it, so aside from a single irritated glance, both ignored the captain and his suggestion.

Unfortunately, they were not agreed on anything else. Alphonse wanted to find a private lodging or, failing that, an inn; Barbara, knowing that an inn or private lodging would mean sharing a chamber, put forward the idea that they ask the White Friars for places in their guest house.

"And then after we are married where will we go?" Alphonse asked. "By then the town will be fuller than a barrel of herrings."

That was true. The captain again advanced the notion of going to the castle, promising that a private chamber would be found for them. Barbara sighed.

"No," she said, "I have had enough of royal castles." She turned her mare's head right, toward the crossroad, and smiled at Alphonse. "Let us go to the inn at the end of the Mercery. We can have dinner there and inquire about lodging."

"You must come to the castle first," the captain said.

In a single practiced movement, Alphonse drew his sword and

swung his shield from his shoulder to his arm. "My lady says she has had enough of castles. Now, sir, you may fight me until you have killed or disabled me or you may let me take my lady to the inn for dinner. If you wish to accompany us to the inn, you may do so. If you wish to accompany us to our lodgings, you may do that too, although I will not permit you to enter therein. I have nothing to hide, no secrets to keep or to ferret out, no desire at all to leave Canterbury before I can see my friend Henry de Montfort and marry my lady in her father's presence—but I will come and go at my own will, not at yours."

There was a moment's tense silence. A guardsman tried to edge his horse between Frivole and Dadais, and Barbara tightened her rein and kicked her mare, who promptly rose on her hind legs and flourished sharp iron-shod hooves at the guardsman's gelding, which backed away nervously. A quick clatter of hooves behind them made Barbara glance over her shoulder, but that was no threat. Chacier was coming back with his sword drawn. Farther back, Clotilde, who had ridden pillion behind Alphonse's servant, was standing in the street, pressing one hand to her lips and holding the rein of the lead packhorse with the other. Then Dadais screamed, lifting his black lips to show long, yellow teeth.

Hurriedly, the captain backed his own horse north on Watling Street, signaling his men to clear an area around the stallion, who seemed about to charge.

"*Pas, pas*, Dadais," Alphonse murmured soothingly, pulling back on the reins, which were still caught in the tips of the fingers of his left hand. "Barbe, go ahead," he said, louder, but in a carefully calm, quiet voice.

She cautiously edged Frivole around the stallion, whose high-arched neck still betrayed tension, and stopped beside Clotilde, turning in time to hear the captain shout the names of six men and order them to follow Alphonse while he rode to the castle for assistance. Alphonse backed Dadais into the side street watching until, with a curse, the captain rode away up Watling Street. Then Alphonse sheathed his sword and slid his shield back on his shoulder. His face was completely blank as, with eyes on the six men ordered to follow them, he soothed Dadais into a more relaxed stand. Then he turned him and passed Chacier, who moved aside and fell in behind. By the time he reached Barbara, however, he was grinning broadly.

"That felt good," he remarked, glancing over his shoulder to make sure that the guardsmen were far enough behind not to overhear him. "I was almost hoping that Dadais, who is not named 'idiot' for nothing, would get away from me and charge.

It would have been a real pleasure to drop that captain in the mud."

Barbara also looked back, assuring herself that Chacier had pulled Clotilde safely onto the pillion saddle. The guardsmen were just behind the packhorses. When she had touched Frivole with her heel and started forward, she chuckled. "That captain has a great deal in common with Dadais, I must say, but it was not his fault, after all. He must follow his orders, and if they are impossible to fulfill, then he cannot help looking like an idiot."

"You were not frightened, I hope."

"Oh, no," she assured him, laughing again. "If the captain had been permitted to use force, Grey would never have allowed you to ride out armed on your destrier."

"You have a touching faith in me, my love, and I do not wish to discourage it, but eleven to two are bad odds, even for me and Chacier—and I am not sure Sir Richard de Grey is aware of my reputation."

"Do not be so silly. Grey could not afford to put even a bruise on you after Henry de Montfort invited you to Canterbury. And Henry must have written separately to him because he did not ask to see your letter."

"So you guessed that. I thought so too."

Barbara nodded but did not reply. She had to give her full attention to her mare, who was less skittish than she had been when they started, but still had enough energy to take exception to a child running in the street and to the slamming of a door. In places the street narrowed too much for Alphonse and Barbara to ride abreast, and he took the destrier forward. Barbara had to hold Frivole well back. The mare did not like to follow and tried to nip Dadais, which would have been a disaster because the warhorse was still shaking his head and snorting, barely under control.

The nameless lane they had been following curved north after a while and ran into the Mercery, but before they came to the end of the quieter street, they could hear the noise of the market. Alphonse muttered a curse. "I will never be able to ride Dadais through there without killing someone," he told Barbara. "Either I must go around, if you know a way, or I must lead him."

Even as he spoke, Barbara was sliding from her saddle. "We must sacrifice our dignity," she agreed, taking Frivole's reins in a firm grip just under the mare's jaw with her right hand and lifting her voluminous skirt to midcalf with her left. "There is no way that will not take us through one market or another. I do not think Frivole will kill anyone if I ride her, but she will kick over half the stalls just for fun."

The precautions were wise; even with them, several disasters were narrowly averted and it was a relief to arrive at the inn that faced the cathedral on the southwest corner of the Mercery. Barbara was so annoyed with Frivole, who had jerked her arm half out of its socket and made her drop her skirt so that one edge was soaked in a gutter running with filth, that she relinquished her without a word of precaution to the hostler who ran out. Alphonse did not need to say anything because Chacier had already thrust his own gelding's reins and those of the first packhorse into another hostler's hand so he could run to Dadais's head.

"That horse worries me," Alphonse said mildly to Barbara, after watching Chacier lead the beast away and then glancing at the men-at-arms who had followed them into the inn yard.

Barbara had just told Clotilde to arrange for dinner and for the innkeeper to set up a private table for her and Alphonse. Her mind was mostly on food, and she waved the maid on her errand before she looked up at Alphonse in considerable surprise. "Is he so intractable that you fear him?" she asked in a carefully neutral voice.

"Of course not," Alphonse replied, his eyes opening and his brows rising with astonishment at the notion of his fearing any horse. "He is not vicious at all. On the contrary, I believe he loves me, and Chacier too, with the idiot devotion of a dog. It is likely he thought he was protecting me back on Watling Street." Alphonse sighed. "He is the strongest and bravest destrier I have ever ridden—and the *stupidest* too. What worries me is whether the three things always go together."

"Strong, brave, and stupid—like you?" Barbara laughed although she was annoyed with herself for not seeing the point, since she knew the horse's name and Alphonse had already commented on his destrier's stupidity.

Alphonse put an arm around her waist and led her into the passage to the door of the inn. "Yes, like me," he said softly. "Perhaps it was not so clever of me to refuse to go to the castle. Henry would have given us our freedom when he arrived anyhow. Now he is going to hear a strange tale about us before we can explain."

"Oh, no," Barbara replied, equally softly, turning and lifting her head so she could speak near his ear.

Her nose almost brushed the line of his jaw, and Alphonse's sharp male smell of sweat, horse, and the oil and metal of armor—a smell that was subtly different from her father's—sent a wave of arousal through her. For a moment she could not speak at all, and the hand she had laid over his at her waist tightened.

In the next moment footsteps echoed under the overhanging second story of two sides of the inn as two of the men-at-arms hurried after them. Barbara could feel Alphonse's hand stiffen under hers, and she let a small sigh of relief spill out. She had escaped betraying her desire for him again by the barest accident. He had taken her silence and the sudden pressure of her hand together with the sound of the men's footsteps as a warning of the way sound carried in the passage.

At the door the innkeeper was waiting, bowing low at the sight of Alphonse's mail and Barbara's rich silk riding dress. He backed into the low-ceilinged, dark room, which smelled of ale and roasting meat and many people. But the place was almost silent, the subdued voices of the few shadowy customers scattered around the heavy tables hardly a murmur, nothing like the raucous noise of a full room.

Nonetheless, the innkeeper did not gesture them toward an empty table; he preceded them to a side door that opened into another small courtyard, walled off from the stableyard. The center of the area was grassed, and beds of flowers brightened the edges around all the walls. Servants were there already, setting up a table and placing two benches. Barbara smiled. Clotilde could always be relied upon to get the best. Sitting in this little garden would be much more pleasant than sitting in the dark inn.

Meanwhile Alphonse had glanced around approvingly, noting that there was no gate in the wall—a reasonable precaution if the innkeeper did not want his guests to disappear without paying. He released Barbara and turned to face the two men-at-arms, who were just about to enter the garden.

"You may come in and look about," he said. "Make sure there is no one waiting to meet us. Check that there is no way out save through the door we entered. Then go. I will give you my word to go out only by the front door, but I would advise you to divide and let two men watch our horses and another two see that we do not climb the wall."

The men retreated hastily into the inn, not being made of the same stuff as the captain, and Alphonse seated himself on the bench opposite Barbara, lifting the tails of his mail so he would not be sitting on the metal rings. She giggled faintly, not loud enough to be heard inside the inn.

"Climb the wall, indeed! I would like to see you do it in full armor, not to mention me in my best silks."

Alphonse shrugged. "I do not like to make people hate me. The men will be in trouble enough with their captain for not having forced themselves into our presence, even though the captain knows quite well they were powerless to do it. However, if they set a guard on the door, on our horses, and on the wall, no one can punish them for a real oversight. So if their captain's bad temper results in their being lash-bitten, they will be angry with him, not with me who gave them good advice.''

Barbara nodded. ''Very clever. And if they escape punishment, those men will certainly be willing to talk to you or perhaps even do you a small favor.'' She smiled. ''I do not think you need worry about too close a resemblance to Dadais,'' she said, then nodded again. ''And I do not think you need worry that Henry de Montfort will think your behavior suspicious. He will understand how you felt about being penned up like an animal. Remember, his brother Simon was taken prisoner at Northampton, and perhaps kept more straitly than we. Simon was only released two months ago. Henry will not have forgotten Simon's fury.''

''I hope you are right,'' Alphonse replied, but his mind was clearly elsewhere, his eyes passing around the garden, deserted now except for them. He asked suddenly, ''Why are we alone here? I do not know English ways, but when the French court is coming to a town, the place is full long before Louis himself arrives. In France an inn like this would be bursting at the seams four days before the king's arrival.''

''It should be the same here,'' Barbara assured him, and mentioned her uneasiness about how quiet the roads had been. ''Half the country should be in Canterbury applying for writs for the king's court.''

''Not if they do not trust any judgment that would be given when the king is under duress,'' Alphonse remarked.

''More likely they would not come because Leicester is known to be in Wales,'' Barbara riposted. ''The king's judgments are notoriously based on favoritism rather than justice, and many prefer Leicester's.''

Although the answer was sharp, her voice held more challenge than anger and Alphonse laughed. ''Not when an appeal to Leicester's judgment is likely to get the favored suitor hanged when the king takes power again, but—''

''*If* such a thing should happen—'' Barbara interrupted.

She was interrupted in turn. ''Sorry.'' Alphonse raised a hand in a fighter's gesture for temporary truce. ''Let us not argue about what may happen. I am more interested in what is taking place now. Remember how I needed to show Montfort's seal at the gate? Can the guard have been told to turn away anyone who does not have a direct invitation?''

''It is possible, but I do not believe it,'' Barbara replied. ''Would there not be a camp near every gate, full of those who had traveled here and been stopped? Even if the guard bade them be gone, most would only move farther out along the road, waiting to importune those of power as they approached the city. And I do not think Leicester would give such an order."

"Then no court has been announced," Alphonse said. "There will be no pleadings of justice. Those who are wanted for the negotiations with Louis have been summoned, no one else. Of course." He nodded with satisfaction. "I should have thought of that. To announce holding a court now might draw defenders away from the coast." He smiled. "We should have no trouble finding lodgings."

Barbara was sure the smile was false, a cover for some idea he did not wish to express, but she gave no sign of her suspicion. She had not the smallest desire to argue with Alphonse about this political situation. To him "king" meant a man like Louis of France, whose faults were too great seriousness and attention to his duties, not carelessness and favoritism and moral cowardice. If they stayed long in England, Alphonse would learn what King Henry was.

However, Alphonse's guess about lodging proved only partly accurate. After an excellent dinner, a question to the innkeeper provided directions to only two merchants who held the living quarters above their shops free for rental. Most lodgings, the innkeeper said, were being held by servants for their masters.

Without giving a reason, Alphonse shook his head at the first place they visited, which was only a few doors south of the inn. Barbara protested that it was a most inviting chamber, large and cool and well lit by several windows. And the horses could remain in the inn stable. Alphonse smiled, lips tight against his teeth, and she said no more. They took the second place, the solar of a grocer's shop on St. Margaret's Lane, diagonally across from the church. This house was also near enough to the inn to leave their horses there, and the large chamber had a walled-off section at the back, furnished with a handsome bed.

Barbara felt like bursting into tears when she saw the place and saw Alphonse nod curtly at the landlord. The separate bedchamber deprived her of any excuse to seek a lodging with the White Friars. She peeped in at the doorway, stared at the bed with dilated eyes, and then backed up precipitately to stand with hands clasped before her near the empty hearth. Alphonse did not seem to notice her odd behavior, although the merchant did glance at her uneasily once or twice.

Alphonse recalled his attention sharply by bargaining hard. The result was that he paid three silver pennies for a week's lodging, which included the use of the apprentice for any light chores of fetching and carrying and of the merchant's own maid for cleaning as Chacier and Clotilde should direct, as well as the right to rent for the rest of the month at the same rate.

Once the merchant had departed, Alphonse bade Chacier and Clotilde bring their baggage from the inn. As soon as he saw them in the street below the front window, he shut the door rather hard and turned on Barbara.

"What the devil is wrong with you?" he snarled. "You made our landlord think that getting into bed with me is equal to being sent to a nether hell. And even if it were, do you expect me to fling you down and force you if you should approach a bed in my presence?"

Barbara barely strangled the hysterical laughter that welled up in her. What she feared was exactly the opposite—that some word or gesture would escape her to betray her own impulse to fling *him* down on the bed. Not that she expected to have to force him; from what she had heard in the past, Alphonse had never failed a lady in need. More comical yet was the fact that Alphonse's pride had been injured because her behavior made the merchant think he was a brutal or ineffectual lover. And funniest of all was Barbara's own deep regret that he, who would enjoy the jest so much, could not be invited to share it.

"I am so sorry," she whispered. "I do not fear you."

"Do you not?" he asked. "Then I beg you to tell me what game you are playing with me."

"I cannot."

Barbara gulped down another gust of hysterical laughter as she spoke the literal truth. She had wondered how to make herself seem remote and mysterious, but she did not even need to try. Alphonse was creating a strange simulacrum of her all by himself. Then the impulse to laugh died. His dark face had grown even darker as blood rose under his skin and his eyes looked suffused.

"Then you do not intend to marry me at all!"

"I do! I do! I swear it!"

He stood staring at her and then said, very softly, "Go into the bedchamber, Barbe, and close the door, and do not come out again until your maid comes to fetch you."

Chapter 10

Alphonse was gone when Clotilde came in, rather wide-eyed and more silent than usual, to tell her mistress she was free to do as she pleased. Barbara could guess where he had gone and spent the remainder of the day alternately feeling sorry for the pain she had caused him and suppressing giggles. She was not jealous of his easing his need on a common whore of the town. He was too proud and too fastidious to be interested in any woman who sold her body to keep food in her mouth and a roof over her head. Alphonse, she thought, grinning, would be outraged; he was more accustomed to being offered bribes for his favors than having to pay for use of a woman. He knew his own worth.

Meanwhile, she was rather grateful for his absence, which gave her the opportunity to have the lodging cleaned carefully, particularly the bed. She was pleasantly surprised to find that it was not as badly infested with lice and fleas and other biting pests as she had suspected, but she bought larkspur powder and camomile and a potpourri of sweet-smelling herbs to work into the bedding before she would allow Clotilde to put her own linens on the bed and pillows. While the bedding was being treated in the garden, the maid was summoned to scrub the frame and leather straps and then to sweep and help Clotilde move a chair and small table to the window in the large chamber.

There, as the afternoon darkened into evening, Barbara sat with her embroidery and ate her evening meal. As she plied her needle, setting a pattern of golden doves perched on a fantastic tree into a wide, dark blue band that would adorn the neck of her shimmering blue silk wedding gown, she regretted that she had not pointed out to Alphonse that she and Clotilde were preparing her wedding dress as fast as they could sew. While the reminder could not have eased the need of his body, it might have cured his doubt. Then she shook her head and reminded herself severely that she did not wish to ease his doubt. If she yielded to her impulse to give him everything he wanted, he would soon not want her.

The reminder was sobering; it would not be easy to quell her generous impulses. When one loves, one wishes to give, Barbara thought, and sighed. She did not linger long after the candles were lit but retreated to the bedchamber. It would be better, she thought, to be able to feign ignorance that Alphonse had been out all night if he did not return.

This thoughtful peace overture was frustrated, however, because he had not come back when she finally rose to break her fast, even though she deliberately lay abed far later than usual. At first she was amused and rather touched, thinking he was deliberately staying away to make her jealous, but by the time she had eaten dinner alone and he still had not returned, she began to feel worried. He was, after all, a stranger in England. It was possible that he had gotten into a fight or fallen afoul of some dangerous thieves.

Barbara had never heard of much crime in Canterbury, where strict watch was kept on those who sold entertainment because the prosperity of the town depended partly on the safe coming and going of many visitors. Some visitors were sincere pilgrims to the shrine of Saint Thomas and would avoid sin, but many did not. They were curiosity seekers on pilgrimage more for change and excitement than for the sake of holiness, and some drank and gambled and lay with women, seeming to feel that the pilgrimage itself would absolve them of sins.

Still, Alphonse dressed more richly than most, which might be an irresistible temptation to those who lived in the underbelly of the town. And the fact that he could not understand any English at all might mark him as a foreigner and increase the temptation. Then Barbara told herself it was ridiculous to worry. Chacier was gone too and must be with his master. She knew she would not be so silly if her father had disappeared for a day. She would have assumed he had been so drunk he was still too sick to show his face.

The strictures did not help much; she felt anxious and uneasy, unable to settle to her work although Clotilde was making good headway on the pale cream-colored tunic that would go under her blue wedding gown. She glanced idly around the chamber and her attention fixed suddenly on the special basket that held Alphonse's mail and curie, which was set near the empty hearth. His helmet sat atop the basket and his shield was propped between it and the wall, but his sword was gone, she noted with relief.

Barbara blinked and looked at the shield again. There was something different about it. She had thought she knew that shield better than her own face and was sure she could pick it out among a hundred others on a field of men battling in a melee. *Or*, four pallets *gules*—yes, that was right. Those were the arms of Raymond Berenger, still carried by Queen Eleanor as well as by Berenger's other daughters. The black bend sinister over the red and gold stripes was right too. Alphonse's father had been Raymond Berenger's bastard. But the bend carried a tilting spear, and that was not right. There had been a crescent, marking Alphonse as the second son . . . But, of course, his father had died, so he was no longer a second son and could choose his own device to difference the family arms.

Barbara stared uneasily at the tilting spear. Her silver mirror had been a tournament prize. She had seen Alphonse win it while carrying her token and still remembered the excitement, mounting almost to madness, she had felt each time she watched him fight. Her *preux chevalier*. But she had been so young then, too young to believe anyone she loved could be hurt. Since then she had learned better.

That tilting spear together with her betrothed's pride and her knowledge of how often he used to fight in tourneys implied an explanation for Alphonse's full purse that sent a chill of fear through Barbara. He always said his living came from his brother, whom he served at court by keeping the interests of Aix before the king and by warning Raymond of any political events that might affect his estate. But now she thought it would be most unlike Alphonse to beg for money to pay for his wine and his gambling and his gifts to women. Barbara realized suddenly why Alphonse understood the rules of ransom so very well; it was because he made the extra money that way—by defeating men at the jousts and in the melee and taking from them horse and armor ransom.

Oh, there was no dishonor in it. In fact, men of high rank

would seek out and defer to a conqueror on the tourney field. But Alphonse was no longer a young man; he was over thirty, in his middle years. He should no longer be fighting to fill his purse. Sooner or later he would fail . . . and men had been killed on the tourney field. Then Barbara took a breath and smiled. If he fought for money, the income from Cruas would solve the problem. Her dowry would pay for wine and moderate gambling—and he would make no more gifts to women if she could bind him tight enough.

That brought her mind back to his absence; he would not have gone out if she had agreed to lie with him. For the tenth time, she laid aside her embroidery and went to lean out of the open window and stare up and down along the street.

Clotilde looked up from her own sewing but only folded her lips in a hard line and said nothing. Was her mistress so foolish as to expect Sieur Alphonse to turn celibate because he had been betrothed? Surely she must know that every servant in the French court had called him Le Grand Sillonneur, and if she would not provide the earth for his plow he would find another field to furrow.

"If only Chacier spoke some English," Barbara said, coming back to her seat. "With no one to explain what he wants, Alphonse might lose his temper."

"Ah!" Clotilde exclaimed, enlightened and relieved that her mistress was not jealous. Then she frowned, also concerned. "You fear Sieur Alphonse has had an accident or is lost—"

"I fear he has behaved like a jackass with too much pride," Barbara snapped, "and has got himself into a fight he could not win."

"I will go out and see if there is news of trouble," Clotilde said, laying aside her work.

"In God's name," Barbara warned her, "do not take any chance that he will discover I have been enquiring about him." And despite her worry she began to laugh. "I do not know whether he would beat me to death or stay away every other week just to teach me a lesson."

At first, Barbara could not settle to work again but watched out the window, fearing she would see Clotilde running back from the cathedral or the hospital Saint Thomas had erected to tell her that Alphonse's body was laid out or that he was dying. After an hour, however, her anguish changed to irritation. By then Clotilde must have asked in all the likely places for news of a corpse or an injured foreigner. If she had heard nothing yet, the likelihood was that Alphonse was at ease in a tavern or brothel and planning to remain there either out of spite or because he was enjoying himself.

Clotilde returned at dusk, wariness of her mistress's mood covering a sly amusement as she reported that she was certain, wherever he was, that *le sieur* had come to no harm. She erupted into open laughter when Barbara grinned and said, "Now how can I best put his nose out of joint? Shall I pretend not to have noticed his absence at all, or should I thank him warmly for his thoughtfulness in keeping out of my way?"

She did neither, however, because when she returned to the lodging late the next morning after attending mass at the cathedral, breaking her fast at the inn, and spending a few leisurely hours examining the wares in the market and shops, she found her father as well as her betrothed waiting for her. The low rumble of male voices in easy conversation had warned her as she began to climb the stairs that Alphonse was not alone, so she came up very quietly and paused a moment on the landing to look in. A single alert glance and the few words she heard told her that all was well between her menfolk, and she entered the room with a small cry of joy.

"How glad I am to see you, father!" she exclaimed, giving Alphonse a brilliant smile before she hurried to kiss the hand Norfolk held out to her. "Pray tell me you are not angry with me."

"Not over having accepted Alphonse," Norfolk said, "but I could have used a word of warning. I almost dropped dead with surprise when my clerk read your letter. After trying for seven or eight years to find a man to suit you, I send you off to France, and in one day there . . . I could not believe my ears. Poor Thomas. I clipped him on the head and called him a dolt and made him read that letter twice more before I believed it said you were betrothed."

Norfolk's voice was amused, but there was a tightness to the skin around his eyes, and Barbara dropped to her knees beside his chair and took his hand. "I was not forced, papa, I swear it, but everything did happen very fast, too fast for me to hope to get a letter to you."

She was wondering how to explain more fully without saying more than she wanted Alphonse to hear, when he got to his feet. "I will go order dinner for us," he said. "I have not forgotten what you said to me about King Louis, Barbe. You had best speak to your father alone."

Barbara looked after Alphonse as he left the room, blessing her good fortune in having set her heart on so clever a man. But she turned back at once to ask, "Have I hurt you, papa?"

"Do not be a goose," Norfolk retorted. "I have been worried sick over what would happen to you when I died. I was certain you would never marry. If Louis did not thrust d'Aix down your throat, I am glad."

Barbara felt her breath catch. Why should her father suddenly speak of dying? Her quick glance assured her that he showed no sign of ill health. Could he be *that* worried about the political situation? To ask a direct question about that would be useless, so she smiled and said, "Oh, papa, did you not guess that Alphonse is the reason I would not marry? I always wanted him. You chose him to protect me when you left me in France. Do you not remember?"

"Of course I remember, but that was business. His brother is overlord of much of the land near Cruas, and I felt he would know the laws and customs of that area."

"And so he did, I am sure, and he did his best for me. But I was a silly little girl and I thought you had chosen him to be my husband. Then King Louis suggested that to settle Cruas without a battle I should marry Pierre, and you agreed, and Alphonse advised me to obey. I did, of course." She smiled up at him. "But then Queen Marguerite had taught me to read, and my head was full of those romances you always growl about. I am afraid that I had already given my heart to Alphonse."

Norfolk snorted cynically, but the tension Barbara had seen in him had eased. She laughed and shrugged. "He was my *preux chevalier*. Papa, he offered to be my knight and fight to protect me from Guy de Montfort . . . Well, you need not look at me like that; I had to give him some reason for coming to France after all those years. And when I said you would protect me, he said he loved me and offered me marriage—and I said yes. You do forgive me for taking him without your permission, do you not?"

He pulled a curl of hair that had escaped confinement and lay against her cheek. "He is a good man, Barbe, and King Louis took care that you had a fair settlement in the contract." Then he sighed and stroked her face. "And, times being what they are, I am not sorry that you will go back to France."

So it was true that her father was expecting serious trouble in England. But from whom? Was it Leicester he feared or was it Queen Eleanor's silly invasion? Barbara took a breath to tell him about the disorganization and inefficiency of those who were planning the invasion then changed her mind, saying instead, "But I will not go at once, papa. Not before my wedding. I want you to be at my wedding."

Worrying about the invasion could do her father no harm, whereas assurances that there would not be an invasion could do harm if she was mistaken. Besides, she needed more information. If it was Leicester he feared, an invasion might not be so unwelcome to him now as in the past.

Norfolk laughed aloud at her plea. "I would not miss your wedding for the world, chick, and I do not think Alphonse cares where he marries you so long as it be soon. I will see about making arrangements."

"Can it be in the cathedral, father?" Barbara asked, and Norfolk laughed again.

"Certainly," he said. "I do not believe the chapter will refuse my request even though their bishop is fled. Chichester will marry you, or London."

"Both!" Barbara exclaimed.

"Why not?" Norfolk agreed, still chuckling. He always enjoyed it when Barbara behaved in what he thought of as a typically womanish fashion, and he did his best to satisfy her desires. "It will be a pleasant change for them, a wedding at which everyone is in agreement."

Although he was still smiling, there was a tinge of bitterness in his last words and Barbara hastily asked, "When can it be?"

He looked arch, and Barbara was already preparing an answer for his expected remark on how eager she seemed to change her state. Before he could speak, however, they heard footsteps on the stair. Gratefully, Barbara rose to meet Alphonse at the door. "You are come most aptly to the time," she said. "My father says he will arrange for our wedding to be held in the cathedral and for the bishops of Chichester and London to perform the service. We were just about to decide on the date."

"Tomorrow," Alphonse said.

"The bishops will not arrive until the twelfth," Norfolk pointed out, grinning, "and neither of them is young. You will have to give them a day to catch their breath." He laughed lewdly. "Hold it in your hand for a little while longer, Alphonse. Let us say the fourteenth—to allow for delays on the road."

"No, the fifteenth," Barbara said. "I do not think my gown will be ready sooner. And also, one cannot forget an event that takes place on the ides of the month."

"I will not forget our wedding no matter what day—" Alphonse began.

Laughing, Norfolk cut him off. "For God's sake, man, do not hand the girl a whip with which to beat you. She is hard enough to manage when she does not hold any advantage. You will make her outrageous."

Alphonse also laughed and said something about using a feint to draw in an opponent. Clearly Norfolk was joking, and that was a tremendous relief. Alphonse had not been at all sure what he would find when he returned; he had half expected that Barbe would complain to her father that he had taken unfair advantage of her and that Norfolk would have him expelled from the country. The sensible half of him trusted her, and had been right. Whatever she had said had calmed her father admirably, but Alphonse was more puzzled than ever. What game was she playing? And why?

Alphonse had found Norfolk at the castle when he went there the previous evening, not knowing where else to go and thinking that he might be better off if he was locked up. Despite the years since they had seen each other, he had recognized Norfolk at once and been recognized too. The earl had demanded his daughter furiously—as if he feared she was being kept from him. No one could doubt he was very fond of Barbe. As soon as he heard that she was in lodgings and Alphonse offered to take him there, he calmed down and said he would wait until morning, since Barbara had probably gone to bed. But he had asked questions half the night about how Alphonse thought a wife should be governed, had almost threatened him about what would happen if any harm should come to his girl, and had finally said outright that he would accept his daughter back if she had any complaint about her husband.

He had made Alphonse swear up and down and back and forth that King Louis had not forced Barbe to accept him. Alphonse had sworn with his courtier's smile in place, thanking God that Norfolk had been fixated on Louis's interest in settling Cruas and had not asked if he himself had used some unfair device to make Barbe accept him. He had also sworn that he loved Barbe, had told the whole story of when and how he learned he cared for her and why he had not earlier asked for her hand. That seemed to impress Norfolk, and when Alphonse explained why he had left the lodging, the earl had at last relaxed enough to roar with laughter. Nonetheless, Alphonse was sure that if Norfolk had not been very uneasy about the future in England, he would have been even more disagreeable about the marriage.

Apparently he had shown none of his doubts to Barbe, or if he had, she was indifferent to them. Alphonse responded with laughter to Norfolk's continued teasing about his unsatisfied lust until the earl gave up, called him a damned courtier, and began to ask questions about Louis. Alphonse told him honestly that Louis could never approve the control of a king by those set beneath him by God, and Norfolk began a recitation of King Henry's offenses.

Alphonse listened with half an ear; he had heard some of what

Norfolk was telling him from Alys, and he was mildly sorry that Henry was a bad ruler. But the catalog of Henry's sins did not change his mind or make him think that Louis's judgment—that a king was subject only to God—was wrong. King Henry was old. In a few years he would be gone. What would really be wrong would be to tie Prince Edward's hands and make him subject to the will of his nobles. That solution to King Henry's weakness could easily breed anarchy, which was far worse than a bad ruler. He made what palliating remarks he could, but he was more alert to Barbe's glance out of the window. He could guess she saw that the shadows were growing short. His stomach said it must be nearly sext, time for dinner.

A lift of Barbe's head summoned Clotilde from her sewing in the doorway of the bedchamber, where she had skillfully effaced herself after she followed Barbe into the room. A good maid, Alphonse thought, and accustomed to living at court, thank God. He replied mildly to a bitter question from Norfolk that, of course, Louis desired to amend injustice and corruption, but not by a device likely to cause worse problems, adding hastily that this was all his own opinion, that King Louis had never made any statement to him of what he thought of England's troubles.

Meanwhile, Barbe bade her maid take from her traveling basket the cloth for dining and two cups and spoons, the silver for her father and the horn for herself. Alphonse's own cup and spoon she took from his saddlebag. He wondered why she stared at the cup so intently, for he did not think it anything unusual although it, too, was silver, beautifully shaped and engraved. He had forgotten that in the design were the date and name of the tourney where he had won it as a prize.

Alphonse's attention was drawn fully back to Norfolk, who was asking about Simon de Claremont, lord of Nesle, and Peter the Chamberlain, the envoys Louis was sending to Canterbury. His answer was interrupted when Chacier came in, leading one of the boys from the inn with their dinner, but he went back to what he had been saying while they ate. After the meal, with a hint of challenge in his voice, Norfolk asked about Queen Eleanor and the king's half brothers and the invasion. Alphonse answered that he did not think it would come soon, if it came at all. And when Norfolk said doubtfully that he hoped that was true, Barbe defended Alphonse energetically, repeating to her father what Hugh Bigod had told her.

After that, although Norfolk seemed thoughtful, he willingly allowed Barbe to divert him to giving her news about Joanna and the children. When he had satisfied her, he heaved himself to his feet and said that if Alphonse was serious about getting married on the fifteenth, they had better get to the cathedral and see about making arrangements. Alphonse agreed with alacrity, only remembering to run back to ask Barbe whether she wanted Chacier to sleep at the lodging. He would not come back, he told her; he would stay at the castle, as he had done the previous night, since she had made it plain she was happier in his absence.

To his fury, she did not seem at all put out but smiled sweetly and said he should keep Chacier with him. Clotilde could do all she needed. But he thought there was a glint of laughter in her eyes, and in the end, he did come back. He saw Barbe as he entered the solar with the last of the day's light; she was bathed in the rosy glow, which touched her cheeks with pink and created dark mysteries in the hollows of her eyes.

''I am sorry to intrude on you when you are at peace,'' he said.

''Your coming is never an intrusion, never unwelcome,'' she replied, setting aside her work and rising.

Her voice had been warm, her first few steps eager, but midway she halted, looking confused, almost frightened, so that he was torn between rage and a desire to comfort her. Instead he told her his reason for coming: Henry de Montfort had arrived at the castle with Prince Edward and other important prisoners and had asked that Barbara visit the prince to tell him of his wife and child.

Frowning, Barbe asked, ''Is Henry de Montfort running errands for Edward? Could the prince not find a time to ask about Eleanor and her babe himself?''

Alphonse then had to admit that he had not seen Prince Edward, who was now treated as a prisoner, lodged on the lowest floor of the keep and heavily guarded. Barbe seemed distressed by that news, and Alphonse quickly seized on her sympathy for Edward to describe his own dilemma, telling her that Henry de Montfort had sought him out in the hall and had hardly greeted him before he began to plead with him to persuade Edward to accept the terms of the Peace of Canterbury.

She stared at him thoughtfully for a moment and asked, ''Have you eaten yet?''

When he shook his head she suggested that they walk together to the inn and eat in the little garden. Alphonse was delighted that she had not agreed immediately with Henry de Montfort that he urge Edward to accept the peace terms. He had been so worried about her reaction to the request that she speak to the prince that he had not yet planned how much to tell her about his disturbing conversation with Henry.

''He will listen to you, Alphonse,'' Henry de Montfort had said eagerly. ''He has always looked up to you.''

"How can I urge Edward to accept terms I have not heard?" Alphonse had asked.

Henry looked uncomfortable and said, "It does not really matter what the terms are. There is no choice. Edward must accept."

"No man *must* do anything," Alphonse retorted stiffly. "At worst he can die for his stubbornness."

"Holy Christus, no!" Henry exclaimed. "There is no threat of harm to Edward. Alphonse, you cannot believe that. It is bad enough that *Edward* looks at me as if I were something that crawls on my belly under rocks. Do not you abandon me also."

There were tears in Henry's eyes, and Alphonse recalled that the young man was in an impossible situation, made responsible by his father for acting as gaoler of a friend. He also reminded himself that he had promised King Louis he would visit the prince and talk to him, which would be impossible if he offended Henry.

"Then I do not understand what you mean when you say that Edward must agree, regardless of what the terms are," Alphonse said more gently.

"It is for his sake," Henry de Montfort said eagerly, "so that he may be free, instead of being locked into a chamber and guarded by four men even when he goes to piss. He hates me, really hates me, who once called me the friend dearest to his heart. And I do not blame him." Henry's voice broke and he dropped his face into his hands. Then he looked up again. "I cannot bear it, Alphonse. When we rode here, I had to shackle his legs under his horse and lead the animal."

"Surely that was not necessary," Alphonse said, his voice cold again. "It was my understanding that Prince Edward agreed willingly to be a prisoner so that his father might be free. If he gave his word—"

A note of near hysteria had come through Henry de Montfort's laugh. "He gave his word to take his father's place as prisoner—and kept that word. But when my father asked him to swear he would not attempt to escape, he said he would gladly swear not to leave England and also swear to return to meet my father at a summoning if he were freed of all other restriction. Could we agree to that?"

Alphonse had not made any direct reply. It was as clear to him what Edward meant as it had been to Henry de Montfort and his father. Instead of giving the parole for which he had been asked, the prince had flung a gauntlet into Leicester's face. By saying he would swear not to leave England, he had refused to accept exile; and when he agreed to come to a summoning if no other restrictions were placed on him, he was threatening to bring an army to that summoning.

"I do not see why Edward should be kept so close," Barbe said, as she walked with Alphonse toward the inn. "He was watched when I was in London in June, before I sailed to France, but he was not locked up."

Alphonse shrugged. "I suppose there is more danger now. The rebellion of the lords of the Welsh Marches and the threat of invasion have no doubt made Leicester more fearful of wider disturbances, particularly if Edward should escape or be freed by his friends."

She said no more until they were settled in the inn garden, but she clearly was not happy about his answer and Alphonse was annoyed with himself for not having told her some innocent lie. As the servants withdrew after laying out the meal, he asked anxiously, "Will you not come and tell the prince that all is well with Princess Eleanor and his daughter?"

"Of course I will," she replied, looking surprised at the question. "Worry will not break Prince Edward, only make him more bitter. I am sorry for Henry de Montfort too. He has a thankless task. I cannot imagine what was in his father's head to put him in such a position. He would have done much better to give the responsibility for keeping Edward to his cousin, Peter de Montfort, or to one of the bishops."

"No one could agree with you more heartily than Henry himself," Alphonse said, stabbing at his trencher of bread with his eating knife.

Barbara laid her own knife down and covered his restless hand with hers, stopping its movement. "What worm is gnawing your belly, Alphonse?"

He looked at her squarely and said, "You know I am not of your opinion about Leicester's right to force the king to bow to the will of his barons. I am not exactly overjoyed to have lost a husband's usual right to demand that his wife think as he does, but I knew you were of Leicester's party before I asked you to give me your hand—and it is stupid to demand a change of loyalty from a wife in any case. One cannot change beliefs as one changes gowns."

"I am of no party," Barbara said, gently pressing his hand before she let go of it. "I am sure I told you that before. Nonetheless, it is true that I think King Henry needs a keeper. He can be led by anyone, and for years he has been sucking the lifeblood out of this realm to feed the band of monsters that sprang from his accursed mother's womb in her second marriage. I am not sorry to see the power in other hands. Since Leicester and his friends are the victors and my father supports Leicester, I am content that he should control the king." She sighed. "Anything is better than more war. All I care for is that there be peace and that my father and uncle and cousins, all of whom I love, do not come to blows."

Alphonse also sighed. "Then you would like Prince Edward to support the peace terms Leicester has proposed even if that means agreeing to give up his right to rule as a king should?"

"Why should *Edward* give up his right to rule freely? Edward will make a fine king." Barbara lowered her voice, which had risen. "I pray nightly that King Henry will drop dead so we can be rid of this strife." Then her expression changed and she said, "Oh, I see. Henry de Montfort asked you to talk to Edward about the peace terms and you want my help."

Alphonse opened his mouth and shut it again. He was appalled at his carelessness and relieved at the same time. He had never felt comfortable about concealing his arrangement with King Louis from Barbe. And, though he did not look forward to the storm that might blast him if she disapproved, he was still glad no longer to need to watch his words. There might not even be a storm if what she had said about being of no party was true.

Seeing that Alphonse had decided not to speak, Barbara asked, "But why should Edward object to the peace proposal?" And then before he could answer, went on, "Are the terms different from those proposed at the parliament in June?"

"I do not know," Alphonse answered. "But I think they must be, partly because Henry would not tell me what they were."

Barbara stared fixedly at the table and then said slowly, "If it is so important that Edward give his public approval to the peace and not merely submit to his father's acceptance of the terms, it must be because the barons' control of the king—Leicester's, really—will not end with Henry's death but be extended into Edward's reign." She stabbed a piece of cheese with her knife. "That is not fair."

"And also unnecessary," Alphonse said. "Edward was not very happy with the way his father ruled, you know. He was careful not to say anything disrespectful, but from remarks he made when we were touring France doing the tourneys two or three years ago, I believe he would amend many of Henry's injustices out of simple good sense. And he does not love the Lusignan brood much more than his mother does."

"Who could?" Barbara snapped. "You would not believe how cruel and greedy they are, and they all but spit publicly on English law." She popped the piece of cheese into her mouth and chewed vindictively for a while. Then her gaze, which had gone out of focus, sharpened. "You will have to agree to persuade Edward to sign the terms, though."

"I do not *have* to do anything," Alphonse said sharply.

Barbara drew in her breath. "I did not mean to give an order." She smiled. "You should know that I am far too clever to give orders to a man if I want a thing done. When I command and stamp my foot, you may be sure that what I demand is the last thing I truly desire."

Alphonse laughed aloud. "You devil! Now I will never know which way to jump when you say 'leap.' "

"Is that not as it should be?" she asked blandly. "Not knowing will leave you free to do as you think best—which you would do in any case, I am sure."

"Flatterer," he growled. "What do you want of me?"

"I want you to dismount from the destrier Dudgeon and think of what is best, without regard for your pride."

Alphonse laughed again. "You mean you *were* giving me an order when you said I would have to persuade Edward to accept whatever terms are offered."

"Will you just hold the reins of the high horse while you listen to me, instead of galloping off on it at speed? After all, you can mount it at any time." Barbara sighed with ostentatious patience. "I do not see why you will not listen. I cannot force you to do anything, can I?"

"Can you not?" he asked, the humor gone from eyes and voice.

"No, I cannot," Barbara said, looking down at her hands. Then, raising her eyes, she added, "And I would not if I could. You were my teacher for too long for me to set your opinion at naught. If I explain and you still do not agree, then I will know there is a fault in my reasoning."

Intense pleasure swamped Alphonse's normal caution, and he nodded. "Very well."

"First is my private reason. I have told you already that my father is not completely trusted. If you refuse to talk to Edward, and if we then marry, I fear that will reflect more suspicion on papa. Second, I fear for Edward. Not for his life or limb, but for him to refuse to agree to Leicester's terms can only make his situation worse, and harsh usage may sour him beyond saving. Edward has a long memory and can be vindictive. Third, we do not know that the terms of the peace will be too harsh. And last, and most important of all, what difference does it make what Edward promises? No oath given under duress can be held binding. I am quite sure either the archbishop or the pope will absolve him."

"Barbe!" Alphonse exclaimed, horrified. "To swear falsely is dishonest."

She shrugged impatiently. "To force a man to swear to his own disadvantage is dishonest too."

"Women!" Alphonse groaned.

"Men!" Barbara retorted.

Barbara was surprised as the word came from her lips. She would not have used that tone to her father; if she had, he would have slapped her. Alphonse only cast up his eyes to heaven and prepared to argue her around to his position. She was beginning to believe that her marriage to Alphonse—if she did not allow jealousy to destroy it and her—might be the gateway to heaven.

Alphonse had been demolishing her first reason, which she admitted was not compelling. As she yielded the ground and saw his satisfaction, she was tempted to yield all. It was Alphonse who yielded on the second point, however, confessing that Edward was already very bitter and that part of Henry's purpose in inviting her to visit the prince was to soothe him. Still, Barbara realized she would never get Alphonse to agree to urge Edward to confirm a peace without knowing the terms. Edward had not contested the terms proposed by the parliament after the battle of Lewes. Perhaps he had yielded to that proposal out of guilt or fear, but Barbara thought it was partly because the agreement only bound him to obey his father and when the king died he would be free.

If the new terms made Edward subservient to the council and bound him—except not to wreak vengeance on those who had defeated him—after his father's death, Barbara was not at all sure that was right. Henry was a hopeless ruler and must be prevented from driving the realm further into ruin, but to try to control Edward was entirely unfair.

"I am sorry, Alphonse," she said as he paused, realizing she was not listening. "I seem to have said something I did not mean at all. Naturally you cannot promise to persuade the prince to agree to anything, no matter what. If you did, he would simply class you among his enemies and ignore you. All I meant was that you should try to soothe him so that he does not refuse to do what would be best for him and the realm out of bitterness and rage."

Instead of answering, Alphonse leaned forward and kissed her. Taken unaware, Barbara pulled him closer, her lips parting naturally under his. His arm tightened around her shoulders and he began to rise so that he could bring their bodies together. With a clash and a clatter, the table went over, cups and flagon spilling their contents amid the scattered cold meats and broken pasty.

Chapter 11

A rush of inn servants in response to the crash saved Barbara and Alphonse from disgracing themselves in the grass. Their meal was quickly replaced, and at first they ate in silence, Barbara's cheeks flaming and Alphonse much tempted to press his luck when the meal was over. After a swallow of wine, however, Barbara made a comment in a cool voice on a neutral topic. A single glance told Alphonse that she was now double-armed and almost angry; he replied pleasantly, and for the remainder of the time they spent together, they kept their talk to safe subjects.

Nonetheless, because Barbe knew the political positions of the parties in conflict so well, she kept sparking ideas in Alphonse's mind. He resisted the temptation to stay in the lodging with her that night, which recurred as he walked her back there. His resistance was supported by the faint chagrin he believed he detected in her manner when he left her at the door and by his need to be quiet and work out a compromise between his promise to Louis to see Prince Edward and his unwillingness to lie to Henry de Montfort. In that he was successful . . . and as for Barbe—Alphonse smiled, his strong teeth very white in his dark face—he had only four days more to wait.

He caught Henry de Montfort at mass just after dawn the next morning and told him that he would like very much to speak to the prince but felt it would be foolish in the extreme for him to espouse the peace terms Henry's father was demanding.

"All that will accomplish is to make Edward angry with me too and even more bitter. What I am willing to do, and that gladly, is try to make him see that you are little happier than he and wish most sincerely to give him more freedom. If I can abate his rage, you can present your terms in the best light yourself."

"I cannot promise him more freedom unless he will agree—"

"Henry, listen to me. I will sound like a traitor, and a fool too, if I urge him to accept terms I do not know, terms you are plainly not ready to tell me."

"I cannot," Henry said unhappily. "The final form is not yet settled, but Edward already knows the major provisions. All I am asking you to do is beg him to consider them."

"Useless. I have told you why. And from what you have said to me, I can guess that Edward is too angry now to be reasonable, no matter who appeals to him. Do you not see that if his rage can be assuaged, he will be much more likely to look at the real merits of a proposal instead of rejecting it out of hand?"

"But what can be done? You do not know what he is like now."

"I can guess," Alphonse remarked. "I have seen Edward in a temper. Still, much can be done, at least to ease the strain between you and him. First, Barbe will tell him that his wife and child are safe and well. That will soften him at once. Then I can remind him in a private way of the misfortunes he has brought on himself by ungoverned rage. I can suggest that if he were more reasonable and gave a limited parole—say for an hour to walk on the walls or any other small liberty you think is safe and reasonable—you might approve it."

Henry de Montfort's bright gray eyes narrowed in thought, but after a moment he shook his head. "No. If he asked for what I could not give, he would be angrier yet."

"Then you tell me what you would be willing to let him do and I will propose that," Alphonse said at once. "Or, better yet, let us keep the first visit very short. Let Barbe soothe him with talk of Eleanor and the babe. I will come back in the evening after you know how our visit has affected him, and we can decide then whether I should speak to him again or not."

"God bless you," Henry said. "I will be your debtor, and so will my father and all England, if you can pacify the prince."

After tierce that morning, Alphonse brought Barbara to the castle. She was shocked when Henry de Montfort asked, although he was plainly embarrassed by needing to do so, that she and Alphonse strip themselves of anything that could be used as a weapon, even their small eating knives. The fact that Alphonse was already unbuckling his sword belt, only shaking his head sadly as he did so, silenced her half-spoken protest. But she found very little to say to Henry after she handed him the bejeweled toy with which she speared her food.

Later her indignation passed as Henry spoke on neutral subjects with Alphonse. She had always liked Henry de Montfort, who had his father's strong conscience without Leicester's pride and stiff righteousness. Then, because he was so uncomfortable and she was sorry for him, she managed to find a faint smile in response to his good wishes on her forthcoming marriage and another when he assured her that he would come with a glad heart to be a witness.

The smile was gone by the time she passed the two guards standing at the head of the torchlit stair, and she could not repress a shudder when one of the guards outside Edward's chamber lifted the heavy bar that locked the door. Inside, her tight grip on Alphonse's arm relaxed. She had feared to see the prince shackled and filthy. The reality was not so bad. What could be done to make the dank chamber, ordinarily a storeroom, comfortable had been done. The floor was thickly strewn with fresh rushes, and the scent of the herbs mingled with them strove with the musty odor from the damp packed-earth floor and stone walls. Three rays of light from loopholes high in the eastern wall penetrated the gloom, which was further mitigated by several bunches of candles tied together and stuck into the wall brackets that were designed for torches.

In these conditions, the huge chair of state in the middle of the room in which the prince was sitting was a mockery that made Barbara gasp. She let go of Alphonse's arm and hurried forward to curtsy to the ground. Her vision was blurred by tears when she looked up, but the face that stared down at her seemed more like a marble effigy than a human countenance.

"My lord, I went to France with Princess Eleanor," Barbara said. "She misses you and worries about you, but she and little Eleanor are in good health and have every comfort and consolation that King Louis and Queen Marguerite can provide. Your mother is well also and wants for nothing."

"I am sure my wife and mother sent some message for me," Edward said, his voice utterly lifeless.

"No," Barbara replied, looking stricken. "I have no special message. Oh, dear, what with my betrothal, which was very sudden, and the fact that I had to come back to England much sooner than I expected, I hardly saw either Queen Eleanor or Princess Eleanor the last few days I was in Boulogne. I did not think to ask for a message. Of course, I did not know then that I would see you, but I am so sorry. I was stupid and cruel. I beg your pardon—"

"You need not," Edward interrupted, a very slight curve now showing on his lips. "I am delighted. I was sure that you would have a message for me demanding that I make peace so that Princess Eleanor could come home."

Barbara was aware that Alphonse had moved closer and guessed he wished to warn her to be careful what she said, but she did not care. "The princess would *never* send you such a message," she cried. "My lord, you must know her better than that. Even if she were suffering terribly—and she is not, I assure you, except for her fears for you—Princess Eleanor would never ask you to do for her what you would not do out of your own sense of right."

"I do indeed know my Eleanor better," Edward said, his lips softening even more toward a smile and his voice taking on life. "I would have known such a message to be a lie, only a new device to break my will. I hope you will forgive me, Lady Barbara, for thinking you would lend yourself to such a scheme."

"I forgive you most readily, my lord." Barbara barely stopped herself from saying that in the prince's situation she might believe worse of the daughter of an enemy. But it was not fair for Edward to blame Henry de Montfort for a crime he had not committed. She smiled slightly and added, "It is true I would not agree to bring false messages for any purpose, but I feel I must tell you that I was not asked to do so, nor was I asked what I was going to say to you."

Edward laughed harshly. "There is no need for that. I am sure my guardian angels will relate the substance of our conversation to my gaoler."

The prince glanced over Barbara's shoulder, and she turned her head and saw two more guards sitting on stools on either side of the door. She felt foolish not to have noticed them earlier or realized there must be watchers even if she did not see them. A quick review of what she had said rather pleased her and she looked back at Edward, but Alphonse's voice made any remark from her unnecessary.

"Henry de Montfort is not happy about the trust laid on him," Alphonse said. "I hope you will not lose your knowledge of him any more than of your lady, my lord."

"Good God! Alphonse d'Aix!" Edward exclaimed. "What do you here?"

Alphonse smiled. He was sure that in his abstraction the prince honestly had not realized who he was.

"I am the partner of Lady Barbe's hurried betrothal," he said, "and the reason for her hurried return from France. She would not marry me without her father's approval, and I felt I had waited long enough for her."

"Betrothal," Edward repeated, then looked at Barbara again and really smiled. "Yes, you did say that. I was thinking of something else and it made no sense to me. Well! That is happy news." He stood up and extended a hand to help Barbara up from her curtsy. "I had thought you both hardened celibates . . . Ah . . . perhaps that is the wrong word, but I did believe you both averse to the married state."

"Oh, no, my lord," Barbara said with a laugh. "I was only averse to marrying anyone but Alphonse."

The prince flashed a glance at Alphonse's face, made an indistinct noise, and quickly gestured to the guards to bring forward the stools on which they had been sitting. Barbara was astonished when the men did not set the stools down until Edward had reseated himself, and further astonished when they kept a hand on each stool until she and Alphonse had actually sat down.

Alphonse had also watched their behavior attentively. Then he looked hard at Edward, shook his head, and said, "Not wise, my lord. Not at all wise. The man who wins most often on the tourney field has a tight hold on his temper and never clings to a grudge over being defeated. Either fault can be his ruin."

"They have already been mine."

Edward's voice broke on the words, and Barbara looked from one man to the other, totally bewildered.

Alphonse's smiling reply—"Nonsense, you will see many new tourney fields"—seemed to her like meaningless soothing, but the prince glanced at him and then away in a flash.

Only then did Barbara realize that the chair of state, too heavy for one man to move without great effort, had been set so that the guards could watch the prince's face. Swift as thought is, that flick of the eyes was swifter; Edward was shrugging away Alphonse's remark, as if that wild hope had not come and gone in an eye-blink, and asking Barbara, "And does your father approve your betrothal?"

Although she had no idea what information had been exchanged between the men, it was clear enough to Barbara that Edward wanted her to talk to mislead the listeners. Without stopping to think of party, she burbled of Norfolk's satisfaction with her choice and King Louis's kindness in waiving the fines for Alphonse and herself to marry as they chose. As she said that, her voice faltered; she had forgotten until she spoke that one of the complaints against Edward's father was that, in his desperate need for money, he levied unreasonable fines. But Alphonse, whose back was to the guards, was grinning fit to split his head and nodding, as if in approval of what she was saying—only Barbara was sure it was another signal to Edward.

"And we are to be married here in the cathedral on the fifteenth," she finished. "I would be greatly honored, my lord, if you would come."

Edward's eyes flashed up to Alphonse's face. The guards could have seen nothing except perhaps a faint puzzlement, but Alphonse wished he could cheer aloud, and he longed to embrace his clever betrothed. Barbe had provided the perfect circumstance to loosen Edward's leash for at least a few hours. Possibly she meant it as a temptation, a reminder of the freedoms yielding could bring, but the device could also be used to ease Edward's violent resentment of Henry de Montfort. If Henry was willing to suggest, or to allow Alphonse to suggest, that Edward be permitted to attend the wedding, Henry's goodwill toward his prisoner would be clear. And Edward's concession would be minimal, merely a promise to return to his prison after the celebration; that would cost him nothing at all.

"I, too, would be greatly honored by your presence," Alphonse said. He paused significantly, nodded again, and added, "It might be arranged."

Now Edward shrugged and lowered his eyes, but before he could speak, a sharp knock sounded on the door. Alphonse stood up and the two guards rushed forward, one to seize the stool he had vacated and the other to reach for the one from which Barbara was rising more slowly.

"What—" Barbara began, turning angrily on the guard. But she fell silent as Alphonse seized her elbow and squeezed it.

Edward laughed aloud as the guards interposed themselves between the prince and his visitors when the door opened. "Oh, for God's sake," he said, "do not be such fools," and turned away to walk toward the back of his prison.

Barbara would have spoken to him, but Alphonse pulled her toward the door. Having been warned, she asked no questions until they had retrieved their possessions and left the castle. She was aware that Henry de Montfort had wanted to speak to Alphonse before they left and that Alphonse had warned him away with a glance at her and a promise to return.

Her voice was angry when they were past the gates and she said, "You do not need to take me to my lodging. Please feel perfectly free to go back and tell Henry what you wanted to say but could not where I could hear."

"You are a little confused, my love." Alphonse chuckled. "Do you not recall that you are the one who is supposed to be conspiring with Henry. I am supposed to be Edward's ally. And, in truth, I thank God you were there and I was able to use you as an excuse to leave."

"So you *were* passing messages to Edward!" Barbara exclaimed, and then added hotly, "Well, I do not care. It is cruel to keep him penned like a wild beast. And what in the world were those guards doing with the stools?"

Although he felt elated by the clear indication that Barbe would not be angry about any attempt he made to help the prince, Alphonse uttered an exasperated "*Zut!*" and then went on to explain, "Edward is penned like a wild beast because he has been behaving like one. The guards will not let him touch the stools, no doubt, because he must have seized one and tried to kill someone with it—likely poor Henry. That is also why the chair of state is there. He cannot throw that."

"Poor man," Barbara said softly. "How desperate he must be. And poor Henry too. I was so angry when he asked for your sword and even my knife. I thought he did not trust your word not to help the prince unlawfully. But if Edward has been behaving like a madman—"

"He has, I am sure, although Henry did not say more than that the prince hated him." Alphonse stopped suddenly in the middle of the street and took Barbara's hands, his dark eyes glowing. "You are a marvel, Barbe. What you said to him was perfect, masterly. You made him understand that Henry was not trying to manipulate him without adding to his rage."

"Now you are confused," she said, smiling. "I am *supposed* to make Edward think well of Henry."

An irritable shout behind them and muffled curses from people who were trying to squeeze by between them and a shop counter made Barbara start forward again. She sighed and shook her head.

"I do not know what I want," she said so softly that Alphonse had to bend toward her to hear. "I cannot bear to see Edward imprisoned, but if he is not brought to some terms, he cannot be freed. As he is now, if he were free, he would surely start the war again."

Neither spoke again until they were at the door of the lodging. Barbara glanced at it and walked on, saying, "It is nearly time for dinner—" Then she hesitated, looked sidelong at Alphonse, and uttered a soft, exasperated laugh. "I do not wish to send you away, but if we go to the inn to eat—"

"I am sorry about yesterday evening," he said, his full lips twitching as he controlled a grin. "I was only trying to praise you for your rational attitude toward Prince Edward." He raised a hand, palm up as if offering the excuse. "If you misunderstood . . . Well, I cannot say I am sorry"—he chuckled softly—"but I will promise most faithfully not to kiss you again when there is a table full of food between us."

"Or at all, if I invite you into our lodging?"

Alphonse tucked an errant curl back into her crespine. The laughter was gone from his voice and he looked troubled, but all he said was "Yes, at least until the fifteenth."

When they were settled with the meal ordered from the inn between them, Alphonse regretted his promise, even though he suspected that Barbe would have refused to go up with him if he had not given it. As a safety measure, he decided that the time had come to clear his conscience.

"Louis did not grant remission of our marriage fines for nothing," he said.

Barbara smiled. "I am not an idiot," she retorted. "No king remits fines without receiving value in kind." Then she reached across the table and touched his hand. "I trust you, Alphonse. I know you would not agree to what could hurt me."

"Nor would King Louis ask what was not honest," he said, covering her hand with his. "I should have told you at once, of course, but we were so busy until we took ship and then neither of us was fit for much talk."

"No." Barbara laughed. "Besides, on the ship I would not have believed that I would live to perform whatever promise you made."

Alphonse smiled in response. "You have already done your part, which was only to tell Edward that his wife and child were well and in no need."

Barbara's thick brows rose to make their little tent on her forehead. "You are a masterly bargainer if Louis remitted my marriage fine for that. I would have done it gladly without recompense."

"But King Louis did not know that. Still—"

Suddenly Alphonse nodded, and a black curl fell over his forehead. Barbara had some difficulty resisting the urge to push it back among its fellows, but the intensity of his stare and the way the corners of his lips tucked back corrected her wandering thoughts. Then he laughed shortly and shrugged.

"Perhaps Queen Eleanor told Marguerite you had come to France to spy for the rebels. I did think Louis yielded your fine more easily than I expected. It may be that he thought he was ridding his court of a clever spy."

Barbara laughed aloud at that. "You seemed to think so too. I do not care, since we are the gainers, unless . . . What did you promise Louis?"

"Nothing of which even Leicester would disapprove. I only promised to discover, if I could, what Edward would consider reasonable terms for peace and, if peace was made with fairness, whether he would keep that peace after his father's death."

"Are you going to tell Louis that Edward will neither make nor keep any peace with Leicester?" Barbara's eyes were wide with distress.

"I have no way to do so, even if I wished it," Alphonse said, "and despite the prince's present mood, I am not without hope. What I wish to do is calm him enough so that he will listen to some decent compromise." He then praised Barbara again for skillfully reducing Edward's suspicions about them, and added slowly, "I think it likely that the terms Leicester has proposed are not fair to the prince. Perhaps the pope's legate will—"

"Do not hope for that," Barbara said. "The papal legate was Queen Eleanor's best hope for pushing Louis into actively supporting the invasion. She is very clever and has subtly convinced him that Leicester and the bishops who support him are contemptuous of the pope. And I must admit that refusing to allow the legate's messengers into the kingdom in June, seizing his letters, and throwing them into the sea was not the wisest way to deal with him."

"I wonder if more damage has been done to Leicester's cause by his friends than by his enemies?" Alphonse remarked dryly. "Certainly after the handling we received at Dover, what little sympathy I had for his ideas was burned away by anger."

"But you cannot blame Leicester for what Richard de Grey did," Barbara protested. "We were freed as soon as Leicester had news of us."

Alphonse was not at all sure that was true, but he saw no sense in arguing the point, which could not be proven and would only mark his political differences with Barbe. He said instead, "Poor Leicester. He is so very good and noble, really, that his few faults stand out like black warts on a handsome face. What you would hardly notice in another man draws one's whole attention in his case. It is not fair, but it is true."

"But—" Barbara began, then stopped and shook her head. Alphonse was perfectly right, as he always was. How many times she had excused indulgence to their children in others, but was enraged because Leicester did not see fault in and curb Guy and young Simon. "I never thought of it," she continued slowly. "How dreadful. Poor man."

"I did not mean to increase your sympathy for him," Alphonse pointed out. "I had better get back to the main point. My Aunt Eleanor did not mention her dealings with the pope's legate to me. In this case, I could wish she was not so clever for even with the legate's approval she will not be able to persuade Louis to help her invade England. He is too well aware of the disaster that followed his father's 'holy crusade' in King John's time—and from the tales that have come down to us, John was far more hated than Henry. Damn!"

"Was that what you were trying to hint to Edward? That the pope's legate might find a compromise? But what has fighting in tourneys to do with—"

"Nothing. I was only reminding Edward that rage and hate are useless. I was not hinting anything to him other than that Louis had not abandoned him. He must have hope. Without hope, all Edward has to think about is his own mistake at Lewes of pursuing the Londoners, who were already beaten, and by his absence allowing Leicester to win the battle. No doubt such thoughts build a black rage in him that makes him desire punishment."

Barbara's eyes opened wide. "So he tries to kill Henry de Montfort and attacks his guards and possibly tries to escape when he knows perfectly well it is impossible to do so . . . And then Henry must put greater and greater restrictions on him. Yes, I see. How clever you are, Alphonse."

"Worst of all, he probably does not realize what he is doing. He is trapped in a round of self-hate, which is covered by hatred of everything and anyone to do with Leicester and makes him provoke them to offend him so that he can hate them still more. If I can break into that with hope, he may be able to think more clearly so that if fair terms are offered he will not reject them out of spite."

"God willing," she said.

Her voice was so warm and the admiration on her face so clear that Alphonse stood up suddenly. "Would you like to ride out?" he asked, then laughed. "If I am to keep my promise, I fear I must also keep my distance."

"I would love to, but I will not," Barbara replied, laughing also. "Otherwise, my wedding dress, which is only rough stitched, is likely to come apart—"

"Oh, do ride out," Alphonse pleaded, laughing also.

"No!" Barbara exclaimed. "Go away, you evil man."

"Very well, cruel woman."

Alphonse made a mournful face, but he was not really sorry. During their talk he had come to a decision about how to present his request that Edward be allowed to attend his wedding, if the guards had not already told Henry de Montfort about what he and Barbe had said. That was what he had hoped for when he used Barbe as an excuse to avoid discussing the visit to Edward with Henry. Then he had felt that the suggestion that Edward attend the wedding should come from Henry himself or should not be made. Now he was ready to push the point himself, but when he returned to the castle he found the place in turmoil. King Henry, Peter de Montfort, the chancellor Nicholas d'Ely, and the rest of the court had ridden into Canterbury.

Before Alphonse could decide what to do, Chacier found him and told him Norfolk was looking for him, and he was soon being introduced to the king's new attendants as Barbe's betrothed and a courtier to King Louis of France. All were eager for news from France, so Alphonse did not find time to hang heavy, and just before the evening meal Louis's emissaries rode in from Dover where they had come to port the previous day. Simon de Claremont drew him away at once to ask for a report on the situation in Canterbury, and approved heartily of Alphonse's plan to pacify Edward, but he admitted that he saw little hope that Louis's mediation would have much effect on Leicester.

Later Peter the Chamberlain, the other French envoy, who had presented Louis's authorization to King Henry, joined them and told Alphonse that, in his opinion, there was even less hope than before he left that any invasion would take place. Louis was as set as ever against breaking his promise to be neutral, and the inefficiency and quarreling of Queen Eleanor and King Henry's half brothers had discouraged the men who had gathered. The invasion force was breaking up; Queen Eleanor's purse was almost empty, and King Henry had written forbidding her to raise funds by selling his lands on the Continent to France. Seeing little hope for the future, the mercenaries were leaving as their pay ended. The knights who had come for the sake of adventure or a hope of lands as reward were also drifting away to more promising opportunities.

Then Alphonse had to repeat to Peter what he had said to Claremont and he heard for the first time that a preamble had been added to the Peace of Canterbury that extended Leicester's new form of government for some undefined term of years into Edward's reign.

There was no question, Peter said, that Louis would utterly reject that provision, and since the pope had already declared null and void the Provisions of Oxford, which were the basis of the government outlined in the Peace of Canterbury, he and Claremont were wasting their time.

The situation did seem hopeless; it depressed Alphonse thoroughly and he wished he could put the whole thing out of his mind. His conscientious countrymen, however, still wanted advice on whom they might approach with Louis's more reasonable opinions. Alphonse named Norfolk at once and explained how he had been kept in Dover so that he had met no one and could suggest nothing else. Even so, he was not able to free himself until the evening meal was being served.

Alphonse was relieved when he saw Henry de Montfort with a large crowd around him. To his surprise, Henry excused himself to those waiting to speak to him, grasped his arm, and dragged him up to his own chamber on the third floor.

"I cannot thank you enough," he said as soon as they were private. "Edward has been like a new man ever since you and Lady Barbara spoke to him."

"I am not sure you should thank me," Alphonse said. "I have now heard of the extension of the Peace of Canterbury any unnumbered years into Edward's reign. I do not blame him for being angry. Edward is neither weak nor foolish. And I merely reminded him that calculation is a sharper weapon than the bludgeon of hate. Are you sure, Henry, that you want Edward thinking about how to get his own way by cleverness?"

"Yes!" Henry de Montfort exclaimed. "That is the whole point. Edward is *not* weak and foolish, so the provision that the king take no action without the consent of the council would become meaningless. The council would not interfere with Edward's rule. Their purpose is only to prevent the squandering of money and the royal estate. Edward would not do that in any case. If only he would stop to think, he would soon realize that the provisions designed to stop King Henry's excesses and foolishness would not really apply to him."

Alphonse looked into the hopeful eyes, the open, almost innocent face; here was honor without the black warts of the father. He shook his head. "That would be true if you were the council, but there are not two like you in the world, Henry." He hesitated, then added, "And Edward is not like you, Henry."

Henry de Montfort smiled. "I know what you mean, but I do not care. If we can prevent King Henry from dragging us all to ruin, we will not try to hold the King Edward of the future to the terms. By then the reform of the courts and the sheriff's office will be set—and I do not think Edward was opposed to cleaning out the corruption anyway. He will not allow it to grow again for his own sake. As to foreign ventures, which cost so much because of King Henry's foolishness, I cannot imagine anyone, even the pope, getting the better of Edward."

"That is true enough," Alphonse agreed, frowning. "You should take it as a warning."

"No, because Edward has looked on us as friends in the past and will do so again." Henry raised a hand to stem the protest Alphonse was about to make. "He is trembling on the edge of agreeing already. I swear it. You and Lady Barbara showed him that I did not wish him ill, and then his father came and pleaded with him in tears to yield. I knew we were near winning when King Henry began to whisper that force would be used—and the prince assured him that no one would hurt either of them."

Alphonse's frown grew deeper. "I hope you do not think another visit from me would push Edward into the decision you desire."

"No, no. I know your coming to him again today would make him suspicious, but tomorrow—" Henry hesitated and looked uncomfortable but went on doggedly. "You know the guards report on what is said to Edward by visitors. I know about Lady Barbara's invitation to the prince and what you said, also. I thank you for that. Would you tell him that I would be overjoyed to allow his attendance at your wedding at no greater price than his promise to return to his chamber in the castle without any delay at my request?"

"Yes, I am willing to do that."

"Then will you hold yourself ready in the morning? I hope it will be possible for you to visit the prince soon after breaking your fast so that you may be free the rest of the day, but if there is other business . . ."

"That does not matter," Alphonse said. "You will find me in the great hall whenever you need me. Lady Barbe is busy with her wedding dress, and I think she will wish to visit the ladies who have come to Canterbury. She will not mind if I do not attend her."

Henry de Montfort again offered his thanks and they parted. Alphonse was uneasy. He could not believe that the small assurances he and Barbe had offered could have had so large and immediate an effect on Prince Edward, and he had tried to warn Henry. There were none so blind and deaf as those who would not hear and see, however, and it was quite clear that Henry de Montfort had deliberately pushed out of his mind the tenaciousness of his prince's nature.

The following morning Alphonse was wakened by Chacier, who then drew aside while Claremont's page said that his master wished to see Alphonse at once. As soon as he was dressed, Alphonse followed the boy to the lodging of Louis's emissaries at the White Friars. There he learned that Barbara's warning about the legate's attitude was all too accurate. The previous morning, Claremont told him, in the Church of St. Mary in Boulogne—in

King Louis's presence—the legate had publicly called on the earls of Leicester, Gloucester, and Norfolk and their accomplices to admit him to England by September 1 or appear before him in Boulogne to show cause why he should not be admitted. He had also set a fixed time for them to renounce formally the Provisions of Oxford, on which the form of government they had devised was based, and to suffer excommunication and interdict if they refused.

"Why? Why now?" Alphonse asked, and related what Henry de Montfort had said the previous evening about not holding Edward to all the terms when he became king.

"Sir Henry believes himself to be in his father's confidence," Claremont replied with a shrug, "but I doubt Leicester would be willing to yield the power to Edward. As to why the legate chose this time—perhaps to prevent the compromise with Edward that young Henry hopes for. All I can say for certain is that the legate wanted the news of his total rejection of Leicester's peace terms to come here before August seventeenth, which is the date set for their formal presentation."

"So that no matter what King Henry swears or before whom he swears it, the legate can declare the oath void."

Claremont nodded. "If his support cannot prevent King Henry from swearing—and the legate knows Henry's malleable nature—his denunciation of the whole rebellion will make revocation of the oath easy. There is more news too, although this is no more than a whisper from one of Queen Eleanor's ladies to her lover. The whisper is that the Marcher lords have been driven back by Leicester and Gloucester. The Marchers have not yet yielded, but probably they will be forced to ask for terms very soon."

"Peste!" Alphonse exclaimed. "I can see my aunt's hand in this. She had the news about the defeats in Wales and set to work on the legate. I suppose by now even she is convinced that no invasion will be possible. It is too bad that King Louis did not wait a few days before sending you. Surely this trip was a waste of time."

To that Claremont agreed wryly. "I thought you had better know everything," he added. "The news may change Henry de Montfort's desire for you to see Edward, but if it does not, Peter and I wanted to be sure you were aware of what has happened."

Having thanked him, Alphonse returned to the castle and his belated breakfast. As he ate he thought about how much to tell Barbe of what he had heard and decided, when he saw a page in Montfort colors bearing down on him, to tell her everything. She had a right to know her father was about to be excommunicated and, more important, Alphonse was eager to hear what she thought about the legate's move.

As he expected, the page took him to Henry de Montfort, but he was not told that it would not be necessary for him to see Edward. Instead, Henry repeated what Claremont had already told him about the papal legate and asked if Alphonse would be willing to break this news to the prince.

"You *want* me to tell Edward that the legate has again condemned the Provisions of Oxford, that he is threatening to excommunicate your father?" Alphonse asked. "Is there not the danger that news of the legate's support will make Edward more stubborn?"

"No, it will not," Henry replied. "The legate's ruling is a death knell to any hope of compromise. Once Edward is aware of that, he will set his mind to accepting the terms as they are."

Alphonse opened his mouth to point out what had leapt immediately to his mind—that swearing would be pointless because the Church would certainly absolve the prince of his oath. But Henry was not stupid. Alphonse had to assume, taking into consideration what Henry had said the previous night, that he did not care whether Edward repudiated his oath in the future so long as he swore it now.

So what he said was "I had this news earlier from Claremont. He also told me that the rumor in France is that your father has all but defeated the lords of the Welsh Marches. Is this true?" Henry nodded but did not speak, only looked enquiring, so Alphonse went on, "Claremont also said that any expectation of an invasion grows less each day. Do you want me to pass this news also?"

Henry clasped Alphonse's hand. "God bless you! I was afraid to ask so much, but from me, Edward would take that news as a taunt." He hesitated and then said, "I do not wish to make trouble between you and the prince. Are you sure it will not make Edward think you are betraying him?" His hand tightened on Alphonse's. "It will be best for him to yield, Alphonse. He will be watched, of course, until he really does accept that we desire only the good of the realm and his good too, but once peace is agreed he will be able to ride and hunt and walk about as he wishes."

Alphonse made one last attempt to warn Henry. "I do not doubt it will be best for him," he said, "but take time and think if it will be best for you."

Henry laughed and let go of Alphonse's hand to clap him on the shoulder. "Of course it will." He beckoned to his clerk, who came to them. "My man will take you down to the prince if you are ready now."

Alphonse delayed only a few minutes to send Chacier to Barbe with the news of the arrival of the court and Louis's emissaries and a warning that he was not sure when he would be free. He bade her keep Chacier by her until she could beg a man from her father to run errands and escort her. "And tell her," he said to Chacier, "that unless the Second Coming intervenes, I will be waiting by the altar of the cathedral at tierce on the fifteenth."

Chapter 12

When Alphonse sent that message to Barbe, he was only offering a jesting apology for not hanging about her as a lovesick swain was supposed to do. Actually, he expected to eat his dinner with her or, if that was not possible, to share their evening meal. He had no idea, even when Edward welcomed him with unusual warmth, that he was about to become a royal attendant.

"I am glad to see you again," Edward said, rising from his chair and stretching a hand to Alphonse. "Your earlier visit did me so much good. I could always depend on you for sound advice without any honeyed flavor."

"As I sincerely respect and love you, my lord—and have no reason either to fear you or hope for gain from you—you might well count on my disinterestedness. Also, I would have come just to talk and give you what ease I might; however, I have news, which I am permitted to tell you." Alphonse hesitated, then said slowly, staring steadily into Edward's eyes, "Some you might think good news and some you will think ill, but I beg you to consider very carefully before you decide what to do, if anything."

"So? Let us have the ill first."

Alphonse tightened his grip on the hand Edward had given him, then let go and stepped back a little. The prince was so tall that, although Alphonse was himself above the middle height, he could not see his face clearly if he was too near. Edward's hair was very dark now, almost black because he had been out of the sun—or perhaps it had only darkened even more in the three years since he and the prince had gone the tourney route together. Alphonse could remember when Edward had first started to attend tourneys; his hair had been dark blond then.

The prince still showed signs of what he had endured over the last three months. He was thinner than Alphonse remembered, and his eyes seemed somewhat sunken; however, the weak lid of his left eye was not lower than usual, as it had been the previous day. Indeed, that eye had barely shown a slit yesterday—a sure sign, Alphonse knew, that the prince was very tired or very sad. Now there was hardly a difference between the two eyes and they were very blue too, which usually meant the prince was up to deviltry of some kind. But playful deviltry was entirely impossible in this time and place, so Edward was planning something.

A prick of conscience was easily dismissed. Alphonse had tried several times to warn Henry that whatever had changed Edward's mood—whether it was his and Barbe's visit or not—was dangerous to Montfort plans. Henry had ignored his warning.

Alphonse moved, as if by accident, so that one of the rays of light from the loopholes high in the wall fell on his face instead of the prince's and Edward was turned, exposing only his profile instead of his full face to the guards. Then Alphonse repeated exactly what Claremont had told him, including the source of the rumor that Edward's friends on the Marches of Wales had been defeated. He saw the prince's jaw square, but he thought Edward looked more thoughtful than defeated.

When he spoke about the emissaries' conclusion that the invasion was a lost hope, however, Edward burst out, "I do not consider that bad news. My mother is mistaken in what she is trying to do. I never favored the loosing of mercenary troops on this land under the control—or lack of control—of Lusignan and Valence."

"I cannot help but agree, my lord," Alphonse said. "If Hugh Bigod had been given the leadership of the invasion—"

"No," Edward interrupted, instantly diverted from the main political subject by his passion for anything military. "Hugh is a fine man and would prevent the mercenaries from ravaging the land, but he is no battle leader. Neither is Norfolk, but for a different reason. Both of them are brave men and good fighters, but Hugh really hates war and Norfolk has a temper—" His voice failed suddenly.

"You will never make that mistake again, my lord," Alphonse said quietly. "I have never known you to repeat a mistake. It is one of your great virtues. Another is your ability to accept the fact that it is useless to beat a dead horse."

Edward stiffened a trifle, and Alphonse went on quickly to tell him about the legate's declaration that the Provisions of Oxford must be renounced and he must be welcomed into England. By the time he was finished, Edward was staring at him with an intensity that Alphonse could only hope the guards would not notice. Both the prince's eyes were wide open and quite brilliant. However, when he spoke, his voice was flat and indifferent.

"I do not think Leicester will agree to the legate's terms, since the form of government specified in the Peace of Canterbury is based on the Provisions of Oxford."

"That was my assumption also, my lord."

After an extended pause, the prince said, "You are a good friend, Alphonse."

"I thank you, my lord," Alphonse replied, "but I hope you will not forget that Henry de Montfort urged me to bring you this news—not that about the troubles in the Marches or the possible failure of the invasion; I offered to tell you of those matters myself—but about the legate's order to renounce the Provisions of Oxford."

There was another long pause before Edward said, "I will not forget." Then he gripped Alphonse's upper arm for a moment and offered his other hand, which Alphonse took and kissed, as the prince nodded, adding, "You may leave me now."

Nothing showed in Edward's face or voice besides the lifting of the weak left lid and brilliance of his eyes, but Alphonse felt the prince was a man set for a desperate dare and braced against great pain. His manner made Alphonse so uneasy that he did not set out for Barbe's lodging as he had intended. That, as it turned out, was just as well because one of Henry de Montfort's pages rushed up to him breathlessly just as he was about to sit down to dinner and begged him to come above and dine with his lord.

When the servants brought up the dishes, Henry acted as would any ordinary host, seating his guest and asking him to choose his cuts of meat and which of the stews he would like served, directing that wine be poured into a silver goblet. After the servants had laid the choices of meat on their trenchers and brought bowls of stew and pottage, Henry sent them away, even his young squires, and began to thank his guest.

Alphonse waved away the thanks sincerely. He was relieved because he expected this would be the end of the matter. He felt his duty to Louis was finished also; he had told the emissaries that at the moment Edward would not truly accept any compromise, no matter what he was forced to swear, although time itself might induce him to do so. Louis's presence with the legate in St. Mary's at Boulogne implied to Alphonse that the French king had virtually given up any expectation of mediating a peace. Since Alphonse's report could only support that intention, there was no more for him to do.

While Alphonse was seeking a polite reason—aside from the oppression this unhappy land laid on his spirit—to go back to France as soon as possible after his wedding, Henry said, "How can I stop thanking you? I am sure it is your influence that convinced Edward to ratify the peace terms."

"Ratify—" Alphonse echoed, but Henry cut him off.

"He told me himself, sent a message asking me to come to him. He was pleasant. He smiled at me and said he knew I had done my best for him. How can I stop thanking you? The guard told me what you said to him about me, how you reminded the prince of my goodwill."

"I will accept thanks for that," Alphonse said, "for I know Edward would not bespeak you kindly if he did not mean what he said, but I certainly did not advise the prince to accept this peace."

"Whether you did or not, that was the outcome of your advice." He smiled at Alphonse's angry protest. "Oh, very well, then it was the outcome of the news you brought." He shrugged and the smile disappeared. "Perhaps it was only the result of seeing you and remembering the joys of freedom. Perhaps it was nothing to do with you at all but Edward's consideration of his father's wishes. I do not know or care why Edward decided to make an oath of peace, but he did and he has asked one single favor of me—that you be one of the men chosen to serve him."

"I? But I am to be married in two days!"

Henry burst out laughing. "You will be excused from night duty, I promise."

Alphonse did not smile in response. "Henry, it is impossible. I am sure you told me that one of the provisions of the Peace of Canterbury is that no foreigner be allowed to hold a place in the royal household."

"But Edward's household is not the royal household," Henry said, smiling.

"That is a distinction without a real difference—at least I am sure that is the way many will see it. They will believe that you object to foreigners whom the king loves but appoint those whom you love."

"You are too honest for your own good," Henry said, and

when Alphonse shook his head impatiently, he went on, "I beg you to do this. It need not be for long, only until my father comes to Canterbury and the details of Edward's regular household are agreed. Alphonse, it is the only thing he asked of me. He is swallowing a bitter potion. Will you not let me give him this one sweet comfit?"

To protest further, Alphonse feared, would waken suspicion in Henry, which would be unfair to Edward, who he was certain did not need a sweet comfit. Most reluctantly, Alphonse agreed to serve, but only without any official appointment. That was the best he could do to retain some measure of freedom for himself and to deflect the anger he was afraid some would feel at seeing a French "adventurer"—no more than a jousting companion of Henry de Montfort—chosen to hold a position that should have been given to an Englishman.

Alphonse grew even more exasperated when he discovered that Edward's submission was to have no immediate effect and that his first duty would be to explain this to the prince. He refused absolutely to serve unless some reward was provided, and then he bargained for the removal of the guards inside Edward's chamber. This concession was granted in exchange for Alphonse's promise not to discuss, or even permit the prince to speak of, present or future means of escape.

He gave the promise gladly and with a strong sense of relief because the request told him Henry was aware that Edward's submission might not be sincere. However he also stated that he would not, under any condition, report on any confidence the prince offered him. Clearly that provision disappointed Henry, and Alphonse again offered to explain to Edward personally why he did not wish to serve so that the onus of refusal would not fall on Henry.

After a moment's thought, to Alphonse's intense disappointment, Henry began to smile again, said he should have known better than to think Alphonse would betray a confidence for any cause, and accepted the terms. Alphonse sighed with exasperation, shook his head, and voluntarily offered not to pass any news to Edward without first clearing it with Henry. That brought a burst of laughter followed by a shamefaced admission that Henry had forgotten that problem, and more grateful thanks. Plunging his spoon vengefully into his stew, Alphonse began to discuss the details of his service to the prince.

Chacier's entrance surprised Barbara and caused her instinctively to draw the folds of her skirt over the silver mirror she had been looking at. She did not realize that her surprise and the swift movement gave an impression of guilt. Chacier's message produced a smile and a brightening of her eyes from a bleak gray to a glinting blue. With the morning meal, Clotilde had brought the news of the arrival of the court, and Barbara had delayed eating for some time, expecting Alphonse to come to break his fast with her and escort her to the castle. When he did not come she had felt sick with disappointment, fearing that this was the beginning of a life in which any better amusement would lead her husband to push her into the background.

Now she realized that Alphonse had not simply been swept up into the general excitement and forgotten her. Indeed, he had not forgotten her at all, despite the demands that were being made on his time. Chacier's answers to her questions awakened the liveliest curiosity in her. So the emissaries of King Louis had summoned Alphonse at first light, and then Henry de Montfort would not even allow him to finish breaking his fast before he called him. Having thanked Chacier and bidden him fetch her mare, Barbara put the silver mirror into her work basket without another glance. She no longer needed its comfort. After the briefest hesitation she laid her work—the end piece for the armhole edging of her wedding gown—atop the mirror. If necessary she could sit up all night to finish it, and if the birds on their branches were not perfect at the very bottom, no one would notice. Right now it was more important to discover what was going on.

Barbara's hope of finding Alphonse at the castle was frustrated. He was still with the prince when she entered, but she was fortunate enough to catch her father before he rode out. When he saw her, he clapped a hand to his head and admitted he had completely forgotten her. Then he stared at her for a moment, smiled, and said that he had better present her at once to the king, who would be eager to hear about Queen Eleanor. One roar canceled the excursion he was about to make; a second sent his older squire off to inform the king of Barbara's presence and to determine whether Henry wanted to speak to her.

Barbara bit her lips and then let herself grin. She had been accusing the wrong man of neglecting her. She was amused because she realized she no longer cared that her father called her to mind only when she was useful to him. So long as Alphonse remembered her, she did not care who else forgot. Then it occurred to her that her father's riding out when there must be state business to transact was very odd, and she guessed that the reception accorded him by the king must have been cold—and that by Peter de Montfort not much better.

Anxiety and anger wiped out the little flicker of resentment she had felt. Of course he had forgotten her! As a small diversion while they waited, Barbara repeated to her father Alphonse's message—that the French emissaries and Henry de Montfort had detained him and that he thought she should ask her father for a man to run her errands and serve as escort—whereupon her father cocked an inquiring brow at her.

"So Alphonse expects to be kept on a short leash," he said, adding absently, "I can spare you five men if you want—"

"No," Barbara said, "two will do. If they are here, I would like Bevis and Lewin."

Norfolk nodded at his younger squire, who ran off to tell the men-at-arms, and asked, "What is Alphonse up to?"

"I have not the vaguest notion," Barbara admitted, "but I do not think any of this is his idea. Both the French emissaries and Henry de Montfort sent for him; he did not apply to them for audience. It may not mean anything, father. He and Henry de Montfort and Prince Edward have been friends for years. They hunted and fought in tourneys together. And Alphonse is Queen Marguerite's nephew and well known in the French court. It is not surprising that the emissaries should ask him for news—"

"Before he had broken his fast?"

Norfolk stared hard at his daughter, and a sharp pang of guilt racked Barbara because she found herself unwilling to tell him about Alphonse's agreement with the French king. In the next moment she realized that her father was staring through her rather than at her, and after another moment he nodded. Before he could speak, however, a royal page was bowing gracefully and inviting them to follow him.

The king was in the castle garden, to which Barbara and her father were admitted by two fully armed guards. One looked at the broadsword at Norfolk's hip, but he did not speak, and the breath that had caught in Barbara's throat eased out. There were other men-at-arms, she saw, standing quietly around the walls. The king, she thought, was little less a prisoner than Edward. She saw him then, seated on a bench in the shade of a small fruit tree, with Peter de Montfort to one side and Henry de Bohun just turning toward her. Seven ladies were also in attendance, one seated on another bench placed at an angle to the king's and six sitting on robes laid on the grass.

Barbara hardly noticed the ladies because she was so stunned by King Henry's expression. The evidence of confinement combined with the effect of her visit to the prince the previous day had led her to expect helpless rage, impotent frustration, or the kind of dead despair that Edward had shown. Henry, however, gave her a sunny smile and extended his hand eagerly. As she sank to the ground and kissed the king's fingers, Barbara almost laughed at herself. She had expected to see in King Henry what she herself would have felt, what she knew her father or Alphonse would have felt, what she imagined any man would feel in similar circumstances. What she actually saw was typical of King Henry, whose incurable optimism—when he was not wallowing in self-pity and hysteria—had brought about the terrible situation in England.

"How is it with my beloved Eleanor?" Henry asked as soon as Barbara raised her head.

"Very well, my lord—except that she frets over your well-being," Barbara replied. "She is treated with the greatest honor and courtesy by King Louis and with most loving affection by Queen Marguerite."

That was no lie. No matter how annoyed Louis was with his sister-by-marriage, his rigid sense of what was owing to his own noblesse oblige and to her position as a foreign queen provided her with honor and courtesy. And Queen Eleanor in need and sorrow was far dearer to her sister Marguerite than when she had been happy. Now Marguerite could feel superior instead of resenting Eleanor's power over her husband, a power Marguerite had never had.

A gleam woke in the king's right eye—the left was half hidden, like Edward's, by a weak lid—and for a moment Barbara was afraid Henry would ask her whether the honor and courtesy of King Louis would be translated into help for him, but he did not. Instead he called for another rug to be spread on the grass and invited her to sit. Then he questioned her on every detail of the queen's health and appearance.

When she had at last satisfied him, he nodded to her and suggested she might like to join the other ladies. Barbara rose at once and gathered up the rug, about to refuse the invitation because none had been offered to her father, who was standing beside her, but before she could speak, the king said, "Wait," smiled a little, flicked a sly glance at Peter de Montfort, and added, "I thought you had gone to France to take up your place in Eleanor's household. Why do you come back so soon?"

"To obtain my father's blessing on my betrothal," Barbara replied smoothly, with a cold smile.

The revelation called forth some feminine sounds, a gasp, a soft exclamation, and from her right a sniff, but Barbara was too intent on King Henry's expression to do more than mentally record what she heard. She was glad to see the sly look on Henry's face change to open surprise, a confirmation of her guess that the king had made the remark about her early return to taunt his gaolers. Henry believed she had been sent as a spy by Leicester to ferret out the queen's secrets and that she had come back because Eleanor was too clever for her.

"How came you to be betrothed in France?" The king's surprise had changed to indignation; his smile was gone when he spoke.

"My lands, sire, a small manor called Cruas with its farms, are beholden to King Louis. I have always been in his gift, but he was kind enough to allow me to come back to England with my father after my husband, le comte de le Pontet de Thouzan le Thor, died."

"Oh," Henry said, smiling again and interested now that she had made clear that his right over her marriage had not been usurped. "I did not know that. I thought your dower would be from your father."

"No, Cruas was my mother's, but it was through my father's care that the lands came to me." Barbara was not about to let pass the implication that her father was not willing to provide for her.

"And she will have something handsome from me," Norfolk put in, his hand on her shoulder. "Not lands. I am not one to break up an estate. The lands will go to my brother Hugh's boy, my nephew Roger."

"Then I take it you are pleased with the man King Louis chose for Lady Barbara?" Henry sounded both sulky and uncertain.

"How could I object to Sieur Alphonse d'Aix, nephew to our queen and also to Queen Marguerite?" Norfolk laughed at the open astonishment in Henry's face. "I was as surprised as you, sire," he admitted.

Henry smiled back, flattered because Norfolk seemed to relish Alphonse's relationship with Queen Eleanor. He spoke of Alphonse, whom he had met during his visits to the French court, and Norfolk replied, also with praise, mentioning that it was Alphonse who had arranged that Barbara have Cruas. Immediately interested, as he always was in personal events, Henry asked for details, seeming to have forgotten the spite that had earlier made him ignore Norfolk's presence. He gestured for Barbara's father to sit down on the bench to his left and listened, smiling and nodding.

Silently blessing Alphonse for providing at least the possibility of easing the king's resentment of her father, Barbara tactfully backed away. She had almost passed the half-circle of seated women when a tug at her skirt made her look down and smile with pleasure.

"My Lord, what a shock you have given me," Aliva le Despenser whispered. "Sit down at once and tell all. I thought you would be weeping and pleading with the king to find a way to free you, not smiling all over your face when you said you had been betrothed."

After a single glance that assured her that the conversation between her father and the king was progressing along pleasant lines and she would not need to step forward again to change the subject, Barbara spread her rug beside Aliva's. Before she sat down, however, she leaned over to kiss the cheek of Alyce de Vere and reached beyond her to press the hand of Margaret Basset. Alyce, who was only sixteen, smiled at her shyly. Margaret, who was double that, lifted a brow.

"I thought you too clever to be caught," Margaret Basset said.

"Oh, did you not hear what papa said?" Barbara replied gaily. "How could I stand against King Louis's will?"

"Barby," Aliva said warningly, "I will catch you in a dark corner and strangle you. You would stand up to God if you opposed His will. Why did you agree to this betrothal?"

In private, Barbara might have confessed the truth to Aliva, but Alyce was too young and Margaret too sharp-tongued for her to admit she loved Alphonse. Aliva's sympathy she might endure if Alphonse proved unfaithful, but Margaret's and Alyce's she did not want. She shrugged.

"It seemed a good thing. Sieur Alphonse has a special relationship to Queen Marguerite, which always provides consideration at court. I am no longer so young—neither is my papa. I must think of the future. The proposal came from Alphonse, so I know I was not forced on him. Since we have known each other for a very long time and I am not rich enough for him to take out of greed, it must be me he desires. He is very clever and was lying in wait to snare me. If I must marry, he seemed best; he is a most elegant gentleman and will always be kind." She smiled and lowered her voice. "Certainly he is a safe haven compared with Guy de Montfort. I am getting too old to keep running away. Suddenly it was too much trouble to run very fast, especially when I had so good a reason to be slow. Wait until you see Alphonse."

As she spoke, Barbara had taken in the faces of all the women: Peter de Montfort's wife, Alice, was seated on the bench to the king's right; her husband was now sitting beside her and watching with no expression at all while Barbara's father talked to the king. Sitting on a robe on the grass beside Lady Alice was Eleanor de Bohun, Humphrey de Bohun's wife, her thin face sour with dissatisfaction. Eleanor was envious, Barbara thought, because Lady Alice had a bench—despite the fact that Lady Alice's age would have made sitting on the ground difficult. Next were two women she did not know, sitting close together and talking in low voices.

In answer to Barbara's whispered question, Aliva said the two women were the sisters of Robert de Ferrars, earl of Derby, who had fought at Lewes for Leicester. Whether Ferrars actually supported Leicester was another question. To Barbara the earl of Derby seemed more like a wild beast, attacking anyone who tried to restrain him, rather than a man of principle who believed in Leicester's cause.

Just then a page in Henry de Montfort's colors came into the garden and spoke to Peter de Montfort, who gestured him toward the king. Although she perked up her ears, Barbara could not hear what he said, but the king nodded and rose, gesturing for the ladies to remain seated. Barbara was pleased when he beckoned to her father as well as Peter de Montfort and Humphrey de Bohun to accompany him.

"D'Aix," Eleanor de Bohun said thoughtfully. "That is a bastard line, is it not?"

Barbara smiled very sweetly. "Yes, but it is noble on both sides. Alphonse is very proud of his heritage. His shield carries the bar sinister across the Berenger colors—by choice. He could have chosen a different device after his father died. It is a powerful family, very powerful. His brother is vassal to King Louis, and held in very high esteem."

Alice de Montfort sniffed. "I suppose you are to be married in Aix?"

"Oh, no," Barbara said. "Papa would never hear of my going so far without the bond of blood being sealed by the Church. And he wishes to give me to my husband in person. I am to be married the day after tomorrow in Canterbury cathedral. The bishops of Chichester and London will both take part in the service."

"The day after tomorrow!" Aliva shrieked.

"Are you with child already?" Eleanor de Bohun asked.

Barbara had turned toward Aliva, laughing. Her head whipped back toward Eleanor, and for a moment she stared, her eyes a cold sleet gray under her heavy brows. Then a corner of her wide mouth lifted with disdain and her nostrils flared and contracted, seeming to reject a nasty stink.

"I had no need to yield anything to make this marriage," she said. "I am a maiden still, I assure you. You are invited, Lady Eleanor, to see the bloodstains on my sheets in the morning."

"Never mind such stupidities," Margaret Basset put in sharply. "Since you have been married already, whether you have a maidenhead is your husband's affair and of very little interest to anyone else. What is important is who is to attend you? Who will make the feast? Who is invited?"

Barbara had to admit with a laugh that everything had happened so fast she had not yet had a chance to speak to her father about what arrangements he had made—if any. This set Aliva to giggling that Barbara meant she had not yet had a chance to tell him what she wanted. Margaret raised her brows at Aliva and said her levity would get her or someone else in trouble someday. To Barbara's surprise Aliva's beautiful brown eyes filled with tears and she looked guiltily down at her hands.

Barbara thought she was the only one who noticed, because Margaret's voice had continued smoothly, now asking Alice de Montfort whether the wedding might be of use in dealing with the French emissaries. Alice grew immediately thoughtful, clearly considering whether, since King Louis had arranged the marriage to his wife's nephew, a grand celebration might not indirectly honor the French king and flatter his emissaries.

"I will certainly mention the possibility to Peter," she said, "and before dinner, so that he can announce at that time the hour of the wedding mass and the invitations to the feast if he thinks the notion good." She nodded at Margaret Basset with approval, then turned to Barbara and asked, "And you will make no trouble, whatever is decided, Lady Barbara?"

"Not of my own will, certainly, Lady Alice," Barbara replied. "However, I must reserve the right to obey my father if he objects to a large celebration. He may be more pressed for money than I realize—"

"And he will get no *aide* for a bastard daughter," Eleanor de Bohun said.

"He will need none," Alice de Montfort retorted sharply. "The king's guests must eat anyway. It will be less costly for Norfolk to add some delicacies to the feast than to pay for a whole wedding, including feeding and lodging the guests at his keep."

Barbara felt almost dizzied by the many implications in Alice de Montfort's remark. She had never thought for a moment of the exchequer bearing the cost of her wedding. For a single instant she had been ready to rise and cheer. Then doubts damped the pleasure she had felt when she first thought her father would be relieved of the expense. Why should Peter de Montfort overlook the opportunity to have her father pay the cost of supporting the court for one day? To flatter the French emissaries? No, that was ridiculous. How could Claremont and Peter the Chamberlain know who had paid for the feast? And why should they care? The purpose must be to *prevent* her father from holding a feast on his own lands to celebrate her marriage.

Barbara was about to lodge a protest against Peter de Montfort taking over the plans for her wedding, but Margaret Basset reached out and pinched her hard. Margaret's hand was innocently behind her by the time Alice de Montfort stood and looked down.

''You were about to say?'' she asked Barbara.

''Only not to set the wedding mass too early, please.'' Barbara smiled. ''I have been so rushed from here to there and back again that my dress is not completely finished.''

''Well, do not run back to your lodging to work on it until I give you leave,'' Alice said. ''You may be needed to support this decision or give your agreement to it.''

''If I ask for leave, Lady Alice, I will ask it of my father,'' Barbara retorted. ''There is none other here who has any right over me, except my betrothed—and he has already given me leave to come and go as I please while he is prevented by business from attending me.''

''Oh, for the holy saints' sake, Alice,'' Margaret exclaimed when Alice drew an indignant breath. ''Do you not yet know it is fatal to give Barby an order? I promise you she will not go if you will hold your tongue until you need it to speak to your husband and Norfolk.''

''Well!'' Eleanor de Bohun got to her feet. ''I had no idea that a hasty little betrothal between two bastards was going to turn into a state wedding. I'm sure you should reconsider, Alice. I doubt my husband will approve of a grand celebration.''

''Do not be such a goose, Eleanor,'' Alice snapped. ''Humphrey will be delighted. Why do you not come along with me now and ask him?''

As the two women started off, a soft, almost tremulous voice asked, ''What will your gown be like?''

The fairer of the two Ferrars sisters had spoken, and she shrank back a trifle when Barbara turned to her rather abruptly. Barbara smiled. ''Not very grand. Not grand enough, I am afraid, but I never expected my marriage to become a state affair. The tunic is a darkish cream color, almost the shade of undyed wool, but with a gloss because it is silk—a gift from Queen Eleanor. The overgown will be blue. It has a wide, low neck and very deep armholes. Actually, it is the embroidery of the armholes that is not finished.''

''We are very good at embroidery,'' the darker sister said eagerly. ''Do send for the work. We would gladly help with it. Oh, I am Agnes and my sister is Isabel.''

Barbara at once exclaimed gratefully. A servant was sent to the lodging with instructions for Clotilde to bring the dress, and the half-hour until the maid arrived was filled with idle chatter. Barbara disappointed the ladies a little; they did not know she had been confined at Dover and thought she would have more gossip about the French court to impart. Still, she was a prized audience because she was ignorant of the gossip in England of the past two months. She listened gladly, although she soon realized that Aliva was strangely silent, except when Margaret prodded her.

When Clotilde came, Margaret rose, shook her head, and said she would go since embroidery was not the greatest of her pleasures. She would see Barby later, she remarked, with a meaningful glance. To Barbara's amazement, Aliva blushed.

Soon Agnes and Isabel were talking enthusiastically to Alyce about what they would wear themselves while they worked away at Barbara's wedding gown. Barbara and Aliva sat apart from the others, quiet until Barbara was sure the younger women were deeply absorbed in their own subject.

"What has happened, Aliva?" Barbara asked. "I can see something is very wrong. Oh, I am so sorry I will not be able to offer you a refuge with my father anymore."

"I could not come, even if you were still living at home and not being married," Aliva said. "The trouble is that Roger—"

"Papa?" Barbara gasped.

As far as Barbara knew, since her mother's death her father had confined his need for women to whores, maidservants, and a girl in a field now and again. Even though Aliva was spectacularly beautiful, just like the descriptions in the romances—blond, with strawberry lips, milk-skin, but brown rather than blue eyes—Barbara could not believe her father would have made a dishonorable proposal to her friend. In the next moment Norfolk was redeemed.

"No. Oh, no." Aliva gave a watery smile. "Your father pats me kindly on the head, just as he does you—when he notices me at all."

"My cousin?" Barbara was almost as horrified to think that young Roger Bigod would offer dishonor to a decent woman.

Eleven years earlier she would not have felt that way; she would have been glad to hear any evil of young Roger Bigod. At that time Barbara had hated Hugh Bigod's eldest son, who was her father's namesake and heir. Young Roger had come to live with her father from the time he was eight years of age, serving first as page and then as squire to the earl. In 1253, a child herself, Barbara had felt he had replaced her in her father's affections. Roger had come and she had been cast out, exiled to France. By the time Barbara returned to England in 1257 she had come to understand that her sojourn in France had nothing whatever to do with young Roger and that what her father felt for her was hers and no one could ever take it from her. Then, having come to know her cousin well, Barbara had grown fond of Roger, who was very like both her father and her uncle.

"Roger was trying to help me," Aliva said faintly. "Simon was forever pawing me and trying to catch me alone. He cannot believe that I would never cuckold my husband, no matter how little I love him. Roger does understand and he knows that Hugh will make no effort to protect me, partly because he trusts me and partly"—she laughed bitterly—"because he does not care. Hugh would be as glad to declare me a whore and put me aside."

Barbara took Aliva's hand but did not say anything. Hugh le Despenser was not an evil man, but to him a woman, no matter how beautiful or clever, was less than a horse—even less than a good dog. One could always get a new woman, and property or goods would come with her, whereas one had to pay for a horse or a dog.

After a little silence, Aliva went on. "Please do not be angry at Roger. I think he simply felt he should continue the good work he had started before you left for France, when you engaged him to keep Guy and Simon away from us. Anyway, Roger took to escorting me about. While he was with me, Simon could only hint, not touch me and try to drag me into dark corners. Only . . . only . . . we began to enjoy being together. We laugh at the same things . . ."

Her voice trembled into silence and all Barbara could say was "Oh, how dreadful—"

Aliva looked up, shocked, and then burst out laughing. Barbara could not help but join her. The remark seemed singularly inappropriate, but it was all too true. Had Roger merely been smitten by Aliva's beauty, the attraction could easily have been a passing fancy. But if they laughed at the same things, just as she and Alphonse did, their desire for each other went deeper than the flesh. If so, Roger might refuse to marry, as she herself had refused—and that *was* dreadful for he was heir to her father's estates and must have heirs of his own.

Alyce turned to the laughter and asked about the jest. Barbara said desperately that she had just admitted that her mare had made her marriage and described Frivole's behavior in the stableyard at Boulogne. The girls laughed heartily, and Aliva pressed her arm. The conversation then became general, and despite her worries about Aliva and her father, Barbara had to concentrate on the light talk in order to avoid making her young companions suspicious. She was relieved when a page came to summon them to dinner.

As soon as Barbara entered the castle, she saw Alphonse at the other end of the great hall, but before she could excuse herself to her companions and make her way to him, a Montfort page plucked him by the sleeve and Alphonse followed the boy to the stairs. Barbara tried to hold back from choosing a seat, expecting every minute that Henry de Montfort and Alphonse would come down and she could join her betrothed; however, Margaret Basset drew her away, refused to listen to her reason for wanting to speak to Alphonse, saying sharply that she could sit beside the man for the rest of her life if she wished and right now to plan the wedding was more important, and led her to a seat beside Alice de Montfort.

Alice told her she had received her husband's approval and Barbara's father's agreement to arrange all matters concerning the wedding. From that moment until the end of the meal, Barbara was deeply involved in a discussion of the details of her marriage and wedding feast. She could not be indifferent or ungrateful about the trouble Alice was taking—nor could she forget for a moment that taking that trouble meant a lack of trust in her father.

Deep in her conversation, Barbara did not notice her father rise from his seat among the other great men at the high table. His bellow made her jump as well as serving its purpose of silencing the hall. The announcement that followed, inviting all present to the wedding, nearly took all power of further movement from her. She finished her meal and rose from the table without really noting what she was doing or where she was. Still bemused by the fact that the entire court, rather than a select group, had been invited to her wedding, she allowed herself to be carried off by Margaret to the garden where Clotilde and the Ferrars sisters were already working on her wedding gown.

About an hour before vespers, when her dress was finished, Barbara sent Clotilde to find Bevis and Lewin, one of whom could fetch her mare and the other walk back to the lodging with the maid. She was idling near the door to the bailey, when a hand clutched at her shoulder and Alphonse's voice breathed in her ear, "Barbe! Thank Mary and all the saints. I have no time, but I must speak to you."

He looked around, then led her toward the back door, saying they would find a quiet place in the garden. Barbara seized his arm and hauled him back, explaining that she had left a whole tribe of chattering women there. Finally she drew him along the hall, sticking her head into one antechamber after another until she found a wall chamber where her father's shield was propped against a bench.

Alphonse promptly kissed her—too briefly for her instant reaction to communicate itself to him—and called her a well of wisdom, which alarmed her so much that the warmth he had generated disappeared. However, it appeared that Alphonse was more afraid of interruption than that his news was so dangerous absolute privacy was necessary. Having explained the outcome of his morning's visits to Henry de Montfort and Prince Edward, he shook his head.

"I went back to Edward after dinner to get his agreement to my terms of service. The only thing he did not like was that I refused any official appointment, but he laughed and admitted he did not think I would let Henry de Montfort fall into the trap of appointing a foreign friend to office when the king is forbidden to do so. He almost kissed me when I told him his reward for agreeing to ratify the peace agreement would be freedom from the guards inside his chamber. That seemed natural enough, but I was not equally happy when he did not even blink over my promise in exchange not to speak myself or allow him to speak of escape. I tell you, Barbe, I know the prince. He is planning something and I am caught between."

"No," Barbara said at once. "With you alone, he may weep or rage without shame or fear of exposure. He may be only a man overburdened by trouble, not a prince with pride and dignity. That was why he took such joy in being freed from those who watched him. He may indeed intend to escape his ratification of the terms, but he will not permit you to be blamed. The prince is not above clever trickery, but I will say in Edward's honor that he carries his own load. He will not drop that burden on you."

"You are right, my love." But Alphonse's sigh was no token of relief. "I have been so harried from field to bank to hedge that I was beginning to see hunters where none were hiding. Thank you. Edward will save my honor, but I am concerned for Henry too. He is too honest and straightforward, and something is going on inside the prince's head. I have this fear that Edward will spring his surprise at our wedding—for the 'thanks' Henry offered Edward for his compliance was permission to attend. The prince will be guarded, but not shackled or held as a prisoner, and all he was asked for was a firm promise to return to his prison as soon as Henry asked him to do so."

Barbara's eyes went wide. "You mean Henry did not ask for Edward's promise not to try to escape?"

"He did not, and I see you know how Edward's mind works. After all, he would not be breaking any promise if he escaped during the wedding and was not there to hear Henry ask him to return to prison. I knew nothing about it because I was not there when the offer was made. I had been sent off to King Henry, who wished to thank me for lifting up his son's spirit. But you know I had nothing—or little, anyway—to do with that. And Edward laughed when he told me of the promise he had made. Now what am I to do?''

The tense pose Barbara had held relaxed. ''Laughed?'' she repeated. ''No, if Edward intended to make trouble for you, he would not have laughed.'' Then she touched his face and smiled. ''I think he was just bedeviling you. I cannot see how he could escape. You must have asked Edward to be your groomsman—'' Alphonse nodded, and Barbara went on—''so papa and I will ride before him, you will ride beside him, and the whole court will be behind. No, he would not ride over me, and he knows my father will be armed and would stop him. Nor would he shame you so deeply''—she smiled—''especially when his friends, the Marcher lords, are so far away, in Wales, across the whole width of the widest part of England.''

''Oh, good God, what a fool I am!'' Alphonse exclaimed. ''I myself told Edward this very morning that the lords Marcher are in no case to help him. He will not try to reach them, but he might talk to people at the wedding.''

''That is Henry de Montfort's problem, not yours,'' Barbara said. ''You cannot be expected to attend Edward at your own wedding. But what do you mean the lords Marcher are in no case to help Edward?''

Alphonse then repeated the news he had had from Claremont about Leicester's defeat of the Marcher lords, and, after a brief hesitation, he told her how the papal legate had threatened to excommunicate Leicester, Gloucester, and her father. ''I did not mean to tell you and worry you,'' he finished, ''but I think your father should know. I intended to tell him myself, of course, only now I am not sure I will be free from one minute to the next.''

''Can they believe the legate's threat will be the stick that makes the ass balk?'' Barbara muttered.

''They? Who? What ass?''

This time it was Barbara's turn, and she hid nothing, telling Alphonse how Peter de Montfort planned to turn their wedding into a compliment to the French emissaries and King Louis.

''Nonsense,'' Alphonse scoffed. ''Marguerite loves me well, but her influence with Louis is limited. Louis . . . ah . . . Louis knows me for what I am, so he trusts me, but there is much about me Louis does not like.'' He paused and chuckled. ''I never thought of it before, but you may be a great political advantage to me in France. Once I am well married and bound to one woman, Louis might come to like me much better.'' Then he sobered and frowned. "No, unless Peter de Montfort is an ass, he cannot think I am of any account to Claremont and Peter the Chamberlain. He must understand that they know me as a clever courtier who has nothing to gain or lose in this trouble in England. So they can rely on me for as fair a picture as I can see, but they will certainly not take as a compliment to themselves or to King Louis any honors bestowed on my wedding."

"Exactly what I thought. So the reason must be to keep papa from using my wedding as an excuse to invite a large gathering of folk to Framlingham."

Alphonse stood still, looking a little to one side of her. Finally he said, "There might be other reasons, but I admit I cannot think of any. Barbe, will you forgive me if I go about and hear what I can hear?"

"Forgive you? I will be grateful."

He took her hand and kissed it. "God has blessed me in your good sense as well as in your charm. If I hear something you should know, I will send Chacier to you."

"Or you can ask for Bevis or Lewin among my father's men-at-arms. They are to be with me as long as I need them."

He kissed her, more lingeringly this time, and she had to push him away to hold back too eager a response. He looked troubled, but she touched his face again and said, with a shaky laugh, "Only two more days. Go now."

But when he was gone, Barbara sank down on the cot, her thoughts spinning back and forth between her concern for her father and her increasing difficulty in hiding her passion. She wondered hopelessly how she could manage to conceal her feelings and still escape hurting Alphonse too deeply. Norfolk's voice from the doorway startled her and she looked up with an intake of breath.

"What are you doing here, chick?" her father asked, coming closer. "Bevis is in the hall, worried to death. He has been looking all over for you."

"Oh, heaven, I forgot about him," Barbara cried, "but Alphonse told me to warn you. The papal legate—"

Norfolk's lips thinned. "I have heard about that. Do not trouble your head . . . but I will thank Alphonse for wishing to warn me when I see him. I suppose he heard the news from Louis's men. Never mind that. Tell me instead how you managed to persuade Alice de Montfort to urge her husband to pay for your wedding."

Barbara stood up and clutched her father's arm. "I did nothing," she said, and she explained how Margaret Basset had suggested the idea of flattering the French emissaries and how eagerly Alice had seized on Margaret's suggestion.

He was shaken with laughter, but got out, half choked, "I swear I will give you in silver every penny you have saved me."

"Father, it is no laughing matter." She tightened her grip on his arm. "Do you not see that either they are trying to bribe you to remain loyal to King Henry, which means they do not trust you, or, worse, they fear that you will gather the doubtful about you for a wedding feast at Framlingham and—"

"Do not *you* begin to take me for a fool," he said harshly. "And do not worry about me."

Chapter 13

Although it was impossible to dismiss her father's troubles from her mind completely, Barbara did not dwell on them. For one thing, she did not take him for a fool and knew him well capable of caring for his own interests. For another, so much happened the next day that she had no time to think about him or even about her own marriage.

First, King Henry and Prince Edward were escorted under heavy guard to the cathedral. There, after mass, in the presence of all the bishops, the French emissaries, and all the people who could be crammed into the great church, both swore to uphold the terms of the Peace of Canterbury. Despite the general desire for a peace among those who attended, the occasion was not joyous. The king had lost, at least temporarily, his usual buoyant optimism; he swore with a lifeless lack of enthusiasm that boded ill for the sincerity of his oath. Worse, Edward's fury and hatred glared from his burning eyes while every line of his tense body screamed rejection of the words he obediently mouthed.

Barbara did not know whether to be appalled or relieved. This silent rebellion almost certainly was what Edward had planned, not any attempt to escape while a guest at her wedding. That was a relief. But as far as Leicester's cause went, the result of the prince's swearing was appalling. She was sure Edward's absence would have been an advantage over the effect produced by his manner, which cried aloud that he was being forced into compliance by some threat too dangerous to ignore.

The prince's frequent glances at his father and the way he touched the king's arm from time to time, as if for reassurance of his father's physical well-being, hinted strongly that the threat was against the feeble old man. Angry as Barbara felt at the implication that Leicester's supporters would threaten harm to King Henry (no matter how often she prayed for the old king's death, to do more than pray was an abomination), she could not help but admire Edward's cleverness. Even the most devoted of Leicester's adherents cast questioning glances at Henry de Montfort and looked uncomfortably at one another. Barbara was also sure that every nobleman present knew of the papal legate's opposition to the peace terms. Thus, Edward's manner was virtually a promise that as soon as his father was out of danger, he would repudiate the oath he had sworn and the Church would support him.

Alphonse was one of four attendants grouped on the prince's right. Once he caught her eyes, for she was well forward in the crowd, standing beside her father near the aisle down which the royal party had walked. He cast his eyes up to heaven over Edward's manner, but she could see he was amused rather than troubled. Barbara stiffened angrily; Alphonse did not care that the rejection displayed by Edward's body and expression of every phrase he spoke aloud might well bring renewed war. But after a moment she dismissed the anger. First of all, Alphonse like most other men seemed to regard war—except on one's own lands—as a kind of pleasant, energetic sport. Second, she was sure what was foremost in his mind was his fear that the prince might use their wedding for his own purposes and welcomed any proof he would not.

Barbara hurried back to her lodging after the painful ceremony, expecting a messenger to arrive at any moment to say that the prince would not, after all, be permitted to serve as groomsman. The messenger arrived, just as she expected, but she had barely time to wonder whom Alphonse would ask to serve in Edward's place when she realized the man was from the king. Long practice as the queen's lady allowed her to ask with seeming calm what King Henry desired, to accept with the same seeming calm an invitation to share the evening meal with the king, and to dismiss the messenger with thanks and a small reward for being the bearer of good tidings.

One must always pretend that a summons from the king was

good tidings, but this summons was so unexpected and so inexplicable to her that Barbara fell a prey to formless fears. For one crazy moment she even wondered if the king had gone mad and thought he had seigneurial rights over her. The contrast of that silly notion with her knowledge of the real Henry was so great that she felt relieved and laughed aloud. Even as a young man, Henry had no reputation as a lecher, and once he married he had been startlingly faithful to his Eleanor. At the king's present age the idea that he would force himself on an unwilling woman was truly ludicrous.

Curiosity and concern, because she could not conceive of any reason for the king to summon her to a private meeting, filled the rest of her day, pushing Alphonse and her father right out of her mind. And though her assumption about the innocence of King Henry's sexual intentions was proved correct—she found Alice de Montfort present when she was shown into the king's presence—the time she spent with him furnished no answers that did not raise even more puzzling questions.

Henry greeted her with smiles and the information that he intended to honor her wedding with his presence. This brought Barbara down again into the full curtsy from which she had just risen as she gave polite but insincere thanks. She enjoyed court functions and had looked forward to a cathedral wedding presided over by two bishops. However, she had not welcomed the information that Edward would attend, although she had tried to soothe Alphonse's worries about the prince's intentions. The addition of the king to the guest list only multiplied the chances for disaster. Despite the defeat of Edward's Welsh friends, could there be plans for royal supporters to rush the church and try to free the king or the prince?

Other equally unlikely notions drifted in and out of her head while she half listened to the king's fulsome compliments throughout the meal—when he was not asking her to repeat what she had already told him about Queen Eleanor. Their talk seemed totally meaningless to Barbara until she picked out one theme: The praise Henry lavished on Alphonse was even more fulsome than the compliments paid her. The king seemed to have fallen more in love with Alphonse than she had. If there was any purpose to his invitation, it seemed to be to urge her to ask Alphonse to remain in England.

To these remarks, Barbara replied as ambiguously as she could, stating that she loved England and adding similar platitudes but also reminding the king that Alphonse owed a duty to his brother that required his presence at the French court. At first she was annoyed with Henry, but then she realized, from

Alice de Montfort's nods and smiles, that the pressure to keep Alphonse in England was not from the king at all but from the Montfort party.

They were toying with the sweet and the sharp at the very end of the meal, when Henry went back to the subject of her wedding, blandly assuring her that his pleasure in honoring the celebration with his presence was increased by his hope of an opportunity for a better understanding with her father. Since a cry of protest would have done more damage than good, Barbara was fortunate in being struck mute by surprise.

Once she was alert, however, the sly gleam in the king's eyes assured her that what he said was no innocent compliment. Henry's political blunders were most often caused by selfishness, sometimes by misplaced generosity or blind affection; they were not owing to stupidity. Doubtless the king knew his compliment would increase the distrust felt for her father by Leicester's supporters. What Barbara could not guess was whether the remark really had anything to do with Norfolk at all.

Henry might have spoken in pure spite, taking revenge on his enemies for using him as a tool for their purposes. That would show his very worst side, the childish pettiness that took no account of the harm done to others—in this case to her father, who honestly loved him and only wished to restrain him to prevent him from harming himself as well as the realm. But there had been no spite in the king's face; the slyness had looked mischievous. So, more likely, it was not aimless spite but an attempt to foment discord among Leicester's party that the king intended.

Barbara managed to murmur some meaningless reply, to which Henry responded by remarking that he and Norfolk had been children together, he five years the elder. Then she remembered how animated the king had been in talking over old times with her father the day before. In addition to his desire to arouse suspicion among his enemies, could King Henry suspect that Norfolk still felt some sympathy for the Royalist cause? It would be typical of the king to think he could win her father to his party by offering him affection and by making him unpopular with Leicester and his friends.

Because she could think of no way to change the subject, Barbara felt quite grateful to the Treasurer, who came to discuss with the king an unexpected diversion of Treasury receipts and exasperatedly gave the ladies leave to depart.

Fury at the usurpation of his power flooded the king's face with red. Barbara was appalled, but to protest would have made matters worse. All she could do was to curtsy right down to the floor with bent head—and that won her a black look from Alice, who assumed she was currying favor. When they reached the great hall, Barbara tried to find her father but had to leave with his servant a message that he come early to her lodging. The servant was a little the worse for wine and told her that Norfolk and a number of others had taken her betrothed out to enjoy his last night of single blessedness.

Barbara was so full of political worries that she did not give a thought to what the servant's remark might mean. She worried more about the king as she got into bed than about the man who would share that bed with her the next night, and she barely remembered in the morning to tell Clotilde to put the oldest and most worn sheet on the bed, just in case her father wanted evidence that she had been a virgin. She was about to send Bevis for her father when she heard him call to her from the solar and rushed out in her shift to tell him about her meeting with the king.

Norfolk put a hand to his head and squinted at her. "You told my servant to get me up before prime, after the night I had, to tell me that the king is a clever mischief maker who may or may not think fondly of me and that the Treasurer can be an idiot in the pursuit of a shilling?"

Barbara ignored the sarcasm. "You should have seen how Peter de Montfort's wife looked at me—"

"I do not need to see it." He frowned. "You are a good girl, Barby, and it was right that you tell me about the king's invitation and why you think it was given. I am glad you have not adopted your Alphonse's way of thinking. He has a mouth like a steel trap. It gapes in smiles, but when the teeth set, what he knows is caught inside for good."

"He is trying to keep faith with two friends who are now in opposing camps," Barbara pleaded. "Do not blame him."

Norfolk smiled. "No. I cannot help but admire him. And you will be safe with him." He drew her close, kissed her forehead, and groaned as he straightened up. "But you worry about me too much. I have told you before that I can manage my own affairs. I would have been as well warned if you told me this after the wedding instead of having me waked at dawn. I am going back to bed."

"Father—" she cried.

But he only shook his head, winced and clutched at it, and went out, leaving Barbara even more worried. The assurances he had offered were rote; his actions contradicted the words. The only reason she could think of for his leaving instead of lying down on her bed to sleep off his wine was so that the ladies who would soon come to help her dress would not know he had come early to speak to her. Now she was almost grateful to Prince Edward for his silent defiance at the swearing. As long as the realm was in danger, no one would dare move against her father. But to hang forever on the brink of war was a catastrophe of another kind.

A knocking at the door of the shop, and Lewin's voice replying, made Barbara flee to her bedchamber. She recalled that she had told her men to arrange that the shop be closed and as much as possible emptied for this one day to accommodate the prewedding guests and those who would accompany Alphonse and herself back for the bedding ceremony.

With that thought came a sudden recollection of what this day would bring. Barbara felt blood beating in her throat. Her breasts filled, the nipples suddenly sensitive to the touch of the fabric moving against them. All anxiety over her father flew out of her head, while the fears she had suppressed about whether she should or could hide her desire from Alphonse swelled into monsters.

The flood of women that soon entered the chamber was very welcome, even those like Eleanor de Bohun who came to prick and tease. One thing was sure—while they examined her garments and questioned her motives and loyalties under the guise of jests, she had no time to think of anything but the subject presented to her. Even remarks on the fine weather, which had now lasted five full days, acquired a double meaning.

A young priest from St. Margaret's Church across the road came up to say a brief mass before the ladies broke their fast. Barbara ate and drank with stolid determination. She had not yet decided what she would do when she and Alphonse lay alone in bed, and she did not intend that any rumor of nervousness on her part come back to him. She was teased for being indifferent then, but that was safe. A man was always glad to learn he was his wife's idol; he would gladly forget any contrary evidence.

The light meal finished, the ladies began to dress Barbara, pulling on her fine silk stockings and tying the garters below her knees—with bows so they would easily come undone. A waste, Barbara remarked, laughing, since today it was the ladies themselves who would untie them to show the bride to the groom's witnesses. A bushel of chaff flew about after that remark.

Her shoes went on then: bright red kidskin, polished to a high gloss, decorated with gilded bands and rosettes, and fastened around the ankle with pearl-set gold buttons. Barbara blinked.

Aliva le Despenser kissed her and murmured they were her gift; she knew, she said, Barbara would not have had time to order new shoes. Then her tunic was fitted on and laced, but the lavishly bejeweled and gilded girdle that was Prince Edward's gift drew surprised murmurs. The girdle would be visible through the wide armholes of the surcoat that was slipped on over the tunic, and every woman in the room would spread word of the costly gift.

That subject carried them along until it was dropped in favor of a good deal of laughter and some envious comment over the attempts to confine Barbara's hair. Unfortunately the mood did not hold after the glittering crespine was finally fastened, the barbette tied, and the fillet set atop. Alice de Montfort's presentation of a gift from King Henry—a gold band set with gemstones to bind around the fillet—renewed the sidelong glances and whispered remarks. Barbara credited the gift to Queen Eleanor, in whose household she had served for many years, but she knew that so intense a show of royal favor was politically significant.

Many of the women present had divided loyalties, however, and the awkward moment soon passed. Then a different kind of uneasiness began to steal over the group. Barbara suddenly realized it was growing late, and she was about to suggest they make ready to go when the outside door slammed open.

"The groom's gift, at last," someone whispered.

The words were a shock. Barbara had completely forgotten the custom of the groom marking his satisfaction in the marriage with a personal gift to the bride. But Barbara knew there could be no groom's gift. Alphonse would never shame her with a paltry trinket, and he had had no opportunity to obtain any better gift. Her heart sank at the idea she would need to explain *that*. Alphonse was not at fault, but she would still suffer the shame of seeming slighted.

"Poor Alphonse—" Barbara began, only to have the words drowned by her father's voice, which came up the stair in an irritable bellow.

Barbara smiled like the sun. All unwitting, perhaps, her father had saved her. As he entered the room her eyes glinted with amusement through tears of tenderness. She did not dare smile at him, for both would have burst into laughter or into tears, both knowing the sacrifice he had made for love of her. He was dressed in the highest fashion in a manner he loathed—brilliant in a gold surcoat, all sewn with red crosses, over a crimson tunic, his broad breast draped with gold chains, which he would ordinarily have worn only to avoid shaming his king when he went on foreign embassies. Even his sword with its plain wire-bound hilt looked strange; although the weapon was unchanged, he had hooked it to a bejeweled and gilded belt girded low on his hips. His shoes were gilded, too—and must be stiff and hurt his feet, Barbara thought—and huge golden spurs were fastened to them. Oh, poor papa!

The women scattered before the earl of Norfolk as he marched forward. Barbara lifted her eyes, wanting to look her gratitude at him, but her breath caught. His smile was fixed; his eyes were anxious and full of warning as he thrust a carved wood box at her and growled, "Bride gift."

Barbara had taken the box instinctively. She almost dropped it at the words. The box was old and very familiar.

"Open it," her father said.

She gasped when she saw the contents; she knew the necklet and armbands well for they had lain in her father's strongbox all her life. They were Celtic gold work and very ancient, fantastically interlaced birds and beasts. Each was collared, and from each collar hung a pendant pearl. The necklet and armbands had belonged to her father's mother.

Barbara's faint protest was masked by the exclamations of the closest ladies, who took her paralysis for joyful astonishment and removed the jewels, holding them aloft to be admired by the whole group. By the time the ladies had pressed forward to see, to touch and comment, and the gauds were fastened around her neck and arms, Barbara had recovered her wits. She managed a broad smile, particularly meant for her father, who grunted with relief, patted her, and muttered, "Good girl."

The rest of the day was one long confusion. The whole party had first to return to the castle because Henry and Peter de Montfort felt it too dangerous for the king and prince to stop in the street while the bride's party joined the groom's. For the same reason, the bridal procession from the castle to the cathedral at the other end of the town looked like the advance of an army, and the cathedral had as many men-at-arms in it as guests. There were so many guards, preceding Alphonse and the prince and hemming them in from both sides, that Barbara never saw her betrothed until he took her hand at the altar. Even then she had no time for the hopes and fears of an ordinary bride. Though Alphonse held her hand very tight and smiled, his eyes were worried.

Another drawback of being honored by the king prevented Barbara from exchanging a private word with her new husband all through the interminable celebration that followed the wedding ceremony. No person save other royalty could be set above the king and prince in honor, so King Henry sat in his chair of state at the center of the table with Barbara at his left hand. Ordinarily Prince Edward would have graced a second table, but for some reason Barbara did not at first understand, the royal pair's keepers wanted Edward and his father together. So Prince Edward sat at the king's right with Alphonse beside him. Being kept apart from her husband was not all bad, Barbara thought. It saved her from touches and looks to which she still did not know how to respond, her head urging an appearance of polite indifference while her heart leapt in natural response. Had she not been distracted with the need to learn what was worrying Alphonse and the desire to tell him about the king's behavior the previous day, she would have been grateful for the separation and have enjoyed the elaborate ceremony.

Each great dish of each course, whether it was a whole roast lamb kneeling in a field of fresh parsley or a huge haddock swimming in a sea of aspic among eels and other lesser fish, was carried around the room to be admired before being brought to the high table and presented to the king. Henry graciously praised the dish and directed it to someone he wished to honor—the first to Alphonse, the second to Simon de Claremont, the third to Peter the Chamberlain, and so on. The noblemen of the king's own household carved and served; then pages and squires carried portions to those the guests wished to honor.

From the first dish of each course, the one carried to Alphonse, Barbara had the first and most delectable slice. The second went to the king. Barbara was startled. Custom decreed that honor be done the king first. She almost gestured the page to set the portion down in front of Henry, who was beside her, as if the young man had misunderstood Alphonse's order, but then she remembered that Henry was not Alphonse's king. Had Henry been setting some subtle trap to make it seem he had won Alphonse's loyalty? she wondered. If so, then Alphonse's flouting of custom had meaning and she must not interfere.

Most likely, she thought, she was seeing goblins in innocent shadows and Alphonse simply did not know the English custom. Nonetheless she smiled apologetically at the king and said, "I hope you will forgive him, sire. He told me he asked King Louis for me out of love. I think he must be trying to prove it, by valuing me above a king."

The excuse was one that appealed to Henry, who was very sentimental, and he laughed, pleased when Alphonse sent the third portion to Edward and the fourth to Norfolk. By then so many pages and squires were carrying dishes to and fro that it was nearly impossible to know the order of service. And when

Alphonse had the second course served in an identical manner, Henry laughed before the portion was set down and everyone laughed with him, for Barbara's excuse had made the rounds of the hall while everyone ate.

Musicians played while the court ate, and between each course there was dancing. Naturally Alphonse partnered his new wife, but neither the wild carol dancing nor the lively tourdion permitted much conversation, and even during the more stately galliard, there were so many intricate steps that separated the partners and brought other couples into their figure that no personal matter could be discussed.

After the first dance, Barbara could barely meet Alphonse's eyes. As soon as he got her on the floor, he had said, "Barbe, I am so sorry—" but could get no further because they had to stand at arm's length. Then the dance parted them altogether, and he did not try again. Twice Barbara started to ask what was wrong, but once she swallowed the words and smiled instead, showing her teeth a little, when another couple came so close as nearly to tread on their heels. The second time she had barely caught her breath and gasped out "What—" when they were whisked apart by the next figure of the dance. Alphonse smiled and kissed her hand every chance he could, but his full lips seemed drawn apart by rictus rather than pleasure and the eyes under his tumbled black curls were so anxious that her heart was wrung.

All Barbara desired was to give Alphonse comfort, but her opportunity did not come soon. Having noted the way the bishops had galloped through the wedding service and the brisk pace maintained both going to the cathedral and returning, Barbara had hoped that the feast would be curtailed to enable the Montforts to return the prince to prison and the king to relative seclusion. However, she soon realized that once inside the security of the castle, whatever fears Peter and Henry de Montfort had had about their charges were gone.

Rather than trying to shorten the feast, Henry de Montfort, at least, seemed eager to extend it. Barbara soon learned that he had given the orders for the many rich dishes and for the elaborate ceremony with which they were served. By his order also, when the dancers tired, players came into the hall to juggle and cavort and a jongleur sang to amuse the guests. Even the guards had been withdrawn, at least from inside the hall, giving the appearance of an ordinary high celebration. Barbara could only grit her teeth and endure.

Eventually the hours passed. There came a time when the most delicate dish could not tempt overgorged bellies or the slowest measure induce tired legs to dance; the wildest antics of the players drew no more than thin smiles or dull murmurs from jaded watchers. The jongleur came forward and sang, waking a spark of interest, but as the light dulled, the audience did too. By then, half the diners were sleeping, some with their heads on the tables, some lying under them. As the jongleur's song drew to a close, Henry de Montfort came to the prince, bowed, and whispered in his ear. Edward stiffened, but he turned to Alphonse without any other protest, said a few words, and squeezed his shoulder. After that, he rose and bowed to his father, and then suddenly, as if moved by irresistible impulse, the prince bent and kissed and hugged the king. When he let go and followed Henry de Montfort, the king burst into tears.

That effectively ended the wedding feast. Barbara had just put out her hand to offer comfort to the king when Alice de Montfort urged her to rise. Barbara saw that Peter de Montfort had hurried to the king before Eleanor de Bohun came up on her other side. As the two women led her down from the dais and other ladies hurried to join them, Barbara saw Humphrey de Bohun go to her father. Norfolk got up at once and Barbara was pleased that he was sober enough to respond without urging or explanation. A last glance over her shoulder as the women escorted her out of the hall showed her that her father and Bohun were urging Simon de Claremont and Peter the Chamberlain to their feet.

Alphonse let out a deep sigh of relief when he saw Claremont and King Louis's chamberlain rise without needing more than an invitation to do so. He had been afraid that they might be too drunk to serve as his witnesses. Although he had watered his wine and spent half the feast with one hand covering his cup to keep the butler's minions from refilling it, Alphonse himself was not entirely sober. And he had been careful only to sip in response to the many toasts, because he knew it was a common jest to make the groom so drunk he would be incapable. The French emissaries had no reason to be wary, however, and a wedding feast for a fellow countryman might have been thought a good time to ply them with enough drink to make their tongues loose. But Peter the Chamberlain and Claremont were old hands at being Louis's envoys; Alphonse knew he should have trusted them.

If he had not been so anxious, he would have done so. Alphonse could not understand why it was so important to him that these men, so close to the French king, be witness to his wedding and bedding. King Louis would accept their word against any other, no matter who tried to find cause to annul the marriage. Ridiculous, Alphonse thought. Who would want to interfere with his marriage? He was allowing the political tensions of this accursed realm to seep into his personal life.

Still he felt sick with doubt. Perhaps he should not have allowed Norfolk to supply the bride gift. But during the celebration Barbe had seemed hardly aware of it, not touching it or drawing attention to it. She had been kind and gracious, not a hint of anger in her face or manner—not a hint of a blush or a doubt either. Stupid, Alphonse told himself, Barbe was no fearful maiden. She was a woman with years of experience in court. But she was worried; her smiles had been as false as his. Why should she be worried?

Even as King Henry was led toward his private chamber, Bohun, Norfolk, and the two French emissaries came toward Alphonse. Others rose to follow, throwing off the shock and doubt the king's emotion had caused them and beginning to laugh and jest as they approached. The increasing levity assured Alphonse that King Henry was gone, and he buried his own doubts and anxieties, smiling and shaking his head at his father-by-marriage who was asking dryly if he needed help to stand.

By the time the wedding party reached the lodging on St. Margaret's Lane everyone had sobered enough to begin suffering the lowering of spirits that follows too much drink. All tried to hide it to spare Alphonse and Barbara, but no one had any desire to linger after the witnesses were assured there was no hidden fault in either bride or groom and they were set into their bed. Somehow jests and laughter sounded hollow, even cheap and ugly, when at the back of every mind was the image of the prince being led away to confinement and the old king weeping helplessly.

Only Barbara and Alphonse were not touched by those visions. For each, this moment was far more important than king or prince, and the little time the witnesses remained was too long in their opinion. The guests were not aware how eagerly their departure was desired because the face of the groom was filled with false merriment and that of the bride was blank. Both knew those expressions were a polite mask; yet though each saw only the other and there was no lack of light, many candles being lit and the bedcurtains drawn back to catch any breeze, neither could read beneath the mask.

The moment the door closed behind the last of the witnesses, Barbara said, "Alphonse, what—"

But he dared not let her finish and he covered her mouth with his, pressing her back, flat on the pillows, and leaning over her so that his greater strength held her in place. He felt her stiffen and ran a hand down her right arm to her wrist, extending his last three fingers to tickle her palm. It was a playful, sensuous gesture—and it also immobilized her right hand and arm so that she could not use it to push him away or strike at him. He felt her shudder, but she made no attempt to free either the right hand he held or her left, which was pinned against her side by his body.

Alphonse was torn between his knowledge that Barbe would never have married him if she did not intend to honor her vows and his jealous conviction that she had unwillingly sacrificed herself to some purpose. In this moment knowledge became a thin wraith beside the solidity of his jealous fear. To release her arms seemed to him still too great a chance to take; he could feel the tension in her, as if she might try to fight him off. He could not allow that. He must possess her. What he was doing now could be excused as playfulness; to take her after she had fought free of him would be rape and unforgivable. But the wraith of knowledge beckoned temptingly. Perhaps, it whispered, she was only suffering last-moment fears; perhaps she had no deeper reluctance that was making her desperate.

He lifted his lips enough to whisper, "This is no time for words. There are better things to do with your mouth."

The invitation gained him nothing. Barbe did not respond to what he had said in any way, but neither did she turn her head to avoid him. And when he barely touched her mouth and then bent farther down and kissed her throat, she shuddered again. He tried the tactic of moving his lips in butterfly touches here and there on her face and neck and breast. She began to shiver continually, sucking in her breath in shaking sobs and letting it out in long, broken sighs. By then Alphonse was almost certain she would not try to refuse to couple, but there was no way to tell whether her reaction to his caresses was owing to eagerness or to fighting her revulsion.

He kissed her mouth again and lifted himself cautiously on one elbow at the same time releasing her wrist. She lay quiet except for her trembling, and he stroked her arm from the shoulder down, touching her breast. A sharper gasp broke the uneven rhythm of her breathing, and when he brought his hand up again, cupped the breast, and brushed the nipple with his thumb, a soft moan—of pleasure or protest?—rose from her throat.

Releasing her lips, Alphonse quickly brought his mouth to her breast to replace his hand. She jerked under him, uttered a wordless cry, and raised her knees. Alphonse pushed them flat and brought a leg over to hold her, which permitted him to slide his hand between her thighs. Carefully, he cupped her nether mouth, pressed gently, released and pressed again, then bent one finger to invade. The broken breathing grew faster, and to Alphonse's surprise he found Barbe's lower lips were full and very wet. Her body was ready for him.

Before he had time to wonder, she cried, "Oh, be done! Take me and be done!"

There was a kind of desperation in her voice; Alphonse knew that was wrong. Love should lie down only in joy. Had Barbe not been his wife, he would have tried to lighten her mood. If he had failed and a mistress took offense because he seemed to make light of her trouble, there would have been an end to the affair. But he could not chance that kind of offense with a wife, whereas obedience to her demand would be easily excused. And he was achingly ready himself so that her words brought him to a state where he could not resist the invitation.

For all her readiness, though she opened her legs for him and even rose a little to meet him when he had placed himself, his gentle thrust did not get far. Poor Barbe cried out once more, this time in simple pain and surprise, and he had to hold still and soothe her before he thrust again. The second time he drove hard and found himself seated. The impediment was fragile, but Alphonse had no doubt of having thrust himself where no man had been before. She was so tight that he almost spilled his seed at once in a mindless physical reaction.

An equally mindless habit saved him, the habit of not taking his own satisfaction until he was sure his partner was also content. This restraint was an absolutely necessary behavior pattern to a man who had little wealth and a very fastidious taste in women, and it had gained him his reputation as an irresistible lover. Instinctively, as the urge to spend came upon him, Alphonse fought it. He lay still and kissed the least erotic part of his partner—her face—not completely aware for a few minutes of who she was. As the worst of his need receded, he remembered that his new wife lay under him, and he thanked God that his many sins had provided him with great skill.

Now he lifted himself, supporting most of his weight on one elbow and caressing her breast with that hand. With the other he stroked her thighs, tickled her ears. Soon she twitched under him and her movement wrung a groan of pleasure from him, but that was half policy. Alphonse knew that open evidence of a man's lust often excited a woman. As if to confirm his thought, Barbe twitched again and he lifted his body a little to give her more freedom. She followed, and when he did not thrust again, she began to push and squirm against him, her breath coming in harsh gasps quicker and quicker until she wailed aloud. He loosed his will then, letting sensation drown him, hardly aware that he too cried out as her voice stilled.

When sense returned, he slid off her and sat up. Her eyes were wide open under their heavy brows, and she looked—terrified. "My God," he whispered, "why are you afraid? Did I not pleasure you at all?"

Chapter 14

The anguish in Alphonse's voice and expression wiped every consideration other than the need to make him happy from Barbara's mind. "Too much," she cried. "You gave me too much pleasure."

The profound relief Alphonse felt over what he knew was an honest confession translated immediately into irritation. "There cannot be too much pleasure in loving!" he exclaimed. "How can you say such a silly thing?"

Barbara did not answer, her sympathy for him already replaced by wariness and by a fear that she had made herself cheap. Had his hurt even been genuine? Or was that another practiced gesture in an old pattern of conquest? No matter if it was, she thought bitterly; she was as weak as any other woman he played like a fish. She dared not try to test the truth of her questions; she dared not hurt him or even give him an excuse to look hurt. To see his pain, real or pretended, reduced her to idiocy.

Alphonse's irritation was as ephemeral as his relief. He was glad indeed that she had come to joy in their coupling; with that as a beginning, he could win her love. But before he could find the path that led to the fulfillment of his deepest desire, he had to uncover her trouble and cure it. Barbe had been desperate when she urged him to couple with her and terrified after coupling. Neither emotion fit any pattern familiar to him.

Alphonse did not find any significance in her silence; his question had been rhetorical, and he had not expected any answer. After a brief pause in which he studied her face, he continued suspiciously, "You have not let some overholy priest convince you that all natural pleasure is sinful, have you?"

"No, of course not," Barbara replied, thrown off balance by the accusation. "You are more in danger of being converted to that view in Louis's court than I am in Henry's."

The answer brought him no closer to an understanding than had her earlier silence, and Alphonse suddenly felt ashamed of trying to manipulate Barbe as he would a harebrained, discontented mistress. If he wanted an answer from a woman he loved, whom he wanted to trust him, he needed to ask a direct question. "Then what did you mean when you said I had given you too much pleasure?"

Barbara had been waiting for that. She knew Alphonse too well to believe he would forget a problem that puzzled him. Fear lent agility to her thoughts, and she had found a suitably ambiguous reply. "I was surprised," she said. "I did not think a broaching could be anything other than painful for a woman, and . . . and it seemed to me from what my friends have told me that, for a woman, love is necessary for pleasure."

Since she had already admitted her passionate response to his lovemaking, she hoped he would take the implication that it did not mean abject devotion, but the ploy was dangerous. If Alphonse asked her outright whether she did not love him, she would have to tell the truth. But she remembered his teasing talk with women and knew he always avoided direct questions and statements. His eyes flicked away, and he did not speak of love, but his next remark was direct enough to catch her off balance again.

"You did not look surprised," he said slowly. "You looked affrighted. Why, Barbe?"

"Because I felt myself helpless in that—that cascade of joy. I was enslaved," she answered, more truthfully than she had intended.

He stared down at her, his face frighteningly without expression for one moment. Then he sighed and let himself drop flat. She had given him an honest answer; it rang true, more especially because of her long freedom from any domination through her senses.

"But Barbe, I was equally helpless, equally enslaved," he said softly. "You must learn to trust me—and I to trust you. What we share, one cannot use against the other."

"*If* we share." Barbara's voice was hard, her memory bringing up images of one woman and then another preening herself under Alphonse's flattery. Had not each of those women heard these same smooth words?

Alphonse misunderstood her completely, associating the reproach with her precoital desperation. "If you were concerned because you felt your anger slipping away while I gave you pleasure—"

"What anger?" Barbara asked, so surprised that she sat up. Then she felt still more surprised when Alphonse's dark skin reddened.

"I should not have let your father provide that bride gift, but—"

"I was not angry." She laughed. "I almost got down on my knees and thanked God for your good sense. Those who love me were near tears, and the envious were licking their lips over my shame when it was near time for the church and nothing had come." She reached down and touched his face, growing serious. "I thank you, my lord. You were generous to abate your own pride so that mine would not be hurt. How could I be angry?"

She seemed sincere, but women set such store on mementos that marked great days in their lives that Alphonse felt he had to probe further. "I will return them to your father, of course, and you may choose what you like, new from a goldsmith," he said.

"Oh. I suppose papa does not really wish to part with his mother's jewels."

Barbara was disappointed. She had always rather coveted the necklace and armlets. No one did work like that anymore, not blandly beautiful but haunting, as if some magic spell was in the pieces if one could only read them aright.

"No, love, no." Alphonse sat up, too, and put his arm around her. "They are for you. Your father wanted to give them to you in any case. But when I remembered—too late, after squandering away the few free hours I had in a stupid celebration instead of trying to find a bride gift for you—he offered to present them as my gift. I only said I would return them because I was afraid if I did not you would always feel cheated of a bride gift. But you will not be. I swear it."

"I trust you for that." Barbara laughed aloud and let her head rest on his shoulder. "No one ever called you ungenerous, Alphonse." Then suddenly she sat up straight and pushed him back so she could see his face clearly. "Was that what you were worried about? Oh, you idiot! You frightened me half to death by the way you looked at me all day, as if some disaster had overtaken us and you dared not tell me."

"I frightened *you* to death?" Alphonse repeated indignantly. "What about the way you looked at me when I took your hand at the altar? I thought you would repudiate me right there in the cathedral."

"What had you to do with my being worried?" Barbara asked, thoroughly exasperated. "The king—"

"I was the groom!" Alphonse interrupted with haughty dignity. "It is generally conceded that when a bride looks frightened at the altar, the cause is the man who will be her husband."

Barbara burst out laughing again. "Well, yes, but you should have known better. We have been friends for more than ten years. I would need to be an idiot to suddenly grow afraid of you."

Alphonse did feel foolish for a moment, not for being concerned about the bride gift but for what now seemed a senseless fear of losing her completely. She was so much at ease with him, not trying to shield her nakedness, her eyes glinting blue rather than bleak gray when a gleam of candlelight caught them, that Alphonse almost laughed too. But then came a memory of her strained voice crying "Be done. Take me and be done." The contrast with what she said was too vivid to put aside. He shook his head.

"It was to do with me when you bade me take you. And you were not crying out in eagerness."

She bent her head, but she could feel his anxious gaze on her and could not lie. "Yes, it was eagerness."

Her blush rose up from her throat to dye her face and ran down to her breast. It was the latter stain that caught Alphonse's eyes and what he saw stifled the hot denial he had been about to utter. As she whispered what he thought a lie, Barbe's nipples had swelled before his eyes. That mute testimony proved her confession was the truth and showed him to be a fool. Alphonse did not think even the most practiced whore could order that response.

"I was ashamed."

The second whisper, even lower, made him put one hand on her shoulder and raise her chin with the other so that he could look straight into her eyes "Not about joining with me," he said. "Never feel shame. No part of you is other than beautiful to me. Nothing you desire is other than pleasing to me."

And nothing different from any other woman either, Barbara thought bitterly, but what she said was "I felt myself to seem no better than a common whore to you, to be so consumed with pleasure of the body only."

"I know very little of common whores," Alphonse replied, "but I doubt they feel any pleasure at all—a good reason why I do not frequent them. Barbe"—his voice took on a pleading note—"do not hide your joy from me or seek to crush it out. I love you. I cannot have true pleasure if you have none. You will turn the need of my body into poison for me."

"Oh, no," she said, "I could not bear that." It was the truth. Barbara knew quite well the quickest way to drive a husband into another woman's arms was to be cold abed. "I want us to be happy as man and wife, and I will gladly learn of you anything that will increase your joy abed or abroad."

He drew her close and she came willingly, swaying forward at his light pull. Alphonse kissed her forehead tenderly, more joyous over this victory than any he had ever won on the tourney field. Neither gold nor jewels nor honor could compete with Barbe's offering. She might not love him, but she had taken away all fear that she resented their bonding. She wanted to be happy and make him happy! Then she was halfway down the garden path that led to the bower of love.

"So you wish to learn of me?" he murmured. "Then we will play *un jeu de la queue leu leu*—do as I do—and we will see who wins the prize."

As he bent his head to kiss her lips, he wondered what she would do. But as his lips parted and hers opened also, as she moved with him to lie down again, as his hand slid over her belly to her mount of Venus and hers found his swollen shaft, he had just time enough, before he drowned in a fiercer pleasure than he had ever known, to remember that she had warned him already. She had loved and trusted him for years. She would do exactly what he urged—anything he did, she would try to imitate.

Barbara was utterly delighted with the course of events. She was relieved of her worst fear, that her inability to conceal her violent response to her husband's lovemaking would make her seem a dull domestic cow. She had seen his doubt when he begged her not to act cold and his pleasure when she said she wished to learn. Enough doubt of her was in him to keep his interest—at least for a time. And for the future there was also hope. Alphonse would surely show her what gave him the greatest delight for purely selfish reasons. Just as surely, she would make those things her special pleasure. It mattered little to her where he kissed her or touched her; all he need do was want her and she was afire.

The theory was excellent, but Barbara found the practice near impossible. Not that she was loath to ape Alphonse's movements, and certainly not that she found any place he touched or kissed unpleasant to her. On the contrary! Everything he did to her brought pleasure, and what she did to him blew up the little flames of delight he created into so roaring an inferno that she soon lost track of any special place or touch. She remembered a tangle of limbs, a warmth and pressure that threatened to split her open and yet so filled a gaping hole in her senses that she struggled to draw it farther in despite the pain. But was it pain? Whatever it was mingled and blended and swelled and swelled until she must burst or die. Was she dying? Was it she crying out in extremis? Surely the voice that groaned in higher and higher tones was not her own. But her throat was sore with cries as shrill as those of a victim on the rack.

''Barbe? Barbe?''

No, she was not dead. Barbara's lips curved as she slowly opened her eyes. Alphonse hung over her, his dark face anxious. ''Mmmm?'' she responded.

He uttered a sigh and dropped flat on his back. ''Thank God I did not cheat you,'' he muttered. ''You took me too far out of myself. I lost my hold.''

The words meant nothing to Barbara at the time. What was important then was that Alphonse said no more and let her drift asleep, a state she craved more even than his love.

Barbara woke first, disturbed by touching a companion in bed, since she had slept alone since childhood. Her heart gave a single giant leap of joy when she saw his face, the features harsher in their stillness and yet more innocent. But the first real thought she had, which overlaid but could not spoil the deep satisfaction she felt about Alphonse sleeping beside her, was that she had never had a chance to tell him about the king. Imagine his being so foolish as to worry about her reaction to a bride gift when they were in the midst of so delicate a political situation! But it was a foolishness very easy to forgive.

Smiling fondly, Barbara eased herself out of the bed, used the pot, and started to the door to bid Clotilde bring her washing water. She stopped abruptly, remembering that she was naked and Chacier might be waiting to attend his master in the solar, and turned to get a bedrobe. As she pulled it over her, she glimpsed Alphonse, still peacefully asleep, and suffered a shock. She had forgotten his service with the prince. Should he be on duty? Before she stopped to think that Chacier would surely have called his master, she was shaking Alphonse's shoulder.

''What time must you be with the prince?'' she asked as his eyes opened.

He shot upright, then sagged back against the headboard of

the bed, rubbing his hands over his face while he yawned and shook his head. "No service today."

"Oh." Barbara smiled sheepishly. "I should have guessed you would ask at least one day's leave. I am sorry I woke you."

But Alphonse had let his hands drop from his face and was staring at her. "That is very interesting, Barbe, that you should say I asked for leave. I did not. Nor did Edward give me leave—though that, I think, was only because we both forgot—I to ask and he to offer. It was Henry de Montfort who said I should have a day's freedom—and he told me the night before last, when we were all making merry at your father's expense. I thought nothing of it, only that Henry was being his usual thoughtful self, but now . . . Did it seem to you, Barbe, that our wedding feast would never end?"

"It surely did. I was half out of my mind with impatience—"

"Oh? Were you?"

His hand went out so swiftly that she was caught and pulled onto his lap before she could resist. She pushed him hard when he had snatched only a single kiss, however, and slid out of his grasp, standing up and saying with icy dignity, "Not for the bedding." Then her brows made their enchanting circumflex on her forehead in response to his hurt expression, and she added, "After all, I did not yet know whether I would like it."

The hurt disappeared from Alphonse's face, replaced by a slightly smug smile. "And you did, did you not, my love?"

She eluded the hands that reached for her again, stepping back and out of the way. "That is not to the point, and you had better get out of bed. Perhaps then you will be better able to think with the head on which you grow hair, rather than that little bald red one between your legs."

"You do me an injustice," Alphonse protested mildly, getting out of bed as she suggested. "Although I do believe that two heads are better than one, I manage to keep the one that thinks and the one that feels in their proper places."

He looked so bland and innocent that Barbara half turned away to get his bedrobe. She was totally unprepared to be seized and kissed and pushed back toward the bed. She almost yielded, her first thought being that they could discuss the political implications of the wedding feast and her summons to the king any time. However, the assurance in his manner set off a clangor of alarms that quickly quelled her desire.

"Alphonse!" she exclaimed. "Stop your teasing and listen." An odd expression, a kind of mingled gladness and exasperation came into his face. Barbara was not certain what it meant, but she felt she had hit the right note when he smiled and let her go.

"Not only was that wedding feast far too elaborate," she continued quickly, "but while you were out cavorting with my father and Henry de Montfort the evening before, *I* was summoned to have my evening meal with the king."

"What?"

Alphonse's face went dark and rigid and Barbara hastily shook her head. "No, no. Henry is not so pure as Louis, but he is no lecher. In any case, his designs were not on my fair body but on yours."

"What!"

The note of horrified incredulity made Barbara laugh. "You are making me doubt which head you think with again, or whether you can think at all, except about futtering. What King Henry said he wanted was for me to convince you to remain in England now that we are married—but although he seemed well pleased with the idea, I do not think it was his own. Peter de Montfort's wife was my fellow guest, and she was there, I believe, to see that the king did her husband's bidding."

Alphonse blinked and said, "Let me piss while I swallow that."

While he went for the pot, Barbara opened the door, called for washing water from Clotilde, and told Chacier to go for food for breaking their fast. When she turned back to the room, Alphonse had pulled on his bedrobe. As soon as he saw her eyes on him, he shook his head.

"I cannot make top nor bottom of why Peter de Montfort should want me to stay in England with the prince."

"Even if he does, why would he approach *me* through the king?" Barbara asked. "Why not ask you himself, or simply forbid you to leave?"

"He would not forbid my leaving. To keep me here unwilling would surely make me refuse to serve his purpose, whatever it may be. And he might not want to ask me directly lest word of that come to Edward, who might then assume I was Montfort's man. To tell the truth, after his manner of swearing to the terms of peace I do not understand why Edward was permitted his promised rewards. I thought all his privileges would be revoked."

"I thought so myself," Barbara said, pushing open the traveling basket in which the linen lay and taking out a drying cloth. "But it may be that Peter and Henry considered his giving the oath—no matter what his manner—a softening of his previous behavior."

Alphonse nodded and went toward the stand where Clotilde was pouring water into a wide bowl. "Yes, you may have the root of the matter there," he said over his shoulder, then turned to face her again to add, "Henry de Montfort is so relieved that Edward is willing to talk civilly with him that he will overlook much. He believes he can win Edward to his opinion."

"Well, the prince did join Leicester three years ago," Barbara pointed out. "Edward knows how ill the realm has been governed by his father, and he is aware of the bitter hatred aroused by the king's half brothers. But when King Henry reproached him for joining Leicester and refused to meet him at all, Edward could not bear it. He left Leicester and since then has supported his father."

"So Henry de Montfort has reason to hope that he can win Edward over," Alphonse said. "Now I wonder less at his indulgence. I see that he is trying to use the carrot and the stick—and quite cleverly."

"You mean that elaborate feast was a taste of what Edward has lost, and the day's leave you have is a reminder to the prince of how dull and miserable prison can be."

"Just so." Alphonse shrugged. "Likely, then, that King Henry's suggestion that we stay in England was urged by Peter de Montfort to further Henry de Montfort's purpose. Yes, why not? Peter took no dangerous chances. It was certainly by Peter's order that we almost galloped to the cathedral and back and the wedding service was overquick. I think it was also by his order that the king and prince were seated together—to prevent anyone from coming near either of them and saying a few words without being noticed."

He dropped the bedrobe off his shoulders, turned back to the bowl of washing water, and began to scrub his upper body briskly. Clearly Alphonse was relieved to find some sense in what had puzzled him and made him uneasy. Barbara was silent while he washed, but when she presented the drying cloth her face was sad.

"Almost no one came to speak to the king or prince," she said, "only the Montforts themselves and Humphrey de Bohun and my father." Her lips tightened. "I suppose all the others were afraid, and I wonder if my father was wise? The king spoke most favorably of papa to me—and Alice de Montfort no doubt carried every word he said to her husband."

"Your father is no fool, Barbe."

She sighed, then smiled. "Quite true. He is always telling me so himself and calling me a fool for worrying about him. Perhaps I am." She took back the drying cloth and asked, "Do you want to dress, or shall we break our fast as we are? Chacier will be back with the food soon."

Alphonse hesitated and Barbara cocked her head questioningly. The corners of his lips curved, and he sighed. "We had better dress or Monsieur Tête à Vide Rouge will begin to do my thinking for me again."

Barbara went immediately to Alphonse's clothes chest, only turning her head after she had lifted the lid to ask, "Court clothing or common wear?"

It had taken Barbara that little while to conquer her disappointment. Now that most of her uneasiness about the king's summons had been laid to rest, she would not have minded a bit letting the empty-headed little red rascal do the thinking. She could not show herself to be eager, however; Alphonse must always be the pursuer, and the harder he had to run the better he would enjoy the prize he won. But one could be too coy, Barbara thought. No, he did not seem disappointed; actually he looked rather smug as he answered that common riding wear for both of them would be best.

"I would like to ride out, if it does not rain," he said, with a sparkle of mischief in his dark eyes. "Let us take food and blankets. We can find a haystack for comfort at this time of year, I am sure. And I need to be out in the open . . . free."

As he said the last words, the amusement disappeared from his expression. Barbara caught up the clothes she had chosen and hurried back to him. "I am so sorry," she said. "I never thought how you must hate being locked up with Edward, as if you were a prisoner yourself."

"No, I do not mind that so much," he said. "What I hate is this state where there is neither right nor wrong. Your uncle Hugh explained some things to me, and Henry de Montfort told me more. And Edward talks about little else—only the subject of escape is forbidden us. There can be no doubt that King Henry ruled very ill; Edward does not deny it. There can be as little doubt that what Leicester desires for this realm is good. But even Henry de Montfort does not deny that only King Henry has the right to rule, no matter how ill he does it. Both sides are right. Both sides are wrong. Both sides know it—and that is the worst of all. There is a heaviness in Edward's heart and in Henry de Montfort's, though he is the victor, that weighs on me."

Barbara kissed his cheek. "It weighs on us all, but should not weigh on you, who have no obligation to this land. Come, for today let us put this grief aside."

They managed to do that. By the time they had eaten, the morning damp had cleared, and they were able to ride out. Barbara discovered why Alphonse had looked both smug and mischievous when he spoke about finding "comfort" in a haystack. The fresh air, open sky, and feeling of freedom lent a certain charm to love play, Barbara admitted, and a gaiety was added by small discomforts, like the prickles and uneven surface of the hay, which once pulled them apart at a near crucial moment. But later on, when they returned to the lodging, there was an equal pleasure in the warm, shadowed softness of their bed where odd gleams from the night-candle gave a kind of mystery to her lover's body and to the intentness of his face.

Over the next week, both Alphonse and Barbara blessed their confinement at Dover for making them too suspicious to stay at the castle. The privacy of their lodgings permitted them to shake off, even within Canterbury, the odd pall that hung over the rest of the court. When they were alone in their chamber they found enough comfort in each other's company and enough to talk about in memories of the past and plans for the future to forget England's troubles.

The discomfort of the court was not owing to fear. Within a week of the wedding, news from Wales confirmed that Leicester and Gloucester had driven the Marcher lords back into their final stronghold and that they had again sued for peace. The desultory negotiations with the French emissaries were temporarily suspended. Leicester had written that he expected to join them in Canterbury very soon, and it did not seem worthwhile to continue the discussions without him.

The very afternoon the earl's letter came, Barbara's father told her that he would leave the next morning for his own lands. Barbara's heart sank at the news. It seemed to her that her father was eager to avoid Leicester, and the only reason she could think of was that he feared Leicester would blame him for leaving his duty to guard the coast to come to her wedding. But when she confessed her fear to Alphonse, he smiled and reminded her that she worried too much about Norfolk. No blame could attach to her father, he pointed out, when all the information that came from France made more certain the failure of Queen Eleanor's plans to invade England.

Yet Barbara knew that Alphonse was troubled too. And when she asked him why, he would not meet her eyes; he only shook his head and said he had no better explanation than what he had already given her—a weight on his spirit. She asked him then if he would like to go back to France at once, her purpose in coming to England having been fulfilled, but he shook his head again, reminding her that he had agreed to serve the prince at least until the court left Canterbury.

He was relieved of that duty, however. Simon de Montfort, earl of Leicester, arrived in Canterbury at the very end of August. That evening he was closeted with his son Henry and his cousin

Peter; the next day he had several conferences with the French emissaries. On the third morning, when Alphonse arrived at the castle to join Edward he was met by a page who escorted him instead to the quarters of the earl of Leicester. The two men knew each other slightly from meetings at the French court, but Leicester was much the elder and they had never even had a private conversation.

Alphonse bowed, and Leicester smiled and gestured him toward a bench that flanked his own chair. "I wish to thank you," the earl said, "for agreeing, against your own inclination, to serve Prince Edward."

"I have no disinclination to serve the prince." Alphonse met the steady gaze of Leicester's large eyes with an equally steady look. "Prince Edward and I are tourney companions of old. I am glad to do anything I can for him."

Leicester smiled again. "I understand it was you who pointed out to Henry that if foreign officers of the household are forbidden to the king, no other royal household should have them either—particularly if appointed by the . . . ah . . . government."

"Yes, but I hope we covered that problem by giving me no appointment. I receive no wages or perquisites and am promised no favors."

"I thank you again," Leicester said. "That was very generous." Now he looked sad and much older than when he smiled, deep lines graven between his brows and down his cheeks. "Unfortunately, Sieur Alphonse, few have so much generosity in them, and most wish to believe everyone as avaricious as they are themselves. There is talk already—I have heard complaints—and so I must ask you to end your service to the prince."

Alphonse was not surprised; he had expected to be dismissed as soon as the page announced that Leicester wished to see him. In the days that he had served Edward, however, Alphonse had come closer to Henry de Montfort's viewpoint. Not all the way; Alphonse was sure the prince could never be brought to accept the principle that Leicester or even a group of barons could interfere with the royal right to rule. On the other hand, he had seen in the prince the beginning of a less passionate rejection of all that Leicester upheld. When Edward's pride and temper were not flayed, he could see the good in a clear statement of the rights and duties of the king and the barons so that fair judgment could be given on the basis of solid law.

Now, although the prospect of freedom from his often depressing service brought Alphonse a wave of relief like a splash of water from a forded brook during a hot ride, he also felt a sharp concern. "My lord," he said, "I hope I have done nothing to cause you to mistrust me. If I have, I hope you will correct me and let me remain as Prince Edward's companion until he leaves Canterbury. I fear—"

"No, no, you have done nothing," Leicester interrupted uneasily. "Nonetheless—"

"Forgive me for speaking so plainly," Alphonse broke in in turn, "but I feel I must remind you, my lord, that Prince Edward does not have a temper than can benefit from being handed a comfit and then having it snatched away. I am sure the court cannot remain in Canterbury much longer, and the prince understands that I wish to take my new wife home to Aix as soon as he is moved. Would it not be best that I continue as the prince's companion for the little time you are to remain here?"

Leicester looked even more uneasy, but he shook his head. "My son was mistaken in urging you to serve the prince. Henry is too much moved by his friend's suffering. I do not desire that Edward suffer either—I hope you will believe that—but neither can I permit the appearance of favoring foreign friends."

Alphonse bowed his head, as much to hide his mingled gladness and sadness as to express acceptance of the earl of Leicester's statement. "Very well, my lord. I have said what I felt must be said, but I am not altogether sorry to be freed of my promise. I would be very glad if you would provide me and my wife, Lady Barbe, letters of passage to permit us to take ship from Dover—" He hesitated, suddenly remembering his promise to try to see William of Marlowe, who was still, with Cornwall, a prisoner.

"I will not refuse you letters of passage if you insist on them, of course," Leicester said, "but I hope you do not intend to leave immediately. Will you not stay until the emissaries return to France?"

Irritation struggled with relief in Alphonse. On the one hand, Leicester's polite "hope" that he would stay saved him from needing to take back his request to leave so he could keep his promise to his brother and sister-by-marriage. On the other hand, it was actually only a pretty covering for Leicester's denial of his request to go home. Oh, Leicester would not "refuse" to provide letters of passage—only there would be so many demands on the earl's time that somehow the letters would not get written until Leicester was good and ready to be rid of him.

The earl's reason for separating him from Edward and yet keeping him in England was plain to Alphonse too. Leicester had been misled by his son into believing he could be used to tempt Edward to further compliance. The assumption was wrong, Alphonse was sure. No doubt Edward enjoyed his company and found some relief in it, but Alphonse knew his service was not even a small factor in the prince's decision on what he would do.

Still, the request that he stay fit in very well with his promise to see William of Marlowe, and Alphonse was just enough annoyed with Leicester's high-handedness to be amused by the earl's misjudgment. He smiled his very best courtier's smile and said, "Just as you like, my lord. To go with King Louis's envoys will save me the cost of passage. But if I am to remain in this country, perhaps—"

The earl held up his hand, and Alphonse paused. "I am not all powerful and cannot do as I please," Leicester said. "I owe you something and will not forget it, but I have pressing business just now."

Alphonse rose at once and bowed; his face showed nothing, but he was thoroughly angry—though not at what the earl would have believed angered him. Leicester's too obvious intention of preventing him from asking a favor troubled Alphonse very little. He was a courtier with long experience. He was well accustomed to the way those in high places tried to avoid being trapped into making promises to petitioners. Although Alphonse felt Leicester could take lessons in tact from even so plainspoken and direct a monarch as King Louis, he also understood that if every request every courtier made was granted all rulers would soon be in a worse state than King Henry.

What enraged Alphonse, and continued to gnaw at him as he made his way into the great hall, was that Leicester had impugned his honor by doubting the promise of strict neutrality he had made to Henry de Montfort and had had the arrogance to imagine him a fool too. So the earl owed him "something," did he? A careful word, "something"; unlike "favor," the word "something" held no implication of good or ill, leaving Leicester free to bestow a favor or wreak vengeance without betraying his word.

Alphonse's temper was so short when he returned to the great hall that he cursed himself for not realizing he might meet someone he knew when he felt a hand on his arm. Nonetheless, he stopped, started to smile a greeting, then let the smile die in his relief.

"Good God, what has happened?" Barbara asked. She wore a half-smile, totally at odds with the tension in her voice, which was so low that no one a foot away could hear.

Alphonse lifted her hand from his arm and bowed over it. "I am free today," he said, smiling as falsely as she. "Can you spare me an hour to walk in the garden?"

"Of course," she said. "I only came to pass some idle time

with Aliva, and she will grant you prior right." She laid her hand on Alphonse's wrist and walked out of the hall with him.

At the bottom of the steps, she glanced around, and seeing no one near, asked whether he would not prefer to ride out, as the garden might also be full of people. He agreed, maintaining the same shallow smile while they got their horses and sent Barbe's men back to the lodging. They went out the closest gate to Winchepe Street, but did not ride far along it, turning right into a tiny lane that, as Barbara guessed, led them to the bank of the Stour, which they followed until they found a quiet grassy spot.

There they dismounted, and Alphonse tied the horses to a tree at the edge of the small meadow. By then he had relieved Barbara's worst anxiety, that some personal blow had befallen them. Afterward, she had listened very calmly while he described his interview with Leicester, until he told her with cold distaste how the earl had doubted his word and taken him for a fool.

"No," Barbara said, now angrier than he. "Leicester did not take you for a fool. He was threatening you."

"Threaten—" Alphonse choked over the rest of the word. Then hot rage welled up in him again; his dark skin flushed and his eyes showed red glints in their depths.

Barbara was terrified by what she had done. Alphonse had had his temper well under control and she had allowed her own anger to reignite his rage. Could Alphonse be crazy enough to challenge Leicester?

She put her hand over his and said, "I did not mean to make you angrier. I wanted to explain that what Leicester said was no planned insult to you. He has been so often betrayed from trusting too much in other men's honor that he has turned right around and now trusts too little in it. And worst of all, you hit him in a very sore spot—his belief in his eldest son."

"You cannot think that Leicester fears Henry will betray him!"

"No, not that," Barbara said, relieved to see that Alphonse's anger was already diminishing as he grappled with a new aspect of what had happened. "It is the same problem again," she continued. "Leicester knows that Henry, the soul of honor himself, expects others also to keep their word in letter and in spirit—remember you yourself were much troubled by his innocence in dealing with Edward. I think Leicester cannot bring himself to scold Henry for this fault, because it is really a virtue, but he cannot trust his son's judgment either. So, since Henry assured him you were to be trusted and no doubt told him that you had warned him of dangers he had himself overlooked, all the more does Leicester fear you have been using his son for some purpose of your own—or, worse, of Edward's."

Alphonse stared at Barbara for a little while, then took her hand and kissed it. ''You are a wonder to me, my love. I do not think that any other woman of my acquaintance could see so clearly into Leicester's—or any other man's—reasons. Some would have listened in silence; others would have cried out in fear or sympathy. I do not know another who could have helped me understand.''

''I have had my own reasons to consider Leicester's nature,'' she said lightly, and then much more seriously, ''Possibly no other woman had the cause I have to desire to help you.''

''You love me!'' he exclaimed, lifting her hand to his lips again.

Barbara swallowed, then laughed. ''Love you or hate you, my fate is bound to yours. You may be sure that I will always do everything in my power to forward your well-being and well-doing.''

''Do you hate me then?'' Alphonse looked down at the hand she had left resting confidingly in his.

''Do not be so silly.'' Barbara leaned forward and kissed his cheek. ''I would not have married you if I *hated* you. I like you very well. I always have. If you want more than that from me, you must win it.''

He caught her in his arms, loosened her wimple with a practiced tug, and began to kiss her throat, murmuring, ''How? Thus? And thus?''

Chapter 15

Passion spent, Alphonse pulled down his own surcoat to hide his nakedness and laid Barbe's over her. She sighed contentedly, eyes still closed, and he lay back and looked at the sky. He must be happy: Barbe was everything any man could want in a wife. She was clever; she desired the same kind of life he did; she was wanton abed—he sighed gently, still aware of the tremor in the muscles of his belly and thighs, for she had drained him until his giving was as much pain as pleasure—but modest in her behavior . . .

There his mind stuck. Barbe was more than modest; she was distant, quiet, and passive, almost as if she was unwilling. Even this last coupling . . . he had misunderstood her. She had not meant what she said as an invitation to make love and had come near to fighting him off until he stirred her body enough, whereupon she burst into so hot a flame that she burned away all sense, all care and caution in him.

Still, she was willing in the end. He *must* be happy . . . but if he was, why was he so uneasy? Why did he feel—not that Barbe did not love him; he could hope to teach her that—that she was hiding something from him, something so important that he could never truly know her and have her until he uncovered the secret.

Without thinking what he was doing, Alphonse lifted himself

on one elbow and stared down at his wife. Slowly her eyes opened and she smiled. He was wrong, he thought; there was nothing hidden behind her eyes now. They were bright under their heavy bars of brow, and her strange beautiful mouth was somehow smiling at him, although the lips were not curved at all. She sat up, too, and leaned against him, both now watching the flow of the river until a boat passed, coming out of Canterbury. As it went by, Barbara exclaimed in horror, wondering whether they had provided entertainment for passing sailors. Alphonse laughed and assured her they had not and explained, when she accused him of making light of her embarrassment, that even absorbed as they had both been they would have heard the cheering and jeering had they been seen.

Once her first shock passed, Barbara found her forgetfulness of time and place quite amusing—until she saw the thoughtful expression on Alphonse's face. Then in her desire to divert him from thinking how easily he could make her forget everything with a few caresses, she said, ''If you really wish to leave England—''

''No, I do not, at least not immediately,'' he replied, and reminded her that he had promised to visit or at least write to Marlowe, his brother's father-by-marriage, who was in prison with Richard of Cornwall.

''I had forgotten,'' Barbara said. ''I am sorry.''

''No reason for you to think about him,'' Alphonse replied easily. ''I have not given him much thought myself. Henry de Montfort said he was still with Richard, so I do not think he is in any distress.'' He smiled at her. ''Should you not dress now, love, while there is no boat on the river?''

She snatched up her clothes and hurried away toward the horses so she could dress in the partial cover of the thin woods. In a more leisurely manner Alphonse drew on his chausses, tied his cross garters, and finally put on his boots. He knew Barbe's hurried retreat was natural; no decent woman would want to dress in the open. Nonetheless, even that natural retreat troubled him, and to occupy his mind he fixed it on William of Marlowe.

''I have bethought me,'' he said, as he reached Barbara, nodding to her request that he tie her laces, ''that what might be of far more benefit to William than an offer to pay a ransom he does not want paid, is for me to go to see his wife and family. Then if I get permission to visit William, I will have news to lighten his heart—I hope—and news to bring back to his wife and to John. I wonder if we could get leave to visit William's keep—''

''Let me ask,'' Barbara said. ''Let me take with me the letter you got from King Louis about Sir William.'' She smiled a tight, flat smile that made her mouth look hard. "Leicester thinks he did me a hurt by depriving me of his precious son, so he will wish to make amends. Moreover, if he does not ask how I came to have King Louis's letter—it might have been obtained by either queen at your brother's request and have been given to me—Leicester might not associate it with you."

She was still angry because Leicester had insulted him, Alphonse thought, pleasantly surprised. "A very good idea," he said, preparing to lift her into her saddle, and suddenly realized that he was still angry himself.

The heat had gone out of his anger, though. What was left was a kind of dislike for the holier-than-thou attitude of the earl of Leicester and pleasure that Leicester might be diddled into granting him a favor. It was not fair, Alphonse knew. Leicester was a good man, a far better one than he was. He should not permit the earl's manner to obscure that. Nonetheless, he felt a definite satisfaction because his principles inclined him to the party opposed to the earl.

"Should we go back to town now so I can get the letter and apply for audience with Leicester?" Barbe asked as he mounted.

"Not this morning," he said. "Let the affairs of the day push me out of the earl's mind. Also"—he smiled at her—"I would like to spend a few hours without thinking of any affairs save our own."

They found the road again and, in a village, an alehouse that had a table in a garden and a chicken roasting for the master's dinner, which he was glad to exchange for a silver penny. His wife added a new baked loaf, a jack of foaming ale, some cooked greens and pottage intended for supper, and a half-dozen near-ripe apples. Barbara and Alphonse sat down on rough stools to enjoy their simple meal, and neither was at all disappointed to see clouds begin to pile up in the sky not long after sext. Rain would be a good excuse to delay their return to trouble.

Thus, when the rain did begin just about the time they finished eating, they cheerfully moved their horses to the shed and themselves to the common room, where they found not only shelter but a battered fox-and-geese board. Half the pieces were missing, but the fox was there and Barbara laughingly accepted thirteen hazelnuts in place of the geese. A second jack of ale and several hard-fought games kept them well occupied during the first heavy downpour and the period of light rain that followed, so that it was past nones and the sun was out again before they left. Alphonse bestowed a second silver penny on the alewife and her husband for their hospitality, and she and Alphonse rode off with good feeling all around.

The light mood lasted until they came to the gates of Canterbury where guards still questioned all who entered about their business in the town. Although Alphonse and Barbara were passed without delay, both suddenly felt impatient with the suspicion and restrictions, and when Barbara again suggested that she get Louis's letter and ask to speak to Leicester, Alphonse agreed. He would have preferred to leave England altogether, but to get out of Canterbury and do what he could for William of Marlowe seemed a good substitute.

Nothing ever was as simple as one hoped, Alphonse thought, when Chacier greeted him at the door of their lodgings with a letter from Henry de Montfort and a verbal message begging Alphonse to meet him at the White Friars monastery at vespers.

"I can set Henry's mind at rest," he said to Barbara, "because of what you told me about his father. Poor Henry, he certainly does not deserve to feel he has done me harm or that I feel bitter toward him. Shall I escort you to the castle? The White Friars is just past it—"

"No," Barbara said. "Just for this afternoon, it will be better if we are not together. And I think I will go to the castle at once. Whenever Leicester has a free moment, I wish to be ready. The sooner I see him the sooner, God willing, you and I can leave this place. Bevis and Lewin can come with me and escort me home too. Then you also will be free to come and go as best suits your need."

At the castle Barbara found a page in Leicester's colors and told him she would like a few words with the earl, if that was possible. The boy ran off and soon returned, begging her to follow him to the earl's apartment. So quick a response, Barbara thought, implied that Leicester's conscience was still tender in regard to her and boded well for a favorable response to her plea. She was pleased as she followed the boy up to the second floor of the keep and threaded her way past groups of talking people toward the far end of the large chamber where Leicester stood with another man on a dais. Barbara was concentrating on how to present her request to Leicester and not at all prepared to be seized and drawn into a window recess before she was halfway down the room.

"So here you are, back in England again," Guy de Montfort said. "And toothsome as ever."

Barbara was certain that he thought he was speaking in a sensuous purr, but her first impulse was to box his ears and her second was to tell him to spit if he had to. She repressed both urges and also the exasperated sigh that nearly slipped out. Guy was by no means his father's favorite, but Leicester was fond of all his children and offending Guy would not be diplomatic.

"Marriage agrees with me," she said. "You had heard I was married to Sieur Alphonse, the brother of the comte d'Aix, had you not?"

"Quick work." He nodded with a self-satisfied smile. "I wondered how you would get around the excuse that, with your mother's life as a lesson, you would never take a lover and chance bearing a bastard."

Barbara looked at him with blank incomprehension. "Whatever can you mean?" she asked. "That was no excuse for anything. It was the plain truth."

His mouth twisted into an ugly sneer. "I have no time for your pretenses. I know and you know you want me. That has not changed, even if you took another man in spite after my father sent you away."

This time her astonishment was so great it made Barbara mute, and she merely gaped.

"But you were stupid to ask to see my father," he went on. "He will not have forgotten that you cast out lures for me and will send you away again."

"That is just what I desire," Barbara got out, "and just what I have come to ask of him—that he give me leave to go away."

Too amused by the conceit of the little toad to be angry, she laughed aloud. That was a mistake; Guy did not like laughter directed at him, even as a protective pretense. Any woman he addressed should plead for his favors or for consideration so that her reputation not be ruined. Before Barbara suspected what he would do, Guy had seized her elbow, pulled her toward him, and then released her arm. The sudden tug unbalanced her. She gave a low cry, and her hands went up in an instinctive move against falling.

If a revulsion against touching Guy as strong as her fear of falling had not made Barbara twist away, she would have looked as if she had tried to fling herself into his arms. Instead, her right hand struck his shoulder, propelling him a step backward, deeper into the window embrasure, while her forward movement was checked. She nearly whirled around to slap his face, but became aware of the shocked stare of a young man standing a few yards away. Distressed as she was, he was striking enough to catch Barbara's attention, with an unruly thatch of flaming red hair and a face almost equally red from exposure to sun and wind. The face was vaguely familiar and the dress very rich, so Barbara dropped a half-curtsy as she hurried past him toward the center of the chamber where any further tricks by Guy would be impossible.

She heard the redhead call out to Guy, who snarled a reply, but the brief delay saved her from another immediate confrontation because she found the page. The boy looked startled when he saw her and asked, "To where did you disappear? I have been looking for you."

"Someone stopped me for a word," Barbara said, relieved when her voice did not come out as a croak or a squeak. "I am sorry. I did not know you intended to take me right to Leicester."

"Well, he was with someone, but said you should wait and he would—" The boy stopped, sighed with relief when he saw Leicester still talking to a short man in clerical garb, and whispered, "Stand here, Lady Barbara. The earl will gesture to you when he is ready."

Barbara nodded to the page and smiled pleasantly in Leicester's direction. He looked bored to death, she thought, which surely meant the cleric was making some political or financial plea rather than talking about a matter of faith. Leicester adored theology and knew more about it than any except the greatest religious scholars, like Grosseteste. However, a cleric making a political plea probably meant she should not need to wait long, and indeed, before a quarter of an hour had passed, the earl had pointed her out to his companion, clearly excusing himself.

The priest retired with a bow, and Leicester gestured to Barbara, who came forward and dropped a brief curtsy. He looked at her severely as he said, "You are quickly returned from France, Lady Barbara, and without permission."

Barbara's eyes opened wide, and then she almost laughed. Her marriage was a matter of the greatest moment to her, but because it had not the smallest significance in the present crisis in England, probably no one had bothered even to mention it to the earl.

"I came to obtain my father's approval of the husband King Louis chose for me," Barbara said. "My father has been too good to me to let me send such news in a letter and disregard his will, even on the order of a king."

"Husband—" Leicester repeated.

He stared at her but clearly without seeing her, and Barbara realized that failure to mention her wedding was impossible. Henry de Montfort might have forgotten to do so even when he talked about Alphonse, because he was concentrating on Alphonse's effect on Edward, but Peter de Montfort would not have dared to neglect mention of her father's arrival and departure or to explain why Norfolk had come to Canterbury. Then as if he had suddenly remembered why she had been sent to France, Leicester looked troubled and patted her on the shoulder.

Barbara flushed slightly, guessing now why he was so reluctant to talk about her marriage. He must be thinking that she had been desperate for a husband, any husband, after he denied her Guy. No doubt he also thought she had come down greatly in her expectations. She was infuriated by this and at the same time amused by the man's blindness. As if any woman in her right mind would take Guy, no matter what his father's position, when she could have a man like Alphonse. The thought restored her good humor, but she was still out of sympathy with Leicester for being so blind and doting a father, so she again explained about her dower lands being in France and her marriage always having been in King Louis's gift.

"One of the reasons I was not willing to go to France while I was Queen Eleanor's lady was that I did not wish to remind King Louis of my existence and perhaps be married out of hand," she ended with an utterly false sigh.

Leicester now looked wary, as if he expected her to make some plea he would need to refuse, but plainly he also felt he had done her harm, and he asked politely, as she had hoped he would, "How can I be of service to you, Lady Barbara?"

"Oh, I am not a petitioner for myself, my lord," she assured him with wide-eyed earnestness. "I have a letter from King Louis requesting that some consideration be given to William of Marlowe, who is the father-by-marriage of a kinsman of Queen Marguerite. Sir William is a vassal of Richard of Cornwall and was taken prisoner with him." Barbara then explained in as few words as she could manage about Alys d'Aix's fear for her father's well-being and then presented King Louis's letter.

A slight relaxation of body and expression showed the earl's relief that Barbara was not going to ask him to save her from an unwelcome marriage or change his mind and offer her Guy. But he was not so relieved that he would agree to anything. He opened and read Louis's brief letter before he made any answer. Then he shook his head, though his voice was regretful when he spoke.

"No exceptions can be made, Lady Barbara. I cannot order that this one man be freed while my own supporters are still prisoners of the lords Marcher."

"I never expected you to free Sir William, my lord, nor, I am sure, did King Louis or Queen Marguerite," Barbara assured him. "And I fear that if you were willing to make the exception, Sir William would refuse freedom. Everyone knows that he wishes to remain with Cornwall, even his daughter, Lady Alys, though she is too distraught with worry to acknowledge it."

"Then what is the purpose of this letter?" Leicester asked.

"What I hope is that you will give me permission to visit Sir William in prison so that when I return to France I can give eyewitness to his good treatment. That, I am sure, will show your goodwill to King Louis, and if it will not content Lady Alys, at least it will lighten her heart enough so that she will cease plaguing her husband, and he will cease plaguing Queen Marguerite, and *she* will cease plaguing King Louis, so everyone will be at least partly content."

Leicester could not help smiling, but Barbara noticed that his eyes were still wary. "That seems much good to be had from a small favor," he said. "Unfortunately the favor is not mine to grant. Although Richard of Cornwall is in my keep at Kenilworth, he is not my prisoner but my son Simon's. However, I will give you a letter for Simon asking that you be allowed to see Sir William. I am sure my son will grant the request if there is no special reason to deny Sir William a visitor."

"Lady Alys and the comte d'Aix will be most grateful," Barbara said. "May I come for the letter tomorrow?"

"I will send it to you—"

"We are lodged opposite the Church of St. Margaret in the house of a mercer," Barbara interrupted sweetly, meeting with a look she allowed to grow more anxious, as if she did not understand the steely gaze directed at her.

"As soon as I can," Leicester ended.

Having no other choice, Barbara curtsied and withdrew, making sure her retreat took her behind Leicester, where he would have to turn to see her. Since the next petitioner was already approaching him, Barbara did not think he would bother, and she allowed her lips to turn down with irritation. What kind of idiot did he think she was not to know an order from him would open his own keep of Kenilworth to her no matter whose prisoner William of Marlowe was? And anyhow, had she not heard that the earl of Gloucester, not young Simon de Montfort, had taken Cornwall and his men prisoner? Not that that mattered. Leicester might not be able to order William of Marlowe freed, but he was certainly powerful enough to arrange a visit and have that request honored.

At least she had managed to deprive Leicester of the excuse that he did not know where to send his letter. She was thoroughly annoyed with the earl, who seemed to have learned all of royalty's tricks for delaying even the most reasonable request, until some profit could be wrung from granting it, without troubling also to learn the graciousness with which Queen Eleanor and King Henry softened their delays and refusals.

"Barby, I want—"

Again her arm had been seized and Guy's confident voice was close to her ear. She tried to wrench away, but this time he was ready and she could not break his grip. In fact his hand tightened enough to hurt her, and he began to draw her toward the end of the room, away from his father. Barbara had no idea whether he intended to stop in the semiprivacy of a deep window embrasure or to seek some more private place, but she was determined to get away. However, she also did not want to draw Leicester's attention, so she let him pull her along. Then, before they reached the door to which he seemed to be headed, she leaned back hard against his pull so that he was jerked to a stop.

"My name is Lady Barbara," she said, and her voice would have made a blizzard seem warm. "I never gave *you* leave to call me Barby, and I will not shame my husband by allowing that intimacy to you now. Let me go."

"You hot bitch," Guy said. "You are the one drawing attention—apurpose, I am sure. All you need say is where I should meet you, and—"

"God forbid!" Barbara exclaimed. "If I never meet you again as long as I live, it will be too soon."

His hand tightened still more on her arm, and the pain made her forget scandal and tear at his hand, her nails digging in hard. He uttered an oath and brought up his free hand, making a fist to strike her, but his wrist was caught by the red-haired young man who had stared at her earlier.

"A gentleman does not bruise a lady's arm or strike her in public," the redhead said with a baring of teeth that was not really a smile, "even when the lady deserves it, and I am sure Lady Barbara does not. Please release her, Guy."

"Mind your own business!" Guy hissed furiously. "I know her. She wants—"

"No!" Barbara exclaimed. "I want nothing from you save your absence." And turning to the redhead she added, "I give you leave and welcome to mind my business at this moment. My arm is my business, Guy. Let it go."

Guy laughed as if she had made a joke, then shrugged and said, "I thought you had more common sense." But he released her arm.

Barbara promptly stepped to one side so she could turn her back on him and curtsied deeply to the redhead. "I thank you, my lord. Would you do me the favor of accompanying me into the hall and waiting with me until my men can be summoned?"

"Women!" Guy snarled, and turned away.

The redhead watched Guy go, his face so expressionless that he might as well have shouted his dislike of the young Montfort aloud.

"You do not really need to come with me," Barbara said, smiling.

"But I will be glad to do so." He really smiled then and said, "You do not remember me. I am Gilbert de Clare, earl of Gloucester. Actually, I do not think we have ever met formally. I remember you because you were the wittiest of Queen Eleanor's ladies. One of the others told me your name and said— Oh, I beg your pardon."

His face got even redder, and Barbara laughed aloud. "Was that the one who said, 'It's a wonder 'er own spit don't poison 'er' or the one who said, 'May one of her little jests only drop on her head like the gift of a pigeon'?"

He laughed then too, and accompanied her right to the stable. They talked easily while her mare was saddled and her men summoned, and he lifted her to Frivole's saddle himself before he took a courteous leave. By then Barbara had connected his name with his sunburned face; the earl of Gloucester had been in the field with Leicester in his recent campaign against the Marcher lords of Wales. Apparently Gloucester did not do his commanding from inside a keep but rode and camped with his men, and his fair skin suffered for his military devotion.

Then, as she rode toward St. Margaret's Lane Barbara recalled why his face was familiar. He was right about not having been formally presented to her; she remembered him because the last time she had seen him, less than two years ago, his face had been as red with fury as it now was with exposure. He had been saying he would refuse to do homage to the king and Prince Edward, claiming that on his father's death he had been unjustly denied his heritage, which had been given to one of the king's half brothers to despoil.

The rest of the story began to come back to her. Gloucester had not been as unjustly treated as he said. He was under age when his father died, and it was King Henry's right to appoint a warden for his estates. But Gilbert de Clare's pride had been hurt by the way the king had made the arrangements, Barbara recalled, and suddenly drew in a sharp breath.

If Gloucester was hot-tempered and proud (which went with his red hair and complexion) and if he was as important a military ally of Leicester's as Barbara believed (she was now recalling recent talk about him among the women), why had Gloucester not been standing beside Leicester on the dais receiving petitioners and adulation? Why was he walking about as if he were no one in particular?

Possibly it was by Gloucester's own desire because he was shy or modest. As the thought came, Barbara rejected it. Aside from that one blush when he almost repeated an unflattering comment to her, nothing in Gloucester's manner indicated shyness or a retiring nature. In fact, his interference with Guy showed either arrogance or self-confidence.

Then might not Gloucester's pride also be hurt by the great attention paid to Leicester while little was paid to him? He was still very young, and Leicester, although inspiring to the young, was also high-handed with them and tactless. For Leicester to allow Gloucester to develop a grudge against him would be dangerous. It was a discomforting thought, particularly when coupled with the dislike Barbara had seen between Gloucester and Guy.

A church bell ringing for vespers startled her, and she looked about and found herself at St. Margaret's Church, opposite her lodging. Her first thought was that Alphonse would be at the White Friars monastery with Henry de Montfort and she would not be able to talk to him about Gloucester. Her second thought was an instant horrified recoil. If she talked to Alphonse about Gloucester, she would sooner or later have to mention Guy.

The bell for vespers rang again, and Barbara signaled to her men to help her down from Frivole. She told them to stable the mare and that she would be in the church attending the evensong mass. The interior was dim, lit only by small, high windows and by the candles at the saint's shrine and altar. The church already held some people when Barbara entered. When the bell rang once again a few more straggled in, passing Barbara, who stood well back and away from the door, near the southern wall. By the time the echoes of the bell had died away, all had found places and become still, patient, faceless shadows waiting to draw into themselves the comfort of the mass.

The familiar, sonorous music of the chanted Latin did soothe Barbara's nervous qualms. Although her mind, more intent on her immediate problem than on her soul's future good, did not consciously make sense of the prayers, she felt a benefit. Her presence in the church helped her come to a decision she knew was right. She must not try to conceal Guy's attentions from Alphonse. If anyone besides Gloucester saw her struggle with Guy—and she had been too much engaged in it herself to have noticed outside interest—gossip might present Alphonse with a far more lurid description of the events than she would.

When mass was over, Barbara returned to her lodging, changed out of court dress into a plain loose robe, and sat down to eat her evening meal beside the small fire Clotilde had lit to chase out the dampness of the late summer evening. The weather had not yet turned chilly and Barbara would have been warm enough without the fire, but the crackling was cheerful and she was grateful for the lift the bright flames gave her spirits.

Alphonse was not as late as she expected, but he plainly considered even the few hours he had spent with Henry de Montfort a waste of time. "I asked him outright whether, if I must remain in England, I could leave Canterbury and attend to some personal business for my brother Raymond," he told Barbara, as Chacier helped him off with his clothes and Clotilde brought a comfortable old robe for him too. "I have a craw full of apologies and excuses, but no answer. Did you do any better?" he asked as he sat down opposite her, letting out a sigh.

"No," Barbara admitted. "Leicester saw me at once—he has a guilty conscience with regard to me, I think—and he even admitted that the small favor I asked might do much good, but he would not grant it."

"Did he refuse outright?" Alphonse asked eagerly. "If he did—"

"No." Barbara chuckled. "You will not find a back door in his refusal that the French emissaries can open for you. Leicester said William of Marlowe is not his prisoner but his son Simon's and promised to write a letter asking Simon to allow us to visit William."

Alphonse groaned and Barbara agreed that she had recognized the delaying device and had done what she could to counter it, first by asking if she could come for the letter and, when he said he would send it, by naming their lodging.

"You did not press him too hard, I hope?"

Barbara asked first if Alphonse wanted wine or something to eat, and when he shook his head went back to his question. "Leicester does not permit persistence in asking. He dismissed me quite definitely before I could approach the subject in a different way—not that I would have done so. It came to me that he has not the skill of putting the petitioner in the wrong with graciousness and thus avoiding blame."

"His manner is not conciliating, which might have won him admiration when he was standing up to King Henry and his brothers, but will serve him ill when directed at his fellow earls and barons."

"My father seems able—" Barbara began, and then hesitated.

Alphonse laughed. "To avoid meeting him?" He raised his brows into a questioning look.

Barbara shrugged. "Papa may lose his temper, which I hope is what he wishes to avoid, but that would not affect his actions in the long run. But I was troubled by something else I saw while I was in Leicester's apartment. Gilbert de Clare, the earl of Gloucester, was there—you remember that he was Leicester's chief ally in the defeat of the Welsh Marcher lords—and he was alone mostly. Everyone seemed to look to Leicester."

"Why should that trouble you? Leicester is the moving spirit in this quarrel with the king. Is Gloucester a longtime friend of yours?" Alphonse asked idly.

"No. Actually I did not remember him at first. I knew I had seen him somewhere—well, one does not forget that red hair—but I could not think who he was. Later he said we had never met formally, but he remembered me."

"Another gentleman against whom I must guard my back?" Alphonse laughed.

He seemed to be amused, but even the jesting implication of jealousy, though warming and exciting in one way, made Barbara uneasy. Alphonse was so calm and indifferent that she wondered whether he was hoping to find evidence of a wandering eye in her so as to excuse his own infidelities. She had been reconsidering her decision to tell him about Guy; now she changed her mind again. If there was gossip, she must be the one to warn him of it before he heard it from others.

"No, not at all," she said, also laughing lightly. "I am afraid the earl of Gloucester, who is quite young, would not take me as a gift. He remembered me as the lady whose own spit might poison her, according to one of the queen's women."

"Yet he accosted you?"

"He thought he was rescuing me from that idiot Guy de Montfort, who for some reason known only to his feeble intellect decided I had returned to England for the sole purpose of making myself available to him."

Barbara was braced for a bellow of outrage or a laugh of scorn, but Alphonse said nothing at all for a moment and then remarked, "He must have a very strong desire for you to flout his father's order."

"Guy has a very strong desire to have his own way," Barbara snapped. "I doubt his desire would be nearly as strong had I thrown myself into his arms when he beckoned to me." Then she sighed and added, "And I am not sure his father did order him to stay away from me. After all, Leicester thought I was safe in France, and he would wish to avoid, if he could, Guy's blaming him for sending me there. Possibly he was also afraid Guy would whine and beg his mother for my recall."

"What happened today, exactly?"

"Nothing."

That was not the truth, but Barbara was disturbed by her husband's lack of reaction. She would have taken it for total indifference, except that she knew, even if he hated her, Alphonse would not be indifferent. She was his wife, his possession, and Alphonse's pride would permit no man to meddle with his possessions. She had a momentary regret that she had raised the subject.

"But the 'nothing' that happened seems to have stuck firmly in your mind," Alphonse remarked, his lips twisting cynically.

"Yes—I mean, no." Barbara swiftly decided to change the slant of her tale and reduce Guy de Montfort to a flea bite compared with a "real" worry. She laughed. "Naturally I was annoyed by that fool's arrogance, but all he is is a puffed-up fool. What made his stupidity stick in my mind was that Gloucester came to my rescue. But Gloucester must have interfered because he wanted to spite Guy. I cannot believe he feared for my safety—after all, we were in a room full of people, and Leicester himself would have come to me if I had let out a single shriek for help."

Alphonse had been looking into the hearth and now turned his head sharply. "Guy de Montfort actually laid his hands on you?" he asked.

About to deny it, Barbara remembered the grip on her arm, which likely as not would show in a bruise. "He grabbed my arm and bruised me. But I gave him as good as I got and tore up the skin of his hand. Everyone will see the scratches and laugh at him."

"I think—" Alphonse began, and slowly started to get up from the chair.

Barbara jumped across the space between them and pushed him back. "You are not thinking at all," she cried. "You are about to act just the way a cat chases a bit of string. If you challenge Guy, you will make something out of nothing. And he is more than ten years younger than you and not near your match in arms. You will certainly kill him or cut him to ribbons if you fight. No doubt everyone except his father and mother will be delighted, but they will still think you punished a stupid boy too severely—"

"Enough," he said, and laughed. "I can see an open challenge would be a mistake. I will say nothing to Guy de Montfort if he does not approach me and if you will promise not to go out without my escort." Before she could answer, he stood up and put an arm around her. ''Come, I will kiss your bruise and make it well.''

He kissed more than the bruise on her arm, but it took some time before Barbara was able to put aside the fright he had given her and enjoy his caresses. She now realized she had grown too accustomed to her father's immediate loud vocal and physical reactions to what displeased him. Alphonse's quiet had almost deceived her into thinking she had succeeded in distracting him from Guy's behavior by dwelling on the political aspects of Gloucester's actions.

Every time she thought anew of the consequences, had she not recognized when she did the fury that raged under Alphonse's outward calm, her body went cold and stiff and poor Alphonse had to begin his lovemaking all over again. It seemed like hours before she was able to relax and let herself drift on the waves of sensual pleasure he created. And she did not fight his response this time as she often did to hide the fact that she was too eager. Still, she was more than usually exhausted after her pleasure peaked and ebbed, and she slept as if stunned.

Chapter 16

Alphonse slept as heavily as his wife, but he woke at dawn by habit and slipped from the bed as he did every morning. He was in the solar before he remembered that he had nowhere to go. First he thought of going back to bed, but he had forgotten to tell the servants that his duty to the prince was ended. Clotilde was on her way to fetch his washing water, and Chacier had already gone out to get food for him to break his fast.

There could be no escape from his troubles by submerging them in Edward's or in further sleep. Alphonse stood in the middle of the room remembering everything that had happened the previous day, most painfully recalling his suspicion after they made love on the riverbank that Barbe was hiding something from him. She had been ten times as hard to arouse last night—after seeing Guy de Montfort. Because she was angry and frightened, as she confessed? Or because she had a secret desire for Guy? Alphonse wondered whether Barbe had taken him as a poor second choice after she realized that Leicester would not sanction a marriage between his son and a bastard, even Norfolk's? Had her swift arguments against his intention of punishing Guy been born of her desire to protect the young man or, as they seemed, the honest fruit of logic and contempt?

He went through the motions of washing, dressing, and eating with the same questions presenting themselves to him in new forms, but in whatever form without answers, until Chacier reminded him it was growing late. Then he looked up from the depths of his cup of ale, swallowing down an impulse to smash in Chacier's face. It was Guy he wished to smash, and he bitterly regretted having promised Barbe he would not challenge him.

Startled by his master's expression, Chacier stepped back and said uncertainly, "Sieur?"

Alphonse shook his head and told his man that he would not be going to Prince Edward again. His servant's immediate nod of understanding and his obvious relief—because he now knew the rage was not directed at him—brought Alphonse the rather surprising realization that he had never before hated an individual as he hated Guy de Montfort. But to explain that to Chacier was impossible. Alphonse looked down into his ale again. Let Chacier believe his anger was directed at a political problem. That was what Barbe had tried to convince him, was it not?

Suddenly part of the tempest inside him stilled. He would not need to sit here with hot coals of doubt burning holes in his belly. Barbe had tried to divert him with the political red herring—Alphonse could not help chuckling in the midst of his misery over the word "red"—of the earl of Gloucester. He could not challenge Guy de Montfort, but perhaps by talking with Gloucester he could get a clearer view of what had happened between Barbe and Guy.

"Bring Dadais, Chacier," he said, then turned to Clotilde. "I must go to the castle for a little while. When Lady Barbe wakes, assure her that I have *not* gone to see Guy de Montfort and will avoid him if I possibly can and that I will return to escort her wherever she desires to go as soon as I can."

At the castle Alphonse discovered without difficulty that the earl of Gloucester was lodged in considerable, if somewhat isolated, splendor in the archbishop's house. This had been empty, Alphonse knew, because the archbishop of Canterbury was in France, neck deep in Queen Eleanor's plans to destroy Leicester, and would not dare return to England until a firm settlement was made.

As he rode across the town from the castle toward the cathedral, Alphonse wondered whether Gloucester would be awake at so early an hour, but he was not left in doubt long. A grizzled steward came hurrying out to lead him into the house very soon after a guard had sent in his name. The steward said nothing unusual, but Alphonse guessed from his manner that the earl was up and about and would be glad of any guest.

Gloucester was still breaking his fast, but he rose politely to greet Alphonse and asked immediately whether he was indeed the Alphonse d'Aix who had taken the prize at Lagny-sur-Marne.

"Well, I have fought five times at Lagny over the past ten years and twice taken the prize there, so I suppose I am the one," Alphonse said, smiling. "But I must warn you that every third man in Provence is named either Alphonse or Raymond, and there must be more than one Alphonse d'Aix."

Gloucester laughed. "I doubt there were two who took the tourney prize at Lagny. Sit, please. Will you eat?"

"No, I thank you. I have broken my fast."

"Wine then? Or ale?"

"Ale, I thank you." Alphonse waited while a servant brought a cup and Gloucester filled it from the jack beside him. Then he said quickly, "And before we are diverted to talk of tourneys, let me thank you for your assistance to my wife yesterday."

"Guy de Montfort thinks he owns the world," Gloucester snarled, flushing redder. "That when he puts out a hand, whatever he reaches for will leap into it." His teeth set and he held up a hand to stop Alphonse from speaking. "As you can see," he said, after taking a deep breath, "you owe me no thanks. It shames me to say it, but when I interfered I was not thinking of Lady Barbara"—the tenseness in his expression eased and he grinned—"although now that I have spoken to her, she would be my first concern, I assure you."

Alphonse shrugged. "Whatever your reason for protecting her, I must still thank you." But he already felt much better than his casual tone implied, not less angry with Guy de Montfort but less fearful that Barbe was deceiving him. So far every word Gloucester had said was completely in accord with the tale Barbara had told, and his next words confirmed it further.

"I do not mean to be rude, Sir Alphonse, but I cannot allow you to feel any obligation. I am certain Lady Barbara would have freed herself in moments."

The words were sweet as music to Alphonse. Clearly Gloucester had seen Barbe struggling to get away from Guy. Equally clearly the young earl was now embarrassed by the urge to annoy Guy that had involved him in their dispute, and perhaps he wished he had not so openly exposed his dislike for Leicester's son. A good courtier could always cover not only his own mistakes but those of others.

Alphonse smiled. "But I doubt she could have gotten away from him without creating a near riot and making everyone in the room aware that Guy de Montfort was forcing his attentions on her," he said smoothly. "Naturally, you would not want

Leicester's name smirched by the disgusting behavior of his thoughtless son."

Gloucester's pale eyes widened for a moment with surprise at so rational an explanation of his behavior. He then busied himself drinking from his cup and refilling it, after which he said carefully, "If that were true, then even less would you owe me thanks." Then suddenly he frowned as the political implications Alphonse had suggested came into focus. "Good God!" he exclaimed. "You are not going to challenge him, are you? To have one of the French delegation—"

"I am not part of the French delegation," Alphonse said, "but no, I am not going to challenge Guy de Montfort. Unless— My lord, by any chance is he famous for his strength in arms?"

"He thinks so." Gloucester grinned. "But unless you have lost all the skill I saw you fight with at Lagny, you could swat him down like a slow-crawling bug."

Alphonse groaned slightly with disappointment. "That is what Barbe said," he confessed. "She said Guy and I were no fair match and that I would be accused of taking a cheap triumph over a young rival."

"Leicester would never allow a challenge anyway, or he would make you put it off until after the peace." A new frown creased Gloucester's forehead. "But if you did not come here to ask my help in your challenge, why are you not with Prince Edward?"

"I have been relieved of that duty by the earl of Leicester," Alphonse said quietly.

Gloucester's mouth opened, then closed. He looked down into his ale cup.

"I was not sorry to be relieved of my duty," Alphonse went on quickly. "Although I have known the prince for a long time and was glad to be of help, it was not a service I desired. And I believe the earl of Leicester relieved me of the duty only to be sure there was no misunderstanding. I refused any official appointment, but you know, my lord, it might still seem to some that Henry de Montfort had placed a foreign favorite in Prince Edward's household."

Alphonse had watched Gloucester carefully, but seeing the young man's relief when he realized that Alphonse had not come to beg for the restoration of his position needed no keen eye. So Gloucester was in considerable awe of Leicester. If Barbe was right about Gloucester's pride, that awe undoubtedly rubbed him the wrong way. Interesting, Alphonse thought; it would not be difficult to drive a wedge between Leicester and Gloucester. However, advancing the Royalist cause by seeding dissension among Leicester's followers was not his affair. Then, to make clear once and for all that he was not in England to seek advancement, Alphonse described his relationship to the comte d'Aix and his services as his brother's agent in the French court.

"But if she was not petitioning Leicester to restore your place," Gloucester burst out, "why the devil did you send Lady Barbara to him when you must have known she would run afoul of Guy there?" Then he blushed furiously and muttered, "I beg your pardon. It is not my business."

Gloucester's obvious embarrassment took the sting from his question and Alphonse said simply, "I did not know that Guy had come to Canterbury with his father, and I do not think Barbe knew either. I had spent all my time with the prince and she with the ladies of her acquaintance. As for what she was doing there, she was asking for permission to visit a prisoner, William of Marlowe."

"Whose prisoner?" Gloucester asked.

"Simon de Montfort's, Leicester told my wife," Alphonse replied. "I only knew he had been taken with Richard of Cornwall—"

"If he was taken with Cornwall he is not Simon's prisoner!" Gloucester bellowed, slamming the cup he had half lifted back down on the table. "*I* took Richard of Cornwall prisoner at Lewes."

"No offense meant, my lord," Alphonse said, raising a brow. "I may not have heard correctly what Barbe told me, or, indeed, she may not have repeated precisely what Leicester said to her. If he said Cornwall was in young Simon's keeping, Barbe would have assumed he was Simon's prisoner. Women are not much interested in precise rules of ransom."

"No offense taken, Sieur Alphonse," Gloucester said, visibly clamping restraint over resentment, "and certainly not against you or Lady Barbara. But visiting Sir William can be no difficulty." The resentment grated in his voice again. "I will be glad to write an order arranging it."

"I will be most grateful," Alphonse said, "but I do not wish to create any difficulties—not that Sir William is a great or important man." He went on to explain briefly the relationship, and ended, "Nonetheless, Leicester did not wish to give Barbe a letter to young Simon."

"Why?" Gloucester asked, frowning.

Alphonse smiled. "I am afraid Lord Leicester is reluctant to allow Barbe or me to leave Canterbury at present." He shrugged. "Perhaps because he thinks I am a secret agent for King Louis, but more likely because he wants me ready to hand as a bribe for Prince Edward's compliance. If so, he overestimates my influence with the prince greatly. However, I would not like to set you and Leicester at odds over a silly misunderstanding."

Gloucester nodded, his color, which had faded as his anger calmed, becoming minimally redder again. Alphonse blessed his own dark complexion, which he knew changed only slightly with his feelings and wondered irrelevantly how a fair-skinned man could conceal anything.

He voiced that question aloud when, some time later, he had returned to his lodging and reached that point in relating his morning's adventures to Barbara.

She laughed and leaned forward to touch his cheek. "Foolish man, most have no feelings but anger to display, and they seldom wish to hide that. It is only younglings like Gloucester, who can still be embarrassed, and men with hearts who need to worry about showing what they feel."

Warmth coursed through him at the tenderness of her touch and words, but she leaned back and looked down at the work in her hands before he could respond, asking, "Are you sure he understood you? A blush can mean anything."

"Oh, yes, he understood. Gloucester may be young, but he is no fool. I think Leicester is making a big mistake in not pushing every task he can onto that young man and keeping him very busy instead of offering him empty honor. Gloucester said he would speak to Leicester and determine whether there was any real reason—beyond those I had suggested—for denying us the right to leave Canterbury and visit Sir William."

There was a minute pause, and then without looking up Barbara asked sharply, "Are you trying to make mischief between Leicester and Gloucester?"

Alphonse laughed. "No. It would be so easy, but why should I?"

"To spite Leicester?" Her voice wavered uncertainly.

"I do not act out of spite," he snapped, "and you should say what you mean to me. If you wish to accuse me of causing a political disaster because I am angry with a lecherous little worm—"

He stopped abruptly as Barbara giggled, looking up at him under her lashes while her head was still bent toward the embroidery in her hands. It was an extraordinarily provocative look and, oddly, removed any lingering doubt in Alphonse's mind about her opinion of Guy de Montfort. Unfortunately, it also increased his anger at Guy, who would have had some excuse for what he had done if Barbara had invited his attentions. To hide the rage, he admitted it.

"It is not pleasant to need to ignore the bruising and insult to my wife by a man—"

"Louse—"

This time Alphonse chuckled. "Very clever, my dear. You mean to imply I can do no more about Guy's marks and insults than I can about those inflicted by a louse and should pay them no more mind. But you know that even if I wished to follow that advice it would be impossible. After what took place in Leicester's chamber, I dare not allow you to visit the court alone without giving you the reputation of a wanton and myself the name of cuckold. Yet, if I attend you everywhere—which, let me say I am willing, even eager, to do—sooner or later we will meet Guy."

"We could stay here," Barbara said.

"You mean be imprisoned in these rooms?"

"There is the town, and the countryside—"

"I am not so sure we will now be allowed to ride out as freely as we did yesterday," Alphonse pointed out. "And the town is small. We would be almost as likely to meet Guy in the market or inns as in the court." He smiled. "I have only promised not to challenge him myself, not to try to stop him from challenging me. However, I do not think I will have that satisfaction. Young Gloucester needs time to think, but when he has it, as I said, he is no fool. He suggested that we accompany him to his keep at Tonbridge."

"Without telling Leicester?"

"No, of course not. Did I not tell you I had warned him about stepping on Leicester's toes by giving us an order to visit Sir William? He will propose the plan to Leicester, offering to make sure that we will not return to France or see what we should not see. Since Tonbridge is only about eighteen leagues from Canterbury, he will be able to produce us within a day if Leicester needs us."

Barbara laid down her work and cocked her head. "Why?"

"Why what?" Alphonse asked, half amused and half annoyed by the astuteness of her understanding.

"Why all," she replied, her brows going up. "Why did Gloucester offer to take us to Tonbridge, since he cannot wish to protect Guy? Why do you wish to accept his offer? And why do you think Leicester will grant Gloucester's request?"

Because he could never resist the little tent that formed on her forehead with two bright eyes peering out, Alphonse jumped up and kissed it, then laughed as she pushed him away and demanded that he answer and not try to cozen her. His gesture had been quite genuine, but her accusation made him remember that she suspected him of Royalist sympathies—and to a certain degree, she was correct.

Alphonse had no intention of playing any active role against Leicester, but he felt that Leicester's wresting of power from King Henry was a violation of the natural order, despite the man's nobility of purpose and character. So he had not struggled to find a polite way of refusing the young earl's invitation to Tonbridge, though he saw trouble could arise from it. Nonetheless, he had honestly warned Gloucester of the danger of a rift between him and Leicester. There was no need to point out any of the details to Barbe, however. Having bent swiftly and stolen another kiss, which his wife yielded but punished him for by nipping his chin, he answered.

"Gloucester issued the invitation because he is young and impressed with my skills on the tourney field. I think he wishes to practice at jousting and swordplay with me. I wish to go to Tonbridge because I have no more to do here and will soon be bored to death. Moreover, I am sure that, as the troops summoned to repel the invasion that never took place go home, and Leicester realizes I cannot be used to bribe Edward, he will become indifferent to where I go and forget me altogether. Then I can take Gloucester's order to Kenilworth and see Sir William. That will fulfill all the pledges I made, and we can go home."

"But why should Leicester agree to let us go to Tonbridge?"

Alphonse shrugged irritably. He had hoped she would not ask that question again, but he answered it. "Because he wishes to be rid of Gloucester, whose skill he trusts on the battlefield but not in matters of state."

To his relief Barbe nodded acceptance to that without comment. She did not seem to realize that Gloucester's proposal held an inherent threat to his relationship to Leicester no matter how Leicester replied to it. If Leicester refused Gloucester's request, the young man would be offended because the earl did not trust him; if Leicester agreed, Gloucester would no doubt feel he was not wanted here in Canterbury. As Barbe stared thoughtfully right through him, Alphonse's relief dissipated. Gloucester's invitation held promise of good too, Alphonse thought, preparing an argument against future wifely accusations: If Gloucester was away from Canterbury, he would not be constantly irritated by being thrust into the background, and his resentment against Leicester would subside.

"I will be very glad to be out of town, away from the court, and at a country manor again," Barbara said, sighing and focusing her eyes on him. "I was just thinking how strange it is that when I am in the country, I am so eager to come to court"—

she laughed suddenly—"and when I am at court, I am eager to go to the country." Then she looked down at her work again. "Of course, this has not been a happy court for a long time."

Not desiring that she apply her memories of the past to the present, Alphonse remarked that boredom in Louis's court was likely to have the same effect, so she would not have to change her ways. She laughed again at that, held out her hand to him, and set her work aside. Something in her expression stirred Alphonse into instant heat, but when he used the hand he had taken to pull her to him, she broke away from his kiss, denying heatedly she had intended an invitation to make love. Then as swiftly as she had become angry, she recovered her gaiety; but she slipped from his arms, shaking her head, called him a lecher, and insisted she had only wanted his help to rise so they could go out to dinner.

Alphonse responded smoothly, but he wondered if he was going mad. He had never in his life misread a woman's expressions and gestures as often and as badly as he did with Barbe. Had love so warped his judgment that he saw only what he wanted to see and thus interpreted her indifference as desire for him? The idea was sufficiently painful that he did not really hear what Barbe was urging on him and only realized that he had agreed to take her to the castle to dine with the court when she bade Chacier tell her men she would not need their company because her husband would attend her.

"I know I seem to have changed my mind," she said, turning to Alphonse again and clearly finishing what she had been saying. "I was the one who first suggested that we stay here so as to avoid Guy. However, if Gloucester thought you desired restoration of your position with Edward so ardently that you would send me to Leicester to beg for it and beg for it from him yourself, will not others think the same? We must show ourselves and show our indifference."

There was nothing at all in the dark eyes that stared at her so intently and no meaning to the nod or the smile that curved Alphonse's beautifully shaped mouth. Barbara felt like wailing aloud. Her desire for him was so strong and so natural that she had not even realized she was offering herself until he drew her up and kissed her. Terror had made her angry until she saw how she had hurt him. She had tried to soothe him with teasing, but he had withdrawn behind a blank mask and she could not tell whether she had succeeded or not. And it hurt to hurt him. It was like stripping the skin from her flesh each time she pretended indifference to his love. Yet it would be more painful to lose him altogether if he became bored with her devotion—or would it?

To remain in the lodging was to confront that agonizing question anew every moment. Barbara was afraid to join the court, afraid that Guy—bad-tempered, arrogant, and convinced of his right to dominate—would accost her in Alphonse's presence. If so, she knew Alphonse was clever enough to get around his promise not to challenge the young man. But much as Barbara feared the consequences of Guy fighting Alphonse, she was growing more afraid to spend a whole day alone with her husband. And then it occurred to her that Leicester would never permit his son to fight a stronger man. If Alphonse did manage to tease Guy into challenging him, she and Alphonse would be sent away . . . but that was what they wanted. So she pressed the point about dining at court and got her way.

Since Barbara was not completely convinced by her own reasoning, she was not very happy with the lesser of the two evils she had chosen until they reached the castle and Alphonse almost collided with Peter the Chamberlain, who was leaving the hall as they entered. He turned about promptly, said Claremont was eager to speak to Alphonse, and led them toward the window embrasures on the opposite wall. There Simon de Claremont greeted them both politely and asked at once what reason Leicester had given for dismissing Alphonse from Edward's service. Barbara hardly listened; she was content. In the French envoy's presence she and Alphonse would be safe from Guy; a fool he might be, but not fool enough to provoke Alphonse under Claremont's nose.

Her attention was caught when the envoy hawked crossly and said he could not understand why Leicester had bothered to plead with Louis to send emissaries if he intended to present peace proposals that were little more than ultimatums.

"Some peace must be made," she said seriously. "With the king and prince his prisoners, one must expect Leicester's terms to demand approval of what he fought for in the first place."

Claremont looked down his aristocratic nose. "I did not know that so many nobles and commons of England took the field and risked their lives to obtain a settlement of Leicester's claims against King Henry for his expenses in Gascony twenty years ago."

"Oh dear." Barbara sighed, then smiled. "Has that problem reared its hoary and ugly head again? But it has been put aside so many times. Surely that cannot really be a sticking point."

"The arbitrators Leicester has suggested are also too one-sided for King Louis's taste."

Barbara's reply was interrupted by a clatter of activity as the servants began to set up the tables for dinner. People moved toward the outer edges of the hall to be out of the way, and Claremont, not wishing to be trapped in the deep window embrasure, drifted toward the long wall on the north. This, to Barbara's distress, brought them face to face with Leicester, who came from the large chamber on the north, followed by his cousin Peter de Montfort and his sons Henry and Guy. Seeing Claremont, Leicester stopped and bowed politely, sparing a nod and smile of recognition for Barbara and Alphonse.

Barbara was relieved when Leicester only exchanged a few words with the French envoy before bowing again and moving away. Guy had sidled around toward her when Henry began to talk to Alphonse, but he retreated with a grimace when his father looked back over his shoulder and summoned him and Henry somewhat sharply. Nor did Guy approach her again that afternoon, but she was not certain whether that was because Claremont graciously invited Alphonse and her to join the envoys' table for dinner or because his father had noticed his intention and reprimanded him.

After the meal was over, several false alarms—when a loud voice or a tunic the same color as Guy's seemed to be approaching—brought Barbara's heart into her mouth. Each fright made her more and more resentful, and there seemed to be no relief in sight. Gloucester was nowhere to be seen, and Barbara jumped to the conclusion that he had been sent away. She later discovered her conclusion to be wrong, but at the time she felt as if a door to escape had been slammed in her face. So the next time the slow circulation in the hall brought her and Alphonse into company with the French envoys she mentioned their desire to leave Canterbury.

Claremont only nodded and shrugged, remarking with a cynical curl of lip that he, too, would prefer to return to France, which made Alphonse explain hastily his promise to his sister-by-marriage. Perhaps Claremont listened more closely than it appeared and presented their complaint when he spoke to Leicester later. Barbara and Alphonse could never decide whether Claremont had supported their case out of pure good nature or simply to annoy Leicester—or whether he had mentioned them at all. It was equally possible that the earl had not needed Claremont's prodding and had, for reasons of his own, been glad to accede to Gloucester's request to let Barbara and Alphonse move to Tonbridge. In any case the very next morning a messenger brought written permission from Leicester for them to leave Canterbury in Gloucester's company.

Chapter 17

In the weeks that followed, Alphonse and Barbara had good reason to congratulate themselves on having escaped Canterbury and the constant reminders of a hopeless impasse. When they first left, Gloucester had believed that some basis for a firm peace would soon be found. The hopes, however, were fruitless. Whether the papal legate's violent antipathy to Leicester and the Provisions of Oxford had influenced the French king or, as Barbara and Alphonse suspected but did not say, some of the emissaries' hearts were not truly in the negotiation, Louis would not support a peace on the terms offered. According to Gloucester, who came and went while Barbara and Alphonse amused themselves at Tonbridge, Leicester made several attempts to find common ground. New names were submitted as arbitrators—men less blatantly supportive of Leicester—and arrangements for the eventual release, under adequate sureties, of Prince Edward and others were offered. Nonetheless, by the end of September, although negotiations were still being talked of, even Gloucester acknowledged that little hope remained of reaching an accommodation approved by Louis of France and by the Church.

This less than surprising news was thrust at Barbara and Alphonse by a mud-splashed, thoroughly out-of-temper Gloucester. The young earl had been summoned to Canterbury to consult on the latest changes in the peace terms. On his return to Tonbridge, he said no more than that at first, but the fact that he had clearly ridden away from the town and continued through a dark, wet day implied to Barbara that Gloucester had been offended. She rose from the bench on which she had been sitting with Alphonse and held out her hand in a warm welcome.

Barbara had become truly fond of the young earl. He had made a firm place in her heart not only because he was good-natured and had an earnest desire to do what was right but because his marital situation was not unlike her father's. He had been married while still a child to the king's niece, Alice of Angoulême. Barbara knew the woman slightly. Lady Alice had spent more time at court than her husband; Barbara had met her now and again while serving Queen Eleanor and did not like her. She found in Lady Alice many of the worst aspects of the pride and contempt for everything English displayed by her father, Guy de Lusignan, King Henry's half brother.

Nonetheless, Barbara appreciated the fact that Gloucester spoke no ill of the lady, who had borne him two daughters. All he had said when she asked, rather apprehensively, if Lady Alice would join them at Tonbridge was that he and his wife now lived apart because she could not bear his association with the earl of Leicester, her loyalty being more strongly bound to the king than to her husband. There was an unspoken hurt under the stiff statement that called to Barbara to offer comfort, and she did.

For his part, Gloucester seemed to return Barbara's affection. Fortunately, he so plainly regarded her as an "older woman," beyond the pale as much because she was like an aunt or older sister as because she was the wife of a friend, that even a far duller husband than Alphonse could not have been jealous. Barbara found Gloucester's attitude both amusing and comfortable.

Gloucester, who had been stamping across the floor as if he were treading on enemy heads, took Barbara's hand and nodded to Alphonse, who had also risen to greet him. Then, in a calmer voice, he said that Louis's emissaries had been recalled to France, and so it was now or never for peace. Barbara nodded sympathetically and Alphonse remarked blandly that it was impossible to get an idea out of King Louis's head once it was in. Soothed by the pretense of his guests that his ill temper was all owing to the probable future rejection of the peace terms, Gloucester sank into the chair by the fireside and said that Leicester planned to make one last effort.

Returning to France with Louis's emissaries—whose advice had been asked, if not always taken, about the new peace terms—was a new group of negotiators. These men had been empowered to bargain, barring a few conditions.

"Which are?" Alphonse asked, pouring wine into a cup from a flagon on a side table and carrying it to Gloucester, who nodded his thanks.

"Security for Leicester, me, Norfolk, and all of our adherents."

"Of course," Barbara said. "Louis could not object to that."

"Then there will be four arbitrators: the archbishop of Rouen, Peter the Chamberlain—"

Gloucester looked at Alphonse who had made an indefinable sound as he imagined how Peter would "enjoy" having so onerous a duty thrust on him. Then, when Alphonse, still wordless, shook his head, he continued and named the bishop of London and Hugh le Despenser as the other two arbitrators, with the papal legate to have a fifth and deciding vote in case the four arbitrators could not agree.

"Louis will not accept those arbitrators," Alphonse said. "The archbishop of Rouen, while not quite as prejudiced as Despenser and London, is known to favor Leicester strongly. The only truly neutral man is Peter the Chamberlain, and he will be outvoted three to one every time he disagrees with one of Leicester's proposals."

"Oh, I know it is hopeless," Gloucester snarled. "I do not understand why we, the victors, should go crawling for approval to—" He stopped abruptly and flushed. "I beg your pardon, Alphonse. Louis is your king."

"But by no means faultless in my eyes," Alphonse said, smiling.

The words were perfectly true, but Barbara knew that they did not mean Alphonse disapproved of Louis's stand with regard to the peace terms. She had no more inclination than her husband to explain this to Gloucester, however. What did concern her was that Alphonse might be classified as an enemy after negotiations ended.

She said, "I am sorry to hear this. Will not the breakdown of negotiations make it impossible for Alphonse to redeem his promise to Lady Alys to visit her father?"

"Good God, I had forgotten all about that," Gloucester exclaimed. "But this last effort for peace will be no overnight matter. Our envoys will be in France for some weeks, I believe. There will be time enough to ride to Kenilworth and see . . ."

"Sir William," Alphonse offered, as Gloucester hesitated, having forgotten the name.

"The man has no political importance," Gloucester went on,

frowning thoughtfully, "and I am sure you would not use permission to visit him to work any harm."

"Indeed, I would not," Alphonse agreed heartily. "To speak the truth, I would gladly be rid of that promise and go back to France with the envoys if I could find any other way to ease my sister's mind."

"Nothing but knowing him free and well will truly ease his daughter's heart," Barbara said. "That is how I would feel if my father were a prisoner. But since that is not possible, I think it more important than ever that you see Sir William with your own eyes, Alphonse, so you can tell Alys whether he was thin or stout and the color of his skin and whether his eyes were sunk . . . You know what she will need to hear to believe him well."

Alphonse sighed. "Yes, I know. And unfortunately Alys is not one easily deceived. To lie and be caught in it would be worse than admitting I could not visit him."

"There is no reason why you should not visit him," Gloucester said. "I can see no harm in it at all. I will give you a letter to young Simon de Montfort, who is his gaoler, and a letter allowing you freedom to travel."

"I would be most grateful, my lord," Alphonse said, then grinned and added, "and you will be free at last of guests whom you may have believed had taken root in your household."

Gloucester laughed. "I wish you *had* taken root. I will sorely miss being black-and-blue from being dumped on the ground by your jousting lance three times a week."

Alphonse laughed also. "And I will miss my lessons on how to manage an army. My brother will approve most heartily of what I have learned."

Although the young earl was clearly pleased and flattered by Alphonse's remark, he made a dismissive gesture. "Seriously, I will be very sorry to see you go and would gladly have offered you a place in my household, but I know your duty is to your brother and that you have lands in France."

Alphonse acknowledged his reluctance to consider leaving France permanently, then tactfully changed the subject by asking whether Gloucester thought it best to send a letter ahead to Kenilworth and what would be the best route to follow. Barbara listened idly, indifferent because she was not, as she usually was, avidly looking forward to any change that would relieve boredom. She had enjoyed being in Tonbridge, yet she had no regrets over leaving, either, so it was not Tonbridge that had held her interest.

Just then Alphonse remarked that he thought Kenilworth was Leicester's main seat and asked whether the earl or members of his family other than young Simon were likely to be there in the next few weeks. The pleasure the mere sound of his voice gave her reminded Barbara why she had not been bored. Then the sense of the question Alphonse had asked penetrated and drove out both the pleasure and the anxiety that pleasure had generated.

"There is a small problem," she said. "If Guy should happen to be at Kenilworth, it would be better if I did not stay there."

"That had occurred to me," Alphonse agreed, voice and face equally expressionless.

Gloucester looked startled at this seeming eagerness to avoid any cause of a quarrel with Guy and then rose quickly and went to the side table, where he refilled his cup. When he turned back toward his guests, his face was as expressionless as Alphonse's. Unfortunately for Barbara's peace of mind, she could see the bright gleam in his eyes from where she sat. He knew from practice fights that Alphonse could not be afraid of Guy. Did Gloucester believe that Alphonse would find it easier to chastise Guy when she was absent? If so, he was wrong. She would remind her potentially bellicose spouse of his promise not to challenge Guy, and she would make him extend that promise to include not prodding Guy into challenging him.

"You must stay here, Lady Barbara," Gloucester offered.

And leave my too attractive Alphonse to wander around the country with his rod at the ready? Barbara did not voice the thought. What she said, smiling, was "You are very kind, Gilbert, but I am afraid that would provide too much fodder for the beasts of rumor. You know they will never believe you and I are only friends. They will grow fat chewing over whether Alphonse encouraged me to lie with you to gain your influence or whether grasping at your favor is my idea and he is so stupid that I have managed to seduce you—or you me—and cuckold him under his very nose."

"The wife of a friend?" Gloucester exclaimed in horror. "I would never—"

"You know it and I know it." Barbara shrugged. "But you are no longer a gangling boy to be discounted. You are a man of power and presence, desirable to many as a lover."

Gloucester gulped his wine and turned around quickly, but his ears were bright red. Alphonse bit his lips, and managed not to choke on laughter over Barbara's skilled refusal of the young earl's invitation. He would not have hurt Gloucester for the world; at the moment, filled with joy at Barbara's clear intention not to be parted from him, he would have been generous to his worst enemy—even to Guy de Montfort.

However, the problem remained; discounting any trouble Guy might make, the main stronghold of the earl of Leicester was not a good place for the beloved daughter of Norfolk, whose behavior toward Leicester might be considered ambivalent. Young Simon had also pursued her and might think it a double coup to hold Barbe as a guarantee of her father's good behavior. Moreover, if Louis's rejection of the peace terms came sooner than expected, Alphonse thought his own safety would be much enhanced by Barbe's freedom to complain to her father and to Gloucester if he should be detained.

Meanwhile, Barbe had said, "I cannot go to Strigul. My father's wife, Lady Isabella, is there and would doubtless hang me sooner than let me in."

"She might indeed," Gloucester said dryly, "since she is strongly suspected of supporting the lords Marcher."

"A plague take that woman," Barbara exclaimed. "I do not think she cares a pin for the right or wrong of the matter. She acts only to spite my father and make trouble for him."

"Perhaps," Gloucester said, "but to be fair, Strigul is surrounded by Prince Edward's friends, and she may have been afraid to appear opposed to them. In any case, I do not think it would be wise for you to seek shelter at Strigul—it is much too far southwest, several days' travel from Kenilworth. You would be safer and more comfortable at Warwick with my vassal, John Giffard, who is castellan there. Warwick is less than two leagues from Kenilworth, and John Giffard is no particular friend of the younger Montforts. He has some hard feeling against them for taking prisoner Alan de la Zouche, who was his prisoner first and whom he had released with safe conduct . . . Ah, no matter. It is done now and must be forgotten."

The very mention of the affront made clear that it had not been forgotten by Gloucester. Probably he was reflecting his vassal's resentment, Alphonse thought, and if so, Warwick would indeed be a safe place for Barbe and a refuge for him too. Alphonse agreed eagerly that Barbe be John Giffard's guest, if he would have her, and Barbara concurred as eagerly; it had occurred to her that since Warwick was so close to Kenilworth, Alphonse could stay with her there and could ride over to see Sir William of Marlowe when he was allowed to visit.

Barbara was unfeignedly delighted with the arrangement Gloucester offered. It would be safer for Alphonse not to need to spend much time in the company of young Simon—and Guy, if he should decide to visit Kenilworth at that time—and safer for her too. She found that she suffered no pangs of jealousy over what Alphonse did during the day as long as he occupied her bed at night and gave such delightful evidence of his pleasure in his place. If he slept elsewhere, she was not certain she would be equally indifferent to his activities. She could imagine herself asking bitter, hurtful questions no woman, wife or not, had a right to ask—since men did not bear their heirs to property, their sins were irrelevant, except to their souls and God's judgment. And that was the answer pride would drive Alphonse to give her if she questioned his faithfulness, whether he was innocent or not.

Pleased with the success of his idea, Gloucester sent a servant for his clerk and dictated then and there the permissions to travel and visit Sir William and his request to Giffard to receive Alphonse and Barbara as guests. The letter to Giffard went out in the morning, but it was the beginning of the second week in October before Alphonse and Barbara left Tonbridge.

They bade farewell to Gloucester—who was himself leaving to meet Leicester at Dover—at the town gate. The two men hugged each other roughly with a faint screech of metal links grinding against metal links. Barbara, still mounted, first kissed the hand the earl held out to her and then leaned perilously from her mare to pull his head closer and kiss his lips. And while he was still looking bemused but pleased, she touched his cheek and begged him to take good care of himself.

"Did you have some reason for giving Gloucester that warning?" Alphonse asked some time later as they were traveling west along the Medway toward the old road that ran due north and south from Lewes to London.

"Warning!" Barbara repeated, startled. "I did not mean—" She shook her head. "I do not know what I meant, just that I felt uneasy in parting from him." She smiled tentatively at Alphonse. "It was very good of you to help me calm him over and over, since I suppose Prince Edward's purpose would be better served if Gloucester became angry enough at Leicester to withdraw his support."

"I do not know that any prince's purpose is best served by having his country torn apart by war, especially a war he cannot control," Alphonse replied. "Edward is learning some salutary lessons. And Leicester does not deserve to lose his friends because he is harassed on all sides and does not have time to think up soothing ways to address a man thirty years younger than himself."

Barbara burst out laughing. "True enough, but you are working on a wrong premise. It is not because he is rushed and harried that Leicester speaks his mind plainly. He never had any tact. I can remember my father's fury over his bluntness. He always said it goaded King Henry into mistakes rather than saving him from them." Then she frowned. "I suppose I should not have warned Gilbert to take care, only he is so young, so brave, and so proud. I am afraid for him."

"And for us?"

"What is there to fear for us?" Barbara looked and felt startled.

Alphonse laughed and shook his head as if he had been jesting. Her surprise made him recall that Gloucester had been careful to speak of the continued unrest in the country only in Barbe's absence. Alphonse had not previously realized that Gloucester had excluded Barbe deliberately. He would not have done so himself, but it seemed foolish to begin telling her horror stories now when they were already on the road.

The battle of Lewes had ended most organized resistance in King Henry's favor; however, it had also made outlaws of the Royalists who had escaped the battle and no longer had homes or lands and had wakened hopes in the unscrupulous that law and order was a thing of the past too. Both the starving and the greedy attacked travelers and their neighbors—the greedy using the excuse that the neighbors were of Royalist inclination. Gloucester thought that the news of the defeat of the lords Marcher in Wales might curb the lawlessness of the greedy. The outlaws, however, were a problem that could not be addressed until a peace was settled on. Then amnesty and methods of redemption of estates could be arranged. Meanwhile, the best Gloucester could do was to offer Alphonse a strong troop as escort. After due consideration Alphonse had refused, saying that more men might reduce the chance of attack by outlaws but would increase their appeal to local lordlings.

Alphonse never discovered whether good luck or good judgment was the stronger factor in protecting them. The result was the same and totally satisfactory. They arrived safely in London before evening. From Alys's letter, Alphonse knew that Marlowe Keep was on the Thames, west of London, very near the Abbey of Hurley. Directions to Hurley were easy to obtain, and they came to the abbey the following evening, also without having been in danger at any time. After some cautious fencing with the abbot, Alphonse was convinced that the man truly held Sir William in high esteem and stated his purpose clearly.

The abbot had good news for them. The furniture and valuables of Marlowe Keep were in the abbey's storehouses. The keep itself was shut tight, being held by a handful of retainers. So far no attempt had been made to take it because the place was so strong. Smiling thinly, the abbot said he had done his best to discourage any offense and, with more warmth, added that his task had been made easier by the fact that Sir William was liked and respected by his neighbors, many of whom owed him favors.

John of Hurley's keep was safe because it was beholden to the abbey, and the abbot had put his own troop into the place when John warned him that he intended to follow Hugh Bigod into the king's army. The Marlowe ladies, who were Alphonse's first concern, were also safe. As soon as word of the defeat at Lewes had come, Harold of Herron, who probably owed Aubery of Ilmer his life and certainly owed him the prosperity of his estate, had taken Sir William's wife, Lady Elizabeth, and her daughter-by-marriage, Lady Fenice, and the children into his keeping.

The next day a lay brother was sent off to discover whether Harold of Herron would be willing to receive Alphonse. He returned that afternoon with a letter from Marlowe's daughter-by-marriage, Lady Fenice, saying that Harold was away from Herron but begging Alphonse to come anyway. Barbara was rather surprised to see that Alphonse was less than overjoyed by the rapid and enthusiastic response. In private, in the visitors' garden of the abbey, he confessed that he was torn between wishing to see Lady Elizabeth and Fenice himself and being somewhat fearful of Fenice's reaction to her husband's imprisonment. Fenice was so timid and fearful a creature, he said, that he expected to be drowned in her floods of tears and begged to accomplish the impossible and free her husband, Aubery.

Barbara thus was braced for an unpleasant day or two providing hope and comfort to a pair of lachrymose ladies. Instead, when she and Alphonse arrived in Herron, they were greeted by a glowing beauty of about her own age and an elderly lady—Marlowe's second wife, Elizabeth—who seemed perfectly self-possessed and smiled at her with singular sweetness. In the light of what Alphonse had told her, Barbara was puzzled by the apparent happiness of both women. She felt she should be repelled by such selfishness, but she could not resist the older lady whose hair, like her own, constantly escaped her crespine and curled wildly in all directions.

As soon as he had assured Lady Elizabeth of her son John of Hurley's safety, Alphonse produced Alys's letter, with its offer of a haven in Aix. Barbara was not at all surprised when it was instantly refused, although she should have been if Fenice and Lady Elizabeth were as selfish as their carefree manner implied. One part of the puzzle was soon solved. Lady Elizabeth made no secret of her conviction that Richard of Cornwall would be able to arrange for his own liberation and that the arrangement would include her husband. Whether that meant the return of their lands or going with Richard to Germany, Lady Elizabeth did not care.

She would be ready and where she would cause no doubt or delay as soon as her husband was released.

Despite the warm welcome she and Alphonse had received, Barbara detected a certain uneasiness in the ladies. She did not seek to probe it, assuming it was because she was Norfolk's daughter. Since it was apparent that Fenice and Lady Elizabeth were safe and well, Barbara expected to leave the next day. Instead, Alphonse made a mysterious excursion from which he did not return until the evening of October 17. And when she asked where he had been, Alphonse looked her hard in the eyes and announced he had felt the need of exercise and had gone hunting, following which he said they would leave in the morning. Barbara blinked only once, thanked him gravely for telling her—hunting was an activity so unlikely because of the forest laws that the statement could not be considered a lie—and blandly hoped he had enjoyed himself.

She did not raise the question again, partly because most of her waking time was taken up with getting ready to leave and partly because she wanted to know whether her husband would redeem the promise in that hard stare. That he did. As soon as they were well on the way the next morning, Alphonse told her without prodding that he actually had been hunting in Barnwood Forest, in company with Harold of Herron, who had bought the right of chase there—and Fenice's husband Aubery of Ilmer. Barbara laughed aloud, understanding at once why two such ladies showed no sign of grief or anxiety over their menfolk; both were safe. She nodded at Alphonse's explanation that Aubery had fled the battle of Lewes on Richard of Cornwall's orders, when Cornwall's capture had become inevitable, to bring warning to those of Richard's vassals who had remained on his lands to guard them. There was, however, a note in his voice that told her Aubery of Ilmer's doings were no longer of great importance to him.

"You have bad news," she said.

"Rumors only," he replied. "Harold of Herron is no devoted Royalist and he has friends among Leicester's supporters. One of them came upon us in the alehouse in Thame where I was brought to meet Harold so he could lead me to Aubery's camp in the forest. He told us that King Louis had objected to the imbalance of the arbitrators but seemed willing to listen to offers of adjustment. But the legate, although he had not yet given a firm answer, had indicated that he was immovable on the subject of renouncing the Provisions of Oxford."

Barbara shook her head. "Whatever else Leicester might be willing to yield, he will not yield that. If all hope of King Louis's arbitration of peace is at an end, will you be in danger because you are French? Perhaps we should not go to Kenilworth. Simon is just careless and arrogant enough to ignore Gloucester's request that you be allowed to visit Sir William and even his order that we be allowed to travel freely."

"There is no danger yet," Alphonse said. "I am certain Leicester has no intention of declaring France an enemy and the negotiations are not yet ended. I would not like to leave without even trying to see Sir William. And he is nobody in himself. A visit to him must be politically without danger and without meaning. Thus, whatever the rumors, I might be permitted to see Sir William."

John Giffard received them warmly in Warwick on the afternoon of October 20 after two and a half days of hard travel. He apologized for the noise and disorder, saying with so little expression that he might as well have shouted his disapproval, that he had been ordered by Leicester to pull down the great stone keep and the work was under way. However, the wooden hall and domestic buildings in the strongly walled bailey were comfortable enough and he was glad to see visitors.

When they had entered the hall and told him their purpose in coming, Sir John was completely of Alphonse's opinion that the sooner he saw Sir William the better. He summoned his clerk, wrote a message to Simon de Montfort at Kenilworth, and sent it off with Gloucester's letter before he instructed his steward to show Alphonse and Barbara to the portion of the solar he had made ready for them.

"Simon is not ill-natured," he said stiffly, "only young and thoughtless. If he has received no instruction to the contrary, his natural response would be to allow the visit."

Before dark the messenger returned: "Lord Simon," he recited, "will be happy to allow Sieur Alphonse to visit Sir William; however, Sir William does not happen to be in Kenilworth at the moment. He has been sent out to certain of Richard of Cornwall's properties, of which he had long been steward, to explain the new management to the bailiffs and make them more cooperative. Tomorrow Lord Simon will send a messenger to have Sir William brought back; Lord Simon expects Sir William to return in about three days. In the meantime, Sieur Alphonse is more than welcome to be a guest at Kenilworth Keep."

Over their evening meal, Barbara, Alphonse, and Sir John Giffard discussed Simon's message, but could come to no conclusion about what it meant. Alphonse had seen how uncomfortable Sir John became when the messenger called the young man Lord Simon, which he could only have picked up from the servants in

Kenilworth or whoever gave him the message. He probed further carefully and discovered that Sir John had been castellan of Kenilworth and had been the man who wrested Warwick from its previous lord—and his "reward" had been an order from Leicester to hand over Kenilworth to young Simon and oversee the destruction of Warwick, his war prize, just because it was too near Kenilworth.

What a singularly stupid thing for Leicester to do, Alphonse thought. Atop the business of the Zouche ransom, Sir John's trust in Leicester's lack of partiality must be badly undermined. Like Gloucester's resentment against Leicester, Sir John's hurt showed where a wedge could easily be driven. However, Alphonse felt it wrong for him to become embroiled in English politics, whatever his sympathy for Prince Edward, and as soon as his curiosity was satisfied, he shifted the subject back to Simon's message.

"What I need to decide," Alphonse pointed out, "is whether to go to Kenilworth tomorrow or not."

"No," Barbara said.

Both men looked at her.

"He has invited me. Will it not seem suspicious to him if I refuse?" Alphonse asked.

"Do you have some reason to believe your husband will be in danger from Simon?" Sir John asked at the same time.

Barbara could have bitten her tongue. It was the green-eyed devil in her that had spoken—and her lust. She had no reason for her "no," only a strong reluctance to let her husband out of her sight.

She could not admit that, however, nor could she even look at Alphonse, so she said to Sir John, "I am not so vain that I believe every man desires me, but Simon has paid me particular attention." She smiled. "I think his attentions were intended mainly to make my friend Aliva le Despenser jealous. Nonetheless, if he should forget Alphonse is my husband and touch his pride with some silly remark, it is not impossible that Alphonse would forget himself and teach Simon a lesson. Whether or not Simon deserved it, Leicester would be angry. Thus, I think the less time Alphonse spends with Simon the better."

Nothing at all showed in Alphonse's face. No man could object to what Barbe had said. She had given him no cause to be jealous of Simon, nor had she implied that her husband was foolish or too hasty; there were remarks made casually or in jest for which a husband in honor must demand a retraction. But unless Simon was a monster or an idiot, a retraction—and an apology too—

would be provided in such a case. Barbe did not want him to go to Kenilworth. Why?

He became certain he would not get a frank answer from her as he listened to her smooth and logical reasons for him to reject altogether—or delay responding to—Simon's invitation. Sir John pursed his lips and nodded more than once, but not one of Barbe's reasons woke a flicker in her eyes or a note of sincerity in her voice. Was it possible that she simply wanted to keep him with her for pleasure? Certainly he gave her pleasure; but then why had she never—no, not once in the months they had been married—come of her own will into his arms. Why each time did he have to woo her anew?

"I cannot refuse altogether," Alphonse said quickly, argument being better than chewing that dry old bone.

"Why not?" Barbe challenged. "You can say you must stay in Warwick because you have a young and foolish wife who—"

She broke off as Alphonse's brows rose and his lips curled tightly in a cynical grimace. "Ah yes, my love, Simon knows you well, does he not? And would he not invite my wife to come with me—that is, if he had not burst with laughing when I said *you* were fearful of being left alone in Warwick." He turned back to Sir John, who was pursing his lips and then pulling them tight uneasily. "But if you are also uneasy, Sir John, why do I not say that I feel it uncourteous to leave you so soon when Gloucester sent me to Warwick and that I will come on the third day?"

Chapter 18

Simon de Montfort looked down from a window of the solar above the hall his father had built in Kenilworth Keep. Alphonse d'Aix was dismounting from his magnificent destrier. Simon was surprised by the unease that gripped him when he thought of the deception he intended to practice on the man he was watching. Although many years had passed since his older brother Henry had taken him to a joust not far from Paris, he now recognized Sieur Alphonse by his lithe movement, his easy grace under the weight of his armor. The admiration he had felt then for Alphonse's style and courage returned, and he also remembered that Alphonse d'Aix was Henry's friend.

Well, what of it? Simon asked himself, watching the stallion paw the ground and shake its head when a groom approached. Sieur Alphonse waved the groom back, pulled his mount around, and seemed to be talking to it. Then the servant who had ridden in with the knight came and took the rein, and Sieur Alphonse turned toward the door of the hall. Simon moved away from the window to go down the stair and greet his guest, but he was filled with doubts about what Guy had asked him to do.

Still, the bones had already rolled; he could not change the symbols on them now. Simon had thought it very funny when Guy first wrote how Lady Barbara had gotten around her vow not to bear a child out of wedlock and had readily agreed to detain her husband when he came to visit the prisoner, Sir William of Marlowe. He had still been amused when he wrote to Guy that Alphonse had arrived at Warwick, that he had sent Sir William away for a while, and that his brother should seek out the lady and enjoy her with all dispatch.

Having recognized Alphonse, Simon was no longer amused, but there was no way to back out of the arrangement with Guy. For all he knew, Guy was already in the lady's arms and it would be far worse to release the husband and have his brother caught committing adultery. No, his father must not hear of Guy's lechery. Worse, if Alphonse caught Guy with his wife, he might even kill him. Simon thought of his father's grief if either disaster took place and set his jaw. He wished he had remembered who Lady Barbara's husband was before agreeing to Guy's scheme, but it did not matter now. Montforts supported each other, right or wrong.

Then, as he came into the hall and walked across the dais, calling "Sieur Alphonse?" Simon thought that if Lady Barbara was set on playing with Guy, in a way he was protecting her husband. As it was, the man would come to no harm. This way, he would never know that he had been cuckolded, and maybe that fool of a woman would get Guy out of her mind.

"Yes, I am Alphonse. Are you Sir Simon?"

"Yes, Henry's younger brother. I am very pleased to meet you. I saw you joust in company with Henry and"—Simon hesitated and then went on in a harder voice—"and Prince Edward."

"They are both fine fighters," Alphonse said smoothly, showing no sign that he had noticed Simon's hesitation.

"But not as good as you," Simon said. "You took the prize."

Alphonse smiled lazily, his dark eyes sleepy under their half-lowered lids. The look was not all pretense. Barbara had given him a parting gift that had kept both of them awake half the night.

"Ah, but they tourney for pleasure," he said easily. "I fight for need. It is the way I make my *pourboire*."

Simon looked shocked; he could not imagine his father and mother allowing one of their sons to pick up scraps at tourneys for a living. Somehow lands would be found to support each of them and to dower their sisters. Then he smiled uncertainly, his eyes on Alphonse's surcoat—a rich gold velvet sewn over with stripes of red, and from left shoulder to right hip the bend that marked the bastardy of his house. The wide black band was embroidered with a tilting lance that glittered even in the dim light of the hall. Simon knew the device was done in real gold. His eyes flicked over the rest of Alphonse's accoutrements and his smile widened; whatever Alphonse said, he was not poor. He felt a trifle contemptuous of a man who would pretend poverty, and that feeling eased his conscience.

"Does that mean you do not wish to show me your skills?" Simon asked, unable to hide a faint note of condescension.

"I hoped I would have no reason or time to do so," Alphonse replied without the smallest sign that he had noticed the contempt. "I expected to see Sir William and then return to Warwick."

"Oh, no, you cannot expect me to allow you to escape without once crossing lances with me," Simon cried.

There was enough sincerity in that cry to make Alphonse laugh. "Not before I see Sir William," he said, and blandly revenged himself by adding, "If I should happen to overset you, I would not wish to be thrust out of the keep without accomplishing my purpose."

"I would not do that," Simon protested, smiling, and then began to apologize for not earlier having him shown to the upper chamber so he could remove his armor.

"But I will need my armor if you wish to try a passage at arms after I have spoken to Sir William," Alphonse insisted gently.

"Forgive me," Simon exclaimed. "I am so pleased to meet you that I feel you are my invited guest. I keep forgetting you have a private reason for being here. I am sorry. Sir William has not yet returned from Cornwall's holdings. He was to go to several different estates, you see. I sent my messenger to the place I thought him most likely to be, but I seem to have misjudged. That would mean the man must try again to find him. Still, it cannot be much longer—a day or two. Surely you can stay that long?"

"Yes, of course," Alphonse answered smoothly.

He felt the trap close, but because he was relatively sure that no bad news about the peace negotiations had come, he could see no reason why Simon would want to detain him. Moreover, the young man seemed relatively transparent. Alphonse had been able to read his surprise and disdain for a man who would speak of poverty with ease, so perhaps everything Simon said was true. Perhaps he really was thrilled to have a well-known tourney fighter as a guest, and perhaps the messenger had not yet found and recalled Sir William.

In any case, Alphonse thought, his best defense was to seem unaware, so he smiled and said he would be glad to change out of his armor but that he had not brought any clothing because he did not expect to be allowed to stay.

"I thought perhaps, despite your kind invitation, that the shorter the visit made by the prince's friend the better."

Simon laughed heartily. "Since Edward has been here many times himself, there is nothing you could learn about Kenilworth that he does not already know. Please believe my invitation was most sincere. You are welcome here for as long as you like. There are guesting clothes in plenty. Come now to my chamber and choose what you like to wear."

Alphonse agreed easily, only asking that a servant be sent to tell Chacier to take the horses to the stable and where to come to take charge of his armor. Simon did so and then accompanied Alphonse to his own chamber and opened his clothes chests. Not unwilling to be thought a man who was interested only in surface matters—of fighting and hunting and clothing—and because he did like fine garments, Alphonse spent some time choosing what to wear. By then Chacier had arrived.

While Chacier helped Alphonse out of his armor, Simon, as if drawn irresistibly to the subject, began to talk about tourneys again and lightly mentioned the riots that had followed several meetings in England. Alphonse was rather surprised, considering the principles the father espoused, to learn that Simon had been more amused than distressed by the destruction of property and injury done the common folk involved. But he wanted to seem stupid, so he did not try to point out to the young idiot that if tourneys got a bad reputation with the burghers, they would soon be banned by all towns. All he said was that he did not like riots because he liked to tourney in a familiar place where he knew the inns and the people and where comfortable lodgings were held for him year after year.

Simon then had the grace to look somewhat abashed and turned the talk to hunting, which Alphonse encouraged. Seizing this opening, Simon promptly offered to arrange a hunt if Alphonse would stay a few days. Without actually agreeing, Alphonse managed to give the impression he would be delighted, and they went down the hall again discussing the types of game each preferred. Eventually Simon invited Alphonse to examine the hunting dogs, and when Alphonse had given well-deserved praise to the kennels and the animals, they moved on to the stables.

The afternoon passed most pleasantly. Alphonse began to wonder whether Barbe's reluctance to let him stay in Kenilworth had poisoned his mind. Simon did not seem at all dangerous. Alphonse was more and more inclined to agree with Sir John that he was young for his age, spoiled and thoughtless but not ill-natured, and hardly an evil plotter. Moreover, Simon had left him alone several times during the afternoon to speak to a servant or attend to a minor estate matter, and Alphonse could not detect a single sign of being watched. The only oddity that struck him was that Simon asked him, after the evening meal, whether he would like a bed partner and offered to collect all the more palatable women in the keep so he could choose among them.

Alphonse refused with warm thanks but considerable firmness. He did not want Simon to think he was merely being polite and find a girl between his sheets. To make clear that he meant what he said, he stated frankly that his wife satisfied him completely and he would have to be separated from her much longer before he sought the kind of relief one got from a common slut.

At the time Simon made the offer, Alphonse was too horrified by the notion that, the two keeps being so close, Barbe might hear that he taken a woman the first night they had not shared a bed to think beyond how to refuse. Later it occurred to him that such an offer was not common custom. A host, seeing his guest look with longing on a maid, might bid her quietly go serve the guest or might wink and nod in such a way that the guest knew he could take what he wanted with no offense. But to suggest displaying all suitable women—that was going too far. And had not Simon looked dismayed by his refusal?

The next day provided enough ordinary reasons for Simon to be eager for his company that Alphonse almost dismissed his doubts. After mass—to miss a day was a grave sin in Leicester's keep and one that was reported to its master even when the sinner was a son—and breaking their fast, Simon begged Alphonse to break a few lances. Alphonse laughed and agreed at once, and when they were armed and mounted they rode to the outer bailey where there was room enough for the destriers to find their stride. Both enjoyed themselves.

Simon recognized that Alphonse's ability was based on skill, not on an exaggerated reputation, because he was not able even once to make his lance catch on Alphonse's shield. His best efforts were slatted off like those of a novice. Simultaneously he swelled with pride because he was not overset even once. Alphonse was particularly pleased with the delicacy of touch he was able to manage, which never allowed Simon to land a telling blow on him and concealed the fact that he was holding back much of his own power. Thus he salved the young man's pride while saving him from overconfidence.

From the thanks he received and the eager way Simon discussed each blow after they removed their armor and while waiting for dinner, Alphonse was certain that Simon sincerely loved martial exercise. It was equally clear that Simon preferred drinking and talking of fighting and hunting with a guest to other duties—not that Alphonse could detect that he had many. Once before and once after dinner a clerk approached Simon with a question and was waved away. Neither time did the clerk seem surprised or dismayed; Alphonse assumed either that the matter was truly minor or that Simon's behavior was not out of the ordinary and the clerk was accustomed to dealing with problems himself. The third time the clerk came was late in the afternoon when Alphonse's fount of small talk was running dry; he thanked God silently when the clerk insisted Simon accompany him and after a petulant protest Simon did so.

Alphonse thought nothing of it; he was too glad to be rid of his young host for a while. Alone, he continued to stroll about in the well-kept garden, thinking idly how strange it was that he should be so soon bored by conversation with a man, many of whose interests he shared, while he had never been bored by Barbe in all the weeks they had done nothing much in Tonbridge. That led him to wonder how soon he could ask Simon again when Sir William would come back . . . or perhaps he should just say he wanted to go back to Warwick and wait there. But since he could not admit that Barbe was there, what excuse could he give for wanting to sleep at Warwick? He chuckled. Simon would scarcely believe he wanted to go to bed with Sir John.

Simon returned before he had thought of any reason and after that Alphonse had enough to do to hide his boredom and irritation as young Montfort went over the same subjects. Still, as he lay on his cot that night wondering how long he would have to endure, he realized he might have been hearing false notes. That aimless and repetitive conversation might indicate a wandering mind rather than silly vanity. Alphonse began to suspect that Simon was worried about something—and not anything directly to do with him—although he might be affected indirectly. Had news arrived of the failure of the final effort to negotiate peace?

If so, he might need to escape from Kenilworth. Alphonse sighed softly. That would not be easy. The walls of both inner and outer bailey were high and well guarded. There could be no question of climbing them, in armor or out of it. In any case he had no intention of leaving his fine armor or Dadais behind. That eliminated stealth. But force was equally useless. The keep was well manned, and for two men to fight their way out was impossible. Worse yet, Kenilworth was virtually an island; the outer walls were surrounded by water on three sides. The gatehouse closed one exit, and the other was over a long causeway. A shout at one end would close the other.

Deception was his only hope. Alphonse was almost certain that

Simon had given no orders yet that he was to be restrained. If Simon were absent or incapable, Alphonse thought, he could simply ride away. Simon would not leave without either telling him to go or making sure he could not go, whichever best suited his purposes. But incapable . . . that might be arranged. Alphonse smiled into the dark, then frowned. He did not wish to do the young man any real harm, so the timing would have to be very neat. Dadais was part of his scheme and would be with him, but Chacier . . . No, there would be no time to go back for him, so Chacier must leave first.

God smiles on the just, Alphonse thought the next morning when Simon told him that his huntsmen had been waiting at dawn with news of a fine boar. He let his eyes light and a smile of pure delight give emphasis to his hope that Simon would let him join the hunt. He enjoyed every minute of the chase too, taking a particular pleasure in getting totally filthy and arranging for every twig and thorn to catch his garments. And when the boar tore and bled all over the clothes Simon had lent him, Alphonse felt a definite impulse to kiss the bristly and ugly snout of his kill.

''Enough is enough,'' he said to Simon when they returned to the keep and he chose new clothes so he could strip off what was now nearly rags. ''You are generous to a fault, but I think I must send Chacier back to Warwick to bring my clothing here. If you intend to let me help you chase that stag we saw in the forest, I think it time to make rags of my own tunics.''

Simon laughed and agreed. He seemed to have forgotten why Alphonse had come to Kenilworth, but Alphonse suspected that was only a convenient pose and wondered whether the young man would find it suspicious if he did not mention Sir William. Still, hunting was a passion nearly beyond reason for many, so he talked eagerly about the stag in the forest and when they could hope to ride in chase.

Laughing again, Simon started to say ''Tomorrow,'' but some idea occurred to him and he shook his head and said, ''No, not tomorrow. I must be here in Kenilworth all day tomorrow. But the day after tomorrow we can hunt, and the day after that also.''

''I love to hunt,'' Alphonse said.

The words were perfectly truthful but committed Alphonse to nothing. Either Simon did not understand that or he did not care because he excused himself to attend to a few ''little matters'' when he had changed out of his hunting clothes. Under his breath, Alphonse blessed him and went out through the gate of the inner bailey with Chacier, giving him grateful messages for

Sir John until he was sure they would not be overheard. Then he told his servant not to return to Kenilworth.

"If a message comes asking why you have not returned, make any reasonable excuse, but do not come yourself. If you must, send some of my clothing here with one of Warwick's servants. I do not think it will be necessary. I believe I will be in Warwick myself some time tomorrow. If I have not come by the day after, let Warwick send a servant with a message to me asking when I will meet Gloucester. My answer will be that I will meet Lord Gilbert in Tonbridge as arranged. If the words are different, you will know I am in trouble."

"Trouble?" Chacier echoed, clearly startled. "But there is no woman—"

Alphonse laughed. "There are other kinds of trouble."

"For you?" Then Chacier shrugged. "This is a crazy country."

After Chacier was gone, Alphonse walked back toward the hall, but the servant's words troubled him. Was there truly any ground for his suspicion that Simon might keep him by force if he could not hold him by temptation? He looked at the open door and turned away, heading back toward the gateway that led out of the inner bailey. He was simply not in a temper to listen to Simon's talk of idle sports if the "little matters" were settled.

By necessity Alphonse crossed from the living quarters toward the great keep itself. The guards at the entrance to the forebuilding tensed, but Alphonse hardly glanced at them. There was little slackness anywhere in Kenilworth at all, but the men who watched the keep were always sharply alert. Alphonse was very certain that Richard of Cornwall and any other important prisoners were there, but he had no interest in them and walked by.

In contrast, the guard on the gate to the outer bailey only smiled at him when he passed through, and he recalled that he had just before gone out with Chacier. So was all his scheming and planning unnecessary? Should he simply ask Simon outright whether he would be permitted to see Sir William soon, and, if not, say he wished to leave? Why did he ever think for a moment that Simon wished to hold him? Only because Barbe did not want him to stay in Kenilworth?

Although it was almost dusk and drizzling slightly, Alphonse turned into the garden. He felt an urgent need to be where Simon's constant chatter could not interrupt him. What ailed him, that Barbe's unease distorted his thinking? To love was not to become a mindless slave with no thought or will of one's own. He walked slowly beside the espaliered trees that grew against the east wall, recalling to mind what she had said, how she had said it. A last leaf pulled from a branch by a small gust of wind blew against his face and touched his lips before it fell, a damp, chill kiss.

No. There was nothing damp or chill in the way Barbe had wished him Godspeed. In fact, he had wondered whether she was trying to drain him out so thoroughly that he would be incapable of coupling again before returning to her. He had *not* been uneasy when he first came to Kenilworth, and his present doubts, he was suddenly sure, had nothing to do with Barbe. Then the thought that had driven him into the garden returned—he had wished to avoid Simon's constant chatter. Simon talked and Simon laughed, but it was from Simon that the unease came. Something . . . Alphonse could not say what, but he had spent nearly his whole life judging the fine shades of meaning in the tones and glances of subtle men, and something about Simon hinted at hidden purposes.

Feeling much better, Alphonse turned and walked back toward the garden gate far more briskly than he had walked away. He was sorry that if his escape was successful he would not be able to see Sir William, but he had much he could tell Alys that would soothe her. Her heart would be lightened by the news that her father was out riding around the country rather than being chained in a dungeon, that Lady Elizabeth and Fenice were safe and comfortable, and that Aubery was free.

As Alphonse lingered by the gate, still reluctant to swallow another undiluted dose of Simon, he saw a party of seven men enter from the causeway. Six of the men were armed; the one without armor did not hold his mount's reins. Alphonse could not make out the faces, but the chance was too good a one to neglect, so he set out across the bailey toward the stable. He reached the door just before the party arrived and began to dismount. As anyone would, Alphonse glanced over his shoulder, spun on his heel, and called out, "Sir William!"

The unarmed man now dismounted, pushed back his hood and looked around. "Alphonse!" he exclaimed. "Of all men! What do you here?"

"I came to England to marry the earl of Norfolk's daughter, but once in the country, I asked and was given permission by the earl of Gloucester to pay you a visit."

The captain of the little troop had thrust his rein into a groom's hand and started toward them, but hearing the illustrious names—both of his master's party—he hesitated. That gave him time to take the measure of Alphonse's easy, smiling manner and see that Alphonse was unarmed. He decided there was no reason to offend this gentleman just as Alphonse smiled at him.

"I know you must wish to hand over your charge, and I do

not wish to delay your relief,'' he said, nodding to the man. ''The guards and grooms know I am a guest here. May I walk to the inner bailey with Sir William?''

''Why not?'' the captain said.

Having smiled his thanks, Alphonse turned his eyes to Sir William. ''I visited the Abbey of Hurley on my way here,'' he said in a bland, indifferent voice, ''and saw Lady Elizabeth and Lady Fenice.'' Sir William's eyes flicked to him and then away. He knew it was impossible for his wife and daughter-by-marriage to be in Hurley Abbey. ''They were in the highest spirits and made my wife very welcome while I went hunting for a few days,'' Alphonse added.

''Fenice is happy?'' Sir William asked, trying to sound indifferent also, but unable to hide a slight tremor in his voice.

''Yes, she is,'' Alphonse assured him. ''Why not? None of the children was hurt, and the abbot is taking charge of everything that he can.'' A great light dawned in William's eyes and he drew a deep breath, but before he could speak Alphonse said, ''I am glad to see that you are well. John went to Alys in Aix, and she was frightened when she heard you were Montfort's prisoner. She begged me to visit you and assure you that Raymond will pay your ransom as soon as you send him news of the amount.''

In fact, until Alphonse issued the oblique warning mixed with the news in those two last sentences, Sir William briefly appeared to have cast off ten years. Reminded that he should not display more than moderate relief, certainly not the kind of joy a man would feel on learning that both his sons—by love if not by blood—had escaped the battle unwounded and were still free, he sighed heavily and shook his head.

''There is no need for ransom,'' he said. ''I will not buy my freedom while Cornwall is still prisoner, and when Richard is freed he will take me with him. You must tell Alys that I am well, very well, and we are very kindly treated here. Tell Alys not to worry.'' He smiled suddenly. ''If boredom does not kill us both, Richard and I will live forever.''

As they talked, they had been walking, surrounded by the armed guardsmen, and had come through the gate of the inner bailey to the door of the forebuilding. Sir William looked at the doorway and sighed again, then shrugged, lifted his hand in farewell, and walked inside briskly, both duty and affection drawing him with little regret back to confinement.

Alphonse turned away without hesitation too. He liked Sir William and was sorry he was bored, but that was scarcely a fate that could wring his heart or inspire him to hopeless heroics. What he felt was a strong lift of spirits. He had fulfilled all his obligations and was free to return home and forget the miseries of this unhappy land. Indifferent now to a few hours more of Simon's talk, whether it covered a plot or mere silliness, Alphonse crossed the bailey and entered the hall.

"So there you are!" Simon's voice rang across the space between the door and the dais with so much relief that all Alphonse's suspicions returned in a rush.

By the time he had walked across and stepped up on the dais to join his host, his expression was empty and his voice mild and lazy. "I could not decide whether to have Chacier pack everything or leave some with Sir John, so I walked down to the stable with him talking about it. If the earl of Gloucester should come to Warwick, which he said he might if he traveled west, I would have to return there and it would be silly to pack and repack the clothes. And since I was in the stable I looked over Dadais's legs. I thought I felt him favor his right fore on the way home from the hunt, but there was no sign of any hurt—"

"Gloucester is coming to Warwick?" Simon asked.

A man interested first in sport and war would have asked anxiously about the horse. Even a man interested in politics should not have been concerned to hear that his father's most powerful supporter might visit his longtime friend and vassal, who happened to be a neighbor. Simon had fallen into the trap Alphonse had laid, so it was possible that Simon's sharp question meant he did not want Gloucester to inquire about Alphonse who had gone into Kenilworth and not come out. But why? In the name of all that was holy, why should Simon want to detain him? Seating himself on a bench, Alphonse shrugged indifference to Simon's question.

"Only perhaps and if and if." He smiled. "But not until the result of the embassy sent to France is known, and there is no news of that yet, is there?"

"Yes, and it is all bad," Simon replied promptly and angrily.

Although he did not elaborate, Alphonse could tell that he had not intended to hide the news and had failed to talk about it only because it was an unpleasant subject to him. Self-indulgent as he was, Simon simply put out of his mind any distasteful news, never thinking that it might have importance to someone else.

"I am sorry to hear it," Alphonse said, sighing pensively and looking away across the hall but in a way that allowed him to catch Simon's face at the far edge of his vision. "As Louis's man, I suppose I must think of ending my stay in England very soon—so it is just as well that I chanced to meet Sir William at the stable and walked with him back to the keep—"

When Alphonse said he had met Sir William, a flash of rage

drew back Simon's lips; a brief struggle with himself produced a grimace that was supposed to be a smile. "But that is scarcely a visit!" Simon exclaimed.

Alphonse turned his head to look at Simon fully. "I told him that my brother Raymond would pay his ransom, saw that he looked well, and he assured me himself that he was well treated." He smiled. "There is nothing more I have to say to him or he to me. We are not plotting any change in government, you know."

Not even a blink disturbed Simon's frozen face or the set smile behind which his teeth were clenched when Alphonse made his jest about political plotting. So that finally eliminated the idea that Simon had a political reason for wishing to keep him from meeting Sir William—not that the idea had ever been very likely. Yet it was clear Simon had intended to conceal the fact that Sir William had come back so that Alphonse would stay at Kenilworth. That meant either that Leicester had ordered his son to detain him or that Simon had some private reason for wishing to do so. There was no evidence that Simon would try to keep him by force if he simply said he wanted to leave, but Alphonse had lost all patience and decided Simon deserved what would happen to him.

"The ransom," Simon said with such open desperation that Alphonse had to make an effort not to laugh at the young man's inability to conceal his thoughts. "I am not empowered to talk about that. Will you not wait until I can write to my father and ask if a figure can be set?"

Alphonse smiled slowly. "I am in no special hurry to leave England—so long as I can have your word that I will not be made prisoner for being a foreigner in time of war."

"Good God, no!" Simon exclaimed. "We are not at war any longer, even within the realm, and certainly England is not at war with France."

Alphonse was not sure whether Simon had deliberately avoided saying "You have my word" or thought what he had said amounted to the same thing. He was pleased by the omission, which cleared even the smallest shadow from his conscience. Smiling again, he said, "I am pleased. There is that stag hunt you promised me, and since you say you must stay in Kenilworth all day tomorrow, perhaps we can have another passage or two at arms."

"With all my heart."

The look of strain disappeared completely from Simon's face and then he frowned suddenly and said, "Did I not hear you say before that you detected a halt in your destrier's gait? Are you sure he suffered no hurt?"

"I do not think so," Alphonse replied, allowing a faint note of uncertainty to enter his voice, "but I would be glad if you would look at his leg yourself in the morning before we joust. That is another reason I wish to run a few courses. If there is some hidden hurt, the shock of a meeting will show it. Then I will have to ask you to lend me a horse for the stag hunt."

"Any mount you like."

Simon gestured widely and began to discuss the merits of the various horses in the stable. Alphonse asked the proper questions to show his interest. Little by little the young man relaxed enough to let his conversation drift away from the safe topics of jousting and hunt. No longer fearful of mentioning his prisoners' names lest that increase Alphonse's consciousness of the time passing in which he had not been allowed to see Sir William, Simon was able to complain about the heavy responsibility thrust on him, which kept him penned in Kenilworth, and in the next sentence remark bitterly that when his mother was at the keep she ruled it and him, except in matters of war.

Alphonse made soothing answers without offering advice or comment. The conversation did not improve his opinion of Simon, but it held more interest for him than the talk of the previous days, and the time until the evening meal and the hour when it was safe to go to bed came swiftly.

Morning saw Simon earnestly examining Dadais's right fore and calling the farrier to do the same. Neither could find any fault—which scarcely surprised Alphonse, who had magnified a weary stumble on the road home after the hunt into a hint of injury—and each agreed that an experimental run in the lists should be the next test. Alphonse and Simon gathered up two jousting lances each and rode to the narrowest area in the outer bailey behind the wall that protected the domestic buildings of the inner yard. There, as he had done the first time they jousted, Simon ordered the few men working around the storage sheds to leave so they would not be tempted to run too close in excitement and startle the horses or be trampled if the horses got out of hand. Then he sat and watched Dadais as Alphonse rode to the other end of the open stretch of ground.

"I can see nothing," he called to Alphonse. Then he asked a question of the farrier, who was also watching, and added, "Nor does the horse leech see anything."

"He feels steady to me," Alphonse called back.

"Then let us run."

Alphonse turned Dadais, signaled that he was ready, and when Simon dropped his lance into position, he touched Dadais with his heels and grunted, "Ha!" more breath than voice. The great horse ran straight ahead, indifferent to Simon's mount thundering toward him. The sun, just risen above the wall, sparkled on Simon's helmet. Alphonse bent his head as if to avoid the glare, and his lance touched above center and to the left of the boss of Simon's shield, held for a bare instant, and slipped off over Simon's shoulder. Simon hit a truer blow, below and on the inner side of the shield. He let out a yell of triumph and thrust hard forward. Feeling his lance catch, he yelled again, but in the next moment the tip came free, Alphonse's shield twisted and lifted, and the two men were past each other.

"Very good!" Alphonse called. "You nearly had me that time. I should have been thinking about you instead of Dadais's right fore." He stopped beside the farrier and said, "He seemed sound at the start of the run, before I had to give my mind to the jousting. Did you see any sign of weakness?"

"None, my lord," the farrier answered in bad French, "but it was a short run. Will you go again?"

Alphonse waved at Simon and then rode toward him. "Did you hear? Your man says he saw nothing but that the run was short. Will you run again?"

"Of course."

"I will take the same position so the farrier can see Dadais clearly."

Alphonse started forward on the words and Simon loosened his rein, then pulled up again as his horse started to move, calling, "Sieur Alphonse." Alphonse turned toward him and he hurried to say, honestly if a bit reluctantly, "I am sure you missed your mark because the sun was in your eyes. It is only right that we change places. The farrier can walk to the other end of the run."

Alphonse laughed heartily. "The sun did blind me a little, but this is only practice and it is more important that the farrier see Dadais's gait clearly. I hope I can count on you not to spread about the news that I missed you and am growing old and weak."

Simon laughed also and rode back to where he had started before. He did not think Alphonse was old and weak, but his confidence had been elevated. He saw Alphonse take a new lance from where it leaned against a shed; that meant nothing, it was the habit of a professional jouster. He shouted his readiness, heard Alphonse's answering call, and spurred his mount, all his attention on the spot on the shield he wanted to hit. He did not notice that Alphonse had struck Dadais far harder with his spurs this time, or that he cried out, "Hai! Hai!" in a higher, more urgent voice.

The stallion leapt into a full gallop, curling his lip so his strong yellow teeth showed in threat and screaming a challenge to the oncoming horse. Simon might have felt the slight check in the stride of his mount, but at that moment a blow of enormous power hit his shield, driving the inner edge into his chest so that his breath was knocked out of him. Simultaneously the top edge of the shield lifted and struck him on the visor, pushing the helmet against his face so hard that his senses swam. The dizziness, pain, and sense of suffocation paralyzed him. In fact, he could not have moved his shield to unseat Alphonse's lance; however, he did not even realize that the dulled point had slid across his shield and lodged against his chest until he felt himself rising and tipping out of his saddle. He cried out, but his voice was the echo of Alphonse's shout. His last thought was that his guest was as shocked and surprised as he.

That last thought was totally mistaken. Alphonse's cry was one of pure triumph. He had not been certain until the very last second, until he saw the placement of the dulled tip of his lance, that he would not pull back and seem to miss completely. But the position was just right and every weakness he had noted in Simon's jousting form—his head too high over his shield, the inner edge tipped too much, his body too far forward in the saddle—tempted him. He struck, throwing himself forward into the blow, prodding Dadais again to get a last desperate effort from him, angling his lance so it would lift against the boss of Simon's shield, and finally shouting aloud in triumph as he saw Simon rise up out of the saddle, lose his stirrups, and crash to the ground.

"My God," Alphonse called to the farrier as soon as he could check and turn Dadais, "is he badly hurt?"

The man had already reached his master, knelt beside him, and lifted the visor. "I see no blood," he cried.

"Stay with him," Alphonse shouted, riding past. "I must catch the horse. I will send help."

"No," the farrier protested instinctively, but then he shrugged. Any man with the sense of a pea would know that the lord's young destrier—unnerved by a threat of attack from a more dominant animal, a severe physical shock, and then the loss of the guiding hand on his rein—would run harder when he sensed pursuit by the older stallion. If the lord had let him alone, the destrier would soon have stopped. But these lords had not the sense of peas, though they thought themselves all wise. Sure enough, the young horse had bolted, rounded the wall of the inner bailey toward the garden, and disappeared from sight. The farrier shook his head and began to unfasten his lord's helmet straps.

As soon as the farrier could no longer see him, Alphonse

checked Dadais's pace. The young stallion also slowed, and in another few minutes Alphonse had him trapped in the angle of the outer and the garden walls. A gesture brought closer two menservants who had been watching.

"Does either of you understand French?" he asked. The older man nodded. "Your master has had a fall," he said. "One of you must run to the hall or the keep and tell the clerk. The other should go around to the back and do whatever the farrier orders. Before you go, just hand me the rein and I will take Sir Simon's horse to the stable."

That much was easy; both men obeyed without question. Now came the last bit, though, which might be the end of the venture.

Chapter 19

After dinner on the day that Alphonse sent Chacier back to Warwick, Sir John Giffard had formal news from the earl of Gloucester that all chance of Louis of France or the Church mediating a peace between Leicester and the king had collapsed. On October 21 the papal legate had issued orders of excommunication against Simon de Montfort, earl of Leicester; Gilbert de Clare, earl of Gloucester and Hertford; Roger Bigod, earl of Norfolk; and all their adherents for contumely in their support of the Provisions of Oxford, which the pope had declared null and void.

Barbara immediately raised the question with Sir John about whether, because of Alphonse's association with the French court, he should try to leave England as quickly and quietly as possible, and then, when Giffard said with surprise that Gloucester's letter contained no such implication, she asked whether the earl could have forgotten about her husband. Sir John assured her it was most unlikely.

''Gloucester is not careless or indifferent about those he has come to like,'' Giffard protested.

''Not in general, of course,'' Barbara said. ''But under these circumstances, perhaps . . .''

Then she shook her head. Alphonse had been gone only three days, but she wanted him back and was trying to find an excuse in Gloucester's message. Unfortunately, it held no excuse. As he should, Gloucester was sending news to his allies and supporters, but his letter held no warnings or sense of urgency. Leicester might have been angry and disappointed over Louis's refusal to mediate a peace, but clearly Gloucester did not feel the same. Nor did Gloucester appear to be much disturbed by his excommunication. Barbara thought he had the inability of most young people really to believe in death and damnation. Not that he lacked faith. He simply felt there was more than time enough before *he* died to change the pope's mind and be received back into the bosom of the Church.

Sir John Giffard and Barbara were still discussing whether it would be wise to send the news to Alphonse when Chacier rode in. He was circumspect in what he said to Barbara, having gauged her reaction from the way her face whitened when she saw him. Chacier had long experience with the screaming terrors and screaming rages of women suspicious of his master's doings, and he knew no explanation he gave would content her. Thus he said only that his master had sent him for clothes. Sieur Alphonse had not yet seen Sir William and intended to stay in Kenilworth one or two more days.

Later, when it was full dark, Chacier caught Sir John on his way to the outer gate where a large armed party—twenty men and a leader claiming to be Sir Guy de Montfort—were demanding entrance. In a few words Chacier told Sir John Alphonse's full message, explaining that he had not given it earlier because he did not wish to frighten Lady Barbe.

Sir John uttered a soft, angry oath and waved Chacier away. There was no reason under the sun why young Simon should want to keep Alphonse in Kenilworth. Yet earlier, the moment Chacier left them, Barbara had told him the servant had not been sent to fetch clothing but to be safely out of the way of some danger. Sir John had been startled by her expression of controlled terror and had soothed her as best he could, not believing a word she said and assuming her a prey to female idiocy. Now Chacier had virtually confirmed what she had said. Surely, then, he must take seriously that, when one of his gate guards had told him that the third de Montfort son was demanding shelter, she had begged him not to tell Guy she was in Warwick.

Thinking her crazed as a moonstruck witling, Sir John had agreed to keep her presence a secret, although at the time he had not believed Guy de Montfort was at his gate. Disseisined Royalists had tried before to win Warwick back, and he had thought the demand for lodging an attempt to get into the keep. He had armed, since he did not know whether the troop would be gone or whether he would need to summon more men to defend the walls. The implications of Alphonse's message, however, caused him to revise his opinion. Probably Guy *was* at the gate. Somehow Alphonse had become a bone of contention between Gloucester and Leicester, and Sir John found himself caught holding that bone.

He made some swift decisions, then leaned out over the wall to shout across the moat that he would be glad to welcome Sir Guy, but because there was no way to identify him in the dark, he must refuse to accommodate the troop that accompanied him. When they rode back into the town, he would let down the drawbridge. He prayed Guy would ride away in a fury, but he had little hope that his prayer would be answered. What he expected was angry and furious protests or possibly threats, but none came. Although the half-moon was partly obscured by moving clouds, it gave enough light to show the troop riding away, leaving two mounted men and two baggage animals waiting. By the time the troop had withdrawn far enough to make a charge at the drawbridge impossible, Sir John had the walls lined with archers and a party standing behind the portcullis, which was not raised.

All the preparations were unnecessary. In the light of many torches it was clear that only Guy and an unarmed man, clearly a servant leading pack animals with loads that could not be men, waited on the drawbridge for the portcullis to rise. Guy made very merry over Sir John's "caution"—the way he said the word implying cowardice—while he dismounted and all the while it took to walk to the hall. Long before Guy allowed himself to be diverted from that subject to answer Sir John's pointed and repeated question about why he was crying out at the gates of Warwick rather than remaining in the comfort of Kenilworth, Sir John had decided he would tell Guy nothing at all.

When Guy finally felt he had drained dry the jest of Sir John's fear of two men and some bundles of clothing, he finally said, "Oh, I have not come from Kenilworth. I was at Hereford on some business for my father. It grew dark and I decided not to ride farther."

The reply was reasonable enough, but when they entered the hall and Sir John noticed how eagerly Guy looked around, he felt a grim satisfaction that there was no sign of any noble presence but his own. His chair with its footstool stood alone by the central hearth. On a table by the chair lay the hunting knife and the oil and sharpening stone he had been using before he had hurriedly pulled his mail over his tunic and gone out to see who was at his gate. The bench, on which Lady Barbara had been sitting with her basket of embroidery silks beside her, was gone.

"I thought you had a guest," Guy said.

"You mean Sieur Alphonse?" Sir John responded. "He only stayed a few days. Then he went on to Kenilworth to see his brother's father-by-marriage, who is a prisoner there. I should imagine he is gone by now. That was . . . let me think . . . three days past? Four? In any case, if you are looking for Sieur Alphonse, I cannot help you. He did not say where he would go from Kenilworth, but I imagine he rode for the nearest port when he heard the news that King Louis had refused to act as mediator—"

"I thought it was his wife who wished to see Sir William," Guy interrupted.

"His wife? He never mentioned her." Sir John looked straight into Guy's eyes. What he said was perfectly true. Alphonse had never mentioned Barbara because she was right there and could speak for herself. "And Gloucester's letter to me," he went on, "clearly said that I should do what I could to forward Sieur Alphonse's purpose to see Sir William."

"Gloucester's letter," Guy repeated. "So Sieur Alphonse came direct from Tonbridge?"

"He certainly came from Tonbridge," Sir John replied. "I cannot swear that he came direct from there. I never asked. Why should I?"

"He has Royalist sympathies," Guy snarled. "Did you not know he was Prince Edward's friend?"

"He is your brother Henry's friend too," Sir John said placidly. "We talked mostly of Gloucester and Henry and jousting while he was here."

"Gloucester is a—"

"Gloucester is my overlord and my friend." Sir John's voice was hard and cold.

Guy's lips curled into a sneer, but he made no direct reply, saying only that he had ridden a long way and was tired. Sir John agreed at once that he had been just about to go to bed himself when the message from the gate arrived. Then, with no expression at all on his face but a good deal of satisfaction in his heart, Sir John inquired politely whether Guy would prefer to have his sleeping pallet set by the hearth or near the wall. He did not laugh at the shocked expression on the young man's face; plainly Guy had expected him to yield his own bed to his guest, but Sir John was not about to give precedence to a third son who was ten years younger than he.

The next morning it was clear that Guy had been chewing the cud of his anger half the night. He slept late and then, instead of leaving at once, demanded to see how the work of dismantling the keep was progressing, claiming he had been ordered to report on it to his father. Sir John was tempted to tell him to get out before he lost his temper, but recalling how plainly he had spoken to Leicester of his opposition to the destruction, he felt a refusal would be unwise. Guy would certainly tell his father that he had not been permitted to see whether the keep was being torn down.

Since Sir John was not eager to have Guy wandering loose around Warwick, he took the young man to the site personally. There he got his revenge by keeping Guy much longer than he really wished to stay, explaining to him, almost stone by stone, how the keep was being pulled down, and laughing inside when he saw that Guy did not understand that the work was being done carefully so the great wall, in which the keep was embedded, would not be damaged.

Finally, no longer attempting to hide his boredom and indifference, Guy interrupted Sir John in the middle of a sentence and insisted he must leave. Irritably, when Sir John asked with seeming eagerness what he would say in his report to Leicester, he stated that he could see that the keep was being demolished as quickly as possible. As a final pinprick, Sir John summoned the master mason and begged Guy to repeat his compliments to that man, as it was mostly his work that was being praised. For a moment Sir John was sorry he had done it; he thought Guy might fall into a fit with rage. But the young man managed to choke out the words. He took no further chances of being outmaneuvered after that, brusquely refusing Sir John's polite invitation to dinner and leaving as quickly as his servant could be summoned and his horse saddled.

Returning thoughtfully from the gate, to which he had insisted on accompanying his guest, Sir John came face to face with Alphonse. His eyes goggled.

"Chacier tells me that he cannot find my wife or her maid," Alphonse said.

"She was hiding from that cow's leaving," Sir John remarked without the slightest hesitation, gesturing toward the gate out of which Guy had ridden. "Come to the hall and I will summon her down. I am glad to see you"—his lips twisted—"I think. It depends on what terms you left Kenilworth."

Alphonse removed his hand from his sword hilt, rather grateful that Sir John had not seemed to notice the threat. He laughed and shrugged. "I hope you will believe me when I say I do not know on what terms I left Kenilworth, but if you do not mind, I will tell the story of my departure only once. May I find Barbe myself and assure her all is well? She is very clever and would have understood that I might be in trouble when she saw Chacier alone."

Sir John agreed with enthusiasm that Alphonse should announce himself, having almost as little taste for joyful vapors as for tearful ones. But announcement was not necessary. As they approached the hall, Barbara came running out and threw herself into her husband's arms. He clutched her to him and bent his head to kiss her temple, her nose, her lips. Sir John watched with considerable interest, then walked on into the hall aware of a mild uneasiness. He pushed it out of his mind before he was forced to consider whether he felt uncomfortable about so open an expression of love or regretted that he was not likely ever to be so greeted by his own wife.

Only a few minutes later they followed him in, and enough of his discomfort lingered to make him question why, after begging him to hide her, Barbara had rushed out like that. "How did you know Guy had not decided to return?"

She laughed aloud. "Because Clotilde and I have been on the watch from one or another window of the upper floor every moment since Guy left the hall. I saw you walk with him to the gate, and at first I did think he was coming back with you. I was fit to get a crossbow and shoot through the window, but then I recognized Alphonse." She laughed again. "How could you think I could mistake him for any other man?"

Her voice faltered on the last few words and her eyes flicked from Sir John to her husband. For a moment she wished she had shot him. There was a confident pleasure in the soft curve of Alphonse's lips that filled her with equal joy and trepidation. She had exposed too much—and that had made him happy, which of course made her happy—and might cost her all her joy. So she raised her brows and added, "I have known Alphonse for over ten years. His size and walk and the fact that his hair is black and Guy's much paler could not be mistaken." Then she turned her eyes to her husband. "Far more important is why you sent Chacier out of Kenilworth. Were you mistaken in thinking you were in danger there?"

"I was never in danger," Alphonse replied, smiling. "I thought, in fact, that Simon was too enamored of my company." He then described his treatment in Kenilworth, ending with his accidental encounter with Sir William and Simon's reaction when told of it. "So," he concluded, "I dropped Simon on his head in a practice joust and came quietly away before he recovered his senses."

"I hope you did not kill him," Sir John said uneasily.

"Oh no, he was only stunned. The farrier had examined him before I left the course. He was breathing well and no blood had come from his nose or ears. Nor did I hear any outcry when I brought his horse to the stable, so I think he was probably showing signs of life already. I am sure I did Simon no lasting harm. The question is why should he want to hold me? It is ridiculous! I am nothing and no one in England."

"You are Prince Edward's friend," Sir John suggested.

"But not so close a friend that Edward could be forced into any action by a threat to me. There are others, much closer to the prince, who are prisoners already and could be used in that manner."

They went on discussing the possibility that Simon's behavior was by Leicester's order and the political implications of the idea, but nothing they said made sense to Barbara—and not much to them either. Guy's sudden appearance and her knowledge of his stubborn willfulness gave her an entirely different notion. Simon and Guy were very close; each was, paradoxically, the other's bitterest rival and greatest support. Had Simon intended to keep Alphonse prisoner until Guy could lay hands on her?

The notion was so wild that Barbara dared not mention it. Both men would think her puffed up with conceit and would laugh at her. But the more she listened to what they said, the more convinced she became that Leicester was not involved in this business and knew nothing about it. Either it was all a mistake—Simon was totally innocent and only wanted the company of a man he admired, just as Gloucester had—or two thoughtless and spoiled young men were engaged in a private game. However, their private game was likely to turn nasty.

"I do not think it is safe for Sir John for us to remain here," Barbara put in at the first pause. It was a polite way of telling Alphonse of her fear of being trapped in Warwick and handed over to Simon or Guy as the lesser of the evils facing Sir John.

"I agree," Alphonse said.

"But where will you go?" Sir John asked, trying to hide his relief at being rid of the bone of contention.

"Home, to France," Alphonse said at once. "We have Gloucester's letter of permission to travel and to leave the country—"

"Our best route would be to ride south," Barbara suggested eagerly, cutting Alphonse off. "We could get a ship at Portsmouth. And it might be wise, Sir John, for you to send messages to my father and to Gloucester. I would not want either of them to worry about us."

She saw Alphonse's dark eyes flick in her direction, but he was looking directly at Sir John when he said, "That makes sense to me, and I think we should pack and leave at once. It occurs to me that even if Simon is still too shaken to act against me, the moment Guy arrives and hears what befell his brother he may try to have me brought back to Kenilworth."

"Yes, and that might be true even if there never was any intention of holding you there." Sir John seized gratefully on the idea, pleased that his knowledge fitted it so well. "Simon might not hold a grudge over a hard fall, but Guy is a spiteful devil and might inflame his brother's pride and convince him he was tricked and ill used. I do not wish to be inhospitable, but I think you will be safer away from here."

No more time was wasted in politeness after that, and little spent on packing, clothing and supplies being bundled any which way into baskets and pouches. Sir John did not suggest that Barbara and Alphonse stay for dinner, even though the tables were being set as they passed out of the gate. He felt kindly enough toward them, however, to make sure that two substantial hampers of food, more than enough for them and the servants and the two men-at-arms, traveled with them. However, they did not pause to take advantage of the bounty for some time, riding fast along the road by the river until they could see Stratford in the distance.

At that point Alphonse signaled for a stop, came up beside Barbara, and said, "I hope you have good reason to trust Sir John."

"Why do you say that?" Barbara asked.

"Why?" Alphonse repeated. "You told him our plans—"

"Oh no I did not," Barbara said indignantly. "I just said we would go to Portsmouth to stop you from asking his advice." She smiled and put out a placatory hand. "After all, Alphonse, you cannot know the country and surely Sir John does—but I know it well too because my father often traveled to Castle Strigul through these parts and because the king and queen also traveled this way to Gloucester."

"I see." He sighed with exaggerated resignation. "It is sad to know your wife thinks you a lackwit—"

"I do not!" Barbara exclaimed. "I think you far too likely to welcome a pursuit so that you can have an amusing little battle. You would not care—"

Alphonse laughed. "So where do we go?"

"Not to Portsmouth, which is fifty leagues or more overland. Nor do I think it safe to travel toward Norfolk or toward London or on any of the great roads. I think we should follow the river to the city of Gloucester where I am sure we can find a ship. I think a letter of safe passage from the earl of Gloucester might have more influence among the ship captains of Gloucester town too.''

''But from so far west, will not the ship take us to Brittany rather than France?''

Barbara shrugged. ''What if it does? Are you not well known to the count of Brittany? But actually it is more likely that the first ship to leave will be a coastal vessel with cargo for London.''

''How clever you are!'' Alphonse's eyes lit with his smile. ''If few ships sail from Gloucester to France, we are not likely to be expected to go there. Gloucester it is, then.'' He began to signal Barbara ahead with Bevis and Clotilde so he could again take up rearguard position with Chacier and Lewin, but then said, ''Wait. Let us muddy the trail a little more.'' He beckoned Chacier and the man closer so they could hear and went on, ''If anyone reports a party leaving Warwick, it will be a party of six. When we were seen on the road we were still a party of six. But if you go ahead with Bevis and Chacier, Barbe, taking two of the packhorses, and I follow with Lewin, Clotilde, and the other packhorse, no party of six will be seen entering Stratford and I hope we will be thought to have left the road earlier to avoid pursuit.''

Barbara elaborated the plan somewhat further by pointing out that if Alphonse struck out west and south from where they were, he would come to the road to Alcester Abbey. Once on it, he could turn back and enter Stratford from the east. He should then head south along the river. She and her party would enter Stratford from the north and take the road west toward the abbey, turn south across the meadows when it was safe to do so, and meet Alphonse on the road.

Although it wasted nearly an hour in traveling time, the plan worked faultlessly. The two parties met a few hundred yards past a roadside shrine on a deserted stretch of road where Barbara's party had waited for Alphonse's to come slowly south. No one had shown the least interest in them. By now all were ravenous, so they stopped in the first likely spot, where a large tree had come down beyond the road making a small clearing. So much confidence had been generated, even in Barbara, who was beginning to doubt her own suspicion that Simon had tried to make her available to Guy, that she did not harry her maid to hurry in serving or urge her husband to eat faster. Alphonse, too, was beginning to believe that even if Simon had wished to detain him, his reason was not strong or important enough to merit pursuit. He said that aloud. Barbara did not reply directly but glanced at the sun, which was dipping into a dense bank of clouds in the west, and remarked that they could never reach Gloucester in daylight and before it rained. They would have to find somewhere to stay for the night. However, when they came to Evesham, the sun was still above the clouds.

Dividing again they entered Evesham separately, this time Barbara with Bevis and Clotilde and Alphonse with Chacier and Lewin. Less time was wasted because they took the same roads in and out of the city, Barbara entering first but spending time in the Chepe while Alphonse rode out ahead. Still, only streaks of westering sun cut the clouds and made long shadows when Barbara's party overtook Alphonse's, and the sun was gone, although the clouds showed red and yellow edges, as they approached the short side road that led to Pershore Abbey. Barbara suggested they stay there; Alphonse agreed with enthusiasm. A long evening with Barbe was more important than any pursuit. His appetite had been whetted by four nights of sleeping alone and by the way Barbe had greeted him at Warwick.

"By all means," he said. "I am very willing to give up the hour or so that remains for traveling and go early to bed."

Unfortunately, the slow smile that curved his lips not only sent a flush of warmth over Barbara but reminded her of how she had betrayed herself by running into his arms when he returned to Warwick. She looked away without answering and no more was said until they arrived at the abbey, where Alphonse explained his needs to the elderly porter. Only then did he learn that the abbot was of that strict variety who would not even permit a woman to enter the abbey itself. A guest house within a special walled enclosure was maintained for that accursed sex.

Alphonse first laughed and said that he would stay in the guest house also, but when the porter replied, in a horrified voice, that it was forbidden for a man to enter that place, he cast a puzzled glance at Barbara, and said no, meaning to add he would prefer to camp in the open despite the chance of rain. But Barbara, who was looking in the direction the porter had gestured, agreed to accept that lodging and bade Clotilde choose a cell in the guest house and make it ready.

Fury strangled Alphonse for a moment, and before he found his voice, the porter was telling him that there was no other hostel until Tewkesbury and that, as he could see by the fact that the abbey's gate was closed in daylight, the area was not safe.

"There is much looting and pillaging hereabout because many were put off their lands by the war and have turned to outlawry," he said. "You should not be on the road after dark. And this news that the king of France will not uphold Leicester's peace will put heart into those who oppose the earl. A party from Wigmore Abbey came in today and one of the brothers told me that there is much stirring in Roger de Mortimer's keep."

"I am sure we have nothing to fear from Mortimer," Alphonse said. "We are of no party, only visitors to this land."

"It is going to rain soon, and there is no sense in chancing an attack by outlaws," Barbara said flatly. "I will see you in the morning."

Alphonse was still so angry in the morning that he was grateful to go to mass in a church that completely screened off the section where women were permitted and to break his fast afterward with the monks. He did not see Barbara again until he was mounted and outside the gate of Pershore Abbey, and when he did, he did not speak a word, only gestured her ahead on the road. His rage was a little abated when he saw the ditches by the road still running with water. The rain had been harder than he thought, misled by muting of the sound of the storm by the thick-walled abbey. They would have been soaked and had little pleasure lying on the ground. And the porter had spoken the truth; there was no other shelter. The area was indeed desolate, mostly wooded with only a few ruined farms, blackened beams marking the sites of houses and sheds and testifying to recent violence. Probably the porter was also right about the lonely track being no road to travel after dark. But they could have stayed in Evesham, he thought resentfully. Barbe had not really been afraid of pursuit; she had known they would be kept separate in Pershore Abbey.

Riding along as silently as her husband behind Chacier and Bevis, who were in the lead, Barbara wavered between frustration and amusement. She had been as disappointed as Alphonse when the porter made clear the guesting arrangements. Separation of the sexes in an abbey hospice was common enough, but for married couples, where there was a guest house outside the abbey proper, such strictness was excessive and she had not expected it. Fear of revealing too much disappointment had kept her from admitting any, and self-discipline—because she knew if she allowed any discussion she would agree to ride on in the dark just to satisfy her lust—had made her rush off to the guest house.

Thus, Barbara understood Alphonse's bad temper. At the same time, she was grateful that he was riding rearguard position. She knew she would have to make her peace with him by explaining that she had never stayed before in Pershore and had no idea the abbot was so strict, but she did not want to do it too soon. The eagerness he displayed to lie with her delighted her; it gave her hope that he had not even tumbled a maidservant while he was away from her bed. However, it also made her fear he would propose they go aside and take their pleasure as soon as she soothed his anger. If she agreed, would he not think her too eager? As eager as she really was, she thought, her mobile mouth flattening even more as the corners of her lips turned down. And if she did not agree, he would be even angrier.

When Chacier rode back to tell Alphonse they had come to a main road, the old high road just north of Tewkesbury, Alphonse did not consult with Barbara. He bade Chacier take the main road, saying acidly—and loud enough for Barbara to hear—that on that route they would be in less danger from mud and outlaws. She cocked her head impudently and giggled, which naturally earned her a black look. But when Alphonse gestured her angrily ahead without speaking, she turned onto the wider, stone-paved road without argument. She was not going to raise the subject of pursuit by Guy or Simon; by now she felt embarrassed over her conceited notion that she was the prize to be taken.

As if to hammer that point home, they drew no attention when they passed through Tewkesbury even though they did not separate this time and the town seemed too full of armed men. But Barbara had had a severe fright when they first approached the town. As they turned a sharp corner screened by woods, she suddenly saw a group of men-at-arms off to the left, resting near the wall and watching the road. Since it was too late to hide and running would only invite pursuit, Chacier and Bevis rode on slowly, giving Alphonse and Lewin time to move forward. However, the armed men made no move toward their horses and continued to look north, past the travelers. Barbara held her breath as they rode by. The seeming lack of recognition could have been a trap. It was not. Clearly the men-at-arms were waiting for someone.

Another group was lounging around an alehouse, and Barbara caught a glimpse of a familiar shield against the wall. She did not turn for a better view; if she was not mistaken and the shield belonged to Hamo le Strange, the bearer would do no service for any Montfort, old or young. However, she preferred not to have to make pleasant, civil conversation with one of the rebel Marcher lords. Nonetheless, the troop added to Barbara's sense of security. No partisan of Montfort would pass unchallenged through Tewkesbury, and she was quite at ease as they rode south toward the city of Gloucester, now less than five leagues distant.

The feeling of relief seemed to grip everyone. Bevis almost certainly recognized someone or something in the group at the alehouse. Barbara saw the tension go out of his shoulders as they passed and later heard the word "Cymry"—Welsh—drift back from a comment he made to Chacier. Perhaps Lewin had passed the same information to Alphonse or he had some other reason to relax; a glance behind showed her that he was half asleep in the saddle. Since even her jealous mind could not conceive of a way he could have smuggled a woman into his cot among the monks, Barbara had to assume he had been wakeful out of rage or frustration. She became almost blind and deaf to her surroundings as she dwelt on a variety of pleasurable plans for teasing Alphonse into a good humor without admitting too much.

She was jolted out of her thoughts when they came over a ridge and Chacier cried out with surprise at the sight of a small troop coming toward them from the direction of Gloucester. Chacier and Bevis were not at fault; the rise of ground had hidden the road beyond it for some distance and the heavy rain had wet the earth between the stones of the road so that there was no cloud of dust to warn them. Barbara pulled back on Frivole's rein when Chacier called out, but not with urgency—her mind had set on all danger being past, and instinct, as often wrong as it is right, told her that pursuit would come from behind, not from ahead—so the mare continued on for a few steps until Barbara also topped the rise. For a moment she sat staring at the oncoming group, not seeing anything to alarm her especially and not considering that if she could see them, they could see her even better.

A shout, wordless, but frightening, made her back Frivole, and Alphonse's Dadais pushed past her. In that moment, the man in the front of the troop spurred his horse hard and pulled his shield onto his arm. Barbara gasped, at the flash of silver on red—Montfort colors—and Alphonse, who had thrust his tilting lance into a similar shield only the previous morning, seized Frivole's cheekpiece and thrust the mare's head around.

"Go!" he ordered. "Back to Tewkesbury and take shelter—with the rebels if need be."

"Come with me," she cried. "Do not challenge them. What need is there to fight? Do not be a fool."

"You are the fool!" he snarled. "We are too close to turn our backs on them. If you are out of the way, I can drive them off. Go!"

On the word, he brought the flat of the sword he had drawn down on Frivole's rump. The mare leapt forward, her neck stretching so suddenly that the reins slid through Barbara's fingers and it was impossible for her to check her mount's stride. Instantly, Barbara could hear behind her the desperate pace of another animal shocked into a gallop. Doubtless it was only Clotilde's mule, but the sound, waking the herd animal's instinct to flee when others fled, added to the terror that noise and pain had caused in Frivole. She became unresponsive to control even as Barbara gathered in the slack of the rein.

As her first panic subsided, Barbara realized it was stupid to try to go back and loosened the rein again. She and Clotilde would only be an added danger to the four men, and Montfort's troop had not been large—only six or seven men. What she needed to decide was whether to call on Hamo le Strange—if indeed it was Hamo's shield she had seen at the alehouse—to come to Alphonse's aid or simply wait near the gate until she saw whether Alphonse or Montfort, whichever one it was, came up the road.

Barbara knew Alphonse expected her only to wait; he had been annoyed, not worried, and he knew she would still have time to throw herself on Hamo's mercy if he failed to drive the troop off. But then, Barbara thought with a sob of terror, it would be too late for Alphonse. He might be injured . . . or dead. However, if she begged Hamo's help, Alphonse would be furious, not only out of pride but because she would have generated a bad political situation, giving the rebels "just cause" to attack Leicester's son.

The decision was not left to her. Scarcely a mile back, the road was filled with a large troop of men coming from Tewkesbury. Since they must have seen her and Clotilde at the same time, it was useless to consider avoiding them or pretending nothing had happened. A gentlewoman and her maid did not gallop madly down a road without an escort for no reason.

"Hamo," Barbara called. "Is it Hamo le Strange?"

"Yes," a man shouted, prodding his horse into a trot as Barbara slowed Frivole. "Lady Barbara!" he exclaimed as they came together. "What—"

"We were attacked on the road—"

"Forward!" le Strange bellowed, not waiting for her to finish, gesturing broadly ahead. "Arm and ride!"

The men at the front of the troop spurred their horses into a run, pushing on their helmets and lifting their shields onto their arms. As they approached, Hamo drove Frivole and Clotilde's mule right toward the edge of the road and shouted, "Tybetot! Stay with her!"

Barbara bit her lip with disappointment. She had hoped to be forgotten in the excitement, but she dared waste no time in argument. She held Frivole on a tight rein, turning her broadside to Clotilde's mule, while a group formed around them. Hamo galloped forward among his men. When the last of the troop passed them, she turned Frivole to follow, saying to the young man Hamo had called Tybetot, "My husband is there," and he nodded and backed his horse so she could start down the road again toward Alphonse.

They arrived not five minutes behind the last of Hamo's troop, but the action was over. From the top of the rise, Barbara saw six men and two horses flying away toward Gloucester. Most of Hamo's troop had followed a little way, but the distance between them and Montfort's men was growing, showing that the pursuit was not in earnest. Closest to her, about a third of the way down the rise, Alphonse was talking to Hamo, his sword already sheathed. Two men lay still and bloody by the side of the road, but both were simple men-at-arms. Barbara was not certain whether she was relieved or disappointed. She was so furious with all the Montforts that she would have enjoyed seeing one of them lying there bleeding; however, good sense told her that the last thing she or Alphonse needed was to be involved in the injury of one of Leicester's sons.

"I have no idea," Alphonse was saying blandly to Hamo when she rode up. "Perhaps he did not know who I was. I cannot imagine any reason for Guy de Montfort to attack me. I was in Kenilworth only yesterday; I had permission to visit Sir William of Marlowe who is a prisoner there—he is Richard of Cornwall's man."

"I know Sir William," Hamo le Strange said.

Alphonse nodded. "He is my brother's father-by-marriage. Having no more to do there, I left Kenilworth the next morning and Barbe and I decided to take a ship at Gloucester—"

"I am afraid you will not be able to do that now," Hamo said. "Guy will take you if you go near Gloucester. Also, I am sorry, but I cannot let you go. You must come to Bristol with us."

"Are we your prisoners?" Barbara asked.

"No, of course not," Hamo said, but he looked uneasily at Alphonse. "I am truly sorry, Sir Alphonse, I must ask you to remain with me, but as much for your good as for mine. God knows what Guy will tell the castellan at Gloucester. He might send troops out to scour the countryside. My troop is strong enough to withstand them, but you and your three men—two lightly wounded already—cannot travel safely now. I know you are Prince Edward's friend. On my honor, no ransom will be asked of you."

Alphonse said nothing, and Hamo looked uncomfortable and shrugged. "I must also consider the good of our cause. Older and wiser heads will have to decide on what terms to release Norfolk's daughter."

He glanced at Alphonse's sword and Alphonse smiled. "You might be able to take it from me while I am still alive," he said, "but I doubt it. And if you do not intend to kill Barbe also, you should consider exactly how you will explain my death to the prince and to Richard of Cornwall."

"You will be taken by Montfort if you leave us," Hamo said

desperately, acknowledging that he really could not hold Alphonse if he decided to fight for his freedom.

"I did not say I wished to leave you." Alphonse lifted his brows in simulated surprise. "I certainly prefer your company to Guy de Montfort's, and I will gladly give you my parole . . . until we reach Bristol."

Barbara let out her breath, eased her hold on her rein and relaxed the muscles in her legs. She had been prepared to drive Frivole between Alphonse and Tybetot, who had managed to press in front of Lewin. The sighs from the men-at-arms did not come until Hamo le Strange nodded and said, "Thank you." Having lifted his hand in a kind of salute, he rode off toward his troop.

Chapter 20

If Guy told the castellan at Gloucester what had happened, they never saw any result of his complaint. A short distance ahead, they took a side road to the east that led to Cheltenham. From there they rode south, stopping at Cirencester for a late dinner and coming, just before the light failed, to Malmesbury. Barbara did not know whether to laugh or cry when they saw the great abbey, but Hamo le Strange told them at once he did not intend to seek lodging there. His men, he said, would camp outside the town; he and Tybetot would find an inn. He looked surprised, but very pleased, when Alphonse said at once that he and his wife would prefer to stay at the inn also, if they were welcome.

Although Barbara had to suppress giggles because Sir Hamo had clearly taken as a compliment what had nothing to do with him, she wished to encourage the idea. Smiling with spurious brightness, she spoke cheerfully of how glad she was the rain had fallen at night instead of making their long ride miserable. Hamo then apologized for tiring her and said he would not have been so inconsiderate if he had any choice, but that he and Tybetot must meet another troop near Bath before dinner the following day.

Barbara assured him that she was accustomed to long rides.

Alphonse, with a warm smile, thanked Hamo for his consideration. Hamo smiled back and continued to ride beside them to the inn. He seemed to feel that all was forgiven and forgotten, and told Alphonse eagerly that he had seen him fight as one of the prince's party at a tournament, describing his own disappointment at not being able to join the party, having broken his collarbone in a fall during the jousts the preceding day. Alphonse laughed and said there would be other times, he was sure—but his eyes just barely flicked to Barbara as Hamo snarled, "Not while our Lord Edward is penned like a beast."

Ordinarily Barbara would have tried to put in a soothing word, but Alphonse was neither careless nor stupid and could not have made that remark by mistake. She heard her husband utter a platitude about hoping the prince would soon regain his liberty. The words were formal and might have been meaningless but Barbara saw Hamo's eyes light and his lips part, saw the effort with which he swallowed what he had been about to say. She thought it might be her presence—at least, the presence of Norfolk's daughter—that had held him back, so, although she was burning with curiosity, she tightened Frivole's rein slightly and slowly fell behind, leaving the men to talk by themselves.

Before anything significant could be said, the inn came in sight. With her ears still cocked toward the men, Barbara began an animated discussion with Clotilde about whether they had stayed there before. After a single glance at her mistress's level brows and the blue gleam of her eyes, Clotilde replied in kind, rambling on, so that Barbara could listen, about whether it would be safe to put their sheets on the inn pallets or whether they should have the servants remove the pallets and use only their own blankets.

They were too close to the inn for the device to work, however. The innkeeper, running out to greet his guests, heard the end of Clotilde's remarks and, with deep bows and great pride, assured maid and mistress that the mattress of the bed in his private chamber was clean and fresh, stuffed with new straw only in September. He then looked doubtfully at the three men clustered together beyond the entryway, who he now realized were not the lady's servants, and stammered that, unfortunately, there was only one bed and the private chamber was very small.

Barbara expected Alphonse to lay claim to the room on the heels of the landlord's remark, but he did not, merely looked inquiringly at Hamo le Strange. It was Hamo who uttered some graceful phrases about Lady Barbara's comfort and said that he and Tybetot would be content with pallets in the large common room. Barbara thanked him warmly, as she must even if she loathed the idea of being alone with Alphonse. By then her husband was beside her, ready to lift her down from her saddle. Her heart skipped a beat at the warning in his eyes and she gasped when he let go of her too soon, just before her feet touched the ground, so that she came down hard enough to make her knees bend.

"My dear," he murmured, putting an arm around her waist, "you are more tired than you will admit. Let your maid help you up to the chamber. Perhaps you will want to lie down and rest."

"Yes, yes, I will be glad to go up." Barbara got out, as she pulled free of his grip and shook her head at Clotilde, saying to the maid, "I am steady now. I do not need help in walking. Do you find our baggage animals and have unloaded what we will need for tonight."

A gesture sent the innkeeper scurrying inside, and Barbara followed close behind, eyes lowered, teeth gritted over the laughter that bubbled up in her throat. She hoped Alphonse would have self-control enough to wait for Clotilde to get their linens and make the bed before he followed. Until that was done, she thought alternately of how cleverly he had provided an excuse for seeking privacy with her and wondered whether she should seize on that excuse to remove her clothing and lie ready for him in the bed. She had not decided the question when a thump on the door brought so shameful a flood of desire on her that she turned her back on the door and went to the small window.

A coarse English voice made her spin around. A thick-bodied woman was handing a flagon and horn cup to Clotilde, saying in broken French, "Drink. Rest. Soon meat, bread, cheese."

Barbara's first reaction was terror. She rushed to the door the woman had closed behind her, expecting to find it locked—but it was not. Carefully she opened it and listened. Male voices drifted up to her—three male voices all calm, although she could not make out any words, and then Alphonse laughed.

Fury replaced terror, the heat of the rage fueled by her burning need, but fury soon supplanted the need as well as the terror and then, slowly, even the heat of the fury ebbed, leaving her bitterly amused at herself for laughing at Hamo for self-deception. Shame for her craving sparked rage again, an old, old rage in response to an old, old pain. Barbara walked slowly toward the bench by the small hearth and picked up from atop her cloak at the foot of the bed the embroidery basket that Clotilde had unpacked among the "necessary" items, as she had done for years. Absently Barbara took out what she wanted and set the basket by her feet. But, with the silver mirror in her lap, in the midst of repeating to herself bitterly that Alphonse did not want her, had never wanted her, she began to chuckle. That was nonsense. Alphonse certainly did want her; she had had frequent and urgent proof of that since the ides of August when they were married.

Idiot, she said to herself, do not go back to being thirteen years old. You no longer fear he does not desire you. You fear he desires every other woman just as much.

As the thought passed her mind, the serving woman opened the door again carrying in a liberal selection of cold meat, poultry, pasty, cheese, bread, and both ale and wine for Barbara's evening meal. The creature was so unappetizing herself that Barbara had to chuckle again. No, Alphonse did not want *every* woman, and it was beyond even her jealous fear to imagine there was any female in this inn more desirable than she. Beyond that, sending up so complete an evening meal was clearly a signal that she was not to come down.

No flicker of anger stirred at that conclusion. She knew Alphonse trusted her social skill. When they were with Gloucester and Sir John, he had always found a way for her to join him, particularly when he hoped to get information in casual talk. He could easily have arranged for her to come down by making a poor selection of food or omitting some essential like bread. But unlike Gloucester or Sir John, Sir Hamo and Tybetot were opponents of Leicester's party—friends of the prince. The signal was political, not personal: it was Norfolk's daughter who was unwelcome, not Alphonse's wife.

Barbara signed Clotilde to take the tray from the servant and send her away. Having made a choice—of what foods she did not know—she said to Clotilde, "Take the rest down and share it with our men."

She felt Clotilde's questioning glance but shook her head irritably, and the maid sighed and went away. Barbara guessed her maid thought she had cleared the way for an unwise, angry confrontation with her inattentive husband, but she could not bother to explain. She was too busy recalling what she had seen and heard from the time they met Hamo's troop near Tewkesbury. While she went over the evidence, she ate slowly and methodically, indifferent to what she chewed and swallowed. By the time Alphonse opened the door, she had come to a frightening conclusion.

She started to jump to her feet as soon as she saw him, felt the mirror sliding from her lap, and gasped with fear that he might see it, guess how she clung to it and fondled it whenever she was troubled, and learn from that how abject was her slavery. She turned away, bending and thrusting the mirror into her basket, under her work, and in the same movement grasped a small log and threw it on the fire. Then she stood up slowly, still looking away, hoping her pretended displeasure would provide a diversion.

A swift glance over her shoulder showed her that the door was again closed and that Alphonse, unarmed, was standing with his hand still on the latch, staring at her. "Well? When is the next war to start?" she asked, keeping her voice low but injecting all the anger she could into it.

"No war," Alphonse said, taking the few strides that brought him beside her. "I thought I would find you abed already. I saw Clotilde go down."

"Are you taking sides with my father's enemies?" she asked, suddenly startled and fearful of a problem she had not considered.

"I am taking sides with no one." His mouth was stiff; his throat worked as the words came through. "Never mind that now. I will tell you later. I have held off long enough. I am dying for you."

The passion that had earlier dried up in the heat of rage burst into flame like oiled tinder at the spark of his words. Barbara's reaction was so strong that she drew in a sharp breath and took half a step backward, one hand coming up. Later she realized he might have feared that hand was to ward him off, for he seized it and pulled her hard against him, kissing her so fiercely that she could not have protested had she been cold with revulsion. As it was, all sense but that of pleasure was swept away. Caution and self-awareness were lost in eagerness, and she allowed her husband to strip off her clothing and helped him strip off his without pretending reluctance.

Both were too eager for lingering love play. He had barely entered when she began to writhe in fulfillment and he, who had watched so many women naked in their joy and held back his own to bring a second and even third renewal to his partner, became entangled and fell with her into that red pit of pleasure. Enchanted by the raw pulse of natural, uncalculated release, he murmured her name—only that, over and over.

That touched her in a way that love words would not, and she did not withdraw herself but lay quietly beside him, letting her hand rest in his. She had forgotten the danger in that gentle afterlove communion. Having begun, she craved, as much as she craved the wilder pleasure of coupling, to offer up everything.

Soft words rose to her lips. She closed her teeth over them and said instead, "A troop came with Hamo, and they were waiting in Tewkesbury, likely for Tybetot and his men, who came from the north—I think, because of what the porter of Pershore Abbey said, Tybetot came from Mortimer's keep in Wigmore. And Hamo said they would meet another troop near Bath. You said there will be no war. But how can you be sure the Welsh Marchers do not plan to start the war anew now they know Louis will not support the peace?"

Alphonse groaned. "Did I not sacrifice myself on the altar of duty? Instead of coming to you at once, did I not sit there listening while those silly young men talked? Did I not even deny myself the pleasure of looking at you during the evening meal for fear your father's relationship to Leicester would stop their tongues?"

"Do not dare to talk to me of your sacrifice." Barbara laughed and sat up. "You may have had a conflict between your lust and your curiosity for the length of a heartbeat, but I know which is stronger in us both. Lust can be wakened and contented any time, but news . . . ah . . . a chance to hear news seldom comes twice. It is I who was the sacrifice"—Barbara sniffed melodramatically—"sent away to bite my nails while my curiosity ate me alive."

"I am glad you understood." Alphonse smiled. "I was not sure the food and drink I chose so carefully would not come flying around my ears when I came up."

But Barbara did not smile back. "I understood and you knew I would. So do not talk about food flying. Satisfy my curiosity. Why are you so sure this gathering of men does not betoken a new attack on Leicester's allies in this area?" Alphonse hesitated, looking troubled, and Barbara stiffened. "Did you think I would forget what I had seen and heard just because you futtered me?"

"I have never known it to affect any woman's memory," Alphonse snapped back, then shrugged. "Barbe, you *are* your father's daughter. If I tell you what I have learned and you get word to him, to my mind *I* will have violated a confidence, even if you do not think so."

"Is there danger to my father?" she asked. "Good God, papa has not come to Strigul, has he?"

"No, no. Not one word was said or hinted about your father. He has nothing to do with this at all."

"If there is no danger to papa, I do not care what Hamo and his friends are doing. I am only curious."

There was no direct danger to Norfolk, Alphonse knew, but indirectly, if the Marcher lords' plot was successful . . . Impossible, he thought, and said, "What you said about the gathering of troops is true, but what these idiots plan to do is free Prince Edward."

"Idiot is as idiot does," Barbara said coldly. "But you are an idiot, not I, if you think you can convince me that Hamo is idiot enough to attack Dover, where Edward is now being held."

"He is not at Dover!" Alphonse snarled, loving and hating his Barbe. Most women could have been diverted by generalities at this point in the conversation, but not Barbe, who grasped immediately at practical matters. He would have to tell her what he had learned.

"Since I could not ask questions without making Sir Hamo and Tybetot suspicious and silencing them completely," he went on, "I could not learn everything, but it seems that Leicester is moving the prince to Wallingford."

"Wallingford Keep? To attack that is almost as hopeless as a march on Dover."

"Perhaps not. From what I have heard from Gloucester and others, the southeast is Leicester's. All who supported the king in that part of the country were imprisoned or are in exile, their lands in the charge of Leicester or an ally. So, for Hamo and his friends to march an army, or even a large troop of men, across to Dover would be well-nigh impossible. But Hamo and Tybetot mentioned a keep called Marlborough, not more than a day's ride from Wallingford, that is ruled by a castellan loyal to Robert Walerand—"

"Walerand is King Henry's man," Barbara murmured. "He still holds Bristol Castle in Henry's name. Leicester has not wasted his strength trying to attack Bristol or Marlborough, hoping such isolated royal strongpoints will come to terms without battle." She frowned. "But Walerand is no wild boy. If he is behind this plan, it must be more possible than it appears to me." She sighed and lay back again, unconsciously feeling for and taking Alphonse's hand. "I do not know what I feel. It was terrible to see Edward caged, but if he is freed, he *will* begin the war again."

Alphonse's hand lay unresponsive in hers. "I hope to God this Walerand will stop the plan," he said. "They must not try to free Edward."

Barbara turned eagerly to him, raising his hand, clasped in hers, to her breast. She had been startled by the way his hand lay limp in hers; now she thought it might be owing to his distress over the hopelessness of the Royalist cause.

"Do you think all chance of opposing Leicester is ended?" she asked. "When we are in France again, will you try to convince Uncle Hugh of that? If—"

"I know nothing of Leicester's chance of holding his power." Alphonse pulled his hand free and clenched it as he sat up. "What I do know is that an attack on the prince's prison—no matter where—will provide his enemies with the best excuse in the world to kill Edward. Who could ever say whether he was killed trying to escape or was struck down by his own friends by mistake?"

"No!"

"You can cry out 'no,' and I know that Leicester is an honorable man and would not give such an order in advance. Still, Leicester is not likely to be in Wallingford Keep to order or forbid, and in the heat and confusion of an attack lesser men might seize an opportunity. I fear the temptation to be rid of Edward, the one man who must be the hope and inspiration for all resistance, will be too great."

Barbara pushed herself up against the headboard. "I do not want the war to begin again, but neither do I want peace at the price of Edward's life. What will you do, Alphonse?"

"What can I do?" He stared at her and shook his head. "Do not you dare, Barbe! Do not you dare try to get word of this to your father, or Gloucester, or anyone. You promised not to do anything if your father was not directly threatened. Le Strange and Tybetot trusted me, and I listened to their plans apurpose."

"To save your honor you will let the prince die?" Barbara whispered, her eyes wide with horror.

Alphonse shook his head. "Thank God my decision does not need to rest on that point. Do you not see that more ill could come from Leicester knowing in advance of this attempt than of it simply happening? Edward has some freedom now, I have heard. If word of an attempt to free him comes, they will lock him up, perhaps in chains. You saw what he was like when we arrived in Canterbury. He might eat himself up and die of sickness, or he might become so twisted with hate . . . Barbe, think of that will of his all turned to hate and deception and then let loose on the realm."

"But that is the whole reason behind what Leicester has done," she said faintly. "To ensure that no king's weakness or wickedness should be visited on his country."

"Then it is better that Edward die." Alphonse stared straight ahead to where coals glowed in the small hearth. "Because I know—and you know too, if you would let yourself know it—that there is no one strong enough to hold together Leicester's government after he dies. Then if Edward is alive, he would be loosed."

Barbara shuddered. "I see that door is closed," she said. "But you must at least point out to Hamo and Tybetot the danger that Edward's current gaoler might be less scrupulous than Henry de Montfort. They may not have seen the danger of a deliberate 'accident' during an attack. Hamo is not a hothead. Perhaps you can convince him that the attempt to free him will do Edward harm. You are known to be the prince's friend. Will Hamo not believe you have his interests at heart?"

Alphonse sighed and rubbed the back of his neck. "I cannot seem to try to sow discord among Hamo's party. If I speak at all, it must be openly, to the leader—Walerand, I suppose. But that will mean losing all chance of simply slipping away when we arrive in Bristol and finding a ship. Once I speak out against the plan to free Edward, I will become an 'enemy'—unless they do give up the idea."

"Then we are going to Bristol, not Marlborough?" Barbara asked.

"Yes, to Bristol, after we meet another party somewhere near Bath. Walerand is mustering the men in Bristol. When all are gathered, they will make night marches to Marlborough in small troops, enter Marlborough secretly, and launch the attack on Wallingford from there."

"We will be safe in Bristol," Barbara said, then looked concerned and asked, "Do you have some pressing duties in France?" And when Alphonse shook his head, she went on, "Robert Walerand would never order harm done to you because you are Edward's friend, and I have my own value as Norfolk's daughter. The worst Walerand will do is hold us as we were held in Dover. I know you hated it, but—"

"Goose," Alphonse said softly, reaching for her and pulling her close, "I would not have minded at all if I could have lain abed with you each night in Dover as I will in Bristol."

She let him kiss her, the corners of her wide mouth lifting as she remembered his various attempts to get her alone when they were in Dover. Then she laughed and pushed him away. "Go mend the fire and bank it for the night." She laughed again as he groaned but threw off the covers and went to the hearth. Her eyes rested on him while he added small logs and then larger ones, laid in a pattern that would collapse slowly, keeping the embers at its heart glowing throughout the night, but she did not really watch what he was doing.

"I do not think Walerand will keep us long in any case," she said as he turned to come back to bed. "If he listens to you, he will put us on the first ship for France—or Spain—as soon as possible to be rid of us and be sure we will speak to no one in England for some time. And even if he does not listen, would not sending us overseas as soon as the attempt to rescue Edward is launched be a good way to ensure our silence during the dangerous time and yet not enrage us?"

"It would," he agreed, innocent as an angel until he slid under the covers and threw himself suddenly atop her, pressing his chilled body to her warm one.

Barbara struggled and protested, but strong though she was

for a woman, she was at a total disadvantage, crushed under her husband's considerable weight. He laughed at her gasps and complaints, arguing that she must pay her share for their future comfort, and slipping bit by bit from warming himself to warming her with caresses.

They did not discuss the matter again that night, and Alphonse had joined the men below before Barbara woke. By the time she came down to break her fast with them, an unmistakable camaraderie was flowing from Hamo and Tybetot toward her husband. Barbara was not in the least surprised when Alphonse told her he had agreed to extend his parole against leaving the company until after he had spoken to Robert Walerand in Bristol.

Some hours later, on the hills above the river between Bath and Bristol, Barbara was surprised and a little frightened when she saw the man Sir Hamo and Tybetot had come to meet. Without thought her hand tightened on Frivole's rein, and the mare obediently backed. Bevis and Lewin closed in front of her, assuming from the action that Barbara was afraid to be seen. That was not true; certainly she had no personal fear of Roger Leybourne, Prince Edward's former steward and friend. In fact, she liked what she knew of him and felt he had been a stabilizing influence on the wild prince in the past. But she also recalled the bitter quarrel between the prince and the man who had so long been his close friend and principal servant. She was aware that the quarrel had been patched over, but with how much sincerity on Leybourne's side?

Barbara thought the prince had been mostly in the wrong, had known it, and had been relieved to come to terms with his old friend. But Leybourne? Not only had he been persecuted and deprived of his lands and honors by the king, but hardly had partial and grudging amends been made when Leicester had won the battle of Lewes and canceled all the king's favors. Might not Leybourne cherish a secret anger against the prince and king who had cost him so much?

Barbara had no time to communicate her fears to her husband, however. Having greeted Hamo and Tybetot and had Alphonse drawn to his notice, Leybourne seized on Alphonse with cries of joy and surprise and rode beside him, talking hard, all the way from the meeting place to Bristol. Barbara followed inconspicuously farther back, thinking it unpolitic to press forward and remind Leybourne that Alphonse had married into Leicester's party before her husband had a chance to state his case. Near Bristol, she was startled by Tybetot and Hamo, who closed in on her from either side, suddenly displaying a surprising eagerness to enjoy her company and conversation. Barbara did not know whether to laugh at their innocence or be annoyed that they thought her stupid enough to be deceived.

She knew they could not suspect her of trying to flee. Bristol Keep blocked off the peninsula on which Bristol town had been built from the surrounding countryside. One had to pass the keep to get to the port, so escape was impossible. And Alphonse had told them he intended to enter Bristol Keep to talk to Walerand and take his chances with what followed. So what Hamo and Tybetot intended must be to keep her and Alphonse apart.

Barbara let them believe her ignorant of their purpose. She rode along with them, talking and laughing—and fretting Frivole so that her mare danced forward and had to be checked. But each time it happened, Barbara came closer to her husband. And each time, she turned in the saddle and called to her escort to catch up.

Perhaps they had never intended to separate her from Alphonse; perhaps they did not realize what she was doing or could not think of a way to stop her without creating a disturbance that would draw her husband's attention. But when they came to the drawbridge Barbara felt it was time to eliminate any chance that she could be held hostage in an attempt to force Alphonse into an action he did not approve. Right in the middle of a sentence, she kicked Frivole so that the mare pushed boldly between two men-at-arms.

Shouts of surprise followed her, but it was too late for Hamo's men to make any move that was not an open threat or challenge. Frivole was already on Dadais's heels and Alphonse had turned around to stare. Leybourne also turned and glared at Hamo and Tybetot while Barbara did her best to look confused and anxious, as if she did not understand what had happened.

Riding alongside Alphonse gave her no chance to exchange a private word with him, however. Leybourne continued to talk eagerly about the prince until they came to the outer gate where they were greeted with an urgent request to go up to the keep at once. Dinner was being held for them, the captain said, and it was already near to nones. No one needed to be reminded of that. Barbara had been surprised when they had not stopped to eat after meeting Leybourne and was by now so hungry that she was glad rather than sorry it would arouse too much suspicion for her to try to draw Alphonse aside. She made no excuse about needing to change her dress, but gave Clotilde her cloak and gloves and followed the men into the hall. There they all disarmed together, washed in the basins held by servants, and went to table.

Barbara was considerably shocked when, as soon as general

greetings and urgent news were passed, Robert Walerand said, "Well, Sieur Alphonse, you have heard from Leybourne what we intend to do. Will you lend us the strength of your arm in breaking our prince out of his prison?"

"No," Alphonse replied. "And it is not because I do not wish to see the prince freed. Show me a way to spirit him free without anyone's knowledge or to settle around him a few men who will provide him with weapons and defend his back while our army fights its way to him, and I will be glad to provide any help I can. For the plan I have heard—no. You cannot succeed. You can only endanger Edward."

Argument and protests broke out. Alphonse listened and ate and drank without responding until the angry noise died down. Then he detailed the threats to Edward's life he foresaw from any attempt to free the prince by force. There was a shocked silence until Leybourne shook his head.

"They would not dare," he said. "And there will not be time. We do not intend to mount a siege. We intend to come swiftly and silently, gain entrance to Wallingford Keep by surprise more than force, and bring the prince out or gain a prisoner or some other advantage for which we can trade Lord Edward's freedom."

Alphonse shook his head in turn. "How much time does it take to strike down an unarmed man? And you know well there is nothing and no one worth trading for Edward's freedom, except Leicester's own life. And if he is there . . ." He hesitated, then said, "I will give my parole not to leave Bristol or try to escape from Sir Robert or whatever deputy he chooses—nor will I permit anyone else to send a message out—until you either have Edward safe or have acknowledged it impossible to rescue him. I say this simply because I need to know what could endanger you, your plan, and your friends and because I wish you to be assured of my silence. I want to know if you have supporters inside Wallingford who will help you enter the keep and help you find Edward in it."

"No," Walerand admitted, "but I do know the guard on Edward is very lax, and Wallingford is not unknown to me—"

Alphonse held up a hand to silence him, not wishing to hear any further details that could make his knowledge more dangerous. "You know Wallingford and think a sudden thrust can win a way to Edward, lax guard or no? Well, perhaps you know more than I. I have never been in Wallingford, but Sir William of Marlowe, my brother's father-by-marriage, spent much of his time there. I have heard him talk of Richard of Cornwall's works on that stronghold, and I do not think you can get past the outer moat and walls unless a way is opened for you by one within." He shrugged. "That is all I have to say, and truly, since I will not go with you, it is better that I hear no more."

Argument broke out again. Hamo le Strange and Robert Tybetot cast angry glances at Barbara, as if they thought it was her influence that had warped Alphonse. She saw the looks in a flickering glance. Mostly she kept her eyes down and went on eating steadily—"modest as a nun's hen," was the saying—because she knew any comment from her would do more harm than good. Finally, Hugh Turberville, one of the Royalists who had taken shelter in Bristol after the battle of Lewes, said sneeringly to Alphonse that it was a bad friend who would not take a risk.

Walerand made an angry gesture at Turberville, but Alphonse only smiled. "I do not mind risking *my* neck," he remarked mildly. "It is *Edward's* neck I do not want to see stretched on the block of my stupidity—especially without his permission. Think about that."

"You mean to say the prince will be angry with us for trying to free him?" Leybourne asked sharply.

"No." Alphonse sighed. "I wish I could say it. I wish I could say anything to turn you from this venture, because I fear, I truly fear, for Edward's safety. But no. Edward will admire your attempt. He will remember it and be grateful, even if you cost him the little liberty he has been granted." He stood up. "I think my wife and I should leave you now. You will be more comfortable, and so will we."

Barbara and Alphonse passed two dull, anxious weeks confined with their servants in one of the towers facing out toward the town. From their window they could not see the inner bailey and thus could not guess what, if any, military action was taking place. Barbara had told Alphonse her fears that Leybourne might harbor a grudge against Prince Edward as soon as they were private. He considered what she said seriously, not dismissing it as woman's nonsense, but decided that it would do no good to try to raise doubts in Walerand about Leybourne. The others were so set on the venture that doubts would not stop them. And Leybourne's participation could not endanger Edward further. Leybourne could not harm the prince inside Wallingford, and certainly would have no reason to do so if they did free him.

Barbara agreed, then sighed and said she had better have kept the worry to herself instead of adding it to Alphonse's load. He looked at her oddly for a moment, but only begged her never to try to spare him. He took great joy in sharing, even troubles, with her, he said, and he smiled, but his eyes were sad. Later she wondered if he had glanced down at the work basket she had been holding. But that was ridiculous—unless he had seen the silver mirror, and why should that make him look sad?

The answer to that question was too terrible to contemplate at length. Alphonse was kind; it would make him sad to know that she still cherished his gift after so many years while he felt his interest in her fading. Barbara pretended the thought had never occurred to her and tried to give her attention to other matters, first to making their quarters as comfortable as possible and, once they were settled, to pleasant ways of whiling away the time.

They were denied nothing but freedom. Lavish meals were sent up to them; a young priest came daily so that their souls would not be in danger of neglect; any amusement they desired was provided. Barbara almost wished that they had been treated harshly, for that would have given her some grievance to occupy her mind. She could not be bored while she was with Alphonse, but his behavior increased her anxiety.

The only subject that could hold her attention away from the foolish, ugly fear that he was slipping away from her was the real concern she felt for Prince Edward. But that was no relief and, worse, it forced her to rethink the political situation. Henry was a terrible king; his foolishness and extravagance had been ruining England. But was what they had since Leicester had begun to rule in Henry's name any improvement? This constant turmoil, these endless rebellions breaking out all over the country—was this better? She began to doubt more and more that any stable government could ever be established under the conditions Leicester had set. Yet the thought of Leicester's fall terrified her because that might doom her father. Her uncle would doubtless attempt to protect his brother as he had been protected by his brother, but Hugh was in France. Could he come back to England to intercede for her father in time? Executions were quick and final.

During the first few days of their gentle incarceration one problem or the other was always just below the surface of Barbara's thoughts. By the end of the week a new puzzle, somewhat less painful and therefore welcome, presented itself. Despite Alphonse's flattering remark that he would have enjoyed imprisonment in Dover if they had already been married—he spoke soothing compliments to women the way a dog wagged its tail when presented with a meaty bone—she suspected that her husband would grow more and more tense and irritable if she did not exert herself to divert him.

Unlike her father, however, Alphonse did not worry at the subject that had made them virtual prisoners. He did not gnaw over what he had said and devise new, cleverer words that would have been more convincing. To her intense surprise, relief at first and then almost distress, Alphonse never mentioned Edward or what Walerand and his allies might be doing. He wrestled and fenced with Bevis, Lewin, and Chacier, sometimes taking all three as adversaries at once. He devised new and amusing rules and additions to the games he challenged Barbara to play. But most of all, like a sleek black cat, he preened himself, seeming to think of little beyond the sensations of his body—and hers.

The frequency and intensity of his attentions, instead of reassuring Barbara, made her more fearful—when she was not too tired to think at all. She had no idea there were so many places on the body that would respond to a man's tongue, lips, and teeth, or that such weird and wonderful twistings and turnings could bring pleasure instead of the pain of broken bones and torn muscles. Some days she was too limp to be afraid, but even then she was troubled because her husband seemed to dismiss so lightly the life of his friend and the good of his cause.

That trouble was cured at the end of the second week of November when Chacier challenged a man entering the tower and was answered with a roar and a blow. Bevis cried a warning of an armed man and then fell suddenly silent. Into both Barbara's and Alphonse's minds came the same thought. If Edward was dead, there was no need to keep Alphonse alive.

Barbara retreated to the wall, catching up in one hand a length of cloth she had been considering for a tunic and reaching with the other for the long spit on which two chickens had been roasted and sent up for dinner. The cloth, thrown over a man's head, could blind him, or could catch a sword arm and make a thrust or parry go awry. The spit could trip a man, or go through his neck and kill him, if an opportunity came for her to get close without being caught and used against Alphonse.

He saw her and said softly, "Courage! God bless you!"

The last words were muffled as he slid into his mail, and he did not look toward her again as he drew his sword and came forward so that whoever came up would have to stop in the doorway and could not swing a sword freely. Moreover, only one man at a time could enter, and there was only a small landing behind the doorway atop the steep, curving stair. But all the preparation was unnecessary.

It was Roger Leybourne's face that showed behind his helmet's raised visor—explaining why Bevis had fallen silent; he had recognized the intruder. Leybourne's sword was sheathed when he stopped in the doorway, but his face was black with anger. "You were right," he snarled.

"The prince is—" Alphonse could not say the word and his deep voice rose like a boy's and broke.

"No, no, not dead," Leybourne said. He put out a hand and his mailed fingers clashed against Alphonse's bared blade. He looked at the sword, then looked surprised, as if he had not noticed it before. Then he raised his eyes to Alphonse's face again. "You are in no danger from us. Indeed, Edward might have died if we had not had your warning. When Tybetot and le Strange burst into the first court at Wallingford, the castellan came to the wall and said if we did not retreat, right out of the country, they would give our prince to us by casting him from the wall by a mangonel. Le Strange laughed and said they would not dare, and they brought Edward out, unarmed and bound. We had to stop our assault or endanger him. When the prince begged us to go . . ."

Alphonse dropped the point of his sword and put his hand on Leybourne's shoulder. "I am sorry, truly sorry. There was always some hope that you would succeed." Then he brought his hand up and down in a light blow. "So, what is done is done. The meat of the matter is that Edward is alive and well. Look forward, man. What is to do next?"

"You do not think the prince is still in danger?"

"God, no! After showing him to all the men in Wallingford, and all hearing him bid you go. No. If harm comes to Edward now, Leicester will have the castellan, and the whole garrison too, skinned alive. But Walerand had better look to his defenses. The earl will consider what you have done a violation of the pact you made with him in August."

"That matter is in hand, of course." Leybourne bit his lip. "We have no right, but we have a favor to ask of you, Sieur Alphonse—not for our sakes but for Edward's."

"If I can help the prince, I will."

"It will delay your leaving for France some time."

Alphonse hesitated, then nodded.

"Would you be willing to go with me and some others to speak with Roger Mortimer in Wigmore?" Leybourne asked. "Force, as you warned us, has failed, but we must have Edward. Without him we are nothing but outlaw barons. With him we are the true supporters of the Crown and many will rally to his standard."

Whatever doubts Barbara had felt about Leybourne's attitude toward Edward were satisfied. Self-interest was the best guarantee of loyalty she knew, and this was an aspect of self-interest that she had not considered. It was not only money and favor that Leybourne needed but the feeling that he was part of the proper ordering of the realm. He did not wish to lead or to be a rebel, no matter how just the cause.

Alphonse nodded. "You must have Edward," he agreed. "I do not see what my speaking to Mortimer can do for you or for Edward, but I am willing to go to Wigmore."

Chapter 21

The guards were gone when they came down from the tower for an evening meal in the great hall, but the back of Barbara's neck prickled and Alphonse kept her close. Later, abed, when she said she had felt watched, he laughed.

"So you were. Did you think we had become trusted allies just because I agreed to go to Wigmore? They know me to be Edward's friend, but they know also I served Edward at Henry de Montfort's order. Since they did not offer the alternative of putting us on a ship, we only had the choice of going to Wigmore or staying here."

"But sending us to France would only have been offered if you *refused* to go to Wigmore!" Barbara exclaimed. "Do you think it will be easier to escape when we are on the road?"

Alphonse laughed again. "No, my love, I am not so silly as to see myself as the hero of an old romance, able to fight my way free of twenty or thirty men. But in fact I do not wish to escape. I do not know this man Mortimer, and I wish to meet him. There may be something I can do for Edward after all."

Barbara sighed. "I do not understand you. This morning you did not seem to care whether Edward was alive. Now you are ready to ride into Wales on the slightest hope you can do something for him."

"Whatever gave you the notion I did not care whether Edward was alive?" Alphonse levered himself up on an elbow to look into her face.

"Are you trying to tell me you gave one thought to his welfare over the time we have been here?"

"Perhaps *one*." Alphonse was smiling as he lay down again. "What good would thinking about him have done? It was not as if by thinking about his fate I could have found a device to save him. All I could have accomplished was to ruin my digestion and make you miserable. My dear, it is like waiting for Louis to make up his mind or waiting for a tournament to start. Concern can only wear me out. I have learned to concentrate on whatever is closest to hand—on you, while we were trapped here." He drew her close. "Did I not please you, my love?"

That was not a question Barbara was prepared to answer, either positively, by responding to his embrace, or negatively, by pulling free. All she could do was say hastily, "But when we left Warwick, you were eager to leave England. You did not then feel you should stay to help Edward."

The pause that followed was so brief Barbara would not have noticed it except that she felt a faint tremor in the arm that held her. Then the arm relaxed, still embracing her but without the tension that implied lovemaking.

"I did not know when we left Warwick that Edward's old friends had joined into a party and were determined to free him," Alphonse said. "I thought from what we heard in Canterbury that they were at odds with one another, scattered and beaten, and would either go into exile or make their peace with Leicester and wait for the prince's release."

"But if Edward is freed, the war will begin again."

"Begin again? Is it not going on anyway, love?" Alphonse asked gently.

Barbara was silent, remembering her own doubts on the subject, and after a moment Alphonse went on, "Whether or not you agree with me that only the king has the right to rule, you must see that Edward is the one hope this country has for peace. Can you not also see that hope will be lost if he is turned into a madman?"

"You think they will punish Edward for this? Put him in the bottom of the donjon and load him with chains?" Barbara shuddered.

"I hope not, but he must be held more straitly for a time. Think what that will do to him, atop seeing freedom so close and snatched away—having been forced to cut off the chance for freedom by his own order."

"But his life was at stake!"

"Ah, but he cannot be sure of that. No more can I, although it is what I feared and warned against. Will he not wonder whether he threw away a last chance to be free? Whether what he did was cowardly? Whether his order will have broken his friends' faith in him? He will tear himself apart. I do not wish to see my friend changed into a monster. And aside from my obligation as Edward's friend, the prince is my brother's overlord in Gascony. I do not think a man twisted with bitterness and hatred would make a good overlord. I want Edward freed while the lessons he has learned will make him reasonable, not mad. So, if there is any real hope of escape for the prince, I will do all I can to help."

"I am worried about my father," Barbara said softly.

She could feel Alphonse shrug. "I cannot help that," he said. "I cannot even agree that there is any need to worry. Norfolk is a wily old fox and will take good care of himself—as he has told you over and over."

Knowing protest was useless and that argument would more likely set Alphonse's intention than change it, Barbara said nothing. Alphonse's own stillness implied that her device was working properly and he was reconsidering Norfolk's fate. She was thus shocked when he pulled her suddenly atop him and laughed.

"We are both talking as if my going to Wigmore will make a difference," he said between kisses on her chin and throat. "Likely it is only a device to keep us both safely in hand without a restraint that would wake enmity in us. It costs Leybourne nothing to take us, after all, and a use might be found for one or both of us. Mayhap I will never get to speak to Mortimer at all."

Alphonse's guess was wide of the mark. Three days later, having followed Roger Leybourne past the abbey of Wigmore and through the poor village, not large enough or rich enough to be called a town, they found Roger Mortimer, baron of Wigmore, waiting at the bottom of the steep ridge on which his keep was set. Barbara did not realize who the leader of the small troop was at first. The man looked almost as wild as the Welsh chieftains she had sometimes welcomed when acting as her father's hostess in Strigul. Mortimer's hair flowed down his back and mingled with the shaggy fur he wore over his armor. His face was more Welsh than Norman too, dark and keen. She knew him when he spoke, however, and remembered that the looks—and the long, love-hate relationship he had with Llywelyn apGruffydd, the Welsh leader—came from his Welsh mother, Llywelyn's aunt.

"I have a summons to appear at Oxford on the twenty-fifth,"

Mortimer called, his voice harsh and loud. ''What has Walerand to say to that, Leybourne?''

''He has sent out a summons to his own men and hopes to bar the Severn,'' Leybourne answered and then, hastily, as if to prevent a demand for more information, he went on, ''I have with me Sieur Alphonse d'Aix, Edward's—and Henry de Montfort's—jousting companion, and his wife, the earl of Norfolk's daughter.''

''Norfolk, eh?'' Mortimer laughed. ''Is he still sitting on his own lands looking out to sea so that he does not need to see what is happening in England?''

''Can you suggest something else Norfolk can do without violating his word of honor?'' Alphonse asked.

His voice was as smooth and lazy as ever, but Mortimer turned his head sharply. ''So . . .'' he began, but did not finish. Instead he nodded at Barbara and said, with an attempt to moderate his tone, ''You are welcome, my lady. My wife will be glad to see you. She misses the company of her sister and the ladies of the court.''

Barbara found a civil smile and reply, but she did not particularly look forward to intimacy with Matilda de Mortimer. Mortimer's brusque nod and his gesture of invitation to the company at large to enter the lower bailey left her free to dredge from her mind what she could remember.

She had only met Matilda once or twice, Matilda never having served the queen at the same time she did, if she served at all. What Barbara recalled of the woman from those meetings was not inviting; Matilda had seemed too much like her proud, envious sister, Eleanor de Bohun, with an additional dollop of bitterness because Eleanor had married an earl whereas Matilda had been given to a mere baron. A damned foolish envy, Barbara thought, because Mortimer was more powerful and necessary than Bohun. Mortimer was so essential to maintaining the English border against the Welsh that Leicester had not dared keep him a prisoner after the battle of Lewes. Mortimer had been freed to prevent his cousin Llywelyn from overrunning the Welsh Marches. He had done that, but he had not kept his other promises to Leicester.

The horses went across a bridge over a deep ditch, through a gate, and into a half-moon-shaped bailey. Barbara was surprised at how small it was, knowing it to be the outer bailey because she could see above her the strong wall that surrounded the inner court and, even higher on a steep motte, still another wall, which enclosed the great keep and two more strong towers. Barbara could feel her heart sink, and she saw on either side of her Bevis and Lewin also looking up, their faces blank to hide their anxiety.

Once inside this fortress, would they ever come out again? Mortimer, she feared, was less dependent on Edward's favor and would be less concerned with offending the prince's friend—and still less concerned about offending her father—than Leybourne or Walerand. Mortimer's escort stopped in the outer bailey, but Barbara shook her head when Lewin asked softly if he and Bevis should also dismount. She felt better when Mortimer made no objection as their whole party, including Chacier and her two armsmen, followed him through the outer bailey, across another bridge, and into the smaller inner court, which held a large hall, two small houses, and all the usual outbuildings, including a kitchen and a smithy.

To Barbara's intense relief, Mortimer dismounted there, grooms running forward to take the horses, and a moment later Matilda de Mortimer came to the door of the hall to speak a formal welcome. Although Barbara's memory of the woman proved partly accurate, she discovered there were ameliorating circumstances. What Mortimer had said about his wife missing the company of her social equals seemed true. Matilda greeted her with considerable enthusiasm, removing Barbara's cloak with her own hands and kissing her cheek. When she had offered refreshment to the company and seen the men unarmed and at ease, clustered around the leaping fire on the hearth in the center of the hall, she drew Barbara with her to the other side and sat with her on a bench, asking eagerly for news.

Barbara thought her a fool at first, knowing she would have learned more from listening to the talk of the men. Then, leaning too much on what Mortimer had said, she guessed that Matilda was hungry for court gossip rather than political news. Later she realized that her hostess was urging her to gossip to extract information about Leicester and his party, and her opinion of Matilda rose. She almost forgot the precariousness of the situation in the pleasure of seeming to spill tales at random while she really picked and chose not only what was harmless but what would lead to more revelations if and when she thought them safe.

By the next day the situation seemed much less precarious. Perhaps because he had less to fear himself, perhaps because he cared less, or perhaps because he trusted his people to bring them back if they ran, Mortimer treated them as guests rather than as prisoners. Barbara was delighted to learn after the evening meal that she, Alphonse, and their servants would have one of the small houses in the inner bailey to themselves. She was less delighted when she discovered that Mortimer, even more than her father, kept men's and women's business separate and expected women to keep well out of the way and be submissively obedient. If she had not known Eleanor de Bohun, who seemed mean and envious without reason, Barbara might have assumed her sister Matilda to be a sweet woman whose husband had turned her sour.

In comparison, Alphonse seemed more precious by the moment, even if he did have the morals of a prowling tomcat. However, not love talk but politics was whispered into her ears in the privacy of their bed that first night. She and Alphonse had discussed thoroughly what each would reveal because, as Alphonse pointed out, it would be dangerous if their stories conflicted. They agreed on almost everything except exposure of the possible rift between Gloucester and Leicester. Barbara was uneasy about that, feeling it came close to treachery, but Alphonse said, with a kind of flat indifference that Barbara now recognized as his form of rage, that he had given no oath of loyalty to Leicester and felt no particular fondness for either Simon or Guy.

Her own anger and disgust sprang to life anew, soothing Barbara's conscience, and she let hints of Gloucester's dissatisfaction slip to Matilda the very next day. Since she could do nothing to stop Alphonse from describing the situation, why should Matilda not gain praise and trust from her husband for discovering information he would be given anyway? Yet, although she was willing to help Matilda, as any woman would help another, Barbara never warmed into friendship for her. There was something harsh and bitter in Matilda that rejected fondness.

Fortunately Matilda was also interesting, which was of considerable benefit because they stayed in Wigmore almost a month, and Alphonse was much absent during that time. Barbara had been frightened the first few times he armed and rode out, despite his assurances, but he returned safely and custom dulls fear. Sometimes he rode out with Mortimer, sometimes with one or another of the group, thus Barbara was not surprised or alarmed when Matilda came to her house soon after Alphonse had left one morning early in December and said Mortimer wished to speak to her. Feeling no more than curiosity, Barbara caught up her cloak and followed Matilda to the hall.

"It is necessary for me to make terms with Leicester," Mortimer said abruptly when she was close enough. "I wish you to arrange a place of meeting and safeguards with him."

Barbara stopped and stared, surprised but also relieved. She had feared daily to see the keep emptied as the men all marched away to fight. She knew, of course, that Mortimer and his allies had not responded to the summons to Oxford on the twenty-fifth of November, and Alphonse had told her that Walerand had not been successful in blocking the passages of the Severn River. That meant Leicester could bring his army across the river into the Marchers' territory and attack them on their own lands. If Mortimer came to terms with Leicester, there would be no fighting, and she had never been certain—partly because she was afraid to ask directly—whether Alphonse intended to go to war with the Marchers.

"Very well, my lord," Barbara said after a moment. "When do you want us to go?"

"Now."

"But my husband has just ridden—" Barbara drew a sharp breath. "No." She shook her head. "I will not go without Alphonse."

"You have no choice," Mortimer said, getting to his feet. "When I say you go from Wigmore, you go, and you do as I bid you do."

Barbara backed up a step, but her eyes were defiant and her voice steady. "You can beat me unconscious and tie me to a horse, but you cannot make me say what you want me to say once I am in Leicester's presence."

Mortimer clenched a fist and raised it.

"Go ahead." Barbara's voice rose in challenge. "Break my nose. Knock out my teeth. Send me thus to Leicester who treats his wife as if she were a jewel. Do you think I will not tell him who beat me? Do you think I will beg for just terms? I will tell him you are not to be trusted, that you are a traitor and a liar—and a murderer too! Where is my husband?"

"My lord," Matilda cried as Mortimer advanced and Barbara backed away, shaking with fear but still defiant. "You will have to kill her husband if you hurt her."

Mortimer knew that himself. He had been much surprised and amused by Alphonse's steady refusal to avail himself of female companionship when they were away from Wigmore for several days. Until this moment he had felt somewhat contemptuous of the respect he detected in Alphonse when he spoke of his wife, which was more often than Mortimer felt necessary. He was furious because it had never occurred to him that Barbara would refuse to obey a direct order from him; but he was not furious enough to forget how desperate his situation was and how little he could afford to make it worse by losing an emissary who could get quickly into Leicester's presence and might have real influence. He stopped and dropped his hand.

"Shut your mouth and listen," he snarled.

Barbara clapped her hands over her ears. ''Where is my husband?'' she screamed.

''Curse you! He is only ridden out. He will be back by nightfall. You must be gone by then.''

''No! I do not believe you! I will not go, leaving him hostage. Since you will doubtless torture or kill him if I cannot make Leicester meet your terms—''

''No I will not!'' Mortimer bellowed indignantly.

''Then why keep him hostage? I will not go without him. I will cry of murder and rape if you put me out.''

''I will kill you!''

''Then kill me!'' Barbara shrieked, knowing either that the words were a toothless threat or that Alphonse was dead already. ''Kill me! I am sure that will ease your terms with Leicester and give pleasure to Leybourne, le Strange, Tybetot, and all the others. Think of their pride in being led by a murderer of women.''

''My lord, bring back her husband,'' Matilda cried. ''She will not listen to anything until she sees him.''

Mortimer turned on his wife with a snarl, and she backed away, but he was too clever a man to be ruled by rage. He swung his head back to Barbara, snarling again with frustration, like a baited bear. There were ways to break a spirit so completely that what was left of the person would be obedient even when far from the master, but that took time and more time for healing—and sometimes left the subject wanting in wits. He needed an emissary who could ride hard and soon, and one who would be convincing in his behalf.

''Sit!'' he roared, pointing at Barbara. ''Watch her!'' he barked at his wife.

Barbara gladly sank down on the nearest bench. She was weak and sick with relief, since Mortimer's behavior virtually guaranteed that Alphonse was alive and probably uninjured too. For some time she just stared blankly at her hands in her lap, but as the shock Mortimer's order had given her receded, she began to feel warm so close to the fire, and she pulled the pin from her cloak, slid it off her shoulders, and folded it across her lap. When she moved, Matilda drew closer.

The movement seemed to release her mind, which had been frozen, but the idea that popped into her head was a surprise. Matilda had understood her desperate, uncaring defiance when she thought Alphonse was in danger or dead. If so, Matilda loved Mortimer. How strange . . . and yet was it so strange? Mortimer was not nearly so bad as his loud voice and wild appearance might suggest. He had not hit Matilda, although many men who could not vent their fury on its real object would have beaten a wife nearly to death for speaking when Matilda had spoken and, worse, for making unwanted suggestions.

Barbara wondered why such an irrelevant idea should occupy her mind, and then realized it was not really irrelevant. If Mortimer was not a monster, then perhaps he had never intended harm to Alphonse. So why did he not send them both to Leicester? That was easy; he liked Alphonse but did not trust him completely. Yet Alphonse trusted Mortimer, Barbara realized. Alphonse had not let her out of his sight in Walerand's keep, but he had gone out, even stayed away from Wigmore several days at a time.

Mortimer returned to the hall but did not come near or speak to her, busying himself with his clerk by one of the windows. Time passed slowly as Barbara worried at the puzzle of why Mortimer had tried to send her to Leicester while her husband was away. Finally she began to wonder whether the plan had been set up between Mortimer and Alphonse to make her think Alphonse was a hostage and thus frighten her into pleading the rebel's case more passionately.

The unwelcome notion stuck firmly in her mind because it fit. Alphonse believed she was of Leicester's party and would need pressure applied to her before she helped the Royalist cause. He also had good reason to believe he was God's gift to women, and she . . . had she not forgotten at least half the time to seem cold and indifferent? So he had reason to believe she would do almost anything to get him back safe. The logic made her so angry that she almost stood up and told Mortimer she would go to Leicester and he could keep Alphonse—for good—but with Mortimer's name came the question of why he had not simply said at once that her husband knew and approved of the plan.

By the time Alphonse entered the hall, the question of whether he had been party to the plan was more important to Barbara than the politics. She was aware of him the moment he stepped into the doorway, but he did not see her at first and walked toward Mortimer, who was still involved with his clerk. Barbara sat still, as if she intended to allow him to speak first to Mortimer. As he came near the hearth, she jumped to her feet and ran forward to confront him. Matilda cried out with surprise or alarm, but Barbara's voice overrode hers.

"Lord Roger ordered me to go to Leicester without your permission, but I would not go."

Alphonse stopped when she stepped into his path, and his face, which had been wearing an expression of lively interest—clearly he had expected that some important news or event had occasioned his recall—went utterly blank. Now Barbara had the answer she had hoped for, and she wished heartily that she had never asked the question. Alphonse had been shocked beyond concealment. He had known nothing about Mortimer's intention and he was very angry. Barbara swallowed, but his eyes had gone past her. He came forward again, catching Barbara around the waist and bringing her with him as he advanced on Mortimer.

"Why do you wish to separate me from my wife?" he asked softly.

Barbara's breath caught with terror. She could feel her husband's arm slipping around in front of her so he could thrust her behind him when he drew his sword, but Mortimer only growled, "Do not be a fool. She would have been back here before you if she had only done as she was bidden instead of screaming that I had murdered you and planned to torture you and God knows what other nonsense."

There was a brief silence in which Alphonse's arm once again encircled her waist and briefly pulled her tight against him. Barbara did not know whom she wished to murder more, Mortimer or Alphonse, the one for betraying her and the other for understanding too clearly and too quickly what her terror meant. She settled on Alphonse as the guilty party in the next moment when he chuckled and said, "Ah, you bade her go, did you? That is not the way to obtain compliance from my Barbe."

"I am not accustomed to pleading with women." Mortimer's lips twisted with contempt.

Alphonse chuckled again. "Pleading would have got you no further than shouting. Barbe, bless her, is not a fool and needs to know why she does something."

Barbara promptly forgave Alphonse all his sins.

"You are proposing I tell Norfolk's daughter why I am asking for a truce to discuss terms and then send her off to Leicester?" Mortimer's voice was strained.

"Hmmm." Alphonse looked thoughtful. "You have a point."

"If Alphonse goes with me," Barbara said, "I will not need to know any more than I do now. I will even promise to say nothing beyond what you bid me say."

"No!" The double shout made Barbara's ears ring.

Mortimer's voice was louder, but Barbara was closer to Alphonse. His objection was as quick and emphatic as Mortimer's. The green fiend that lay coiled inside her rose up and hissed, *He wants you gone. He wants to be loose of you.* She knew it was ridiculous; everything that had gone before—Alphonse's fury at the idea Mortimer wished to separate them in particular—gave the lie to the jealous thought. Nonetheless she shook her head furiously.

"I will not go and leave my husband a hostage."

"I am not a hostage," Alphonse said before Mortimer could speak. "Be reasonable, Barbe. I have been living in Wigmore and riding out with Mortimer and his men for weeks. I have seen too much. But he is protecting me as much as himself. If Leicester asked questions and I refused to answer, might not he begin to regard me as an enemy?"

"Thank God you are a man of sense and not an idiot woman," Mortimer said.

Alphonse cocked his head inquisitively. "When another man says I have sense it means I am doing what he desires. And that reminds me that I must ask, before I urge my wife to go, why you tried to send her away without telling me."

"Because you are besotted of her," Mortimer said, his lips curving downward as if he had bitten a very sour apple. "Anyone can see it. I cannot send an army to protect her. Speed is of importance. And I did not want to argue with you about the cruelty of exposing her to the winter weather and making her ride so far and so fast and the dangers of sending her across this wild land with so few—"

A double burst of laughter from Alphonse and Barbara cut him off.

"That I am besotted is perfectly true," Alphonse got out, "but you have mistaken the reason and the result. I am besotted *because* I can trust Barbe to ride as hard and as long as is necessary and not to cry for more protection than she really needs. So where do you want her to go?"

"Worcester," Mortimer said. "Leicester is gathering the feudal host at Worcester. I would prefer that he come no farther west with his army. That is why I want my message to get to him as soon as possible. All I want Lady Barbara to do is to carry the message. I thought she could gain admission to Leicester's presence more easily than a common petitioner. She does not need to plead my case."

"I am not unwilling to plead for peace," Barbara said, her demon crushed, at least temporarily, under the weight of evidence that her husband did not wish to be rid of her.

Mortimer shrugged angrily and turned away to look out of the window. Alphonse touched Barbara's hand, but he spoke to Mortimer. "Will you trust me, my lord, to suggest the limits Barbe must set on her pleading?" The dark head turned; eyes as black as Alphonse's locked with his, then slid away. "If she offers more than you are willing to yield," Alphonse continued, "Leicester will believe you have deceived him, perhaps to gain time. He will feel ill used and angry and be unwilling to grant any compromise.

But if she offers less than you are willing to yield, will not the earl think he is making a good bargain?''

Mortimer's gaze came back to fix on Alphonse's again. ''You are a clever devil,'' he said softly, ''but if I offer too little, Leicester will not be willing to talk at all.''

''There will be a fine line between what is worth some delay to talk about and what is not. What do you say—''

''Would it not be better to talk of this in private?'' Mortimer said quickly. ''Or perhaps we have said too much already—''

''No.'' Barbara smiled. ''Even if I wished to betray you, all I could tell was that you planned to yield more than the proposals I presently carry—and, after all, will not that be a temptation to listen to you in person to see how much more can be wrung from you?''

Mortimer stared at her for a long moment, then looked back at Alphonse. ''I would strangle her if I were you. She thinks too much. That is dangerous.''

''But I enjoy danger.'' Alphonse's eyes glittered.

Barbara's broad brows lifted so that she seemed to be looking down her long, elegant nose. ''There is no danger for my husband. It is said that two heads are better than one, and as we are flesh of a flesh and bone of a bone, being made one by wedlock, it is as if the two heads were on one body. My thinking is only for my husband's good. Would I bite off my own right hand? So neither would I do him harm.''

Because her absolute refusal to abandon her husband under threat was proof that what Barbara had said was true, Mortimer was silenced. He grunted and his eyes flashed to his own wife, standing silently off to one side. Barbara smiled at him again.

''I will leave you, then, to pack what I will need so you can talk to Alphonse in peace.'' She laughed aloud. ''I will swear not to ask a single question of my husband about what you say, if that will ease your mind. But I must ask of you—is there a limit to my time of staying with Leicester? And what am I to do if I am kept over that time?''

''As far as I am concerned, you need do nothing but obey Leicester's orders.'' Mortimer lifted his brows and added a purposeful exposure of his teeth. ''You may tell him that I will wait five days for a reply.''

''Worcester is how far?'' Alphonse asked.

''A day's ride,'' Mortimer replied.

''About fifteen leagues,'' Barbara said simultaneously.

''Then five days altogether, from the time Barbe leaves here, is reasonable,'' Alphonse said. ''It may take her longer than usual to get to Worcester and return if the weather is bad. Also, Leicester may be too busy to see her at once, and to expect him to answer within moments of receiving the proposals seems too much.'' He looked at Barbara. ''Tell Leicester that Lord Roger will wait three days before he moves—from the day you arrive in Worcester.''

Mortimer seemed startled by what Alphonse had said, but Barbara was too relieved to wonder about that beyond the brief thought that Mortimer was far more direct a person that she had thought. That could be no problem for Alphonse, however, and she did not try to linger to hear Mortimer's question and Alphonse's response. She simply felt grateful, as she hurried across the small courtyard to the house in which she had been living, that she would not be expected to ride all the way in one day. She could do it, but it would mean changing horses and riding constantly rather than resting and warming herself while the animals rested. Still, she changed at once to her warmest, thickest clothing and bade Clotilde pack several changes and wrap them in oiled leather traveling bags. There was no misery like riding in cold, wet garments.

Alphonse came in while Barbara and Clotilde were still discussing whether she would need more than one court dress. ''Only one,'' he said. ''You must not seem to be ready to stay for any reason. So far as Leicester is concerned, we were taken prisoner by le Strange, have been held prisoner ever since, and I am a hostage for your swift return. You can devise any pretty threat you like for wishing to hurry back to me. Leicester dislikes and distrusts Mortimer so much by now that he will believe you even if you tell him Mortimer has threatened to send my balls after you if you do not come back fast enough.''

She turned on him, her mouth flat and thin with irritation. ''You expect me to lie to Leicester?''

''Is our being prisoner really a lie?'' Alphonse asked softly. ''Perhaps we could have escaped if we tried; more likely we would have ended locked up in the keep. That I do not wish to escape has no bearing on that.''

Barbara shrugged without speaking. She was less annoyed about telling Leicester a specious truth than by the reason Alphonse had given for her eagerness to return promptly to Wigmore. However, to admit the irritation would merely make Alphonse laugh and mark the words as important.

''Do you want Leicester to wonder why Norfolk's daughter has been a contented guest of the rebels since the end of October?'' Alphonse went on. ''Or perhaps you want a reason to linger where Guy de Montfort is?''

''Ugh!''

The spontaneous and involuntary reaction made Alphonse laugh aloud, and Barbara stuck out her tongue at him, but she wrinkled her nose and admitted, "I had forgotten Guy might be there."

He came closer and put his arms around her. "And I want you back," he murmured. "I am a thousand times a fool because I grow more hungry for you the more I have you. I cannot even hide my reluctance to be away from you for a day . . . or a night. You heard Mortimer laugh at me for being besotted. Come back soon, dear heart."

Chapter 22

Alphonse's words kept Barbara warm all through the cold ride, and she drove her escort along beyond Leominster, where they wanted to stop for the night in the priory, across the empty, hilly country, where Bevis and Lewin rode with their bared swords in their hands, as far as Bramyarde. There, with the black hulks of the Malvern Hills rising threateningly before her in the dusk, Barbara agreed to stop. No doubt had yet unsettled her eagerness to be back in Alphonse's arms at the earliest moment possible, but she knew that riding farther was purposeless and stupid; the gates of Worcester would be shut long before they could arrive, and it would be far too easy to stumble into one of the army camps, where anything might happen, depending on the type of captain and the discipline of the men.

She was glad she had come so far, however, because she wished to give an impression of haste and urgency. To further this purpose, she told Clotilde that she would wear the same mud-stained garments the next day and bade the alewife in whose house they lodged to wake them at first light. They left before sunrise, followed the alewife's man's instructions for finding the pass, and arrived well before the dinner hour at Worcester, passing the gate into the crowded, seething town with a motley of wagons bringing in supplies.

Getting into the keep was a different problem entirely. When Barbara saw the strict watch being kept, she regretted her stained dress, fearing she would not be believed if she announced herself either as Norfolk's daughter or as a messenger from Mortimer. She was hesitating, one moment turning her mare toward the center of the town to find an inn and change her clothes, the next turning back because she realized that arriving decked in her finest would give the wrong impression, when shouts and groans announced the lowering of the drawbridge. Barbara rode forward eagerly, hoping Leicester himself would come out of the keep. She was not alone in that hope. Others waiting near the road pressed forward, and Barbara soon feared she would not be able to get close enough to catch his attention. Her luck was even better; first over the bridge came a horseman with a head so red she could not mistake it.

"Gilbert!" she screamed. "Gilbert, it is Barbara. Help me!"

Gloucester's sword was out, his horse leaping off the bridge driven by sharp spurs, before his eyes found her. By then the crowd in front of her had melted out of the way of the charging horse, and Gloucester could see Barbara was in no immediate danger. He pulled his horse up and shouted, "Where is Alphonse?"

"Hostage for my carrying a message from Mortimer to Leicester," Barbara called out. "Can you bring me to the earl?"

Gloucester sheathed his sword and rode close enough to speak in an ordinary voice. "I can try," he said, his lips thinning. "What happened? I heard from Sir John at Warwick that you were on your way to Portsmouth."

"Did you hear the rest?" she asked quietly as they went back across the drawbridge to the castle, pausing for Gloucester to order that her maid and two men just behind them be allowed to enter. But the dark passage under the walls echoed sound and was filled with arrow slits and pour holes through which words might pass. Barbara shook her head when Gloucester looked at her, expecting her to continue.

"What rest?" Gloucester asked after they passed the gatehouse. "Sir John wrote that Alphonse had seen William of Marlowe after a short delay, no more than that."

"Let us dismount before we talk, Gilbert," Barbara said. "I am too tired to shout at you from horse to horse."

The bailey was full of men rushing about, but Gloucester, with Barbara and her party following closely, rode straight through the crowd, leaving a trail of curses behind. At the stable, Barbara told Bevis and Lewin to stay with Clotilde, then laid her hand on Gloucester's arm and smiled faintly as she said she could trust herself to him. He flushed slightly but covered her hand with his and started toward the gate to the inner ward.

As long as they were moving, no one could hear more than a few words and Barbara thought it the safest time to tell her story. She explained how Simon de Montfort had tried to hold Alphonse in Kenilworth and the ruse Alphonse had used to get away—which brought a brief crow of delight from Gloucester. He did not think it funny, however, when she said that she and Alphonse had been attacked on the road by Guy and, in fleeing, she had fallen into the hands of Hamo le Strange.

''Alphonse could not fight them all,'' she said defensively.

''Four against forty are no odds for a sane man, no matter how good, and Tybetot was holding you so Alphonse would hardly blink an eye unless he were bid.'' Gloucester patted her hand, then looked concerned. ''Were you ill used by le Strange?''

''Not at all, except that he took us to Bristol and we were confined there—although with the greatest courtesy—by Robert de Walerand. Not, to tell you the truth, that I even thought of protesting against going with Hamo. Rebel or not, I liked his company better than Guy de Montfort's.''

Gloucester's hand tightened over hers and Barbara said no more until they had passed into the inner bailey. But before they entered the forebuilding to go up the stairs to the hall of the keep, she asked, ''Gilbert, is Guy here?''

''No, but he is expected, which is why I decided to stay in the town.''

Barbara sighed. ''Too bad. But it is better than his being here now.''

She was quiet again as they passed the guards at the entrance of the forebuilding, but she glanced back at them as she started up the stair. More guards stood at the inner end of the passage from the stair landing through the thick wall of the keep. One put out a hand to stop her, but dropped his arm when he saw Gloucester just behind.

''Why so many guards?'' she asked softly as they crossed the room.

''King Henry is here now, and after the attempt to free Edward—had you heard of that?''

''Yes, Leybourne told us about it when he came to carry us off to Wigmore,'' Barbara answered, and then, before Gloucester could ask any questions, she added, ''Thank God I found you. Who knows how long it would have taken me to get past all the guards if I had not.''

''Oh, the common guards have not been told to keep me out.''

Gloucester's voice had a thin edge. "But I am not so sure my influence will be enough to get you in to see the earl, who holds himself very high these days."

The question of Gloucester's influence was not raised, however. Mortimer's name held enough magic to provide Barbara with an immediate audience the moment she said she had been sent with a message from the lord of the Welsh Marches, and since she clung to Gloucester's arm, he entered with her. Leicester exclaimed about her worn and travel-stained appearance, but she only said shortly that she had ridden as fast as she could from Wigmore because her husband was being held hostage for her immediate return. Then she drew from under her cloak the pouch that had been concealed there, and handed it to the earl.

"I beg you to give me an answer at once, my lord," she said. "I was told that Mortimer would wait no more than five days from the time of my setting out before he moves, and I have been two days on the road already."

"Before he moves?" Leicester laughed harshly. "Where can he move? The Marchers are alone in rebellion. Even his cousin Llywelyn has seen reason and made treaty with me."

The words hit Barbara like a blow. No wonder Mortimer had looked surprised when Alphonse bade her say he would wait five days before he moved. Alphonse must have known how hopeless Mortimer's situation was, yet he had hidden it from her. Alphonse was apparently deep in rebel plans. Simultaneously she felt Gloucester's arm stiffen under her hand. He said nothing and she dared not take her eyes from Leicester's face to look at him, but Gloucester's tension implied that something Leicester had said was false. Barbara swallowed nervously; she could not believe that. The earl of Leicester did not lie. Still, if he was sure Mortimer could not resist, why make any terms? And if he would not make terms, why let her return to Wigmore?

The sensible court-trained part of Barbara told her it did not matter if Leicester would not let her go back to Wigmore. Alphonse was not really a hostage; Mortimer would not harm him, even if he did not regard Alphonse as a friend and ally, because doing so would make his situation worse. And if Mortimer yielded to Leicester, it could not be long before she and Alphonse were reunited . . . unless Guy convinced his father that Alphonse was not Mortimer's prisoner and should be treated as an enemy. Even then her father could— No, that would only make trouble for her father. Leicester *must* at least agree to talk to Mortimer. Barbara swallowed again and wet her lips.

"My lord," she said, "I know nothing of where and how Mortimer can move, but that is a wild and empty land and he looks more like a Welsh chieftain than a Norman gentleman. I can tell you nothing definite because I was never in the inner keep at Wigmore and never heard any of the talk among the men there. My husband and I were lodged in a house in the outer ward. All I can tell you is that there was much coming and going every day and I saw many armed men."

"The same troop passing in and out on patrol."

"My lord, I am no fool." Barbara kept her voice even, but now she was annoyed as well as frightened. "I was held in Wigmore for near a month. Do you really think I would not recognize the same men passing, even if they were dressed differently each time—and why should Mortimer do such a thing? Surely he did not believe a month ago that he would be in so hopeless a position. Surely he would have done something more practical in that time than send one troop back and forth to befool a woman."

"You plead his case very well," Leicester remarked.

"I do not plead his case at all," Barbara said. "You are my father's ally. I tell you what little I saw and heard."

Leicester frowned at her. "How did you come to be taken prisoner by Mortimer?"

"Not by Mortimer, my lord," Barbara said quickly, suddenly realizing why Leicester had been looking at her so strangely.

If Leicester did not recall why she and Alphonse were in the west and thought they had been riding around on the border of Wales, he had a right to be suspicious. She reminded him of her husband's desire to visit William of Marlowe and explained that they had been traveling south from Kenilworth to find a ship at Gloucester and had been caught by Hamo le Strange on the road. Leicester listened without expression. When she had told her tale, carefully omitting any mention of his sons, he nodded and asked if she had anything more to tell him—as if his presence should have awed her into some confession.

"Nothing," Barbara sighed. "Nothing except what every woman has said from the beginning of time—I beg you, my lord, to find some way to avoid the shedding of blood."

Leicester made no direct answer to that beyond a brief hesitation and look of sadness. Then he nodded briskly and waved her away, his eyes going to the pouch he still held. As he opened it, he began to walk away. Barbara felt Gloucester stiffen again and turned toward him. His eyes were fixed on the earl's back and his mouth was tight with fury.

"It was through my mediation that the treaty was made with

Llywelyn," Gloucester muttered, "and I am not even invited to hear what Mortimer proposes."

The voice was so low and Gloucester's attention so clearly elsewhere that Barbara was not certain she was supposed to have heard what he said. She did not think Leicester had intended to offend his young ally, but to say that he was absorbed in his own thoughts and had forgotten Gloucester was there would scarcely improve matters.

"If you wish to talk over this matter with Leicester," Barbara said, pretending that Gloucester had stayed with her to be polite and hoping if he followed Leicester and asked what was in the parchment he would naturally be included in the discussion, "I will just sit down by the fire and wait."

"Do not be ridiculous," Gloucester said, his eyes still on Leicester who had beckoned his cousin Peter de Montfort and two clerks to him. "I am not needed or wanted."

Barbara began to wonder how often this had happened before and whether the slight could have been deliberate—but that was impossible. She drew a breath to speak, but Gloucester shook his head at her and she was grateful to be silent because she had not the slightest idea what to say.

"You must eat and rest," Gloucester said, finding a smile for her. "Will you come with me to my lodging in the town, or shall I try to find a place for you here?"

Barbara hesitated. Perhaps if they remained in the hall, Leicester would notice Gloucester and ask him to join the conference. But if he did not, she thought, staying there would be a constant irritant, reminding Gilbert that he had been ignored. Besides, if Leicester sent especially for Gilbert, that would be best. All in all, it would be better to go.

"If Guy comes, he will come here," she said. "I will be safer in your lodging."

The excuse satisfied Gloucester, who promptly caught a squire—Barbara did not know whose—and bade him tell Leicester, as soon as he was free, that Lady Barbara could be found at the earl of Gloucester's lodging.

The interlude in Gloucester's lodging was pleasant for Barbara; however, putting the blame for her retreat on Guy did more harm than good. It reminded Gloucester of a variety of unpleasant incidents involving Guy, which he related all through the dinner they shared. Later Barbara felt guilty because she had not tried to soothe him and talking about Guy kept fresh in mind his present hurt, but she disliked Guy so much that she had enjoyed the tales and actually encouraged Gloucester's open resentment and anger.

They had barely finished eating when Leicester's messenger arrived to say his lord's answer to Mortimer was ready. The message did not include Gloucester. It did not exclude him either, however, and Barbara said several times she was sure that Leicester had meant it for both of them. But Gloucester had not gotten over his hurt feelings, and he refused to accompany her to the keep uninvited. She was afraid to insist. If Leicester was not welcoming, the affront might be aggravated—and she herself forgot all about Gloucester when she arrived at the castle and Leicester told her that he would discuss terms of submission only if Mortimer and his allies came to Worcester themselves.

"You have some objection?" he said, when Barbara's lips parted.

By the time he finished the question she had reminded herself that Leicester was already suspicious of her, and she shook her head.

"And you wish to return to Wigmore yourself?"

"My husband is hostage for my return," she said.

"Are you afraid for him?" Leicester's voice was much gentler.

"I am afraid," Barbara repeated, and put out her hand to take the pouch he held.

The words were not lies. True, she was not afraid that Mortimer would harm Alphonse if she did not herself return to Wigmore, but she was certainly afraid that Mortimer would reject Leicester's conditions and might drag Alphonse and her into an outlaw life in the hills or seal them into Wigmore to fight to the death. Also, she felt vaguely guilty, as if she should have done more, although what more she could have done she did not know. Leicester would certainly not have listened to any plea she made for Mortimer and his friends.

"Are you lodging with Gloucester?" Leicester asked then.

"No," Barbara said. "I will set out for Wigmore at once. Our horses are well rested. There are four hours of daylight still. I should be able to go as far as Bramyarde."

"Child, there is no need to start at once. You have three days before your husband is in any danger. I will order that lodging be found for you here."

"Oh, please let me go!" Barbara exclaimed. "I cannot stay here!"

She was thinking that Guy might turn up at any moment and in the mood she was in she would stick a knife in him if he annoyed her. Leicester, of course, associated her reaction with her earlier confession of fear; he patted her shoulder and begged her to calm herself. Recalling some of the emotional outbursts of his wife, Barbara bit her lip—and he misinterpreted that too and said soothingly that if nothing would content her but to leave that day, he would send an escort with her as far as Bramyarde so that she would not be in danger riding the trail through the hills at dusk.

For that, Barbara offered heartfelt thanks, and for providing messengers to find her servants and carry her farewell to Gloucester. She was still thinking kindly of Leicester when they arrived at Bramyarde. But she found she could not sleep after she lay down, wrapped in her fur cloak, on her own folded blankets before the fire in the same alehouse she had slept in the night before. Leicester nagged uneasily at her mind. Suddenly what Leicester's first messenger had said in Gloucester's lodging came back to her. He had spoken of "his lord's decision," not the king's, and that recalled to her Gloucester's remark that Leicester held himself very high these days. Gloucester had also said the king was there, in Worcester.

Barbara sat up and opened the pouch she had laid under her blankets where it could be safe and serve as a rough pillow. In the light of the fire she examined the seal on the folded parchment within—Leicester's seal. Was the earl no longer even pretending that the orders he gave came from King Henry? If the safe conducts she carried were from Leicester rather than from the king, would that permit the earl to violate them—on the king's order? And if she raised those questions with Mortimer, which honesty urged, would she destroy all chance that peace would be made?

When she reached Wigmore late the next afternoon, Barbara was taken at once to Mortimer and recited the verbal message she had been given as close to word for word as she could manage. Roger de Mortimer, Roger Leybourne, and a third lord of the Marches, Roger Clifford, were to appear on December 12 at Worcester to discuss the terms of their submission to Leicester. The three men were to come without any armed troop; however, they were granted safe conduct—Barbara offered the pouch—to leave Worcester freely whether or not terms were agreed.

A dead silence in the private chamber closed off from one end of the great hall followed her little speech. Barbara was not surprised. To offer safe conduct only out of Worcester, rather than to their own borders, was like giving a prisoner permission to run free when he wore a chain that allowed him three steps. If Mortimer and his allies refused the terms Leicester offered, there was a whole army to chase them down and capture them between Worcester and their own lands.

The silence was so complete that Barbara heard a stifled sob so soft a whisper would have drowned it. Mortimer heard it too; his head jerked infinitesmally toward the farthest corner of the room where his wife stood. He did not complete the motion but opened the pouch and drew out its contents. His head was bent toward the parchment, but Barbara did not think he saw what he held, and before she thought, she cried out, "Do not break the seal before looking at it."

Every head turned to her, then to Mortimer, whose eyes had already gone back to the parchment. "The king is in Worcester," he said, "but this is Leicester's seal." He stared into nothing briefly, then nodded at Barbara. "I thank you."

Barbara shivered, and Alphonse, who had been standing close beside her, put his arm around her and said, "You must be chilled to the bone by that long ride. These braziers do not warm the room enough. Come, I will take you out to the fire in the hall."

She went willingly, although she was still wearing her heavy cloak and had not shivered from cold. Nor did she care that Alphonse's purpose was to get her out of Mortimer's chamber politely so that the men could discuss their problem in private. She wanted to be out of that chamber. Mortimer and his wife were not her friends, and if fate saved them, it might doom her father. But somehow that bleak thanks for pointing out one more danger, which Mortimer gave courteously because he knew she had intended to be helpful, mingled tragically with Matilda's soft sob in her mind.

"Do you wish to go back?" she asked Alphonse.

He had been guiding her past servants and men-at-arms toward a bench by the hearth, but he started slightly at her question as if his mind had been elsewhere and shook his head. "No," he said, changing direction as he spoke and moving toward the door. "You are tired, love. Let us go instead to our house where you can change your clothes and rest more comfortably."

Barbara agreed with a sigh of relief. Although she doubted that the servants and lesser captains, who spent much of their time in the great hall, knew the exact situation, all seemed to sense impending disaster. There was an uneasy tension in the hall. Small knots of men gathered to whisper anxiously together and glance over their shoulders to catch the expressions of the greater men as they came and went. Some of those brief, worried glances had been directed at her and Alphonse as they came from the private chamber. Barbara tried to look calm and indifferent, to offer neither hope nor despair, but she could feel eyes following her as she crossed the hall.

Neither she nor Alphonse spoke again until he had shut the

door of their small house behind them. Clotilde looked up from laying out garments on the bed and smiled. Part of the weight of despair Barbara had felt lifted, but not all. Against her will she felt anxious about those she should regard as enemies.

"What will Mortimer and Leybourne do?" she asked.

Alphonse put his arms around her and kissed her. "I missed you," he said, then smiled over her shoulder at her maid. "Clotilde, go and ask Lady Matilda, whenever she happens to come into the great hall, if you can bring an evening meal here for Lady Barbara."

"Will I help you change first, my lady?"Clotilde asked, half laughing.

"No, you silly woman," Alphonse said before Barbara could reply. "I will help her change. Just go away."

"Yes, go," Barbara said.

Since Clotilde would put a desire for coupling on the most tactful device, Barbara thought it clever of Alphonse not to waste time concocting a more delicate suggestion to be rid of her. She did not think it necessary; although Clotilde loved to gossip, she usually made sure of what she should and should not reveal. However, these secrets were not Alphonse's own, and Barbara accepted his caution as reasonable. Thus, when he kissed her again, she embraced him warmly—until she heard the door close, when she expected he would let her go.

To Barbara's surprise, his kiss only deepened and his hands began to move over her body. She pushed him away with considerable energy. Partly she was chagrined at worrying about his allies when he seemed not to care, partly she was ashamed because she had seized on an excuse openly to welcome and enjoy his caress, but mostly she was infuriated by the same cause that bred Gloucester's resentment: She had ridden four days through wet and cold, fearful of danger, had suffered all the hardships of winter travel, and was not to be told what resulted from her labor.

"If you do not wish to tell me anything about Mortimer's plans, then say so," she cried. "Do not try to cozen me with kisses."

"Do not be ridiculous," Alphonse muttered, snatching her back into his arms. "I will tell you anything I know later. At present I do not care if Mortimer and all his friends and the prince, too, plan to be snatched up to heaven in a fiery chariot."

"And what if the plan sends them down to hell?" Barbara asked, leaning away from his kiss so she could speak.

"With my goodwill!" Alphonse exclaimed, beginning to laugh. "Anything that will rid me of them so I can fix your attention on a matter more important to me just now."

The lure of believing herself more important to Alphonse than politics was irresistible. Barbara also laughed and allowed her hands, which had been braced against his chest, to slide over his shoulders. It was not so dreadful to be cozened with kisses, she thought, as he pulled the pin from her cloak and let it fall to the floor.

Chapter 23

"You are not a very efficient maid," Barbara murmured later. "Not only did it take you much longer than Clotilde to get my clothes off, but you forgot to warm the bed."

"I did not forget," Alphonse said, tipping his head back so he could look haughtily down his nose at her. The attempt was seriously compromised because he did not let go of her and, close as they were, his eyes crossed. "Can you not recognize a clever device? Think how the cold sheets made you cling to me, even climb atop me." He chuckled. "And you cannot complain of being cold for long. Did I not warm you well—and quickly?"

"I can complain about anything I choose," Barbara retorted. "You might think me unreasonable—" She stopped suddenly, reminded of Gloucester's complaints about Leicester and said aloud, "I wonder if Gloucester is unreasonable because he has given Leicester reason to distrust him."

"What?" Alphonse lifted himself on one elbow.

Realizing that what she had said might lead Alphonse to believe the rift between the earls was greater than in reality, Barbara described her encounter with Gloucester.

"Gloucester said he had mediated Leicester's agreement with Llywelyn?"

"Why do you sound so surprised?" Barbara asked. "The Clares

were lords Marcher and had lands in Wales from the time of the first William."

"How should I have known that?" Alphonse asked. "The only place I knew Gloucester held was Tonbridge. To speak the truth I was not interested to find out about his other lands, but even if I had been curious I would not have asked. Would not Gilbert have suspected I was looking for a position?"

She thought he was trying to draw her off the subject of the rift between Gloucester and Leicester and made a dismissive gesture, her brows drawn together into a thick, straight line. "But do you think Gilbert has given Leicester cause to suspect him?" she insisted.

Alphonse sighed and dropped back flat. "In a way, yes, in a way, no. The problem is like a snake biting its own tail. It seems to me from this and that I have heard that there were reasons from the beginning for lack of perfect trust. Gilbert was not originally of Leicester's party, for example, and there were, and still are, disagreements between them about prisoners and ransoms. So Gilbert cannot help but wonder whether Leicester is suspicious of him. And he may be, but even if he is not, as you yourself have said, Leicester is so much older, with so much more experience, it is natural for him to make decisions without consulting Gilbert, who is about the age of his third son. Each time Leicester ignores Gilbert, however, he exacerbates Gilbert's doubts. Gilbert is young and passionate, but he respects Leicester too much to argue. Thus, he sulks. Leicester sees him sulk, which increases his suspicion. And so, round and round, with the snake's teeth digging into its own tail, the tail thrashing in pain, causing the teeth to dig in so much harder, causing more pain—"

"And on and on forever," Barbara said sadly. "Where can it end?"

Alphonse did not answer, and Barbara shivered. Then he drew her back into his arms and said slowly, "I am sorry, my love, but I think the end was decreed when Leicester insisted the form of government he established in the Peace of Canterbury must be extended into Edward's reign. That made the prince his implacable enemy, and everyone knows it. Everyone also knows that any oath extracted from the prince is worthless because it is given under compulsion. Edward will turn on Leicester the first chance he gets. So the prince is a standard for the rallying of every enemy Leicester has . . . or makes . . . forever. If he is pushed too hard, Gloucester will turn to Edward."

Alphonse was surprised when Barbara did not react with more than a resigned sigh. She had told him more than once that she did not care for party, only that there be peace and her father and uncle both be safe, but she had also spoken strongly about the king's unfitness to rule. Thus he could not decide whether to speak to her about the idea that had come to him: Mortimer, he thought, might use the fact that Gloucester had lands in Wales and his dissatisfaction with Leicester to save himself and his friends.

Barbara herself made it unnecessary for Alphonse to mention the subject by saying, "You must remind Mortimer that Gilbert now knows we are prisoners in Wigmore and will be displeased if we are detained longer." Then she sighed and added, "I am so sorry for Mortimer and for his poor wife, who will be dragged down with him, but I do not see that our remaining with him can do the slightest good. I think it is time for us to go to France."

Since it was not Alphonse's habit to look a gift horse in the mouth, he accepted Barbe's turn of subject. They had a delightful evening—a pleasant meal together, which Clotilde brought from the kitchen; serious yet soothing subjects to discuss, like whether they should retain Alphonse's lodging in Paris or try to buy a house; and whether Barbara should seek a place as a lady of Queen Marguerite, which had many political and financial advantages, or keep her total independence and come to court only as Alphonse's wife, which led to a discussion on whether the interests of Alphonse's brother and Aix might conflict with those of Queen Marguerite. The talk lifted Barbara's spirits so much that she had almost forgotten England's problems when they went to bed—and had a delightful night.

The talk had its effect on Alphonse, too, increasing the conflict between his desire to protect his wife by taking her away from the torments of this divided realm and his desire to help Edward escape his imprisonment before he was irretrievably embittered. For himself, he had rather enjoyed taking part in the dangerous attempts Mortimer had made to block the Severn so that Leicester could not attack in force, and he had also enjoyed riding deep into Wales to try to arrange a meeting with Mortimer's cousin, Prince Llywelyn.

The failure of both efforts had not affected him much because he had not believed Edward could be freed by force or that any effective resistance could be made against Leicester without Edward as its leader. Now he felt a trifle guilty over his indifference to Mortimer's fate and to the pain it gave Barbe, and her remark that they could do no good by staying in England took on force. In all honesty, Alphonse had to admit that anything he could do to help Edward could be done as well or better by anyone else.

Thus to remain in England was mere self-indulgence—and Barbe was paying the cost of his amusement.

The next day, therefore, Alphonse sought Mortimer in the great hall and, when he did not find him, asked for admission to his private chamber. There he found Leybourne and Clifford as well. All three looked at him with the dull eyes of men who have not slept. "I have two suggestions to offer," he said. "The first is that when you bring Barbe and me to Worcester—"

"And why should we allow you to benefit from our misfortune?" Leybourne asked bitterly.

Alphonse lifted his dark brows. "I did not think I needed to explain that there is no purpose at all in holding us any longer. I am worthless to Leicester and you could not get any ransom—or any favors—for Barbe from Norfolk. You must plead your case with Leicester before you could even get a message to Norfolk. Moreover, you do not know Norfolk if you think he would ask mercy for you or pay ransom. More likely, when Norfolk heard Barbe was a prisoner, he would come roaring to Leicester's support and demand you all be hanged."

Mortimer made an angry gesture at Leybourne. "You are not a prisoner, Alphonse, and you know it. When we leave for Worcester, you may come with us or ride where else you will. It cannot matter. Roger is only at his wit's end."

"And I am trying to extend his wit," Alphonse said, his lips thinning in irritation. "You must treat us as prisoners so that you may yield us up openly, where all may know of it. Freeing us—you may say we were the only prisoners you could bring in the short time you were given to obey Leicester's summons to Worcester—will show your good intention of freeing all your other prisoners and will cost you nothing at all."

A spark of interest showed in Leybourne's eyes. "By God, that is clever."

"Not really," Alphonse said. "I beg your pardon all, but I fear you are so deep in the rut of defeat that you are not thinking, just chewing the bitter cud over and over. Which brings me to what I had intended to say when I began. I think it would be most to your benefit to release us to Gloucester, not Leicester."

Mortimer's mouth twisted. "It is Leicester we must find a way to cozen."

"I do not think you can succeed again. Leicester is a generous enemy but not a fool. You have twice failed to fulfill agreements with him. What can you now offer that he will believe? No, your one hope, as I see it, is to try to gain Gloucester's sympathy—"

He was interrupted by harsh laughter and looked around at the three faces with surprise. Clifford said, "I am afraid Gloucester does not love us much. We raided and looted his Welsh lands—''

''Recently?'' Alphonse asked. ''Since you fought him in June and July?''

''No, not since then.''

Alphonse smiled. ''Then the 'insults' he has suffered from Leicester are fresher in his mind and far more painful than any damage you may have done to his purse. Remember, I told you of the cracks in the alliance between Gloucester and Leicester. Barbe says these are wider now. If you can use the excuse of handing us over to Gloucester to speak to him, you can say you are sorry that, because he is an enemy to your overlord, the prince, you were forced to attack him even though he is a fellow Marcher lord.''

''And what good will that do?'' Clifford asked angrily. ''Will we not seem like beaten dogs, licking his hand for favor?''

''Not if you speak with dignity and ask no favor. You must say, of course, that you released my wife and me to him at our request. The apology will pave the way for me to speak well of you to Gloucester, to say you are not unruly robber barons but only fixedly loyal to your prince, and to suggest to him that Leicester does not understand the problems of the Marches and that the punishment he proposes to inflict on you—whatever it is—will increase those problems.''

Leybourne shifted on his bench. ''You have seen and heard a great deal since you met Hamo on the road . . .'' His voice was apologetic, and he did not seem to know how to finish the sentence.

''What could a prisoner have seen or heard?'' Alphonse asked, then smiled and added, ''And surely if I had given my parole and been free to go about the keep or even ride out with a guard, you would make me swear an oath to be silent about what I had learned by chance. Gloucester would not wonder at that or question me. He is a most honorable young man.''

Mortimer sat up straighter in his chair. His eyes were bright now and his expression thoughtful. ''You offer us a thin thread of hope, but a thin thread can trail a thicker line behind it. We should have some way of passing information to each other privately without compromising your position—if we survive this submission.''

''I do not think I will be in England much longer,'' Alphonse said. ''I suspect that Leicester will order me to go home to France. And I have no excuse to stay.''

Alphonse sounded sincerely regretful, and in a sense he was. He knew he would enjoy the kind of intrigue he foresaw—slowly convincing Gloucester that the good of his country rested with Edward, not Leicester, followed by some exciting adventures in arranging the prince's escape, and capped by some hard fighting when Edward's forces confronted Leicester's. This was exactly the kind of enterprise he most enjoyed. However, he knew Barbe would not see it his way. She was too deeply, too personally, involved and would suffer if he embroiled himself in these events. And half the fun would be gone from the enterprise if he could not talk it over with her.

At the end of the following week, Alphonse was patting himself on the back because the meetings with Gloucester and Leicester had proceeded smoothly just as he had hoped—in some ways even better. Leicester's terms of surrender were harsh: Mortimer, Clifford, and Leybourne's estates were forfeit for a year and they were to be exiled to Ireland for that time. However, the severity was not unexpected, and the Marchers had already bemoaned to Gloucester the certain overrunning of their lands during that time by the Welsh. Gilbert had made no promises, aside from granting them a month's grace before leaving for Ireland, and agreeing to speak to them again before they set sail.

Gloucester had been very thoughtful after Mortimer and his two friends left Worcester, however, and pointed out to Alphonse that whoever Leicester appointed to oversee the Marcher lords' estates—most probably one of his sons, he remarked with a grimace—had no particular reason to guard the property too carefully. That meant Gloucester's lands would be overrun along with theirs. Alphonse, who already knew this, nonetheless exclaimed sympathetically. And, Gloucester went on, he had less faith in Llywelyn's promise not to raid than in the Marchers' promises to abide by this new agreement. Not that Llywelyn was himself likely to lead the raiding parties, Gloucester admitted. However, he was even less likely to hunt down other raiders. Alphonse laughed and agreed. Frowning thoughtfully, Gloucester, who had been treated with considerable respect by Mortimer and his friends, had talked at length to Alphonse about working out a way to avoid exiling the lords Marchers to Ireland and at the same time prevent them from starting the war a third time.

Of equal advantage was that Leicester had not been as inflexible as he might. His strict view of abiding by legal forms outwardly, whatever the reality, led him to grant the Marchers' plea that they could not go into exile until the king and also the prince, their particular overlord, had given them permission to leave the country.

Mortimer and his friends had been taken to see the king on

December 13. In Leicester's presence, Henry was sweet and smiling and seemed utterly indifferent, approving the conditions, which he called most merciful, almost without listening. More important, on December 14 they were given safe conducts to visit Edward, who had been moved to Kenilworth, carrying with them copies of the agreement.

Before he left Worcester, Mortimer sent a servant with a note for Chacier to give privately to Alphonse with this news and with repeated thanks for the jolt of hope that had freed him to see new paths through the morass of defeat. There was a hint, too, that Mortimer would be very glad of Alphonse's future help, if he could see a way to give it.

What else, Alphonse wondered, would be included among the rolls or sheafs of parchment that were supposed to detail the terms of surrender to Edward? Did the prince speak any Welsh? Mortimer certainly spoke a few words. Would that be enough to make plans for Edward's escape? Perhaps they would not need to be sly. Henry de Montfort, again saddled with overseeing the prince after the fiasco at Wallingford, might be too trusting and allow them to talk in private.

Alphonse called himself a fool for being flattered by Mortimer's praise, but he still felt frustrated at being excluded from the stirring events that might take place. Nonetheless, he had already had one mildly unpleasant confrontation with Guy, who was now also in Worcester, so he held by his resolve and told Gloucester that he and Barbara wanted to leave for France.

Gloucester was disappointed, insisting that winter was a bad time for sailing. He had welcomed them into his lodging and told Alphonse flatly that he enjoyed their company enough to play host as long as they were willing to be his guests. When Alphonse reminded him that he was not beloved of either Guy or Simon de Montfort and that his presence only added to the friction already existing between Gloucester and Leicester's younger sons, Gloucester said angrily that it was time those two strutting cocks were shorn of their combs.

Alphonse could not resist saying, "That is dangerous," which he knew would only increase Gloucester's determination to deflate the pride of the younger Montforts. But then he felt guilty at mixing a batch of trouble he would not have to drink, and he added, "I do not wish to be a cause of conflict, and it is not fair to Barbe. You and I do not need to hide away, as she feels she must when Guy is nearby. It is better that we go."

"If you must," Gloucester said discontentedly. Then he brightened and proposed, since a summons had been issued for a parliament in London on January 20, that Alphonse and Barbara accompany him there.

To this Alphonse agreed readily and with thanks. They would have a better choice of ships from London than from any place other than one of the Cinque Ports, and several of those were closed to them because one or another of Leicester's sons had been made governor. As soon as Leicester had left Worcester, they set out for London, but when they arrived there, Gloucester complained bitterly that Christmas was less than a week away and he had no one with whom to make merry. It was ridiculous for them to leave, possibly to be caught aboard a ship on Christmas, waiting for good weather, when he would also be alone. He looked so young and pathetic that Barbara's heart was softened and she agreed that they should go on to Tonbridge with him.

When they arrived in Tonbridge, however, they found that Gloucester's complaint was not literally true. His younger brother Thomas was waiting for him at the keep. Not that Gloucester had deliberately lied to them, for he cried out in surprise, "Why are you here instead of at St. Briavels?"

"I have come to hold Christmas with you, brother," Thomas de Clare said, his sharp blue eyes flickering to Alphonse and Barbara, who sat their horses to the earl's left.

Gloucester smiled and said, "This is Sieur Alphonse d'Aix and his wife, Lady Barbara, Norfolk's daughter. They have also done me the kindness to assuage my loneliness." He dismounted then and embraced Thomas, adding, "I am sorry if I sounded unwelcoming. I was only surprised. I am very glad to see you, Tom. I would have had to send for you if you had not come. But it is too cold to talk out here. Let us all go in."

Alphonse had dismounted while Gloucester was speaking and helped Barbara down. "If you will permit," he said to Gloucester, "Barbe and I will go to our quarters. I am sure Barbe wants to rest and change her dress."

"Your usual chamber should be ready," Gloucester said, nodding his thanks, and the next moment laughed at Barbara, who had looked at her husband, and added, "Now do not take his head off, Barby. It was a nice, polite excuse to give me and Thomas some privacy, and might even have been true. Thomas would not know you can ride me into the ground and that you do not care a bit about your dress."

"You," Barbara said, laughing also, "were not supposed to notice that look. And what a shocking lie—to say I do not care about my dress!"

Alphonse flung up a hand, as he might have raised a sword to stop a practice bout of swordplay. "That is a hit, Gilbert!" he cried. "You must see that by denouncing one lie she has affirmed the other. Now, before she makes worse fools of us all, I had better take her away."

Gloucester smiled and nodded. "But do not be long. When you are settled, you will find us in the hall."

Some time later, when they rejoined the earl and his brother in the hall, they found interesting news also. Thomas now smiled warmly at Alphonse and Barbara. When they had seated themselves, he repeated to them that he had come east to spend Christmas with his brother because he had a letter from Mortimer, signed by Leybourne and Clifford, to say that no man of theirs would offend against Clare lands—until they were forced to give up command of their men by Leicester's order—because they no longer considered Gloucester an enemy.

"I was not sure whether I should believe them," Thomas said—and Barbara could have wept because the eyes were so old and wary in the face still rounded with youth—"but I thought I should test their good faith by absenting myself from our lands for a time."

"I think you did exactly right," Alphonse said in response to Gloucester's questioning look. "I am sure you warned your marshal, or whoever you left in charge of the keep, to be extra alert."

Thomas nodded and said grimly, "And I rode over to Strigul and spoke to Norfolk's man, who promised to come up on any attacker from the rear and do what damage he could."

"So," Alphonse went on, "if they do attack, they will win nothing and prove themselves no more than greedy curs. But I do not believe it. I think they desire your goodwill, Gilbert."

"I think so too," Gloucester agreed, "since they could accomplish nothing by seizing St. Briavels, but why do they desire my goodwill?"

"To protect them against Leicester," Alphonse said, and squeezed Barbara's hand, which he had been holding, hidden in the folds of her skirt between them on the bench.

"Please," Barbara protested, "if I hear another word about the earl of Leicester, I will rend my garments, put dried leaves in my hair, and leap into the moat. Can we not, for an hour or two, talk of something that does not depend on him?"

Alphonse squeezed her hand again. He could have kissed her for her ready grasp of the situation and even more for her instant response. Gloucester looked a little surprised, because Barbe was usually eager to talk politics, but he obligingly changed the subject to the coming amusements during the twelve days. In a little while, when Barbe was talking to Thomas, Alphonse was able to go up to Gloucester's chair and murmur in his ear that Barbe did not think it wise to talk too much about Leicester in open hall.

Gloucester's eyes flickered to her and away, and his hand closed briefly on Alphonse's arm. Alphonse felt guilty about that, knowing that Barbe would murder him if she guessed how he was twisting her words to a purpose she did not approve. He intended to explain to her why he seemed to be encouraging Gloucester's suspicion of Leicester, but by the time he and she parted from Gloucester and Thomas to go to bed, he had changed his mind. Why argue with Barbe about a few words she would soon forget? The next day would be Christmas Eve and would be given over to getting in the Yule log with attendant giving of food and drink. On Christmas Day they would doubtless ride to the church at Penshurst and much time would be spent in prayer. And the feasting and merrymaking would begin when they rode home.

The outer bailey would be open to all that day, and no one would go hungry or thirsty. Whole oxen, sheep, and hogs would be roasted in open pits. Tubs of pottage and every other sort of dish would be stewed up from the Christmas dues that had been carried in for days by the tenants. Every troupe of players for miles around would converge on the castle. The subject of Leicester would be dead and forgotten, Alphonse thought, by the time the due solemnities of Christ's birth had been celebrated and the joyous feasting and dancing of the twelve days was past.

They did not need to talk at all that night, he decided, as Clotilde removed Barbe's clothes and Chacier helped him disrobe. Barbe was already in the warmed bed, staring at the gathered curtain, as the servants went out, and he reached for her before she could speak. She stiffened, as she always did. Against her resistance, Alphonse pulled her close. She tried to turn her back, but he held her, stroking her shoulder and arm, kissing her ears, nibbling on the lobes, tickling them with soft breaths. He did not think about what he was doing; he was a practiced lover. He began to touch her breasts at the first sign of yielding, and she warmed further, not even so slowly that she tried his patience. Still, he could have wept. She was in every other respect perfect. Why must there be this bitterness underlying the sweetest part of their marriage? Why did she not come to him willingly? Why?

On January 10, Thomas de Clare left to return to his duty in St. Briavels. The same day, Barbara and Alphonse set out for London with their host. Gloucester had his own house in London and was not worried about lodging, but Barbara had written to her father and hoped to spend some time with Norfolk before the full business of the parliament began. The morning was clear and not cold, although a little damp. However, as they rode north, the mist thickened rather than clearing, and by noon it was raining. Gloucester politely asked if Barbara wanted to find a place to stay, but she and Alphonse were both eager to go on. As it grew colder, Barbara said, the rain could change to snow. If that continued for long, they could be trapped in some small village.

The decision was fortunate. Although the snow did not begin until late that night, the rain started to freeze on the ground as they entered London. They were all grateful to find fires blazing in every hearth in Gloucester's house when they arrived. The next day was worse, all hail and sleet, with snow again during the night. To walk was difficult; one could never tell when a foot would go through the top layer of snow and slide on ice. To ride a horse was to court disaster. Barbara was disappointed to find that her father had not arrived before the weather changed, but glad when he did not come while traveling was dangerous.

The cold held for five days longer, packing the ice and snow hard. Gloucester was disturbed because so few of those summoned—especially the northern lords—had appeared to attend the parliament, but he pushed the worry aside to enjoy the winter sports with his guests. They played like grown children, fastening bone runners to their boots and sliding about on the frozen swamps near the city and careening down snowy slopes on wide boards.

Norfolk arrived in London on the seventeenth, and Barbara, who claimed she was one large bruise from falling on the ice and off her sled, was content to spend most of the next two days with him by the fireside in his lodging. He told her he was not happy with the settlement Leicester was forcing on the king and prince. The king needed restraint—Norfolk had no quarrel with that—but the prince was another matter. Aside from provisions to protect those who had fought to prevent the king from ruining the country, Norfolk did not agree that Edward should be bound to the new form of government. He had answered Leicester's summons to the parliament only because its purpose was to liberate Edward from his confinement—and, he said, he had told the king exactly what he thought.

''Leicester intends to liberate Edward?'' Barbara repeated. ''But, papa, the moment the prince is free he will—''

''I am not a fool.'' He laughed at her. ''There will be eyes on him, and his household will be of our choosing. But he will be free to walk around where he likes—he has been locked up since that business at Wallingford—and ride out to hunt or to visit a fair. We will one day have a madman for king if Edward is kept in prison too long."

"So Alphonse says," Barbara murmured thoughtfully, and then quickly, before she told more than was safe about what she suspected the lords Marcher might be planning, she turned the subject and asked how the king had responded to what her father had said.

She felt sick with guilt over concealing anything from her father, but she knew nothing for a fact—and she would be betraying Alphonse's confidence if she spoke. Bitterly she thought that half her pleasure in her father's company, the last she might have of it for years, was being ruined by Leicester's hope for good government. So far, from what she could see, Leicester's victory had produced more grief and trouble than the hope of better government was worth. But she was somewhat comforted by her father's response to her question about the king's reaction: Henry was less inclined to view Norfolk as an enemy now than he had been in the past. She was also somewhat surprised by the number of times her father began a statement with "Joanna says."

Over the course of their conversations, her guilt about being eager to leave England and its troubles behind her abated. She put together the "Joanna says" with the fact that her father was pleased to see her but did not, as he often had in the past when she had been at court, complain that he had missed her. Although she did have to suppress a twinge of jealousy, she was truly glad to learn that he was not pining with loneliness. Discreet questions elicited the information that he had spent much of his time with his heir, young Roger. And Joanna, softened by his obvious fondness for Hugh's eldest son, gave him as much female company as he desired. Despite feeling just a bit left out, Barbara was greatly relieved to know that her departure for France would not leave her father alone and sad.

Leicester himself appeared in London the next day, accompanied—unfortunately, for Barbara and Alphonse—by young Simon and Guy. She avoided the court—which was no sacrifice, because none of her special friends had come—but one day, by sheer bad luck, was accosted by the brothers right outside her father's lodging. No harm was done; little more than salacious teasing on Guy's part and insults on Barbara's passed between them. Then Norfolk, hearing their voices, came to the window, saw Guy reaching for Barbara's rein, and her whip hand rising. He roared with anger, and the brothers departed with more haste than dignity.

Barbara was not afraid for herself, but she realized the situation could easily become dangerous. She managed to prevent her father from pursuing Guy and Simon, but she was not sure that good sense would prevail if Norfolk should see her insulted again or, worse, if Guy should attempt physical persuasion where her father could see him. The incident left her badly shaken, and she made the mistake of flying into her husband's arms and pouring out the story as soon as she returned to Gloucester's house, without noticing that Gilbert had entered the hall soon after she did.

Naturally Alphonse and Gilbert they wanted to rush out immediately, find the brothers, and bring them crawling to kiss Barbara's feet as they begged her pardon. Only by bursting into tears—an event so unusual for her that both men were shocked into agreeing to do anything she wanted if she would only stop—was she able to get them to listen. Even then, it took considerable time for her to make them agree that the simplest solution would be for her and Alphonse to go away.

"It is ridiculous to have a confrontation with Leicester over what his foolish sons probably think no more than a merry prank. I do not like it. You do not like it. But Simon and Guy hardly realize they have done wrong."

"Then they should be taught," Gloucester said.

"Someday," Barbara pleaded, "but not now, just when a parliament is called. Do you think Guy or Simon will admit what they have done? Will they not claim that you and my father seek some political end by missaying them? And may not their indulgent father believe them—not because he wishes to believe ill of you, Gilbert, but because he cannot bear to believe ill of his darlings?"

"Perhaps Gilbert should not involve himself," Alphonse conceded, "but I am your husband. I do not like to look like a fool or a craven, which is what I will look like if I run away."

"Look like to whom?" Barbara snapped. "Who will ever hear of this if we ourselves do not spread the tale abroad? Do you think Guy or Simon will admit they insulted me in front of my father's door and ran away like frightened children when he shouted at them? And how can anything you do fail to involve Gilbert? Are you not a guest in his house—"

"Yes," Gloucester put in. "You have said it yourself, Barby. I am already involved, so there is no sense trying to keep me out. I—"

Barbara put her hands to her head, and Alphonse took her into his arms, burying her face against his chest and saying hastily, "No, love, no. You are quite right."

Meanwhile, he winked over Barbara's head at Gloucester, who said grudgingly, "Oh, very well. Tomorrow I will send someone to inquire about a ship."

Gloucester clearly expected that Alphonse would talk her out of her intention, but in fact he did not try. He knew it was wrong to force Barbara into a situation in which she must constantly fear being a cause of conflict, but he resented violently not being allowed to teach a lesson to those two spoiled cockscombs. Moreover, he was eaten with curiosity about whether the poor response to Leicester's summons to parliament was owing to the bad weather or to some deeper reservation in the barons of the realm that portended ill for Leicester's hold on England.

Thus nothing more was said about the subject of leaving England. Gloucester went out soon after he agreed to find a ship to take them to France, and the next day Norfolk came to tell Barbara he was going home. He said it was plain that no valid decisions about Prince Edward or anything else could be made, since only Leicester's closest allies had responded to the summons. He had more important things to do, he told Gloucester, and better ways to spend his money than idling away his time in London.

When Norfolk was gone, Alphonse realized that whatever was to happen in England could not take place soon. Meanwhile, he could not force a confrontation with Simon and Guy without causing trouble for Gloucester, and unless he did that, Barbe could not walk the streets or visit a friend without fear. So he sought out Gloucester and told him that he now thought he and Barbe *should* go. And when Gloucester protested, he pointed out Barbe's situation. Gloucester opened his mouth to say something else, but flushed and clamped his jaw. Then he shrugged and nodded and went down to the lower floor where his men-at-arms were quartered. Alphonse was disturbed by his young friend's expression, but when Gloucester came up, he seemed to have cast off his worries.

Any doubts Alphonse might have had about whether to stay in England to stand by Gloucester in any trouble were put to rest on Saturday, January 24, when a messenger from the king's court delivered an order bidding him to leave the country within a week. Because he had already decided to go, he told no one about the order and swallowed his outrage until Monday, when Gloucester came in with a sheet of parchment in his hand and a grin from ear to ear on his face.

"You and Barbara cannot go away to France," Gloucester said. "Barby is forbidden to leave the country."

"What!" Alphonse exclaimed. "That is impossible!"

Gloucester shrugged and handed over the parchment, and Alphonse read aloud from the list of those prohibited from taking ship at any port, " 'Barbara, the natural daughter of our beloved

Roger Bigod, earl of Norfolk—for that she would be at risk of falling into enemy hands—is forbidden to travel abroad.' "

"But an order expelling me as a foreigner with 'no known purpose in the country' came on Saturday," Alphonse protested.

"Expelling you?" Gloucester repeated and then burst out laughing. "Those puling cowards!"

"What puling cowards? What are you talking about?"

"I am talking about Simon and Guy. They are the only ones who have any reason to be rid of you. They must be at the bottom of the order expelling you, from whomever it comes. Why did you not tell me?"

Alphonse's lips hardened with anger. "I guessed it might be their doing, through some complaint to their father. Why I did not tell you is simple enough. It seemed foolish to cause more bad feeling when you had already sent your man to see about a ship." He paused, then added softly, "But I will not leave England without Barbe. Not if I have to—"

Gloucester took a deep breath, as if a weight had fallen off his shoulders. "Of course you will not go without Barby. As of today you have a purpose in this country. You are a member of my household, and you are the marshal entrusted with the arrangements for my party in the tourney to be held at Dunstable on Shrove Tuesday."

The rage disappeared from Alphonse's face, and he began to laugh. "So that is why Simon and Guy wanted me gone now, without delay. They did not wish me to fight in your tourney. Am I right?"

Gloucester nodded. "Oh, yes, you are quite right. Simon and Guy de Montfort will lead the party opposed to mine in the tourney."

A grin as broad as Gloucester's split Alphonse's face. "If you have challenged them, Barbe will flay us both," he said.

"It was not a challenge," Gloucester stated, his blue eyes as wide and innocent as a baby's. "It was a mutual agreement."

Chapter 24

Barbara was very angry when she heard that she had been prohibited from leaving England while Alphonse was to be expelled. She was so angry, she was almost as enthusiastic about the tournament as Gloucester and her husband. Her fear that Alphonse might be injured in the fighting was, in this case, overmastered by her knowledge of his skill. She herself had seen Guy fleeing him down the road, and she was certain Alphonse had spoken the exact truth, or less than the truth, when he said he had dropped Simon on his head in a practice encounter at Kenilworth.

Nor was Barbara much worried about the political repercussions of Gloucester making Alphonse a member of his household to circumvent the order to leave the country. Like Gloucester and Alphonse she had concluded that the two orders had not come from Leicester, although he might have set his seal on them. She did not mention her thoughts aloud, lest the men think her vain, but she was convinced the orders had somehow been arranged by Guy so that she would be left open to his advances. Not that she believed Guy had the smallest sexual desire for her any longer. By now his only purpose was to humiliate her and Alphonse.

At first she could hardly wait to see Alphonse and Gilbert beat

Simon and Guy to bleeding hulks. She stopped hiding in the house and went out, even to court, although never alone. With Gloucester or Alphonse beside her, she looked calmly down her handsome nose or lifted her lip in a sneer if either of the brothers approached, knowing she was giving as much pleasure to her male escorts as she was herself taking. After the first few meetings, however, she grew a trifle uneasy because she detected a kind of gleeful satisfaction under Guy's fury. On February 2, she discovered the basis for that glee. Four men-at-arms came to Gloucester's house to arrest "Alphonse d'Aix, a foreigner who had overstayed his time in England."

They never got inside the house, of course. Gloucester's men, who had been warned this might happen, laughed in the captain's face, and Gilbert's master-at-arms brought out an impressive document, written boldly on a large sheet of parchment and sealed heavily with Gloucester's personal seal and the great seal of England, which stated that Sieur Alphonse d'Aix was a servant of the earl of Gloucester and had the right to remain in England and travel throughout the realm freely on his master's business and his own for a year and a day. The parchment was handed over, it being only one copy of many, to be passed upward to whoever had ordered Alphonse forcibly deported. Another copy, Gloucester's master-at-arms informed the surprised captain of the arresting officers, was in Sieur Alphonse's possession, and still others were deposited in secure places to be ready in case of complaint.

When the attempted arrest was reported to Alphonse and Gilbert, they nodded wisely at each other and began to discuss what Simon and Guy would try next to ensure their victory at Dunstable. That was when Barbara began to have second thoughts. She realized that, unless Alphonse and Gilbert killed them, the result of the tourney would have little effect beyond increasing the Montforts' hatred. Far from ending their efforts to get their revenge, defeat would only make those efforts more furtive. Thus, it was almost a relief to her when, two days later, Gilbert received an invitation to speak to Leicester.

"I wonder who was cozened—or bribed—to complain to Leicester that you did not obey the order to leave," Gloucester said to Alphonse after he told Leicester's messenger that he would come and sent him back to his master. "Or do you think the complaint will be that I have taken a foreigner into my household?"

"I will come with you, if I may," Alphonse said mildly. "You will be able to defend your right to choose your servants, of course, but I would like very much to speak for myself on the subject of the attempt to separate me from my wife."

"I want to come, too," Barbara said. "I want to make very clear that I approve the separation no more than does my husband."

Gloucester looked from one to the other and smiled. "I do not need protection," he said, but his expression was grateful.

"I will be no protection to you," Alphonse remarked dryly. "To speak the truth, what I have to say may grate most unpleasantly—"

"That is exactly what I am afraid of," Barbara interrupted sharply. "You are both going to stalk into that audience like dogs with your hackles up. I like what was done no better than either of you, but I am not so blind with bad temper. Remember that Leicester himself may be quite innocent. Who knows what tale has been told him? I think it is time that I complained of Guy's persecution."

Both men, who had started to protest during Barbara's first few words, reconsidered. Gloucester, who did feel uneasy about confronting Leicester for taking Alphonse into his service after a writ against him had been issued, was aware that Barbara's argument would deflect any blame from him—whether Leicester believed her or not. Alphonse felt a spurt of pleasure in her willingness to back him in any argument and, particularly, in her willingness to speak aloud her affection for him; plenty of wives would be overjoyed if their husbands were exiled. Barbara hoped that her complaint against Guy would induce Leicester to revoke the prohibition against traveling so that she and Alphonse could leave England, which would eliminate any chance for future mischief by his sons.

They were all so certain that Leicester intended to reprimand Gloucester for shielding Alphonse that they were considerably surprised when he merely acknowledged Alphonse's and Barbara's presence with courteous nods. Peter de Montfort, who was standing with his cousin, also smiled at them. Barbara and Alphonse glanced at each other behind Gloucester's back. The looks questioned without words whether it was possible that Leicester had not even known of the orders concerning them.

"I asked you to come, Gilbert," Leicester said, pleasantly but with a kind of authority that implied Gloucester could not have refused, "because I thought it only right to tell you in person that the king has forbidden any tourney to be held at this time."

"But this is the best time of year for a tourney," Gloucester protested, so bewildered by the unexpected tack that he answered the literal words rather than the meaning. "The crops are all harvested; there is yet no young growth in the fields to be trampled; everyone is idle and looking for entertainment . . ."

"Yes, yes," Leicester said as Gloucester faltered to silence. He sounded impatient, like an adult explaining something obvious to a child. "But do you not see that the gathering of a large crowd of idle armed men is the last thing we want when we are negotiating for the prince's release? I cannot permit it."

"*You* cannot permit it?" Gloucester's voice rose till it cracked.

"Now—" Leicester began.

"I thought you said the *king* had forbidden it," Gloucester interrupted, his voice lower now and steady.

"Do not act like a spoiled child, Gilbert," Leicester said. "You may have your amusement another time—"

"The king has a right to command me." Gloucester's face was now as red as his hair, but an unfortunately ugly clashing shade. "You, my lord, have not. I never heard or agreed that one of us was to be set above the other. I have deferred to you in the past because I felt you to be wise and impartial. No armed men under my command will prevent Edward's release. I will have what you call 'my amusement' on Shrove Tuesday, the date set by agreement with your sons, and I will cry craven on any man party to that agreement who does not come."

"My sons will have no part of this tourney because that is my order and because they have more care for the peace and good management of this realm than you." This time it was Leicester's voice that was rough and angry.

Gilbert laughed harshly, his mouth ugly with tension. "If you believe that, you are the only man in the realm who does. I will be at Dunstable on Shrove Tuesday—"

"You will obey my order!" Leicester bellowed.

"Simon!" Peter de Montfort protested, coming forward and gripping Leicester's arm.

Simultaneously, Alphonse had come closer and said in Gloucester's ear, "A good jouster does not lose his temper. Anger leads only to a fall. Turn your back on him and walk away. He will look a helpless fool yelling after you."

As he spoke, Alphonse gripped Gloucester's shoulder and tugged at it lightly. The young earl resisted for a moment, but on the last few words he turned smartly about and marched down the hall toward the door.

Behind him Leicester shouted, "I warn you that you and any man who comes with you and disobeys the writ will be cast into a place where you will enjoy neither sun nor moon—"

Barbara, who had been following close on the heels of her menfolk, looked back as Leicester's voice stopped abruptly. She saw him drop his head as if ashamed and shake it when Peter de Montfort asked a question. The tightness in her throat and chest eased a trifle. She was not certain whether Peter had asked if he should go after Gloucester to apologize or if he should order them taken prisoner, but clearly Leicester had decided no action should be taken.

Then she hurried on again, fearing to be left behind because Alphonse did not dare remove his attention from Gloucester to look for her. They found their horses in the courtyard, saddled as they had left them, ready for trouble—although they had not guessed the kind of trouble they would find—with Chacier and Gloucester's master-at-arms alert at their heads. Without exchanging a word they mounted and rode out of the gate, through the middle bailey, and over the drawbridge across the moat.

Only when they were on the road that led to Candlewick Street did Gloucester say, "I never knew what cowards Guy and Simon were. I was not surprised when they tried to strip my party of you, Alphonse. I was sure they thought that having you gave me an unfair advantage." He smiled. "I was a little worried about that myself, and wondered if I should ask you not to take part in the melee." Then he frowned again. "But to run whining to hide under their father's gown to save themselves a few bruises . . . I would not have believed that."

"Nor should you," Alphonse said. "Do not confuse vanity with fear. It is their pride that is tender, not their flesh. I think Guy and Simon would fight to the death without quailing or turning tail—but a tourney is not to the death, and they would have to live with the sneers over their defeat. Their fear of being laughed at, not any fear of being hurt, was the cause of telling Leicester."

Barbara was grateful to Alphonse for trying to quiet and warn Gloucester, who was still very angry at having his chance of revenge on the young Montforts for many petty slights snatched away. If Alphonse had not helped Peter de Montfort cut short the quarrel with Leicester, such bitter words could have been said as to throw Gloucester into the Royalist camp with no more ado. But if both men had lost their tempers enough to utter threats, Leicester could have had them all arrested right then.

Gloucester's high complexion still flew storm signals, and Alphonse was urging him to save the rest of what he had to say. Once on Candlewick Street, with its shop counters protruding into the road and crowds of buyers, hawkers, and walkers, they had to ride single file and would have needed to shout at each other to be heard.

Barbara followed, thinking hard. She did not underestimate her husband or believe he wanted a true reconciliation between the two earls. Alphonse wanted to find for Gloucester a safer and less violent path to the prince's party than an open quarrel with Leicester. She was shocked to discover the thought gave her a strong sense of satisfaction. That would never do. If Gloucester changed sides, active war would break out; she did not want that. She had better suggest that the blame for canceling the tourney did not lie altogether on the shoulders of the Montforts.

As soon as they had reached Gilbert's house and were in the large hall, before Alphonse or Gloucester could speak, Barbara asked, "Why are you so sure Simon or Guy told Leicester to stop the tourney?"

Both men turned faces blank with surprise to her, Gloucester's hand arrested in the act of pulling out his cloak pin.

"You did not make any secret of the tourney," she went on. "And anyone with a flicker of sense could see there would be trouble when armed men with grudges met. More than one must have told Leicester it was dangerous to allow a tourney at this time. Likely the fault was mostly mine for coming to court apurpose to tempt Simon and Guy into immoderate behavior while clinging to you for protection." This time Barbara shook her head to silence loud exclamations of protest and continued, "What I did made the bad feeling between you apparent to all. I do not love either Guy or Simon de Montfort, but I know they are not cowards—except in one thing."

"And that?" Gloucester asked, his head cocked to the side as he finished pulling the pin from his cloak.

"They are terrified of their father's disapproval, not because they fear to be punished but because they are aware of his love—and aware they are unworthy."

Gloucester looked as though he had had a heavenly revelation, but he did not speak at once. He gestured for Barbara and Alphonse to come with him nearer the fire, swinging off his cloak and handing it blindly behind him. A servant caught it as he opened his hand.

"It fits," he muttered, "and it explains many things."

Barbara had pulled off her gloves and passed them to Clotilde, who had come running up. She rubbed her hands briskly together and held them out to the heat as the maid removed her cloak, but her eyes flicked from Gloucester's thoughtful face to Alphonse's. They stood in a small semicircle, Gloucester by his great chair, which had been placed before the high-leaping fire, Barbara beside the bench to the right of the chair, and Alphonse between them. Barbara noted that her husband wore his "court face," his lips faintly curved in the hint of a smile, the whole expression alert and pleasant but totally unreadable.

Then Gloucester laughed. "You are very clever, Barby," he said, "but that does not amend the fact that Simon and Guy are nasty pieces of work and need a good lesson."

"But not at the cost of open defiance of the king's writ forbidding the tourney," Alphonse said. "All that can accomplish is to provide Leicester with a good excuse to lock you up."

Gloucester did not look at all startled by what Alphonse had said; Barbara realized the idea was not new to him. "I may have provided that already," he said sourly.

"Oh, no." Alphonse shed his own cloak and walked past Barbara, stopping beside her but closer to the fire. When he turned to Gloucester again, his face was shadowed by the brightness behind him. "I am sure Leicester did not intend to provoke you. He will not use your natural response to his unfortunate manner as an excuse to arrest you. If he wanted to do that, he would have done it before we left his presence."

"I do not mean today's quarrel." Gloucester glanced at Alphonse and then looked away, into the fire. "You remember that before we left Worcester I gave Mortimer and his friends leave to delay their departure for Ireland by a month. I did not tell you before because it did not seem to matter, but Leicester took exception to my lenience. He accused me of taking his enemies under my protection."

"Well," Alphonse said, "perhaps it might not be a bad idea to leave London . . . ah . . . quietly."

"But not to go to Dunstable," Barbara put in.

"I must go to Dunstable, Barby," Gloucester said. "I will not hide like a scolded puppy. If the king's writ is delivered there and the tourney forbidden in Henry's name, I will not defy the writ. But this has nothing to do with you anymore. If there will be no tourney, then Alphonse's purpose here is ended, and I think the time has come for you to leave the country—"

"No!" The male and female voices, though different in pitch, sounded exactly the same note of determination.

Gloucester looked from one to the other and laughed.

"I am forbidden to leave anyway," Barbara said.

"And I am no puppy either, to be chased from my bitch by a bigger dog," Alphonse added.

"That is not in question," Gloucester said. "Had Leicester known about either of those orders, he would not have greeted you as he did. Tomorrow I will write to Leicester to ask about having the prohibition against travel for Barby removed."

"No." Barbara shook her head energetically, and the young earl vented an exasperated sigh.

"This is not your stinking stew but mine," Gloucester said. "I mixed it and cooked it. Why should you eat it?"

"Oh, Gilbert—" Barbara began, but Alphonse cut her short,

gesturing with one hand and squeezing her shoulder with the other.

"Wait, Barbe," he said. "Gilbert's idea is not such a bad one—"

"I will not go off to France alone and leave you two here to brew up more trouble," Barbara protested.

"No, no." Alphonse laughed. "We could not do without you, my love. What I was about to say is that if Gilbert uses that prohibition as an excuse to write to Leicester, he will learn at once whether a reasonable request will receive a reasonable answer. If it does, it would be stupid for Gilbert to annoy Leicester by rushing out of London, especially to Dunstable."

The reasonable request, sent off the morning of the next day, received no answer at all, which was puzzling. The lack of response might have been alarming rather than puzzling, but after dinner Gloucester received what could be looked on as a gesture of reconciliation from Leicester—a long report detailing the proposed exchange of property between the prince and himself. The exchange was designed to break Edward's power in the west, so that he could not begin a new war, but at the same time not deprive the prince of a decent income.

Gloucester looked at the parchments spread over the table in his bedchamber with some distaste and repressed his impulse to carry them out and show them to Alphonse. Although he knew the report had been sent to soothe him by implying he was important and must be included in the negotiations, he also regarded Leicester's gesture as a warning. A significant portion of Gloucester's own property was in the west. Once Leicester had control of what had been Edward's lands, he would be in a far better position to suppress any rising against him. Gloucester sat and stared at the closely written sheets of parchment. Did he really want Leicester breathing down his neck in the Marches? Worse yet, he and Leicester's sons were young—Leicester himself was not. When the earl was dead, the lands would go to his sons. Gloucester grimaced as he thought of having Simon or Guy as a neighbor.

His glance lifted from the parchments at which he had been staring unseeingly and settled on his writing desk. Within it there lay a letter from Mortimer, which had come the day after the attempt to arrest and deport Alphonse. The letter was a request for another postponement of his departure for Ireland; Mortimer said his wife had fallen ill with strain and grief and he wished to stay until she was more settled. Gloucester knew quite well that Mortimer's request was only a device to avoid exile; if he granted it, every other lord Marcher would also beg to stay in England. He had been about to write a curt refusal. Now . . .

He thought again about Simon and Guy as neighbors in Wales and ground his teeth. Even if they did not attack him, they would almost certainly upset the delicate balance of the relationship he had maintained with the Welsh. Mortimer had been a good conduit to Llywelyn before Leicester had offered Llywelyn better terms to turn on his cousin. But Gloucester knew Llywelyn. That he accepted Leicester's terms would not necessarily make Llywelyn Mortimer's enemy. So if the situation changed—if power in the west shifted out of Leicester's hands—Mortimer would be useful again to bargain with his cousin.

The question was rapidly becoming, Gloucester thought, whether it was better to endure the rapacity of Leicester's favorites or the king's favorites. He pushed away the parchments, then pulled them closer but did not read from them. Whatever property was confiscated, whatever was "temporarily" placed in Leicester's hands, only his sons and a few very close friends would profit. It had not been that way in the beginning. The Council had agreed to control the king's extravagance and dismiss his favorites; the power and responsibility had been evenly distributed. Only since the battle of Lewes, since Leicester had taken and kept the king a virtual prisoner, had the earl, little by little, made himself all powerful.

Again Gloucester suppressed an urge to talk over the subject with Alphonse, which reminded him that Barbara still did not have permission to leave the country and that she and Alphonse clearly intended to accompany him to Dunstable. It was stupid and unnecessary for them to do so, but Gloucester understood why they insisted. He had stood by them when they were in trouble, and now they intended to return the favor.

Irritably, he reached for a clean sheet of parchment. He would think about Alphonse and Barbara later. Right now he had to decide what to write to Mortimer—and if he was not going to refuse Mortimer's plea to remain at Wigmore, decide to whom he should entrust the letter. He did not want Leicester to intercept it because— He broke off the thought, rather relieved at not needing to complete it and delighted that the solution to both his problems had interrupted an idea too dangerous to formulate before he obtained more information. Alphonse could take his letter to Thomas at St. Briavels, and Thomas could send it on to Mortimer.

He started to get up at once to explain his brilliant notion, then laughed aloud and sank back in his seat. The letter had to be written first. Gloucester took a quill from the writing desk, fished around for the small, sharp knife that was always kept in it, and trimmed the quill, his lips pursed. If Alphonse was going to carry the letter to St. Briavels, there was no chance at all that it would be lost or taken from him; he would destroy it before he was captured—or Barby would destroy it for him. Thus it would be safe to write . . . what? It would be safe, but what did he want to say?

The quill cut, Gloucester unstoppered the ink horn, dipped the point, and drew a short line on the bottom of the nearest piece of parchment to test it. Then he paused. Mortimer would see at once that the letter had not been written by a clerk. Would that make him read too much into anything that was said? A man did not trouble himself to write unless he wished to keep very secret what was written. Should he call his clerk? No. Gloucester smiled. To write in his own hand would solve the problem of what to say—he need say nothing that would commit him to any act. It would be sufficient to write good wishes for Mortimer's well-doing. That plus the extension of Mortimer's leave to remain in England for another month would be enough.

He began to write, then stopped and smiled. And now he had his insurance that Alphonse would not refuse to go to St. Briavels. He could give Alphonse a word-of-mouth message for Thomas: to arrange a meeting between him and Mortimer during the early part of March. Alphonse would surely understand that he would not wish to commit that message either to writing or to a common messenger. And his clerk was old; it would be cruel to send him all the way to Wales in winter weather.

Chapter 25

For the first few weeks after she and Alphonse arrived at St. Briavels, Barbara enjoyed being the lady of the castle. Though the keep was in good order, many of the amenities provided by a woman were lacking. Thomas de Clare had no wife, and the widow of the old castellan had retired to a convent when Thomas took hold for his brother. Within a day of arriving, Barbara was hearing from Clotilde of menservants in rags because the cloth readied for their new clothes had never been cut or sewed, of wool carded and spun but not bleached or dyed because no one knew what its purpose should be, of waste and mismanagement of food because Thomas was often away and there was no one to say what part of a slaughtered animal should be served, what part salted or, if there was more soft curd than anyone wanted to eat, that the excess should be pressed into hard cheese.

Absently, her mind on the more serious problem of what she should do about her husband's intention to ride back and meet Gloucester at Dunstable, Barbara allowed Clotilde to shepherd her to the trouble spots and settled the household problems. Realizing later what she had done, she apologized for interfering to Thomas, who had comically got down on his knees and begged her to continue. Thus, she almost accidentally became the lady of the keep.

The occupation the task had given her was fortunate because she was totally unsuccessful in stopping Alphonse from leaving for Dunstable. When, in the privacy of their bedchamber in the west gate tower, she protested to Alphonse that Gloucester did not want him at Dunstable and that he had not yet given Gilbert's message to Mortimer, Alphonse laughed at her.

"Thomas will give the message to Mortimer, if he responds to Gloucester's letter before I return here, but I expect to be back from Dunstable by the twentieth or twenty-first of February."

"You will only encourage Gloucester to fight," she said bitterly.

"No." Alphonse cupped her face in his hand. "I swear I will not. And though I do not wish to crow like a cock on a dung heap, if I am with Gilbert, the young Montforts are less likely to plead with their father to allow the tourney to take place. Not that I think their appeal would move Leicester, but why take the chance? And the last thing we need is another confrontation, so I hope to keep Gilbert from losing his temper again, if I can."

"And if you cannot? You will both end up in prison."

"Not I. The worst Leicester will do to me is expel me from the country." He burst out laughing again at the expression on her face, lifted her from her seat beside the small hearth, crushed her to him, and kissed her.

Taken by surprise, Barbara clung to him. When their lips parted, he said playfully, "I could swear from your sour look that you do not wish to part from me. Confess! Tell me you love me!"

For once Alphonse had struck the wrong note. Later Barbara asked herself whether he was awkward and off balance because she was more important to him than other women, but at the moment the teasing infuriated her. She pushed at him, and his arms tightened brutally. When she failed to free herself, she tilted back her head and lifted her brows.

"If you intend to 'press' a confession out of me, you are wasting your time. I told you before we married that I had loved you since I first laid eyes upon you—like every other woman."

He was hurt; the warmth and laughter disappeared from his voice and eyes, and though he made a light answer, he released her quickly. Then he had mumbled that he had forgotten to tell Chacier he thought a stirrup leather was wearing and should be replaced before they rode out again, and went away. Still angry, but more because her sense of fairness was in direct conflict with her jealousy, Barbara let him go.

She could not think of a way to open the subject of his remaining in St. Briavels again either, because she did not really fear any harm would come to him in Dunstable. Had she been truly afraid, she would have used other devices, even admitting that she was jealous if it was the only way to keep him safe. But she could not try to force Alphonse into what he would believe was abandonment of a friend in need just to keep her private green-eyed devil at bay.

Besides, he soon returned to her, seemingly cured of his hurt, in fact in a singularly good mood. Barbara guessed he might have put together her remark about every other woman with her reluctance to let him out of her sight to come to a conclusion too close to the truth. To betray her jealousy would be worse than letting him know she really did adore him. Thus, she was more yielding than usual when he began to caress her abed, and she let him ride off to Dunstable the next day with no more than an astringent reminder that he had promised to keep Gilbert from fighting, not goad him into it.

Alphonse left St. Briavels on February 12. On the sixteenth, a messenger came from Mortimer with thanks for the extended leave to stay and a warning that he had yielded two of his fortified manors in Wales to Montfort's deputies. If Thomas was wise, the messenger said, he would warn his brother that Montfort had sent far too few men. Mortimer, the message continued, was not sure whether this was a sign of weakness in Leicester or a sign that the earl did not wish to defend Mortimer's property. Whichever was true, one thing was certain: The Montforts would not try to protect Gloucester's nearby Welsh estates from raiding.

"And what am I to do about this?" Thomas said to Barbara when he had dismissed the messenger to find a meal for himself in the kitchen. "No rider from here could reach Dunstable by tomorrow, and I have not the faintest notion where Gilbert will go afterward."

"You are not really worried about the lands, are you?" Barbara asked.

Thomas shook his head. "What Mortimer says is very likely true, and I may send an extra troop to each manor, but Mortimer sent this warning to bring Gilbert west. You know Gilbert intends to meet Mortimer in March, but if I now suggest that meeting to Mortimer's man, will it not sound as if Gilbert is too eager? But if I do not use this messenger, I may not find it so easy to discover where to send the invitation later. Mortimer is moving often and keeping his whereabouts secret to reduce the chance he might be arrested despite Gilbert's order."

Experience with an uncle and a father who moved often and rapidly around the country had taught Barbara the answer to that problem. "Mortimer cannot guess how uncertain Gilbert's plans are. He will not know that Gilbert may be out of your reach, so thank him for his warning, tell him you are sending it on to Gilbert, and ask him to send a man again in six days—unless he wishes to tell you where he will be at that time—because you are sure Gilbert will want to thank him for the warning, perhaps in person."

"Now that is a clever notion." Thomas smiled at her.

"It is possible too," Barbara added, "that before the six days are over, Alphonse will be back here with news of Gilbert's whereabouts, if he has gone elsewhere than Tonbridge or London."

In fact it was on the sixth day, only a few hours before Mortimer's second messenger arrived in St. Briavels, that Barbara and Thomas learned Gilbert had gone to London after leaving Dunstable. They did not learn it from Alphonse, however. Alphonse had gone with Gloucester to London. It was Sir John Giffard who came with the news—and with a hundred men and more to follow.

In response to Gloucester's invitation to the proposed tourney, Sir John told them, he had gone first to Dunstable. While there, he had heard of the capture and arrest of Robert de Ferrars, the earl of Derby, for lawlessness.

"Good riddance," Thomas muttered. "Who has Ferrars for a friend needs no enemies. That man is like a wild beast. Whatever he wants, he takes, without regard to law or loyalty."

"But will the arrests stop with Derby?" Sir John asked. "Leicester said publicly that he hoped Derby's arrest would prove that all men, whether or not they were his supporters, were equally subject to the law. If they had taken property—even in lieu of ransom from those who had been their prisoners—they must be prosecuted."

"That is not going to sit well with many," Barbara remarked tartly. "But I cannot believe Leicester could be so unreasonable. There have been so many years of disorder. To speak of prosecuting every crime is crazy."

"Not if Leicester is seeking a legal excuse to rid himself of anyone who is not blindly obedient to his will and his vision," Sir John pointed out bitterly.

There was a brief, tense silence, then Thomas cried, "But if Gilbert thinks that too, why did he go back to London?"

"For my sake, curse me," Sir John groaned. "I went to Gilbert when I heard what Leicester said. In fact, I have taken land in lieu of ransom, as you know, Thomas, and I have had various other disagreements with Leicester. Then"—he nodded at Barbara—"there was that trouble with your husband. You could not know, but Guy rode up to Warwick at the end of October, foaming at the mouth, and accusing me of being party to making an attempt on his life. He said your husband laid an ambush for him, backed by a troop of the prince's friends."

"That is not what happened!" Barbara exclaimed, and gave a brief explanation of the attack by Guy's larger party on their smaller one and how Hamo le Strange had become involved. "But surely Guy cannot blame you for what happened outside of Gloucester. How could you know he would go to Gloucester?" she pointed out.

Sir John shrugged. "One can be blamed for anything at all, when an excuse for blame is sought. Anyway, Gloucester said I should take my men and come here and he would try to find out exactly what Leicester planned. I argued until I was blue, but he would not listen to me."

Thomas only shook his head, but his young mouth looked so hard and grim that Barbara could have wept. Her anxiety increased when, over the next few days, she realized Thomas and Sir John were quietly making ready for war. She feared any moment to see Gilbert and her husband come flying down the road pursued by an army, but no one came except the serfs whose service was due and Mortimer's messenger. The messenger reported that Lord Mortimer did not wish to be offensive and did wish to speak to Gloucester in person, but he could not help fearing this suggested meeting was a trick to take him prisoner, like Derby, and he wanted hostages for his free coming and going to and from the place of meeting.

Thomas threw up his hands in despair. He was offended that Mortimer would not trust his brother's word of honor and wanted to refuse outright. Then recalling that they might be on the verge of a war, he realized he could not afford to cast away any ally. Sir John agreed, and began to ruminate on what was best to do. Barbara, eager to fix her mind on any problem that did not include a pitched battle between Leicester and Gloucester in which her husband was involved, came to a quick decision; she urged Thomas to offer her and Alphonse as hostages to Mortimer.

"I cannot do that," the young man cried, looking horrified. "Gilbert would kill me if I suggested that his guests be turned into prisoners."

"Not if the offer came from the guests. And who else can Gilbert send? Besides, I am not at all sure Mortimer will accept us; he may not think we are of enough value to Gilbert—but to make the offer will gain time. The messenger will have to go and come back again. I am sure Gilbert will be here by then—"

Her voice faltered. She was beginning to have visions of Alphonse dead on the road instead of fleeing before an army, but both visions turned out to be false. In the late afternoon of February 27, one day before Mortimer's messenger made his fourth appearance, Gloucester and Alphonse rode into St. Briavels. They were cold and muddy, but that was the worst danger they had suffered on their journey. The red-brown stains on their armor and surcoats, which had made Barbara bite her lip when they shed their cloaks, were rust, not blood.

At first everyone asked questions and no one answered, but once mail and wet cloaks had been shed, dry clothes donned, and the whole party settled around the roaring fire, little by little everything was made clear. Gloucester had had no open confrontation with Leicester, but neither had he obtained any assurance that Sir John—or anyone else—would be pardoned for past offenses. He had thus been very glad to use the excuse of danger to his Welsh lands to leave London for St. Briavels. Then Thomas brought him up to date on Mortimer's demands.

''Hostages!'' Gloucester exclaimed. ''After I have put myself at risk to delay his banishment to Ireland—''

''Gilbert,'' Barbara interrupted, ''do not take at face value anything Mortimer does or says. I cannot swear that fear of capture has not overpowered his real knowledge that you can be trusted, but equally I cannot swear that the hostages you send will not serve some far cleverer purpose than ensuring Mortimer's safety. In any case, do not take as an insult what cannot have been meant as one.''

''Cannot?'' Gloucester asked, but more curiously than angrily.

''Oh, Gilbert, a man who wishes to insult another does not send messengers back and forth a half-dozen times. Mortimer made the first moves toward reconciliation too. And you may as well know that by my advice and urging Thomas has already offered him hostages—me and Alphonse.''

Gloucester looked at Alphonse, who was sitting beside Barbara. He had taken her hand in his own and, after she spoke, raised and kissed it. Then Gloucester looked back at Barbara.

''I think you should know, Barby, that Alphonse has already confessed to me that you were not really held as prisoners at Wigmore. I must tell you also that I am no longer satisfied with the earl of Leicester's control of the king, the prince, the government—everything. I may be forced to oppose him openly, and that would perhaps make me your father's enemy.''

''Why?'' Barbara asked. ''Papa does not approve of everything Leicester does either. He only opposes the king's extravagance. I do not think my father will regard you as an enemy unless you attack him—on his own lands.''

''You may be sure I will not do that,'' Gloucester said, smiling.

"And I think Barbe has proposed the perfect answer to Mortimer's request," Alphonse remarked, bringing the subject back to the hostage question.

Gloucester grumbled that he could not use his guests as hostages, but Alphonse only laughed.

"If Mortimer will accept us," he said, "you may take it as a clear sign he *does* trust you and has asked for hostages for some reason we cannot yet guess. Mortimer is no fool, you know, and must realize that he can have no hold on you through us, who have neither blood bond with you nor military value to you, unless you are a man of honor."

Gloucester made another protest about exposing those under his protection to danger, but Barbara could see that he spoke more for form's sake than out of conviction. And, since he was actually quite certain that Alphonse and Barbara would only exchange one host for another, it did not take much longer to bring him to agree to the arrangement. The talk then moved on to expedients to be considered if Mortimer refused the proffered hostages.

Having gained her original objective, which was to do what she could to isolate Alphonse with Mortimer in case Leicester and Gloucester came to war, Barbara could relax. She took up her work basket and drew out her embroidery—this time a neckband and front, to be sewn into a court gown for Alphonse. Listening to the men's talk, she pulled out the tail of the front somewhat carelessly. The cloth caught on something heavy, and the basket shifted, nearly tipping off Barbara's knees.

Only as she caught the basket with half the yarn and bits of cloth toppling out did Barbara remember that she had replaced the silver mirror in it when Alphonse left St. Briavels. Color flooded her cheeks, and she bent her body concealingly over the basket. A swift downward glance showed only a glint of silver; a quick tuck, and the betraying symbol of her enslavement was out of sight. Barbara chose a length of yarn, took the needle from the cloth, and straightened up. When she raised the needle to thread it, she dared take a quick look at Alphonse. He seemed unaware of her, intent on the men's talk, which had now shifted to the question of a meeting place both Gloucester and Mortimer would consider safe.

A short, fervent prayer of thanks passed through her mind and brought a sudden inspiration. "There is a better place to meet than a town," she said. "Llanthony Abbey."

"Too close to Gloucester," Thomas protested.

"No, I meant the older one, in the vale of Ewias. It is right at the foot of Black Mountain."

She then described the place, which she remembered vividly, although she had been there only once, when King Henry and Queen Eleanor had made a tour of especially holy foundations. The original Llanthony Abbey was isolated and primitive, a poor, neglected mother of the flourishing daughter abbey near Gloucester. Sir John groaned when Barbara mentioned how few visitors ever dared the bare, narrow track that threaded the hills to the place and the correspondingly limited and Spartan accommodations, but Gloucester nodded and laughed.

''I think I am going to dismiss my marshal and appoint you instead, Barby,'' he said. ''You have a very fine grasp of where places are and the purposes to which they best lend themselves.''

''No, I have not,'' Barbara protested. ''But Llanthony is truly very holy. No one would dare commit an act of treachery there. Even Mortimer will feel the sanctity; possibly he knows the place already, and he will understand. To betray a man in Llanthony would be such an offense against God that even Mary's mercy would be strained to forgive.''

There was a slight pause, and then Gloucester said, ''I hope Mortimer is as sensitive as you.'' He smiled faintly and looked around at his male companions, each of whom nodded approval of Barbara's proposal. ''Well, we have our offer for meeting ready. We have only to learn whether Mortimer is interested enough to take a risk.''

''Then I will bid you all to have a good night,'' Alphonse said, standing up and holding out his hand to Barbara. ''You may have nothing better to do than sit and swill wine, but I . . . Well, wife?''

A spate of male humor covered Barbara's first moment of shock. So he had seen the mirror! She should have known Alphonse would not so completely ignore her sudden physical movement if he had not seen the mirror and her stupid attempt to conceal it. If only she had not tried to hide it. Now what could she say?

Suppressing a horrid vision of Alphonse pulling out the mirror and laughing at her if she carried the basket to their chamber, she stuffed the embroidery back into it and pushed it under the bench. One of the men asked a question, and she answered with a laugh—the sound seemed forced and she had not the faintest notion whether her response was appropriate, but no one seemed surprised. Then Alphonse put her cloak around her and pulled the hood over her head. Their dash across the bailey through a sleety rain to the west gate tower dispelled some of Barbara's shock but brought no inspiration, and she swallowed desperately as she turned to face her husband when he closed the door of their chamber.

''Barbe,'' he said, throwing back his hood, ''I had to talk to you in private before Gloucester began to tell you what he hopes his meeting with Mortimer will accomplish. I am very grateful to you for always seeming to support me and to approve the choices I make, but I know your sympathies were with Leicester and I do not want you burdened with secrets you feel it wrong to keep."

Barbara stood with one hand on the edge of her cloak, which she had been about to remove, and stared at him without answering. He had not seen the mirror. He had not been moved to leave the hall by guessing how much she desired him. She should have been overjoyed; instead she was furious.

Alphonse stared back at her, frowning. "Barbe?" he urged softly. "You do understand that Gloucester may break with Leicester—"

"I am not an idiot," she snapped, pulling off her cloak. "I heard him say so."

Alphonse dropped his cloak on the chest by the wall and came forward, reaching for Barbara's. She almost threw it at him. "Sorry," he said. His voice was meek, his eyes wary. "I seem to have committed a most infantile sin, making too clear to a woman that she has changed her mind."

"I have not changed my mind!"

"No, of course not."

She stamped her foot and in the next moment burst out laughing. What a fool she was to sulk. She had lost nothing. A brief feeling of puzzlement filled her. Why should she be angry at having escaped exposure of her slavish devotion? But the silence was stretching, and she said quickly, "Oh, you monster, to hold your temper like an angel so I will be filled with remorse. And to say you committed a childish sin, implying that you had come to expect better of me than of other women . . . Monster of deceit!"

Alphonse put her cloak with his and came back toward her with hand outstretched. "No, I am not, Barbe, but I want to be sure you are clear in your own mind where this is leading. I value your loyalty to me more than I can say, but I do not want you to feel you have betrayed your friends to honor your marriage bond."

Barbara sighed and gave him her hand. He pulled her close and she dropped her head to his shoulder. "I will not blame you, if that is what you fear." She sighed again. "Mostly—as women so often do—I have spoken without really thinking of the result, but I do not regret it. I have seen that Leicester is losing the trust of those who supported him. Even when what he does is plainly just, like curbing the earl of Derby, he is suspected of evil purposes."

"It is because he does not have the right to rule, because he is no more or less than any other earl. Thus, whatever order he gives is resented. A king is set by God above other men, so they do not take offense when he commands them. Leicester knows this as well as any other, so he places his trust in those who are bound to obey him by nature—his sons and his blood kin."

"Which makes the resentment of others worse and worse." Barbara shivered. "But what else could he have done?" she cried. "The king was destroying us!"

"Come, sit down, love." He led her to the bench by the small hearth, threw more wood on the fire, and sat down beside her, pulling her close again.

"God knows what Leicester should have done," he went on. "In his place, I would have gone to Prince Edward after the battle of Lewes and asked him to persuade his father to let Edward rule in his stead. Then, with sufficient safeguards for my own and my allies' safety—and they would need to be good safeguards because Edward holds grudges against those who have bested him and has a sly way of twisting words to mean what he wants them to mean—I would have left the prince to rule without any restriction other than ancient law and custom." He shrugged. "But Leicester still thinks of Edward as a foolish boy, needing the guidance of those older and wiser. He made the same mistake with Gloucester."

"Must it come to war again?" Barbara whispered.

"There is one small chance of avoiding another war. If Edward is freed and enough of the country rallies to him, Leicester may make a peace that simply protects him and his friends and, as he has done twice in the past, curse the fickle English and withdraw to France."

Barbara lifted her head from Alphonse's shoulder. "Do you think that likely?"

He hesitated and then said, "No. If Edward is freed, Leicester will move as fast as he can to retake him, and he will bring an army to the task. I do not think there will be any chance to negotiate. Of course, if he has lost so much support that he cannot raise an army—"

"He is weakest here in the west," Barbara said.

Alphonse smiled. "Gloucester is right. You would do very well as a marshal. Yes, love. That is why we are all here in the west."

"If, God forbid, war should be necessary, I do not think papa would come all the way to Wales—"

"No, I am very sure he would not," Alphonse assured her. "Nor will he be given any cause. Do you not remember that Gilbert just said he would not attack your father's lands? He knows your father is as little trusted and as little satisfied with Leicester as he. Gilbert will do nothing to antagonize Norfolk. I am sure he will avoid damage to Strigul as he would avoid a plague.''

They sat in silence for a few minutes, Barbara again placing her head confidingly on Alphonse's shoulder. He held her comfortingly while he looked at the flames, leaping high as they caught on the fresh logs. Though he did not look at her, he saw only his wife. She had told him so many times that she cared nothing for party, only for the safety of those she loved. Now he was coming to believe her. She trusted him; she clung to him; she was loyal. He even had reason to believe she was jealous of him. So what was she hiding from him? She kept some token, which she carried everywhere with her. Chacier had mentioned how she hid something from him, and he had seen her do it more than once himself.

''Barbe—'' he said.

She turned and put her arms around his neck. ''And what of you?'' she murmured. ''Will you be safe? Are you pledged to Gloucester?''

Had she read his thoughts and deliberately diverted him from the question he had finally found courage to ask? He put aside the impossible suspicion and tasted the lips so close to his. After a moment, Barbe shivered, took his head gently in her hands, and broke the kiss.

''Alphonse, answer me.''

Grateful for the respite—his courage had melted with her kiss and he no longer wanted to know about the token she kept hidden—he said, ''I have given no oaths—I cannot, being my brother's man, as I am—but . . .'' He drew a breath, and voice and face hardened. ''Yes, I will do anything in my power to free Prince Edward, and if it comes to war, I will fight as Gloucester or Edward order.''

Tears filled her eyes and rolled down her cheeks. He expected her to pull away, but she did not. Instead, still weeping, she pressed her mouth to his and then whispered against his lips, ''Love me. Love me while we may.''

Chapter 26

On the next day, the last of February, Mortimer's messenger came again to say his master would be satisfied with the hostages Gloucester offered. On the first of March, a day that presaged spring one moment with brilliant sunshine and renewed winter with vicious winds and spitting hail the next, Alphonse, Barbara, and their four servants rode away from St. Briavels with the messenger. They went not to Wigmore but to Weobly, a strong fortified manor no more than four leagues from Hereford but well back along a narrow, easily defended road.

Mortimer came out to greet them like old friends, his long hair flying in the wind. He struck Alphonse a fond blow on the shoulder and then, most courteously, apologized to Barbara for the absence of his wife, who had remained to hold Wigmore for him if she could. Barbara replied politely, if not very truthfully, that she would miss Lady Matilda, and said with far greater sincerity that she hoped with all her heart that Lady Matilda would be left in peace. During the days that followed, she was glad enough to have no company other than Clotilde, even though Mortimer often drew Alphonse away to the second hearth in the great hall where she could not hear their talk.

Had Alphonse been of the same mind as Mortimer, Barbara might have been bored, but her amused expectation that she would hear everything was fulfilled. Alphonse had always enjoyed discussing his plans, ideas, and experiences with her. Sometimes he laughed, but more often he listened soberly—and took her advice. She thought with comfort that she could never lose him entirely. Even if he took another lover, he would always give her his confidences.

Not that there was much to confide in pillow talk at Weobly. Alphonse did most of the talking in the four days before they set out for Llanthony, explaining how and why Gloucester had decided to break with Leicester. Mortimer was very nearly convinced to trust the young earl and join forces with him before they came to the abbey; he had no difficulty making a final decision soon after they arrived.

Hardly had Gloucester greeted them when he drew them out of the sharp wind into the abbey's barren refectory. He stood just beyond the door, holding Barbara affectionately by the hand, and told them he had received an order to yield up Bamburgh Castle into Leicester's hands. "Why?" he asked, clearly not expecting any answer. "I gave oath that the castellan would return Bamburgh to Prince Edward's keeping when a settled peace was made—to Edward's keeping, not Leicester's. If Leicester does not think it safe to put Bamburgh back in Edward's hands, why should he hold it rather than I?"

"Because he intends to hold every royal stronghold in England, and every other that he can wrest from its lord on one pretext or another," Mortimer said. "But he has the council behind him and the poor, captive king. If you do not obey, you will soon be in prison, like Derby. What will you do?"

"Lord Mortimer," Alphonse said, half laughing and half reproving. "You are inciting to riot. From all I have heard, Derby deserved his fate. Let us not make ourselves like him."

"So I should yield Bamburgh, as I gave up the tourney at Dunstable?"

Alphonse cocked his head at the tone of Gloucester's question. It was more teasing than angry. He shrugged. "No, of course not. But there are reasons enough not to comply with the order besides outright defiance. You cannot go to Bamburgh and order the castellan to yield it up until you drive off the Welsh raiding parties. That was why you came to Wales. And surely it would be wise also to persuade Mortimer here to make an agreement that will protect your Welsh lands from his men before he leaves for Ireland."

Gloucester laughed. "That is a better reason for this meeting than any I have come up with, in case Leicester should hear of it. But I cannot imagine any but squirrels and wolves are likely to notice us." He smiled at Barbara. "You could not have chosen a better place—that is, if we do not all freeze or starve to death. I was unfortunate enough to have dinner here and stupid enough to take off my cloak."

"I warned you," Barbara said, then shivered. "But I was here in the summer."

"Well, I have done my best. If we sit close," he gestured to the benches on either side of the rough table on which low braziers of burning charcoal had been set, "we may catch a little of the warmth before the wind that seeps through the cracks in the walls carries it away."

"My lord," Mortimer said without moving, "you made no answer to Sieur Alphonse's suggestion. If instead you have already sent a defiance to Leicester, there may not be time to sit. He will be marching west with his army while we are all scattered—"

"I am glad to hear you say 'we,' Lord Mortimer, even when you think I have brought nothing but a call to arms." Gloucester gestured to the benches again. "I have news from good friends. There is, as yet, no army marching toward us. Leicester is intent on 'making the peace,' which will permit him to grasp every bit of Edward's property. The final swearing is set for the tenth of this month—five days—"

"If you are hoping for delay, you will be disappointed," Mortimer interrupted, his voice rough. "Edward will swear to the terms that Leicester is offering. When you gained permission for us to visit him in Kenilworth, I fulfilled my promise to you. I told him to agree—and I made some signs. He thinks his promise is part of a plan to free him, and I meant to keep that promise too, but in five days—"

"The prince is no fool," Alphonse said. "He will not expect any attempt at rescue while he is in Kenilworth, so far from his friends. And he does not wish to escape to France—I know that."

"And his promise will open the door," Gloucester said.

"You do not believe Leicester will truly allow him any liberty, do you?" Mortimer asked bitterly.

"Such liberty as he allows the king, who may walk and ride abroad—surrounded by Leicester's men. But"—Gloucester grinned at them triumphantly—"two, at least, of the men who guard the prince will be ours."

"Can you arrange that?" Mortimer asked, trying to hide his skepticism.

Gloucester laughed aloud. "I have nothing to do with arranging the matter. It is Leicester himself who arranged it." Then his mouth hardened. "He has written me a letter flavored with honey, saying that part of the prince's agreement is that his household be purged of any 'suspects'—though suspect of what Leicester does not say. What he does say is that my brother Thomas would be welcome to be one of the men serving the prince."

"But Thomas would be hostage, in Leicester's power," Barbara cried.

Gloucester covered her hand with his, but his eyes did not leave Mortimer's. "Yes, Thomas would be hostage," he agreed, "which means that our plan to free Edward must work or it will cost me my brother—or my own freedom."

"He is so young—" Barbara whispered.

"That is one man," Mortimer interrupted, his impatience with a woman's weakness showing in his voice. "Who is the other?"

Gloucester turned his head now and smiled at her, but his eyes were very worried. "Barbe is right. Thomas is young, and that is my excuse for sending with him someone older."

"Who?" Mortimer insisted.

Gloucester hesitated and Barbara was surprised when, instead of looking at Mortimer, he continued to watch her apprehensively, but his answer explained it. "Alphonse," he said.

Barbara gasped and Alphonse laughed. "You could not have made a better choice," he exclaimed. "If by ill luck we fail, I could perhaps remove the worst of the evil consequences. I could confess to having corrupted poor young Thomas, and I could put the blame on you, Lord Mortimer."

Mortimer grunted. "Thank you." His tone was caustic.

Alphonse laughed again. "You cannot be in worse trouble with Leicester than you already are, and he will believe you made a plot to free the prince. If he does not suspect Gilbert of that, you may gain another chance."

"You are a brave and generous man," Mortimer said.

"No I am not." Alphonse grinned and shook his head. "You must know from my advice that I do not believe in taking risks."

"Liar," Barbara muttered under her breath.

Alphonse's dark glance flicked to her, but it was Gloucester's worried face his eyes fixed on. "No harm can come to me. Leicester will not want to offend my aunt, Queen Marguerite, since he still hopes some day to wring approval of his government from King Louis. And Leicester knows she will go weeping to Louis with the tale of any punishment meted out to me. Louis will have to act angry and demand my freedom because he does not want to offend my brother. So the worst Leicester can do is to expel me from the country—and you can send Barbe after me if that happens."

"And where will Barbe go in the meanwhile?" she asked waspishly.

Mortimer seemed ready to tell her to hold her tongue, but Gloucester chuckled. "Barbe will, of course, go to court with her husband." He lifted her hand and kissed it. "I cannot believe there will be any danger for you. You are Norfolk's daughter, and Alphonse would of course deny having revealed this plot to you. And you are our excuse for Alphonse to come and go freely from Edward's guarded household—and to pass information on to me. Well, will you do it?"

Barbara thought of her father. Then she thought of the caged prince growing madder and madder, filled with hate. Leicester would die sooner or later, and the power he had gathered into his hands and molded to his use would fall apart; Henry de Montfort was good but had not his father's strength. Then Edward would break free and loose the rage and hate that filled him—most likely on innocent and guilty alike. But the guilty, and her father would surely be counted among them, would not even escape with their lives. Fines would not content Edward. Not even her uncle would be able to save her father. Edward might have grown so mad by the time he freed himself that he would blame her uncle for fleeing the battle at Lewes or for not coming with an invading force . . . Barbara shuddered.

"Yes, I will help you free the prince, if I can."

The feeling in the court, when Barbara and her companions arrived in Westminster, was strange. There was an outward air of triumph on March 11, as the "release" of Prince Edward was announced in Westminster Hall. According to the harsh terms of the peace, Leicester was utterly victorious. The king and his son agreed that the form of government established at Canterbury in June 1264 was to continue. All who took part in the battle of Lewes, and who were repudiated at that time by the king, were to be received back into Henry's favor. Edward, although released from captivity, swore to accept the purging of his household, the replacement of his own servants by those of Leicester's choosing; he must aid no invasion of England and swear also not to leave the country for three years. If he did not abide by these oaths, he might be disinherited—and on and on.

Under the surface of compliance, there were layers on layers of hope, fear, doubt, and distrust. Recalling the swearing that had preceded her wedding in Canterbury, Barbara did not know what to expect, but doubtless Leicester had heard enough about that swearing to take no chances. Neither Prince Edward nor King Henry appeared; only formal letters of sworn acceptance of the terms were read and recorded, in which both king and prince undertook to seek no absolution from their oaths.

"How ridiculous," Barbara said later to Aliva le Despenser, who had accompanied her back to Gloucester's house in London and now sat knee to knee with her by the fireplace in the solar. "They do not need to seek absolution. The new pope absolved them of all forced oaths when he was still the papal legate, and he absolutely forbade the new papal legate to accept any treaty of peace with Leicester."

"I think my husband would like the king and prince to die," Aliva whispered.

Barbara hesitated, surprised. She would never have expected Hugh le Despenser, justiciar of England, to voice such a thought. Barbara did not like Hugh. His rigid righteousness demanded perfect obedience from all lesser mortals, particularly from that sinful and aberrant type of being called womankind—and he was not averse to using a switch or a leather belt to get what he thought was right. Nonetheless, Hugh le Despenser was not the man to condone murder.

"He might like it, but he would never do any harm to them," Barbara said.

"Oh, yes, you are right about that. Hugh is too holy to commit a crime without an order. But he is worried sick and has been ever since the Marchers got Gloucester's permission to delay their exile." She held up a hand before Barbara could speak—or, more significantly, not speak. "I do not want to hear anything about Gloucester. What I do not know, I cannot tell—and you know Hugh can make me babble."

Barbara was silent for a moment, sick at heart. "Then you must have something to tell him," she said. "Why not say I talked of how kind Gilbert is to me, and of how all the women's tasks in St. Briavels had been left undone after the old castellan's wife had retired to a convent, so I was utterly taken up with that work. You can say that no one came to visit Gilbert at St. Briavels—that is true—and that he kept Alphonse with him to practice jousting and swordplay. That is less true, but they certainly spent a good part of their time pounding at each other. Men are all mad, I think. They come in all black-and-blue with bruises, caroling of how much they enjoyed themselves."

Aliva did not smile at Barbara's attempt to lighten the mood or lift her eyes from her hands, which were clasped tightly in her lap. "I will tell you what I have heard," she said. "Hugh is angry because your father has not come to court. He says Norfolk is currying favor with the king, just waiting for a chance to stab

Leicester in the back. Your cousin Roger has not come to London either."

Barbara was appalled by the dark flush that rose up Aliva's throat when she spoke, but she leaned forward and patted her friend's hands. "Papa must have forbidden him because he did not want to seem to send a deputy."

"Do you really think so?" Aliva's eyes flashed up, then down again.

"I do," Barbara said, "but you must not think about Roger, love. You have your duty and he has his. For his sake and that of some innocent girl, I must hope that he does not think about you. Papa will soon choose a wife for him."

"Not soon!" Aliva exclaimed. "He is only twenty, and I think your father will wait until the situation in the country is more settled. Oh, Barby, so many people are angry at Leicester. They say he wants to eat up everyone's land. The castellans of Richmond and Montgomery and Shrewsbury and others, too, never came to yield up their castles as they were bidden. And Hugh was furious when he heard that the king's clerk, the one who went to take back the land Derby had seized from Peter de Montfort, was taken prisoner himself, and the land is still in the hands of Derby's man. Hugh is not only angry; he is afraid. Why should he be afraid if his friend Leicester is so all powerful? No, no. Your father will not choose a girl for Roger yet."

"Love . . ." Barbara pleaded, but Aliva looked away.

"I will tell you everything I hear," she repeated stubbornly, "and give you free leave to repeat it to anyone you think can make use of it."

That was how Barbara learned that Leicester had given his sons permission to reschedule the tournament he had canceled at Dunstable in February to be held on April 20 at Northampton. Despenser had argued with Peter de Montfort about the wisdom of that decision—ignoring the presence of his meek and silent wife—and thus Barbara learned that Leicester intended to bring Edward west with the army if Gloucester did not come to the tourney.

Barbara knew Gloucester would wish to accept the challenge of the younger Montforts, partly out of a desire to fight them and partly in the hope of using the disorder, which always seemed to accompany tourneys, to free Edward. But the countryside around Northampton was loyal to Leicester, and Barbara feared that the prince would be caught and returned to his gaoler even if he did escape. In the west, Edward's own allies were more numerous than Leicester's and escape might mean real freedom. Gloucester must be warned to stay away from the tourney at Northampton so that Edward would be moved west, nearer his friends.

The news Aliva had passed was important enough that Barbara had to repress an impulse to rush off to Westminster palace and ask to see her husband. To do so would have shrieked aloud that she had something of great importance to tell him. Alphonse had leave from his service to Edward to visit his wife two nights each week, so only a dire emergency could require that she ask he be excused from service.

Fortunately Barbara only had to wait one day or she might have burst with impatience. She even waited until their belated evening meal had been laid out for them and Chacier and Clotilde had left Gloucester's own bedchamber, which Thomas had invited them to use. The lines of tension that for two weeks had added years to Alphonse's eyes and mouth disappeared when Barbara told him her news.

"We have it," he said softly, heaving an enormous sigh. "We have a chance to free Edward. This is worth sending a letter to Gloucester."

Barbara glanced longingly at her slice of pasty and cup of wine; she was hungry and wanted to eat before she wrote, since the letter could not go until morning, but she got her writing desk without protest. She addressed the letter to Isabella Bigod, Norfolk's wife, at Strigul, but Lewin, who would carry it, was ordered to take it to Gloucester at St. Briavels. If disaster befell Lewin and the letter was delivered to Isabella, she would probably burn it without reading it because it was from Barbara, whom she abhorred. Also, the letter, though dictated by Alphonse, was in Barbara's hand and written as if Isabella had demanded it.

"As you commanded, madam," Barbara wrote, "I will send such news as I have regarding the earl of Leicester's intentions toward the earl of Gloucester. My husband tells me that there is no sign that any trap will be laid for Gloucester during the tournament at Northampton. Alphonse thinks Leicester means this tourney to be a peace offering—a replacement for the one he canceled in February. Alphonse also thinks Gloucester will be able to make peace with Leicester if he wishes to do so, and very likely Leicester will be more careful of offending Gloucester in the future. However, Gloucester will certainly be required to yield Bamburgh and to enforce the exile of the lords Marcher. Alphonse has not spoken to Leicester himself, but Peter de Montfort and Hugh le Despenser have both asked him what Gloucester desires and told him at length why all of Edward's property must be held by Leicester or a direct deputy appointed by him and why the Marcher lords must go into exile. Alphonse has also heard that even if Gloucester does not send an early answer, the whole court will move to Northampton to await his coming to the tourney. Alphonse says that if Gloucester does not come, Leicester will take it as an act of defiance. Leicester will then send out summonses for the feudal hosts of Worcester, Hereford, and Gloucester to assemble and will march west at once. The better to rouse the country against Gloucester, Leicester will bring the king and the prince west with him."

The words were innocent, a simple recounting of news and rumor, but even if Barbara's device was suspected—many knew that Norfolk's wife would not ask her for anything or even deign to command her—and her letter was seized and read by Leicester, what she said would seem a simple warning to Gloucester. In a sense it was; Alphonse explained that he wished to let Gilbert know that the door to reconciliation with Leicester was not yet shut. However, the warning was really a mask for the news in the last line of the letter.

The closer the prince was to the holdings of the lords Marcher, the better was the chance of keeping Edward free after his escape. And the need to free Edward was very great. As long as Leicester had Edward and the king in his power, he could make any order he gave seem legal. Thus, in the king's name he could raise a feudal host to attack Gloucester, whose own allies would be forced into the "king's" army by law and custom, virtually guaranteeing that Gloucester would be defeated. However, if the prince was free and could send out conflicting orders, saying that his father was under duress—which most knew but could not prove—serious questions would be raised about the legality of Leicester's orders. Any who wished to avoid the conflict could ignore Leicester's call to arms and later plead confusion between the two royal orders for their inaction. Many, more daring, would take arms and join Gloucester's force to fight for Prince Edward, again with the excuse that the prince's writs had confused them.

"I suppose Leicester had to allow Edward to come to Northampton," Barbara said as she handed her little knife and the splintered quill to Alphonse to have its point mended. She picked up her slice of pasty, saying hastily before she bit into it, "The prince's love for tourneys is widely known."

"Well"—Alphonse chopped the splintered point from the quill, glanced at her and then down again—"if Edward is not present at the tourney, all pretense that he has regained his freedom will be ended. Then Leicester's seizure of the prince's lands would seem gross theft—and that would add to the growing resentment." He handed back the quill, resharpened and neatly split.

Holding the remaining piece of her pasty away from the parchment, which she secured with her left elbow, Barbara dipped the quill in the ink horn, wiped the excess ink off on the edge of the horn and added, "Written this third day past the ides of March by Barbara d'Aix, *née* Bigod." Then she handed the parchment to her husband and said, "But it seems mad to me for Leicester to take Edward west."

"Leicester has only poor choices." Alphonse shrugged and was quiet for a while as he read over the letter. "What a barbarous French you write," he remarked.

"Gloucester will understand it much better than what you think is French," Barbara snapped.

He laughed at her and handed the letter back to be folded and sealed, saying thoughtfully as he watched her, "The whole point in this mockery of liberating the prince is to pacify those who are horrified by seeing Leicester swallow Edward's property and power. Thus, the prince must seem to be truly liberated. No one would believe Edward would remain behind of his own will if the king really wished to fight Gloucester."

"And if destroying Gloucester is not truly the king's will, those who lose nothing by a quarrel between Gloucester and Leicester will not answer the summons to war."

"That is just right, my love," Alphonse replied. "And with whom can Leicester leave Edward? He dare not seal him into Kenilworth again. He needs all his sons and trustworthy allies if he cannot count on a good response to the summoning. So Leicester must take Edward. He may have visions of the prince managing to call together an army, even with the limited freedom he is allowed, and attacking him from behind."

"You were counting on this, were you not?"

"We were hoping for it, yes," Alphonse replied. "From Gloucester or Hereford or almost any of the western keeps, it is only a short flight to the Welsh hills. But I think your duty must be considered done, dear heart. Now you had better go back to St. Briavels."

"No." Barbara answered before she knew why, only realizing after she spoke that she had not felt the tightening in her gut that marked the thought—is he tiring of me?

Alphonse smiled slightly. "I do not wish to be parted from you either, but Simon and Guy will be in Northampton. We have been fortunate that they were both busy bringing Edward's orders to submit to the keeps he yielded to Leicester, but they must be in Northampton if they are the challengers in the tourney. I will not be able to protect you because I will truly be a prisoner with the prince while we wait for Gloucester. You cannot lodge alone. It would be dangerous."

Barbara had hardly heard him. She was taken up with surprise at her lack of fear. Jealous—yes, that nasty pricking was there—but she felt no real fear of loss. She watched her husband, leaning back and swirling the remains of the wine in his cup as he spoke. He was at ease; he was content; he did not need to measure every word he said. He might be drawn by a well-shaped body, 'ovelier features, a purer skin—but it was to her fireside he would return with his troubles and his laughter. She smiled.

''Do you want Guy to abduct you?'' Alphonse asked with sudden sharpness.

Startled, Barbara shook her head vehemently. ''I like the idea of encountering Guy and his drunken armed band even less than you do, but I *must* follow the court. Aliva le Despenser and I are together almost every day, so her husband would know I was gone, and Leicester would hear from him. Would my absence not imply I had been waiting for this news and had gone to tell . . . someone?''

''If you leave at once, before any announcement of the tourney is made—''

''No, that might get Aliva in trouble. If Hugh remembers she was there when he was talking about the tourney with Peter, he will beat her for betraying him.''

''What a stupid man!'' Alphonse exclaimed, his full lips curving down with disgust. ''That is only a path to a worse betrayal.'' Then he shook his head. ''But no business of mine, which is to convince my wife, in a different way, that she is more precious to me even than the escape of the prince and I had rather see that enterprise fail than hear she had been insulted by Guy de Montfort.''

But Barbara had sat up suddenly, grinning from ear to ear. ''I have thought of the perfect solution. I will seek shelter with Aliva and complain to Hugh le Despenser that Guy annoys me. He will not dare allow me to be affronted while I am his guest, and might even whisper a word in Leicester's ear.''

''Are you sure?'' Alphonse rose and took her chin in his hand, tilting her face up and kissing her. ''I mean it when I say I would rather take the chance of sharpening Leicester's suspicion than of endangering you.''

''Hugh might refuse to have me as a guest,'' she admitted. ''I will let you know as soon as the move to Northampton is announced. I will send you a note.'' She put the writing desk aside and got up. ''Yes, that will solve all the problems. If Aliva cannot offer me lodging, I can say I cannot stay alone in so crowded and dangerous a town. That will be my excuse, and yours, too, for my going. I will, of course, go to St. Briavels, but I cannot say that to Aliva. Now, where *can* I say I will wait for you?"

"I do not know the country," Alphonse said, "but it should be somewhere that implies you do not know that Leicester intends to travel west."

"St. Albans," Barbara said at once. "It is on the road from London to Northampton, so I will seem to expect you to come back, and it is a large, very rich abbey where guests may have every luxury."

Alphonse pulled her against him. "I cannot think how I lived without you for so many years. I do not wish to do without you even for a few weeks. So smile prettily at Despenser and keep your eyes and voice down. Perhaps you can cozen him into forgetting what you really are so he will be willing to invite you."

Barbara had no need for any pretense, however. By the end of the week, news of the court's move to Northampton was on everyone's lips. It was safe, when Barbara dined with Aliva and her husband, for her to broach the topic of her desire to accompany Alphonse and to confess her fear of Guy de Montfort. Hugh invited her to stay with them almost before the words were out of her mouth, and Aliva looked startled but very happy. Later, however, she began to look less and less happy and finally suggested they ride into London to buy a length of cloth. When they were safely alone by the mercer's counter, Aliva having sent the shopkeeper to fetch another bolt, she warned Barbara that Hugh had made the offer because he wanted to be able to watch Alphonse.

Barbara patted her hand. "I am delighted to learn that poor Alphonse may be allowed to visit me. We both feared he would be held on as short a leash as the prince, but Hugh may watch us all he likes. Neither Alphonse nor I will do anything he might disapprove while in Northampton."

When she spoke of Despenser's disapproval, Barbara was thinking only of communication with Edward's friends or Gloucester's allies. She had for the moment forgotten that they might do other things that would displease Despenser, because she had forgotten all about Guy. He remained totally absent from her mind over the next few busy days as she prepared to leave for Northampton and during the journey, too.

Spring was finally in the air. Although showers were frequent, their damp was compensated by the beauty of the rainbows sparkling on every new blade of grass and newly unfolded leaf. And the sun that lit the rainbows was growing warm enough to drive off the damp swiftly. Barbara was absorbed by the miracle of rebirth, amused by the presence of her friend, charmed by an accidental meeting now and then with her husband as the cortege moved and halted, now this portion now that coming forward or falling back; she had not a single thought for the unpleasant ugliness that was Guy de Montfort.

Because Barbara had forgotten him so completely, she agreed eagerly to accompany Despenser's party to the great hall of the castle after dinner the day they arrived in Northampton. She had news for Alphonse, if she could find a private moment for a whisper. She had heard Despenser say that orders had already been written to the sheriffs of Worcestershire, Gloucestershire, and Herefordshire—before the date when Gloucester was due to answer the challenge of the tourney—to summon the *posse comitatus*, the whole armed forces they commanded. Did this mean that Leicester was sure Gloucester would not arrive and was simply saving time? Or was that army to be a trap laid to capture Gloucester on his way home—if he was not mortally injured "by accident" at the tourney?

Barbara was sick with fury over the implications of the information Hugh had dropped. So swiftly did she set out to greet Alphonse, when she caught sight of the tall prince whose head topped the many people in the hall, that she left Aliva behind. That was not intentional; she knew Aliva would deliberately immerse herself so completely in conversation with the prince himself or with his other attendants that she would not hear anything Barbara said or notice what she did. Her sudden movement and Aliva's soft gasp of dismay—she had just caught sight of young Simon de Montfort—drew Despenser's attention. He saw Alphonse wave at his wife and start toward her, noticed Aliva following Barbara, and after a moment's hesitation, he also moved toward the prince's party, not on Barbara's heels but at an oblique angle.

He was, thus, just behind and a yard to the right of Guy de Montfort when Guy pushed aside John FitzJohn, who was also moving toward Edward and his attendants, and stepped right into Barbara's path. William Muntchenesy caught Lord John's elbow to steady him and both began to protest Guy's rude behavior, but Guy only reached toward Barbara and said, "I have been waiting for you. Come."

The shock and disgust Barbara felt on finding herself almost breast to breast with Guy was all the greater because he had been expunged from her mind until that moment. She was already angry about what seemed like treachery on Leicester's part, and when Guy touched her, her temper shattered, destroying any idea of caution. She swung her arm in an arc and smashed her clenched fist into the side of Guy's nose.

"Lecher!" she shrieked at the top of her voice. "Take your hand from me, you filth!"

Half stunned, with blood streaming from his nose, Guy bellowed with rage and reached out to grab her shoulder, but she had already jumped back. Unfortunately Aliva was so close behind that Barbara bumped into her and could not altogether avoid Guy's touch. Instead of falling on her shoulder, his hand landed on her breast and tightened. Barbara cried out and twisted away, but his fingers caught on the fabric of her gown. Barbara thrust at his hand, and Guy instinctively gripped harder. Simultaneously, John FitzJohn seized him by the left arm and Despenser by the shoulder, and both men tried to pull him away. Barbara's tunic and surcoat seams tore under the strain, leaving her thin shift the only covering over her left breast. With loud exclamations of shock, FitzJohn and Despenser released their hold on Guy.

Because he had been resisting them, Guy staggered forward, completely off balance, crashing into Barbara, who stumbled back. Feeling himself falling, Guy let go of Barbara's gown to take hold of some more stable support. The check to his forward movement came from another source, however. A large hand seized his hair and pulled him away from Barbara. Soon as he was upright, his hair was released, he was spun around, and a fist as hard as steel crashed into his chin. Guy went down like a stunned ox.

Alphonse bent to pick him up and hit him again, but Prince Edward had grabbed him by one arm and Thomas de Clare by the other. They pulled Alphonse away from Guy, both shouting to let be. Aliva had caught and steadied Barbara, who had pulled up her tunic and was holding it in place, though her surcoat still hung loosely over her waist.

The noise and violence suddenly became a breath-held silence broken only by Guy's groan. Alphonse said, "Let me go to my wife," and the prince and Thomas released him. He stepped over Guy's prone body and pulled Barbara into his arms. Despenser bent over Guy, who was beginning to stir, and the tight crowd that had formed opened to admit Leicester and young Simon, who helped his brother to his feet.

"Who committed this outrage?" Leicester asked.

"Guy," Alphonse answered before anyone else could speak. "I merely stopped him from assaulting my wife."

"In public?" young Simon sneered. "Nonsense."

A low but very ugly sound, a growling snarl, came from the crowd. Leicester looked at the angry, unfriendly faces—even his strongest allies, Despenser and Muntchenesy were clearly angry and disgusted, and FitzJohn made a gesture of contempt.

"Guy—" Leicester began, but Barbara pulled free of her husband before he could finish.

"Do you think I ordinarily come to court with my breasts bare?" she asked furiously, showing her torn dress to the crowd, which was growing larger by the moment. "Guy said he had been waiting for me, ordered me to come with him, and when I shook my head he grabbed my breast. Ask Lord Hugh and Lord John, who tried to pull him off me. Do I lie, my lords?"

"You hot slut—" Guy began.

Whereupon Leicester turned on his son and slapped his face. "Out," he said gesturing to the door, and then to Simon, "See that he stays in his quarters today. I will talk to him in the morning."

"I hope your talk will induce him to keep his hands from my wife," Alphonse said.

Edward had stepped forward and put a comforting hand on Barbara's shoulder. "When my father ruled, even princes did not meddle with decent wives in this country, my lord earl," he said to Leicester.

"Your father still rules," Leicester snapped.

Edward laughed. "Perhaps, but his son no longer has the power to protect his subjects."

"There is no need for personal protection," Leicester said. "There is the law—"

"I should have let him rape me and then sued him?" Barbara shrieked.

Leicester's face twisted with mingled anger and distress. "The fault is mine," he said. "Guy wished to marry this lady, and I forbade it."

"No, my lord," Barbara spat. "Guy never offered me marriage. I only told my father that tale because I was afraid he would kill Guy and break the peace."

"I think you misunderstood," Leicester said coldly. "Guy is young and impulsive. You hurt him. Now I think it would be best if you were not constantly in his sight."

"You would separate me from my husband and remove me from public sight?" Barbara cried. "Why? So that I can be taken and abused at your son's will and no man the wiser?"

"Good God, no!" Leicester exclaimed. "I am sure it will be the prince's pleasure to release your husband from his household. He may then carry you home to France where you will be safe."

"If we are not taken on the road, so I can be murdered and my wife enslaved," Alphonse said. "And do not make light of the threat. Guy tried it once already not far north of Gloucester—"

"That is how we came to be taken prisoner by Hamo le

Strange,'' Barbara put in. ''We would have been safe in the town had not Alphonse had to fight Guy and I to flee north for safety.''

''You will have no more trouble from Guy in public, in private, on the road, or anywhere else,'' Leicester said, his mouth grim. ''Again, the fault is mine. I did not realize the boy was obsessed. The problem will be corrected. To be certain you are safe—''

''You will send an escort?'' Alphonse looked around at the watchers. ''Where will we arrive, I wonder, my wife and I? And who will ever know what has become of us?''

''*I* will send an escort,'' Despenser said, cutting off an explosion of rage from Leicester. ''From the time you leave my lodging, the men will obey no orders except those you give, Sieur Alphonse. And we will say nothing of your destination. You may order the captain to take you where you will after you leave Northampton.''

''I thank you, my lord.'' Barbara bent her knee in a curtsy. She did not like Hugh le Despenser, but she knew his narrow sense of honor. What he promised, he would perform honestly.

Her sense of satisfaction in getting back at Guy upheld Barbara until Alphonse had escorted her into Aliva's solar. They were alone. Aliva had wanted to accompany her friend home, but Despenser forbade her, saying it was her duty to stay behind and heal whatever damage the incident had done. Barbara had smiled and kissed her, assuring her she needed no female support. Now, however, the shock that rage and glee had kept at bay made her knees tremble and presented a side to the incident she had not before considered.

''I am so sorry, Alphonse,'' she whispered, raising stricken eyes to him.

''Sorry?'' Alphonse repeated absently. He had stopped not far from the door, his eyes fixed ahead unseeingly, his mind clearly busy. Then his eyes focused and when he saw the expression on her face, he moved quickly to take her into his arms. ''Sorry for what, love?''

''You warned me about Guy, but I forgot all about him, and now I have lost Prince Edward a friend—''

''No, dear heart''—he kissed her lightly, and when he lifted his head he was wearing a broad smile—''I did that, and I did it apurpose. Had I wished to avoid the confrontation, I needed only to cry out that you were fainting and hysterical and have carried you away the moment I took you in my arms. In fact, you miracle of a woman, it is I who should beg your pardon for exposing you to more insult and anguish—but I knew you would do just the right thing.''

Barbara was silent for a moment and then said in a lowered voice, "You wanted an excuse to return to Gilbert in Wales?"

"My work here is done. I am as familiar as I need to be with the way Edward is guarded and the workings of his household. What plans could be made have been made. Thomas has a new way to get word out, and I would prefer to explain the possibilities for escape to Gilbert and Mortimer myself. Some matters must be left to chance, but one thing is essential: There must be no war, no open break between Leicester and Gloucester, until the prince is free."

"Because without Edward's influence, Gilbert will be defeated."

"We are sure of it. Gilbert is a fine soldier, but he can raise troops only from his own lands. Few except the lords Marcher, who are already declared enemies to Leicester, will join him. The case will be very different if Edward raises his own banner. So the prince has ordered me to persuade Gilbert to hesitate and negotiate while openly preparing for war. That will fix Leicester's attention on Gilbert, which Edward will encourage by acting meek and docile."

"Meek and docile? But what he said in the hall—"

"Gave the impression that he is trying to sow dissension from within the court."

"And therefore has given up the idea of escape."

Knowing that Alphonse and the prince had been deliberately baiting Leicester gave Barbara a brief flash of regret. For a moment she saw the earl as a noble old stag beset by yapping, snapping hounds. The regret did not last, however. Leicester might be noble, but he was also blind, still offering excuses for the inexcusable Guy.

"I doubt we can befool Leicester that far." Alphonse's voice broke into Barbara's thought. "But we do hope to soften his suspicion, which is why Edward does not wish to send me away himself. Unfortunately, Leicester has been so careful not to seem to interfere with Edward that we were not certain how to induce him to dismiss me." He grinned and kissed her again. "And then you arranged it all."

Barbara could not help laughing. "You make it sound as if I planned to have my dress torn off by that clod."

"Did you not?" Alphonse asked lightly.

"I would not even have quarreled with him if I had not already been angry about something else," Barbara said, suddenly reminded of why she had run into Guy without seeing him. She then hurriedly told Alphonse about Leicester's orders to the sheriffs for May 3. "Is it a trap? Would they have taken Gilbert on his way home if he had come to the tourney?"

"I cannot swear, but I think part of the price Leicester would ask for a reconciliation would be that Gilbert not go west again, leaving the Marchers to Leicester's mercy. Of course, if Gilbert made and kept such an agreement and went, say, to Tonbridge, there would be no way to spring any trap. So Leicester is not being dishonest."

Barbara sighed. "Then you are fortunate, for if I had thought of that I would not have been in a rage with Hugh le Despenser. I would have stayed beside him, where Guy would never have accosted me, and—"

"Someone is answering the prince's prayers," Alphonse said, only partly in jest.

"Not unless we can get to Gilbert." Barbara stepped out of her husband's encircling arm and bent over the basket of clothing. "Surely you are not going to order Despenser's men to ride with us to St. Briavels?"

"No. We will have to go to London first and pretend to be looking for a ship. As soon as Despenser's men are gone, we will simply pack up and ride west. Our journey will be longer that way, but this is a good time of year to travel and there is no great hurry. We only need to get to St. Briavels before Leicester comes west to join his army on the third of May."

Chapter 27

Gilbert welcomed them back to St. Briavels with delight for their company and enthusiasm for their news—although there was one piece that Alphonse told him, which he heard with mixed feelings, about which Barbara knew nothing. While they were in London Alphonse had not "pretended" to look for a ship; he had in earnest sought one going to France that would carry a message from Prince Edward to Queen Eleanor. Alphonse had hidden his action, not for fear his wife would betray him but because he wanted to save her from worrying about her uncle being involved in the invasion the prince was now urging. Alphonse knew Barbara would have to know about the invasion soon, but he hoped she would not hear about it until her uncle was out of danger. Edward's message urged that no grandiose plans be made; all that was needed was the arrival of a diversionary party, a hundred men or so, to confuse and delay Leicester.

By May 3, Leicester had arrived with the king and prince in the town of Gloucester. On the fifth, the earl of Gloucester marched his army into the forest west of the town. He camped on a hill, and the campfires of his men lit up the countryside by night. However, the army did not raid, and the next day Gilbert sent a party to Leicester with a long complaint about the subjection of the king, the unfair distribution of castles and prisoners, and the exaltation of Leicester's family.

Although Gilbert made no request for an accommodation, Leicester assumed that was a mark of his youthful pride. The fact that Gloucester was restraining his men and had stated the causes of his dissatisfaction implied that Gloucester was having second thoughts and wished to make peace. If it occurred to anyone that the bill of complaint might as well set forth Gloucester's reasons for breaking with Leicester, no one mentioned it. On May 7 Leicester sent four of his supporters—the bishop of Worcester, Hugh le Despenser, John FitzJohn, and William Muntchenesy—to Gloucester's camp with Gloucester's own men to settle the differences. Gloucester's men also brought some interesting information from Thomas de Clare.

Two different councils with diametrically opposite purposes—one to discuss the differences between Leicester and Gloucester, the other to make plans for Edward's escape based on the information Thomas had given Gloucester's men—were held on May 8. As a result of the latter, Alphonse, who had been with Gloucester, although he had kept out of sight of the delegation from Leicester, rode from Gilbert's camp to St. Briavels that night and gave Barbara a pleasant surprise when he slid into her bed after midnight.

"But I will be away again tomorrow," he sighed, nibbling her neck and ears. "I need to take four or five fine horses to Gilbert. The horses will be sent to Thomas, and he will offer one to the prince, who will thus have a good reason to try the paces of each. Edward can then ask to try the horses of his escort for comparison. When he has tired them all, except for his chosen mount and the one Thomas is riding, he and Thomas will gallop away."

Barbara was so distracted by his wandering lips, by the hand that toyed with her breast and the other that strayed between her legs, that she only sighed, "Oh, marvelous," and Alphonse laughed and gave all his attention to what was, at the moment, most important.

The next morning, however, after they had been to mass in the chapel and had broken their fast in the hall, talking freely of the sad state of Thomas's mounts and the need for fresh horses for him, Barbara asked Alphonse to come back to the south tower for a moment to try on a new gown she was sewing for him. Once alone in the bedchamber she said, "Edward may gallop away on one of the fine horses you send to Thomas and he might outdistance his escort, but the whole of Leicester's army will gallop after him as soon as one of that escort returns and cries the alarm."

"The prince will not have far to go to reach Gloucester's forces."

Barbara stood quite still staring down at her clasped hands. "I thought the plan was for the prince to escape so that he could collect an army. Is Gilbert's army strong enough to win a battle against Leicester?"

"No."

Alphonse could have laughed aloud for joy but did not for fear of offending her. He was more sure of her love every day. It was fear for him that was marked by those tight-clasped hands, and he could not help smiling when he lifted her face and kissed her. "But we do not intend to fight a battle," he pointed out. "Gilbert will hold off Leicester only until Edward's escape is ensured. Then we will all drift away into the hills and regather elsewhere. Do not worry. Probably I will not be engaged, or Gilbert either. You will hear from me in a ten-day or less."

Alphonse did not realize that Barbara did not believe him, that she assumed his good humor was only a mark of his reckless joy in fighting, so that he was doubly delighted by the warmth with which she greeted him when he returned to St. Briavels, this time accompanying Gloucester, only two days later. Second thoughts diminished Alphonse's delight in Barbara's growing love for him. Much as he loved her, much as he wanted her, the closer they came to open war the more Barbe's presence was a burden.

For himself Alphonse had no fear; he recognized the chance of death in war, and though he did not want to die, all the more since Barbe had become his, he did not fear dying. Nor had he any reason to be afraid of anything else. He could move about with Gloucester's army to avoid Leicester's and he could fight when the armies did meet.

A woman did not have his alternatives. Barbe would be confined to one keep or another, and any of them might be the focus of an attack. Knowing her, Alphonse was sure she would try to defend any place in which she was set. He shuddered at the thought. If she were taken, she would be a proven rebel and denied even a pretense of Leicester's protection. After the open quarrel with Leicester in Northampton, Alphonse was certain that if Barbe were not thrown to the men who had captured her refuge, she would be handed over to Guy's tender care. He wanted her away from Wales, away from the battles that would soon take place, and free of any hint of association with the rebels.

How to send her away was not as simple as the decision that she would be safer under her father's protection. A crisis for the Royalist cause was rapidly approaching, and Alphonse did not want to discuss the dangers of a defeat with Gilbert before the prince had actually escaped.

The reason he and Gilbert had returned to St. Briavels was that Leicester was no longer in the city of Gloucester. On May 9, news had come—probably simultaneously to Gilbert and to Leicester—of an invasion of Pembroke by the king's half brother, William de Valence, and the earl of Surrey. That same day, before Alphonse had arrived in Gilbert's camp with the horses, Leicester had moved the entire court, including Thomas and Edward, to Hereford.

Had Barbe still seemed strongly attached to Leicester's cause, Alphonse might have used that as an excuse to send her away. Instead, she seemed as eager as any of them for Edward's escape. As soon as she was sure that he and Gilbert were unhurt and had seen to their needs for clean clothing and refreshment, she coaxed them to walk in the garden. Once there, safe from the ears of those who constantly passed to and fro in the hall, she began to ask anxious questions about whether the move to Hereford would delay the plans to free the prince.

"You cannot move your army to Hereford, Gilbert," Barbe said. "To follow Leicester with your army would make him too suspicious and might put your negotiations with him in doubt. What lands do you have near Hereford to which we could move?"

"We!" Alphonse exclaimed. Then he nearly swallowed his tongue because her mention of lands near Hereford had suggested a solution. "You are quite right, my love. Gilbert cannot take his army to Hereford, and he cannot leave the army either."

"Why—" Gloucester began, and almost at once shook his head. "No, I cannot leave the army and myself chase after Leicester to Hereford. I am afraid every man who has answered my call would take that to mean I was about to accept Leicester's terms and that there was no purpose to remaining under arms. But what choice does that leave us?"

"Wigmore," Alphonse said. "Wigmore is only about six leagues from Hereford, and you cannot doubt Mortimer's willingness to shelter the prince. And Weobly is in just the right place to provide troops—without the movement of a single man, which might come to Leicester's ears and make him take extra precautions—to lay an ambush that can hold off Edward's pursuers."

Gloucester bit his lip. "Damn you!" he burst out. "You will give Mortimer all the sport and all the glory."

"Oh, no." Alphonse began to laugh. "Mortimer is going to love me even less than you do. He is going to leave Wigmore as soon as possible—as if he were withdrawing from Leicester."

"He will kill you if you say that to him!" Gloucester said in a hushed voice.

"Which is why I am not going to say it. Barbe will carry the message."

Barbara gasped as a fear she thought she had conquered caught her by the throat. Did he want to be rid of her? Alphonse's face told her nothing. Then a single glance at her, while Gloucester, with lowered head, continued to gnaw his lips, betrayed a hidden well of unholy glee. Her chest ached for a moment, but almost at once she took comfort. She had been included in that hidden laughter; it was Gilbert who was being cozened. As she came to that conclusion Gloucester shook his head.

"Well, Mortimer will not murder Barby for carrying a message, but neither will he leave Wigmore just because you and I send a letter saying he should."

"That is why I will follow Barbe with the horses for Thomas the very next day. Once Mortimer is past his first rage at the idea of appearing to run from Leicester, I will be able to reason with him. I think I can make him leave Wigmore."

If Alphonse's primary purpose had been to move Mortimer from Wigmore, he might have been disheartened by the reception he received. True, Mortimer did not actually challenge him or spit in his face, but that might have been because he did not come out to greet Alphonse when he first arrived, very late the night of May 12. For a while Alphonse thought he would have to sleep in the outer bailey, but sound carries well at night and faintly, beyond the wall, he heard a high-pitched voice arguing with the guard. Eventually Barbe, who had preceded him as planned, arranged his admission.

Even the next morning, however, Mortimer was clearly not prepared to pretend fear of Leicester. Since Alphonse had actually accomplished what he wanted—by moving Barbara to a place far less dangerous than St. Briavels—he found no difficulty in being indifferent to Mortimer's anger and content with what he had achieved.

Sensibly, Alphonse did not raise the topic of Mortimer's leaving Wigmore. Instead, he apologized to his host in a voice denoting urgency for, without his permission, having left several horses to be cared for in Weobly. Then he disclosed the original idea for Edward's escape and engaged Mortimer in devising a method for getting the horses to Thomas, who was in Hereford Castle with the prince, and in arranging a path of communication so they could revise the plan for Edward's escape.

As Alphonse suspected, Mortimer already had friends and partisans, merchants and priests, who came and went freely in the town of Hereford and who would not be suspected if they entered the castle or even approached the prince. Before the day was out, a plan had been arranged. The next day, May 14, Mortimer and Alphonse rode to Weobly to enlist the cooperation they needed. In Weobly they learned that a convention reestablishing "cordial" relations between Gloucester and Leicester had been written out and sent to Gloucester on the twelfth.

With smiles of delight wreathing their faces, Mortimer and Alphonse agreed that five men dressed in Gloucester's colors should deliver the horses to Thomas at Hereford Castle within the next few days, as if they had been sent by Gloucester soon after he had received the articles of convention.

"Perhaps we should not send the men with the horses until Saturday or even Monday," Alphonse said, his smile fading, his eyes half lidded, calculating. "That might serve as a hopeful sign to Leicester and encourage him to wait a few days longer before despairing of Gilbert's acceptance. And another thing: The prince was born in June—I remember because his birth date fell on a tourney day once, and all who won gave him their prizes."

"I think you are right about Edward being born in June, but what is that to do with anything?"

"It is to do with the reason for Thomas to offer him a horse," Alphonse said, nodding with satisfaction. "I was always troubled by the fact that there was no good reason for the offer—except the usual one of pleasing a prince. But why should Thomas de Clare, Edward's gaoler, wish to please the powerless prince? I always feared the offer would wake suspicion and Thomas's suggestion that Edward choose the one he liked best give all away. This is better. Any good-natured, fortunate young man, in receipt of more horses than he is likely to need, might offer even a powerless prince a gift in celebration of his birth date."

"And it will be typical of Edward that he should ask to try the paces of all the horses to choose the one he likes best."

Alphonse laughed aloud. "Very typical, indeed. The prince does tend to look even a gift horse in the mouth. I think we should also tell Thomas to grumble a little behind Edward's back about that."

"And you think it is important that I be gone from Wigmore before Edward escapes? If I left that day, would not that draw attention to where I was going—presumably to meet Edward—and make Wigmore safer?"

"My lord," Alphonse said, showing no surprise at the sudden change in subject, "you must do as you think best, of course, but if I knew that you were at Wigmore and that you left on the day the prince escaped, I would smell a long-dead fish being dragged across a trail to deceive. But, if Leicester—puffed up with the false notion that he has defeated you—hears you left your stronghold within a week of his coming, he will think you have run to join the invaders or run from him. He will dismiss you from his mind."

"Courtier!" Mortimer said, his lips twisting. "It was no 'false notion' that Leicester defeated me."

"It *was* false because Leicester had the resources of the king to draw upon, and you had much less. I am a courtier and not averse to saying what I must in the most pleasant words I can find, but I am no liar."

Laughing harshly, Mortimer said, "Well, I will go, and I will send word to Clifford and the other Marchers to call in men and supplies. Clifford is about six leagues from Hereford—due west. His activity might lay a false trail."

"Very good, especially as the men and supplies will be needed."

"Who will give the signal to the prince to flee and lead the troop that will block pursuit?"

"I, if you will trust that task to me," Alphonse said.

Mortimer nodded. "You have been a good friend to us, and with nothing to gain for your risk."

"I have more to gain than you think," Alphonse replied with a smile; Mortimer, like most men, was suspicious of generosity without a cause. "Edward is lord of Gascony. My brother has wide lands in Gascony, and I hold a small estate there. Raymond and I can only profit from Edward's goodwill. Moreover, I do not want for my brother such a lord as Edward might become if he were kept leashed until Leicester dies—and I am sure Leicester's power will die with him. Not one of his sons could hold it. Henry is not ruthless enough, and Simon and Guy . . . Well, you might have heard that I have a personal spite against them."

"Yes, every tongue in Northampton was wagging, and I still have friends to tell me gossip." Mortimer sounded amused. "I heard Guy has been kept as close beside his father as if shackled to him ever since."

Alphonse nodded, but he did not smile. "He will be loosed when Edward escapes. And for that reason I hope you will agree to let me send my wife east to her father."

"But if she tells Norfolk about the plan to free the prince—"

"She would not," Alphonse assured him. "But I agree that one must never trust a woman. We can set the time of her leaving so that no matter how hard she rides she could not reach Norfolk before Edward is free."

"Then to send her east is an excellent idea." Mortimer spoke with considerable enthusiasm; sending Barbara to her father would free him of responsibility for her safety. Then his enthusiasm faded and he looked troubled. "But this is no time for a woman to travel across England with a maid and two men-at-arms. Even if I or Gloucester could spare a troop, she would be in worse danger with them than without. And, truthfully, I do not wish to send twenty or thirty trained men-at-arms away at this time."

"That was not what I intended," Alphonse said quickly. "I will take her to Wigmore Abbey and ask that the monks send an escort with her to the next nearest holy place that is not . . . ah . . . tainted with rebellion against Leicester's rule. Her father can send for her, but I am not sure where—"

"Evesham Abbey," Mortimer interrupted. "The abbot of Wigmore will send his men that far if I ask it. It is well away from Hereford and Gloucester, where I would suppose the fighting will center, and I have heard it hinted the abbot is proud and will yield none who take refuge—even to Leicester's sons. She will be safe there until Norfolk's men come for her, and the abbey is rich and powerful, so Lady Barbara will have every comfort."

Now all that was necessary was Barbe's agreement. Alphonse said nothing of that to Mortimer, merely thanking him for his help and advice and returning to the subject of how the prince should be signaled to begin his dash for freedom and where the troop to hold off pursuers should wait. Alphonse knew Mortimer would have thought him mad to seek his wife's concurrence rather than simply giving her an order. But Alphonse did not at all object to the prospect of wheedling Barbe into doing as he asked. To bend her to his will—and make her enjoy yielding—gave him a pleasurable sense of power. More important, although he did not like thinking about it, her initial objection to leaving him would soothe that faint uncertainty he still felt about her. Barbe seldom resisted him now; she came willingly, even eagerly, into his arms. Nonetheless he was aware of some shadow on the brightness of her love—and there was that token she hid from him.

Alphonse was, therefore, not altogether pleased to win an easier victory than he had expected. He had managed, by asking Mortimer to take him over the territory that would be covered in Edward's escape, to delay their return to Wigmore until the ladies had separated for the night. Barbe, who knew they intended to return, had undressed but was in her bedgown, still sewing by the fire in the small guest house when Alphonse came in. She jumped to her feet.

"I heard horses some time ago. You are late. I was worried."

Alphonse caught her to him. "If I had known you were awake, I would have come sooner. I disarmed in the hall, not wishing to disturb you."

"Then you have eaten already?"

"Yes, but I would like a cup of wine—" He felt her stiffen in his arms and chuckled. "You are altogether too clever, my love. How do you know that I do not really want wine but talk?"

She pushed him gently away and stared at him, heavy brows level, lips flat. "If you do not want to leap into bed, there is trouble. You never want food or drink when you have been away from me—unless this time you are futtered out already—" She stopped speaking abruptly and walked to a table near the wall where a flagon of wine, a flask of water, and two horn goblets stood.

Alphonse made a small sound as he choked down joyous laughter. She was jealous! But by the time she turned toward him, cup in hand, his face was perfectly sober. "Not trouble," he said, "but a problem I wish to discuss with you without Mortimer overhearing."

"You do not trust him?" Barbara whispered, stopping with the cup of wine half extended.

"Of course I trust him, but there is something I wish you to do that you will not like. Mortimer would never tire of the jest that I feared my wife and pleaded with her instead of bidding her obey me and knocking out her teeth if she did not. But," he added plaintively, "I like you better with your teeth, so—"

Barbara started to laugh, then frowned and thrust the wine at him. "What is it that I will not like?"

"I want you to go to your father and stay with him until the prince is free and Leicester makes terms."

"You want to be rid of me."

This time Alphonse let himself laugh aloud. "I will show you soon enough whether that is true." Then he sobered and came close, taking the cup from her hand and setting it back on the table. He put his hands on her shoulders. "Dear heart, I will miss you bitterly. You have no idea how bitterly—"

"Then why send me away?"

"Because you are a danger to me. Edward will come here after his escape. We hope, of course, that none will follow, but there is always a chance that someone faithful to Leicester will espy him and pass the news to those who will be sent out searching. The prince will stay here only long enough to rest, but you kno[illegible] Leicester will not care. He will use word that Edward stopped here as an excuse to attack Wigmore, and this keep will not be well defended. Mortimer will take most of his trained men with him. If Wigmore falls and you are taken in an enemy stronghold, when you are believed to be in France—''

''I see,'' she said, staring hard at him, but he wore no courtier's face for her. The fear he felt at the thought of her being taken was written in his eyes and the tension of his mouth. And Barbara was herself afraid. After what she had said to Leicester, she did not think being Norfolk's daughter would protect her. She looked down and sighed. ''And I cannot go to St. Briavels because that is another likely target for attack and also will not be well manned.''

Alphonse was a trifle put out at hearing Barbara state his arguments. He had expected her to refuse to be parted from him, as she had in the past, and had been prepared to reason and wheedle her into compliance. Now he had little left to say. ''I am delighted that you see the situation so clearly.'' He hoped the compliment would be convincing, but his voice sounded flat to him, and he thought he detected an amused spark of blue in the cold gray depths of Barbe's eyes.

''Only . . .'' Her lips had no curve, no hint of a smile softening them. ''Would it not be even more dangerous for me to ride all the way across England with armies marching about? Have you forgotten that Leicester is sure to call up the whole knight service of England once the prince is free?''

''Ah, no.'' Alphonse misunderstood the straightforward question and thought that Barbe had pretended to agree only to cut the ground from under his feet. He rebraced for argument with considerable pleasure, making his first move by drawing her close, and kissing her. ''We will have two strings to our bow,'' he began, and went on to tell her how Mortimer would arrange with the abbot of Wigmore Abbey to have her escorted to Evesham. ''I doubt any captain of Leicester's army would interfere with a lady escorted by holy brothers, but if it should happen, you need only say you parted from me in anger when you discovered I intended to join with the rebels.''

She pulled her head back, away from the lips that were seeking hers again. ''And then how could I protest if such a captain wished to deliver me into Leicester's hands?''

Alphonse laughed, her protest having confirmed his guess that her agreement had been part of a design to circumvent his purpose. ''Mortimer will confide to the abbot Guy's lust for you,'' he said, ''giving that as your reason for seeking the protection of the Church. The brothers will not give you up to any but your father's men.''

While he spoke, Alphonse had slid one arm around her shoulders; his other hand was busy unloosening the belt of her bedgown. He was already aroused and turned so that his body was fully pressed against her and she could not mistake the hardness of his shaft. She had been untying his shirt strings, but she stopped and laid her hands flat on his chest as if to push him away. Alphonse was a little troubled by a renewal of the resistance she seemed to have abandoned, but his lips closed on hers, just as she said "My father's men!" and he was relieved, assuming she did not understand the rest of the plan.

Shock at hearing her father brought into the discussion first held Barbara immobile. In that instant she was convinced that the whole purpose in sending her away was to involve her father in the rebellion against Leicester.

"You will be safe in Evesham as long as you wish to stay there," Alphonse murmured, his mouth moving against hers, giving a sensual effect to the practical words. "You can send Bevis and Lewin to your father and ask that he send a troop to escort you. I cannot believe he will wish to be involved in fighting against the prince, so he will be able to spare a strong troop to take you safely to Framlingham, or wherever he is staying."

Almost as the suspicion about entrapping her father formed, she rejected it. There would be real danger for her if she were captured. Still, doubt mingled with the intense pleasure Alphonse's kiss created. The movement of his mouth against hers as he explained made it very hard to think, but that very fact renewed her suspicion. Resentment got all muddled up with her need to draw Alphonse to the bed, where all doubts would be allayed as the emptiness in her was filled. The need, growing with his caress, fed the doubt; the doubt fed the need. For her own pride's sake, to assure herself she was not totally enslaved, Barbara found the strength to ask, "When?"

"I am not certain." He bent his head and kissed her throat where the loosened bedgown had fallen away. "We must first get the horses to Thomas, and he must arrange that the prince be allowed to try them out where there is room to gallop—that is, beyond the walls of Hereford." He nibbled at her throat again before he murmured, "Not less than a week or more than three weeks from now, because the prince's birthdate is in June."

Her arms were still braced against his chest but she did not push him away. She could not; her bones felt like limp strings, but she managed to say, "I meant when must Bevis and Lewin leave Evesham?"

"The sooner the better after you arrive there."

Barbara let her hands slide down her husband's body, over his hips, down to his firm buttocks. If he did not mean to set the trap for her father at once, she could take what she wanted before beginning a quarrel. Doubt of her own motives made her resist a moment longer to make sure. "You mean," she whispered, "you want me to send for my father's troop after I arrive in Evesham?"

"After . . ." Alphonse relaxed the guard he had been holding on himself while he made sure she would not send her men out too soon. Barbe would not deliberately betray the plan to free Prince Edward, but it was better if she could not do so by accident—and did not suspect his uneasiness. "Yes . . . after," he whispered, his eyes half closed, one hand pulling her even tighter against him as he moved his hips.

The very tip of his tongue made a little circle in the V where her collarbones met, and she sighed and reached for his belt.

Chapter 28

Four days later, the opinions of each had become fixed. Alphonse was certain he had manipulated his wife into doing as he wished, and Barbara had resolved on going to Evesham, but not one yard farther. In part, her decision was influenced by the impossibility of remaining in Wigmore. Mortimer had left his keep the day after he returned with Alphonse. What he told his wife—or perhaps because he told her nothing—seemed to have turned her to stone. She avoided Barbara and Alphonse whenever she could and hardly squeezed a word between frozen lips when they were forced into proximity, as at meals. The austere guest house of an abbey would seem a high revel in comparison with the scarcely controlled fear and rage in Wigmore.

Barbara could not face that reminder of what she was concealing from herself. Buried under layers of jealous fear that Alphonse simply wanted to be rid of her, of angry suspicion that he had become so caught up in the game of politics that he was willing to use his own wife as a pawn, of a kind of pleasure in being clever and independent enough to go her own way despite her love was her terror for him. To hide from herself the knowledge that he would fight for Edward, that he might be injured or killed or captured with the prince, she concentrated on her surface dissatisfactions.

Several times Barbara thought longingly of doing just what Alphonse still believed she would do—seeking her father's protection. Being a guest in Evesham might be better than living with Matilda de Mortimer, but the thought of going home to her father and to the loving support Joanna would give her was a glimpse of heaven denied. She refused to think about it, knowing if she consulted with Bevis and Lewin, they three could concoct a plan for getting her to Framlingham without casting doubts on Norfolk's loyalty. The truth was she could not go so far away from where the fighting might be. She needed to be where a day's hard ride would bring her to her husband if ill befell him.

On May 26 a messenger on a lathered horse rode into Wigmore soon after dinner. By nones, Alphonse was lifting Barbara down from Frivole's saddle in the courtyard of the guest houses in Wigmore Abbey. Out of deference to the porter, who was waiting to show Barbara to her quarters, he did not kiss her as he would have liked to do, only took her hand. Then the porter turned his back, and Alphonse lifted her hand to his mouth and gently touched the tips of her fingers with his tongue.

"How I will miss you," he murmured.

"You could come with me," Barbara said, closing her fingers around his hand.

"You know I cannot," he replied, frowning. "I have given my word."

Barbara opened her mouth to say "A word that can make you dead," but she knew the protest was useless, and said instead, "I know."

"I will come for you as soon as I am freed from my promise," he said. "When you are settled, write and tell me where you are." He leaned closer and whispered so the monk could not hear, "Write to Gilbert. I will be with him or he will know where I am." He raised her hand and kissed it again, then pulled loose. "God help me, I miss you already."

He turned away quickly, as if he must wrench himself free to make the parting briefer and thus less painful. It was a technique he had honed to perfection, but this time he was caught in his own snare. When he was mounted and looked back, Barbara was calmly walking away with the porter, not standing and waving or weeping or simply staring after him. Doubt stabbed deeply, presenting to him every likely and unlikely reason for her indifference, except the idea that she was not indifferent at all and had turned away to hide from him the tears streaking her face. Had the notion occurred to him, he would have dismissed it as ridiculous. To his mind there was no reason for Barbe to hide her fear and her tears, and thus her love.

They were man and wife and had a right to love openly; to Alphonse that was one of the greatest joys of the married state. He had grown very tired of concealment, of lies, of the uneasiness of needing to look calmly into the eyes of cuckolded husbands. He did not need to vow he would seek no other woman; not once since Barbe had agreed to be his wife had he desired any body but hers. So Alphonse was agonized because she had not watched him go, had not tried to cling to the sight of him—as he would have turned and turned again to cling to the sight of her—as long as possible. He suffered all the way to Weobly, where another message from Thomas, which drove personal considerations from his mind, was waiting for him.

"One of the horses sent by my brother has too hard a mouth," Thomas wrote. "I will send a man to return it to you on Thursday. He will meet you west of Wydmarsh Gate where the land rises into little hills. Wear a white hat so that my man may know you. If you wave it, he will come to you at once and your business may be done quickly."

Thursday. That did not give them much time. Alphonse spent a minute wondering whether the early date for trying the horses and choosing one had been set to gratify Edward's impatience to have a new horse or to make more difficult any plan of escape. In the next minute, he dismissed the question. He and Mortimer had devised the plan before the horses were delivered, but there was still much to do in a shorter time than expected. Parties had been leaving and returning to Weobly for a week, as if a nervous Mortimer was scouring the countryside. That did not change, except that the parties leaving were larger and those that returned had fewer men and horses and most of the men rode awkwardly.

Alphonse went out of Weobly with a party that headed east after dinner on Wednesday, May 27. They traveled some distance, then turned sharply north into a little wood. There they waited for anyone who was following to take up their trail, but no one came to the edge of the wood or into it. When they were sure there were no watchers, they found a group of serfs mounted on farm horses and bade them ride back to Weobly manor. After the serfs were on the road going west, they turned east again within the wood and finally, before the wood ended, south. They crossed the road into another, smaller wood and left a man where he could see a good way up and down the road. Bearing southeast now, the party came out on hilly grazing land. Here they stopped while men who knew the area examined the small wooded copses and hidden valleys. They returned to report the land empty, except for a few shepherds, and rode away again prepared to watch through the night in case Thomas's message was a trap. At dusk Alphonse, Chacier, and one other man rode south toward the top of the final rise. To the north of the broad slope they saw a boy seated on the ground beside a tethered horse. From his saddlebag Alphonse took a broad-brimmed white traveling hat and put it on. The boy stood up and waved.

"No change," the boy said as soon as Alphonse and his men had ridden close enough to hear ordinary speech.

"Do you ride back?" Alphonse asked as he dismounted.

"Now that you are here, no. If you had not come, I was to go back at dawn."

The boy's face was alive with curiosity, but Alphonse said nothing to satisfy it. He unloosened his saddle roll, threw the boy a blanket, and pulled one around himself. Chacier and the man-at-arms also dismounted; Chacier took bread and cheese from his saddlebags, which he shared with his master and the boy. No one spoke at all, and after eating they all lay down. By the time full dark had blanketed the hill, the boy was asleep. Alphonse sat up and touched Chacier, who felt about until he found the small hollow he had marked while they ate. He pulled most of the grass from it. On the bare earth, he lit a little fire. The man-at-arms walked to the top of the hill and lay down where he could watch the road below without being seen.

Through the night men came and went, reporting on the gathering of the troop that had left Weobly in small groups and made their way to a tiny copse, no more, really, than a windbreak, below the hill east of the road. In the quiet of midnight, Alphonse heard the bells ring for matins and by the time the faint peal for lauds came, together with the light of false dawn, Alphonse calculated that at least fifty men were in place. Then he ate more of the bread and cheese, washed it down (with a mild expression of despair at English taste) with a few swallows of ale, and lay down to sleep. Chacier woke him about an hour after tierce.

"A party of five has just ridden into the meadow and dismounted," he said softly.

Dadais had already been moved as close to the top of the rise as he could be without showing up against the skyline. Chacier's horse was well down the hillside, ready for the dash to warn the troop to block the road after the prince had passed. The boy and the man-at-arms were gone. Alphonse climbed to the top of the hill, crouched behind some low brush, and looked out. In the distance, he could make out the walls of Hereford. Just below was the road, snaking back toward those walls. On the left of the road was the mingled lush green, glittering wet, and tall brown stalks of rushes that marked marshland. To the right the marsh had filled in to form a wide, flat meadow. Between the meadow and the town was another of those little copses that dotted the countryside.

The spot could not have been better chosen, Alphonse thought. Most of what took place in the meadow would be hidden from watchers on the walls, and any sounds they made would be blurred, too. In the time he had taken to get into position, one man, taller than the others—obviously the prince—had clearly tried one of the horses and found it wanting. He was thrusting the reins of the magnificent animal into the hands of a much smaller, slighter man—no doubt Thomas. The way their hands moved indicated that Thomas was protesting Edward's decision and urging him to try the horse again. Edward gestured the animal away and moved to mount another.

He rode the horse in a circle, guiding it with reins and knees to turn and lift. Then he seemed to call something to the waiting men and spurred the animal into a gallop. He rode madly to the edge of the meadow, turned, and rode back again just as the other four men started to mount to follow him. But he did not dismount immediately; he rode the horse back and forth until Alphonse, although he could not see it at that distance, knew the beast was tired and lathered with sweat. Alphonse settled down to wait. Edward had two more horses to wear out.

By the time Edward dismounted from the fourth horse, Alphonse could see his four companions grouped together as if they were bored and paying little attention to him. Thomas approached, leading the animal the prince had first rejected; they seemed to have words, and Thomas turned away sharply as if angry. He mounted the rejected horse and Edward mounted the last untried animal. Both began to circle, as Edward had done with all the other horses. The other men hardly looked at what was taking place.

Swallowing a burst of excitement, Alphonse flung himself into Dadais's saddle and rode to the top of the hill. Edward promptly set spurs into his mount, which broke into a gallop. Thomas hesitated a moment, then followed suit. Alphonse started Dadais down the hill, waving his hat as Edward came to the edge of the meadow, where he had previously turned his horse to go back. This time he headed into the road instead, crouching low over the saddle, spurring and slapping the horse to wring more speed from it. A length behind, Thomas's big black stallion thundered. The last thing Alphonse saw before he was too far down the hill for an overview was Edward's three other companions mounting the exhausted horses left with them.

Edward flew past, then Thomas. Alphonse turned Dadais into the road and fell in behind, intending to keep his armored body between the lightly clad escapees and their pursuers—if the pursuers ever caught up. He could hear shouts behind him, but only a few voices, faint with distance. That meant there had been no troop guarding the prince closer to the town. Even as he shook his head in disbelief at the credulity of Leicester, the voices behind him faded out entirely. Clearly they had seen the hopelessness of chasing Edward on exhausted horses and were riding back to Hereford to summon help.

One patch of woods loomed up on Alphonse's right; beyond, on the other side of the road, was another. On the grass verge between the wood and the trees, Chacier waited, wearing a white hat. Edward rode on without slowing, Thomas behind him. As soon as they were past, Chacier started after them while Alphonse slowed Dadais to wait for the men who began to pour out of the wood. Five men rode south out of the copse. They would go along the north bank of the Wye until they could ford the river and continue south, laying a false trail. The rest of the troop blocked the road completely, riding slowly north. When the distance between the troop and the three was about a quarter of a mile, Chacier spurred his mount, which overtook Edward's and Thomas's tiring horses. Alphonse watched Chacier take the lead, then turned to signal, and the first ten men rode off to the right, driving their horses up the hill as fast as they could go. At the top they would divide, five riding due east and five curving back as if to go around Hereford and head south.

The main body of the troop continued on the road for another quarter of a mile. There a second signal sent another ten men left on a narrow track. Alphonse knew that was where Chacier had led Edward and Thomas. They would soon come to a branch of the Wye, which they would ford. At the ford, the men following them would form two parties; eight would cross behind them, three would continue on along the south bank of the tributary west toward Wales.

Alphonse pulled Dadais aside and the troop rode past him. He was relieved when the last man passed the track; to be too close might draw attention to it. But he wanted to be in sight so that the attention of the pursuers would focus on his troop rather than on the side path. He was just wondering whether to order the men to stop when shouts from the rear warned him that pursuers were finally coming.

One wordless yell made the men pick up speed, as if they still hoped to get away. Alphonse glanced over his shoulder to make sure the oncoming men were gaining. A second shout brought the troop to a halt, the men putting on helmets and raising their shields as they brought their horses to face the pursuers, except for two who had been ordered to ride on as fast as they could. With any luck, someone in the oncoming troop would see them and believe Edward and Thomas had fled toward Leominster.

Alphonse had just time enough to see the men from Hereford sweep past the track the prince had taken before he shouted a third time and gestured with his drawn sword. At the touch of the spur, Dadais leapt forward toward the lead man in the pursuing party, who suddenly screamed, "Traitor! Traitor!"

Before he remembered that he carried a blank shield, wore no colors, and could not be recognized with his helmet on, Alphonse aimed a tremendous blow at the oncoming rider. Until Edward was safe and raising an army, he did not want his name associated with this venture. Then he saw the leader's head was slightly turned. It was not he who was being called "traitor" but the two fleeing away up the road. Simultaneously, he recognized Henry de Montfort's shield.

Alphonse cried out in distress; but it was too late to avoid the encounter or even check his swing. All he could do was turn his sword so that the flat of the blade, rather than the edge, hit. His shout had some effect too. Henry started to lift his shield to catch the blow. He was too late for that, but he did deflect Alphonse's sword upward so that it landed on the thick rim of his helmet. Alphonse heard the loud clang of metal on metal, saw Henry reel in the saddle, and then was past him, into the body of the oncoming troop. Furious at his bad luck and unable to look back to see what had become of Henry, he slashed right and left. A shriek and a grunt told him of a hit and, probably, a miss. He did not turn to see. From the noise, he knew the men of his own troop were right on his heels. He caught a slashing blow on his shield, pushed outward to hold his attacker's sword, and delivered a vicious chop to the man's shoulder. Dadais shouldered the slighter mount aside, and Alphonse burst through onto the clear road.

Off to one side he saw a group of four men, one struggling feebly as a second, riding behind, supported him in the saddle, and two on either side protected them. Alphonse checked Dadais; then as they passed, riding back toward Hereford, drove his horse between them and two members of his troop who clearly intended to pursue.

"Let them go," he shouted. "Let them take their wounded back to Hereford."

A few more blows were struck, but essentially that was the end of the fight. With their leader injured, with one half of the troop not knowing what the fight was about and the other half appalled by the thought of trying to take their own future king prisoner, with the facts evident—that they were outnumbered and that catching the two who had fled was plainly impossible—the offer of safety while they gathered up their wounded and returned to the town was too good to ignore.

Both troops, holding shields and swords ready but striking no blows, withdrew a cautious distance while the dead and wounded were separated and carried to either side. Then the men of Hereford turned south. If any had thought of turning back suddenly and catching the prince's guards unaware, they soon put the idea out of their minds. Most of Alphonse's troop followed them for more than a mile—well beyond the track the prince had taken, but they did not know that. Then they sat in the road watching until the last of the men of Hereford passed out of sight. Those who did not follow bandaged the hurt and tied the dead onto their horses. None were left behind to be questioned or identified as Mortimer's.

After Alphonse's troop had reassembled, they rode north again. Well before they reached Leominster, however, the troop broke up into small groups, most headed back to Weobly across country. Alphonse and Chacier alone passed through the town, where they stopped to eat a belated dinner, and then rode on. Although they did not hurry their meal, they heard no excitement, no criers calling out important news, and the gate guards did not even glance at them when they rode out. Alphonse bit his lip. Surely Henry de Montfort had not been so seriously injured he was unable to send out messengers to order the prince be apprehended.

Alphonse reviewed the blow he had struck and how Henry had acted when he last saw him, and concluded he could have done no permanent harm. So why— Then he shrugged. Alphonse accounted himself clever with words, but could not devise just how he, in Henry's place, would phrase an order to capture the prince when the whole country had been told that Edward was free. Most likely Henry had decided Edward was beyond his reach and instead of taking action himself had sent the news to his father so that Leicester could decide what to do. That, Alphonse thought, was typical of Henry—or was it because Henry was not certain he wanted to recapture the prince?

When that idea first occurred to Alphonse, it came lightly, as near to a jest as one could come about so bitter a subject. He was thinking only in terms of Henry's own weariness of spirit at having thrust on him a second time the heavy and unwelcome responsibility of controlling Edward. Later, near to midnight, when he finally rode into Wigmore and was told by the gate guard to go directly to the prince in the near tower, he began to be uneasy. And his welcome from Edward, who was still wide awake, brought to mind a different reason for Henry's reluctance to recapture him.

Although Edward took Alphonse into a crushing hug and thanked and complimented him for his part in the escape, the prince also asked quite sharply why Alphonse had taken so long to arrive in Wigmore. Every line and twitch in Edward's face was clearly visible because the small tower chamber was brightly lit. Torches flared in three wall holders and large candlesticks had been carried in and placed on either side of the small hearth.

With a slight sinking of heart at what he saw in the prince's face, Alphonse answered calmly that he and his servant had stopped to eat in Leominster to provide evidence of two armed but harmless travelers, who were certainly not the fleeing prince, if someone asked questions about men arriving from the south. Then he had taken a slow and circuitous route to Wigmore. His answer satisfied the prince, but more, he thought, because Edward recognized and forced down his own unreasonable suspicion than because of the inherent logic of the answer.

It was then, seeing both the half-mad suspicion and the iron will that controlled it, that Alphonse began to wonder whether Henry de Montfort had welcomed the prince's escape because he knew it would soon be too late. Long before his father could be brought to loose Edward's bonds in fact rather than pretense—if he ever could be—the prince would be irretrievably mad and all the more dangerous because he would not seem mad. He would not gibber, probably not even rage, but he would see only evil and ill intent in every living being, even in those who were most loving and devoted to him.

"What now?" Edward asked sharply. "How long must I stay here?"

Alphonse started. The words, implying that Edward was afraid he was now in Mortimer's power, hit too close to the uneasy thoughts they had interrupted. "Pardon, my lord," he said, "I am tired. I was half asleep. As to how long you stay, that is a matter for you to judge. Lord Mortimer is at Ludlow. He will await you there or come here on your order or meet you at any other place you designate."

A brusque nod showed that Edward had accepted the information, but there was no sign of relaxation. One part of Edward, Alphonse guessed, still suspected he was to be used, a tool in other men's hands for purposes that were not his own, but another part was busy with saner, tactical considerations. These were the lands of Edward's lordship, and Alphonse was sure he knew exactly where Ludlow was—well under four leagues from Wigmore, Alphonse had been told—and was calculating the reasons why Mortimer had chosen the place and the advantages and disadvantages of accepting Mortimer's choice or designating a new place. What he said had nothing to do with the place of meeting, however.

"Thomas told me," Edward remarked, his left eyelid drooping more than it had a moment earlier, "that his brother will answer my call to arms. Is that true, or is it the hope of a young zealot?"

"It is true, but there is a price."

Edward sighed as he said, "There is always a price," but the rigidity of his stance relaxed a trifle.

Alphonse relaxed also, knowing he had struck the right note. Certainly at present, and perhaps forever, Edward had lost all faith in professions of loyalty and generosity; to offer such reasons for supporting him, especially in his current weakness, would only stimulate his suspicion. Bargains, however, he was willing to credit as rational bases for action. The prince confirmed Alphonse's thought by glancing around the small tower chamber and pointing to a stool that stood beside the cot holding a flagon and a cup in lieu of a table.

"Bring that to the hearth and sit down," he said.

While Alphonse took the flagon and the cup in one hand and carried the stool over with the other, Edward threw a few more small logs on the fire. Then he laughed. "Lady Matilda was both shocked and grateful when I refused her chamber, her bed, Mortimer's chair of state, and a passel of servants to wait on me and chose instead to lie in the tower alone."

"You mean she thinks you wished to do her honor for her husband's sake." Alphonse spoke over his shoulder, as he set the stool down and placed the cup and flagon on the floor between the two stools. "That will do you no harm. She is very devoted to Mortimer," he went on, as Edward seated himself and he followed suit.

The prince uttered a snort of laughter, filled the cup, and drank about half, offering the remainder to Alphonse. He accepted the cup, drank off what was left, and handed it back.

"I imagine," Alphonse said, "that a luxurious prison might gall the spirit as badly as fetters in a stone cellar gall the body. I am sure, though, that any extended experience of the fetters on the body might make me think less ill of the gall of luxury."

"Still trying to bring me to forgive Henry?" Edward said, his voice thinner and harder. "You need not worry. I appreciate fully that he could have made my life much more miserable—even though fetters in a cellar would not have been politic or suited Leicester's purpose of seeming virtuous and magnanimous." He filled the cup again but did not drink; then, staring down into it, he asked softly, "Why did you take part in my rescue, Alphonse?"

"Not, I am sorry to admit, out of my pure love for you, my lord," Alphonse said, smiling. "I am afraid I became involved partly by accident and partly because I have a personal grudge against Guy de Montfort." He sighed. "Not very uplifting reasons."

Edward raised the cup and sipped. Over the rim his eyes seemed to Alphonse to be sadder but less mad. Alphonse shrugged, hiding his intense pleasure at having said the right thing in the right way. He had guessed that to speak of his own grudge would make his support both intensely personal and totally comprehensible to the prince, who could hold a grudge with the best. Alphonse uttered a short laugh and spoke again. "Yet Guy is also my benefactor, in a way."

"A parable?" Edward asked, his lips twisted, his voice flat and dangerous.

"Oh, no." Alphonse laughed again. "Pure fact. If Guy had not pursued Barbe with dishonorable intent, which she was afraid to confess to her father lest he squash the little louse and enrage Leicester, she would not have fled to France. I would not have seen her again and been reminded of how desirable she was and that our lands run well together. Thus, it is owing to Guy's lust that I have a wife entirely to my taste. In so much he is my benefactor."

Edward laughed, the sound full and natural, and Alphonse took that as an invitation to tell the whole tale. His emphasis was on Guy's attempts to cuckold him, first by invitation and, when Barbe refused, by guile and by force. Naturally, he mentioned in passing that Barbe would not involve her father because he and Leicester were already in disagreement and that she and Alphonse had become friends with Gloucester because he had defended Barbe from Guy.

Although he made no comment on it, Alphonse knew the prince had noted his remarks about the distrust between Leicester and Norfolk. He surely had other evidence of the strain in that relationship, but Alphonse was satisfied that his casual mention of the daughter's anxiety was an interesting confirmation that Norfolk was no inveterate enemy.

Edward, however, was more interested in another casual comment. "Friends with Gloucester, are you?" he remarked. "I hardly know him. He did not come to court and some two years ago refused to swear fealty to me—"

"He refused to swear because he had not yet received title to his father's lands," Alphonse interrupted. "Is it not true that he was denied that title on a point of law—a point that was waived for others, some younger than he—that he was under age? Is it so strange, then, that he should refuse to swear on an equally technical point of law?"

Edward said nothing, staring down into the cup of wine he still held. Alphonse hesitated. This was one of the nastiest sticking points of the rapprochement between the prince and Gloucester. He knew it had to be brought into the open before the prince and Gloucester met, but he had already made a mistake by seeming to have accepted Gloucester's interpretation of events without waiting to hear Edward's defense. He wished he were not so tired that his head felt thick.

"Gloucester told me," Alphonse went on in a more uncertain voice, "that he had been shamefully treated by your father when he came to France as his father's heir. My lord, as Gloucester's lord to be, and as an impartial judge—did he lie?"

The prince's blue eyes, almost equally wide open with surprise, regarded Alphonse thoughtfully for a long moment, assessing that challenge. "I do not know what happened in France," Edward said slowly, "but it is true that my father put Gloucester's lands into the hands of a warden instead of giving him livery at once." He shrugged. "That brought two years' revenue from rich lands into my father's always-empty purse."

Alphonse felt tears of relief sting his eyes. Clearly, even without the healing that freedom and the exercise of power might bring him in time, Edward was not totally ruled by resentment and suspicion.

"I think Gloucester could have understood and accepted that," Alphonse said. "Not acknowledged that it was right or just, but not felt so deep a bitterness—had he not been humiliated by the king's handling."

"My father was a little sore himself from ill handling," Edward snapped.

Another mistake. Alphonse passed a weary hand across his eyes. "My lord," he said, "I know that, and I never would have mentioned it, except that I feel you should know what is still a key to Gloucester's good or ill will: He has not been treated with respect. Leicester dealt with him as if he were a foolish little boy when he protested what he felt were injustices. That was a grave mistake. Gloucester is a *man* with power and strong opinions. He is, perhaps, not quite so strong a man of his hands as you in single combat, my lord, but he is a remarkably astute battle leader. Still, Gloucester *is* young and is easily offended."

"He is only four years younger than I," Edward said.

Alphonse stared, but Edward was looking into the cup again

and the profile he could see told him nothing. Alphonse thought with a sinking heart that his warning had been misunderstood. He drew a breath and tried again. ''Gloucester is four years younger by the passing of the seasons, but a hundred years younger in the grief that has taught you patience.''

Edward did not answer that, merely drained the cup of wine he was holding, refilled it, and handed it to Alphonse who drank in turn.

''And what will you do now?'' the prince asked, with another abrupt change of subject.

''Whatever you command,'' Alphonse replied and then, desperately, added, ''which I hope will be to go to bed tonight. Tomorrow I will be ready for any more vigorous enterprise.''

Chapter 29

For several days, Alphonse did not know whether his talk with Edward had borne fruit. Much earlier—in fact, the following morning, when he woke on a pallet on the floor of the uppermost tower chamber at Wigmore, where Thomas de Clare sat sleepily grumbling on the edge of a cot—he realized all at once and with a considerable shock that he had been outmanipulated by Edward. The prince had deliberately kept him talking after he mentioned he was half asleep from exhaustion, not only because he was himself tense and wakeful but because he knew he was more likely to hear the bald and undecorated truth that way.

Alphonse's pride suffered a blow when he realized how easily he had fallen into the trap laid for him. Not that he could have avoided talking if Edward demanded he do so but because he had not understood sooner what the prince was doing. When he reviewed the conversation, however, he began to grin. Sly as a leopard, Edward had been called. Perhaps he was, but he was now as much a victim of his own slyness as his prey had been. Alphonse knew he had said exactly what he had intended to say, if not with his usual tact. And because Edward himself had set the conditions to draw out blunt and unvarnished statements, his lack of tact had been excused and his words had gained more force.

The satisfaction was tempered by being unable to judge the result. Later that morning, when Alphonse breakfasted with Edward, Thomas, and Matilda, the prince seemed already less haunted and less in need of a constant application of will to control himself. He was no less suspicious, however. He cast out several lures to catch any hint that he was not utterly master of the situation, but found no takers. When he asked Thomas whether he would return now to his brother, the young man replied that he had taken Edward's service and would do as Edward bade him. Mortimer's wife was, by her husband's direction, instantly ready to obey any order, to strip Wigmore of troops, to go with Edward herself, to serve as messenger or hostage, or to fulfill any role by the prince's will. And Alphonse, when he was asked if he now wished to be released to go home to France, was no longer too tired to think and smiled lazily.

"Not at all, my lord. I am useless as a battle leader, for I was never trained in that art and I have no troop to bring to your support. Still, I hope you have enough value for my personal skill at arms to make a place for me at your side in the coming battles. I still have my little personal grudge to settle, and I am most likely to settle it to my satisfaction if I am beside you."

Edward smiled, a show of teeth with little humor, but his eyes were clear and direct on Alphonse's own as he promised that the "settlement" would be presented to him on the battlefield if possible. Actually, Alphonse cared little about Guy de Montfort. If he did meet him in battle, he would kill him with no regret, but to Alphonse, Guy had become too despicable to merit a deep and bitter hatred. Guy was an adequate excuse, however, not to ask to leave Edward at the present moment and not to give his true reasons for wishing to stay.

None of the reasons was particularly complimentary to the prince: The primary one was that Alphonse suspected Edward was still unbalanced enough to hold a grudge against him if he "abandoned him in his need." The second was that Alphonse regarded the coming fighting with lively anticipation, if with no real seriousness. The war was a matter of life and death to Edward, he knew; for himself it had as little true meaning as a tournament. Alphonse hoped Edward would win because he felt what Leicester had done in wresting the rule of a realm from its king was wrong—even if the king was unfit to rule. Third, he did not like Leicester's young sons. Fourth, this was all an amusing adventure to him. And last, he had to fill the time until Barbe wrote and told him where to meet her, and fighting with Edward was as good a way to fill it as any other.

"So you may stay beside me, and welcome," Edward was concluding. ''And though you are no experienced battle leader, my dear Alphonse, you have your own wisdom. Now, tell me, what do you think about my going to Ludlow?''

Alphonse smiled again, but he called himself a fool for allowing his mind to wander while the prince was talking to him. Fortunately he had heard enough to sense the hook trolling for an opinion of Mortimer, and to avoid it.

''How can I have any useful thoughts on that subject?'' he asked, opening his eyes to demonstrate his surprise at the question. ''It was my idea that Lord Mortimer should leave Wigmore to make this place less suspect as your first haven, but that is where my contribution ended. I am totally ignorant of the country and the people here. It would have done me no good to ask Lord Mortimer's purpose in choosing Ludlow because I would have been none the wiser when I heard it.''

''My lord,'' Lady Matilda put in, ''my lord explained to me why he chose Ludlow. I was concerned because it is my cousin's property and her husband, Geoffrey de Genevill, has gone to Ireland. There is no mystery in the choice, only that Ludlow is close, large, and strong enough so that the addition of my lord's troops to the garrison would not be too obvious, and with Genevill gone there would be nothing surprising or notable if my cousin should shut the keep against all comers, including Leicester or his sheriff.''

''You and your cousin are both de Braose, are you not?'' Edward asked.

''We are indeed, my lord.'' She smiled. ''We are both named Matilda de Braose.''

Edward smiled too. ''And both courageous women as befits your heritage.''

The gallant remark, a little spark of the old Edward, raised Alphonse's hopes that reason would conquer the prince's irrational suspicions. His decision to go to Ludlow, made that morning, improved those hopes, as did his seemingly warm and grateful greeting to Mortimer when they arrived at Ludlow later in the day.

From what Alphonse could judge, Edward's spirits rose and lightened as soon as he began to make active plans. Over the next few days, the prince was able to discuss with Mortimer, at least with outward calm, the all-important problems of inducing men to rally to his banner and the form their campaign must take. Now, Alphonse thought, if Edward could handle Gloucester with tact, there might be a good chance of success.

So far all signs were favorable. Thomas had been sent, not with an order but with a courteously worded invitation to his brother to join them at Ludlow.

To Alphonse's intense relief, Edward was every inch the prince when he greeted Gloucester but with it courteous and attentive, his manner admitting Gloucester's importance without diminishing his own. Some delicate subjects could be barely touched on and set aside—such as the fact that both had made sworn agreements with Leicester and violated them—with a glancing reference to Leicester's almost overpowering attractiveness and growing tyranny. Both were equally guilty, which gave them a kind of bond of sympathy.

As the goodwill each brought to the meeting became apparent, tensions eased. Nonetheless, there were some bad moments—particularly when Gloucester demanded of Edward a promise to uphold the good laws of Magna Carta and to exclude all foreigners from king and council.

"You put me in a hard position," Edward said with gentle reasonableness. "My uncle, William de Valence, is even now in Pembroke fighting Leicester. Am I to exile him as thanks for his service?"

"I did not ask that his lands be reft from him or that he be forbidden residence here," Gloucester replied. "He may hold what is his in peace, as long as he obeys English law. What I asked is that we who know the ways of this land be the counselors who advise the king and that no foreign law take precedence over English people."

"I have no quarrel with that," Edward said. "But how will you take your assurance? Must I swear oaths and sign letters—"

"No!" Gloucester exclaimed, his color rising as he remembered how many oaths and useless proclamations had been wrung from Edward. "You are my lord, and if I cannot trust you, I cannot serve you. Give me your word, with your hand in mine, that you will observe the good old laws and ban from the king's council those who scoff at them, and I will be content."

Edward's hand came out without the smallest hesitation and Gloucester laid his own in it. "I swear," the prince said.

Later in the day, as Edward, Gilbert, and Mortimer settled down to discuss the military objectives that must be attained and their priority, a genuine feeling of respect and cooperation began to emerge. Edward's drooping eyelid lifted; Gloucester's normally ruddy complexion lost the pallor of discomfort and concentration; the lines of bitter hopelessness on Mortimer's face smoothed as his mouth relaxed and his eyes lit.

Alphonse felt a surge of enthusiasm himself and a prick of hopeful superstition. For once, forces totally outside of their control seemed to be working for them. Leicester himself had inadvertently done Edward a good turn. Conveniently, on May 30, two days before Gloucester arrived in Ludlow, Leicester had announced the prince's escape by proclamation and summoned the whole feudal army of England to assemble at Worcester to fight the invaders in Pembroke, where he assumed Edward had fled.

Once the proclamation was spread abroad, no one could doubt that Edward was free and intended to fight. On the next day, Mortimer's men had carried letters under Edward's seal all up through Cheshire and Shropshire. The letters repudiated as forced the prince's agreement to yield his lands to Leicester and summoned his vassals, not to join the invaders but to free the king from Leicester's tyranny under his son's banner. By June 2, when Gloucester arrived in Ludlow, a small army was assembling north of the village on the east bank of the Teme.

Counting on the news of the prince's release to restore their enthusiasm, Mortimer had also sent out summonses to his vassals and invitations to his fellow lords Marcher to join the prince. Most, like Mortimer himself, were so stained with rebellion that they had little to lose, but Edward's recognition gave a new legitimacy and a new hope to the war they were waging. They responded swiftly and were assembled near Wigmore by June 2.

To show his trust in Edward and to display his own goodwill, Gloucester had left at Leominster that portion of his army which he had brought with him. They were only four leagues from Ludlow, however, and as ready to move as the other forces on June 2. In addition, Gloucester had other troops encamped or holding keeps and manors in various positions southward all the way to the river Usk. Messengers came frequently up the chain of armed camps and brought, during the night of June 2, an essential piece of news. Although he had summoned his army to Worcester, Leicester had not yet left the town of Gloucester, perhaps because he hoped that Edward would be retaken on his way south to join his uncles in Pembroke.

There were other possible reasons for Leicester's inaction, but no one wasted time speculating on why he did not move; it was enough that his behavior gave them a chance to achieve what Mortimer had failed to do in his last rebellion—close off the crossings of the river Severn. Unless the whole country rose at Leicester's summons, in which case the Royalists' cause was hopeless anyway, most of the forces loyal to Leicester would come from London and the southeast. These men must be kept from reaching Leicester, a general objective too clear to all to raise a single contrary opinion. What pleased Alphonse, who quite properly had taken no part at all in the discussion, was that the method of achieving that objective had also been agreed on with refreshing unanimity.

On June 3 the leaders left Ludlow, separating to join the men who had come at their orders. They had agreed to meet at Worcester to take the town and destroy the bridges over the river Severn. If the crossing of the Severn was blocked, no army could reach Leicester, and he would be isolated with a relatively small force and no strong base west of the river.

Alphonse rode at Edward's side, thanking God that he had had the foresight to ask for a formal release from his promise to serve Gilbert when he had been sent with Thomas to join the prince. To ask for his freedom during the making of the pact between the prince and the earl might have added another bone of contention, small perhaps, but even a trifle was too much when a mixed force such as the prince now headed was in the field.

The contest for Worcester was brief, so brief Alphonse almost felt cheated. Leicester's supporters closed the city gates and cried defiance to Gloucester's army, which arrived first, but when the prince's banner was unfurled on June 5, the chief men of the city came out to make submission. Of course, the bridges had already been torn down—Edward had driven away the defenders and ordered demolished those north of the town, and Gloucester had burned the wooden portions of the bridges at the western gate—so there was not much purpose to resistance.

The prince could have ordered the sacking of the town for spite, but he did not. There was no need this early in the campaign, Alphonse thought cynically; the men were not yet starving for loot. There was also goodwill to be gained by accepting the town's submission graciously and demanding nothing beyond the right to replace the garrison of the keep, which was readily granted. No major victory could be claimed, but the event made clear the benefit of being an army under a royal banner instead of lawless rebels against Leicester; everyone's spirits rose.

With one accord the army turned south, destroying bridges and leaving guards at most good fords to prevent the enemy from crossing the Severn. On June 7 new orders from Leicester made clear that news of the barring of the passages of the Severn had been carried to him by those faithful to his party. The feudal host was commanded to gather at the city of Gloucester rather than at Worcester. That Leicester had partisans was no surprise and little disappointment; none of the Royalist leaders deluded himself that the whole country was ready to abandon the new government.

Control of the Severn was also established with varying ease at different places. Delegations came eagerly from some towns with bridges or fords to greet Edward; the folk of other places, perhaps remembering a bad master protected by the king or the prince, resisted loyally in Leicester's name. There was enough danger and fighting to keep Alphonse interested, and with each success Edward became a more genial companion. So, for two weeks, until they reached the town of Gloucester and settled down to besiege it, Alphonse very nearly forgot he was married. When the first sorties against the walls failed and the dull preparations for a full attack began, Alphonse did now and then wonder where Barbe was.

The thought occurred to him only when he was very bored; he knew that not enough time had passed for her messengers to reach Norfolk, for his troop to cross the country and recross it with her to take her to her father, and then for her messengers to come all the way back to him. Thus, bored or not, it was too soon for him to think of asking leave of Edward. He did not even have the excuse that he was anxious about her. All the news coming from England implied Barbe's journey was sure to be peaceful and safe. No armies were gathering and marching.

Information had come in day by day as the messengers Edward had sent all across England returned. The bits and pieces could be added up many ways to make a sum good or bad as one chose to see it. The news was bad in the sense that few men from the country at large were rushing to join Edward; but it was good in the sense that no feudal host had responded to Leicester's summons. Most men were simply too confused or too cautious to support either side. Were the orders of the king, though he was clearly only a puppet in Leicester's power, of more legality than those of the prince, who was free? Moreover, was it safe to obey any orders since there was no clear sign that either party would achieve a final victory?

On balance, Alphonse considered the news better for Edward than for Leicester. Most of Edward's power was here in the west, and many of the men who had been his vassals had responded to his call, bringing their subtenants who were resentful of Leicester's high-handed "seizure" of the prince's land. Clearly Leicester recognized the prince's advantage. He had not stayed to fight at Gloucester but had moved north to Hereford. If the feudal army had come at his summons, Edward would have been caught between the two forces, but no feudal army had formed. Whatever forces Leicester could command in the east were still far away, but Leicester did not wait passively in Hereford. He had taken the poor tired old king with him and was now advancing on Monmouth.

Mortimer had enough relatives, friends, and allies among the Welsh to have good and accurate information about Leicester's activities. It was soon clear that the earl was trying to bring the Welsh prince Llywelyn into the war. Leicester had offered Llywelyn a very favorable treaty for his support.

Edward cocked his head when Mortimer made the report. His face was brown, his eyes bright, although the day had brought no advance in their siege of Gloucester city. "Should I send an emissary to Llywelyn to warn him against alliance with Leicester?" Edward asked.

"No indeed!" Mortimer exclaimed. "The treaty, signed or unsigned, will do you no harm, and you should not imply my cousin's act *could* affect you. You will need to be completely free when you deal with him in the future." His dark eyes gleamed at the thought of the renewal of the long contest between himself and Llywelyn on new terms—terms that might now be slightly favorable to him. "Whatever you do," he went on, "Llywelyn will accept Leicester's treaty." He laughed. "Why should he not? He will make sure there are clauses in it that will permit him to violate it if he needs to do so. And to prove goodwill, he need only send Leicester a few archers. I assure you, my lord, he will do nothing more."

Gloucester, who knew the Welsh almost as well as Mortimer did, told Alphonse the advice was good. The question of whether Edward could resist trying to influence Llywelyn became moot, however, when Grimbald Pancefot of Gloucester offered to open the city to him. The town was overrun, but by agreement not sacked. For a few days Alphonse's boredom was alleviated as attacks were launched against the citadel, but the entertainment did not last long. The castle had been shorn of most of its defenders when the townsmen fled, and surrender was inevitable. On June 29, Robert de Ros, who held Gloucester castle for Leicester, yielded.

That Leicester knew the castle could not long resist once the town opened its gates was clear from the reports about his actions. A messenger from Thomas, who much to his disgust was in Wales making sure no large army formed there, reported that Leicester had sent messengers to his son Simon. The young de Montfort was ordered to abandon his attack on Pevensey and bring the whole army he had collected to his father's support at once. One messenger had been taken, Thomas wrote, but others were sure to have crossed out of Wales safely.

A few days later another messenger came. This time Thomas's letter did not begin with complaints of being overprotected and pleas to join the prince. Instead it gave news that Leicester had been repulsed by several of Gloucester's keeps in the valley of the Usk. Having tested the defenses and found that conquest would require more time and more men than he had, Leicester had moved south toward Newport. Thomas thought the earl had hoped to take that town, cross the channel to Bristol, and so pass behind Edward's army. If so, his messenger reported with grim satisfaction, the move had been checked.

During the third week in July news came that Leicester had turned north again and was making for Hereford. Edward, however, had traveled north ahead of his enemy. A week earlier an outraged deputation had come from Winchester to report that young Simon, because they would not give him without payment everything he desired, had sacked the city. The prince promptly secured Gloucester, garrisoned it with troops that had long been faithful, and put the rest of the army on alert. When, a few days later, word came that Simon had passed Oxford and was marching due north, the prince was ready to move too. Edward assumed, since Simon had not turned toward the city of Gloucester to attack him, that he had new orders from his father about joining forces. Because the Severn was unfordable in the south and all the bridges were gone, Edward expected an attempt to cross near or north of Worcester, where fording the river was possible. He returned there to guard against the passage of either father or son across the Severn.

Early on July 29 a report came from one of Mortimer's friends in Hereford that Leicester had arrived in the town on the twenty-seventh. By then, Edward was certain an attempt to cross the river would have been made, but a close watch had been kept on the east bank of the Severn north of Worcester and no sign of young Simon's army—not even of small units to test for fords—had appeared.

In the tower chamber of Worcester Castle he had claimed for private use, Edward had been wondering aloud to Alphonse, who because he had no other responsibilities like provisioning and commanding his own men had become a constant companion, whether Simon could have doubled back and somehow crossed farther south. Listlessly, Alphonse remarked that he did not think Leicester's son likely to expend so much thought or effort. Spoiled and selfish as he was, Simon probably had decided to stop to rest or amuse himself.

"Not if he knew his father to be in need," the prince argued. "Leicester's indulgence has bought him his sons' love, and—" He stopped abruptly, expecting a half teasing, half serious reminder that his own father was scarcely a model of severity, but Alphonse said nothing. Edward stared. Several weeks' worth of visual and aural cues had finally pierced his self-absorption to add up to a clear picture of Alphonse as a very unhappy man.

"What is wrong?" he asked. And then with a touch of reserve, for the prince had learned to be wary of generosity, "Is there anything I can do to help?"

"I seem to have lost my wife," Alphonse replied. His voice was even, his face was without expression, but sudden tears glittered in his dark eyes.

"Lost your wife!" Edward's voice shook with horror for he loved his own gentle princess deeply. "Man—" he came and put a hand on Alphonse's shoulder. "I have been busy, but not so busy I could not mourn with you."

"I do not mean that she is dead, my lord. No, not that." Alphonse found a smile and went on to explain how he had arranged for her to go to Evesham where her father was to send for her and that she was to send a message back to let him know when she had arrived safely and where he should meet her. The smile disappeared and his voice shook when he said, "But no message ever came."

"Norfolk is across the whole width of England," Edward said comfortingly. "And a messenger can get lost, injured, or even killed."

"Yes, but I cannot believe only one man would have been sent in these times, and for two or more to be injured or dead without any chance to pay for a message to Norfolk or me—I cannot believe that either. I have tried to tell myself that Barbe's messengers might have somehow missed us and been following behind, but we were at Gloucester so long. Could even a stranger to the country have failed to find us? And many of Norfolk's men are not strangers to that country."

"Strigul," Edward said, naming Norfolk's great keep in Wales in acknowledgment that Norfolk had servants who knew the area well. He bit his lip, then asked, "You think she was taken on the road? Made prisoner?"

Alphonse shook his head. "If ransom was desired or she was taken as a hostage, would I not have had word of it either from her captor or from Norfolk?"

He stopped speaking and turned away abruptly, unable to admit to Edward—so secure in the perfect adoration of his loving Eleanor—that he did not fear for Barbe's safety. He felt unloved, abandoned, afraid that she had found in her father's keep the man who had given her the token she hid from him. Over the weeks, as he realized how much time had passed without a message from her, he forgot the moments of warmth, the fear she had shown for his safety, the unfailing and unstinting support she had offered in public even when she differed with him in private, the signs that she was jealous of him.

Instead he found himself seeing again and again the furtive motions with which she concealed her love token, and he began to accept the wild suspicions that crawled in his head: She loved her cousin, Roger Bigod, with whom marriage was plainly impossible because of consanguinity and because she could bring nothing to so great a match. Or she had formed an attachment for some poor knight too far below her high, if illegitimate, birth. That was why she had not wanted to go to Framlingham in his company; that was why she put aside the joy of having her aunt at her wedding, of marrying in her own home among her own people. She had wished to spare her lover or to spare herself. All her talk of political danger for her father was only a white cloth over the filthy desire she hid.

There had been a little silence while Edward thought over what Alphonse had said and decided it was true that Alphonse would have heard if Barbara had been taken as a hostage or for ransom. But what else could have happened to the lady? Suddenly he frowned like a thundercloud.

"You told me Guy de Montfort desired her," he said, "but I thought Guy was with his father. Good God, Alphonse, Evesham is not far from Kenilworth, not more than ten leagues—"

"What!" Alphonse spun around, gray with shock.

"Yes, and if Guy were riding from Gloucester, he might well pass through Evesham on his way to Kenilworth." Even as he spoke, Edward caught at Alphonse who was heading out of the room, his face twisted. "Wait," he insisted. "Let me order a troop to go with you."

Alphonse hesitated, then shook his head. "Thank you, my lord, but no. A small troop could not break open Kenilworth to free my wife, so there is no sense in weakening your force by even a few men when they can serve no real purpose."

But Edward still held Alphonse. "A word. I am a fool for putting such an idea into your head. We have heard no hint that Guy traveled east from Gloucester when Leicester went to Hereford. I will not give you leave to go until you promise me you will not go to Kenilworth." Edward's lips twisted into a caricature of a smile. "Man, do not look at me as if I were a monster. If Lady Barbara is in Kenilworth, she is safe. My aunt may be indulgent to her sons, but not in matters of the flesh, nor would Leicester himself condone lewd behavior. Go to Evesham and ask the brothers when your wife left and with whom. If she has been taken, come back to me, and we will devise a way to obtain her freedom."

Chapter 30

Late on the same day, Barbara walked slowly down one path of the visitors' garden in Evesham Abbey. She was by now as familiar with every bed and bush of this garden as with the garden of Framlingham. With the thought came a surge of homesickness so strong that tears stung her eyes. More and more as time passed and Alphonse gave no sign that he cared whether or not he ever heard from her, she longed for her father and the comfort of Joanna's company.

By the beginning of July, after the city of Gloucester surrendered to the prince, she had expected every day to see her husband appear in the visitors' courtyard or to hear that he had sent an irate message asking where she was. But the days passed and neither Alphonse nor a message came. Day by day the pleasure drained out of Barbara. She remembered that she had agreed to send word where Alphonse was to meet her, but she had never known her husband to wait passively for what he wanted. If he wanted her, he would have sought and pursued her.

Most likely Alphonse had forgotten all about her, Barbara thought angrily. He was playing at war— She swallowed hard Perhaps he had been wounded . . . killed? No. That was ridiculous. Mortimer or Gilbert would have sent her word if harm had come to her husband. No, he was not hurt; doubtless he had found another woman. She would go home. Tomorrow she would go home without a word to him, without sending for a troop of her father's men. It would serve Alphonse right if she were taken prisoner—

Barbara laughed aloud at her own silliness, although tears still stung her eyes. She would be a far greater sufferer than Alphonse if she were taken prisoner, especially if he was in no hurry to get her back. Biting her lips against sobs, she turned her back on the rose trees and walked quickly to the bench near the tiny pool at the center of the garden. Furious with herself for becoming trapped in a weary round she had sworn she would not think about again, she sat down and pulled a wide band of pale blue ribbon from her basket, found the needle, and threaded it with a deep red silk.

Grimly, Barbara fixed her eyes on the pattern of little lions with curled-up tails chasing each other along the ribbon. Red was a favorite color of her father's and the blue would match his eyes. She sewed steadily, keeping her mind on her work and on the small events that were news in an abbey, until the lowering sun, just above the top of the garden wall, shone full in her eyes and blinded her. She turned her head and sighed. The sun would drop behind the wall in a few minutes. It was time to go in.

Barbara snipped her thread, pulled the needle free, and fixed it firmly into its carrying cloth. She could not leave it in the satin ribbon, where it might pull and leave a hole or catch on a thread and snag it. By habit she counted the pins in the cloth before she put it away; she had been used to lose pins, which dropped to the bottom of her basket and worked their way through the woven withies, and replacing them irritated her father who always felt it unjust to spend so much for such tiny things. She smiled, recalling the many times she had tried to explain to him that greater craft and patience were needed to make a pin than a sword.

Memory of her father's likes and dislikes made Barbara put a hand to her crespine. There was not a wisp of breeze, and she had been sitting quite still; how had tendrils of hair worked themselves out? Impatient, she began to push them back into the net, and felt her finger catch and tear one of the delicate knots. Uttering a word no lady should say, especially in an abbey, Barbara scrabbled in the bottom of the basket and pulled out her silver mirror. For the moment she was her father's daughter and the mirror was no more than a thing she had had "forever." But with the mirror a finished piece of work came from the basket—a panel of brilliant violet silk now embroidered with little dark purple snakes climbing silver trees bearing golden apples. As the frontlet she had made for Alphonse's gown unfolded, the pain hit. Barbara sat for a long moment with her hand poised over her basket, thinking of the weeks of work she had done to make Alphonse laugh.

"Damn you, Barbe, have you no conscience at all!"

His voice came from her right, from the entrance to the garden from the men's wing of the visitors' quarters. Barbara uttered a shriek of surprise and joy, dropping the mirror and frontlet into her basket, jumping to her feet, and whirling to face him. The mail hood of his hauberk had been thrust back so she could see his face plainly, and his distorted expression stopped her dead. He was angry enough to beat her, she thought, her breath catching. She backed away from the pool, and his mouth grew harder yet. Barbara had never had such rage directed at her in her life—except by her father's wife, who wanted her dead. Aware only of the need to put something between her and the threat, she caught up her basket, holding the open side against her breast so that the solid bottom faced outward.

"Put that down," Alphonse said, his voice a caricature of its usual gentleness.

Barbara was so frightened that she did not even think of running into the women's quarters, where Alphonse could not come. She knew the brothers would not interfere with a husband lessoning his wife; she had forgotten that though wife beating was acceptable, they would not tolerate a man's invasion of the chambers reserved for women. She tried to swallow but her mouth and throat would not move; her arms would not move either, so she could not put her basket down as ordered. She stood like a statue, having not the slightest idea that she projected an image of rigid defiance.

When Alphonse took another step forward, however, Barbara jerked back as if the distance between them were fixed by some solid matter. "I said—" he began, and moved more quickly. She took two quicker steps too, and then her heel tangled in her skirt and she fell—still frozen with the basket tight against her breast.

She landed in a bed of thyme. Low-growing and springy as it was and with the earth beneath the plants stirred and loosened so that it was soft, she was not hurt beyond the thump that bruised her backside, shoulders, and the back of her head. The violent jarring and slight pain broke her paralysis; more important in reducing her terror was the note of anguish in her husband's voice when he called her name as she fell.

"Barbe," he cried again, as he bent over her.

"What have I done? Why are you so angry?" she asked, fury at the unnatural terror she had felt making her voice sharp.

He did not answer, only stared down at her. His rage broken by shock and anxiety over her fall, Alphonse could not summon it again and bury himself in it to protect him from a far greater pain. Her questions flayed him. Why was he angry? Because by refusing to go home she confirmed his belief that she was keeping herself out of the way of a lover. Was that wrong? Was it not modest and prudent of a good wife to avoid temptation? Her behavior was perfect. She had sworn faith and loyalty, and faith and loyalty she had given him. But he did not want a perfect wife; he wanted love.

Disgust rose like bile in his throat as he suddenly understood why he had so eagerly accepted Edward's unlikely notion that Guy had seized her. Rather than believe she had an old love, still so powerful that she could not face it, he preferred her to be a prisoner, perhaps raped and beaten. Whatever she was, he was worse. Alphonse straightened and backed away.

Staring up at her husband, Barbara watched wide-eyed as the rage in his face was replaced with horror and then pain as if her questions had stabbed him. Then his eyes had gone dead. She drew a sharp breath, willing to bring back the fury if she could erase what she now saw.

"Wait," she cried, rolling over and struggling to her feet. "I am sorry if some plan of yours was overset because my father did not send his men for me, but I could not let you make a tool of me to trap him into war. You are my husband, but I owe my father for the years of nurture—"

"Trap your father?" Alphonse interrupted, looking back over his shoulder. He turned toward her, his black brows knitted into one line above eyes that held a reborn gleam. "What the devil are you talking about?"

"Did you not hope that the coming of my father's men and their turning away without joining Leicester would make all believe he had abandoned Leicester's cause?" she asked somewhat uncertainly.

Alphonse blinked and his mouth fell open. Barbara recognized that ploy, and it annoyed her. In any case, the crisis was now past and her fear with it. She walked forward to the bench and smacked her basket down. Alphonse closed his mouth and swallowed.

"You can make yourself look foolish by imitating a frog if you like," she said irritably, brushing at the twigs caught in her skirt, "but you cannot convince me that you are foolish—or innocent."

"I am innocent of that plot," Alphonse said, but he did not look at her; his eyes were on the basket. "My mind, it is clear, is not half so devious as yours. But what a marvelous idea! If only

I did not have these stupid scruples against tricking those with whom I have made bonds of blood into actions that might be dangerous.''

The sarcasm of the words and what he said rang true, but his voice and expression were wrong. He should have grown angry again; instead he sounded almost indifferent, as if he were thinking of something more important. He was still staring down too, as if fascinated. Her gaze now followed his, and she saw he was looking at the basket. Suddenly she remembered how he had told her to put it down as if it were horrible. That was ridiculous. It was an elegant basket, beautifully shaped and richly patterned. And he had been too angry to care if her work spilled out when he hit her.

''What are you looking at?'' she cried.

''What have you in that basket?'' he asked.

''Are you mad? My work is in it.''

''And your love token! Is that not so?''

Barbara was stricken mute by so unexpected an accusation. She stared into her husband's face, where emotions she herself fel too often showed plainly. She had acted too cleverly it seemed a being indifferent. He was jealous! But the knowledge gave her no joy as she realized she had inflicted on Alphonse all the ago nies she herself had felt. Alphonse had never shown her any thing but love, and she knew he would not—even if he did play with other women. He was, and always would be, kind. She hac been cruel.

''I have no love token,'' she said softly, stretching a hand t him.

''For God's sake, do not lie to me!'' Tears glittered briefly ir his eyes, and then he shrugged and turned half away. ''I have seen you hiding what you carry under your work in that basket or pulling your skirt over it, a dozen times since we were mar ried.''

Barbara choked, swallowing down a hysterical peal of laughter The mirror! She had forgotten all about it. But if she showed it he would know she was enslaved. She caught at her achin throat, torn between his pain and her own, not realizing her ges ture looked like one of fear.

''You need not be afraid. I am not accusing you of fouling you honor or mine,'' he said bitterly. ''I know you have not seen you lover. Perhaps you should and you will discover I am not so ba a substitute—''

Rigidly repressing another impulse to laugh at this comical dis play of hurt pride, Barbara said soothingly, ''You are a substitut for no one. I have never loved any man but you, which I told you when you first asked me if I would marry you."

Now there was contempt in his face. "Do not drag out that tired old lie again. I will not hurt you. I have no cause for complaint about our marriage. You are doing your duty to me nobly."

All temptation to laugh died as Barbara realized something deeper than Alphonse's pride had been hurt. He would soon hate her, she thought, terrified. She took a quick step, bent, and upended the basket so everything tumbled out onto the bench. Then she caught up the mirror and thrust it into his hands.

"There!" she cried. "There is the token of love I have carried since I was thirteen years old. Do you not recognize it, you great fool! It is the mirror you won in a tourney and gave to me."

Alphonse stood with the mirror in his hands, gaping as she picked up everything, ostentatiously shook out every piece of cloth so he could be sure nothing was folded into it, refolded it, and replaced it in the basket. She held up the comb, the only other item that was not necessary in a work basket.

"This is my father's gift to me. You may send it to him and ask him."

Wordlessly Alphonse shook his head. Clearly the comb had been designed to match the mirror—and he did, indeed, recognize the mirror, although he had not seen it for many years. Its form and decoration had been seared into his memory as an ugly, awkward little girl carried it about and showed it to everyone, innocently implying that he was her lover. He remembered vividly, even now, how he had told her in very plain language that she must stop what she was doing, that he did not love her or intend to marry her. She had sent the mirror back to him, and it had lain on a chest in his chamber, silently accusing him of cruelty until he had sought her out and returned it, explaining that he did not regret having given her the mirror. He wished to be her friend, although he was not fit to be her husband.

"Well, then," Barbara said with cold indignation recalling him to the present, "do you wish to reexamine the contents of my basket or the basket itself in case there is some hideous secret woven into—"

"Do not you dare!" Alphonse roared, thrusting the mirror into her hands so hard that she hit herself in the solar plexis and gasped. "Do not you dare try to make me a guilty fool! You hid that mirror apurpose, as if it were a shameful thing. What game are you playing?"

"I cannot see any reason to stay here and listen to you seek reasons to be angry with me," she said, drawing herself up and dropping the mirror into the basket. She reached for it, but Alphonse caught her wrist. She shrugged and her eyebrows rose into the little peaked form on her brow that marked puzzlement and scorn. "Oh, very well. I will leave the basket with you. When you are through with it, you can send it—"

He pulled her so sharply that she fell against him. Because her head had been lifted and tilted a little back in a posture of haughty disdain, her chin struck his chest, slamming her mouth closed and angling her head perfectly. Alphonse clasped her tight and kissed her brutally hard. The step forward he had taken to reach her had opened the split front of his hauberk, exposing the arming tunic underneath, and she felt a familiar protrusion against her groin. She pushed against his chest, although not hard enough to break their kiss, which pressed their lower bodies even tighter together. The bulge pressing against her grew even harder, but there were strange gurgles in Alphonse's throat.

She wrenched their mouths apart. "You wretch!" she gasped. "You are laughing at me."

"At you, at me, at the world," he admitted, laughing openly. "But a certain lady, who has managed—she thinks—to avoid answering a perfectly fair question has no right to call me a wretch." Barbara opened her mouth and he silenced her, but this time the kiss was as brief as it was hard. "However," he continued, as soon as their mouths parted, "you never said a more sensible thing than that I was a fool to spend time talking. Off with you, quick, so we can be out of this place at once and find lodgings before dark."

"Lodgings? But—"

"Barbe, do not start new games!" He chuckled evilly, spun her about, and sent her toward the women's section of the abbey with a smart slap on the buttocks. "If you do not leave me at once, the poor brothers will need to purify their whole visitors' quarters. You know we cannot stay here."

She caught up the basket as she flew by, laughing herself. Alphonse was exaggerating; carnal congress in the visitors' quarters would not require purification, but the act would be a shocking ingratitude to the brothers who had housed her for two months without questions. Besides, Alphonse would have to sneak into her bed after everyone else was asleep and then sneak back to the men's section before anyone woke. That would lend a spice of guilt to their lovemaking, and Barbara knew a spice of guilt could provide a fine flavor for the mild pleasure of the marriage bed—but not tonight. She and Alphonse had been apart too long. They needed no spice to whet their appetites. They needed a long, unbroken night and a lazy morning to play and rest and play again.

"Quick, Clotilde," she called as she ran into the large chamber where they took their meals—but the maid was not there.

Barbara had to bite back another word the monks would not have approved. She hesitated, wondering whether she should run out to the courtyard to seek Clotilde or go along to her chamber and herself begin packing. Fortunately, a lay brother came in and Barbara asked him to tell her men to make the horses ready to leave and send her maid to her, explaining breathlessly that her husband had come to fetch her and wished to go at once.

She thought he looked surprised, and turned away before he had a chance to speak. Another time she might have been annoyed at his unquestioning acceptance of her husband's right to order her to leave a proven shelter late in the afternoon; just then she was too glad not to need to give a reason that she was grateful. A few minutes later another reason for the servant's surprise came to her: Clotilde was already in her chamber and most of her clothes were packed away, only her riding dress lying on the bed.

"I saw Sieur Alphonse going through the courtyard like a storm wind," the woman said, smiling at her astonishment. "I did not think he would be willing to stay here, confined to separate beds, after being parted from you for so long."

Barbara had no answer for that and could only ignore Clotilde's suggestive leer. Nor was she willing, for the sake of dignity, to allow any delay. She dressed quickly and even helped the maid carry out the traveling baskets, most of her mind busy with what she could say to the abbot. However, that was a task she did not need to face. She discovered Alphonse was taking care of that matter as soon as she came out into the courtyard.

Since Alphonse had expected to ride on as soon as he learned with whom, when, and in what direction she had left Evesham, Chacier had not even unsaddled their mounts. A word from his master, after his first meeting with the abbot, had sent him seeking Bevis and Lewin with orders to make ready to leave. Thus when Barbara came out into the courtyard, her men were waiting with the packhorses, Frivole, and their own mounts saddled and ready near Dadais. Chacier came forward to lift her to her saddle and tell her that Alphonse had gone to the abbot to make their farewells and leave a gift.

He came out more quickly than she expected, mounted, and said, "Since you did not see fit to obey me, I will now take you to your father myself."

Until they were outside the gate, Barbara hung her head as if ashamed and did not speak. As soon as they were safe from being overheard, however, she looked up brightly and said admiringly, "What a clever excuse. It explained why you were angry when you learned I was still here, and because you were angry the abbot would not try to persuade you to stay at least the night. But where are we going?"

"To your father," he replied, grinning. "I would not lie to the holy abbot, would I?"

A rich burst of pleasure filled Barbara. If Alphonse was taking her to Norfolk himself, he must have long leave—or even better, have parted permanently from the prince. Her delight was so strong that she could not bear to have it snatched away, so she did not ask for confirmation of her hope. Instead she teased him by widening her eyes and asking, "Will you drag me all the way to Norfolk tonight? I thought—"

"Did you? Did you also think of a good lodging that we can reach before sunset? If not, you will find yourself used like a greensleeves in the nearest ditch."

Barbara laughed, but although the setting sun gilded the road where it did not cast long shadows of the bordering trees, behind them, to the south, there were serried ranks of swollen clouds. That presaged heavy, steady rain during the night and possibly on into the next day. Had the sky told a different story, Barbara might have chosen to sleep out. Blankets on the grass in the shelter of a rough tent were preferable in the mild summer weather to the pest-ridden rooms of most inns. She might even have ignored signs of a sprinkling; a brief shower could not interfere with the urgent need that had been awakened by her husband's presence. But a pouring rain, seeping through the fabric of the tent and soaking the ground they lay on, would surely dampen any but the first fine fervor. And if it rained very hard, Chacier and Clotilde would have to come into the tent also, which would put a limit to some of the games she had in mind.

"A ditch will not do," she said, pointing to the clouds.

"I had noticed," Alphonse said. "I had to bite my tongue not to ask the abbot where to stay, but I thought you would know. Surely you have traveled this road with your father."

She was silent for a moment, thinking, then smiled. "Stratford," she said, remembering a place her father would ride hard to reach on his journey to and from Strigul. "There is a bridge across the Avon there as well as a good ford, and nigh by the gate to the bridge is an inn that has an upper chamber. The alewife thinks herself better than the common kind—I do not know why, but she speaks good French—and she keeps that chamber for the gentle born, and keeps it clean too."

"How far?" Alphonse asked.

"I do not know," Barbara admitted. "We did not come this

way but rode west through Alcester to Worcester and then south."

"How far is it from Alcester to Worcester?"

"An easy day's ride, under ten leagues."

"Stratford cannot be very far then, but I am not certain we can reach it before the sun sets."

"Well, we can look at any other place we pass."

They did not even stop at the next village. Offensham was little more than a cluster of huts. Bevis asked about the distance to Stratford, but even the ragged priest did not know. Evesham was as far abroad as he had been. The sun was down and the clouds were almost overhead by the time they reached Bidford. There was an alehouse there, but Bevis came out very quickly and shook his head.

"No good, my lord," he said, "and for a better place she only named the priory at Cleeve. But at least I learned that we are halfway to Stratford and on the right road."

"Then let us ride," Barbara urged. "The light will last, if the rain does not catch us."

They beat full darkness and the rain to Stratford but not by much. Large drops, gleaming fitfully as they caught the light of the night torches, were splatting on the hardened mud of the inn yard as Alphonse lifted Barbara down from Frivole and drew her under the eaves.

"If there is someone in the chamber," she said, "I will try to buy them out—do you mind?"

"Not at all, my love," Alphonse replied. "I am sure you will be successful, since I will prick them out"—he patted the hilt of his sword suggestively—"if they do not like the bargain you offer."

He was smiling and his voice was soft, but Barbara drew a sharp breath. She was always astonished by how much threat her husband could convey without recourse to a loud voice or violent gestures. All she could hope was that no guest of great importance lay in that chamber. She had the feeling that Alphonse would evict the king himself. She shook her head and murmured some words of caution, but even while she was trying to think of an excuse to offer the alewife for taking the upper chamber from guests already settled in, she realized that very little sound was coming through the open door. She squeezed Alphonse's hand.

"It is so quiet. Surely that means there is no meiny in the common room."

He nodded. "You are right, but—"

He was interrupted by the alewife, who came running out,

curtsying and begging pardon for being slow to welcome them. "I did not think anyone would come so late," she said. "Come in, come in."

Barbara frowned. It was not really very late; travelers often rode until dusk, especially in summer when the mild weather and long, light evenings tempted them to cover more miles. She remembered that the outer gate to the inn yard had been closed and barred. Lewin had had to dismount and shout for a stable boy, who had asked the number of their party before he opened it. That was why she had been so sure the inn would be full of guests. How odd.

She had no time to comment, however, because the alewife had recognized her when they entered the common room and she began to apologize all over again, curtsying to the ground to Norfolk's daughter. Barbara had to tell her she was married, which called forth another spate of words and curtsies to Alphonse. Then she called her husband and berated him for not having already brought the best from the kitchen for an evening meal, and she wiped the top of a table with her apron and curtsied Barbara and Alphonse onto the benches, ran away to bring cups of wine, assured them their meal would be laid out at once, and ran away again when her servant came in with the traveling baskets to see that the room was made ready. She knew, she said, still talking as she backed away, that Barbara would desire her own sheets on the bed.

"No," Alphonse said softly before Barbara could ask. "Despite the good woman's nervousness, I do not see that there is any immediate danger here." He gestured with his head at the folk eating and drinking at other tables. "Those are decent merchants and craftsmen from the town. They would be guarding their houses or the walls if they expected trouble tonight."

"Yes, but it is strange there are only townsfolk," Barbara pointed out. "I have never been here when there were not at least a few men in travel-stained clothes."

"I agree that trouble is brewing somewhere in this area." Alphonse shrugged and grinned. "But not in this inn tonight—and tonight is all that interests me now."

Since it was all that interested Barbara too, she dropped the subject to tell the innkeeper, carrying a tray of food toward them, to take the dinner up to the chamber where they could eat in private. Clotilde and Chacier only glanced at their master and mistress for the expected sign that they were not wanted and then gave their attention to the servant carrying in their own meals. Bevis took a swallow of the ale and said it was as good as ever. Chacier made a face and asked for wine, and Lewin began to argue that ale was better with food. Half listening, Barbara sighed. She felt as if several hours had passed since she first sat down. The alewife's man came down the stair empty-handed. Barbara glanced at Alphonse who had started to drum his fingers on the table. His wine stood untouched. Again they waited, but the alewife did not appear.

Suddenly Alphonse rose and stalked up the stair with Barbara right on his heels. She thrust herself ahead of him entering the room, not certain whether she would fling herself between him and the woman or shove her officious hostess out the door with her own hands. Fortunately the alewife was just pushing a sack of heated stones into the bed to drive the damp from the sheets. She straightened as Barbara and Alphonse came in and looked bewildered—which made Barbara realize that no more than a quarter of an hour could have passed since they entered the inn. She bit her lip and turned to Alphonse.

"I am sorry your hauberk binds," she said. "Let us take it off at once, and I will see to a better fitting of the arming tunic to-morrow."

Alphonse opened his mouth in protest at the idea of his mail galling like that of some young or inexperienced knight who fought seldom. His armor had been worn so long and so hard that, from battering in battle and the adjustments of armorers, the steel rings had been subtly bent and twisted until they lay on him like a second skin. But he too had seen the alewife's surprise and realized that impatience had made the time she was above-stairs readying the chamber seem much longer than it really was. So he shut his mouth and allowed Barbara to undo his belt and pull off his surcoat.

The alewife finished with the bed and came to the tray of food which had been set on a table. She reached for the flagon to pour wine into the empty cups. Alphonse drew his lips back from his teeth.

"We will serve ourselves," Barbara said hastily, and moved toward the woman making shooing gestures with her hands and glancing significantly at Alphonse.

The alewife blinked, looked suddenly suspicious, and then left the room very quickly. Barbara burst out laughing. She was about to complain that the woman almost certainly now thought Alphonse was her lover rather than her husband, but he grabbed her and kissed her, then thrust her away and began to struggle out of his armor. Still laughing, Barbara started to undress herself, having a strong suspicion her clothing would get torn if she was not ready before her husband.

Had her shift had any ties, her suspicion would have proved

correct; fortunately, Alphonse could pull that light garment off in one swift motion without damage as he backed her toward the bed. They fell together, and the jolt seemed to snap the leash on which she had held some wild beast within her. She uttered a soft cry, her nails scoring his buttocks, her legs going around him and gripping as he found her nether mouth and thrust blindly. He groaned as he was lodged as if he had been stabbed instead of she and heaved away as if he would escape his confinement. But Barbara's powerful legs contracted, and he slid into the warm and welcome prison once more. She held him fast, rocking against him, tearing at his back when he once tried to hold her still. Despairingly, he closed his eyes and threw back his head, but Barbara's high, wavering cry brought his release, and he let his seed spring as he closed her mouth with his.

They rolled apart laughing over their haste, and Alphonse bruised his hip on the heating stones, which made them both laugh more. After a while they gathered strength enough to get up, use the chamberpot, find their bedrobes in the travel baskets, and begin to eat. Somehow neither had much to say.

Barbara knew she should use this moment, while echoes of past pleasure still coursed in the blood and glances and smiles exchanged promised new pleasure to come, to urge Alphonse to send a message back to Edward that he would not return. Surely Alphonse's departure could work no hardship on the prince. If Edward could spare him for long enough to go to Norfolk, he could spare him for good. The argument was sound, but she dared not use it; she could not bear that any discord sour the sweetness of the moment or blur the memory of the piercing joy he had given her.

Alphonse's thoughts echoed hers, although the subject was different. He had not forgotten the question she had avoided. Why had she hidden his own mirror from him? But he pushed it out of his mind, salving doubts with remembering how eagerly she had come to him, the feel of her full breasts pressed against him, her legs gripping his thighs, the heave of her body in response to his. He had been with too many women to be fooled by pretense. Barbe desired him and enjoyed him.

Naturally, with this trend of thought, they were in bed again before the meal was finished. Eventually they did talk while they finished eating, but each had made essentially the same decision, so Barbara asked for details of the prince's escape and Alphonse gave them eagerly. He also told her that Edward's imprisonment had left him dangerously sensitive and suspicious, and that was why he felt he could not yet ask to go back to France. And before she could begin to argue, he changed the subject to their campaign down the Severn and the great importance of keeping Leicester penned in the west. If Edward could bring him to battle without support, though Leicester was a great soldier, he could be defeated.

Talk of war made Barbara shiver with fear; her father was safe and so was her uncle, but to her horror she realized she would throw both into battle to keep Alphonse out. The wish would do her no more good, she knew, than would pleading or arguing with Alphonse, but the fear made Barbara push away the remains of her cheese. To change the subject, she commented that it was fortunate the meal had been cold to begin with. She did not understand why that made her husband drag her back to bed, although between sucking her breasts and tickling her lower lips until they were hard and wet he murmured something about proving her hot, not cold. It did not matter at all; she was as eager as he and she made no objections to what he was doing.

That time Barbara did not even remember their bodies coming apart. Alphonse remained awake just long enough to pull the cover over them, but he as well as she slept hard, unaware of the crashing thunder and violence of the wind, which banged the shutters against the window frames until Chacier, hearing the noise from downstairs, crept up and fastened all tight. When he told Clotilde in the morning that their lord and lady had not stirred, although their bedcurtains were lashing about them, she looked at the rain outside and agreed that they doubtless needed their rest, hoping they would sleep until the weather improved.

She did not need to worry. Although Alphonse wakened later than usual because the room was so dark, he realized morning had come. Hearing the rain, he decided there was no need to hurry. He thought lazily that it was most fortunate that he had gathered sense enough before he left to tell the prince he would follow Barbara if he learned she had left with Norfolk's men. Time was no problem. Then he tickled her awake and into playful passion again. Relaxed and happy, they slept again, to be startled awake by Clotilde's voice just beyond the curtain.

"My lord, my lady," she was whispering urgently, "two men have just come in with news that an army is marching toward the ford."

Alphonse leapt out of bed, pulled on his bedrobe, and ran down the stair. Barbara jumped out the other side, caught up the shift, which lay near the bed, and pulled it on, then used the pot while Clotilde brought her other clothes. She was fastening the last laces when Alphonse came up again with Chacier on his heels. Alphonse's eyes were blazing bright.

"I cannot believe our good fortune," he said, ripping off the bedrobe and yanking on the shirt Clotilde was holding. "The men who brought the news are merchants from Chipping Norton who were overtaken on the road by foreriders of the army. Most of their goods were seized—all they got were promises to pay—and they are somewhat bitter now that the relief of coming away with their skins in one piece is wearing off. They were eager to talk."

Alphonse was silent a moment as Chacier slid his arming tunic over his head. Barbara came forward to fasten it while Chacier readied his hauberk.

"Barbe," he continued, "it is the army Simon de Montfort was ordered to bring to his father. I cannot believe he has idled away two weeks coming from Winchester to this place. Edward did not seem to think he should take longer than four days from there to Worcester."

Barbara nodded. "It is no more than thirty-five leagues. A man can go ten leagues a day if he must."

She stepped back as Chacier brought his master's armor and Alphonse bent forward into it, arms outstretched, then straightened and wriggled his head through the neck opening. "The prince has been racking his brain to discover what clever device Leicester and Simon were planning to use against him, when he was not blaming the men he left along the northern Severn for somehow allowing Simon and his army to sneak past."

Chacier had pulled the hauberk straight and smoothed the places where the links had caught against each other to form little ridges. Barbara brought Alphonse's sword and belt from the chest atop which they lay. She looked down at the buckle as she fastened the belt, trying to remember which of them had put it on the chest, and when. All she remembered was the thump when Alphonse loosened it and it fell to the floor. Then his hand was under her chin, lifting her face.

"They are going to Kenilworth, Barbe. The merchants are sure of it." He bent and kissed her eyes shut. "Do not look at me as if I were leaving you forever. I will only be gone a day or two. You know I must tell Edward about this . . ." His voice faded uncertainly, and Barbara's eyes fluttered open; she hoped her misery was causing him to reconsider, but he was not looking at her. "Do you know how far it is from Kenilworth to Worcester?" he asked eagerly, his mind plainly on considerations that had nothing to do with her.

Barbara lost all impulse to weep; disappointment and fear were both replaced with a sharp urge to kick her husband where it would do the most good. Her restraint owed nothing to affection; it was dictated largely by her fear that, armed as he was, he would only feel enough to make him laugh at her. Men! Nothing was more important to them than playing at war and politics.

"Less than ten leagues," Barbara snapped, stepping back out of his reach.

"Marvelous woman!" he exclaimed, wondering suddenly if she really knew all these distances; such knowledge was most unusual in a woman. Perhaps she just did not wish to confess ignorance. He could not say that aloud, but he could ask admiringly, "How do you know these things?"

"You would also know them if you had spent ten years traveling all over the country with the queen," Barbara replied waspishly. "One must know how long a journey will take to send a maid or man ahead to be sure of a good place in the queen's chamber or good lodging or a bath to be ready before the great dinner. Or simply to fill one's head with something other than gossip. There was a time when we often went to Kenilworth, and Worcester is a royal city and the next natural stopping place."

While they were talking, Chacier and Clotilde had stuffed bedrobes and clothes into the baskets and strapped them closed. Alphonse looked around at the faint grunt his servant uttered as he lifted two baskets to his shoulder and started for the stairs.

"I will escort you back to Evesham," he said to Barbara. "I would really like to send you on east, but there is too much danger of stragglers from the army. I think you will be safe in the abbey."

"I will be safe enough," Barbara said, still barely restraining herself from kicking her single-minded mate. "There is no need for you to escort me and delay your news to the prince by another hour or more. There is a shorter route between Stratford and Worcester—I told you of it yesterday. Go out the west gate on the road to Alcester, then west again, and you will come to Worcester. You cannot miss the way."

"Beloved!"

Alphonse caught her in his arms and hugged her so hard the rings of his mail hurt her. He was too involved in his own calculations about how soon the prince could move his men to hear the sarcasm in her voice. All that came through to him were the words, so he believed that despite her original prejudice toward Leicester's cause she was now as eager for Edward's success as he. More marvelous yet, for he had had no time to explain, she understood how precious time was. Even a few hours might make the difference between catching Simon's army outside of Kenilworth and having a good chance of defeating and dispersing them or having them disappear within the great fortress. Edward simply did not have enough men to besiege Kenilworth and fight

Leicester. One reason the prince had not yet moved to attack the father was his fear that the son would come up behind him and catch him between two armies.

''I will send Chacier with you, too,'' Alphonse said, after a grateful kiss.

''There is no need,'' Barbara said, pushing him away. ''You may need Chacier, and I will be going in exactly the opposite direction from Simon's army and away from where he must know the prince to be also. No one will be interested in a woman and her maid traveling with a small guard. Go, go quickly. You do not have a moment to waste.''

''There is no other woman alive your equal!'' Alphonse exclaimed fervently, taking every word she said at face value. He kissed her hard once more and was out of the room and down the steps before Barbara had raised her hand to straighten her fillet and cap.

Chapter 31

Barbara did not begin to weep until she was safe again in the same chamber of the abbey's guest house she had left only a day earlier. Fury had sustained her over the first part of the return journey, a fury intensified by the miserable weather. She had replayed the parting scene between herself and her husband many times, finding more elegant and more cutting things to say to him each time. She had replayed the scene once too often, until she realized that nothing "clever" she said could have penetrated Alphonse's mind. She would have had to slap him or, better, hit him with a war ax to fix his attention on her. Then she had begun to laugh over the way Alphonse had misunderstood her. He was not usually obtuse—far the contrary—but his mind had been so fixed on the need for speed in returning to Worcester that he had believed what she said and had been quite sincere in calling her wonderful.

Despite the constant drizzle through which Barbara and her escort rode, they had been able to maintain a much faster pace returning to Evesham than going to Stratford. Having twice been over the road, every turn and hill was familiar. When Lewin called a warning to his lady to ride on the verge because great ruts were hidden by mud, Barbara realized they were passing through the village of Offensham and would soon be at the abbey.

Still amused by the way her mind and Alphonse's had been so far apart, she thrust all thought of him away while she decided what to say to the abbot about coming back to the guest house. If armies were moving about, even if they were not too close, she had to warn the abbot of it, but it was better in these times and this place not to claim connection with either party. Thus when the abbot granted the interview she requested, she told him that the way east had been blocked by an army on the move north, toward Kenilworth, and that her husband had felt it necessary to return to his duty.

The abbot thanked her heartily—but did not, she noted, ask to what duty Alphonse had returned. She later learned from another visitor, who had been in the courtyard and had seen the messengers going out, that the abbot had sent word to those at distant farms and into the hills to the shepherds to protect the flocks and themselves as well as they could. After the village had been warned, the gates of the abbey were closed, although it was not yet dark, and the brothers gathered to sing a special mass. From the back of the church, Barbara listened to the abbot pray for the safety and well-doing of all men and ask God, out of his mercy and in the face of their wild and sinful natures, to infuse the contenders in this war with a desire for peace and reconciliation.

That prayer seemed so hopeless to Barbara, especially after what Alphonse had said about the darkening of the prince's spirit, that she fled to her chamber and, at last, yielded to fear. She cried herself to sleep and woke the next morning drenched with new tears, believing herself a widow. Unable to bear the thought of Clotilde's attempts to comfort her, she put on the riding dress, which the maid had cleaned, and fled to the mute and merry companionship of Frivole.

The mare had already been carefully groomed, her legs and belly brushed free of mud and her flanks gleaming. For want of something more sensible to do, Barbara sought in the saddlebags for the ribbons used to decorate the animal for great celebrations and began to braid them into the mare's mane. First the sight of the gay colors brought new tears to her eyes, but then the sun came out and made her more hopeful. Young Simon de Montfort was not the great military leader his father was. Perhaps his men would be disorganized and not prepared for battle. If Simon were taken prisoner and his army disbanded, with little hope of other help might not Leicester be brought to consider terms?

The lift in spirits made her able to break her fast. She spent the morning braiding the mare's tail—with Frivole a ticklish and dangerous job that allowed no wandering of the mind. The mare tended to lash out with her heels unexpectedly just to see her groomer jump. She would then turn her head and raise her lip, producing an expression so like a human sneer that Barbara suspected she kicked not because she was hurt or startled but with malice aforethought.

Bevis and Lewin, who had often attended Barbara when she served the queen, had seen this battle with Frivole before and came to enjoy the show; however, they were also clearly puzzled to see her decking Frivole as if for celebration. So, to prevent them from thinking her completely mad, after dinner she gave the afternoon to rehearsing the mare in the fancy steps and rearings and bowings she had used in court processions in happier days. She collected quite an audience, nearly all the abbey guests, who were only too glad to while away dull hours and forget the danger that might be abroad in the countryside.

That danger was not acute, however. During the evening meal the abbot sent word to his guests that the lay brothers who had gone out to give warning had seen no armies or armed men, not even troops of foragers, in the area. Instead of cheering Barbara, who knew whatever action took place would be much farther north, that news only reminded her of her fear. She lay awake with pounding heart most of the night, and when she slept, toward morning dreamed of death and loneliness again—and learned that dreams were not to be trusted, that they were devil-sent torments, because Clotilde woke her out of the very depths of her nightmare to say that Chacier had brought a message from Alphonse and was waiting for her in the refectory.

''He is—'' she faltered, sitting up, a hand at her breast.

''Eating his dinner like a starved boar,'' Clotilde told her mistress sharply, wiping the tears off Barbara's cheeks with the hem of her sleeve and blocking her attempt to get out of bed. ''And cheerful with it too, so you needn't fear any harm has come to Sieur Alphonse.''

Relief seemed to lift Barbara out of bed and into her clothes. Quick as she was in dressing, she found Chacier already the center of a rapt circle to whom he was announcing the prince's rout of the army Leicester had summoned from the east. Knowing Alphonse's servant, Barbara was sure that he had been told to spread the word, and when he rose, bowed to her, and handed her a thick folded parchment, she signaled for him to continue with his news. Slipping the letter into her gown to lie next to her heart, she found a place and began to eat the food her maid brought her, listening as eagerly as the others to Chacier's tale.

She noted with a tiny surge of anxiety that Chacier gave the news of Simon's coming to Kenilworth without saying how that news had reached the prince. If Alphonse had been telling the tale, that omission would have had no meaning, for Alphonse never drew attention to himself—except while actually fighting. Possibly Chacier followed the same path through habit, but more likely he had been warned not to pinpoint his mistress as having any special connection with the disaster that had overtaken Simon de Montfort. The caution, then, meant that Alphonse believed Leicester or his supporters might have sympathizers in the abbey.

While one part of her thought that out, another heard how Edward had ordered all the forces that could reach him before vespers on the last day of July to come to the main camp outside of Worcester. As soon as it was dark, he and his chief vassals had left the city. The army, which had been alerted earlier, was ready, and as soon as its leaders were in place, marched east through the dark to Alcester. Turning more northward, they had continued by small lanes and over fields and meadows to within half a league of Kenilworth and had then stopped to rest. Just before dawn they had attacked Simon's army and found most of the men still asleep, unarmed and unprepared. When Chacier began to describe, with considerable enthusiasm, the slaughter and looting that followed, Barbara got up quietly and went into the garden. Alphonse's letter would also contain details, she was sure, but not gory ones.

She was not disappointed. Alphonse wrote first about the prince's warm thanks and said he had seized the opportunity to tell Edward that he hoped, after this battle had been fought and won, he would be permitted to take ship for France. The prince had agreed at once, and he had letters of transit in his purse, all signed and sealed. Barbara breathed deep with joy and offered up a brief prayer of thanks before she read on, even more eagerly.

"The only reason, my love," the letter continued, "that I did not come myself instead of sending this letter with Chacier, is that I have been busy making arrangements for the payment of some fat ransoms. You will not believe that Simon could be more foolish than he seemed in taking so long to come west, but he outdid himself after arriving in Kenilworth. He must have known the prince was not far off, and one would think he would by now have taken Edward's measure, yet he seemed to think that he was perfectly safe. He sent out no patrols, which would surely have seen us marching through the open land despite the dark, nor did he set any special watch. Worst of all—we are still puzzling over the reason for such madness and thanking God, Mother Mary, and all the saints for removing whatever wits that young fool ever had—neither Simon nor any of his principal men went into the keep. They stayed in the village, and we caught them also abed. I captured, in naught but their shirts, the earl of Oxford and William Muntchenesy and two other young gentlemen whose names I will not write because I took those two in the inn, not the priory, and they had not even braies on.

"The one misfortune we had was, in the tumult and rush of naked men, we missed Simon himself. Apparently he knew where were kept the little boats used to row about for pleasure on the lake that fronts Kenilworth Keep. Perhaps he crept out through a window after we set guards on the doors, or his ears were keener than those of his friends and he fled without warning them before we reached the priory. All we know is that a boat was missing and though we found his armor, sword, and shield, Simon himself escaped.

"As you can imagine there is considerable confusion here. Not only are there so many prisoners of high rank that we are having some difficulty in finding places that are safe and suitable to keep them, but very violent feelings have arisen between some captives and captors. I barely prevented Muntchenesy from spitting in Gilbert's face, and Mortimer, for some reason I did not bother to ask, grabbed Adam de Neumarket by the throat and all but throttled him. Gilbert and I had much ado to pull him off. Thus I cannot simply turn my prisoners over to Gilbert and have him send me whatever ransom he decides is just.

"Another thing, I have traded one of my braies-less young men for your aunt Joanna's eldest son, Baldwin Wake. He was slightly wounded, not dangerously but enough to keep him from swinging a sword. Since he will not be able to fight for a time, I hope, if I can find a moment's peace to plead his case to Edward, that I can get Baldwin paroled to his mother's custody. But the prince is buried in all kinds of business and is not—for many reasons, some of them very good—inclined to show too much softness. I will have to remain here for a few days longer."

Barbara dropped the parchment in her lap. Was it only for Baldwin that he remained in Worcester or had he been wounded? She jumped up and ran back to the refectory to pull Chacier away from his eager audience and ask anxious questions.

Chacier laughed. "With what would they have wounded him? A pillow? Most were naked and had not time even to snatch up a sword. Nay, my lady, he has not a scratch."

The answer seemed easy and natural, and Barbara told herself that Chacier would not have left his master if he was in any danger. Chacier added, too, that he had been told to stay in Evesham. First Barbara's heart lightened; then it sank again as she realized Alphonse must have given that order with the sole purpose of reassuring her. There was no other reason for him to deprive himself of his servant.

She shook her head. "No, I do not need you here," she said, and then, not wanting to throw her husband's generous gesture in his face, she sought an adequate reason to send Chacier back against his master's orders. Memory pricked her, and she scanned the letter again, soon finding the familiar name. "Besides," she added, "you must carry a message about one of your master's prisoners. The earl of Oxford is married to my friend Alyce. She is very young and will be frightened. I would like you to ask Alphonse to let Oxford write to his wife, and to set a ransom and let him go if Oxford will give his parole and the prince will agree."

The alacrity with which Chacier seized the excuse she offered troubled her a little, and when he had left, riding Lewin's horse, which was fresh, she blamed herself for not going back with him. Upon which she burst out laughing. Alphonse would have murdered her if she had added herself to the problems he already faced. Worcester, overcrowded with prisoners and those rushing to Edward's standard after his victory, must be like a sow with an overlarge litter—everyone pushing and shoving for a place to eat and a quiet corner in which to sleep. The image in her mind—alas for dignity—of a heap of squirming piglets with the faces of Edward's graver supporters, like John Giffard and Roger Leybourne, sent her giggling for her work basket and then out to find a shaded bench in the garden.

From time to time over that day and the next, Barbara did have to take out Alphonse's letter and reexamine the strong, steady strokes of his pen to assure herself once more that he was not hurt, that business more important than affairs of state—substantial profit to his purse—were what held him in Worcester. She was not aware of having bad dreams either, except that she found herself waking suddenly several times during the night. In the early dawn of August 3, she jerked awake again, sighed with exasperation, and was just about to turn over and try to go back to sleep when a scratch on the door brought her out of bed, holding the light blanket around her.

A brother so ancient that she could have offered no temptation to him even if she had come naked to the door was just raising his hand to scratch again. "The holy abbot sent me to tell you that he has had a message from the earl of Leicester. His lordship is on his way here to hear mass at lauds and to ask that prayers be said for him."

"Leicester," Barbara breathed, "but why—" She did not finish the sentence.

She knew well enough why the abbot had sent word to her of

Leicester's coming. Chacier's tale had made clear to all that her husband was of the prince's party. The abbot wished to be rid of her. If she were in Evesham Abbey, the earl might ask to take her hostage. The abbot would have to refuse, and he did not wish to risk incurring Leicester's anger.

"The father abbot," the old monk continued, "will send a man to see you safely out of the town, if you wish."

Barbara nodded curtly and asked the monk to wake her men and bid them make ready to leave. She prodded her maid awake, thanking God she had ordered Clotilde to pack everything the very day Chacier had come in the childish hope that being ready to go would bring her husband sooner. As Clotilde sat up and groggily rubbed her eyes, she explained the situation.

"But you owe the abbot nothing," the maid protested, climbing to her feet and looking about for Barbara's shift. "Whatever he likes or dislikes, I do not believe he will give you up to Leicester, and the earl is too holy to try to force him. If you are taken by a troop of the earl's foreriders—"

"Dress yourself," Barbara urged, taking the shift from her maid's hand and pulling it on, then finding her tunic and yanking that over her head. "There is some danger of being captured, but not much. I do not think Leicester's men would wish to burden themselves with two women fleeing the town. Just to be sure we have something to distract them, take the best of Alphonse's clothes in your saddlebags and I will take my own and my jewelry. Then, if we must, we can cut the baggage animals free. I hate to lose the tent and the sheets, but soldiers will always stop to examine loot."

"But why must we go at all?" Clotilde insisted, coming to tie the laces of her mistress's gown. "You warned the abbot about Simon's army. He owes you a favor and should be willing to protect you."

"Silly woman," Barbara whispered, "if Leicester has crossed the river and escaped the prince, he can go east and raise a new army. Does it not occur to you that my idiot husband will doubtless feel he must stay and support Edward through this new danger? If I bring warning, perhaps Edward can catch Leicester before he escapes this area. And if I can speak to Edward and seem fearful and shaken, perhaps he will leave my husband behind to protect me."

"Sieur Alphonse will kill you," Clotilde warned.

But Barbara did not want to think about that, and shook her head so angrily that the maid was silenced. She stuffed the sheets and covers into the one open basket and took up that one; Barbara took the other and they crept silently down the corridor and out across the courtyard to the stable. There they found Bevis and Lewin busy saddling the horses. They looked at their mistress, but she raised a hand imperiously for silence, and neither of them spoke. Lady Barbara had never yet gotten them in trouble. Both nodded grimly when they saw Clotilde stuffing everything of value into bags that could be fastened to their own mounts. Abandoning the baggage animals would serve as a bribe to any troop too numerous for them to fight. Just as Bevis was lifting one lightened basket, the abbot's secretary came into the stable leading his own saddled mule and carrying two plain hooded cloaks of unbleached wool just like the one he wore.

Barbara sighed with relief and called herself a fool for not having thought of that simple disguise herself. No man under Leicester's personal command would dare pursue or lay hands on a man in holy orders, so the chances were very great that they would be allowed to pass without pursuit if sighted at a distance. Of course if someone saw that she was riding a mare rather than a mule, or if they should be unfortunate enough to come face to face . . . Barbara put the thought aside as she was lifted to Frivole's back and put on the cloak. Before she pulled the hood up, she looked at the lowering clouds in the barely lightening sky and smiled. Was it a small sign of God's favor that no keen-eyed trooper would wonder why a brother should cover his head on a fair day? However, Barbara saw no sign of any armed men as the abbot's secretary led them from the abbey through the town to the road that ran north to Alcester. At Barbara's exclamation when they did not turn west along the river, their guide came to ride beside her.

"It is better for you to go north before you go west," he said. "The earl of Leicester crossed the Severn at a ford near Kempsey last night. Most of his troops are nigh on Evesham, but there may be a rear guard or small troops of laggard soldiers. The holy abbot thought it would be dangerous for you to go that way. I will take you north along the river to Harmyngton and show you a track that will bring you out on the Alcester to Worcester road halfway to Worcester.

His face was without expression. Barbara was somewhat startled by the information he had given her. Because he did not expect her to be able to pass what she knew to anyone opposed to Leicester? She gestured to her men and reined Frivole in so that Bevis and Lewin could ride on either side of the monk. The secretary threw a startled glance back at her, and she smiled and nodded, slowly and deliberately. He seemed about to speak, but he did not, only shivered and hunched into himself, and Barbara knew he understood that her men would kill him if they were attacked.

But they were not attacked. In fact, they saw no one except two farmers driving loudly creaking carts south on the road. They kept the abbot's secretary with them when they turned into the rough track at Harmyngton, but let him go after they had traveled another two miles. Barbara thought, and her men agreed, that any trap the abbot had set to give them to Leicester would surely have been sprung while they were closer to the earl's army. The secretary looked disgusted while they discussed it and said it was God's care that had kept his innocent blood off their hands, for if they had met the earl's men it would have been by accident and not by his doing.

He was so indignant that Barbara believed him, but the inconsistencies of his behavior made her think, as they rode along, of the conflicts caused by honor, loyalty, and the need to protect something more precious than one's own property—God's property. For a while as she speculated on how the abbot's loyalties might be divided between Leicester and the prince, Barbara kept a sharp lookout, but there was little to see. The track wound through a forest and was overhung with trees in full leaf so that they could not see more than a few yards in any direction. Soon they all relaxed, feeling they were too far north to be troubled by stragglers or foreriders from Leicester's force. Then they came to a tiny village. The place seemed to be deserted, but Barbara knew that serfs often hid when any party of riders came; the quiet did not make her wary. In the next instant, horsemen burst from concealment and they were surrounded.

Clotilde shrieked just as the nearest man shouted, so that Barbara did not hear the name he called. She looked in the direction he had turned his head, gathering herself together to speak suitable lies with haughty calm. The mass of captors parted to allow a big black destrier to pass, and Barbara bit her lip, her tiny hope of seeing a familiar face gone. Her captor had his helmet on, presenting only an inhuman metal facade. The solid bottom hid all sign of mouth and chin, and the dull light did not even strike a glitter of eyes through the barred visor. Then the horse sidled.

Barbara stared for an unbelieving moment at the shield presented before she threw back her hood and joyously cried aloud, "Lord Mortimer! It is I, Lady Barbara."

The single word Mortimer said as he pushed back his helmet visor was not in the least welcoming, and Barbara had to choke down a laugh and clear her throat. She told him at once from where she had come, when she had left Evesham Abbey and why, and what she had learned from the abbot's secretary.

''Women!'' Mortimer snarled. ''Always meddling. You fool. Even if the prince had not enough troops to block every ford, did you think he had no spies? We knew Leicester had crossed.''

He hesitated, cast a fulminating glance at her, then called to a squire and bade him ride back and tell the prince that Leicester intended to hear mass at lauds at Evesham Abbey. His sharp words had brought tears of shame to Barbara's eyes, but she felt much better when she heard him repeat her message. He might call her fool, but he had not known where Leicester was until she told him. His troop was all mounted, she saw, and guessed that they were riding southeast as fast as they could in the hope of finding the earl.

Her guess proved accurate when Mortimer went on, ''Beg Prince Edward to make all haste. I will send word to him as soon as I sight Leicester's army. And if by God's will the earl has not yet left Evesham Abbey, I will try to hold the bridge at Bengeworth.'' He waved the squire away and turned on Barbara. ''What am I to do with you?'' he asked.

''I will gladly go on to Worcester if you think that best, my lord,'' she said, with a fleeting notion that she might meet Alphonse along the way.

''Impossible,'' he growled. ''You would be stopped every mile by the troops afoot on the Alcester road—which you well deserve—but your husband, who is a good man and who is besotted upon you, God alone knows why, would never forgive me if you were misused by some stupid captain who did not know you.''

''I am very sorry, my lord,'' Barbara said meekly, suddenly feeling that she did not want to meet Alphonse after all.

She remembered Clotilde saying he would kill her for leaving Evesham and recalled that she had laughed at herself for thinking of going to Worcester, knowing how angry he would be to be burdened by her presence. How much more of a burden would she be to him if he knew she was abroad and unprotected when a battle was about to be fought? Her glance flicked around, as if she were seeking some magical haven, and was caught by an ale stake protruding from one of the huts. Immediately she remembered Bevis ducking the ale stake as he came out of the alehouse at Bidford, saying they could not lodge there and that the alewife had no better lodging to recommend than Cleeve Priory.

''I can go to Cleeve Priory,'' she burst out.

''But every foot you travel with us brings you closer to Leicester's army,'' Mortimer snarled.

''No closer than I would have been in Evesham Abbey,'' Barbara reminded him.

Mortimer hawked and spat, then said, ''I have no more time

to waste on you. At least Cleeve is on the east side of the river and north of where I hope to cross. You can ride along with us. If we meet Leicester and must fight, flee north if you can."

He did not speak to her again, but gestured irritably to the center of the troop, where she would be best protected. Mortimer's bark was worse than his bite, Barbara thought, as they started out. They rode hard, coming back to Harmyngton sooner than Barbara expected. Men and women scattered fearfully as the troop rode into the village, but that they had been working peacefully rather than hiding in the woods or behind barred doors was a good proof that no other armed force had passed. Better yet, the small bridge at Offensham was undamaged and unguarded.

Mortimer came up to her as soon as she had crossed. "We part here," he said, more courteously now that he had more hope. "If you ride north along the river, you will come to Cleeve Priory. I hope you will be safe. Perhaps God has kept Leicester mouthing prayers so long that he has not yet crossed the river. In any case, I think we will be between you and Leicester's force."

"Thank you, my lord," Barbara said. She raised her hand in parting and followed Bevis, who had already led the pack animals onto the track along the river.

"And be sure you *stay* at Cleeve Priory," Mortimer roared after her, "so your husband will know where to find you and not be worried sick."

By the time Barbara was settled at Cleeve, Alphonse was already worried sick. He was among the party riding with Edward when Mortimer's squire found the prince. The army had moved faster than Mortimer expected, and Edward's own divisions were across the bridge at Alcester when the young man delivered his message.

"Leicester has stopped to hear mass?" Edward pulled one ear as if he distrusted his hearing. Then his eyes narrowed suspiciously. "Did the abbot send this news?" he asked.

The squire laughed. He had been present when Alphonse brought the news about young Simon going to Kenilworth. "No, my lord," he replied. "This time it was Sieur Alphonse's lady who carried the good word."

"Barbe?" Alphonse exclaimed.

The squire repeated what Barbara had said about leaving the abbey.

"Then it is true," Edward said. He spared a glance at Alphonse. "She will be safe with Mortimer, safer than in the abbey with Leicester there." He seemed to dismiss Alphonse from his mind as he went on to the men clustering around him, "We cannot go back; we would be blocked by Gloucester's men. I will send word for Gloucester to turn south at once, before crossing the bridge, and we can go down this side of the river and cross at Cleeve. Let Gloucester meet us . . ."

He hesitated, and the squire said eagerly, "There is a village near the west bank of the river north of the little bridge at Offensham. The fields around that village would serve for mustering the men."

"My lord," Roger Clifford said, "I know that place. The crossing at Cleeve is not far north of it."

Edward smiled. "Well, God does not wish us to be lost and has provided two who know their way." He nodded at the squire. "It is too late for you to rejoin your master in time to fight with him, you know. So, since you know the road to the Offensham bridge, lead Gloucester to the fields you spoke of." He raised his hand as the young man rode off, then looked at Clifford again. "Now I need a man—"

"My lord," Alphonse interrupted desperately. "I—"

Edward looked over his shoulder and after a minute pause beckoned Alphonse forward. "Never mind, Clifford," he said, "I will send Alphonse. He was over that road only a few days ago. You may ride ahead, Alphonse, and tell Mortimer the new order of march. Bid him do his uttermost to keep Leicester from crossing the river and tell him to send me word if I must come south to support him instead of crossing at Cleeve. If you find any trace of Leicester's army on this side of the river before you meet Mortimer, you must let me know. If there is no need for haste in your return to me, I give you leave to place Lady Barbara in whatever safekeeping you think best on your way back."

Edward did not seem aware that Alphonse might wish to thank him. He turned his horse at once, and Alphonse started forward, shouting for Chacier, who had been riding with other squires and armsmen behind the group of noblemen. Alphonse had little attention to give to anything else until he had disentangled himself from the advance portion of the army. Once he and Chacier were free and cantering south, however, he began to distract himself from worrying about Barbe by thinking about what Edward had done.

The prince certainly knew how to get the best out of any man. Because he wanted the squire to lead Gloucester, Edward had taken the time to explain that the young man would be useless to Mortimer if he tried to return to him. It was also possible, Alphonse suspected, that Edward did not trust the squire to ride back to warn him if he found Leicester's forces east of the river instead of trying to find his master.

Then Alphonse's lips curled mischievously. The prince knew when he had met an irresistible force too. Edward had gracefully given him permission to do what Edward knew he *would* do—with or without permission—thereby giving him cause to be grateful and willing to serve rather than sullen and resentful. And, Alphonse thought, the smile turning into a grimace, by giving his permission Edward had also placed an obligation of honor on him. If Leicester had broken through Mortimer's forces, he would have to carry back that warning—leaving Barbe to whatever fate could overtake her in the tail of a beaten army.

Alphonse had to fight a terrible desire to rake Dadais with his spurs and gallop south at top speed. He could not set so wild a pace because there were other travelers on the road, ordinary travelers—merchants with loaded packhorses and farmers with cattle and sheep or a wagon loaded with hay. They pulled aside, sometimes with curses but not with unusual fear, when they heard his horse thundering behind them or saw him coming. That had to mean they were not aware of any army or any preparation for battle nearby. He was comforted, and he found more comfort still when he saw that the same was true of two villages he passed, tiny places where men looked up gaping from their work and women clutched their children to them to be out of the horses' way but had yet no reason to flee their unprotected homes.

More people crowded the road as he neared Bidford, and Alphonse had to moderate his pace further, but he was not so frantic now and his patience was not tried by going through the small town. Even from a distance he could see that the bridge over the Avon was carrying travelers in both directions. Then there was no fighting within miles of the town. Even foraging parties or foreriders would have sent frightened fugitives scurrying to the stronger place for safety. The traffic on the bridge would all have been going into the town.

South of Bidford the road turned west as much as south, but the next village was as peaceful as the others Alphonse had passed farther north. The first sign that there might be something to fear was that the gates of a religious house he passed were shut. That must be Cleeve, Alphonse thought. If Barbe was there, she was safe and would be safer still when Edward brought his army south to ford the river at Cleeve. Fleeing the temptation to seek her out, he dug spurs into Dadais and sent him down the road at a full gallop. The road beyond the closed priory gate was deserted, as he expected. That did not trouble him or make him cautious. Because he desired it to be true, he assumed that the abbot of Evesham would have sent warning to another religious house.

He did find Mortimer without incident, and called his name in answer to a challenge.

"Are there new orders?" Mortimer asked.

"None new. To hold the bridge as you said you would," Alphonse replied. He reported the proposed movement of Gloucester's troops and told Mortimer that Edward would come south as far as Cleeve. If Leicester had not crossed to the east bank, the prince would ford the river to the west to join Gloucester's army there. Finally he asked about Leicester's action since the squire had come to the prince.

"I have already sent another messenger to Edward," Mortimer said. "I sent some men creeping into the lands around Evesham Abbey and one came back to say that, having heard mass, Leicester has given order that the men . . ." He stopped and then went on as if he did not believe his own words. "Leicester's party has stopped to eat and rest."

"To eat and rest?" Alphonse echoed. "Without securing the bridges? At Evesham? But the river bends so they are trapped on three sides. Oh, doubtless they have settled on the ridge to the north—"

"No," Mortimer interrupted, looking worried and puzzled. "If God has not smitten Leicester with utter madness, I do not understand what he is doing. His army is in the fields near the abbey. The king and the noblemen are in the abbey. I would judge Leicester does not yet know that we destroyed the army his son had gathered. But if he hopes to trap the prince between his army and Simon's, should he not be driving northeast as fast as he can?"

"In such matters I am no judge," Alphonse said. "But if you think Leicester is setting a trap, I should go to Cleeve and tell the prince not to cross back to the west side of the river."

"What trap can Leicester be setting?" Mortimer asked. "I have sent men east and south and set lookouts on the hills. There is no sign of any army moving but Prince Edward's. I suppose you must go back and report to the prince that Leicester is still sitting still, but—" He stopped suddenly and said, "Cleeve?" then laughed. "I had almost forgot. I met your wife."

"Your squire mentioned her," Alphonse said stiffly.

Mortimer shook his head. "Women are fools, but she meant well and has caused no harm. She is safe. I remembered her when you mentioned Cleeve because I sent her there and bade her strictly stay there so you would know where to find her. Well, then, you need not trouble your head about her."

Alphonse vaguely heard Mortimer say something about not knowing the river was fordable at Cleeve and mention the bridge at Offensham, but his mind echoed "I bade her strictly . . ." He nodded when Mortimer stopped speaking and said a proper farewell, but he felt like choking the man instead. Imperious orders had the unfortunate effect of making Barbe contrary. But not at such a time, Alphonse told himself. Barbe might often be rebellious, but she was not a fool. She would not, just to spite Mortimer, go wandering around the countryside when she knew armies were marching. And he had not seen her on the road going north to Alcester, so she must be safe in the priory.

He started north, more annoyed with Mortimer than with Barbe. To Alphonse it was disgusting that one should wish to force obedience rather than induce another to obey and to enjoy obeying. By the time he rode past Offensham awhile later, the irritation had faded. His way of using people differed from Mortimer's because of their different duties and places in life. He was accustomed to persuading those more powerful than himself to do what he wanted and had come to enjoy subtly bending others to his will. Mortimer was accustomed to taking and giving direct orders—and very properly too; in war there was no time to convince or be convinced—only to act at once.

The thought of war made Alphonse uneasy all over again so that when he came to the gate of Cleeve Priory and saw that the prince's foreriders were not yet in sight, he hesitated. He had time enough to make sure Barbe was at the priory before riding on to meet Edward, he decided. If he did not, he would be worrying about her all through the fighting. However, when the porter told him she was, indeed, within, he felt ashamed of his desire to see her. He would have turned away, but the porter begged him to enter, asking whether Lady Barbara's news was true and gesturing to Chacier to lead the horses in so the gate could be shut. The man was so terrified when Alphonse told him that Prince Edward himself would soon be at Cleeve, that Alphonse began to soothe him lest he start a panic. While he was speaking, Lewin came out of the stable, saw Chacier, waved, and rushed off before Chacier could speak.

Alphonse, knowing Lewin had run to tell his lady that her husband had come, hesitated and had to ask what the porter had last said. The man wanted reassurance that the battle would not spill over onto the priory. Alphonse said he did not believe it would, since the prince intended to cross the river, but admitted that no man could foresee all that would happen. Just then Barbe herself came running across the courtyard and flung herself into his arms. He held her as he said, with clear and growing impatience, that prayer and keeping the gates shut was the best advice he had, and at last the porter turned away.

"I cannot stay," he said to Barbe when the man was gone.

Her eyes were like slate, dark and dull. "Do not be angry with me, not now," she begged and pulled at him.

"I am not angry," he said, but he felt her hand tremble and he followed where she led. Just inside the garden wall he stopped. "Barbe, I swear I am not angry, but Edward will be here very soon, and I must go with him."

She stopped and turned to face him. Her face was bone white, the only clearly visible part of her now, because the clouds were so heavy. In the brief silence while she looked at him, thunder growled in the distance. He bent and kissed her.

"I love you," he said. "I will not be long away. By dark, I will be here again."

"Or never come."

He smiled. "Oh, no. You will not be rid of me so easily."

She threw her arms around his neck and kissed his lips, his eyes, his cheeks, his lips again. "You fool! I would as soon be rid of the heart out of my breast as be rid of you."

He flicked the tip of her elegant nose with his finger to show he was teasing and asked, "Then why will you not tell me why you hid from me my own gift to you?"

He wanted to remind her of her success in beating him at his own game, in keeping secret information from an expert at extracting it. Most of all he wanted to make her smile. Instead she looked stricken.

"Forgive me, husband," she whispered. "I am a sinful woman, so jealous that I have hurt you because I love you too much. I did not want you to know I was enslaved—but not for pride, at least not that. I only hoped you would more eagerly seek the doe that fled than the dull cow in your own byre."

"Barbe!" he cried, but before he could express his joy a voice like a trumpet rang out. Alphonse looked over his shoulder toward the outer gate, shocked, realizing that the dull, distant roar he had mistaken for continual thunder had been the noise of the army passing down the bank of the river beyond the priory. "I *must* go." He smiled. "Now, do not fear for me. We are so much the stronger that I may never even strike a blow."

That was a lie, but hope eased the strain in her face and he felt such a lie could be no danger even before a battle. It could be no sin in the eyes of man or God to soothe the fear of a loving woman. Then he kissed her hard, took her arms from his neck, put her hands together and kissed them, pushed her away, and ran—more to escape her haunted eyes than to save time. He did not look back, afraid that he would return to comfort her if he saw her following him out of the garden, weeping, even though he felt her anxiety was foolish. As he mounted and rode out the gate, he shook his head. Barbe should trust his skill and strength. But with love came fear; he understood. Did he not fear for her when he knew she must be safe?

He could not bear her suffering, yet what could he do? He was a man, not a milksop, and he had to fight. And then he remembered that Barbe had been only enough concerned when he intended to fight in the tourney to urge him to do nothing foolish. It was war she feared, he thought. Poor girl. If Leicester had delayed a day in crossing the Severn, instead of sitting down to eat a meal at Evesham today, he and Barbe would have been on their way to a port. He had finished the arrangements for the ransoms and had decided to tell Edward he would leave when news of Leicester's move had come. But if they lost this battle, he would not be able to abandon Edward—if he and the prince were not bound together literally by prisoners' chains.

The thought made him start a brief prayer to preserve him from such a fate, but he never finished. His way was blocked by a river of footmen cutting him off from the water. God alone knew how long it would take him to cross, he thought, and then recalled Mortimer telling him of a bridge at Offensham. He turned Dadais away from the men and rode south again. After being stopped for identification several times, he crossed, turned north, and was challenged once more, this time by a troop wearing the colors of the earl of Gloucester.

"I am Alphonse d'Aix," he shouted, "in Prince Edward's service. Can you tell me where I may find the prince or my lord of Gloucester?"

"Not far." The horseman pointed. "In the river meadow just beyond the trees."

Alphonse followed a rough trail to an open area where a group of horsemen sat together. To the left, in the direction from which Alphonse had come, brush and young saplings had been cleared away so that the road was visible. Footmen were filling the meadow; beyond them a troop of horse clattered down the road. Alphonse rode across, bowed in the saddle to the prince, and lifted his hand to Gloucester.

"As always, Alphonse, you appear the moment you are needed," Edward said. "How far to Evesham?"

"No more than one league from here, my lord. And Mortimer

said to me that Leicester has not seized the high ground north of the town. We should make all haste—"

"That is where the horsemen are going," Edward said, but he sounded pleased, not impatient.

Alphonse laughed. "I should not try to teach an expert to suck eggs," he said. "I am no trained battle leader."

"It takes no trained battle leader to know the advantage of holding that ridge," Gloucester remarked.

There was a brief, uneasy silence. The earl of Leicester was a great soldier, yet he had not sent his army up to hold the ridge. No one knew why. And no one knew why Leicester had stopped to eat and rest in Evesham, which was a natural trap.

"Mortimer's second message was that we outnumbered them, and I have sent the banners we took from Simon with our forward troops of horse." Edward smiled when he said that, his right eye like blue glass and the left glinting under its drooping lid. "Let Leicester think his son is coming. I would not want him to cut short his meal or leave before we serve the subtlety."

Gloucester's destrier snorted and pranced. Alphonse thought his hand had moved uneasily on the rein. Before the earl could speak, however, Edward had continued, "Will you hold the right center, Gilbert, and send a good man to the river on that side?"

"Yes, my lord. Sir John Giffard will hold the far right. Leicester will not pass him."

Gilbert started to give further details about how he would arrange his battle, but Alphonse did not listen. He thought instead of how quick and clever the prince had been in distracting Gilbert from his trick with the banners of Leicester's allies. He had made a little mistake, Alphonse thought, in believing Gilbert would enjoy the deception—no, he had not! Edward had known exactly what he was doing. If Gilbert had seen those banners without being told, he would have been far more distressed.

Dadais sidled and Alphonse curbed him automatically, while he swiftly looked for what had startled his horse. Roger Leybourne and his two squires were riding away, and Alphonse realized he had missed the rest of Edward's battle plan while he was thinking about Gilbert. It did not matter. He had no troops to lead; he needed only to follow the prince wherever he went. Edward set off toward the road and Alphonse grinned. At least with Edward he would be in the heart of the battle, not sitting on the ridge and listening to his leader yell orders as he once had done when he went to war with Louis.

Chapter 32

As events transpired, Alphonse did not follow Edward into battle. Because he was well known to all the leaders and was free of responsibility for any troops, Alphonse was the ideal messenger. It was he, when the army was in place and beginning to grow impatient as the wind rose and the thunder growled louder and louder, who rode off to tell each commander not to be tempted to rush down on Leicester's men as soon as they appeared. He had started with Sir John Giffard, on the right, and had just given Edward's order to Roger Leybourne on the left flank, when the shouting of a charge rose over the wind and rumbling in the sky.

"There was no trick," Leybourne bellowed. "Look! Leicester is charging straight up the hill, hoping to force a way between Lord Edward and Gloucester."

Alphonse turned Dadais, for his back had been toward the valley. He could see Edward beginning to move and knew he could not reach the prince before the armies met. He would have to fight his way through. His right hand went out, and Chacier put his lance into it as he settled his shield more firmly. Then Leicester's men crashed into Edward's. Leybourne shouted his battle cry and spurred his horse. Alphonse had never led a battle, but he knew Leybourne intended to hit Leicester's force in the middle and take the pressure off Edward's front lines. He raked Dadais lightly with his spurs and set off too.

The horse's power was enhanced by the downward tilt of the land, and the first man he struck fell from his mount, not pierced by the lance but swept aside. Another was shouldered away by Dadais's speeding bulk, his lance jolted harmlessly skyward. Alphonse steadied his own weapon just in time to slide it across the haft of a third man's spear. A twist to avoid his blow failed. The man screamed as the steel head pierced his side. In instinctive response Alphonse thrust hard to drive the point in farther and then let go because there was no way to pull the lance out. From the corner of his eye he saw the wooden shaft rise up and knew his opponent had fallen. A waste, he thought. War was all waste. In a tourney that lance would have a blunt head, and the man he had struck would be cursing the need to pay ransom—but he would be alive to fight again.

The thought did not distract Alphonse's body. He tilted his shield to slat off a lance that came at him and drew his sword, struck at the man whose lance he had cast off. He felt the jar as his weapon landed but had no time to judge the harm his blow had done. Dadais was past too swiftly, but his pace was slowing.

Off to his left he heard Leybourne's battle cry again, and urged Dadais to the right. Because of the angle at which they had come, they had struck Leicester's column well below the place where his men had met the prince's. Alphonse knew he would have to move uphill to find Edward. Once more he struck and passed. Then Dadais was barely moving and Alphonse caught a sword on his shield, hammered at the helm of the man in return, and saw him fall. He was exchanging blows with a man whose shield was quartered silver and red when someone thrust between them shouting curses. Alphonse drew away, guessing there was a private quarrel there.

As if the thought had summoned him, Guy de Montfort burst past the duelers. Alphonse shouted a challenge with the first pleasure he had felt in this battle and struck, warded off a blow, struck again, and parried the return thrust hard enough to drive Guy's hand outward, which gave him a chance to bring his weapon down against Guy's helmet. He heard a muffled cry, but knew his blow had not been strong enough to do more than dizzy Guy a little. Indeed, the young man slashed at him with commendable force. Alphonse caught the blow on his shield and forced Guy's arm up and out, but the return cut he readied was never delivered.

A voice just behind him cried, "Do not strike me! I am Henry of Winchester, your king! I am too old to fight!"

For one moment, longer in mind than in reality, Alphonse's left knee quivered, ready to prod Dadais in an instinctive response to go to the old man's aid. Then the flat of Guy's sword struck the point of his shoulder. Had he turned Dadais, the edge would have caught his neck from behind just below his helmet and killed him. As it was, pain speared up into his head and down along his arm. Alphonse gasped, the point of his sword tipping down as his grip weakened. Guy spurred his horse to push past Dadais and reach Alphonse's unprotected back, but the older stallion knew his work and screamed and bit the younger destrier, who hesitated.

The king shouted again, and Guy struck again. Alphonse got his sword up to parry but held his return blow as if he did not trust his sword arm, pulling his shield in toward his chest. Meanwhile, his right knee was prodding at Dadais and his left spur pricking the stallion's flank. The horse turned to the left and surged forward. Guy cried out with triumph and cut violently, expecting his sword to pass over the curve of Alphonse's shield and slice into his chest. With an even louder shout, Alphonse tilted his shield over, catching Guy's weapon and forcing it down while he brought his own sword up and over in a slash that cut into Guy's shoulder. Guy shrieked as Alphonse felt a resistance go soft. He raised his sword again, standing in his stirrups and taking the chance of being knocked from his saddle in his angry desire to add power to his stroke. He was very eager to deliver a killing blow before Guy toppled from his horse. Triumph and rage mingled in a hot flood as he struck down with all the strength in him—just as a new rider thrust between him and his victim.

Alphonse could not stop the blow, and he shouted with shock as he saw the intruder's shield. The stroke intended for Guy had hit Henry de Montfort. Henry did not cry out, but he reeled in the saddle. It was Alphonse who cried out again as he pulled his sword away and saw bright red stain Henry's dull mail. He was so appalled that his sword hung useless for a long moment, but Henry did not strike back, only kept his horse between Alphonse and Guy, who had fallen forward on his stallion's neck but still clung to the saddle. Alphonse could not tell whether Henry was incapable of attacking him or unwilling to do so, but he did not wish to harm his friend further. He turned Dadais so swiftly that the stallion collided with Chacier's horse and the blow Chacier had launched went awry. No harm was done. Alphonse struck Chacier's opponent so hard he fell at once. Then he drove Dadais past, turning again. Henry and Guy had drawn back, and a defensive circle was forming around Leicester's banner. Off to the side, he heard "I am your king, Henry of Winchester. Do not harm me!"

This time Alphonse was not even tempted to pause. Let him die, he thought. Let him die, and this war will be over for good.

As if drawn by a cord, Barbara had followed Alphonse as far as the garden gate. She went no farther, but stood watching him run light-footed under the weight of his mail and mount Dadais in a leap as if he were a young knight proving himself. Under the fear she felt for him was a great relief, a great gladness that she had nothing left to hide. There was a joy in it, like being naked before her lover.

The smile he had given her when she confessed her jealousy held such delight—pure, astonished delight that had not a jot of smug satisfaction. For how long? the green-eyed demon inside Barbara asked. At the jealous thought, with tears streaming down her face, she chuckled. But pain like a knife stroke came with the answer: Perhaps as long as he lives—if he does not live out this day.

When the priory gate shut behind Chacier and Alphonse, Barbara turned and leaned against the garden wall, sobbing bitterly. Then wearily she straightened her body and wiped her face. At least he had left in joy. A clear mind and a light heart were as strong a defense as armor and shield, her father had told her once when criticizing a friend's wife who moaned and wailed whenever he went to fight.

Before dark. Alphonse had said he would come to her before dark. But the storm was so near and so violent that it was dark already. Barbara laughed again, then clapped a hand to her mouth. There had been a hysterical shrillness to that laugh that frightened her. Her hand dropped and she looked up at the clouds, hanging lower and blacker every moment. The storm would be dreadful. Perhaps it would put an end to the battle. Perhaps Leicester would escape in the dark and the wind and reach Kenilworth and lock himself in. Then there would be a long siege, and Alphonse would be bored to death by a siege. He would take a polite leave of Edward if the prince besieged Kenilworth.

She walked back to the guest house, almost smiling again. Somewhere inside was a little knot of doubt that said she was selfish to hope for such an outcome, that all of England would suffer if the war dragged on. But all of England would suffer if Leicester were defeated and King Henry were free to rule at his own will again, to throw lands and money down the maws of his voracious family or squander them on harebrained, fantastical adventures in the hope of winning his younger son a crown. Barbara shuddered and hurried inside the guest house.

The realm could not be tormented by Henry for long, she told herself. He was old, and Edward had nothing of his father's softness to the Lusignans. And Leicester's rule had not been so different. The earl had spouted righteous rules and texts, but instead of Henry's favors to his cruel and rapacious half brothers, Leicester heaped confiscated estates on his careless and greedy younger sons. At least Henry had tried to disarm his critics with grace and charm; he did not explain weightily why he was right to be wrong. A gasp—half laugh, half sob—escaped Barbara and she hid her face in her hands for a moment.

Thunder rumbled again, muted by the walls of the guest house, but with the wind stilled, the air seemed thick and heavy. Barbara lifted her head and walked with determination to her small chamber. Before dark, Alphonse had said. At this time of year that meant she could not hope to see him before compline. She had been awake since before dawn and lay down on the narrow cot in her clothes in the hope that she could sleep away some of the long hours.

At first her hope seemed vain. She lay still with her eyes closed for a while, trying to keep all thoughts out of her head. When that failed, she began to count sheep as she had been taught as a child, but the meek curly-fleeced ewes turned treacherously into shouting armed men waving swords as they leapt the gate. She turned to her right side and stared at the wall, trying to find figures or patterns in the rough stone to beguile her, but a red streak, like blood, kept drawing her eyes, so she turned her back and lay on her left side. Clotilde sat near the door, sewing, holding her work at an angle to see better in the dim light. At first Barbara found that soothing, but soon the cock of Clotilde's head made her seem to be listening. Without wishing to, Barbara began to listen too, so intently that she thought she could make out the faint sigh of her maid's breathing, a tiny creak coming from the corridor, a buzzing—no, that was inside her own ears.

Barbara closed her eyes to hear better in the dark, listening harder and harder as the sounds receded. She felt peaceful as the dark grew thicker, so dense that it even muffled sound—and then her ears betrayed her. Where she had had to strain to hear, noises now rushed at her, ugly noises, human shouts and wails. Barbara tried not to listen, not realizing that she had been asleep and thinking in the confusion of waking that what she heard were the sounds of the growing storm making their way through the walls of the guest house. Her eyes snapped open. Those were not dream noises; Clotilde was on her feet, shutting the door against the sound of voices in the corridor.

"Wait," Barbara cried, jumping up. "The cries! Someone is wounded. Alphonse! Alphonse!"

She ran out into the corridor, jerking to a stop as she came fully awake and realized Alphonse would never wail. The sudden stop saved her from colliding with a man-at-arms, who turned with a snarl, his bared sword inches from her breast. Barbara shrieked, a man's cry, thin and tremulous, blended with hers, and before either faded, a deeper voice overrode both, exclaiming, "Lady Barbara!"

"Leybourne," Barbara gasped, then reached for the door frame to support herself and whispered, "Alphonse?"

"Hale and well and enjoying himself when I last saw him, but, Lady Barbara, here is the king."

"Sire!" Barbara cried as she sank into a curtsy and in the next instant leapt up, stretching out her hands as if to lend support. "Oh, heaven, you are wounded, sire."

Henry clutched at the hands held out to him, letting go of Roger Leybourne's arm, to which he had been clinging. "Leicester's men wanted me to be killed." His hands trembled and his voice held a mixture of resentment and disbelief. "They dressed me in this common mail and gave me a blank shield and a helmet without even a crest. Leicester intended that I should die if he did."

"My dear lord," Barbara said gently, completely forgetting in her pity for his hurt and bewilderment how often she herself had wished him dead. "Will you not come into my chamber and lie down until more fitting quarters can be readied for you?"

The king cast a frightened glance at Leybourne, whose lips tightened as he said, "You may do as you please, sire. We have taken a wrong turn and are in the women's dormitory, but a short exception will be made for you, I am sure. Rest in Lady Barbara's chamber if you like. I will go and find the prior's guest house."

As she and Leybourne led the king into the room and seated him on the cot, Barbara guessed he had been brought to Cleeve so that Leicester could not run off with him. Her guess was confirmed when she saw men-at-arms take positions along the wall of the corridor.

"As soon as the prior's guest house is ready, I will come for him," Leybourne murmured.

"First send the infirmarian to dress his wound," Barbara said. As Leybourne nodded and went out, she gestured to Clotilde to shut the door, then knelt down beside the king. "Will you allow my maid and me to help you out of your armor, sire?"

Henry looked at the closed door of the chamber, at Barbara on her knees, at Clotilde, who was curtsying. "Why did Roger Leybourne bring me here, away from my son?" he whispered.

Barbara smiled, although her lips felt stiff. Dazed and confused as he was, it was apparent that Henry only remembered a long-ago quarrel between Leybourne and Edward, which he had made worse, and that for a short time Leybourne had become Leicester's supporter. He seemed to have forgotten that the quarrel had been settled.

"Leybourne is a most faithful servant to you now, my lord, and a loyal friend to Prince Edward," Barbara said. "Perhaps you did not hear how Lord Edward came to escape from Leicester, but Roger Leybourne was among those who helped. And he has loyally fought for Lord Edward since May. Truly you may trust him."

"Leicester, my own brother-by-marriage, wanted me dead," Henry said. "Whom, then, may I trust?"

Part of Barbara felt so exasperated she could have screamed. Did Henry not remember the many offenses he had given Leicester? Did he expect to be loved despite his insults, his efforts to deprive his sister of her dowry, his accusations of treachery? But tears of pain and fatigue and bewilderment rolled down the king's face, catching in glittering points on the gray stubble of his unshaven beard. That Henry, who was always so particular about his appearance, should be unshaven told how hard the old man had been driven. Despite herself, Barbara almost wept for him, despite her knowledge that he was the cause of all the trouble, the cause, perhaps, that her husband might be bleeding out his life in the mud. No, Leybourne had said Alphonse was well, and Henry's blue eyes looked into hers like a lost child's. Barbara put a hand on his.

"Oh, no, my lord," she soothed. "I cannot believe that Leicester wished any harm to come to you. I do not say he has not been wrong in how he acted, but that is because he deceived himself that he was doing what was best for your safety and honor. No one wishes to harm you. I am sure the earl gave you plain armor to save you from being seized by this one and that one and becoming the center of the battle, where you might be hurt." She patted his hand. "Come, my lord, let us take off your armor. You will be more comfortable."

He agreed faintly, and Clotilde helped lift him while Barbara pulled the skirts of the hauberk out from under him. Then they had to lift the mail shirt over his head, easing it carefully over his cut shoulder. Barbara had just repeated the process with the arming tunic when a scratch on the door heralded the arrival of a breathless infirmarian. Barbara stepped back to allow him to look at the wound, and in a few moments he began to assure the king that the hurt was small and would soon be well, but to dress it properly he would prefer that the king be carried to the infirmary.

Although Henry looked very frightened and clutched at Barbara's hands when Clotilde opened the door, he relaxed as soon as he saw the Cistercian habit and endured the monk's examination patiently. When the infirmarian wished to move him, however, he looked anxiously at Barbara, who could not resist the appeal. She asked if she might be allowed to accompany the king. This drew a spate of apologies from the infirmarian, who explained that women were not allowed in the infirmary, even that portion segregated for guests.

In his excitement at having a king as a patient, his desire to do exactly what Henry wanted, his conflicting fear of breaking the rule, and his distress at being in the women's dormitory, the infirmarian spoke so quickly and disjointedly that Henry did not understand and became even more confused. At that moment Leybourne returned. The king grabbed Barbara's hand and would not let go.

Eventually Barbara and the infirmarian accompanied Henry to the prior's guest house, arriving not a moment too soon. As they left the dormitory, three brilliant flashes of lightning split the sky, making the courtyard brighter than the sun at noon, and as they reached the door of the guest house, came a crash of thunder so loud that all, even the warrior Leybourne, cried out. All hurried within as a cascade of water, like a river tumbling over a cliff, fell from the sky. In the bedchamber one lay brother was tending a small but lively fire while another was warming the sheets of a large, handsome bed. The infirmarian's novice was also waiting, and the crowd of clerics seemed to calm the king so that he agreed to allow them to undress him and put him to bed. While that was being done, Leybourne drew Barbara down the stairs to the chamber below.

"I will go back now," he said. "I have left a troop who will defend the priory against stragglers if any should try to enter. You need have no fear. Leicester's army is destroyed. The battle was all but over when I left."

"Over—" Barbara began, but Leybourne had turned on his heel and walked away.

She followed for a step or two, her hand outstretched, unable to unlock her voice. If the battle was over, why should Leybourne ride back when one could scarcely see through the pouring rain? Why had not Alphonse come if the battle was over? The fear swelled so that her knees shook too badly to walk, and she had to stop. When it receded, she still went no farther. Leybourne would not even hear her if she called to him; the noise of the storm was terrible. And even if he heard her, he was unlikely to wait in the rain to explain. Besides, what could he tell her if he did wait? He had already said Alphonse was "enjoying himself."

Enjoying himself? Did that mean he no longer wished to return to France soon but would seek out more wars to fight in? Barbara stood staring at the empty doorway until the infirmarian's novice approached and asked her to come to the king. She followed without thinking, sank into a curtsy, and murmured something proper and meaningless.

"It is very strange of your father to bring you to a battle," the king said querulously.

"My father is not here, sire," Barbara replied, only half absorbing what was said to her. "I was with my husband, Alphonse d'Aix."

Vaguely she recalled that the king had been confused when Leybourne brought him into the priory, and she thought he had forgotten she was married. She lifted her head as she spoke and saw that though Henry was still pale, he seemed perfectly composed. And the half-smile he wore, the sidelong glance he cast at her under the drooping eyelid, set off alarm bells in her head. Before she could say more, he told the second lay brother to bring her a stool so she could sit and talk to him. As Barbara rose from her curtsy, Henry said he was hungry, and the lay brother replied that he would bring some warm soup and went out.

The delay had given Barbara time to think. A closer examination of Henry's face as he sat propped among pillows made her doubt that the extra droop of his eyelid was owing to slyness. More likely, she thought, remembering the way his hand trembled when he gestured her to rise and the querulous voice, the slackness was owing to exhaustion. If he wished to talk, however, her long training as a court lady bade her never to lose an opportunity to lay an obligation on royalty.

"Alphonse was one of those who helped Prince Edward escape," Barbara went on as soon as the servant was gone. "For safety he sent me to Evesham Abbey, but I took fright when I heard that Leicester was coming there and—and fled here to Cleeve."

Henry's expressive face grew sad and he put out his shaking hand to grasp hers. "How dreadful for you, my poor Barbara, to have your husband on one side in a battle and your father on the other. And how dreadful for them if they should have met on the field."

Barbara was touched by the sincere sympathy and murmured,

"You are very kind, sire," before she remembered how often she had railed against the way the king's warmth seduced those who should have known better, and a wave of irritation replaced her gratitude. Simultaneously the sense of what Henry had said about her father caused a new clangor of alarm bells, and she added quickly, "But your kindness is wasted. My husband and father could never have met. My father did not answer Leicester's summons and took no part in this battle. You must know, sire, that he has never approved of much that Leicester did and was very angry when he heard the terms of the Peace of Canterbury."

"But he did not repudiate the Provisions of Oxford," Henry said, withdrawing his hand.

"My lord, you yourself approved the provisions in their first form. It is the earl of Leicester who has distorted them into something different from what was first intended." Barbara felt a pang of guilt over those words, but she knew no power on earth could reconcile Leicester with the king now. It was better that the earl bear the onus and that her father, who also had the good of the realm at heart, should be free and restored to power so that some good might be salvaged from the wreck of Leicester's plans. "You know my father loves you," she went on. "I cannot tell you how often he has told me of your mischief together as boys and how your kindness saved him from his father's anger. There was something about a horse, but I have forgotten exactly how it came about . . ."

She let her voice drift away invitingly and hid her sigh of relief under a chuckle as Henry promptly began to retell the well-known story with details and embellishments that Barbara had not heard before. By the time the king's soup was brought, Henry was more relaxed. Barbara served, holding the bowl so the king could eat in comfort, presenting the napkin when it was necessary, and talking gently of great state dinners in happier times. Now and again she managed to insert a reminder of occasions when her father had supported Henry, but she was careful that the remarks seemed to be made only in passing. If Henry noted what she said, he gave no sign of it, and when the bowl was empty and Barbara had held a basin for him to wash his hands, he dismissed her. He said only that he wished to rest, but he smiled warmly at her, patted her hand, and called her a good girl.

At first as she walked down the stairs, Barbara was disappointed, rethinking the conversation and wondering whether she should have been more direct in her father's defense. By the time she reached the outer door, she felt less dissatisfied. Had she harped on her father's break with Leicester, every suspicion in the king's devious mind would have wakened to combat her claims. And to have pointed out her father's reasons for supporting Leicester would have forced her also to point out the king's mistakes—a very foolish thing to do at any time.

No, she had done just right, she thought. She had soothed the king, made him feel safe and happy, and made clear that her father had withdrawn his support from Leicester—whether or not that was true, it would be true now. Best of all, she had tied her father's absence from this battle to his love for the king, and Henry always wanted to be loved. If anything could ease the king's spite against a man who had opposed him, it was the notion that the opposition had ended out of love. She could trust her father to say and do what was proper as soon as he knew—Barbara drew in a sharp breath. She had to send him the news of Leicester's defeat and what she had said to the king at once.

Becoming aware of her surroundings, Barbara found she was standing at the door of the prior's guest house, looking into the courtyard. Now she saw with relief that the rain had diminished to little more than a drizzle, although there were still distant flashes of lightning and rumbles of thunder. She ran hurriedly across the courtyard to her own chamber in the guest house. There she wiped dry her hair and gown while Clotilde ran out to buy from one of the lay brothers two quills, some ink, and a sheet of parchment. Taking a candle to the guests' refectory, she sat down to write her letter while Bevis and Lewin made ready to carry it to Norfolk.

The light grew brighter as she wrote, covering the parchment tightly with every detail of her conversation with Henry after writing the news of Leicester's defeat. The storm was passing, but Barbara was too intent to notice the change in the light even when she had to move her head to avoid the last rays of the setting sun, which glanced in through the narrow window. She reread her letter, adding a small point between the lines or in the margin, while the shaft of sunlight disappeared as the sun sank below the priory wall. The light from the window was so strong now that she absently pushed the candle aside.

All Barbara was aware of was a growing sense of relief. She had realized that being among the first to know of Edward's victory would give her father time to gather his strength as well as to make peace overtures. If the king did not insist on punishing Norfolk—and she felt strongly hopeful that she had laid a ground for forgiveness there—the rest could be left to Edward's good sense. The prince knew he would have to come to terms with most of those who had supported Leicester. Since her father had not fought at Lewes or Evesham, the prince would be willing to accept a new oath of fealty from Norfolk and perhaps a minor fine instead of waging a war to disseisin so powerful a man. Barbara closed her eyes for a moment as she breathed a prayer of thanks; she was sure her father's peril was over, but another point came to mind and she opened her eyes to add that information to the letter.

A shadow fell across the table. Barbara looked up, about to order sharply that her man stand out of the light. Instead she sprang to her feet so quickly that she knocked over the bench she had been sitting on. She stretched frantically over the table, but could not reach Alphonse, who was standing behind the bench on the other side, staring at her as if he could not remember who she was or could not think what to say.

''Are you hurt?'' she gasped, throwing aside the quill and rushing around the end of the table, nearly tripping on the overturned bench.

''A little bruised,'' he replied. ''That is all.''

His voice was flat; his skin was gray; his head was turned to her, his eyes fixed on her, but she thought he saw something far uglier. ''My love, my heart,'' she whispered, coming to him and taking his hand, ''what is wrong?''

The affectionate words brought more sense into the eyes fixed on her, and she stretched up and kissed his mouth. He wrenched his hand free of hers, but only so that he could clutch her to him. He held her hard, dropping his head and burying his face in her headdress. She felt him shake and heard uneven breaths that might have been sobs, but the strength of his grip reassured her. Though painful, it was a joy to her, confirming without words that he had told the truth and was not injured. After a little while, he drew one more long, shuddering breath and let her go.

Silently Barbara pressed him down to sit on the bench with his back to the table and, when he had eased himself down like an old man with sore joints, sat beside him. She took his hand again and stroked it gently, lifted it and kissed his fingers—and had to set her teeth because the hand—dark-stained, she now saw—smelled of blood. But she did not jerk away. She laid the hand against her cheek lovingly and waited without speaking.

''The war is over,'' he said at last. ''Leicester is dead and all his supporters with him—Peter de Montfort, Despenser . . .''

Barbara bit her lip to hold back an exclamation. So Despenser was dead! Aliva was free—and rich. And she would be in no danger even as the widow of a rebel because young Roger Bigod would rush to her defense, and Roger, who had not fought at Evesham and was the son of a faithful king's man, would also be safe. Her attention was jerked back to her husband. He had been naming others killed and then had fallen silent and pulled his hand away from her and rubbed it over his face.

"I do not think I have ever seen so many nobles dead," he went on. "And Leicester"—he shivered—"it was not right. He was a good man. I thought him wrong to set his will over Henry, who had been anointed king, but if I had caught the one who cut off his head and hands—"

"Oh God," Barbara breathed and shivered too.

"Edward was pleased." Alphonse's voice was even flatter, and he stared straight ahead at the wall.

"Edward is a good hater," Barbara said bleakly, then called herself a fool. What kind of comfort was that remark to a heart-sick man? She touched her husband's cheek to draw his attention and went on, "It is a dreadful thing, but not all bad. You know, Alphonse, once Edward has his satisfaction for an injury, he does not hold a grudge. Leicester's death and the manner of it may make the prince less harsh to the living."

Alphonse turned his head and really looked at her, then nodded slowly. "It will take time, but I think you may be right." But he shivered again. "War is no tourney," he said. "I hate it. Henry de Montfort is dead too."

"Oh, I am so sorry," Barbara cried, caught her breath at Alphonse's expression, and whispered, "By your hand?" She was horrified at the thought that Alphonse could kill his own friend in the heat of battle.

He shook his head and told her how he had been trying to kill Guy and Henry had come between them. "I wounded him. If I had not, perhaps he would have lived. They pulled Humphrey de Bohun and Peter de Montfort's two sons out from among the dead—and Guy . . . Guy survived too."

"Too bad," Barbara remarked, "but that is proof that the wound you dealt Henry made no difference. You wounded Guy also, and he lived. Not that I really care. He is nothing, less than a worm without his father's power to back him."

Alphonse's full lips tightened, and he shook his head again. "He is dangerous. I do not know why, but I feel he is. Not to you or me, but I have a—a feeling of ill intent that hangs about him. I almost stabbed him when I found him alive beside Henry's body. I should have. He will do some great evil . . . But I could not bring myself to kill a helpless man."

"You did what was right. Whatever Guy is or does, there can be no good in smearing yourself with filth." Barbara sighed. "The priests tell us that God works in mysterious ways and that we should not try to understand Him, and they assure us that God is stronger than the devil, but Satan looks after his own too. Let us forget Guy. He will not touch you or me again.''

Alphonse lifted his shoulders and let them fall, but did not answer. Barbara hesitated, anxious over the unaccustomed expression of despair in her husband's face. Rarely did Alphonse take any matter, except what concerned his family, deeply to heart. She searched her mind for something cheerful to say, decided that cheerfulness was not appropriate, and at last murmured, ''At least Henry was not despoiled.''

''No.'' Alphonse's voice took on more life and he looked at her again. ''And there Edward held no grudge. He was truly grieved. He even ordered that Henry's body be taken to the abbey in honor and swore that he would himself attend his internment.''

''I am glad of that,'' Barbara said and, seeing that he looked less distraught, thought she had better warn him of their illustrious fellow guest. ''Do you know that the king is here?'' she asked.

''Here!'' Alphonse exclaimed, opened his mouth, closed it firmly, and opened it again to say urgently, ''Barbe, I have taken my leave of Edward. To say the truth, I do not wish to see him again, at least for some while. We have a few hours of light left. Let us go.''

''But you are tired and sore,'' she protested.

''I will be worse tomorrow,'' he told her, then found a wry smile. ''And if I must lie up for a day or two, I want you near me.''

Barbara got up at once, recalling that in the priory she would not be allowed to stay with her husband in the men's part of the dormitory. ''You are not hurt?'' she asked again. ''It will do you no harm to ride?''

He smiled at her. ''I swear it.''

''What of Dadais and Chacier's horse?''

''Tired, but for the few miles to Bidford, they will do well enough.''

''Sit here and rest, then. I will tell Clotilde to pack what little we have taken from the travel baskets.'' She turned and, seeing her letter lying on the table, swung back to Alphonse. ''I must send Bevis or Lewin to my father with the news. I would like to send both men so that he will be sure to get my letter, but—''

''Send them,'' Alphonse said. ''So few fled the field that we need not fear large bands of stragglers. Any who did escape will be intent only on getting home without notice. We will not be attacked on the road, and I have the prince's letters to ensure our safe passage. The news of Leicester's death will have run before us. No official will dare disobey Edward's order.''

* * *

They did not stay at Bidford. The alehouse was full and foul and the light was holding. They rode on at the best pace Dadais could keep—Chacier had put the baggage on his own horse and rode one of the pack animals—and they came to Stratford just before the gates were closed at dark. Because the terrible rain had washed the blood from Alphonse's armor and since he was with a woman and her maid, the gate guards had a good enough excuse not to ask whether he had been in the battle, despite his own and his destrier's obvious weariness.

Alphonse was too tired to wonder why he was not challenged for being a fugitive rebel so he could be brought back to face the king's justice, but Barbara knew. She had seen the ugly side of Leicester's rule, had seen his tyranny grow, but the common folk, especially the burghers of the towns, still loved him. The battle was over; their champion was dead. They would bow to the rule of king and prince, but if they could secretly help Leicester's partisans by looking the other way, they would do it.

More silent proof came: The inn in which they had stayed before welcomed them back without questions about the two missing armsmen. Barbara had a good reason ready if the innkeeper or the alewife asked why she wanted a bath carried to their chamber when there was a bathhouse in the town. But neither mentioned the bathhouse, where marks of battle could not be hidden from public view and would betray a fugitive from Leicester's army. Nor did the alewife blink when Clotilde asked for the name of the nearest apothecary. The maid was ready to say that her lady's flux was painful, but she had her directions as if she were asking the way to the privy or the well.

The eagerness of her host and hostess to serve her and the little extra comforts they brought to her door with the evening meal she had ordered—a new, fuller pillow, a small flask of usquebaugh, and under a napkin, strips of old, soft linen for bandages—their looks of wordless sympathy too, drew a few tears from Barbara. The unspoken sense of loss in the innkeeper and alewife brought back to her all of Leicester's dreams of justice and good government. But the dreams had foundered because they had no sound base. Leicester had no *right* to rule, so he gave power only to those he could trust through love or blood—and that was exactly what the king had done. The king's reasons were less sound, but the act was the same.

Barbara bit her lip and wiped the few tears away. The king, she feared, would never change, but Edward was different now, truly a man, and would curb his father's worst excesses. She was almost tempted to offer that reassurance to her host and hostess, but she did not. They probably would not have believed her, and, worse, she would have deprived them of the satisfaction of striking a last blow for Leicester by helping one they thought to be his man.

She warned Clotilde and Chacier to be careful of what they said, even in French, and to avoid all mention of Leicester or the king. Then she bade Clotilde to see to Chacier's comfort and salve any hurts he had—he was falling off his feet—and go to bed. She went to add hot water to the tub in which Alphonse was soaking. His eyes were closed and he did not stir. She dipped a folded bandage into the hot water and laid it on his shoulder, which was turning blue. He stirred and sighed but did not open his eyes. Quietly Barbara got the warming stones from the hearth and warmed the bed.

Alphonse opened his eyes when she came around the screen that shielded the tub and kept in the heat from the small fire. "The water is getting cool again," he said and, as Barbara turned toward the pot on the hob, added, "No, do not get more water. I had better go to bed or I will fall asleep here." He smiled at her. "Give me your hand."

Barbara thought that he wanted her help in rising from the tub and braced herself against his pull, turning her head to look for the thick, soft drying cloth.

"Do not play that game with me any more," Alphonse said, pulling her down and toward him so sharply that she stubbed her toe on the tub and almost fell into it.

"What game?" she asked, catching herself by one hand on the tub to keep upright.

"The fleeing doe," he snapped. "I am tired to death of chasing coyly retreating temptresses—"

"And of dodging attacking lionesses too?"

"For Mary's sweet sake, Barbe, will you not believe I love you and do not desire any other woman, whether she flees me or runs after me? I am no green boy who needs assurance that he is desirable. I want peace. I desire only a woman who is one heart and one mind with me."

"I am of one mind and heart with you—you know that—but you have had a war to keep you occupied. Oh, Alphonse, I do not think you play with women to salve your self-esteem. You do it to keep amused when you are bored."

"That is not true—at least, it has not been so for many years. I did it to fill the emptiness that was in me because I could not have you."

Barbara stood up. "I am playing no games with you. I was only reaching for the drying cloth, not turning away. I have confessed my love and I will not pretend that confession was a lie—but I wish you would not lie to me either. Come, get out of the tub. You will take a chill.'' Her voice was flat and her face expressionless as she reached for the drying cloth again.

Alphonse got up slowly and let her dry him. When he was in the bed, propped up by pillows, he ate the evening meal she put before him. Having emptied his ale cup and put a hand over it to stop Barbara from refilling it, he broke the long silence.

''Barbe, I was not lying. I am not trying to tell you that I soaked my pillow with tears every night or that I had no joy in the women I took. But I told you no lie. Soon after you married Thouzan le Thor I knew I had made a terrible mistake in not taking you when you offered yourself. But what could I do? Pierre was my friend. I could not cuckold him in his absence. And besides that, I *loved* you. I did not want you only for my bed. Your body is lovely, but it is the least part of you.''

''I am glad to know you enjoyed your consolations,'' Barbara said, and snatched up the tray. ''I will try to remember,'' she added over her shoulder as she carried it to the door, ''that my body is the least of my value to you when you seek another, newer and lovelier.''

''God have mercy!'' Alphonse groaned. ''Why are jealous women so stupid? Think what you are saying. Think of the women I took as lovers. Were they all beautiful? With which did I keep faith the longest?''

Barbara stood stock still, clearly remembering—and she could remember everything about each woman Alphonse had been rumored to love while she was at the French court with him. Then she set the tray outside the door and came back. She named the women, and over two of the seven he shook his head, saying he had never had any relationship with those. Of the others, he had had one mistress for two years, another for more than a year, and the three great beauties for a month or two each.

''I parted from Melisande, who, if you remember, was ten years older than I, because what had started as a game to both of us was becoming serious to her—and my heart was already full of a girl with the mane of a horse.''

He reached out and tangled his hand into the thick curling mass. Barbara guessed he was about to pull her into an embrace, as much to divert her as to display his affection. She had no desire to loosen his grip, but had no intention of permitting him to abort the conversation without satisfying her curiosity.

''You cannot tell me you left Madame Janine for fear of injuring her heart. She had none.''

Alphonse's expressive brows rose. "True enough. Janine broke off our affair, not I. She did not tell me why." He smiled and his black eyes glittered with amusement as he continued blandly, "And the others—may God bless and keep them all, the silly hens—were so taken up with their own beauty and thus so boring that I could hardly keep awake in their company long enough to futter them."

Barbara burst out laughing. He had courted each so briefly that what he said must be true.

He looked at her with eyes made round like those of one afflicted with eternal innocence and added, "A man can close his eyes and imagine any body he likes"—the eyes narrowed into laughing slits—"but one cannot enjoy that body if he has been bored asleep. I have no trouble keeping awake in your company"—his voice took on a plaintive note—"even after a hard battle and a long ride when no entertainment is offered."

Laughter sputtered out of Barbara again—but what he said that time was true too. A man could close his eyes and see any body he desired, but it was impossible to hold a truly interesting conversation with oneself. She felt warm and more content than ever before—not that she really believed the green-eyed devil was dead, but for now he had been defeated.

Still laughing, she pulled off her bedrobe. "I think you are quite mad, all bruised and battered as you are, but if it is entertainment you want, I will provide it in full measure so that you need seek no other body."

He caught her and held her away, and now, as only a few times before, she saw his naked soul—hopeful and vulnerable. "Barbe," he said softly, "I love you. Do not use coupling to hide your heart from me."

She bent and kissed him. "My love, my love, I cannot help being a jealous woman. It is my nature. But I will try not to plague you."

He laughed suddenly. "Plague me! Do!" he exclaimed. "I am getting older. I have fewer offers already. Can you not understand how flattered I will be when I am fat and toothless and you still believe me too desirable?" Then the laughter was gone as suddenly as it had come and the bare soul looked out of his eyes again. He drew her against him and murmured, "Do anything but withdraw from me. I cannot bear that there be anything between us."

"I have no more secrets in my heart," Barbara whispered. "I love you too. I have always loved you." He sighed with content, believing her at last, and she touched his face tenderly, then firmed her grip so he could not jerk away and nipped his chin. "And since you and I are both as naked as fish, if you will only let me into the bed, I can get warm and there will be nothing between us but love."

AUTHOR'S NOTE

In the Author's Note I wrote for *The Rope Dancer*, I commented on the problem of describing the conditions in which medieval people lived, and whether it was inaccurate and unscholarly not to detail the filth, cold, heat, lice, and other discomforts. I explained my infrequent and glancing references to those conditions as reasonable because the people of the period did not find them nearly as noxious as we would. Now I wish to comment on a problem coming from the other direction—that is, modern metaphor.

A medieval person would never have thought or said, "I love you with all my heart." Aside from the fact that the characters in this book spoke mostly what we call Old High French, they were more likely to associate love with the liver, "lights" (lungs), womb (stomach), or belly than with the heart. However, an author must consider her readers' suspension of disbelief as well as historical accuracy. If my characters were to cry, "My lights and liver are broken!" or "I love you with all my womb!" or "My belly yearns for you!" I suspect the romantic mood of the reader would be broken while he or she had a good "belly laugh." Thus, I use the modern idiom, regardless of accuracy.

There are other reasons to omit a known fact from a work of fiction. There are, for example, too many kings in this book—King

Henry of England, King Louis of France, and King Richard of the Romans. Because King Richard may be known to readers of my earlier works as Richard of Cornwall and because his winning (largely by bribery) the title "king of the Romans" has no effect whatsoever on the events that take place in this book, I have chosen to refer to him here as Richard of Cornwall.

Also in this book I have mingled historical and fictional characters more closely than I usually do. Roger Bigod, earl of Norfolk (d. 1270), was a historical personage, as were his brother Hugh Bigod and Hugh's entire family. The story of Norfolk's unhappy marriage is also true. In 1226, at the age of twelve, Roger was married to Isabella, sister of the king of Scotland. Clearly the marriage was not successful, although many marriages arranged for political or financial reasons were, and in 1244 the earl began a procedure to set aside his wife. Norfolk's case was not accepted, and in 1253 an ecclesiastical court ordered him to take back Isabella.

I must point out, however, that there is no record of any illegitimate child; Lady Barbara, Sieur Alphonse, and all their relatives (aside from the Bigod family) are totally fictional as are any influences they are said to have had on historical events. The events, however, including the escape of Prince Edward and the movement of troops before the battle of Evesham are historical and as accurately related as possible; the people with whom Alphonse and Barbara associate, such as the earl of Gloucester, John Giffard of Brimsfield, Lord Mortimer of Wigmore, and the young Marcher lords, are also historical personages; only Barbara's and Alphonse's involvement in those events is fiction.

Naturally the description of their wedding is fiction also. I am afraid I have glossed over one custom in medieval weddings that was quite different from our own by avoiding all mention of any gift except the groom's gift to the bride. Actually, everyone gave gifts at medieval weddings; not only did the guests give gifts to the bride and groom, but whoever made the wedding gave gifts to all the guests. This custom could be a source of great anguish to the giver of the gifts, both because of the financial strain and because the gifts were graded in value by the status of the guest. Violent enmities could be provoked by presenting the wrong gift to the wrong person. I wished to use this custom as a plot device but, unfortunately, the book was rapidly growing too long and too complex and I was obliged to abandon that idea and mention the custom briefly here.

Another fiction is the mention of Lagny-sur-Marne as the site of regular tournaments. One great tournament was held in that town to celebrate the coronation of Philip Augustus as king of

France in November 1179. I have no evidence that any others were held at that site; however, tournaments on the Continent were better regulated than those in England and not as likely to end in general riot and destruction of property. Thus, it is possible that a French town with a tradition of being a tournament site might be eager for the trade and money brought in by a large gathering of the nobility and might welcome such events.

Last, but not at all least, is the difference in attitude between a modern person and a medieval person toward the central political conflict of the book—the control of a bad king by those better fit to govern. No contemporary person in the Western world (and few anywhere else these days) would have the slightest hesitation or doubt about supporting Simon de Montfort, earl of Leicester. This simply was not true in medieval times, however. Joanna Bigod states the medieval case in the first chapter of this book, and Alphonse d'Aix presents the typical nobleman's opinion. In the last few pages of the book, also, I point out why Leicester's movement had little chance of success even after the victory at Lewes. There is evidence that the rapidly growing middle class had more "modern" opinions and many merchants and craftsmen supported Leicester's government, but in 1264–65 wealth and power—and thus the ability to wage war—still lay in the hands of the nobility, and it was their ambivalence that destroyed Leicester's hope of reform.

I hope, without much confidence, that I have managed to make these medieval attitudes comprehensible and believable. If I have not and any reader has questions or comments or simply wishes to write to me for any reason, my address is

Roberta Gellis
P.O. Box 483
Roslyn Heights, NY 11577